KNITORIOUS MURDER MYSTERIES BOOKS 4 - 6

A Knitorious Murder Mysteries Collection

REAGAN DAVIS

SEQUOYAH
REGIONAL LIBRARY SYSTEM

116 Brown Industrial Parkway
Canton GA 30114

Carpe Filum
www.CarpeFilumPress.com

ISBN: 978-1-7772359-8-7 (ebook)

ISBN: 978-1-990228-11-7 (print)

A Knitorious Murder Mystery Book 4

Twisted Stitches

REAGAN DAVIS

COPYRIGHT

ISBN: 978-1-7772359-0-1 (ebook)

ISBN: 978-1-9990435-9-9 (print)

FOREWORD

Dear Reader,

Despite several layers of editing and proofreading, occasionally a typo or grammar mistake is so stubborn that it manages to thwart my editing efforts and camouflage itself amongst the words in the book.

If you encounter one of these obstinate typos or errors in this book, please let me know by contacting me at Hello@ReaganDavis.com.

Hopefully, together we can exterminate the annoying pests.

Thank you!

Reagan Davis

CHAPTER 1

"Megan!"

The disembodied voice comes from nowhere. Just loud enough to hear, but not loud enough to recognize. There's nobody around. This is the third time in fourteen hours the voice has called my name. Am I hearing things? Is this a neurological symptom?

The voice called out to me when I walked Sophie last night, again this morning during our morning walk, and just now, while I load groceries into my trunk at the Shop'n'Save in Harmony Hills.

I make a mental note to search the internet when I get home, in case this is a symptom of a stroke, or a brain tumour, or something.

Returning the empty cart to the cart corral, I see Mr. and Mrs. Willows across the parking lot. They're getting into their older, oversize, white pickup truck that Mrs. Willows affectionately refers to as "The Beater." They see me too. We smile at each other and exchange waves. Could one of them have called out to me?

Like me, Mr. and Mrs. Willows live in Harmony Lake. They have a farm on the outskirts of town.

It's not uncommon to run into other Harmony Lake residents in Harmony Hills. Harmony Lake is a small town with limited amenities. Most of us who live there make regular trips to Harmony Hills to visit the big box stores, medical facilities, and other businesses and services we don't have on the other side of the Harmony Hills mountains.

Standing in an asphalt parking lot with no shade, at noon on a July day, with the heat from the hot pavement radiating up my sundress, makes a hot summer day feel downright scorching. I start the engine, turn the stereo down and the air conditioning up.

A few uncooperative curls insist on hanging rebelliously around my face as I twist my hair into a bun and secure it with the hair elastic I wear on my wrist.

I pull down the sun visor and open the mirror. With my sunglasses resting on top of my head, I check the mirror and wipe a smudge of mascara from below my left eye. I squint into the bright, midday sun as I grab the lip balm from the cup holder, and smear some on my lips. Ready! I return my sunglasses to my face and turn up the stereo so Beyoncé and I can sing Crazy in Love together.

Merging onto the highway that will take me through the mountains and home to Harmony Lake, Beyoncé fades out and Mr. Brightside by The Killers takes its place.

"Destiny is calling meeee. Open up my eager eyes 'cause Iiiiii'm Mr. Brightsiiiiiide..." I'm dueting with Brandan Flowers when I check the rearview mirror and notice a small white car following way too close.

I'm in the left lane. I turn on my indicator to let the driver know I'll change lanes and get out of their way. I check the mirrors and shoulder check to make sure it's safe. As I press my foot into the gas pedal and begin to move over to the right lane, the driver of the small white car guns the engine and slams into me from behind.

I grip the wheel tightly to maintain control of the vehicle and stay in my lane.

That was intentional. Why did the car rear end me?

The driver revs the engine again and veers right.

The car is beside me now.

There's an exit coming up. The last exit before Harmony Lake. I need that exit. If I miss it, I'll be stuck on the highway with this crazy driver for twenty minutes until we get to the Harmony Lake exit.

I accelerate again, hoping to pass the car and veer across to the right lane toward the exit. When I press the gas pedal, the other driver accelerates, too, and won't let me pass.

The car swerves toward me. I steer left to avoid it and almost hit the concrete median that divides the north and south lanes.

Why is it trying to side-swipe me?

Easing my foot off the accelerator, I change tactics. If I slow down, maybe it'll pass me. Then I can switch lanes behind it and get to the exit before we pass it.

As I slow down, I look to my right and see the driver of the white car is wearing a disguise. One of those fake-nose-fake-glasses-fake-moustache disguises that makes you look like Groucho Marx, paired with a fuzzy wig-hat combo like the ones you find at a party store.

Why would someone drive around incognito, intentionally hitting another car on the highway?

The driver's side window in the white car lowers about halfway down. The wind from the open window causes the driver to take a hand off the wheel and adjust the hat-wig disguise. I look at the road and accelerate again, hoping to pass the car. I'm running out of time. I turn my head to the right, and the driver is pointing a gun at me!

A gun!

7

POP!

The impact shakes my car and rattles my nerves. I wrestle with the steering wheel and manage to keep control, narrowly avoiding the concrete median.

What the?!

The driver shot at me. Whoever is in that car is trying to kill me! My grip on the steering wheel is so tight, my knuckles are white. I look to the right and make eye contact with the shooter, and they lower the gun.

Clunk!

The shooter lurches forward immediately, following the distinct sound of metal against metal. The disguised head almost hits the steering wheel. Someone rear-ended the car. The shooter recovers, looks right, guns the engine, and glides across the highway, just making the exit.

The car is gone.

It's over.

What just happened?

I barrel instinctively down the highway toward home. My heart is racing. There's a lump in my throat, and a knot in my stomach.

Honnnnnnk!

Mr. Willows is beside me in his big white truck, gesturing at me to pull over.

I indicate, check my mirrors, turn my head to check my blind spot, then pull onto the left shoulder. I should have pulled over to the right, but I choose the path of least resistance.

Mr. Willows pulls up behind me. He appears at my window and cranks his fist.

Thankfully, I'm old enough to remember when cars had crank windows and understand his hand motion. I lower my window.

"Are you OK, Megan? Is it in park? Put it in park."

I nod. My vision blurs as my eyes fill with tears, and I

unclench my hands from the steering wheel and put the vehicle in park.

Mr. Willows reaches through the window and turns the key, shutting off the engine. Then he pushes the button on the dashboard that turns on the hazard lights.

I inhale deeply and take my foot off the brake.

"Is she OK? Was she hit?" Mrs. Willows is beside him now with her face in the window.

"I'm OK," I mutter. "I need to get out." I open the car door and try to get out, but the seatbelt stops me.

Mrs. Willows reaches across my lap and unbuckles it. Clutching the car door for support, I stand up. My stomach roils. I take the two steps to the concrete median, grab on, heave the top half of my body over it and throw up on the paved shoulder of the north bound lanes. The wind is at my back, and I'm grateful I put my hair up before I left the grocery store.

"Henry! Get her some water!" Mrs. Willows shouts as she rubs my back. "*Shhh*," she says quietly. "You're OK, Megan, you're safe."

With his cell phone to his ear, Mr. Willows nods in acknowledgement and jogs toward the back of his truck.

"Why don't you sit down?" Mrs. Willows suggests as she guides me back toward the car.

I sit sideways with my feet hovering above the pavement. Mr. Willows reappears with a bottle of water. He removes the cap and hands it to me.

"I hit him! His car will have rear end damage." I'm not sure if Mr. Willows is speaking to me or to the person on the phone. "I rear-ended him as soon as I caught up to them. He was chasing her." He uses his hand to cover the microphone on his cell phone. "The police are coming, Megan. It's going to be OK." He speaks to me in a quieter voice than he uses on the phone.

In the moments before the police arrive, Mrs. Willows tells

me that she and Mr. Willows saw the whole thing. According to her, the driver of the white car followed me onto the highway. She thinks the driver targeted me. She doesn't believe it was road rage because she says I didn't do anything to the other driver. She says she got the car's license plate number.

Good. I want to know who tried to kill me.

CHAPTER 2

POLICE ARE EVERYWHERE. Panicky and shaky, I stand up beside my car. A police officer introduces himself. Bruce? Bryce? I hear him speak but can't retain much.

A paramedic appears and asks if I 'm having difficulty breathing. She asks if I have any neck pain. She asks a bunch of other questions while she checks my blood pressure, and pulse, and fusses over me.

"We gave her some water!" Mr. Willows bellows from the next lane where he's speaking to a different police officer.

The police close the highway. Standing in the middle of the open road, I suddenly feel vulnerable and afraid. Between the mountains on either side of me, and the northbound traffic still flowing, albeit slowly, I wonder where the shooter is. Are they out there? Aiming a gun at me?

Heavy shoulders, long arms, I mentally repeat to myself while taking deep breaths. Heavy shoulders, long arms is a mantra I learned in a yoga class in my twenties. It helps release the tension in my neck and shoulders.

"May I sit down?" I ask no one in particular.

My officer, we'll call him Bruce, nods and leads me to his SUV. He opens the back doors, for airflow he explains. I sit sideways in the back seat and watch my feet dangle above the lane of the highway. I don't look up because directly in front of me is my black, crossover SUV with a bullet hole in the passenger-side door, just below the window. A few centimetres higher, and the bullet would have found me. If the shooter had been in a larger car, or if I had been in a smaller one, the bullet would have gone through the window, and into me.

Thank goodness Hannah wasn't with me.

My belly roils again.

Hannah is my daughter. Her nineteenth birthday is next month, and she's home from university for the summer. If it weren't for her summer job as a camp counsellor, she could have been sitting in the passenger seat of my car only centimetres from where the bullet now rests.

Bruce asks me questions. I tell him what happened. He diligently takes notes as I speak.

"Have another water, Megan." Mrs. Willows has a soft, comforting voice.

She twists the cap and hands me the bottle. I sip it and try to distract myself with the sensation of the lukewarm liquid in my hot, dry mouth.

I force a smile. "Thank you."

I left the first bottle of water she gave me in my car. Bruce says I'm not allowed to retrieve anything from my car. My cell phone is in there.

Mr. Willows comes over, a police officer following him. "Don't worry, Megan, I phoned your husband. I told him what happened and that you're OK." He uses his arm to wipe sweat from his brow. "And I phoned your boyfriend too." He smiles. A police officer taps him on the shoulder, and Mr. and Mrs. Willows turn and follow him.

"It's not how it sounds," I say weakly to Bruce, shaking my head. "I don't have a husband and a boyfriend. Well, technically I guess I do, but not really..."

"Don't worry about it," Bruce says without looking up from his phone.

Good. I don't have the mental bandwidth to explain it to him right now.

When Mr. Willows says he called my husband, he means Adam, my almost-ex-husband. When he says he called my boyfriend, he means Eric. We've been seeing each other for about six months. Eric is also my tenant. He lives in the apartment above my yarn store, Knitorious, in Harmony Lake.

"What happened? Someone *shot* at you? Are you OK?" Eric has a hand on each of my shoulders.

Where did he come from?

I look up at him and nod.

He looks at my car. His eyes dart from the rear-end damage, to the blinking hazard lights, to the bullet hole in the door. He utters a curse word under his breath. He turns back to me, puts his hands on either side of my face, and tilts my face upward. Looking in my eyes he asks, "Are you sure you aren't hurt? Holy crap, Megan. Someone *shot* at you!"

Tears sting my eyes and stream down my face. I stand up and let Eric hug me. He holds me tightly and rubs hard circles on my back. He's strong and solid. Safe. His heart rate is elevated; I feel the quickened thumping through his black polo shirt.

Mrs. Willows runs over, rummaging through her purse. She hands me a tissue. While I thank her, Bruce approaches us. Eric pulls out his badge and shows it to Bruce.

Eric is a detective sergeant with the Harmony Lake Police Department. He must have used his credentials to get past the roadblocks.

"Husband or boyfriend?" Bruce asks, shaking Eric's hand.

"Boyfriend," I hear Eric say as they walk toward a non-uniformed officer who's approaching them.

Eric and the officer seem to know each other. They slap each other's backs and shake hands enthusiastically. I resume my seat in Bruce's SUV, and sip my water, trying to ignore the compulsive thought that someone is watching me.

"Adam is blowing up my phone with texts," Eric says when he comes back to where I'm sitting. "He says you aren't answering your phone."

"My phone is in my bag. In the car." I nod toward my car behind him.

Eric turns and looks at my car and the bullet hole again. Cops surround it. "They won't let you get it right now. I'll text him and let him know you're OK." He starts typing into his phone.

"Tell him he needs to pick up Hannah. She finishes work at six."

He nods and finishes typing. "Connie and April are texting me too. They want to come here." He shakes his head. "They shouldn't come here."

April is my best friend. Connie is my mother-friend. She's been like a mum to me since I moved to Harmony Lake. The three of us are close. Thanks to an app on our phones, we always know where the other is. If they don't get a response, they will come here. Even with a response, they might come here.

"Can you text them and tell them I'm fine, ask them to stay in Harmony Lake, and tell them I'll text them when I can?"

Eric extends his hand, offering me his phone. "Do you want to text them? I don't mind."

I take the phone, but my hands are shaky, and my mind draws a blank when I try to type. "I can't. Not right now." I hand his phone back to him.

He takes my shaky hand in his steady hand. He rubs the top with his thumb, then raises it, and kisses it.

"I'll send a group text. They won't stop texting until they get a response."

I slide along the back seat of Bruce's SUV, and Eric slides in next to me, leaving his right foot on the road.

Even with the doors open, it's hot in the police cruiser. But it's covered, and I feel less exposed, so I put up with the stifling hot air and perspiration forming on my face.

"There," he declares. "I set up a group chat with you, me, Adam, Connie, and April. I told them you're fine, you can't get to your phone right now, but you'll text them as soon as you can."

"Thank you," I say. "And thank you for coming. You didn't have to."

"Yes, I did," Eric replies. "There's nowhere else..." His voice hitches at the end of his sentence, and he rubs the back of my neck. "I should thank Mr. Willows for calling me. Will you be OK for a minute?"

I nod. Eric slides out of the SUV and walks over to Mr. Willows. I can't hear them but watch them shake hands and smile. Mrs. Willows hands Eric a bottle of water and hugs him.

Several police officers are also walking around with open bottles of water. How much water do the Willows have in their truck? I bet they just bought it at the Shop'n'Save. I make a mental note to drop off a case of bottled water to them when I stop by to thank them for helping me today.

Bruce comes over and asks me if I'll need anything from my car.

"You're keeping it?"

Duh! Of course, they're keeping it. It's evidence. It has a bullet in it, for goodness' sake.

After Bruce explains that my vehicle and The Beater will be taken into evidence, I tell him I need the tote bag from the front seat, and the groceries in the trunk.

"Can I leave soon?" I ask Bruce. "I have frozens in the trunk. They're in insulated freezer bags, but they won't stay frozen forever."

"I'll ask," he says.

He walks over to the non-uniformed officer, who seems to know Eric. While they talk, Eric comes back from talking to Mr. and Mrs. Willows.

"Adam wants to know what to say to Hannah when he picks her up," Eric says. "Also, he wants photos of your car for the insurance claim."

Adam always knows what practical things need to happen in every situation.

"He has to tell her the truth," I dictate to Eric. "She's an adult, and she'll hear about it from someone else anyway. Tell him to reassure her I'm fine but to be honest."

"Got it." He snaps a couple of pics of my car, and his thumbs type a response to Adam.

Eric's phone chimes several times in a row.

"What's going on?" I ask.

"The group chat is growing," he explains without looking up. "Connie added Archie, April added T, and Archie just added Ryan."

Archie is Connie's boyfriend. T is what we call Tamara, April's wife. And Ryan is Archie's son.

"And April just named the group chat, Modern Family." He looks at me and smiles.

Bruce and the non-uniformed officer join us. After dispatching Bruce to go through my tote bag and groceries, Eric's friend, Detective Darby Morris, says we can transfer them to Eric's car and drop off my groceries at home. We agree to meet him later at the police station in Harmony Lake, so I can finish giving a statement, and he can talk to Eric.

Why would he need to talk to Eric?

CHAPTER 3

"Why does Detective Morris want to talk to you?" I ask, adjusting the air-conditioning vents on the passenger side of Eric's car until I feel cold air hitting my face and blowing the loose curls.

"You know how this works," he reminds me as he slowly navigates his car out of the crime scene and through the roadblock. "We always start with the people closest to the victim and move out from there. Statistically, Adam and I are the most likely to try to kill you." He waves to the officer who just moved the barricade, allowing us to leave.

His last sentence doesn't sit well, and I'm not sure if the wave of nausea I feel is because of what he said, car sickness, narrowly escaping a bullet, or all of the above.

"I'm sorry, that came out wrong," he clarifies. "I'm trying to say, Darby's doing his job. He has to eliminate everyone so when he finds the person who did this—and he will find them—there are no holes in the investigation that the shooter can slip through."

"OK," I reply. "How do you know Darby?"

"From the academy," he replies. "He's a nice guy. We came

up the ranks together. I couldn't have chosen a better cop to investigate your case."

"*He's* investigating it?" I ask.

It never occurred to me that Eric wouldn't be the investigating officer.

"This happened in Harmony Hills, not Harmony Lake," he explains. "Even if it did happen in HLPD's jurisdiction, I couldn't investigate it. Our relationship would be a conflict of interest. It could jeopardize a conviction."

"That makes sense," I agree. "But I know what to expect with you. I know you'd be honest with me."

"Darby's a good cop. Your case is in good hands." He glances at me. "And I'll still be here, every step of the way. As your boyfriend, not as a cop."

We drive in silence until we get to the off-ramp. We pass the time with Eric clenching and unclenching his jaw, the way he does when he's working, and me repeatedly telling myself I won't throw up again.

"You haven't asked me anything," I observe as we exit the highway.

"Nope," he agrees. "And it's not easy. Trust me, I want to ask you so many questions."

"I don't mind answering them," I offer.

Eric shakes his head. "We can't talk about it until after we've both been questioned. It would compromise the investigation." He glances at me. "I don't want to do *anything* that could jeopardize this case, Megan."

"Me neither."

"Is the house armed?" Eric asks as he backs his car into my driveway.

"Yup," I reply.

My house has a state-of-the-art security system. Adam

had it installed after someone broke in and laid in wait for me, shortly before he moved out. The security system was a negotiation tool—he agreed to move out if I agreed to have it installed. It works in conjunction with Oscar, the digital voice assistant that sits on the end table in the family room.

"Can you open the garage for me?" he asks.

I rummage around in my bag until I find my keys, point the key-chain remote toward the garage door behind me, and push the button. The door opens slowly.

"Why are we parking in the garage?"

Eric never parks in the garage. Not even when it's snowing.

"Just in case," he replies, maneuvering the car backwards into the garage.

In case of what?

"Do you think I'm still in danger?"

He turns off the car and reaches for the keys in my hand. I expect him to close the garage door, but he doesn't.

"Just being overly cautious," he replies. "It's what I do." He smiles, puts his hand on my knee, and looks me in the eye. "You're safe. Trust me. You're the safest person in Harmony Lake right now." He removes his hand from my knee. "Can you disarm the house?"

I pull my phone out of my bag and, bypassing the dozens of unread text message notifications, disarm the house.

"Done," I say.

"I'm going to clear the house. You stay here. Keep the car doors locked. If I'm not back in six minutes, call 9-1-1."

I look at him, concerned. "The house was armed. There's no one in there except Sophie."

Sophie is my corgi. She's overdue for her midday walk. She must have to pee so badly her little legs are probably crossed.

"I don't expect to find anyone in there. I'm being extra cautious," he explains. "Six minutes. Got it?" he asks.

I nod. "Got it."

Eric gets out of the car, closing the door quietly behind him. He motions for me to lock the car. I guess he doesn't want the chirping of the remote lock to alert the fictional intruder, who's not in my house, that we're here.

He unlocks the door that leads from the garage to the laundry room and enters the house, carefully closing the door behind him.

I check the time on my phone so I can keep track of six minutes. Such an oddly specific number. Why not five minutes? Or ten? I make a mental note to ask Eric how he determined six minutes.

One minute down, five more to go.

Poor Sophie. She hasn't been out since breakfast. She must be so uncomfortable. I bet she's on the other side of the laundry room door, tippy tapping her little paws, desperate to empty her small bladder. I could quietly let her out and take her to the front lawn so she can pee. That's what I'll do. It's cruel to make her wait any longer.

I get out of the car and leave the door slightly ajar. Gingerly, I walk over to the door and open it just enough for a corgi to slip through.

"Hey, Soph," I whisper, bending down to rub her head. "Do you need to pee?"

I stand up.

Something touches my shoulder.

A blood-curdling shriek leaves my mouth.

My heart thuds so hard, I'm sure it's visible through my dress.

Another shriek, but not mine.

I pivot away from the hand on my shoulder and see my neighbour, Phillip Wilde.

We're screaming at each other.

Sophie barks, adding to the cacophony.

We both clutch our chests and stop screaming.

"You startled me!" I hiss.

I gesture for Phillip to follow me out of the garage where we can speak at a normal volume, and Sophie can find some grass to do her business.

"I'm sorry, Megan. Your scream scared me. You're jumpy. But I guess after what happened today, you're bound to be on edge."

We turn to leave the garage and the laundry room door bursts open. Eric charges into the garage, his gun drawn.

Phillip and I let out high-pitched squeals.

Seeing the horror on our faces, Eric aims his gun toward the ceiling. "What happened?" he demands.

"Nothing," I blurt out. "I let Sophie out, and Phillip startled me. Then I startled him. Please put that away."

This is the second time today I've looked down the barrel of a gun, and that's two times too many.

Eric holsters his gun. "Why are you out of the car?" He looks intense.

"Sophie needs to go outside. She hasn't been out since this morning."

"Sophie wasn't part of the plan," he says sternly, shaking his head.

"Neither was getting shot at, but here we are." Sarcasm is one of my go-to coping mechanisms when I feel defensive.

"I saw you pull up," Phillip interjects, halting our exchange. He looks at me. "I heard what happened to you in Harmony Hills, and I thought I should mention something that might be relevant." He looks at Eric.

"I'm listening." Eric says this when he's interviewing witnesses.

It's not his case though.

I'm not surprised Phillip already knows about what happened. Harmony Lake is a small town with a thriving network of gossipers whose efficiency is matched only by their commitment and enthusiasm.

"Willows says the person who chased you was driving a small white car." Phillip reaches into his pocket and pulls out his phone and unlocks the screen. He opens an app, types something with his thumbs, and starts swiping. "Last night, and then again early this morning, there was a small white car hanging around our houses. I didn't get any photos of it, but it looked like this." He turns the phone toward me.

I reach for Phillip's phone. "May I?" I ask.

He nods. "Of course."

"This is exactly like the car that chased me, bumped me, then shot at me." I extend the phone toward Eric without looking up at him.

I feel nauseous again.

"Are you sure?" Eric asks.

Not knowing which one of us he's asking, Phillip and I both nod.

"It was parked across the street when Kevin and I went for our walk at about 10 P.M. last night. Then, when I left the house this morning at 6 A.M. to receive a delivery at the shop, it was parked two houses down." He points to his left. "This morning, I took out my phone to take a picture, but I think the driver saw me, because they sped off."

Kevin is Phillip's chihuahua. Phillip owns Wilde Flowers, the florist shop next door to Knitorious. He often receives deliveries at unreasonably early hours.

It's the same car. I know it is. The knot in my stomach agrees with me. It's too coincidental that last night, and this morning when I heard someone call my name, this car was hanging around the neighbourhood. And it happens to be identical to the car that just chased me on the highway.

None of this is random. The shooter targeted me.

Why didn't I notice the unfamiliar white car? Clearly, I'm too comfortable in my surroundings. Living in a cozy, tight-knit community has given me a false sense of security. I don't like the idea of always being suspicious of my surroundings. I blink away the tears that are welling up.

"I'm taking the frozens in," I confirm with Eric, who's instructing Phillip to phone Darby Morris right now.

Eric nods. "Yeah. I'll stay out here with Sophie until she's done."

"Thank you for coming over and letting us know, Phillip." I touch his arm.

"We've got to have each other's backs, right?" He smiles.

I reach into the car and pop the trunk, take the insulated freezer bags into the house, and put the frozen and the refrigerated items away.

THE GROCERIES ARE PUT AWAY. The reusable grocery bags should go in my trunk, but my trunk, along with the rest of my car, is with the Harmony Hills Police Department. I stash the bags in a drawer by the front door.

Eric is still outside with Phillip and Sophie. Phillip is talking on his phone; I assume to Darby Morris.

I brush and floss my teeth, then wash my face. I decide to leave my hair up. It's too hot to wear my thick hair down, and it was down the three times I heard the shooter call my name. Maybe if I wear it up, they won't recognize me. I release the messy bun, shake out my curls, then twist my hair into a French twist and secure it with a few hair pins.

I slip out of my sundress and drop it in the laundry hamper, on top of the sundress I wore yesterday. I pull the olive green, sleeveless, wide leg, capri summer jumpsuit from the hanger in my closet and put it on.

I look completely different from last night and this morning when my hair was down, and I was wearing a dress. If I am being stalked by someone with a gun, hopefully they're nearsighted enough to not recognize me.

I retrieve my ear pods from the nightstand beside my bed and put them in, then I head across the hall to Hannah's room.

I reach for the overnight bag on the shelf in Hannah's closet, open it, and put it on her bed. I pull out my phone and text Adam.

Me: Can you talk?

This is our code for, "I need to talk to you without Hannah overhearing."

Three dots appear on the screen. He's typing. I wait for his reply to pop up.

Adam: Give me two minutes.

I open and close Hannah's drawers, refolding and adding items to her overnight bag as I go. Two minutes later, my phone rings. Adam's number is on the call display.

"Hi," I say.

I stop packing and sit on the edge of Hannah's bed.

"Are you OK, Meg? We've been waiting to hear from you all afternoon."

"I'm shaken, but I'm not hurt. Is Hannah with you?"

"She doesn't finish work until six, right?"

I check the time on my phone. It's 3 P.M. I thought it was much later. Every hour of today feels like it's a day long.

"Right. Sorry. I didn't realize the time. Adam, can Hannah stay with you tonight?"

"Of course, she can stay with me. But she's almost nineteen, we'll have to ask her if she *wants* to stay."

I shake my head even though Adam can't see me. "No, she has to stay with you." My voice cracks, and I stop talking and compose myself.

Sophie jumps up on the bed and lies next to me with her front paws on my lap. Automatically, I stroke her. She's trained me well.

"OK, Meg, she'll stay with me." He's uses his gentle, reassuring voice. "Why don't you both stay here, with Sophie.

The condo has good security, and Connie and Archie are only an elevator ride away. You can share Hannah's room, or I'll sleep on the sofa and you can have my room."

"I don't want to be near Hannah." That sounds wrong. I realize as soon as the words leave my mouth that it sounds like I don't want to see my daughter. "That's not what I mean," I try to explain, frustrated with how difficult it is to find words when I'm emotional. "It wasn't random. It wasn't road rage, or anything like that. Whoever did this to me, they know my name and they know where I live. I don't want to lead them to Hannah. What if they make a mistake and think she's me? It could happen. From a distance, and from the back, we have the same hair…" I try to swallow the sobs, overcome with emotion at the thought of this causing harm to my daughter.

"Is someone with you? Eric or April or someone?"

I nod, while I collect myself enough to speak.

"Eric and Phillip are here."

"Good," he replies.

Adam offers to come by the house and pick up Hannah's overnight bag. I don't want him to bring her here after work in case the shooter is lurking around the neighbourhood. I don't want him to come by before he picks her up, because I want to see her. We agree that I'll drop off her overnight bag after Eric and I go to the police station.

Adam and I end our call and I look in the overnight bag to remind myself what still needs to be packed. Toiletries. I gesture for Sophie to get off the bed, then get up to collect and pack Hannah's toiletries.

Eric is standing in the doorway.

He opens his arms. "Come here."

CHAPTER 4

"It's nice of Darby to let us do this in Harmony Lake," I say, playing with the Newton's cradle on Eric's desk. "He could've made us drive to Harmony Hills."

"He's a nice guy," Eric replies, retrieving a piece of paper from the printer behind him.

He signs the piece of paper, then logs off his computer.

We're sitting in Eric's small, minimalist office while we wait for Darby Morris to join us. Darby is walking around the station, greeting fellow officers he doesn't see often because he's with a different police force. Eric says it's a small community. It seems like a friendly community, too, judging by how happy the Harmony Lake officers are to see their colleague from another town.

"I don't think it's a good idea for you to stay at home tonight." Eric looks at me, and I'm distracted by the honey-coloured flecks in his brown eyes. "You and Sophie can stay at my place."

"If the shooter knows my name and where I live, they probably know about Knitorious too. Would it really be safer there?" I ask. "Anyway, I have a really good security system. Sophie and I will be fine at home. And they know the police are looking for them. They'd be dumb to hang around my house."

"Fine. I want to sleep over tonight," Eric declares.

"That's presumptuous," I tease, sitting back in my chair.

"I don't mean to sleep," he clarifies poorly. Now he looks flustered.

I raise my eyebrows and smile, amused by his discomfort. It's a welcome, temporary distraction. "Wow, I didn't know you could be this forward."

"You know what I mean." He's blushing. "I want to be nearby. Just in case."

There's that phrase again, "just in case,"

I nod. "OK."

"I'll drive home and pack an overnight bag while you're talking to Darby."

"Aren't we talking to Darby together?" I clarify. "He said he wants to speak to you too."

"He'll want to talk to you alone first," Eric explains.

I nod.

"Hello, again." Darby Morris extends his hand and I shake it.

Darby is a big man with a booming voice. He has a voice for radio, deep and soothing. He's about six feet tall, the same height as Eric but thicker. His presence is more physically imposing, and everything about him seems louder and larger than Eric. When Darby smiles, his whole face smiles, and I can see his smile in his dark brown eyes. I can't imagine him sneaking into a room.

Eric stands up and comes out from behind his desk. They shake hands and slap shoulders in the friendly way that men do. Eric grabs the piece of paper he printed earlier and leaves his office, closing the door behind him.

Darby takes Eric's seat behind the desk, opens his leather folio, slides a black fountain pen from the pen loop and posts it.

"Nice pen," I comment.

I have a few fountain pens myself and am always excited to encounter another enthusiast.

We spend a few minutes talking about his Kaweco AL sport pen—it was a birthday gift from his second wife. They're divorced now, but he's still fond of the pen. He lets me hold it and try it. After a brief discussion about our pen collections, the ice is broken, and we get down to business.

"Start at the beginning," he says.

"The beginning of today? Or the first time I heard them call my name?"

"You heard them call your name?" His mouth is agape, and he sounds stunned.

I nod. "I think so. Three times."

"Start there," he specifies.

I tell Darby everything, starting from hearing my name last night with Sophie. He's easy to talk to and asks a lot of questions as I disclose more information.

When we're finished, Darby opens the office door, and Eric comes in. I leave so they can talk, closing the door behind me on my way out.

I find a seat in the lobby and go through the texts I've been ignoring all day. After I reply to the Modern Family group chat, then individually to April and Connie, I put my phone back in my bag and pull out my knitting.

I'm working on a teeny, tiny baby hat for the local hospital. The charity knitting guild that meets at Knitorious once a week has chosen the hospital as its current project. The hospital always needs little hats, mitts, and blankets. Some hats are so tiny, they fit on an orange. Each hat knits up quickly. I already have a small pile of them ready to give to the charity knitting guild.

I'm casting on the brim of a purple hat when Eric comes out of his office. With a sigh, he sits in the chair next to me and runs a hand through his short, brown hair, causing it to stick out every which way.

"You weren't in there very long," I observe, putting my knitting away.

"Nope. Are you ready to go?"

I check the time on my phone, 6:30 P.M. Hannah and Adam should be home by now. "Ready when you are."

We interrupt Darby's conversation with a group of fellow officers and say goodbye.

"Call me anytime, Megan." He hands me his business card. "I'll be in touch as soon as I know anything."

"Thank you," I say, accepting his card. "I do have one question." I pause, waiting for his acknowledgement before I proceed. "Mrs. Willows said she got the license plate number of the white car. Does that mean you know who you're looking for?"

He shakes his head. "The car was stolen yesterday from a residence in Harmony Hills. We're looking into it, but whoever did this to you likely doesn't have an association with the car or the owner. They probably chose the car because it was generic looking and convenient."

I smile and nod. "Thanks. I'm sure we'll talk soon."

ON THE DRIVE to Adam's condo, I realize talking to Darby helped a lot. Telling the whole story, out loud from beginning to end, made it less confusing in my own mind. It also helped me recall small details that seemed meaningless a few hours ago, but I now realize might be significant.

Eric, on the other hand, seems distracted. He hasn't said a word since we left the station.

"Are we allowed to talk now?" I ask. "I mean, now that we've both given statements?"

He nods. "We can talk. But if Darby asked you *not* to talk

about something specific, then we can't talk about what he asked you not to talk about."

It takes me a moment to untangle what he said. "He didn't ask me to hold anything back," I confirm. "You seem distracted, what's wrong?"

He sighs. "They're looking into my old cases. Just in case."

I'm starting to hate that phrase, "just in case."

"Just in case what?" I ask. "Does Darby think what happened to me today has something to do with one of your cases?"

"No," Eric replies. "But there's no explanation for someone targeting you. You don't have any enemies, you don't live a high-risk lifestyle, and this wasn't a road rage incident. He's exploring every possibility."

"I'm sure it has nothing to do with you."

"What if it does?" he asks. "What if someone is seeking revenge against me by targeting you?"

"Does that happen? Has it happened to other cops you know?"

He shakes his head. "There's always a first time."

"If someone is angry at you, they'd go after you directly. Or a family member, not someone you've been dating for all of six months. I really don't think that's the motive."

"I hope you're right," he says.

"OH MY GOD, Mum! Are you OK?" Hannah meets me at the door and hugs me before I can step inside Adam's condo.

"I'm fine, Hannah Banana. How are you? How was work?" I brush a few stray curls behind my daughter's ear and admire her pretty face.

"What happened?" Her voice is quick and chirpy, her eyes are wide. "Tell us everything."

"I will," I assure her. "As soon as I come inside and take

off my shoes." I take her overnight bag from Eric and hand it to her. "Put this in your room, please."

Hannah backs up so I can step inside, and I see that when she said, "Tell us everything," she wasn't just referring to her and Adam. Connie and Archie are sitting on Adam's sofa, and April and Tamara are sitting in chairs.

"Hi," I say to everyone. "I wasn't expecting a welcoming committee." I smile.

"There was no stopping them," Adam whispers as we kiss cheeks.

Adam and Eric greet each other before Adam excuses himself and rushes toward the kitchen. He's wearing the apron Hannah gave him for Christmas. It combines two of his favourite things, golf and cooking. It says, "Golf is like cooking, you slice it, chip it, and throw it on some greens."

I slip off my sandals and walk into the living room.

"Come here, my dear." Connie stands up and extends her arms. "How are you?" Her blue eyes become moist, and she blinks away the tears.

Connie and I have a long tight embrace. She strokes my hair while I inhale the floral scent of her perfume through her sleek shoulder-length grey hair.

Connie is my mother-friend, and I am her daughter-friend. We met when Adam, Hannah, and I first moved to Harmony Lake almost seventeen years ago. We became instant friends and soon after we became family. I lost my mum just after Hannah's first birthday. Hannah was born when I was barely twenty-one, so when Connie and I met, I was young, newly married, a new mum, and grieving. I'd wandered into Knitorious to replenish my yarn stash because I was knitting through my grief during Hannah's naptimes. Connie welcomed us, nurtured us, and filled the mother and grandmother-shaped holes in our hearts. At almost seventy years young, she's the most beautiful, smart, and sophisticated woman I know.

Connie is the original owner of Knitorious. I started working for her part-time about five years ago. A few months ago, she decided it was time for her to retire and move out of the upstairs apartment. She moved into a new condo with her boyfriend, Archie, and I took over as owner of Knitorious. So, now I own Knitorious and Connie works for me part-time. We've come full circle.

"I'm fine," I assure her. "That bullet wasn't meant for me."

The more I think about it, the more certain I am that bullet wasn't meant for me.

"At least you didn't find a dead body," April teases, referring to my knack for stumbling across recently deceased neighbours.

"She almost was the dead body," Eric mutters behind me.

I shoot him a look of disapproval. I don't want to freak out Hannah any more than absolutely necessary.

April and I hug. Physically, April and I are opposites. She's tall and lithe, I'm short and curvy. She has stick-straight blonde hair, I have brown curly hair. She has blue eyes; I have hazel eyes. She has a year-round sun-kissed glow; I have fair skin.

We've been best friends since we met at a Mommy-and-Me group over sixteen years ago. Her daughter, Rachel, and my Hannah are the same age and best friends. They both attend university in Toronto but are home for the summer.

April and her wife, Tamara, also have a son, Zach, who's sixteen, plays hockey, and eats them out of house and home, according to his mothers. April and Tamara are the owners of Artsy Tartsy, the bakery up the street from Knitorious. Tamara is a talented pastry chef, and they spoil me rotten with baked treats.

Finally, I hug Tamara, then Archie. The last time I had a line-up of people waiting to hug me was my wedding day twenty years ago.

I sit on the sofa next to Connie and tell everyone what

happened. They get the heavily edited, abridged version. I don't detail the fear or dread I felt. I don't mention puking over the concrete median, and I overstate the distance between the bullet hole and the window. To hear this version of events, you'd think the shooter was a myopic, bumbling idiot with no depth perception and horrible aim.

"Hannah, my lovely, would you do me a favour?" Connie implores after I'm finished telling my story. She smiles and looks at Hannah over the frames of her reading glasses. "I've had a senior's moment. I left the garlic bread on the kitchen counter. It's wrapped in foil." Connie produces her keys and holds them out toward Hannah. "Would you be a dear and get it for me?"

Nothing Connie does is an accident. Mark my words, she left the garlic bread on the counter in the kitchen on purpose, so she could send Hannah to retrieve it and give the grown-ups a few minutes to talk.

Hannah jumps up from her chair. "Sure!" She takes the keys from Connie and heads toward the door.

"We're having spaghetti Bolognese," Adam explains. "Connie made garlic bread, and April and T brought salad and dessert."

"I didn't know we were having a family dinner," I say. "If I'd known, we would have brought something." I look at April and Tamara. "Are Rachel and Zach joining us?"

"Both working," Tamara replies. "This family dinner was kind of impromptu." She smiles.

"What about Ryan?" I ask, looking at Archie.

"Out with Lin, I'm afraid," Archie responds.

Lin is Ryan's girlfriend.

Hannah leaves and the door clicks behind her as it closes. Connie's unit is in the next building over, so we have about ten minutes before Hannah returns with the garlic bread.

"Now, my dear." Connie puts her hand on my knee. "Tell us what *really* happened."

33

CHAPTER 5

I FILL in the blanks and provide more details than I was comfortable disclosing with Hannah here.

"Now that I've had a few hours to go over it, re-tell it to Darby, and to you, I really don't think the shooter was aiming for me," I say.

"Then why is there a bullet hole in your car? And why is your back fender destroyed?" Eric asks. "It's pretty obvious who they were aiming for."

"That's not what I mean." I shake my head. "You had to be there. You didn't see the look in the driver's eyes when we made eye contact. They lowered the gun and looked... sorry... and shocked. Kind of like when you recognize someone and wave at them, but then when they look at you, you realize they aren't who you thought they were, so you kind of slink away." I look at Connie. "Does that make sense?"

"Yes, my dear," she replies. "But you're in shock, and perhaps you're seeing what you want to see, hmm?"

"Maybe," I submit.

"Just in case, maybe you should stay with us tonight," April offers.

Just in case is the phrase of the day in Harmony Lake.

"Thank you," I reach out and touch April's hand. "But I'm staying at home. Eric is staying with me, and Hannah is staying here." I smile.

"Well, I've spoken with Marla, and we'll take care of the store. There's no need for you to come to work until this is sorted," Connie tells me.

"Thank you." I smile at her.

I haven't even thought about the store. Knitorious was closed today. It's closed every Sunday and Monday. It's in good hands with Connie and my other part-time employee, Marla. I'm relieved and grateful to have so many friends who have my back.

Hannah returns with the garlic bread, and after Adam warms it in the oven, we have a lovely dinner and talk about anything and everything except what happened to me today.

Dinner is followed by a yummy dessert of Blueberry Squares, made by the lovely Tamara. Blueberry squares are my favourite summer dessert. I love them so much I learned to make them so I wouldn't spend every day of every summer asking Tamara to please make more blueberry squares.

After dinner, Eric helps Adam clean up and load the dish-washer. In the living room, I can hear the low drone of their voices, and the occasional chuckle from the kitchen.

Over the past few months, Adam and Eric have become good friends. It started when they bonded over their mutual love of golf and has evolved. Now they watch sports together and even meet at the pub sometimes for a pint and wings. Is it weird when your boyfriend and almost-ex-husband are friends? Yes, but no weirder than Adam and I remaining friends and having breakfast together every Sunday.

Our Sunday breakfasts started as a way to have a family meal with Hannah during the school year when she's in Toronto. We alternate between my house and his condo, but

Adam always cooks. We Facetime with Hannah while we eat, and the three of us have a virtual visit. Now that she's home for the summer, we still have our weekly breakfast, but Hannah joins us in person instead of on a tablet screen.

Adam and I met in university when I was eighteen. By the time I turned twenty, we were married, and I became pregnant soon after. I was focused on being a mum and member of the community, while Adam's ambition to make partner at a large law firm meant he worked sixty-hour weeks and brought work home on weekends. One day, we realized that aside from our last name, and Hannah, we had nothing left in common.

We tried to reconnect and make it work, but years of apathy and neglect had taken their toll, and ultimately, we decided it would be best for all three of us to end our marriage. The love is still there, but it's changed. It's not the romantic love that a marriage needs to be happy.

We see each other more often, now that we're apart, than we did when we were married. It hasn't been easy, but we're figuring out how to be friends, and we have a much better relationship now.

Adam has practiced family law for most of his career, and he has seen some horrible, nasty divorces. He's determined to make sure we don't devolve to that level. We're hell-bent on coming out of this as friends and as a functional family unit.

"Are you sure you're OK, Mum?" Hannah asks as I slip into my sandals.

"Of course," I tell her. "Everything's fine." I give her a tight hug.

"If everything's fine, why do I have to stay at Dad's?"

"Just in case."

CHAPTER 6

TUESDAY, July 7th

I apply a lot of product to my damp hair and spend almost half an hour blow drying it with a big round brush. By the time it's dry, my arms ache from pulling the brush though my hair and holding the blow dryer at the correct angle.

I plug in my flat iron and decide what to wear while I wait for it to heat up. I settle on my black pedal pushers with my pink and white, sleeveless, button-down gingham shirt.

After another fifteen minutes of ironing and combing my hair, my arms are tired, and my hair is as straight as it's going to get. I hold up a hand mirror to check the back of my hair one more time before I unplug the flat iron. My hair is about four inches longer when it's straight than when it's curly. If I didn't know better, I'd think this was someone else's hair. Good. That's exactly the look I'm going for.

I don't usually straighten my hair, especially in the summer when the humidity works against my efforts. But today, I'm determined to look as different as possible from the Megan who heard a voice call her name, took part in a high-speed car chase, and was almost shot yesterday.

When I get to the kitchen, there's no sign of Sophie or Eric.

Assuming he took her for a walk, I drop a pod of Wild Mountain Blueberry coffee in the coffee maker.

"Good morning," I say as Eric closes the door behind him and arms the house. "Coffee?" I hold up my mug.

"I already had one, thanks." He slips off his flip flops. "You look different. Did you straighten your hair?"

I nod. "What do you think?" I run my fingers through my smooth locks, then bend down to rub Sophie who's pawing at my knees.

"You're beautiful no matter how you style your hair," he replies.

"A very diplomatic answer," I point out.

"Well, it's true." He winks. "What made you decide to change your hair?"

"Honestly? I'm trying to look different from yesterday. If someone is watching me, I don't have to make it easy for them."

"Megan, you're safe," Eric says softly. He takes both my hands. "The person who did this won't get the chance to do it again. Darby's going to find this person, and until he does, I'll be right here."

"Aren't you dressed a little casual for work?" I step back and take in his beige walking shorts and Toronto Blue Jays t-shirt.

"I'm not working," he explains. "I have a lot of time owing from the overtime I've worked." He shrugs. "I'm using some of it."

"You don't have to take time off for this," I tell him. "I'm fine on my own. I have nowhere to go anyway, so I'll just be sitting here, biding time."

"I'm taking the time, Megan. I wouldn't be able to concentrate at work, anyway. I need to be here."

My phone dings and I pick it up off the kitchen table.

April: How do you want your eggs?

"Is it Darby?" Eric asks.

I shake my head. "April."

Me: What do you mean?

April: I'm picking up breakfast. I'm at Tiffany's. It's almost my turn to order.

Me: Scrambled please!

April: Eric's eggs?

I look up at Eric. "How do you want your eggs?"

"Excuse me?" He looks confused.

"April's picking up breakfast at Tiffany's. How do you want your eggs?"

"Ah," he nods. "Over easy, please."

Me: Over Easy

April: Got it! See you soon.

As soon as I lock my phone and put it down on the kitchen table, it rings.

I pick it up and look at the call display.

"Darby?" Eric asks.

I shake my head. "Adam."

"Good morning," I say.

"Hey, Meg. How are you? How was your night?"

"Good. All quiet here. How's Hannah?"

"I just dropped her off at work. I think she's more worried than she lets on, but she's OK. I told her I'll pick her up after work. She said she might call you on her break."

I swallow a mouthful of coffee. "OK. I should be around all day if she calls." I shrug.

"I called the insurance company about your car," Adam continues. "They need a police incident report number for the claim. Also, they're arranging for a courtesy car, so you should be able to pick it up later today or tomorrow. I'll call you when I know more."

"I'll ask Detective Morris for the incident report number and get back to you," I tell him.

"I asked him myself, but he won't give it to me. He says he can only give it to you."

"You spoke to Darby Morris?" I ask.

"Briefly, on the phone. We're meeting this morning. He wants to ask me a few questions."

Adam's done all this before 9 A.M. All I've done is straighten my hair. I feel like a laggard. Adam excels at taking care of practical details. The administrative tasks required after yesterday haven't factored into my thinking yet.

"Thank you, Adam, for taking care of everything. I really appreciate it."

We end the call and I retrieve Darby's business card from my wallet. I send Darby a text requesting the incident report number while Eric disarms the house and opens the door for April.

"That smells so good!" I call from the family room.

"Good morning, Megster!" She hands Eric the bags of food and gives me a tight hug.

April likes to come up with punny nicknames for me. This morning, it's Megster.

"Good morning!" I say. "This is a nice surprise. Why aren't you at the bakery?"

"T told me to take the morning off and come see you. Zach's home for the summer, and we're trying to keep him busy with work, so he's filling in for me this morning. It's good for him."

As we enjoy our breakfast, my phone dings.

Darby Morris: Hi Megan. I have an update on your case. Would it be OK if I stop by in about an hour?

"It's Darby," I say. "He wants to come over in an hour. He says he has an update." I look from Eric to April.

Eric nods. "You said yes?"

"Right!" I reply. "I'll reply right now."

Me: Great! See you in an hour.

Darby sends a follow up text with the incident report number, and I forward it to Adam.

40

We finish our breakfast, and April leaves so she can make the most of her morning off by treating herself to a pedicure.

DARBY SITS on the living room sofa and opens his leather folio on the coffee table in front of him.

"Would you like a coffee, or tea, or something?" I offer.

"No thanks," he replies. "I just finished a coffee in the car. Your hair is different. It looks good."

His powers of observation increase my confidence in his investigative abilities.

Sophie jumps onto the sofa and parks herself next to Darby. He has her approval. Automatically, he reaches out and rubs her head. He's a dog person, which makes me like him even more.

"This is Sophie," I say, introducing Darby to the corgi. "If she's in your way, you can tell her to get down."

"She's not in my way," he replies, scratching her chest. He looks up at me. "I have good news…"

"You arrested the shooter?!" I blurt out, interrupting him.

"Not that good," Darby says. "However, we have found the car involved. It was abandoned in an industrial complex in Harmony Hills. We located it last night."

"The gun?" Eric asks.

Darby shakes his head, then looks at me. "The disguise you mentioned was in the car. We found a trench coat, hat and wig, and Groucho Marx glasses. The forensics team is processing the car. They've found fingerprints, and they're checking the disguise for DNA. We're waiting for the results, but in the meantime, Megan, does the name Hayden Lee mean anything to you?"

Hayden Lee. I gaze at Darby intently while I scan my memory bank for any reference to Hayden Lee. I'm sure this is the first time I've heard the name.

I shake my head. "No. I've never heard that name before. Sorry."

"Don't be sorry," he says. He pulls a sheet of paper from his folio. "Is this man familiar?" He extends the sheet of paper toward me.

I lean forward and take it from him. I sit back and tilt the paper so Eric can see it from the chair he's sitting in next to me.

The headshot looks like it could be a driver's license photo or a mugshot. I examine the man in the photo. Nothing about his straight black-brown hair, almond-shaped brown eyes, or bronzed skin is familiar.

I shake my head again and look up at Darby. "I've never seen this man before." I hold the photo closer to Eric.

"I've never seen him either," Eric says without taking the photo.

I put the photo on my lap, but Darby reaches for it, so I guess he wants it back.

"Is he the shooter?" I ask, handing the paper to Darby.

"I can't say for sure. He tested positive for gunshot residue, though."

"That means he fired a gun, right?" I ask.

"That's right," Darby confirms. "I just can't say for certain it was aimed at you."

What are the chances it was a different gun aimed at someone else?

"When did you find him?" Eric asks.

"Last night when we found the car."

"In that case, I assume you won't be interviewing him." It's a statement, not a question. Eric's jaw is clenching and unclenching like it does when he's working.

Darby shakes his head. "I'm afraid not."

"Can one of you fill me in please?" I look from Darby to Eric.

"GSR, gunshot residue, only lasts about four to six hours

on a living hand," Eric explains, leaning toward me. "You were shot just after noon. They found the car and the suspect last night. More than four to six hours after your car was shot."

I'm struck with a sense of comprehension. "The man they found with the car was dead." It's a statement not a question. "GSR lasts longer on a dead person?"

"Occasionally more than eight hours," Eric replies.

I look at Darby and clutch my chest. "Oh my, did the man shoot himself? Was he so distraught after what happened on the highway that he took his own life?"

"Doubtful," Darby clarifies. "We haven't found the gun. It's unlikely he shot himself then disposed of it."

The shooter wasn't working alone.

CHAPTER 7

"I ONLY SAW ONE PERSON."

"I know you did. So did Mr. and Mrs. Willows."

The other person might be a behind-the-scenes person, like a silent partner. Or maybe they were lying down in the backseat where we couldn't see them.

"What do you think this means?" I ask.

"It's too early to speculate," Darby explains. "The forensics report should help fill in some blanks."

Using lots of words but revealing very little information seems to be Darby's superpower.

"But this person, Hayden Lee, had an accomplice, right? An accomplice who shot him and took off with the gun?"

"I never said Hayden Lee was the deceased individual we found with the car," he clarifies.

"So, he wasn't?" I ask pointedly. "Hayden Lee was not found dead with the car?"

"I didn't say that either, Megan." He shakes his head.

We're going in circles. He's determined not to tell me anything, and not wanting to frustrate myself anymore than I already am, I give up.

"What about this person?" Darby reaches into his folio

again and slips out another sheet of paper, this one is in a plastic Ziplock bag. "Is this woman familiar?" He extends the plastic bag toward me.

I lean forward and take the Ziplock bag from him.

It's a headshot of a woman. An unfamiliar woman. The paper looks aged. The edges are worn, and the page has creases in it, as though it was folded in quarters.

I'm sure I've never seen her before. I'd guess she's a few years younger than me. She has brown hair and brown eyes. Her hair is pulled back. Her skin is fair. She has a thin face with a long nose and a long chin. Her features are angular, and her eyebrows are thick and well-groomed—on fleek as Hannah would say. There's a snippet of a hand on her shoulder, like this photo was cropped from a larger photo with at least one other person in it.

I shake my head. "Sorry, I've never seen her before." I hand the photo to Eric.

"She's not familiar at all," he says, handing the photo back to Darby.

"How does she fit into all this?" I ask, not hopeful for a clear response.

Darby sighs. "I'm not sure. We found the photo with the car. It was on the deceased's person."

A shiver runs up my spine when I realize the photo I just held in my hand was possibly found in a dead man's pocket or clutched in his cold, lifeless hands.

Darby's phone vibrates on the coffee table. The force of the vibration causes it to spin in circles.

Eric leans over and touches my shoulder. "Lemonade?"

I nod. "Yes, please. I'll get it, you stay with Darby." I start to get up, but his hand stops me.

Darby picks up his phone, flips it over, and looks at the screen.

"I've got it. You stay here." Eric removes his hand from my shoulder and looks at Darby. "Lemonade, Darby?"

Darby checks his watch. "Sure, a small glass would be nice." He presses the screen on his phone and holds it to his ear. "Hang on one second." He's talking to the person on the other end of his phone, not to me.

Eric leaves the living room and walks into the kitchen.

"Would you like some privacy?" I ask. "I can leave the room while you take your call."

Darby shakes his head. "I have to take it. It will only take a minute. I'll step outside."

He leaves, closing the front door behind him. Eric is still in the kitchen; I hear the clinking of glass as he gets lemonade for us. Darby left his open folio on the coffee table when he stepped onto the porch. The living room window overlooks the porch. I can see Darby, and he can see me. He repeatedly shifts his weight from one foot to the other, then turns to face the street. His back is to me.

Quickly, I pull my phone from my pocket. With my gaze fixed on Darby's back, I lean forward and pull the Ziplock bag out of the folio, just enough to see the upside-down photo of the mystery woman's face, and snap a photo. I slip it back into its leather slot, slide out the photo of who I assume is Hayden Lee, and snap a photo of it. I nudge it back into its slot and lean back in my chair.

I'm about to check my phone to make sure the photos are recognizable, when Darby turns toward the window. I smile and wave, then look down at my phone as if I'm scrolling social media. Darby ends his call and comes into the house. At the same time, Eric returns from the kitchen with a tray carrying three glasses of lemonade. He puts the tray on the table between our chairs.

"Thank you," I say, lifting a glass and placing it on the coffee table in front of Darby.

"It's good," Darby says after taking a sip.

"I appreciate you getting the police incident report

number so quickly this morning," I say to Darby. "Adam needed it for the insurance claim."

"He mentioned that," Darby replies. "Are you and Adam divorced?"

"Almost." I nod. "Our divorce should be final by October. That'll be the one-year anniversary of him moving out."

Notice I didn't say the one-year anniversary of our separation. We separated months before he moved out, but we faked it publicly until Hannah finished her senior year of high school. The last thing she needed as a high school senior was the distraction of our marital problems, or our family status being a hot topic of gossip in our small town.

"You're friendly for exes," he observes. "Neither of you says anything negative about the other. You get along well. I don't get along that well with any of my ex-wives." He chuckles, smiling.

"We try." I smile back. "We have a daughter together. Hannah is eighteen, and she's our priority. We're determined to stay intact as a family unit. It hasn't always been easy, but Adam and I are learning to be friends and co-parents."

"How do you get along with Adam?" Darby nods toward Eric.

"He's a friend," Eric replies, nodding. "We golf together and watch the occasional game together."

"Really?" Darby screws up his face and sounds incredulous.

"Why is Adam handling your insurance claim? If you're almost divorced, your finances are separate, no?"

I tilt my head. "For the most part we have separate financial lives, but there's still some crossover. I do the books for his legal practice, for example. And we still have some joint investments together. I think both cars are in my name. Our insurance situation is complicated. We have insurance for my house, his condo, my store, his law practice, both cars, and

Hannah is insured as a driver on both cars. It's simpler, and more cost effective to keep our insurance together. Which is fine with me, because I trust Adam to deal with it. I know he'll make sure we're adequately covered, getting the discounts we're entitled to, and the premiums will be paid on time."

"What about life insurance?" Darby asks. "Does Adam handle that too?"

I see where this is going, and I don't like it. If I die before our divorce is final, Adam would own all of our joint assets outright. He wouldn't have to divide them with me. He would also benefit from my life insurance policy.

"Adam didn't do this," I say matter-of-factly. "First, he was in Harmony Lake when I was accosted on the highway, and second, disguise or no disguise, I would recognize him. I made eye contact with the shooter, remember?"

Darcy raises his hands in front of his chest, defensively. "I'm not suggesting Adam chased you, rear-ended you, or shot at you."

He's suggesting Adam could be behind it, though, that he could be the unseen second person who was working with Hayden Lee.

"He thinks Adam has something to do with this," I say as Eric closes and locks the door behind Darby Morris.

"He has to consider every possibility, Megan. He has to eliminate every suspect."

I walk over to the living room window and watch Darby back out of the driveway. "Adam has nothing to do with this." I'm certain this is true.

"I don't think he has anything to do with it either." Eric puts a hand on each of my shoulders. "But statistically…"

"You and Adam are the people most likely to kill me. I know," I finish his sentence. "At least he hasn't found a link between what happened to me and any of your old cases." I'm grasping for something positive in Darby's visit.

"So far," Eric clarifies. "He said they haven't found a link *so far*."

"He won't," I reassure him. "I'm sure this has nothing to do with you, either."

I sink into the living room sofa with an audible sigh.

Eric sits in the chair across from me. "Did you make good use of your time alone with Darby's open folio?" He looks at me with raised eyebrows as he puts the lemonade glasses on the tray.

Impressed and shocked, I grin. "You did that on purpose? You got the lemonade because you heard Darby's phone vibrate. Were you hoping he'd leave me alone in here?"

He shrugs slowly. "I thought it might be a possibility."

"Do you want to know?" This might not be Eric's case, but he's a cop nonetheless, and I don't want to risk telling him anything that might compromise him.

"It's probably best if I don't know the details." He winks.

We search the internet for information about Hayden Lee. He's not outwardly active on social media. He has a Facebook account that hasn't been updated in two years, but his profile picture confirms that the man in the photo Darby showed me is, in fact, Hayden Lee.

His friend list is private—he has thirty-seven Facebook friends—and his only posts are a handful of changes to his profile picture. There are no comments or likes that I can use to snoop his online contacts. We don't find social media accounts for him on any other platforms, and a Google search yields nothing. He's an under-the-radar kind of guy.

Eric suggests that Hayden could use the account for private messaging, even though it looks like the account is inactive. He also speculates the lack of Hayden's online presence could be because he was incarcerated and had no access to the internet. He can't say for sure, though, unless he looks him up at the station. I suggest that for all we know, Hayden Lee could have loads of social media accounts in fake names with fake profile pictures. Social media is an inexact science.

Sophie whimpers at the front door. It's time for her midday walk. I try to convince Eric to let me take her, or at least to let me accompany them while he takes her. He says he knows he can't make me stay home, but he'd feel better if I did. I agree to stay home. The midday heat and humidity will probably make my hair frizzy anyway, and after all the time I spent on it, I don't want to risk it.

As I attach her leash, the doorbell rings.

Eric looks out the living room window. "Phillip."

I unlock and open the door. Those are definitely Phillip's legs and feet, but his top half is hidden behind a huge bouquet of summer flowers.

"They're beautiful!" I say, standing aside so Phillip can step into the foyer.

"They're yours!" he says walking past me and placing the vase on the coffee table in the living room. "It's your July bouquet. It was on my to-do list for the end of the week, but after the day you had yesterday, I thought you could use some flowers to brighten your day." He fusses with a few of the individual blooms until it's just right.

In January, Eric and I attended a fundraiser with a silent auction. Businesses from Harmony Lake donated items for the silent auction, and Phillip donated a floral arrangement every month for a year. Eric bid on it and won. Now I get a beautiful arrangement of flowers delivered every month.

"Thank you," I say to Phillip while admiring the flowers. "They're beautiful! You've outdone yourself." I inhale deeply, the scent is intoxicating. I look at Eric. "Thank you to you too."

Eric smiles and picks up Sophie's leash. "Phillip, can you hang around for a few minutes? I'm just about to take Sophie for her midday walk, and I'd rather Megan wasn't on her own."

Really? In my locked and armed house?

"Go ahead." Phillip waves dismissively at Eric and Sophie.

"Lemonade?" I ask Phillip after I lock the door behind Eric and Sophie.

"Sure," he replies, following me into the kitchen.

I place two glasses on the counter. "I assume you've spoken to Darby Morris?"

"Twice." Phillip holds up the first two fingers of his right hand. "Yesterday afternoon on the phone, then last night in person."

I retrieve the lemonade from the fridge and close the door. "Did he ask you how many people you saw in the white car? The Willows and I only saw one person, but Darby said something that suggests a second person might be involved."

"I didn't see anyone." Phillip shakes his head. "I saw the car from a distance. It was two driveways away. When I took out my phone to take a picture and walked toward it, the driver sped off. I told Detective Morris about the bumper sticker though." Phillip picks up his lemonade and takes a sip.

"Bumper sticker?" This is the first I've heard of it.

Thinking back, I didn't see the back end of the white car. It came up behind me, then beside me, then sped off to the right, but I was too focused maintaining control of my car to watch it exit the highway.

Did Mr. and Mrs. Willows see a bumper sticker? I need to ask them.

"What did it say?"

"It said, **Stay alive, don't knit and drive**, and it had an illustration of a ball of yarn with two knitting needles sticking out of it."

We sell those bumper stickers at Knitorious.

CHAPTER 8

THE WHOOSH of chilled air flowing through the vents in Eric's car breaks the silence on the short drive to Knitorious. The only cars in the small parking lot behind the store belong to Phillip, Connie, and my other part-time employee, Marla. The empty parking lot is not indicative of how many shoppers are inside the store.

It's July, and Harmony Lake is in the thick of the summer tourist season. Most tourists who find their way to Knitorious don't drive to the store, they stumble across it while strolling along Water Street, or they stop in every year as part of their annual pilgrimage to our cozy town. We locals also tend to drive less during tourist season because the throngs of tourists make driving hazardous, frustrating, and slower than walking.

Eric needs to stop by his apartment to pick up more clothes, then he wants to "swing by the station." His words, not mine. Torn between taking me with him, and leaving me home on my own, I decided for both of us, and here we are. I'm sure Connie and Marla are fine, but it's nice to check for myself. I feel guilty leaving them to cope on their own when the store is busy.

Connie and I have texted a few times today, and she insists everything is under control. I know Connie, and even if everything isn't under control, she wouldn't tell me because she wouldn't want me to worry. This also gives me a chance to look at the store computer, find out who might have purchased that bumper sticker, and when.

Eric parks in the spot closest to the back door, despite usually parking at the far end of the parking lot.

He holds the back door open for me. I walk in first, and he follows, letting the door close behind him. He gestures for me to climb the stairs to his apartment ahead of him.

"You go ahead," I tell him. "I need to check a few things in the store."

He sighs.

It hasn't even been a full day yet, but I think guarding me is exhausting him.

"Can you come upstairs with me, and I'll go into the store with you after?"

"I'll be fine," I insist. "No one other than you knows I'm here. And I told you, I'm sure I'm not in danger, I'm sure they were chasing the wrong person."

"Until we have evidence to back up your instincts, let's not take any chances. Please?"

"I'll stay near the back of the store, away from the door and windows." I nod and smile, hoping he'll agree with me.

"Near the harvest table?" he asks.

I nod. "Yes, I'll keep a low profile."

"Fine. I'll be down in a few minutes. I'll leave the apartment door open. If anything happens, yell."

"Got it."

WALKING into the store feels like coming home. I'm in my element. Knitorious is my happy place. The spacious store has dark wood floors and yarn-filled, white shelving along the walls. The counter is in the centre of the store. Behind it, and in front of where I'm standing, there is a long wooden harvest-style table with ten chairs where we teach classes and sometimes sit for knit night. In front of the counter, and off to the side, there are two sofas, two overstuffed chairs, and a coffee table arranged in an intimate, cozy sitting area for knitting. As far as yarn stores go, Knitorious is classic yet contemporary, just like Connie, the original owner.

I count seven customers milling around the shelves of yarn, petting and squishing skeins that get their attention. Connie is at the counter, ringing up a customer.

"Megan!" Marla dumps an armload of yarn into the arms of her unprepared customer. She wraps her arms around me. "I'm so happy to see you. Thank goodness you're OK."

"Thank you, Marla." I smile. "I'm fine. I'm sorry I couldn't come in today and help out. You and Connie have your hands full."

Connie turns at the sound of our voices. "What are you doing here, my dear?" She turns back to her customer, hands her a paper bag, and wishes her a good day.

"Eric needed to pick up a few things, so I thought I'd stop by and say hi. I can help out for a few minutes."

"Don't be silly," Connie chides, approaching me with her arms wide open. "I'm happy to see you, though." We squeeze each other tightly.

"I can't stay long. I need to look up something quickly on the store computer."

Marla is called away by her customer, who's barely able to contain her armful of yarn, and Connie needs to get back to the counter where another customer is waiting to complete their purchase. I walk over to the wall of knitting notions where we display the novelty knitting items. Mugs, bumper stickers, t-shirts, knitting bags, enamel pins, and more. Knitters love collecting novelty items related to their hobby.

We have two versions of the bumper sticker Phillip described. A white bumper sticker with black letters and a black yarn ball, and a black bumper sticker with white letters and a white yarn ball. I grab one of each and walk over to the counter.

Carefully, I reach around Connie and remove the laptop computer from the shelf under the cash register. "I'll be at the harvest table if you need me," I whisper to Connie.

"OK, my dear," she sings as she bags yarn and needles.

We don't keep records for every purchase made by every customer. But if a customer pays by credit card, the name on the credit card is included on the store copy of the receipt. Likewise, if a customer signs up for our email list while they're paying for their purchase, their name and email address will be listed on the store copy of the receipt. We don't ask people to sign up for our email list because, as a customer, I hate it when stores do that. But we keep a small sign at the cash register, telling we have an email list and they're welcome to join it if they'd like to be notified of sales, new yarns, and class schedules.

I search all sales over the past year for the supplier from whom we purchase the bumper stickers. They also supply us with other novelty items, but the bumper stickers are their only items priced at $5.99, so I narrow the search to sales over the past that include items from that supplier for $5.99.

Ten results. Four of them paid by credit card. Only one name is familiar, Rita McConnell. She's a local yarn dyer. Her yarn line is called, *Life's a Stitch*. We carry some in the shop.

I quickly jot down the four names and put the piece of paper in my tote bag. I close the laptop and return it to the shelf under the counter.

"If you don't need me, I'll get going," I announce.

"We don't need you." Connie looks away from the shelf where she's tidying yarn and smiles. "Not today, anyway. You get going. And stay safe, my dear!"

"It was good to see you, Megan," Marla calls from the front of the store.

I wave to Marla, pick up my tote bag, and turn to leave.

"Oh, Megan! Before I forget…" Connie walks toward me, and I meet her halfway. "We were expecting a yarn delivery from Rita today, you know, from *Life's a Stitch*? Anyway, she's having car trouble and can't get here. She's not sure if she'll get here this week."

"Small world," I say. "I was just looking for something on the computer, and her name came up. She's in Harmony Hills, right? I can probably pick it up from her. I have to go to Harmony Hills to pick up the courtesy car when it's ready."

"That works out well for everybody." Connie brings her hands together in front of her. "I'll text you her address and phone number, and you can work out the details with her. We're running low on her sock yarn, so the sooner the better."

A customer interrupts us to ask Connie what gauge means. I excuse myself and leave the store through the back door. I walk across our shared parking lot to Wilde Flowers and ring the bell at the back door.

"Oh, hey, Megan." Noah smiles.

Noah is Phillip's assistant, or apprentice, or both. I'm not exactly sure what his title is.

"Hi, Noah." I smile. "Is Phillip around? I need to ask him a quick question. I'd come in, but I'm pretending I'm not here."

Visibly confused, he shrugs. "Hang on, I'll get him for you." Noah closes the door, and I stand in the parking lot, waiting for Phillip.

"Why aren't you at the harvest table?" Eric throws up his hands in frustration.

He locks the back door at Knitorious and joins me outside Wilde Flowers' back door.

"I was going straight back to Knitorious to wait for you at

the bottom of the stairs." I smile. "I just need to ask Phillip something."

"I panicked, Megan. You weren't in the store. Connie and Marla said you left."

"I'm sorry, I'm not used to all these security measures and constantly checking in with you whenever I move more than a few feet in any direction."

He puts an arm around my shoulders and kisses my forehead. I get a lot of forehead kisses. Eric is almost a foot taller than me, and it's easier to kiss my forehead than to bend down to my level.

"How about this, if you need to switch locations, even for a few minutes, shoot me a text so I don't have a small heart attack when you aren't where we agreed. Will that work?"

"I can do that. I'm sorry you were worried."

The click of the door gets our attention.

"Hey, Megan, what's up?" Phillip asks, joining Eric and I in the parking lot.

I reach into my tote bag and pull out both bumper stickers. "Familiar?"

Phillip points to the bumper sticker in my left hand and nods. "This one. White with black writing. That's it exactly."

"Thank you, Phillip," I say.

"No worries," he replies. "I've got to go. A Bridezilla is having a meltdown in my sitting area because flowers smell."

"Really?" I ask.

He nods. "She loves flowers but hates the smell. Apparently, if we can send people to the moon, I should be able to engineer scentless flowers for her wedding day."

"Good luck with that," Eric says.

Phillip returns to his Bridezilla, and Eric and I walk to the car.

"What was that about?" he asks.

I shrug. "Weddings are stressful and bring out the worst in some brides, I guess."

"Not the Bridezilla." He shakes his head. "The bumper sticker. Why did you want Phillip to choose a bumper sticker?"

I tell him about Phillip's bumper sticker revelation.

"I'm going to ask Mr. and Mrs. Willows, too," I tell him. "Then I'll know for certain whether the car that was creeping around my house and the car that ambushed me are the same car."

"Megan, this could mean whoever was skulking around your house and calling your name, visited the store and interacted with you. And they blended in. Nothing about them made you suspicious."

"When you say things, they sound scarier than when I think them."

He puts his hands on my shoulders. "I'm not trying to scare you. But you need to be scared enough to be extra cautious until Darby figures this out."

"Do you think it could be someone I know?" I ask.

"I don't know," he admits. "But if they were in the store and made a purchase without making an impression on you, something about them avoided your radar."

This doesn't sit right with me. I know the evidence says otherwise, but I just can't shake the feeling that bullet wasn't meant for me. I don't want to dismiss Eric's concern, so I stop myself from once again lamenting that I trust my instincts and the evidence must be wrong.

"If you weren't a cop, and you wanted to stalk someone in your car, and try to kill them in a drive-by shooting, would you remove your bumper sticker first?"

"I wouldn't have a bumper sticker," Eric replies. "But if I did, maybe I'm so used to it that I forgot it was there. Or maybe it's too difficult to remove, and I decide not removing it would be less obvious."

I pull one of the bumper stickers from my tote bag and slap it on the back of his black Dodge Charger. His eyes bulge open, and his jaw drops. He looks mortified. Is it wrong that this amuses me?

I peel the bumper sticker off his car and hold it up. He sweeps his hand across the paint. I know he's checking for damage, but it kind of looks like he's soothing and reassuring his car.

"Magnetic," I say. "Some bumper stickers are magnetic now."

CHAPTER 9

I ADJUST the vents like it's the only way to convince the air to change from uncomfortably warm to cool. I know it doesn't work that way, but I'm impatient. Especially when I'm the wrong temperature.

I buckle my seatbelt and rummage around my tote bag, searching for the piece of paper with the names of the customers who purchased bumper stickers.

I snap a photo of the paper with my phone. "We've sold ten bumper stickers in the past year. I only have names for four of them. The other six were cash purchases." I text Eric the photo. "Knitorious isn't the only retailer that sells them. The one on the white car could have been purchased online or at another store."

"It's not my case," he reminds me, "but I'll forward this to Darby."

We pull out of the parking lot and wait for a crowd of tourists to cross in front of us before we can turn right onto Water Street.

Water Street is to Harmony Lake what Main Street is to other small towns. It's our main drag, our downtown, and where many of the town's businesses and stores are located.

Most of the buildings on Water Street are on the north side. The south side is a strip of park in front of the boardwalk and lake front.

The town is nestled snugly between the lake on the south and the Harmony Hills mountain range on the north. Nature left no room for expansion but provided the town with the perfect foundation for a tourism-based economy. The Harmony Hills mountain range has two popular ski resorts that keep the town full of skiers and snowboarders in the winter, then again in the summer with city-escapees who flock to the lake.

Except for fall and spring, the town is full of tourists. During the busiest weeks, like this week, I think there are more visitors than locals in Harmony Lake.

"Why are we going to the station?" I ask. "I thought you were taking time off?"

"I want to look up Hayden Lee," Eric replies matter-of-factly. "It'll only take a minute. I keep some extra clothes in my office. I need to bring them home and wash them anyway, so I'll use that as an excuse. No one will know why I'm really there."

"But it's not your case," I tease, shaking my head.

"I have a vested interest." He winks at me, and my stomach does a small somersault.

Approaching the police station, it's obvious something is happening. The parking lot is a hub of activity with cops rushing out of the station and into cars. A line of cruisers with lights flashing files out of the parking lot and speeds westward.

"What's going on?" I ask.

"I'm not sure," Eric replies, steering onto a back street, then entering the station parking lot at a different entrance, where he won't interfere with the mass exodus.

We get out of the car, and Eric uses his fob key to open a back door to the station.

"What's happening?" he asks the first person we see when we're walking down the hall.

"10-24 Hav-a-nap Motel," the officer responds as he rushes past us.

We stop walking and watch the hastening officer. The radio on his uniform crackles, and a voice says something.

He turns around and looks at Eric. "And a 10-44," he says, then exits through the same door we just entered.

"I don't speak police code," I remind Eric.

"The first code was shots fired," he explains, "and the second code was homicide."

"That's you!" I declare. "You investigate homicides. Are you going?"

He chews the inside of his cheek, still staring at the door. "I'm not working," he reminds me. "But I could swing by and check it out."

I nod. "Uh-huh. You could."

"You'd have to wait in the car." He looks at me. His eyes narrow, like he's challenging me. "If we go, I mean. We don't have to go. I'm not on duty."

He wants to go. He wants to go to this crime scene like I'd want to go to a knitting festival if I found out there was one at the Hav-a-nap Motel.

"I can wait in the car," I assure him, tapping my tote bag. "I have lots of knitting to keep me busy."

"Let's go!" He grabs my hand, and we race to the door.

ABOUT A BLOCK from the Hav-a-nap Motel, we stop at a police barricade. Eric talks to the officer and confirms there isn't an active shooter before we drive through.

We pull up at the side of the motel and park between two patrol cars.

There are cops everywhere. Some in cars and many on foot, securing the area and doing police stuff.

"Stay here." Eric unbuckles his seatbelt. "If for any reason you have to leave the car, text me. You know how crime scenes work, you can't wander around or touch anything."

Sadly, I do know how crime scenes work. We've attended several together in the short time we've known each other. Yet, every time I find myself in the periphery of a murder, I'm shocked. And each time it happens, I tell myself this will be the last dead body I see. What are the odds of finding myself in the vicinity of yet another murder? But here I am.

I nod. "Got it. Don't worry."

Eric exits the vehicle, and I plug in my phone and shuffle my playlist on the car stereo. I pull out the baby hat I'm working and start the crown decreases while Tom Petty and I belt out "Mary Jane's Last Dance" together.

Baby hats are tiny—especially the newborn-sized ones—and soon I'm binding off this hat and casting on for the first matching mitt.

Out of the corner of my eye, flailing hands get my attention. Carlo Viscardis is waving at me with both hands. I raise my hand and wave back. Once acknowledged, he stops waving and uses one of his hands to remove the cigarette pursed between his lips.

I put my knitting on the driver's seat, turn off the car, and remove the keys from the ignition. "Hi, Carlo! How are you?" I lock the door behind me. I already miss the air conditioning.

"I've been better, Megan," he says.

"Of course, it was a stupid question," I say, rubbing his shoulder reassuringly. "What happened?"

"I dunno." He shrugs and takes a deep drag from his cigarette. "I was working behind the desk. A woman came in and asked for me. She said we have a 2:00 appointment, but she was early. I told her I don't have any appointments today. She said the name of the company she was from—I can't remember it now, and I already gave her card to one of the cops—and I said, 'I remember someone from your company phoned. I told them I'm not interested. Sorry for the misunderstanding. Have a nice day'. I had to go, you know? It's tourist season. The motel is fully booked. Everyone needs something. We're perpetually understaffed..." The pace of his words increases, and his hand gestures become more animated as he describes his interaction with the woman whom I assume is the victim.

I inhale deeply and put my hand on Carlo's upper back. "Breathe," I remind him.

He nods. He has one more long drag from his cigarette and flicks the butt off into the distance. "I'm tryin'."

"You might be in shock," I tell him. "Why don't we go into the air conditioning and get you some water?"

Carlo nods.

I get my tote bag and phone from Eric's car and follow Carlo into the motel office. Carlo sits on a stool behind the counter, and I send a quick text to Eric letting him know I've relocated to the motel office. Feeling quite proud of myself for remembering to do that, I slide my phone into my back pocket.

"Will the vending machine take my card?" I ask. "I think you should have some water."

Carlo takes a set of keys from the desk and slides them over to me. "The plain white card."

I take the keys to the vending machine across the room and slide the white card into it. I push the code for water, and like magic, a bottle of water falls into the tray.

"Get something for yourself, Megan," Carlo says.

"Thanks, Carlo," I respond, pushing the code for Diet Coke.

I hand Carlo his water. "What happened when you told the woman you didn't have an appointment with her?"

"She said she was sorry for the misunderstanding, and her

assistant must've made a mistake. Then she left. Then, like less than a minute later I hear *pew*." He shoots a finger gun when he makes the *pew* sound. "Then I heard a scream."

"The victim screamed?" I ask.

That would be horrifying.

"No." He waves his hand in front of him. "A guest screamed. She ran out into the parking lot after the *pew*"—he fires another finger gun—"and screamed when she saw the victim laying in a pool of her own blood."

"Graphic," I say, sipping my Diet Coke.

"It was," Carlo agrees. "I ran out after I heard the scream. I called 9-1-1 from my cell phone."

"Did you happen to see who did it?" I ask, knowing the police have already asked him.

He shakes his head.

The door to the motel office opens, and Carlo and I jolt.

"Hi, I'm Eric Sloane." Eric extends a hand to Carlo.

Carlo shakes his hand and looks Eric up and down. "You're a cop?"

I can see why he's confused. A Toronto Blue Jays t-shirt, walking shorts, and flip flops isn't Eric's usual professional outfit choice. His gun is the only indication he's with law enforcement.

"Yes, I'm with Harmony Lake PD," Eric replies. He looks down at his attire. "Sorry, I wasn't supposed to work today." He looks at me. "Can I speak with you for moment?"

I shrug. "Sure." I look at Carlo. "Excuse us." I follow Eric outside. "I texted you. I told you where I was." In case I'm about to find myself on the receiving end of a lecture for leaving the car.

Eric nods. "You did. Thank you. I appreciate it." He looks around to make sure we're alone, then he moves closer so he can speak quietly. "You can say no," he warns me, barely above a whisper. "I will completely understand if you say no."

I raise my hand in a stop motion. "Just ask me. If I don't want to do it, I won't do it."

"Will you look at the victim?"

"Why?" I cringe visibly.

"She's familiar."

I suck in my breath and cover my mouth with my hand. "Oh no! Is it someone I know?"

"No, not that kind of familiar. She's not a friend or anything, but I think I've seen her before, and I think you were with me."

I hand him my Diet Coke, and he takes a swig. Why is he being vague? Why not just tell me where and when he thinks we've seen her? Must be a cop thing, not leading the witness or something.

"Fine," I agree. "I'll look."

A flurry of activity surrounds the grey Volkswagen sedan. The driver's side door is open. A police officer is taking photos of the car from different angles. As we get closer, I take a deep breath and lower my gaze. Eric holds my hand, and I walk behind him looking at my feet because I don't want to see her until I've prepared myself mentally. When we stop walking, I stay behind him.

He turns to me. "Ready?"

"Ready." I look up, and he moves aside.

She's sitting in the driver's seat. Her arms are splayed to her sides, palms up, like she's about to catch a giant beach ball. I can't tell what colour her shirt is. Or was. Before it was blood-coloured. Her face is turned slightly to the left. She was probably looking at her killer. Her brown eyes are open, and her eyebrows are on fleek. I've admired those eyebrows before. Recently. I look at the rest of her face. Angular features, long nose, and chin.

I inhale sharply. "That's her!" I hiss to Eric.

He nods. "It is, right?! I thought so, but I needed you to confirm it."

He leads me away from the Volkswagen, to a less busy corner of the parking lot. I pull my phone from my pocket and open my photos. It's the third most recent photo on my phone. The photo Darby showed me of the woman. The photo he said he found "on the deceased's person." I show Eric the photo.

"Definitely," he says, nodding. He looks from my phone to me. "There's more."

"More?" I ask.

More what? More victims? I'm not sure what sort of "more" to brace myself for. More doesn't sound good.

He raises his right index finger. "Stay here. I'll be right back."

After being absorbed briefly by the crowd of officers surrounding the Volkswagen, Eric emerges wearing latex gloves and carrying a woman's wallet.

"Her driver's license," he says, lowering the open wallet so I can see it.

I look at her driver's licence photo and confirm it's the same woman. Then I look at her name.

Meaghan Martelle.

CHAPTER 10

"THIS CAN'T BE A COINCIDENCE!" I insist, pointing to the driver's license.

"We don't like coincidences in murder investigations," Eric responds.

His phone rings; he pulls it out of his pocket and looks at the screen. "My boss. I have to take it."

His boss is the chief of police.

"I'll wait in the car," I reply.

On my way to the car, I lower my sunglasses from the top of my head and cover my teary eyes because I'm overcome with relief and guilt. Relief because I'm more certain than ever that I wasn't the intended target of yesterday's bullet. Guilt due to the relief I feel because today's bullet found its intended target, and my sense of safety is at the expense of someone else dying.

With the air conditioning blowing full blast, I sit back in my seat, close my eyes, and allow myself a sigh of relief. My eyes open when the driver's side door opens. Eric gets in and helps himself to the bottle of diet coke in the cup holder between us.

"What did your boss want?" I ask.

"To know if I'm back on the job, or if she should request a detective from a nearby force."

"What did you tell her?"

"I told her I need five minutes. I wanted to talk to you first."

"You should work the case," I say without hesitation.

"Why?" he asks.

"Because this case, other-Meaghan's case, is related to my case. When you find her killer, you'll find out who tried to shoot me and why." To avoid confusion, I decide to refer to my name-doppelganger as other-Meaghan.

"Officially, the cases aren't linked," Eric explains. "The name and the M.O. are coincidental at this point."

M.O. is *modus operandi*. A suspect's established method of committing a crime. In this case, shooting the victim in the victim's car in the middle of the day. These are the kinds of things you learn when you date a cop. I get to learn crime investigation lingo, and he gets to learn the characteristics of various knitting fibres. We're a hoot at parties.

"You and I know they *are* linked, and when you find the evidence that links them, you'll have access to my case because you and Darby will exchange information. That's how it works, right? Instead of him working my case and you working other-Meaghan's case, all three of us would be working both cases."

Eric nods. "Pretty much, except officially *two* of us would cooperate on both cases."

By "two of us," he means him and Darby.

"Will you be allowed to work this case? Yesterday you said my case would be a conflict of interest because of our relationship."

He takes a deep breath and thinks for a moment before he responds. "Your case happened outside my jurisdiction, so there wasn't an option for me to work it, anyway. But yes, in your case, our relationship would be a conflict of interest that could jeopardize a conviction. But I don't know other-Meaghan, and at this point there's no tangible evidence connecting her case and yours, so there's no conflict here. If I find evidence linking them… Well, I'd cross that bridge when I get to it." Eric shrugs.

"Why are you hesitating? Don't you want to work other-Meaghan's case?"

Eric raises his sunglasses and rests them on his head. "Of course, I want to work it. It happened in my jurisdiction. But, if I'm working all hours to solve this murder, who will keep you safe until Darby solves your case? I can trust another detective to work this case, but I can't trust someone else to keep you safe."

"You don't need to keep me safe." I take a deep breath. Eric is a show-me-the-evidence kind of guy, and I have no evidence to back up what I'm about to say. "I know you think it's wishful thinking when I say the shooter lowered their gun yesterday because they realized I wasn't their target. But I know that's what happened. I'm certain I was the wrong Megan, and other-Meaghan was the right Meaghan. Now that she's… gone, it's over. Whoever did this has no interest in me. My instincts haven't lied to me yet."

"What makes you sure you were the wrong Megan, and she was the right Meaghan?"

"Because the shooter was careful to confirm which Meaghan they shot today," I explain. "Unlike yesterday, the shooter got out of their car this time."

"Why do you say that?" Eric asks, squinting at me.

I shrug. "That's what it looks like. She was shot in the chest. Right in the heart. Either their aim was much better than yesterday, or other-Meaghan was shot at close range, which means the shooter got close enough to confirm her identity and make sure they didn't miss this time. Whereas with me they called my name from a distance to see if I'd look. Also, other-Meaghan was lured here, and the shooter waited until after she got out of her car, went into the motel, then came back to her car. They were either working up the nerve to do it, watching her to make extra sure she was the right target, or had to wait because there were too many witnesses or something. I'm not sure about the last part, that's for you to figure out. But the whole scene seems carefully planned. More carefully planned than yesterday."

"How do you know she was lured here?" He looks amused and impressed at the same time.

"Carlo told me. He said she blamed her assistant for the error. Someone else, maybe her assistant, put this appointment in her calendar. She was set up. He also said she was early for the fake appointment. It's possible other-Meaghan got here before her killer, and that's why she was shot after she went into the motel. Maybe she was about to leave when the killer got here."

He sighs. "I'm glad you choose to use your powers for good. My job would be a lot harder if you worked for the other side." He pauses for a moment, then concedes, "Let me suggest another possible theory."

"I'm listening," I say in my best Eric-voice, mimicking what he says when he questions witnesses.

Without much success, he attempts to suppress a grin. "Let's assume, for the sake of my theory, that you are the right Megan. When the bullet missed you yesterday, the shooter lost the opportunity to make another attempt. It happened in the middle of the day, there were witnesses, the police are looking for them, I took time off work to be your personal bodyguard, and pretty much everyone in Harmony Lake knows what happened and is on high alert."

"OK." I shrug at his statement of facts.

"Harmony Lake is a small town with limited resources. An incident like this"—he gestures vaguely to the organized chaos of the crime scene around us—"uses most of them. The handful of cops that aren't here, are dealing with issues related to the tons of tourists in town. What if other-Meaghan was killed to create a diversion? To separate you from the herd so the killer can try again."

I like my theory better because no one wants me dead.

"I get what you're saying, but I think it's far-fetched. I can't think of anyone who would want to kill me. I've wracked my brain trying to come up with someone who hates me enough or is angry enough to want me dead."

"It doesn't work like that." Eric shakes his head. "A motive that justifies murder to one person might seem trivial to another. We don't know what kind of suspect we're dealing with or how mentally unhinged they are."

"I think your five minutes are up," I remind him.

He checks the time on his phone, then taps the back of it impatiently with his finger. "I think I'd be too distracted to work this case effectively," he admits. "I'd be worried someone is trying to kill you the entire time."

"You'd be distracted either way," I implore. "If you're babysitting me, your mind will be on other-Meagan's case." I pause and try to come up with a solution that will make everyone happy. "How about this? Set up whatever safety protocols you want, and I'll follow them until the case is solved." I smile. "I know Darby is a good cop and you have faith in him, but you're the best cop. I know with access to Darby's information and the evidence from other-Meaghan's murder, you'll solve both cases."

Flattery can't hurt, right? Besides, it's true.

He continues to tap the back of his phone while he considers my suggestion. "Fine," he finally agrees. "I can remove myself from the case if it doesn't work out. I'll text my boss."

Upon realizing he's significantly underdressed, Eric informs me of the first part of his plan. Drop me off at home, have a quick shower, and change into clothes more appropriate for a detective sergeant. He texts a couple of his colleagues, gets out of the car to converse with a few uniformed officers, then we leave.

On the drive home, he advises me that a patrol car will be stationed outside my house when he's not there. He makes me promise to keep the house locked, the blinds and curtains closed, and the security system armed. I promise. I even cross my heart and hope to die, but he isn't amused by my dark humour.

He asks me not to walk Sophie but to take her to the front lawn on her leash and stay where the officer in the patrol car can see me. I agree. My enthusiasm when he tells me we'll need a safe word confuses him because, apparently, we have different definitions of what a safe word is. Eric explains that our safe word is 143. Not a word at all, but I don't mention it. I need to use it every time he texts or phones to check on me. If I don't use it every time he texts or phones to check on me, he'll assume there's a problem and send help. I prefer my definition of a safe word.

BEFORE HE SHOWERS, Eric takes Sophie for a quick walk and assures me he'll be within earshot and eyesight of the house. While they're gone, I take my safety into my own hands and make a few changes to the alarms and locks on the house.

While Eric showers and gets dressed, I make him a couple of sandwiches for the road. It's after 4:00 P.M. and we haven't even had lunch yet. While I'm packing them, a succession of dings emanates from my phone. First Connie, then April, then practically everyone else in town. They've heard about the shooting, though they're light on the details. Someone heard the victim is a man, and someone else heard it's a woman. Someone heard it was Carlo, and someone else heard it was a false alarm because a rogue guest fired a starter pistol. I pretend not to know anything and neither contribute to the conversations nor correct any misinformation.

"Very professional and police-y," I say when Eric emerges, wearing beige dockers and a black polo shirt with the Harmony Lake PD logo embroidered on the chest.

My phone dings. "Sandwiches." I hand him the container, then check my phone.

Adam: If Hannah is staying with me tonight, can I stop by and pick up some clothes for her? Also, she says she needs her rain boots.

Me: Of course!

Adam: Be there in about fifteen minutes.

"The patrol car isn't here yet," Eric says, peering through the slats of the blinds in the living room. "I'll eat these while I wait."

"While you were getting ready for work," I tell him, "I gave you access to the alarm system. If you check your email, you should find a link with your username and passcode. When you work late solving other-Meaghan's case, you won't have to rely on me to disarm the house when you get back. Also, you can check the app whenever you want and see for yourself that the house is armed when you're not here." I smile smugly.

"Thank you." He smiles, checking his email on his phone.

"But, wait! There's more," I say. "I've set you up as a user on my Oscar account. If you follow the link in your email, you can download the app and use it to lock and unlock the house."

"Wow." He looks shocked.

"I promised I would take my security seriously until this is solved. I want you to be able to focus on your job without being distracted."

He smiles. "This is really thoughtful."

"I have one more surprise for you!" I declare. "I've added

you to my Find My Friends App. You can see where I am, well, where my phone is if you need to find me."

He sits on the arm of the sofa and pulls me into him. "Thank you." He kisses me. "I promise we'll go back to normal when this is figured out. You came within centimetres of dying yesterday, and I won't let that happen again."

CHAPTER 11

A SERIES of three light knocks at the front door interrupts us.

"Adam," I say, not sure if Eric can hear me over Sophie's excited yelps.

"I recognize the knock," he replies, walking to the door.

"Did you make a sandwich for me too?" Adam asks, rubbing Sophie and watching Eric bite into a turkey breast on rye.

Sadly, he's not joking.

"No," I reply, shaking my head. "You can make your own sandwich." I jerk my thumb toward the kitchen.

Adam walks into the kitchen to make himself a sandwich. Eric eats his sandwiches while he texts whoever is responsible for sending a patrol car to my house, and I go to Hannah's room to collect her clothes for tomorrow. I place the bag with Hannah's clothes on the table by the front door and retrieve her black and pink polka-dot rain boots from the hall closet.

Plate in hand, Adam sits down at the dining room table. "Before I forget, Meg, the insurance company called. You can pick up the courtesy car at the rental place tomorrow. I'll email you the confirmation information."

"Thanks," I say.

Adam's phone and my phone ding almost in unison.

"What the heck, Meg?" Adam sounds panicked. "Why is Hannah asking if you're dead?"

I grab my phone from the table and unlock the screen.

Hannah: Mum are you OK? Someone said you died at the motel today? Dad is Mum OK?

I curse under my breath.

Me: I'm fine!

I snap a selfie as proof of life and send it to the chez Martel group chat with me, Hannah, and Adam.

"I think other-Meaghan's name was leaked," I whisper, tilting my phone upward so Eric can read it.

He curses out loud.

Our phones ding again.

Hannah: Your hair looks so good today! You straightened it. *Followed by a hairstyle emoji and a heart emoji.* **But why do people think you're dead?**

I love my daughter and her eighteen-year-old priorities.

"Yes, Meg, why do people think you're dead?" Even with a mouthful of food, Adam's voice oozes sarcasm.

"A woman died today at the Hav-a-nap Motel. Her name was Meaghan Martelle, but spelled differently than mine," I explain.

Adam swallows his mouthful of sandwich. "That can't be a coincidence!"

"That's what I said!" I reply, while also typing a response to Hannah's text.

Me: The woman who died at the motel has a name similar to mine. It's a misunderstanding.

Hannah: Creepy! *Followed by a ghost emoji, scared face emoji, and headstone emoji.*

"He's here!" Eric declares. "I have to go. I'll text you soon. Remember the safe word."

"Be careful." I kiss Eric goodbye at the door and lock it behind him when he leaves.

"Remember the safe word?" Adam's eyes are so wide his forehead almost disappears.

I wave away his comment. "It's not the kind of safe word you're thinking of."

While Adam continues to text with Hannah and make sure she's OK, I find a photo online of Mark Twain's famous quote, "The reports of my death are greatly exaggerated," and proactively text it to the Modern Family group chat. If other-Meaghan's name was leaked, it's only a matter of time before someone else is mistakenly told that it was me who was shot.

"Hannah's fine," Adam reassures me. "I'm picking her up in less than two hours, but I think she's good."

I nod. "I hope so."

"Does Eric going back to work mean Darby arrested whoever tried to kill you?"

I shake my head. "No, but other-Meaghan's murder is too similar to what happened yesterday, so Eric went to work to find evidence linking the two incidents."

"What do you think is going on?" he asks.

I tell him my mistaken identity theory, then I tell him Eric's theory about other-Meaghan being a distraction because I'm the right-Megan.

"Wow," Adam replies. "There must be theories in between yours and Eric's."

"Since you mention it," I say, "Darby's theory is that you're the mastermind behind my attempted murder. He hinted that you're in a hurry to kill me before our divorce is final so you can own our joint assets and benefit from my life insurance."

Adam nods. "I'm familiar with Darby's theory. He told me. Of course, I'm a suspect, Meg. Let's face it, it's usually the spouse, especially when the marriage is ending. I'm fully cooperating with the investigation, and I'm sure he'll eliminate me. Anyway, I'm not the beneficiary of your life insurance anymore, remember?"

Not sure what he's talking about, I shake my head. "No."

"Last fall, after Hannah turned eighteen, we made some changes. If one of us dies, the life insurance proceeds go into a trust for her. She'll get access to it slowly until she's twenty-five, then she'll get access to the entire thing."

"Sounds vaguely familiar," I admit. "Do I have copies of this?"

Adam nods. "Check your emails from then, but I'll re-send them to you. It was a busy time, Meg. I was in the process of moving out, you took over the house, I bought the condo, you took over the store, I started the law practice, Hannah went away to school, there was that murder investigation. We signed a lot of paperwork last fall. I'm not surprised the insurance slipped your mind."

This doesn't eliminate Adam's motive to kill me, but it lessens it.

"Maybe it's a serial killer with a very specific victim profile," I speculate. "They only kill women whose names are a variation of Megan Martel."

"Maybe it's a bizarre coincidence," Adam counters with logic. "Maybe this other-Meaghan's murder has nothing to do with what happened to you, and maybe what happened to you was a one-off attack by a crazy person who thinks you cut them off, or took their parking spot, or something."

I wish that were true.

AFTER ADAM LEAVES to pick up Hannah from work, I open my laptop and type Meaghan Martelle into the search engine.

According to the internet, other-Meaghan lives in Harmony Hills. Her social media accounts are full of smiley photos with her husband, Wayne. He looks about ten years older than her. They look happy, but everyone on social media looks happy. People don't post images of themselves at their worst; they post images of themselves living their best life. Posts that make the rest of us feel like we're the only one not living a perfect, photo-ready life.

I don't see anything about them having kids together, but according to her social media accounts, other-Meaghan is a proud stepmother to Wayne's tweenagers from a previous marriage. The boys are about ten and twelve.

Another coincidence to add to the list: other-Meaghan is also a business owner. She owns a concierge company called, *Just Task Me!* Their tagline says they are *a hotel-style concierge service for your business and life.* They pride themselves on *providing world class service with small town care.* No task is too big or too small and they have price plans ranging from one-off services to monthly retention plans for large corporate accounts. They'll do everything from picking up your dry cleaning to planning your six-hundred-guest wedding.

I'm digging deeper into other-Meaghan's online life when my phone dings.

Eric: How's it going?

He's been gone for an hour. I wonder if he's planning to text me every hour.

Me: Good. How about you? 143.

143 is code for I love you; each digit represents the number of letters in each word. Eric's sense of the romantic can verge on corny. I'm still getting used to it.

Eric: Good. Will text later.

I continue my fall down the rabbit hole of other-Meaghan's life until my phone rings. Adam's name is on the call display. My heart skips a beat.

"Is everything OK?" I ask, instead of using the more traditional greeting of *hello.*

"We're fine," he replies. "I only have a minute. Hannah forgot something at work, and we had to come back. She just ran inside to get it."

"What's up?" I ask.

"She's shook about what happened today and yesterday, Meg. She wants to see you. She wants to stay at home tonight."

I want to see her too. But I also want her to be safe. There's a patrol car at the bottom of the driveway, the alarm is on, and Eric is checking in regularly. If Adam and Hannah are here, there would be three full-grown people in the house. Who would be stupid enough to try anything risky under these circumstances?

"Bring her back here," I suggest. "We'll have dinner together and talk to Hannah about everything that's going on. I have some burgers in the freezer, we can throw them on the barbecue and make a salad or something."

"Sounds good," Adam replies. "She's almost back at the car. We'll see you in a few minutes." He ends the call.

I close my laptop and find the burger patties in the freezer. I'm slicing tomatoes when I hear Adam's distinctive, three light knocks at the door.

"The cop out front wouldn't let me pull into the driveway until Hannah and I showed him our driver's licences and explained why we're here," Adam tells me. "And that's after he saw me leave less than an hour ago. He takes his assignment seriously."

"Hi, Mum!" Hannah hugs me, and I hug her back until she wiggles out of my embrace. "Your hair looks so nice." She combs her fingers through my unusually straight hair.

"Hi, Hannah Banana," I say. "How was work?"

"It was fine. Actually, it was pretty boring until someone told me you *died*. What's going on?"

I delay answering her and walk into the kitchen while I think of a response. "Honestly, honey?" I ask, picking up the knife and continuing to slice tomatoes. "We don't know." Honesty is the only option. Hannah's smart and she'll sniff out a lie. She's also an adult now, and I need to treat her like one. "Eric says what happened today at the motel and what happened to me yesterday aren't connected." I plate the tomato slices and reach for an onion to slice next.

"How can they *not* be connected?" Hannah asks, crossing her arms in front of her chest. "Like, no one ever gets shot here. Like ever. And all of a sudden two people are shot in two days? And their names are practically identical? And they were both in their cars? They have to be connected."

I like to think she gets it from me.

The Harmony Lake rumour mill is extra efficient today. The victim's name and the knowledge that her car was involved are already making the rounds.

"Eric went back to work to find out for sure." I look at her. "Can you set the table, please?"

While Hannah opens the cupboard and gets plates, Adam announces he's going outside to the back deck to turn on the barbecue. He slips out of the patio door, sliding it closed behind him.

"So, you're staying here alone?" Hannah asks. "Eric can't be here and at work at the same time."

"He'll come back here after work," I explain. "It'll be later than usual, that's all. There's a police officer outside, and the house has a good alarm system. This is probably the safest house in town. I'll be fine." I smile.

"I'm staying with you," she insists, getting cutlery and closing the drawer. "Dad can stay too."

The sliding door opens, and Adam comes inside to retrieve the burger patties and barbecue utensils.

"Right, Dad?" Hannah asks.

Adam looks at her confused. He shrugs.

"You'll stay here with Mum and me tonight? In the guest room?"

Behind Hannah's back, I look at Adam wide-eyed and shake my head. He looks from me to Hannah.

"Let's talk about it when the burgers are done, OK, Princess?" He winks at her.

I can't think of anything more uncomfortable than all four of us in the same house overnight. Tomorrow's breakfast would be the most awkward meal ever.

"It might be safer for you to stay at dad's," I say after Adam returns to the barbecue.

She looks at me blankly. "You just finished telling me how safe it is here." She raises one eyebrow exactly the way her father does when he makes a solid argument.

I sigh. "You're an adult, now. I can't tell you what to do." I carry the plate of sliced tomato and onion to the table. "Stay home tonight. I'll ask Eric to stay at his apartment. I don't want you to feel uncomfortable." Also, I don't want me to feel uncomfortable. Eric's never spent the night when Hannah is home from school.

Hannah shrugs. "I'm fine with it, Mum. He's a nice guy. And if anything happens, he has a gun and knows how to use it. Besides, Dad's girlfriend sleeps over, so why shouldn't Eric?"

Excuse me? Adam has a girlfriend?

OVER DINNER, we decide that Hannah will sleep at home in her own bed, and Adam will sleep at his condo in his own bed. Two out of three Martels are relieved and happy with this arrangement.

After dinner, Adam walks Sophie and Hannah has a shower. Shuffling off toward her washroom, she grumbles about how messy it is being a day camp counselor to a bunch of kids under age six during a heat wave.

When Adam and Sophie get back, I'm washing and blocking the baby hats and mitts I've made so I can drop them off to the charity knitters at Knitorious tomorrow. They usually come by the store on Wednesday afternoons to sit and knit and plan their charity projects.

"If you or Hannah need anything, just call me," Adam says as I take off Sophie's leash.

"Thank you," I say.

"Do you want me to hang around for a while? I don't mind."

I shake my head. "No need."

"I'll come by in the morning and take Hannah to work." He turns to leave, then he turns back. "Have you made arrangements to pick up the rental car?"

"Not yet," I reply.

"I have to drive into Harmony Hills tomorrow to meet a client. If you want, I can drop you off at the rental place."

"That would be great! Thank you. I was going to ask April to take me, but if you're going anyway…"

With that settled, Adam leaves, and I finish washing and blocking the baby hats and mitts.

I reply to another text from Eric, assuring him that everything is fine at chez Martel. Then, feeling smug about remembering to use the safe word every time we've texted, I settle onto the sofa to knit and watch TV.

"What should we watch, Hannah Banana?"

Hannah emerges from her room freshly showered and wearing jammies. She curls up next to me on the sofa. Sophie jumps up and snuggles on our laps.

"I don't care," she shrugs.

I hand her the remote and continue knitting. She opens the on-screen program guide on the TV and begins scrolling.

"So, does Dad's girlfriend sleep over when you're there?" I've been itching to ask her about this.

"No." She doesn't look away from the on-screen TV menu. "I haven't met her."

"He told you about her?" I probe.

She shakes her head. "Not yet."

"Then how do you know she spends the night? Or if he even has a girlfriend?"

Hannah stops scrolling and looks at me. "There are two toothbrushes in his toothbrush holder." She pauses. "He only has one mouth."

She inherited her flair for sarcasm from Adam and her keen sense of deductive reasoning from me.

"Maybe he never threw away his old toothbrush," I theorize. "Your dad's a smart guy. If he didn't want you to see it, he would've moved it out of sight."

"Maybe," she concedes, "but it's in his washroom, and I don't usually go in there. He wasn't expecting me to stay over last night. With the excitement of everything that happened yesterday, he might not have had time to prepare." She raises her right eyebrow again. "Also, in the last few weeks, I've picked a few long, straight hairs off the headrest in his car." She looks at me. "Really long. Light. Maybe strawberry blonde or light auburn."

I sigh deeply, overcome with pride at my daughter's observational skills but hesitant to praise her for spying on one of her parents.

I wonder if Darby knows about Adam's secret girlfriend. If Hannah is right, and Adam does have a girlfriend, would that give him a motive to kill me? I'm dating someone and I don't want Adam dead. Well, maybe sometimes, for a fleeting moment when he says or does the wrong thing, I *think* I want Adam dead but not literally, more in a metaphorical sense. It would make more sense if it's Adam's girlfriend who wants me dead—she wouldn't have to deal with her new boyfriend's ex-wife, and his net worth would benefit from the exclusive ownership of our joint assets.

CHAPTER 12

WEDNESDAY, July 8th

Getting ready for the day is faster when I don't spend forty-five minutes blow drying and flat ironing my hair. I rake my fingers through my damp curls in a useless attempt to tame them, then apply SPF to my face, neck, and arms before applying my usual moisturizer. I decide to wear my floral, off-the-shoulder maxi dress. Light and flowy. On the way out of my room, I look in the full-length mirror, relieved to feel safe enough to look like myself again.

After sleeping on it, I'm still convinced my attempted shooting was a case of mistaken identity, and other-Meaghan was the real target.

Unfortunately for the shooter, they chose the wrong Megan Martel both literally and figuratively. They have no idea how determined I am to find out who they are and make sure they're held accountable for their actions.

"Your curls are back!" Eric declares from the kitchen table where he's drinking coffee and working on his laptop. "Does this mean you're not worried anymore about someone watching you?"

"I'm certain no one is watching me," I reply confidently.

I put a mug under the coffeemaker and drop a pod of French vanilla coffee into the machine.

"Sophie and I are going for a walk." Eric gets up from the kitchen table, and Sophie perks up and wags her tail when she hears her name and the word "walk" in the same sentence. "I have a late start today. I'll work from home until I have to leave for the autopsy."

"Do you always attend autopsies?" The thought of watching an autopsy up close and in person creeps me out.

"Depends on the case," Eric replies. "I want to be there today for the bullet. To make sure it gets safely from the coroner's office to the lab and to hear the coroner's initial opinion."

"Why is the bullet so important?"

"It could be the best way to link other-Meaghan's case to your case. Darby has the bullet from your car door. If both bullets have the same unique striations, it would prove they were fired from the same gun."

"The same unique what?" Sometimes he forgets I'm a civilian.

"Striations are the scratches left on a bullet after it's fired from a gun. Kind of like fingerprints for firearms. If the striations on the bullets match each other, they were fired from the same gun. When we find the gun, we can compare the striations on the bullets to the barrel of the gun to confirm it's the right weapon."

"What about real fingerprints?" I ask. "Maybe the shooter left fingerprints on the bullets when they loaded the gun."

"It's rare to find fingerprints on a bullet after it's been fired. Sometimes a partial print, maybe, but it's unreliable," he explains.

There's no doubt in my mind that both bullets were fired from the same gun.

I remove my full coffee mug from the coffeemaker and watch Eric attach Sophie's leash.

"I'll be back soon. The patrol car is outside," he reminds me.

I smile. "No problem. Hannah will be up in a few minutes, and her dad will be here soon to drive her to work."

"DAD, ARE THEY IN YOUR CAR?" Hannah is panicking because she can't find her rain boots.

"That's right!" I nudge her shoulder. "Dad came to get them last night before he picked you up at work. He thought you were staying at his place. I bet they're still in his car."

Adam tosses his keys to Hannah from the kitchen table where he's sitting with Eric, eating a bagel he toasted for himself when he got here. He also made himself a coffee. In one of my insulated travel mugs. He left this house less than twelve hours ago. He's here more often now than he was when we were married. I'm still getting used to our family's new normal. Some days are easier than others.

"Be right back," Hannah announces, closing the front door behind her.

"Why does she need her rain boots, anyway? It's sunny. Is it supposed to rain?" Adam has developed a habit of speaking with his mouth full, and it takes all my willpower to resist mentioning it.

"She's taking her campers to visit the pigs today. The pig pen is muddy, and she doesn't want to ruin her shoes," I explain.

Hannah comes back, confirms her boots are in the back-seat of the car, and collects the rest of her gear for work.

"We better get going or you'll be late for work, Princess," Adam says to Hannah as he puts the rest of his bagel in his mouth and gets up from the table. Carrying my insulated mug in one hand, he walks to the door and turns to me. "I have to go to the office and take care of a few things. I'll pick you up at ten."

"We'll be ready," I confirm.

Everyone says goodbye and wishes each other a good day, and Adam and Hannah leave.

"Hannah thinks Adam has a girlfriend!" The words explode out of me as soon as I lock the door behind them. I've been dying to bounce this off someone.

"I thought he might." Eric narrows his eyes.

"You did? Why?"

"The last few times we golfed I caught him reading texts with a goofy grin on his face. He usually ignores his phone when he's golfing unless it's Hannah. These texts don't have Hannah's ringtone."

"Oh, you mean you're listening to your *instincts*?" I clarify. "You don't have actual evidence."

"I know what you're doing." He smiles. "I believe in being overly cautious. Trusting my instincts on something like Adam having a girlfriend isn't the same as you trusting your instincts about someone trying to kill you. If my instincts about Adam's girlfriend are wrong, no one dies or gets hurt."

"Are you sure about that?" I ask.

He looks concerned. "What do you mean?"

"I understand why Darby considers Adam a suspect, even if I don't agree with him. But wouldn't Adam's girlfriend be a suspect too? If she exists. She'd benefit if I wasn't here, wouldn't she? She would have at least as much motive as him."

Eric takes my hand. "I'm sure if there's a girlfriend, Darby knows about it and is investigating her." He tucks a stray curl behind my ear. "I'll mention it to him anyway, in case Adam hasn't mentioned her and Darby hasn't uncovered her in his investigation."

"Thank you," I say, hugging him.

"Where are you going at ten?" Eric asks.

He's not going to like this. "To the rental place to pick up the courtesy car."

"In Harmony Hills?" he asks.

I nod. "I'll be fine. No one wants me dead, and April is coming with me."

He sighs. "This isn't part of the safety plan." He sounds defeated.

"I'll text you if I have a problem, and you can find me on the app if you're worried."

"Where else are you going?"

Why does he assume I'm going somewhere else?

"To pick up yarn at a dyer's house and to Shop'n'Save to replace the water Mr. and Mrs. Willows handed out on Monday."

"After that you're coming home?" He sits back in his chair and crosses his arms in front of his chest.

I nod. "Yes. Right after I drop off the yarn at Knitorious and the water to the Willows."

"You're killing me, Megan," Eric mumbles, shaking his head.

To give him some space while he works, I settle in the dining room with my laptop where I check the store email and text with Connie to make sure she and Marla will be OK on their own at the store again today.

"A cop outside and a cop inside. How much security do you need?" April jokes when Eric opens the door for her.

"More than she thinks," he quips, putting on his shoes.

Passive aggression and sarcasm squeezed into only four words. Very efficient.

"I'll be fine. Please don't worry." I kiss him goodbye.

"I'll keep her safe. Who would mess with this?" April flexes her long, graceful arm.

"Have a good day, ladies." He smiles, then looks at me. "Be aware of your surroundings. Text me or call me if there's a problem. I'll text you in an hour."

I nod, then lock the door behind him and arm the house.

"Get a load of this." I tell April about Hannah's hunch that Adam has a girlfriend.

We're in the midst of listing every woman we know who has long, light auburn or strawberry blonde hair when we're interrupted by three light knocks at the door.

"Speak of the devil," April says.

CHAPTER 13

THIS SUV IS HUGE. It makes my crossover SUV look like a toy car. Clumsily, I climb up and hoist myself into the driver's seat.

"Not my most elegant moment," I say to April, who has no problem gracefully sliding her tall body into the passenger seat.

"It's a marketing conspiracy, you know," she replies.

"What do you mean?"

"This car." She gestures around her. "The car company pays the rental company to upgrade your rental, so you'll get used to driving a bigger, more expensive car. Then when you get your own car back, it'll feel like a downgrade, so you'll trade in your car to buy one just like it." She shrugs one shoulder.

April is full of conspiracy theories, and I love it.

"You might be onto something," I admit, adjusting the seat and the mirrors.

When we get to Shop'n'Save, I intentionally park near the store entrance, far from where I was parked on Monday when I heard the voice call my name. I show April the spot where I was parked on Monday and where I saw Mr. and Mrs. Willows parked.

I load the case of bottled water into the trunk and heave myself into the driver's seat of the giant SUV. Eric sends me our first check-in text of the day, and I reply. To make sure I don't miss his next check-in text or any texts from Hannah, I spend a few minutes trying to sync my phone with the computer in the SUV. No luck. April tries for a few minutes, and she can't figure it out either, but somehow her phone manages to connect itself, so at least we'll have some decent music to listen to on our travels. She puts Rita's address into the GPS on her phone, and we make our way over there to pick up some yarn.

THE OUTSIDE of Rita's house is lovingly maintained. In addition to knitting and dyeing yarn, she seems to be a dedicated gardener.

"Hi, Rita!" I say when she opens the door. I gesture beside me to April. "This is my friend April Shaw."

Rita and April greet each other, and Rita invites us into the house.

Rita is an older lady. I'd guess early seventies. She's shorter than me, and her short, salt and pepper hair is more salt than pepper. She's wearing a muumuu with a busy pattern in tropical colours. My mother would have called it a house dress. Her reading glasses hang around her neck on a beaded, macrame leash.

We follow her past the living room and through the kitchen to a sunroom at the back of the house. It's so sunny that I'm tempted to lower my sunglasses to my eyes. There are plants everywhere. I sit on the bright teal cushion that covers the rattan sofa.

"This is lovely," I say. "It feels like being outside without being outside."

"Thank you," Rita replies. "This is my favourite room. It's for friends and family only." She smiles sweetly at us and offers us some iced tea.

Talking to Rita feels like talking to my grandmother. She gives off a maternal, nurturing vibe.

When Rita leaves the room to get the iced tea, April leans into me and whispers in my ear, "I think I know why this is her favourite room and why it's for friends and family only." She points to our right.

I follow her finger and spy what I think is a marijuana plant in the corner of the room, in front of two windows.

I whisper, "Is that…?"

"It sure is," April replies before I can finish the question.

It's not difficult to imagine Rita as a younger woman in the 1960s and 70s immersed in the hippie lifestyle.

Rita returns with iced tea and a plate of homemade cookies and brownies. I drink the iced tea but decline the baked goods because I'm driving. I'm not sure if they include any special ingredients, and I'd rather not ask.

"I hear we're both having a bad car week," I say.

"Your car was stolen too?" she asks.

"No," I clarify, shocked. "My car was damaged in… an accident. I thought your car broke down?"

She shakes her head and swallows a bite of brownie. "My car was stolen. Right out of the driveway. After breakfast on Sunday, I went outside to water and deadhead the begonias, and it was gone."

"Wow," April says. "Have the police found it? Did some kids take it for a joyride?"

"Yes and no," Rita replies. "The police found it the next day. Apparently, it was involved in some kind of incident. The insurance company says they can fix it, but the police won't release it to them. They said it's evidence in a serious crime."

This sounds too familiar. What are the odds that Rita's car is small and white?

"Rita, is your car a small, white, two-door compact?"

She nods.

"Did it have any bumper stickers by chance?"

"Yes!" She sounds amazed. "Coincidentally, I bought the bumper sticker at your store."

I reach into my tote bag and pull out the two bumper stickers I've been carrying around since yesterday. I hold them up and smile.

"That's it!" she points, enthusiastically at the white bumper sticker in my left hand. "My bumper sticker was exactly like that one."

I extend my left hand toward her. "Keep it. In case yours was damaged," I say, handing her the bumper sticker.

"How did you know to bring this?" She looks impressed and confused at the same time—the face I make when someone does a magic trick.

Starting with the moment I saw the small white car in my rearview mirror, I tell Rita what happened to me on Monday and about Phillip noticing the car near our houses on Sunday night and Monday morning.

"You poor thing! That's awful. I hope the police have found the person who did it."

"They're working on it," I tell her.

"The person who shot at Megan from your car and the person who stole it are probably the same person," April observes as she helps herself to one of the cookies on the plate and takes a bite.

"Did the police show you any photos?" I ask Rita.

She shakes her head. "No, but the officer who I've been dealing with is coming by this afternoon to talk to me. Maybe he'll have some photos with him."

While April compliments Rita on her chocolate chip cookies and tells her that her wife is a pastry chef, I unlock my phone and answer the latest text from Eric. Then I open the photos and find the one of Hayden Lee.

"Do you know this man?" I ask, interrupting their conversation and holding my phone in front of Rita's face.

She puts on her reading glasses and looks at my phone screen. "Not personally." She looks at the photo intently for a moment, then adds, "But I see him around. He cuts the grass at the house across the street. In the winter, he shovels the driveway." She removes her glasses and lets them fall around her neck.

April is eating a brownie now, and she and Rita are talking about whether a brownie without nuts should even be considered a brownie. While they talk, I process what I've learned from Rita so far.

If Hayden Lee was across the street on a regular basis, maybe taking Rita's car was a crime of opportunity, like Darby said. Maybe it's an eerie coincidence that I happen to know the owner of the car that stalked me, chased me, and hit me. But Eric says investigators don't like coincidences. And this coincidence is causing a knot in my stomach, which makes me think there's more to it.

There's no way Rita is involved in what happened to me. We hardly know each other. And if she was the mastermind behind my attempted murder, she wouldn't have reported her car stolen the day before the incident happened. Everything makes less sense, the more I think about it. How does other-Meaghan fit in to all this? Does she fit into this at all, or is she a coincidence too?

I unlock my phone again and find other-Meaghan's photo. This time, I wait for a break in April and Rita's conversation before I hold up the phone toward Rita and ask, "Do you know this woman?"

"That's my Meaghan," she replies, smiling.

CHAPTER 14

"YOUR MEAGHAN?" Did I hear her correctly?

"Yes. How do you know her?"

April leans forward, looks at my phone screen, then looks at me. "Is that other-Meaghan?" she mumbles under her breath.

I nod.

I look at Rita. "I've never met her. Someone showed me this photo. Your Meaghan and I have the same name, sort of. Our names are pronounced the same but spelled differently."

Rita must not know other-Meaghan is dead. There's no way she'd be this cheerful if she knew other-Meaghan was murdered yesterday.

"Is Meaghan your daughter?" I ask.

"No." Rita chuckles. "She's like a daughter to me, though. We're very close."

Then why don't you know she's dead?

"You speak to her often." It's neither a question nor a statement. I'm not sure how to proceed or what to say next.

"Almost every day," Rita confirms. "Except yesterday. Yesterday my sister picked me up and drove me to her place for my nephew's birthday. Since I don't have a car right now, she offered to pick me up. She doesn't like to drive at night anymore, so I stayed over. I got home about an hour before you and April arrived."

Oh my. She has no idea. I'm speechless. I have no idea how to tell her or whether I should tell her.

"You don't keep in touch on your cell phone when you're not at home?" April asks.

Good one, April.

"I don't have a cell phone, and I don't want one. The world was friendlier before all this technology. Meaghan is always nagging me to get a cell phone, but I've lived over seven decades without one, and I'm doing just fine, thank you very much. Besides, everyone else has one. If I have an emergency, everyone else will use their cell phones to get help."

"You're not wrong," I tell her.

From somewhere in the house, a phone rings. Rita doesn't move.

"Aren't you going to answer it?" I ask.

"They can wait." Rita smiles. "I don't answer the phone when I have company. Technology is meant to be our slave, not the other way around."

I lean forward and touch her arm. "Rita, you should answer it. It might be important. April and I don't mind waiting."

Rita walks briskly out of the room. I'm anxious the ringing will stop before she gets to the phone. I relax a little when I hear the mumble of her voice a few rooms away.

"She has no idea," April says quietly.

"I know."

"She's probably finding out right now."

"I know."

"We can't leave her."

I nod. "Do you want to comfort her or call her sister?"

"I'll call her sister."

We sip our iced tea and wait. Minutes pass. Rita doesn't return so we decide to go to her.

We find her in the living room, sitting in a wing chair with the cordless phone to her ear. Tears stream down her face, and she nods into the phone as if the person on the other end can see her. We stand nearby with a box of tissue until she hangs up.

It takes several minutes, much hugging, and many tears before Rita is able to speak. She tells me her Meaghan is dead.

"I'm sorry," I tell her. I say it again every time she tells me anything about the phone call.

April asks where she can find Rita's sister's phone number. Rita directs her to an old-timey Rolodex in the kitchen.

While April calls Rita's sister, and Rita cries and processes the shocking news, I look around the living room at the many framed photos. Other-Meaghan is in at least half of them. One photo in particular gets my attention. It's the photo of other-Meaghan I have on my phone. Except it's the entire photo, not the cropped version I have of her head. It was taken at Niagara Falls. Other-Meaghan, Rita, and Wayne are leaning against the railing with the Falls behind them.

"Who took this?" I ask, holding the framed photo.

I'm hoping to distract Rita from her shock for just a minute and maybe remind her of a happier time.

"A tourist." She smiles weakly. "Wayne hates that photo. He's a photographer, and it drives him crazy that the best photo ever taken of the three of us was taken with a cell phone. A random German tourist snapped a single photo, and it was perfect."

"Why did you visit Niagara Falls?" I ask.

"Meaghan arranged that weekend as a surprise for me. To celebrate my first anniversary of being cancer-free."

Just when I think this can't get sadder.

At some point during the story, April finishes talking to Rita's sister on the phone and joins us in the living room. She tells Rita that her sister will be here soon, and we'll stay with her until she arrives.

"I hope you're still cancer-free," I comment.

"So far so good." Rita knocks on the wooden table beside her. "That was my second bout of breast cancer. I've been in remission for almost five years now."

Knocking on wood is a superstitious action to ward any bad consequences that could happen when you mention something happy or lucky in your life. It's a counter measure to prevent being jinxed.

"I'm glad to hear it."

"As awful as it was, I kind of met Meaghan because of my cancer, so something good came from it."

"Really?" I ask. "Tell us about it."

Rita tells us that when she was undergoing cancer treatment the first time, she was tired, weak, and absent-minded. Running errands one day had left her exhausted. She was making trips back and forth from her car to carry her purchases inside when she accidentally locked herself out of the house. She made several attempts to get in through the various windows and doors she could reach but with no luck. Other-Meaghan was visiting the house across the street and saw Rita trying to get in. She came over and helped.

"She knew exactly what to do and who to call." Rita sounds like a proud mother. "Within half an hour, she had a locksmith here, the door was open, and she was helping me carry and unpack my purchases. She even stayed and made me lunch. She began coming by to visit and check on me regularly after that. And she had someone run errands for me so I wouldn't go to the stores while my immune system was compromised. She even drove me to and from my treatments."

"She sounds like a wonderful person," I say. "Was Meaghan across the street at the same house? The one that has their grass cut by the man who might have stolen your car?"

"That's right. Karla's house."

"How do Karla and Meaghan know each other?" I ask.

"Karla Bell is Meaghan's best friend and business partner. She's lived there for years. She bought that house from the original owners. What was their name again? A lovely Scottish couple, blah, blah, bagpipes, blah, blah, poodles…"

While Rita enlightens April with the history of people who've lived in the house across the street, I zone out and get lost in my own thoughts.

The *Just Task Me!* website didn't mention anything about another owner. I'm sure other-Meaghan was the only owner mentioned. Maybe Karla Bell is a silent partner. Behind the scenes, like whoever was working with Hayden Lee. Speaking of Hayden, in light of the fact that he maintains the property at other-Meaghan's business partner's house, his choice of car seems less random and more intentional than it did a few minutes ago. Is Karla Bell his partner in crime? Was he trying to point the finger at Rita by choosing her car? What an odd choice of person to frame for a crime. She's elderly, frail, and loved the victim.

My phone dings. Eric's latest check-in text. When I look at the screen, I notice the time and realize Sophie needs to go outside. I decide to phone him. I excuse myself and step out onto the porch.

"How's your day?" I ask when he answers the phone.

"Busy. How's yours?" He's in the car. I can tell by the echo of his voice.

"Unfolding differently that I'd planned. I'm stuck in Harmony Hills for a while. Are you near home? Do you think you could stop by and let Sophie out?"

"Sure. I'm on my way to interview witnesses, but I'll visit Sophie on my way. Is everything OK? You sound odd."

"I feel odd," I admit. "You know how you don't like coincidences in murder investigations?"

"Yeah."

"I can't turn around today without bumping into a coincidence. I've come across so many, I might have to write them down, so I don't forget."

"Coincidences that I need to know about?" he asks slowly.

"Definitely, if you don't know about them already. I should go. Thank you for putting the dog out."

"Are you sure you're OK, Megan?"

"Honestly, I'm fine. My brain is just full of new information. 143. I'll text you later."

We end our call and before I go back inside, I have a long stare at the house across the street. There are no cars in the driveway. The doors and curtains are closed. From where I stand it looks like no one is home.

It strikes me as strange that Karla Bell hasn't come to see Rita in the three hours since Rita got back from her sister's house. Karla and Rita are both close with other-Meaghan. Even if Karla and Rita aren't close with each other, wouldn't their shared grief be reason enough for Karla to reach out? Assuming Karla knows other-Meaghan is dead. I suppose it's possible she doesn't know yet. Rita only found out in the last thirty minutes.

"I never married or had kids. I was way too busy for that. I always thought I'd have time later. Then one day, there wasn't any later left," Rita is telling April when I return from the porch. "When you've been alone as long as I have, you get set in your ways and almost don't want to change to accommodate someone else. Meaghan was the closest person to a daughter I've ever had." Rita chokes up and takes a moment to compose herself.

"Was Meaghan from Harmony Hills?" I ask. "Did she grow up here?"

Rita shakes her head. "No. She moved here for a job after university. Her upbringing wasn't very happy. Her parents had a lot of issues. She was shuffled from pillar to post and raised by various relatives until she finished high school. As far as I know, she hasn't spoken to her family since she moved away from them. They say the universe has a way of helping children find their parents. Meaghan was a mother-less daughter, and I was more than happy to be her surrogate mother."

Rita and other-Meaghan's relationship reminds me of my relationship with Connie. "You were lucky to find each other."

"Are these their kids?" April asks, pointing to school photos on the mantle.

"Technically, they're Wayne's kids. He was married before. The boys are from his first marriage, but Meaghan loved them and cared for them like a second mother."

"So, Meaghan and Wayne didn't have children together?" April asks.

"Not for lack of trying," Rita replies, picking up a photo of her and other-Meaghan from the table beside her and gazing at it lovingly. "They tried for a baby after they got married. Wayne is quite a bit older than Meaghan, and she didn't want to wait to start a family. They tried but it didn't happen for them."

"That's too bad," April commiserates.

Rita nods. "It was hard on them. Meaghan didn't like to talk about it, but they just stopped trying one day. It definitely caused some stress in their marriage. For a while, I worried she might leave him. But instead, she shifted her focus from starting a family to building a successful business. After their fertility issues, she put all her time and energy into making that business what it is."

"With Karla?" I clarify. "She and Karla put all their energy into the business?"

"Mostly Meaghan," Rita asserts. "Karla handles most of the day-to-day responsibilities. Meaghan handled the big-picture stuff. She was always trying to land big clients and find exclusive services to offer to them. That business was very important to Meaghan. If it weren't for *Just Task Me!* and her hard work, she and Wayne wouldn't have most of the comforts they enjoy. The house, the fancy cars, the travel, *Just Task Me!* paid for all of that. Meaghan was proud of her success."

"She sounds ambitious," April comments.

"She's driven, that's for sure," Rita says then catches herself. "I mean, she *was* driven."

We sit in silence until her sister arrives.

"We have to get going," I say to Rita after her sister settles in the chair next to her. "Rita, I'm so sorry for your loss." Rita stands up and we hug.

April says goodbye to Rita, hugs her, and offers her condolences again. "We can let ourselves out."

At the front door, April and I slip into our sandals and step out onto the front porch where we each take a deep breath. We're almost at the car when Rita calls to me from the porch.

"Megan! Don't forget the yarn!" She holds up her index finger and ducks back into the house.

Right, the reason I came here today. I completely forgot. Learning that Rita's car was the car that stalked me and chased me, then the revelation that other-Meaghan was like a daughter to her has left me a bit dazed and confused. The garage door behind me opens. I turn to see Rita standing in the garage.

Rita's garage is her dye studio. The space has been reno-vated and fitted with the equipment and dye pots she needs to work her magic.

Rita points to two large plastic storage bins near the door. "Those two are yours."

I open the trunk to the SUV and silently load the large bins inside. I've been lifting and carrying bins of yarn for over five years, and the weightlessness of even the largest tub of yarn still amazes me. I smile and wave at Rita after I close the trunk. She waves back from inside the garage as the door closes.

I'm preparing to thrust myself into the driver's seat when a familiar car slowly rolls up the street and comes to a stop outside Rita's house.

"Isn't this a surprise! What on earth brings you here, Megan?"

"Hi, Darby," I wave. "Rita is a yarn dyer. I'm picking up yarn for the store." Tired of waiting for me, April gets out of the passenger side of the SUV. "April Shaw, this is Darby Morris. He's the detective who's working my case."

Darby rushes over to April with his hand extended.

She shakes his hand. "It's nice to meet you, detective."

"P-please call m-me Darby." He's stunned by her beauty. I've seen it before.

"Alrighty then, it's nice to meet you Darby." April rewards him with a wide, toothy smile.

He looks like he might melt, or faint, or something.

"Well, it's nice seeing you, Darby," I say, opening the car door, "but we have to go."

Almost imperceptibly, he shakes his head and looks from April to me. "Actually, Megan, I was going to call you after my meeting with Rita. I have some updates on your case. Can we meet later?"

"Of course," I reply. "What time?"

He looks at his watch. "Let's say 5:00? I have a few calls to make before we meet."

"That works for me," I confirm. "Should I meet you at your office?"

"No," he shakes his head. "I'll come to you. I'll be in Harmony Lake anyway, so it works out well."

"Great! See you later." I scale the SUV and plant myself in the driver's seat.

My mind is cluttered with new information that I need to sort out.

CHAPTER 15

"Nothing about that visit was what I expected," April declares as we leave Rita's subdivision and turn onto the main road.

"I know, right? I don't even know where to begin processing everything," I reply.

"Let's start at the beginning," April directs. "Rita is growing marijuana plants in her sunroom. At first, I was shocked, but after she told us about her two battles with cancer, it makes sense that she might have them as part of her treatment."

"Was there any in the brownies or cookies?" I ask. "I'm driving and didn't want to risk it, so I didn't have any."

April shrugs one shoulder. "I don't think so. I had them and I feel fine."

"Her car is the small white car that stalked my house and chased me. And the person who probably shot me mows the lawn across the street from Rita's house. Those are *huge* coincidences."

"You mean, other-Meaghan's business partner's house?" April asks rhetorically and with a good dose of sarcasm.

"It's too coincidental that Rita knows other-Meaghan and loves her like a daughter," I surmise.

"There are no coincidences," April informs me. "There's only the illusion of coincidences. Whoever is behind your incident and other-Meaghan's murder wants everyone to believe there are coincidences so they can hide behind them. They're distracting the police with a succession of unrelated events and circumstances that appear to be unrelated but aren't."

"That's deep," I concede. "As close as Rita and other-Meaghan were, I don't think Rita knows everything about other-Meaghan's life. She knows that other-Meaghan and Wayne had marital issues when they stopped trying to have a baby, but she didn't seem very clear on the details, you know what I mean? She said they just stopped trying one day, and she was worried they might get divorced, but she didn't mention any details."

April nods. "Rita could know more than she lets on and doesn't want to share the intimate details of other-Meaghan's marriage with us."

"Possibly," I agree. "Rita's relationship with other-Meaghan reminds me of Connie and me. I love Connie like a mother, and I know she loves me like a daughter. I also know she worries about me, so I don't always tell her everything. I tell her enough that she can enlighten me with her sage wisdom and stay in the loop, but I leave out details that I think will worry her." I look at April briefly while I turn right to merge onto the highway that will take us to Harmony Lake. "You, on the other hand, get all the details."

"So, if Rita is other-Meaghan's Connie, we need to talk to other-Meaghan's April," she concludes.

"Karla Bell," we say in unison.

"IT'S THE TONER, that's how they get you," Mr. Willows warns us. "Inexpensive printers are everywhere, but it's a trap. They give them away because they know they'll make their money on the toner." He taps his temple with his index finger.

"Like lightbulbs!" April declares with wide-eyed enthusiasm. "You know, they can make lightbulbs that will never burn out. But they don't because if they did, they wouldn't be able to keep selling us lightbulbs."

"Exactly!" Mr. Willows brings his fist down onto the Willows' kitchen counter.

Before the conversation turned to consumer conspiracies, Mr. Willows was telling us that when I waved to them in the parking lot on Monday, he and Mrs. Willows were coming from Electric Avenue, the big box electronics store in the Shop'n'Save plaza. They were shopping for a new printer.

WHILE MR. WILLOWS and April exchange conspiracy theories and enable each other's distrust of "they" and "them," Mrs. Willows and I go outside to the SUV. I carry the case of water into their farmhouse and deposit it on the kitchen table.

"I wanted to thank you again for everything you did for me on Monday. Thanks to you, everyone at the scene was fully hydrated," I say. "Also, here's a skein of yarn from *Life's A Stitch* fall colour line up. You're the first knitter in Harmony Lake to see this colour." I hand her a skein of *Pumpkin Spice Everything* from one of Rita's yarn bins. Mrs. Willows is an avid knitter.

"Thank you, Megan!" Mrs. Willows says, squeezing and petting the skein of yarn. "There's no need to thank us. You would've done the same."

"Mrs. Willows, did you notice anything unique about the car that attacked me?"

"Unique how?" she asks. "It was unique how determined the driver was to catch up to you and hit you."

"Anything about the car specifically? Other than the license plate number I mean. How many people did you see in the car?"

"We only saw one person, but we didn't get a good look at them. We were behind them. Before the craziness started, I did comment to Henry about the clever bumper sticker on the back of the white car. I teased him about getting one for The Beater."

"Do you remember what it said?" I ask.

"I sure do," she replies. "**Stay alive, don't knit and drive**. And it had a cute cartoon ball of yarn."

I reach into my tote bag and pull out the bumper sticker that I didn't give to Rita.

"Like this one?" I hand her the black bumper sticker with white letters.

"Exactly! Except the one on the car was white with black letters." She extends her hand to give it back to me.

"You keep it." I wave her hand away. "For The Beater." I wink.

Mrs. Willows and I wait patiently while Mr. Willows and April discuss how our cell phones are always listening to us and big marketing companies use our conversations to decide what ads we see on the internet.

I reply to a check-in text from Eric and notice the time on my phone. When they come up for air, I remind April that we have to be on our way. We say goodbye, and I walk quickly to the SUV before either April or Mr. Willows comes up with another conspiracy theory they need to discuss.

I APOLOGIZE to Sophie for missing her lunchtime walk while I toss some left-over chicken into some left-over salad for a late lunch. While I eat, I text Eric to let him know I'm home, then I text Connie to make sure Knitorious is running smoothly in my absence. Of course, it is.

I miss my routine. It's only been three days, but I feel like what happened on Monday has upended my entire life. I should be at Knitorious. I want to be at Knitorious. I love my job and it's our busy season. I haven't had a coffee from Latte Da since Saturday, and I think I might be having withdrawal symptoms. I'm driving an unfamiliar SUV I don't like, Eric has practically moved in, Adam is here more than either he or I like, and there's a patrol car blocking my driveway. Sophie is used to going to work and seeing people, but instead, she's stuck in the house all the time except when she gets short walks within earshot and eyeshot of the house. I feel like a background character in my own life right now.

I finish my salad and tidy up. I'd planned to drop the yarn, and the baby hats and mitts off at Knitorious, but when I check the time, I decide against it. If I run into anyone and stop to chat, I'll be late for my meeting with Darby. Instead, I settle on the living room sofa and knit on a sock while I reflect on the events of the past few days and try to make sense of them.

"Is that your courtesy car?" Eric asks as soon as he steps into the house.

"It sure is," I reply.

"Do you like it? How does it drive?" He sits next to me on the sofa and kisses my forehead. "Hi." He smiles.

"Hi." I smile back. "It feels like I'm driving a battleship. It's way too big, and I can't get my phone to connect," I complain. "Why are you here? Don't you have witnesses to interview."

"We're meeting Darby at five, right? Where else would I be?" he asks as though he's reminding me of something I forgot.

I don't recall Darby mentioning that Eric would be joining us.

"If you're busy with the case, I can meet Darby alone and fill you in later."

"I want to be here. You first, then work, remember? Besides, Darby and I need to talk about the cases," he replies.

Does this mean they've found evidence connecting the cases? I'm about to ask him when an unfamiliar notification sound comes from his pocket. Eric pulls out his phone and unlocks the screen. "The coroner's preliminary findings just arrived in my inbox." He looks at the screen for a moment, then tucks the phone back into his pocket.

"I thought it was your hourly alarm to check on me," I tease.

I might be teasing him, but I'm impressed he remembers to text me every hour in the midst of everything else he has going on.

"I don't need an alarm to remind me to think about you." He smiles. "I think about you all the time. You only know about it once an hour because I text you." He winks. "What I need is an alarm to remind me to think about something else."

I'm about to lean in and kiss him when my phone dings.

"Is that your hourly alarm to answer my text?" Eric jokes.

"Give me a minute to come up with a reply as romantic as yours," I jest as I reach for my phone.

It's true. Eric is more romantically inclined than me. Spontaneous romantic gestures and saying sweet things comes naturally to him whereas I tend to express my feelings through humour and awkwardness.

April: All set for tomorrow. I'll meet you at the store at lunchtime.

"It's April," I say, typing a reply to her text. "She's confirming our plans for tomorrow."

"What's happening tomorrow?" he asks.

"I'm working in the morning," I reply. "I'm going in early because I didn't have time to drop off the yarn that I picked up today. Connie and Marla deserve a morning off, and I need a dose of my normal life. I'm only scheduled to work half the day. I'll leave at lunch."

Eric looks at me with narrowed eyes, and the muscles around his jaw clench and unclench. "To tell you the truth, I'm surprised you've humoured me this long. What are you and April doing in the afternoon?"

Saved by the bell. I smile and wave to Darby through the living room window when I get up to let him in.

CHAPTER 16

DARBY SITUATES himself on the sofa and opens his leather folio. I snap my fingers and motion for Sophie to remove her front paws from his knee. She complies, then jumps up onto the sofa and sits next to him.

"It's OK," Darby says to me while he looks at Sophie. "Sophie knows I like it when she sits with me." He scratches between her ears, and they both look quite pleased with the arrangement. Darby turns to me. "It was a surprise running into you at Ms. McConnell's house this afternoon, Megan."

"It was a surprise running into you too," I reply. "Almost as big a surprise as finding out it was Rita's car that was lurking around my house and chased me on the highway."

He raises an index finger. "I never confirmed that the car your neighbour reported and the car on the highway are the same car."

"No, you didn't," I agree. "I did."

"How?" he asks, sitting back and crossing his arms in front of his chest.

"The bumper sticker," I reply. "Phillip and Mrs. Willows both identified the bumper sticker, and Rita confirmed her car had the same bumper sticker. She bought it at my store months ago."

"Impressive," he says, sitting up straight and uncrossing his arms. "What else did you and Ms. McConnell talk about?"

"You first," I insist. "You said you had information about my case?"

He nods and flips the pages in his folio until he finds what he's looking for. "For starters, you're right about the white car. We believe the car that your neighbour reported stalking your house, and the car that attacked you, are the same car. We also believe the car we found later that evening is the same car. The paint transfer on both vehicles is a match."

"I think I understand, but can you explain, please?" I ask.

"Of course. When the white car made contact with your vehicle, some of its paint was transferred to your car, and some of your car's paint was transferred to the white car. Our forensics department was able to confirm that the paint samples from both vehicles match."

"I understand, thank you."

"We believe Hayden Lee is the person who shot at you. In addition to the gunshot residue on his hand, we were able to match his DNA to trace DNA collected from the wig-hat and Groucho Marx disguise that were found in the car with him. No other DNA samples were found on the items."

"So, it *was* Hayden Lee who was killed in the white car?" I ask.

Beside me, Eric mumbles, "Good," under his breath. Darby either doesn't hear it or chooses to ignore it.

"Yes, it was." Darby nods. "And the bullet the coroner removed from his chest was fired from the same gun as the bullet our forensics team removed from your car door."

Hayden Lee was shot in the chest, too, like other-Meaghan. Another coincidence or the same shooter?

"Who killed Hayden Lee?" I ask.

"We're working on it," Darby assures me. "But for now, your case is closed. We've solved it. We know who did it."

"But we don't know why," I remind him. "Or who Hayden was working with."

"We don't know for certain he was working with anyone. As for the motive"—he shrugs—"it's nice to know why people do the things they do, but sometimes we never know. Sometimes all we have is speculation."

"What do you speculate Hayden's motive was for shooting at me?"

"I don't know," Darby admits. "I'm hoping it will become clearer as I continue to investigate Hayden's murder."

I nod. "You said my case is 'closed for now.' What does that mean?"

"It means if the investigation into Mr. Lee's murder ties into your case, I'll re-open it."

I step out of the room to get refreshments and give Darby and Eric a few minutes to talk. When I return, Eric has an open file folder on his lap, and he's shuffling through papers.

"I haven't read the full report yet," Eric says as he leans forward and passes a sheet of paper to Darby, "but the bullet the coroner removed from other-Meaghan was fired from the same gun that shot Hayden Lee and Megan's car."

"Other-Meaghan?" Darby asks.

"That's what we've been calling my Meaghan Martelle. I mean my case. To avoid confusion."

Darby nods.

"Does anyone else think it's more than a coincidence that Rita and other-Meaghan were close, and it was Rita's car that was involved in my incident?" I pause for a response. Nothing. "Or that Hayden Lee was the groundskeeper across the street from Rita's house?" I attempt another dramatic pause. No reaction. "At the house owned by other-Meaghan's business partner and best friend?" I look back and forth from Darby to Eric.

"How did you find out all of this?" Darby asks. He looks at Eric. "Did you tell her this information?"

Eric shakes his head and smiles.

"April and I were at Rita's house today, remember?" I jog his memory. "Rita told us."

"What else?" Eric lifts his chin toward me and smiles as he clicks the top of his pen and prepares to take notes.

"Something happened between other-Meaghan and Wayne a few years ago. I don't know the details, but it had to be significant because it coincides with other-Meaghan pivoting her life and changing direction. She and Wayne stopped trying to have a family, and she became hyper-focused on her business."

"Wayne and other-Meaghan seemed happy. Everyone I've talked to says they were loving and had a close relationship."

"Lots of marriages that appear happy aren't." Sadly, I speak from experience. "Did any of them mention Wayne and other-Meaghan starting a family?"

Eric shakes his head. "They had custody of his kids fifty percent of the time. From all accounts she loved them, and they loved her. I'm told she was a doting, proud stepmother."

"Rita mentioned that other-Meaghan loved Wayne's kids. Rita even has photos of them in her living room. Also, according to Rita, other-Meaghan and Wayne tried to get pregnant right after they got married. She said other-Meaghan wanted children badly, and they tried for a long time. Rita said one day, abruptly, they just stopped trying and other-Meaghan didn't like to talk about it. She didn't sound certain, though. I get the feeling Rita doesn't know the whole story."

I wait while Eric jots down a few notes.

"Anything else leave an impression on you?" Eric asks.

"Lots of things, like why isn't Karla Bell mentioned on the *Just Task Me!* website? Rita said Karla and other-Meaghan are BFFs and business partners, but other-

Meaghan is the only person on the website who's mentioned by name."

"Some people like to keep a low profile. They're happier behind the scenes," Eric replies, shrugging.

"Like whoever was working with Hayden Lee?" I ask.

"You're right, she's good," Darby says to Eric. Then he looks at me. "Eric said you have a way of getting people to talk to you. He said when you speak, I should listen. I should have realized it when you had me talking about my fountain pen collection and how I feel about my second wife within five minutes of shaking your hand."

I think I'm blushing.

Pretty soon, it's 6:30 P.M. and the thud of a car door closing in the driveway gets our attention. Adam is dropping off Hannah after work. He backs out of the driveway as she enters the house. I introduce her to Darby, and she says *hi* to us, then sweeps out of the room like a Tasmanian devil. She's going out with her friends tonight, and she's in a rush to shower and get ready.

As he closes his folio and starts to stand up, I ask Darby quietly, "If my case is closed, does that mean you've eliminated Adam as a suspect? And his girlfriend?" If there is a girlfriend.

Darby looks at me. "I have found no evidence linking Adam or anyone associated with Adam to your case," he says quietly, neither confirming nor denying the existence of a girlfriend.

Darby must have kids. He seems aware that I don't want Hannah to hear us. While Darby puts on his shoes, he and Eric talk at the door, and I clear the remnants of refreshments and dishes from the living room.

I rejoin them when their voices take on a less official tone. "Do you have kids, Darby?" He bends his thumb and holds up his right hand. "Four?" I ask.

He nods. "Four. My oldest is seventeen and my youngest is five. Two girls and two boys spread over three wives."

"Wow," I say. "You're a busy man."

"Not too busy." He grins. "How about your friend, April, is she busy?"

"She's married," I reply.

"I don't mind," he chuckles, but I'm not sure he's kidding.

"Happily," I add.

A few of Hannah's friends picked her up, and they're on their way to Harmony Hills to see a movie. She wanted to take the giant SUV and was disappointed when I told her she can't drive it because the rental company doesn't allow drivers under the age of twenty. Apparently, when she's a lawyer, she'll confront such blatant examples of age-based discrimination and make the world a fairer place. Oh, to have the idealism of an eighteen-year-old.

Eric is working from home tonight. He says he wants to read the report the coroner emailed and go through the information about my case that Darby promised to send tonight.

We order dinner from Ho Lee Chow and eat in front of the TV. I'm half-watching a *Forensic Files* marathon and eating my second helping of Cantonese lo mein. Eric is beside me on the sofa, eating and reading on his laptop.

"Do you want the rest of my lo mein?" I ask.

"Sure," he replies, extending his plate toward me without looking away from his screen.

I scrape the rest of my noodles and vegetables onto his plate and get up to get myself another helping of Moo Koo Gai Pan.

"I thought you were full?" Eric asks, still looking at his computer screen.

He takes a forkful of food from the plate he's balancing on his knee.

"I'm full of lo mein," I clarify. "Do you want anything while I'm up?"

"Egg roll, please," he replies.

"Whatever you're reading must be interesting." Carefully, like I'm playing Jenga, I place the egg roll on his plate as close to the middle as possible, so I don't throw off the delicate balance and cause it to crash to the floor.

"I'm working on other-Meaghan's timeline," he explains. "I'm piecing together where she was and who she was with in the days leading up to her murder." He moves the plate from his knee to the coffee table in front of him and tilts his laptop so I can see the screen. "Something else you and other-Meaghan have in common." He points to the image on the screen. "She used the calendar on her phone, but she also used a paper planner. Some appointments and errands that she had were only in the paper planner, not in the calendar on her phone. Why do you think she'd do that?"

"Could be lots of reasons." I tip the screen so I can see the image. It's a two-page spread from other-Meaghan's planner; the day she died and the day before. "May I?" I ask, gripping the laptop.

"Sure." Eric nudges the computer toward me.

With the laptop on my lap, I look carefully at other-Meaghan's planner pages. Her writing is enviable. Neat, legible, and consistent.

"I can tell you why I do it," I finally reply. "I plan my week in advance. Every Sunday I transfer the appointments from the calendar on my phone to my planner. If something comes up through the week and it doesn't affect anyone else who has access to my online calendar, I don't bother adding it to my phone. I just write it in my planner. My planner is my main calendar, the one I reference on a daily basis."

"That makes sense." Eric nods. "But other-Meaghan

shares her online calendar with other people, so she could also be omitting certain appointments that she doesn't want them to know about."

"True," I agree, "but depending on where she keeps her planner, those people would see it, anyway. Though, looking at her planner pages, she seems to be the only person who writes in it most of the time." I gesture to the neat handwriting on the two-page spread. "The handwriting is consistent and in the same ink."

"Except for this one." He points to an entry on the Tuesday page of the spread: *2 P.M. Hav-a-nap Carlo HL.*

"Someone else wrote that," I point out. "The handwriting is completely different, and it's written in blue ink. Carlo said she blamed her assistant for the mix-up. Do you know who wrote this appointment in her planner?"

Eric shakes his head. "Not yet. She doesn't have an assistant. Her employees have titles like, 'concierge', and 'event planner.' No one admits to being other-Meaghan's assistant or knows who she was referring to. But they all insist they didn't write this appointment. I might ask for handwriting samples tomorrow."

"Does the forensics department have a handwriting analysis expert?" I ask.

"I don't know. I don't think so," Eric admits. "It's less about having the handwriting analyzed, and more about watching their reactions when I ask for the sample and then watching their demeanour while they write. It's not tangible evidence, but it might help me decide who to focus on."

"Smart," I say.

"I try." He smiles.

"May I look at her other planner pages?"

He nods.

I scroll through the photos of other-Meaghan's planner, both admiring how organized she was and taking mental notes of a few planner hacks I might try in my own planner.

My planner is my brain on paper and, if anything ever happens to me, the right people would be able to use it to piece together a lot about me and my life. They'd know where I was, when I was there, who I was with, even what I ate, and what I was thinking about.

Other-Meaghan seems to rely on her planner to the same extent. She has pages of lists organized by location. Tasks at home, at the office, and errands. Her tasks are colour coded. She has charts for tracking personal things, like how much sleep she gets, which books she's read, and which ones she plans to read next. She also has charts to track business goals, like how many new clients she's signed and how many subscribers are on the *Just Task Me!* email list. I have planner envy.

"Did you notice these stars in the corner of every day this week?" I ask, pointing to the small, hand-drawn stars in the upper corner of each page.

Eric nods. "They seem to coincide with the weeks Wayne's kids are with them."

"I thought they might," I reply. "That means she died during their week. The kids would've been at their house when Wayne found out."

"He phoned his ex-wife to come and stay with them while he talked to us," Eric confirms.

"Have you eliminated Wayne as a suspect?"

"Not yet," he replies. "You know the spouse and the people closest to the victim are always at the top of the list."

"If Wayne wanted to kill his wife, wouldn't he choose a week when his kids were with their mother?"

"Not if he wants us to think it couldn't be him because he wouldn't do it with his kids around. People do extreme things to look innocent, and someone who is capable of murder probably isn't worried about traumatizing their children."

"Well, I'm not sure if this means anything, but it's interesting," I say, pointing to a hand-drawn box on one of the planner pages. "Other-Meaghan planned her meals in advance. She drew one of these boxes on each daily page and the letters B, L, & D inside the box probably mean breakfast, lunch, and dinner." I point to the box on today's page. "Tonight, she planned to have barbecued chicken skewers and pasta salad."

"Lots of people plan their meals in advance, don't they? You do."

"I know," I agree, scrolling through the photos until I land on a daily planner page from the previous week. "But other-Meaghan only planned dinners for the weeks Wayne's kids were with them. All the weeks with stars have dinner plans, and all the weeks without stars only have breakfast and lunch plans."

"Hmmm." Eric takes the laptop from me and puts it on his lap, scrolling through the photos of planner pages. "Why would she do that?"

"Maybe when it was just her and Wayne, he was responsible for cooking dinner. Or maybe they threw together whatever they had on hand and called it dinner."

"Or maybe they didn't eat dinner together if his kids weren't around," Eric suggests.

"Rita said other-Meaghan was ambitious. Maybe she worked through dinner on those nights. Who knows? I just thought it was interesting."

"It is," Eric agrees.

CHAPTER 17

Thursday, July 9th

I'm an early riser. Not intentionally, it's just how I'm made. My internal clock likes to wake me up with the sun. Sometimes before the sun, depending on the time of year. I'm used to being the first person awake in my house. I don't mind. The quietude of the early morning gives me time to ease into the day without feeling rushed. This week, however, Eric wakes up before me every morning. It's amazing how he's able to function through the day, considering how little sleep he gets.

This morning is no different. I'm up bright and early, showered, slathered in SPF 60, moisturized, and dressed. I want to look respectable today but still dress appropriately for the never-ending heat wave we're stuck in. I chose my black, sleeveless shift dress, and black high-heeled sandals. I completed the look with the gold, floating-heart necklace Hannah and Adam gave me for my thirty-fifth birthday.

When I open the back door, Sophie launches herself into the backyard like she's being released from prison. She lets out a few high-pitched barks and prances around the yard proudly when her fearsome canine presence causes the birds to scatter from our lawn.

No sign of Eric. Weird. I check the dining room. No Eric. His messenger bag and laptop are still here, so he hasn't gone far.

I open the cabinet above the coffeemaker and start to go through the basket of coffee pods, then stop myself, and put the basket back in the cabinet. I'm saving myself for a coffee Frappuccino with extra whipped cream from Latte Da. Last night I promised myself it will be the next drop of caffeine to pass my lips. I haven't had one since Saturday, and I intend to savour every drop.

Closing the cabinet door, I see it. A sticky note stuck to the coffeemaker. It would've been impossible to put a pod in the machine without noticing it. *Gone for a run, back soon,* in Eric's barely legible scrawl. That's one mystery solved.

While Sophie eats her breakfast, I nudge my sleeping daughter and tell her I'm leaving for work. I remind her that her dad will be here soon to take her to work, and I'll pick her up tonight. She acknowledges me, but I don't think she hears me, so I send it as a text in the chez Martel group chat.

I jot a quick message on a stickie note and stick it on Eric's laptop, *Gone to work xo.*

"Ready, Soph?" As we leave, I warn her about the change in altitude she's about to experience getting into the giant SUV.

AFTER SAFELY DISEMBARKING from the giant SUV, Sophie and I —mostly I—retrieve the plastic bins of yarn from the trunk and put them on the pavement. As the trunk closes, I hear a voice call my name. Not again. Please, not again.

Something touches my shoulder, and I almost jump out of my skin!

"You scared the life out of me, Phillip!" Perturbed, I swat his hand.

"Sorry, Megan. I called out to you, but you didn't hear me." He bends down to rub Sophie before she pops a vein trying to get his attention.

"Oh, I heard you," I say. "I thought I was having a flashback."

"Right. I'm sorry. I didn't think."

"Don't worry about it." I toss my keys on top of the plastic bins and bend at the knees to pick them up.

"Here, let me help you with that." Phillip bends at the knees and picks up the keys I just dropped.

"Thanks," I say, lifting the featherweight bins.

At the back door, Phillip unlocks it with my key and holds it open for me. Sophie runs inside, and I drop the bins in the kitchenette.

"Did you get my text?" I ask.

"Yup. I'll throw a couple of arrangements together for you and drop them off later this morning. What time do you need them?"

"April and I are leaving at lunch."

"No problem," Phillip assures me. "Do you know where you're going? Do you have her address?"

I shake my head. "I was going to ask our mutual friend, Rita."

"I'll give it to you. I've had quite a few orders for her. Just don't tell anyone where you got it." He smiles.

"Thank you, Phillip." I twist my keys out of the lock and head into the store.

THIS IS the first walk Sophie and I have had together since Monday morning. I've missed our walks.

We take our time meandering through the park, stopping

every few steps for Sophie to sniff the next tree we encounter, and enjoy the warm breeze off the lake. It's not even 8:00 A.M. and the temperature is already approaching the threshold of uncomfortably hot.

I REFRESH Sophie's water bowl. "I'll be back in a few minutes, Soph. I really need this coffee," I tell her as I place the full bowl on the floor.

Keys and phone in hand, I leave through the back door and head down Water Street toward Latte Da where I join my fellow caffeine addicts at the end of the long line. My phone dings. It's the chez Martel group chat.

Adam: Shoot! Sorry, I was driving and just saw this. Meg, I thought you were driving Hannah to work today. I'm in court all morning. It's in the family calendar.

We really got our wires crossed this morning. I haven't checked the calendar since Sunday. Adam, Hannah, and I still share an online calendar. If one of us has an appointment that affects another Martel, we're supposed to tag each other so we get a notification. I didn't receive a notification about Adam's court date.

Me: No worries! Good luck in court.

Adam replies with a thumbs-up emoji. I step out of line to go back to the store and get the car so I can drive Hannah to work when my phone dings again.

Eric: Hannah showed me the texts. I can take her.

I step back, reclaiming my place in line.

Me: Are you sure? I know you're busy.

Eric: I have to go to the station and it's on my way.

Me: Thank you! You're a life saver.

Eric: Just another benefit of me staying here. Winky face emoji.

I like it when Eric stays over. Occasionally. But he's been at my house three nights in a row, and I'm not used to it. Especially with Hannah home. I appreciate him looking out for me; it gives both of us peace of mind, but I think it gives him more peace of mind than me. I understand he's a cop, and his urge to serve and protect is strong, but I'm beginning to worry that he likes this arrangement a bit too much. I get the feeling he'd be happy to extend his stay as long as necessary, and I'm not sure we share the same definition of necessary.

"Hey, Megan, how are you?"

Hearing my name brings me back to the here and now.

"Hi, Carlo, I don't usually run into you here."

"I don't usually come here," he replies. "I was next door at the pharmacy and came in to grab a coffee. I didn't realize you were in front of me until you stepped out of line, then back in."

"Thought I had a crisis," I explain, "but it was averted. How are you doing after everything that happened on Tuesday?"

He sighs. "Not great. That's actually why I'm here. I haven't slept in two nights. My doctor called in a prescription to help me sleep. I just picked it up next door."

"I know that feeling," I sympathize. "Sometimes it's hard to turn off the brain, right? I'm sorry you're struggling."

We shuffle forward with the rest of the line.

"Every time I close my eyes, I see her. In the car. Eyes open. Arms out. Blood soaked."

I nod. "It's traumatic. There are people you can talk to. Experts who can help you process everything."

He nods. "My doctor referred me to someone. I have an appointment early next week."

"Good," I say.

I place my order, pay with the app on my phone, and move down the counter to wait for it. A couple of minutes later, Carlo joins me.

"That's not the only part I keep reliving," he says. "I relive the brief conversation we had when she came into the office, and even the conversation I had with her assistant on the phone the day before."

The day before? The day before was the day Hayden Lee tried to shoot me. I don't know why, but I assumed the appointment with Carlo was booked before that. Days or even weeks before.

The barista hands over my coffee Frappuccino with extra whip and I thank him. Then I turn to Carlo.

"Her assistant phoned you on Monday to book the appointment?" I confirm.

A different barista hands Carlo his coffee. I wait while he thanks her, then we turn and walk out of the café together.

"Yeah. She phoned me the day before." He starts sauntering up Water Street in the direction I need to go, and I saunter with him.

"Do you remember what time?"

"Seven minutes after four in the afternoon," he replies confidently.

After the shooter's bullet missed me on the highway.

"That's pretty precise, Carlo."

"It's on the call display on the motel phone, Blocked Number with the time right underneath it," he explains. "Also, it's kind of embedded in my brain."

"Are you sure it wasn't other-Meaghan who called you?"

He looks at me with a furrowed brow and puckered mouth. "Who?"

I shake my head. "Sorry, we've been calling the victim other-Meaghan." He still looks confused. "To avoid confusion because my name is also Megan."

"Right. That makes sense." He nods. "It wasn't the same voice. The person who called me was definitely a woman, but it wasn't the same voice. I'd bet my life on it." We stop walking in front of The Pharmer's market, and he adds, "Also, they had different laughs."

"Oh?" This piques my interest. "You made them laugh?"

He swallows a sip of coffee. "Not intentionally," he clarifies. "The woman on the phone said someone from her company wanted to meet with me to discuss the motel's concierge needs. She said offering concierge services could increase bookings, improve online reviews, and even earn the hotel some extra money. I said, 'That's great and all, but this is our busy season. I barely have time to pee. If I'm going to find time to sit down with anyone, it'll be candidates for all the housekeeping positions I have to fill.'" He shrugs. "She giggled."

"Why did other-Meaghan laugh?" I ask.

"Her laugh was more like an embarrassed chuckle," he specifies. "I told her we didn't have an appointment, that I declined her offer on the phone. That's when she said, 'I'm sorry. My assistant must've put it in my calendar accidentally.' Then she said, 'If you change your mind and we can do anything for you, please call me.' That's when she handed me her card. I took it and said, 'If you decide to offer housekeeping and turn-down service, I'm in.' She did a nervous chuckle and left."

"I'm sure they'll catch whoever did this," I assure him.

"I am too," he agrees. "The detective seems really determined. Anyway, I'm parked in the lot behind the pharmacy. I'll see you later, Megan."

"Bye, Carlo. Take care."

CHAPTER 18

WITH LESS THAN five minutes until it's time to open the store, I take Rita's empty yarn bins to the kitchenette and leave them by the back door. It's the only way I'll remember to take them with me when I leave.

All of her yarn is unpacked, added to inventory, and shelved. I even remembered to include the skein I gave to Mrs. Willows.

The fall yarn colours are creeping into the summer yarn colours and slowly taking over the shelves. It might be early July, but knitters tend to knit in advance. Many are knitting items they plan to wear this fall, and even to give as Christmas gifts for loved ones. Because of this, the prominent colours in the store are always a little off-season.

I take the baby items I knitted for the charity knitting guild out of my bag and place them on one of the shelves under the counter. Then I grab my phone from the counter and type a quick text to Eric.

Me: Did Hannah get to work OK?

She was due to start an hour ago. I assume if there was a problem, I would have heard about it by now. But it doesn't hurt to check.

Eric: All good. I even got her there a few minutes early.
Me: Thank you. 143.

"It's showtime," I say to Sophie in the same sing-song voice Connie uses when she says it.

As soon as I unlock the door and turn the sign from CLOSED to OPEN, the first customers walk in the door. Oh, how I've missed this, even though it's only been two days.

There's a difference between *wanting* to do something and *having* to do something. Normally, I would enjoy two days away from work during the busy season—if it were by choice. But because I was compelled to take the time off, I resented not being here. I think the same might be true about Eric. Normally, when we spend a lot of time together, I'm happy he's around, and a little sad when it's over. But our current togetherness is forced on us by reasons beyond our control, and that makes me feel pressured. It's no one's fault, but I hope we can get back to normal soon.

"Good morning, my dear!" Suddenly Connie is behind the counter, stashing her purse underneath.

I've heard that time flies when you're having fun, but it feels like the store has only been open for an hour.

"Is it lunch time already? It feels like I just unlocked the door." I reach for my phone on the counter and check the time. She's early.

"I decided to come in early and help out," Connie explains, already ringing up a customer's purchase.

"You didn't have to do that," I tell her. "It's your morning off. You should have your feet up. I'm fine on my own."

"I wanted to come in. Besides, the store is a two-person job right now. It's tourist season."

"Well, thank you for coming in, but if you want to take a break at any time, please do."

I'm about to put my phone down on the counter—I regret not choosing a dress with pockets—when it dings. Eric.

"Here we go again," I mumble as I type a reply to his hourly check-in.

"Do I sense trouble in paradise?" Connie asks flippantly, but her concerned facial expression betrays her.

"Not trouble," I assure her. "More like a rough patch. Not really rough. A bump in the road. A small bump. A speed bump." I wave dismissively.

"Don't do that." Connie points her finger at me and waggles it.

"What?" I ask, genuinely unsure what she's talking about.

"That thing you do where you dismiss your own feelings so no one will get upset."

She's right. It is what I do. Before I can respond to her accusation, my phone dings again.

Eric: If I stop by the store, do you have a few minutes to talk? Or is it too busy?

He doesn't say it's important, but I get the feeling it is. Usually, if he needs to talk, he suggests a time when we can meet and talk uninterrupted.

"What's wrong?" Connie asks. "Is it Hannah?"

I shake my head. "No, it's Eric. He wants to talk. I think it's important."

"Then talk to him," she urges.

Me: Of course, but we might be interrupted.

In between helping customers and ringing up sales, I explain to Connie how I feel like I'm not in control of any aspect of my life right now. She's a great listener and always provides thoughtful advice gleaned from experience.

"It is not selfish to put your *needs* ahead of other people's *wants*. In fact, it's necessary so you can take care of your family and your business." Connie is profoundly wise. "Selfish is when you put your wants ahead of someone else's needs. You're not doing that. You never do that. Eric doesn't do that either. You both get so caught up trying to make each other happy that sometimes it has the opposite effect."

"I don't know what I'd do without you!" I throw my arms around Connie, and we sway together for a moment while a customer waits to ask a question.

"He's behind you," she whispers in my ear, then she lets go and helps the patient customer.

I turn around and smile.

"Wow," he says. "That dress is very flattering." He stands up from greeting Sophie.

"Thank you." I take his hand and lead him to the harvest table at the back of the store. "Is something up? I got the feeling from your text that this couldn't wait."

"I'm not sure." He sounds confused. "First, can you look at this and tell me if it's familiar?" He reaches into his messenger bag and pulls out a plastic evidence bag containing a partial skein of yarn.

"It's yarn," I state the painfully obvious. He hands me the bag. I squish it and look at the messy tangle of coral-coloured yarn inside. There are some brown stains on the yarn and few dried brown clumps in the evidence bag. Mud, I assume. "All yarn looks familiar to me. Can you be more specific? Where did you get this and why is it in an evidence bag?"

He takes a seat at the table, and I pull out a chair and sit next to him.

"Forensics was processing the car we believe other-Meaghan's murderer drove, and they found this under one of the seats," he explains.

"Was the murderer's car stolen?" I ask. "Maybe the yarn belongs to the car's owner."

He shakes his head. "It doesn't. They have no idea where it came from." He looks around for eavesdroppers, then moves in closer. I move in closer, too, so he can speak quietly. "I think it was planted for us to find. Even if the murderer is an avid knitter, it's unlikely they took their knitting with them on this particular errand."

"Unless their knitting is always in their bag and it fell out and went under the seat," I suggest. "It's happened to me more than once."

"No needles," Eric replies. "Knitting is usually attached to needles, isn't it?"

I nod. He's right. I look at the yarn. "It looks like a worsted weight, maybe an Aran." If I could touch it, I'd know the weight for certain because I'd wrap it around a needle and count the wraps per inch. I look up at him. "Was there a ball band or tag with it? Have you had it analyzed?"

"No identifying information," he answers my first question. "I'm taking it to be analyzed now, but I thought I'd ask your opinion first because the forensics people won't be able to tell me anything for a day or two."

I look at the yarn again and squeeze the bag. "This is just a guess. I could be completely wrong," I warn. "I'm just thinking out loud here." I look at Eric, waiting for him to acknowledge my disclaimers before I say anything else.

He nods, so I continue, "I think it's a blend of fibres. I can't say which fibres exactly, but the halo makes me think there's alpaca or angora in it. Looking more closely, it could even be a DK weight, but the halo makes it look thicker. It could have acrylic content. Sometimes acrylics have a halo. This is a bright colour. The dyer probably used an acid-based dye to achieve it." I nudge the bag toward him and look up. He's busily jotting down notes.

"What does halo mean?" he asks, putting down his pen.

"Do you see the bits of fuzz around the yarn? It kind of looks like the yarn is a bit furry or shedding? That's the halo. Some people call it a haze. The amount of halo varies by the type and breed of animal the fibre is from."

He makes notes. I wait.

"Can you explain about the acid-based dye?"

"There's a trend now for knitters and dyers to be as environmentally friendly as possible, so there are more yarns than ever using eco-friendly methods to process and dye fibre. It's difficult to achieve a colour this bright and rich with most plant-based and environmentally friendly dyes, though that's changing. This bright coral colour is likely achieved with an acid dye."

He writes. I wait.

"Did it fall in the mud?" I ask.

"I have no idea. There was mud everywhere. Mud in the car and mud around the car. But it wasn't rainy and there was no mud in the area the car was found. There also wasn't any mud in the Hav-a-nap parking lot." In a whisper, he adds, "Does Rita McConnell carry yarn like this?"

Is Rita a suspect?

"Rita has several different yarn bases, and she likes to introduce new colours every season. This doesn't look like one of her regular colours. She mostly dyes sock yarn. This yarn is thicker than sock yarn. But she's been dyeing yarn for decades, so this could be similar to something she's offered in the past."

He closes his notebook and clicks his pen. "Thank you."

"You're welcome." I sense he has more to say. "What else?"

He sits up and looks around. So do I. While we were talking, Marla arrived at the store, and she's helping Connie serve customers and ring up sales. I feel a little less guilty for abandoning Connie.

"Can we talk in the back?" Eric jerks his head toward the door and gets up from the table.

"Sure." I stand up and push in my chair, then follow him into the back room.

He closes the door behind us.

"What's wrong? You're acting weird and it's scaring me."

He takes my hands. "Nothing's wrong. There's no reason to be scared." He smiles. "I was reading the information that Darby sent over about your case..." He stops talking.

It's like he can't find the right words.

"Getting a little scared again," I say.

"*If* Adam has a girlfriend, I know who she is," he confesses.

"*If* he has a girlfriend, you know who she is." Obviously, Adam has a girlfriend.

"No matter how I said it, you'd make the connection that there's a girlfriend."

"OK." I nod. "Why is this urgent? Is she relevant to my attempted shooting?"

"No. I'm uncomfortable knowing about it without you knowing I know. It feels like a secret, and I don't want us to have secrets. I don't want you to think I'm in cahoots with your ex to keep something from you."

In every case Eric investigates that I somehow manage to get tangled up in, we reach a point where the collision of our relationship with his job tweaks his insecurities. I have to reassure him that we won't break up because of his job.

Part of the reason his first marriage ended was the strain of his job on their relationship. Now, because of his job, he's privy to information about my ex that I don't know. I understand why he'd worry that keeping it from me could cause a problem between us. It wouldn't, but I understand his concern.

"Are you OK?" He looks concerned.

I nod.

I'm tempted to ask Eric what her name is, but I know he'd tell me, and I don't want to put him in a compromising position. He's already in an unfair position, stuck between his girlfriend and her almost-ex-husband who also happens to be his friend. I understand now that my case would have been a conflict of interest for Eric in more ways than one. I take a deep breath and exhale audibly.

"Thank you for telling me," I finally say. "I appreciate your honesty. I don't care if you tell Adam I know. I don't want you stuck in the middle," I say blankly.

I'm still dumbfounded by the revelation and can't snap out of it.

"I'm not worried about upsetting Adam." Gently, he tips my chin upward and looks in my eyes. "It's understandable if you have feelings about this, Megan," he says slowly and gently. "You and Adam were married for twenty years. It must be hard for you to see him with someone else."

Wait! WHAT?!

"No." I squeeze his hands. "That's not it. Not at all," I reassure him. "I couldn't care less if he's seeing someone."

"Are you sure?"

"Positive," I reply. "It's the secrecy. I don't like secrets. Why would he keep his girlfriend a secret? I can kind of understand him not telling me, but why wouldn't he tell Hannah? This woman leaves things in his apartment, but he won't acknowledge her existence to his family."

This isn't the first secret Adam has kept. When we were newly separated, he had a relationship with a married woman, and instead of finding out from him, I found out from blackmailers. His secret turned out to be deadly and was the reason I met Eric.

Eric still looks worried. He's not convinced.

Even in heels, I'm shorter than him, so on my tippy toes, I comb my fingers through his hair and kiss him. A knock at the door interrupts us. "Honestly, I'm fine," I whisper as I lower myself to my natural height.

He reaches behind me and opens the door.

"Sorry to interrupt," Connie croons. "Phillip is here to see Megan." Grinning, she turns and walks away.

CHAPTER 19

"They're beautiful, Phillip. Thank you,"

"No worries," he replies, fussing with the two floral arrangements on the harvest table. He places two enclosure cards with envelopes on the table next to the flowers and presses a third card into my palm. "The information we discussed." He winks.

"Thanks," I say.

"I have to get back to the shop." Phillip turns to leave.

"Email me the invoice, and I'll e-transfer the money," I call after him as he leaves. He doesn't acknowledge me.

"Are the flowers related to your plans with April this afternoon?" Eric asks.

"Maybe," I reply coyly. "Do you want to know?"

He raises his hand in a stop motion. "I don't think I do. You can fill me in later if I need to know. But judging by your black outfit and the bouquets of lilies, I think I have a pretty good idea."

I smile. "You are a detective," I tease.

"Please be careful," he implores. He gathers his bag and puts it over his shoulder. "I'll text you in an hour."

"About that," I say. He stops and looks at me. "Can we

ease up on the regular texts? If anything happens, I'll get hold of you."

"I guess," he shrugs. He sounds disappointed.

"Darby closed my case. The man who shot at me is dead. I miss texting you because I want to, not because it's part of a safety protocol. And it must be inconvenient for you to stop whatever you're doing and text me every hour of the day."

"Fine," he agrees curtly. "But texting you is never an inconvenience." Awkward pause. "Are we ditching the safe word, too?"

"Would you mind? You still have the Find My Friends app, right? If you're worried, you can look at that."

He nods. His eyes are downcast, and the rest of his face is expressionless. His feelings are hurt. My capacity for guilt is strong, and I fight the urge to reinstate the hourly texts and the safe word.

When Eric leaves, I write a quick note on each enclosure card, label the envelopes and place them in the bouquets. I place the bouquets on the top of Rita's empty yarn bins by the back door.

My phone dings.

April: Ready?
Me: 10 minutes. I have to walk Sophie.
April. K. I'll be there in 10.

"FLOWERS OR BINS?" April asks, surveying the pile of stuff by the back door.

"Up to you," I reply.

She gathers up the bouquets and steps into the parking lot. I follow her with the empty bins. We load everything into the trunk and hit the road.

"Our appointment is at 4 P.M." April checks her watch.

"That gives us almost four hours to make our first two stops. Where to first?"

"Rita's house," I reply.

We breeze down the highway with the air conditioning blasting cool air at us, singing along to various Cold Play songs.

When we pull up to Rita's house, her garage is open. I place the empty bins in the garage in the same spot they were in when I picked them up yesterday.

"Rita?" I call into the deserted garage. Surely, the open door means she's around here somewhere.

April and I look at each other, and she shakes her head. We try the front door. We ring the bell and wait. Nothing. I knock and try to peer into the window next to the door, but the curtains are drawn, and I can't see through the tiny slit where they meet.

"Do you have a knot?" April asks, referring to the knot in my stomach that has a history of revealing itself moments before I stumble upon a dead body.

I shake my head. "No knot. Shall we try the back of the house?"

Turning the corner of the house, we're greeted by a back gate left ajar. We stop and take a deep breath before walking through, bracing ourselves for a worst-case scenario.

"Rita?" I call out as I step from the side yard into the back yard.

"Over here," she calls back.

Thank goodness. My shoulders drop about two inches, and my jaw relaxes. Behind me, April releases an audible sigh of relief.

"Your garage door is open," I remind her. "I put your empty bins inside."

"Oh, thank you, Megan. Hello, April." Rita stands up from the patio chair she's sitting in. "I was tidying up in there and cleaning out my dye pots. I'm just taking a break before I get back to it."

"How are you doing today?" April asks her.

"Still in shock, I think," Rita replies. "But trying to stay busy."

What's that smell? It's familiar but I can't place it. My nostrils twitch as I chase the scent, trying to remember what it is.

"These are for you." April hands her one of Phillip's bouquets.

"We're sorry for your loss," I add.

"Thank you." Rita takes the flowers, then picks up a joint from the ashtray behind her and takes a long drag.

That's the smell!

"Ladies?" She extends the joint toward us.

"No, thank you, I'm driving," I reply.

"Not for me, Rita, but thanks," April says.

We follow Rita into the house and make small talk while she decides where to put the flowers. Then we follow her out to the garage and watch as she surveys her space.

"Do you use acid-based dyes, Rita?" I ask.

"Yes, but I like to use all sorts of dyes. Sometimes, I even use Kool-Aid," she replies.

"Just out of curiosity, what type of dye would you use if you wanted to achieve a really vibrant coral colour?"

"Are you looking for a custom dye, Megan?" Rita reaches up to a shelf and pulls down a few photo albums.

"No," I reply. "I was talking to someone at the store this morning about dye techniques, and we were discussing how to get vibrant colours. That's all."

"Vibrants aren't really in demand right now." She flips through the first photo album. "Vibrants haven't been popular for a few years. Muted colours and jewel tones are really having a moment, though." She stops flipping and turns the album toward me. "This is the brightest coral I've ever dyed."

It sure is. I look at the photo album of yarn samples, and the colour Rita is referring to is beyond vibrant. It's neon. "Wow, that is bright."

Rita shrugs, "The eighties. Neons were a thing back then."

"May I?" I gesture to the album in front of me.

"Sure! There are decades of pinks, corals, and salmons in there."

April and Rita make small talk while I flip through the pages, looking for a yarn similar in colour and texture to the yarn Eric showed me this morning. A few come close, but none are exactly the same.

"I have two more albums in that colour family," Rita tells me as I close the album of yarn samples.

"No, thank you," I reply. "Actually, we should get going. We're going to drop flowers off for Wayne."

"That's nice of you." Rita rubs my arm. "You didn't even know her."

"I didn't know her," I agree, "but I feel a connection to her. You know, with our cases being linked and everything, and you sharing so much about her with us yesterday."

"They are?" Rita sounds astonished. "What happened to Meaghan and what happened to you are connected? Wayne didn't mention that. I was there last night and this morning. He didn't say a word. He didn't say much of anything. He's struggling."

"Well, he has a lot on his mind. And the police might not have told him. Our cases might be connected, but there's no connection between Meaghan and I personally."

At least not that I've uncovered yet.

"WHAT WAS THAT ABOUT?" April asks as we drive away from Rita's house. "I've never seen you wear anything bright coral."

"Eric showed me a yarn sample earlier," I explain.

I tell her about Eric's visit to the store this morning, including the part about Adam's girlfriend and putting an end to the hourly texting regimen.

"Adam could have lots of reasons for keeping his girl-friend a secret," April says. "Like, maybe they're not seeing each other anymore, and the toothbrush is a relic of their brief relationship."

"Maybe," I cede. "And I think Eric's feelings are hurt because I asked him to stop checking on me constantly. Like I rejected him or something."

"He'll get over it." April waves her hand dismissively. "You two are way too careful about each other's feelings. It's painful to watch. You both constantly try to do whatever makes the other one happy."

"Thanks a lot!" I'm taken aback by her honesty.

"I'm always honest with you, Megaroo."

"I know," I admit. "I wouldn't have it any other way. Connie told me pretty much the same thing."

In 200 metres, the destination is on your right. In response to the GPS voice, I slow the giant SUV and look for Wayne and other-Meaghan's house number.

"This one," April says, jabbing the window beside her with her index finger. "The man out front must be Wayne."

I drive past the house and turn around, then pull up across the street two houses up from Wayne and other-Meaghan's house.

"Far enough away?" April asks, unbuckling her seatbelt.

"Just a minute," I tell her. "I need to work up the nerve. This is hard enough when it's someone I know, but offering condolences to a complete stranger feels... I don't know... intrusive."

"We'll keep it short and sweet," she reassures me. "We'll follow his lead."

The man is rummaging around the trunk of a minivan. His head is inside the vehicle. I can't see enough of him to be sure he's Wayne Martelle.

"I love her hair!" April points to a petite lady with pink hair coming out of the Martelle's house.

"It's nice," I agree. "Lot of maintenance, though."

April nods. "She must have to tone it constantly to keep it that pink."

The pink-haired woman opens the trunk of the vehicle next to the mini-van, then turns and talks to the man whose head is in the back of the mini-van.

"That's him," I confirm when the man ducks out of the trunk to talk to the woman.

"Handsome," April remarks.

"I guess," I reply.

I hadn't noticed before, but looking at him now, April is right. Wayne is handsome in a classic way. He's tall with a head of thick dark hair streaked with silver and a thick moustache. He exudes a modern-day Clark Gable vibe.

"Let's go." Before I can respond, April is out of the car and standing on the road.

As we approach the Martelle's driveway, the pink-haired woman goes back into the house.

The Martelle's live in a mid-to-late-eighties large ranch bungalow. It has a brick exterior and attached garage. The houses in the neighbourhood are similar but not identical, like the cookie-cutter houses you find in new developments. I'm guessing the size of the lots alone make this an expensive neighbourhood. The landscaping on the street looks professional and well-maintained. My father would refer to this part of town as well-appointed.

"Wayne?" I call from the bottom of the driveway.

He turns around.

"Yes."

April steps in front of me. "I'm April Shaw." She extends her hand, and Wayne shakes it. "This is my friend, Megan." She steps aside and gestures to me.

Good thinking, April. It hadn't occurred to me that walking up to this newly widowed man who doesn't know me and introducing myself with his wife's name might freak him out. Wayne and I shake hands.

"Hi," I say. "We're sorry to hear about Meaghan." I hand him the flowers.

"Are you from the media?" he asks suspiciously. "I'm not talking to the media or giving interviews."

"No," I assure him, "nothing like that. I'm a friend of Rita's. I didn't actually know your wife, but through Rita, I feel like I know her, and I just wanted to give you my condolences."

He takes the flowers. "Wait, are you Megan Martel? The lady with the same name as my Meaghan." His eyes narrow, and he looks at me closely.

I nod. "That's right. I guess Rita has mentioned me?"

"She has and so have the police." He shakes his head as though he's organizing the information it contains. "Now that I look at you, I recognize you. The police showed me your photo. They asked if I knew you. They said you were involved in an incident that might be related to my wife's murder."

I have his full attention now. "Did they tell you any details?" I ask.

He looks to the left without moving his head. I suspect he's trying to pick out specific details from the chaos of the past couple of days.

"You've had a lot to deal with this week," I say. "It's understandable if you can't keep it straight."

"They told me bits and pieces, but I'm not sure I took it all in. When someone says your wife is dead, everything they say after that is just noise."

I reach into my tote bag and pull out a business card. "If you want to ask me any questions, or anything, here's my number." I hand him the card.

He looks at the card blankly, then looks at me. "Would you have a few minutes now? Maybe you can come inside, and we can compare notes."

I look at April and Wayne quickly adds, "I'm sorry, is that weird? You don't know me. I'm a strange man inviting you into my house. I'm not crazy or dangerous or anything. My assistant, Felicia, is here too."

"It's not weirder than us showing up here unannounced, having never met you before," I assure him.

"We'd love to come in," April adds.

Wayne closes the trunks of both vehicles, and we follow him toward the house. Approaching the front door, I wonder if his assistant, Felicia, could be the same person other-Meaghan was referring to when she told Carlo her assistant accidentally wrote the appointment in her planner.

CHAPTER 20

"Please, have a seat." Wayne gestures toward a sitting area.

The inside of the house doesn't match the outside. The architecture is sleek and modern. The main floor is a large, open concept space with the functionality defined by the placement of the furniture. The walls are white, the art is abstract and colourful. The kitchen is white with stainless steel appliances and a breakfast bar with white stools. The floor is a dark hardwood. Everything looks expensive and carefully curated. Unlike my house, this house does not have a lived-in feel. Everything seems to be where it belongs, the surfaces have no clutter, and there are only a handful of family photos. It's like being in a show home. The professional photography and the concierge businesses must pay well.

I sit on the end of the modern sofa, and April sits next to me.

"Coffee? Tea? Anything?" Wayne asks. "Whatever you drink, we probably have it. Meaghan liked to keep the kitchen stocked. Always ready for company."

"Water?" I ask.

"Same for me," April says.

"We definitely have that." Wayne steps behind the large kitchen island. "So, your incident happened on Monday, Megan? Am I remembering correctly?"

I nod. "Just after noon. On the highway between here and Harmony Lake," I explain.

"What exactly happened?" Wayne hands April and I each a glass of water.

I give him the semi-abridged version of events. I don't tell him about hearing someone calling my name, and I don't tell him about the car prowling around my house. I leave out the part where I throw up into oncoming traffic, and I don't mention Eric.

In the interest of full disclosure, I probably *should* mention that the detective investigating his wife's murder is my boyfriend, but I don't want Wayne to think Eric sent me or feel uncomfortable talking to me. Besides, he shouldn't reveal anything to me that he hasn't revealed to the police.

"What a strange coincidence that it was Rita's car," Wayne observes.

Is it a coincidence?

I nod. "We were stunned. This whole week has been one coincidence after another."

Suddenly, the petite, pink-haired woman is standing behind the kitchen island fussing, one stem at a time, with the flowers we gave Wayne. I'm glad Phillip isn't here to see his creation rearranged. He would not like that.

"Felicia," Wayne says to her. "Do you have a moment? I'd like to introduce you. I think you'll definitely want to hear this."

Felicia wipes her hands on a white dish towel and walks over to us.

"Felicia Tam, this is April Shaw," Felicia and April shake hands and mutter, "It's nice to meet you," practically in unison.

Wayne gestures to me. "And this is Megan Martel."

Felicia looks like she's seen a ghost. Her facial muscles go completely lax, and she stares at me unblinking. I stand up. "Are you OK, Felicia? Do you want to sit down?" I gesture to where I was sitting.

Felicia shakes her head. "You look nothing like her," she mumbles, then she blinks rapidly and takes a breath. "I'm sorry. It's nice to meet you."

We shake hands.

"It's nice to meet you too. It's been a crazy week," I sympathize.

Felicia sits in a chair across from the sofa, and I reclaim my seat next to April.

"Hearing your name threw me for a loop," Felicia explains, her eyes gleaming with moisture. "I don't know why, but for some reason, I expected you to look like her." She shakes her head and smiles. "I know it doesn't make sense."

"I assume the police didn't show you my photo, then?" I ask.

"No," Felicia replies. "They only showed me one photo. A man."

There's my cue. I reach into my bag, pull out my phone, and find Hayden Lee's photo in my camera roll.

"This one?" I hold the phone out so she can see it.

She leans forward and squints. Wayne also leans forward to look.

Felicia nods. "That's him."

Wayne nods. "Hayden Lee."

"Do either of you know him?" I ask.

Wayne and Felicia shake their heads. "The detective asked us if we knew anyone called Hayden Lee. Or if Meaghan might have known him. When Felicia and I talked after we were questioned separately, we put two and two together and figured the mystery man in the photo was Hayden Lee."

"Do you know him?" Felicia asks me.

I shake my head. "I'd never seen him before the police showed me this photo."

"How did you get that photo?" Wayne asks.

"Detective Morris left me alone for a minute with his stuff. It was sitting right there, so I took a photo of the photo." The last part is slightly untrue, but I'm not about to explain how I went through a cop's papers so I could photograph evidence. "Once I knew his name, I could've lifted a photo from his social media profile, anyway," I add to justify my behaviour.

"You have Detective Morris?" Wayne asks. "We have Detective Sloane. If the cases are connected, why wouldn't the same detective work both?"

"I think it's jurisdictional," April explains. "My Megan was shot at in Harmony Hills. Your wife's incident happened in Harmony Lake. Different police forces."

I swear she's telepathic and senses my discomfort about disclosing my connection to Eric.

I nod. Please don't ask me if I know Eric Sloane. If I'm asked outright, I won't lie. If I disclose our relationship now, it would be suspicious that I didn't mention it earlier.

"How is Hayden connected to both you and Meaghan?" Felicia asks.

Once again, I tell the abridged version of what happened on Monday.

"The police believe he's the person who shot at me. I didn't recognize him because when I saw him, he was wearing a disguise."

"Do they think he shot my wife too?" Wayne asks. "Have they arrested him?"

I shake my head. "Hayden Lee is dead."

"What?" Wayne looks like I slapped him across the face. "Do you know when he died? Was it before or after my wife was killed?"

"Before," I confirm. "My understanding is they found him on Monday night when they found Rita's car."

"Then he couldn't have killed Meaghan," Wayne mutters, his fingertips on one hand pressing against the fingertips of his other hand in front of his chin. "Did the police tell you how the cases are connected?"

I nod. "Detective Morris visited me last night. He said the bullet from my car door matches the bullet that killed Meaghan." I do not mention that the bullet from Hayden Lee was also a match. I'll let the police tell Wayne more about how Hayden died.

"I bet that's why Detective Sloane wants to see me today. He's probably coming over to tell me the same thing."

"If you're expecting a visit from the police, April and I should make ourselves scarce," I say.

I don't want to risk running into Eric. I know I'll cave and tell Wayne we already know each other. I feel like they're more likely to talk to me if they don't know about my personal relationship with the investigating detective. Besides, if Eric thought it was relevant, he would've mentioned it to Wayne already.

Wayne checks his watch. "He won't be here until four. Plenty of time."

There's a break in the conversation while everyone processes the new information.

"I'm a suspect, you know," Wayne proclaims, breaking the silence. "In my wife's murder, not your incident. At least, I don't think I'm a suspect in your incident. I didn't do it. I love my wife. And I was out with friends when she was killed. Dozens of people saw me. Yet, I still feel like a suspect."

"Nobody thinks you did it, Wayne," Felicia reassures him.

"The police do," he argues.

"The spouse is always a suspect," April reminds him. "They start with the people closest to the victim and work out from there."

"Word for word, that's exactly what Detective Sloane said," Wayne replies.

Of course, it is. He's said it to April and me more than once.

Eager to change the subject and get a glimpse into other-Meaghan's home life, I say, "Rita tells me you have kids, Wayne. She showed me some pictures of your boys. How are they coping with the news about their stepmum?"

"They were here when I found out." Wayne takes a deep breath. "It was awful. I completely fell apart. I couldn't deal with my own reaction or theirs. Luckily, Felicia was here, and she took care of them until my ex-wife could pick them up."

"I'm sorry," I say.

"How are they doing now?" April asks.

"They didn't go to school yesterday or today. My ex is keeping them close. They were emotional, and she was worried about the other kids asking them questions or telling them rumours about what happened." He wipes his palms on the legs of his jeans. "She brought them by yesterday for a visit. And they're coming over again for dinner. My ex-wife is bringing a lasagna. She said she was going to phone their school today to get some referrals for counselling. I haven't talked to her yet, so I'm not sure how that went."

It sounds like an amicable co-parenting situation.

"I'd love to see some of your photography work, Wayne," April suggests. "Back in the day, before two kids and a bakery took over my life, I was a photography hobbyist."

"So was Meaghan," Wayne replies. "That's how we met. I was teaching photography at the community college, and Meaghan was one of my students." He smiles. Then his smile is replaced with panic. "It wasn't unethical," he adds quickly. "It was a part-time special interest course, not a degree course. I wasn't a professor or anything."

Is it me, or is Wayne overly worried about being interpreted as predatory? First when he invited us in, and now when he explains how he met other-Meaghan. Is he sensitive because of the age difference between him and his wife? Has he been accused of being creepy before? Is he hyper-sensitive right now because the police are dismantling his life? *Is* he predatory?

"Did she stick with the photography?" I ask. "Is the photography business something you and Meaghan did together?"

"No, she ran her business and I run mine. I have Felicia to help with my business, and my wife had an office full of staff for hers. Meaghan could've been a professional photographer, though. Her work is beautiful. Her eye for scale and composition was amazing."

"I'd love to see her work, sometime," I say, hoping sometime can be now.

"No time like the present." Taking my hint, Wayne stands up.

Following him down the basement stairs, I wait for him to assure us he's not creepy, and it's safe to go into the basement with him, but he doesn't.

CHAPTER 21

Upstairs might be the main floor of their house, but the basement is their home. This is where the family lives.

The basement is above ground — the house is built into the side of a hill. The large, bright, sun-filled family room leads out to the backyard through a wall of sliding glass doors. There are kids' toys strewn about, books and magazines piled on the end tables, TV remotes scattered across the coffee table, and a basket of folded laundry on the floor in the corner. Two video game remotes lay on the floor in front of the TV. The walls are dotted with framed photos of family and places.

"Please excuse the mess," Wayne says.

"It's not messy," I correct him. "It's lived in."

"Well then, you'll love the rest of the 'lived-in' basement," he informs us. "Most of Meaghan's work is in her office."

While Wayne proudly explains the story behind each framed photograph in other-Meaghan's office, I half-listen to him and half-look around at her space. Papers and files are stacked high beside the computer on her desk. She definitely worked from home. I'm reminded of Adam's desk when we were married. He'd leave his office in the city every day and continue working in his office at our house after Hannah went to bed and on weekends. Rita described other-Meaghan as "ambitious," which I now suspect is a euphemism for workaholic.

Her work habit is likely the reason she didn't plan dinners in her planner for the weeks the kids weren't here. She probably worked through dinner.

"It's a beautiful landscape," I agree after Wayne finishes telling me the story behind the framed photograph. I gesture to other-Meaghan's desk. "Was Meaghan left-handed?"

"She was. You can tell that from looking at her desk?"

"I suspected it. Her computer mouse is on the right, though, so I wasn't sure."

"Very observant. How can you tell?" he asks.

"Her files are on the right of her computer. Her desk is full of files and stationery and such, but there's a planner-sized gap on the left with the cup of pens."

"You're right. Her planner was always in that empty spot on her desk when she was home. Always open. She planned her entire day. Even the smallest tasks were written in her planner." I follow him to a bookshelf along the wall. "Planners past," he says, running his hand along the spines of Meaghan's previous planners.

Other-Meaghan's collection of past planners takes up two entire shelves of the built-in bookcase. If each planner represents a year, she kept planners dating back to when she was in high school. Amazing.

"I completely get this. I call my planner my brain. I don't know how I'd get anything done without it. My life would be a mess. I notice it's not on her desk now. I guess she took it to the office on Tuesday?" I probe.

"To the office, to meet clients, even to lunch, and on vacation. She took it everywhere with her. Made notes constantly." He sounds nostalgic. "The police have it now, for obvious reasons, but I hope they give it back so I can add it to the shelf of planners past."

"I'm protective of my planner." It's sort of true. "I don't like anyone else to write in it. Was Meaghan like that? Did she let anyone else add things to her planner?"

"Occasionally, I think. I know for sure that Karla has. Karla knew Meaghan well enough to know that if it wasn't written in her planner, it wouldn't get done. But mostly, my wife wrote in her own planner. There was rarely a need for anyone to write in it because she always kept it nearby."

"Rita mentioned Karla," I say. "They were best friends and business partners?"

"Business partners, yes. But I like to think I was my wife's best friend."

The mention of Karla's name seems to trigger some animosity in Wayne. He either dislikes Karla, the relationship between his wife and Karla, or both.

Wayne takes us on a guided tour of all the photos on the walls and surfaces throughout the basement. They were taken by either him or Meaghan, and all of them have a story or memory behind them.

While April and Wayne discuss camera equipment, I ask Felicia how long she's worked for Wayne.

"About four years now," Felicia replies. "Like Meaghan, I was a student in one of his photography classes. At the end of the course, he mentioned he needed a photography assistant and invited the class to apply." She smiles. "I was the lucky candidate."

"Do you have a photography business of your own, or does working for Wayne keep you busy?"

"I do sell my photography, but my work is fine-art photography. It's a harder sell and less reliable than the wedding and event photography Wayne does. One day, I hope to earn a living selling my work."

"I'd love to see it," I say.

Felicia shows me a selection of her work on her phone. She's talented. She photographs everyday items and people, but she photographs them in a way you've never seen them before. You recognize the thing, but at the same time it's like seeing it for the first time. Like seeing the world through someone else's eyes.

One of her photos is a man fishing off the end of a pier on Harmony Lake. The photo is taken from a very low angle, the camera could be sitting on the dock. It creates the illusion of the dock being much longer than it is. The texture of each wood slat is so vivid, I swear I can feel my fingertips touching them. I've walked up and down that pier dozens of times in my life, and I've never noticed the detail in the wooden slats that Felicia captured in this photo. The lake is calm. It's early morning, and the sky is hazy. The remaining fog on the lake shrouds the fisherman, making him look ethereal.

"Felicia, these are incredible." I'm easily moved by art. Almost any form of creative expression stirs me. "I especially love the pier on Harmony Lake."

"You recognize the pier?" Felicia answers my question with a question. "That's my goal. I want to show things and people we look at every day, but not from the perspective we're accustomed to seeing them. I want the observer to experience them how I see them."

"Goal accomplished," I tell her. "Is that photo available for sale?"

Felicia nods enthusiastically. "Yes, and I have other photos from Harmony Lake too. It's one of my favourite places to photograph. There's just something about it, you know what I mean?"

"I sure do," I assure her. "It's a special place. Would you send me a few with a price list?" I reach into my tote bag and hand her a business card.

"Sure!" She slips my card into her back pocket. "Can you

wait a few days? There's a lot going on here, and Wayne needs my help."

"Of course," I sympathize. "There's no hurry. Do you help out with more than Wayne's photography business?"

"I'm kind of a jack-of-all-trades," she replies. "If they need me to run errands, I run errands. Pick up the kids? No problem. Wash a soccer uniform an hour before the big game? I've got it covered." She shrugs. "It's a kind of other-duties-as-assigned situation."

It sounds like Felicia is the photography assistant-nanny-housekeeper who helps keep the Martelle family running smoothly.

"You don't mind doing all those other non-photography things?"

She shakes her head. "Not at all. The Martelles make me feel like family. I wouldn't want to work anywhere else."

Felicia's voice hitches, and her eyes fill with tears at the end of her sentence.

"I'm sorry for your loss." I rub her arm. "Were you and Meaghan close?"

She waves her hand in front of her face to fan away the tears and nods. She composes herself, then says, "We were. She was a good friend. I ended a long-term relationship last year, and Meaghan was one of my biggest supporters. She helped me pack my bags and sat with me while I cried. She was special."

"I wish I has known her." I think other-Meaghan and I might've been good friends if we'd had a chance to get to know each other. It's sad getting to know someone after they've died.

Felicia looks at the time on her phone. "I don't want to be rude, but I have to move some stuff from Wayne's van to my car before I leave for an appointment." She disappears into Wayne's office and reappears a moment later with an armful of photography equipment. She stops behind Wayne and April. "Wayne, I'll be outside rearranging the cars."

Wayne nods in acknowledgement and continues talking to April about digital versus film photography.

"Let me help you." I relieve Felicia of some items she's struggling to hang on to.

"Thank you," she says. "Actually, if you come out to the car with me, I can give you one of my business cards for my fine-art photography."

Felicia pushes a button on the key chain, and the tailgate of Wayne's minivan opens automatically. I place the equipment I'm carrying in Wayne's trunk, next to the bags and boxes of stuff already there. It's a tight fit with Wayne's golf clubs taking up most of the space, so I hoist his golf clubs out of the trunk and stand them up on the driveway.

"Thank you," Felicia grunts as she releases her armload into the space freed up by the golf clubs. She pops her trunk and begins organizing the items inside to make room for the stuff she needs to transfer over.

"My daughter has the same rain boots," I say when I see the black rubber boots with pink polka dots in Felicia's hands.

"Your daughter's boots are probably cleaner though." She bangs them together over the driveway, knocking clumps of dried mud off them, then stands them upright on the driveway.

"Pigs?" I ask.

"Pigs?" Felicia answers my question with a question. She does this a lot.

"My daughter's boots are just as muddy. She's a counselor at an animal-themed summer camp, and her mud is from the pig pen," I explain.

"Scouting," Felicia replies. "I was at Princess Diana park on Tuesday, scouting locations for a wedding we're working this Saturday. The mud is from the trails and wooded areas."

"Ah!" I nod.

Princess Diana Botanical Gardens—often called Princess Diana Park, or PDP by the locals—is a popular destination for wedding photos. The park is beautiful, the gardens are well-maintained, and there are lots of gardens and locations to choose from.

"You must work at Princess Diana park a lot," I observe. "Wouldn't you already know which locations to pose the wedding party?"

"Yes and no," Felicia says, picking and choosing items from Wayne's trunk and moving them to her trunk. "The time of day is important. The sun affects the lighting and the shadows. I like to see a location beforehand, at the same time of day we'll be working, and pick and choose the best locations. Also, because there will be so many wedding parties competing for the best spots on a Saturday in July, I like to have more locations than we'll need since the best ones might have wedding parties already queued up."

"That makes sense," I respond. "Wayne is lucky to have you. Speaking of Wayne, will he be able to work on Saturday? I mean faking a smile and photographing happy newlyweds less than a week after his wife died sounds painful."

She hands me a box of kids' toys. "That's why I'm taking this equipment with me. I'll set up and organize everything so Wayne can just show up, take the photos, and leave. I suggested he cancel, or let me take care of it, but this wedding is for one of Meaghan's clients. Meaghan planned the entire event, and Wayne doesn't want to let her down."

As my heart breaks for Wayne, I look down at the box of kids' toys in my arms. A selection of plastic outdoor toys like the ones I would buy at the dollar store for Hannah when she was little. Bug catchers, a butterfly net, a small pail and shovel, various sized balls, and a myriad of other inexpensive toys that last long enough to entertain the kids for a while but usually break soon after you buy them.

"Do you have kids?" I ask, looking at Felicia.

"No, I'm happily single and child-free," she clarifies. "Those toys are to keep kids busy at photo shoots. Kids can get really bored when they're part of a wedding party. Waiting in between photos isn't easy for them. The toys occupy them. You can put them in the backseat."

"Rita told me that Meaghan wanted kids. It's sad she didn't get to experience that," I point out.

"I started working for them just after all that happened," Felicia replies. "I don't know the details, but it was a sensitive topic for Meaghan. She didn't talk about it, and whenever the subject of babies came up, I could feel the tension between them."

Felicia and I chat while she finishes organizing both trunks. She tells me about the most and least beautiful wedding dresses she's seen in her role as photography assistant. As she returns Wayne's golf clubs to his trunk and closes the door, April and Wayne come out of the house.

"We've got to get on the road Megabot, or we'll be late for our appointment." April smiles.

Felicia gives me her card so I can follow up with her about the Harmony Lake pier photo I love, and we thank her and Wayne for talking with us. I remind Wayne that he has my card, and if he wants to talk, he can call me.

"WHAT DO YOU THINK?" I ask after we drive by and wave goodbye to Wayne and Felicia, who are still standing on the driveway.

"I think one of them probably just asked the other that same question," she replies.

"Yeah," I agree. "I get the feeling Wayne is doing a little sleuthing of his own. Can't blame him though. I was a murder suspect once, remember? I did everything in my power to prove my innocence."

"I don't think he did it," April says matter-of-factly.

Stopped at the stop sign, I look at April. "What? Did I hear you correctly? You *always* think it's the spouse."

She gives me a one-shoulder shrug. "I don't know who killed other-Meaghan, but I don't think it was Wayne."

"Why not?"

"I don't think he could do it alone," April asserts. "I spent a lot of time talking with him, and it sounds like either other-Meaghan or Felicia do pretty much everything for him."

"Are you suggesting he's not smart enough to murder his wife, or he's too lazy?" I ask.

"Lazy," she clarifies. "I think other-Meaghan and Felicia shared the mental and emotional labour of running the household and Wayne's business. I think his ex-wife and other-Meaghan shared the mental and emotional labour of organizing and sharing the kids."

"You're right," I concede. "Felicia told me about the other-duties-as-assigned part of her job, and she does a lot of non-photography work for the Martelles."

"For Wayne, it's a pretty sweet setup," April points out.

"Yes, it is," I agree. "Too sweet to risk ruining it by killing his wife."

CHAPTER 22

ON THE ELEVATOR ride to the eighth floor, April and I finish comparing notes about Wayne and Felicia. Neither of us picked up any romantic energy between them. We also didn't sense any unrequited attraction from either Wayne or Felicia toward the other. Sexual and romantic chemistry are difficult to hide. We decide jealousy or lust are unlikely motives.

"I got more of a brother-sister vibe than anything," April says as the elevator door opens. We stop at the reception desk and wait for the receptionist to finish a call. "April Shaw for Karla Bell at 4:00 P.M." April and I smile at the young, heavily tattooed and pierced receptionist.

"Have a seat. I'll let her know you're here." She points to the waiting area across from her desk.

"*Just Task Me!* is a hip, young company," I whisper after we're settled into the bright yellow, art deco side chairs.

"These chairs cost more than every piece of furniture T and I own," she whispers in reply.

"Coffee? Tea? Water?" Stealthily, the receptionist came out from behind her desk and is suddenly standing in front of us.

"Water, please," we say in unison.

The receptionist nods and walks away briskly.

"April?" A blonde woman walks toward us with her hand extended, ready to shake.

We stand up. "Karla?" April extends her hand and they shake.

Karla aims her extended hand toward me and raises her eyebrows.

"Megan," I say, then shake her hand.

She stares at my floating heart necklace, then looks me in the eye. "Are you married to Adam by chance?"

"Sort of," I reply cautiously and a little shocked. "Do you know him?"

"I picked out your necklace." She points and nods her chin toward my neck and chest area. "It was your thirty-fifth birthday, I think?"

"It was," I confirm. "You have quite a memory."

But more importantly, let's talk about why Adam outsourced my birthday gift. I have questions.

"It was a lot of years ago," she agrees.

Well, that feels like a passive-aggressive dig at my age. Both innocent and insulting at the same time. I rely on my instincts and on my first impression of new people. My first impression of Karla is confusion. Is she a nice person or not?

We follow Karla down the hall, and she turns to me. "Do you still have the Louis Vuitton tote bag Adam gave you for your fifteenth wedding anniversary?"

"I sure do," I reply. "Do I have you to thank for that gift too?"

How many of my gifts did Karla choose? Was she the only personal shopper he hired? What other parts of our marriage did he delegate? How did he know Karla? I assumed if my husband gave me a gift, my husband chose it. Did Adam lead me to believe he chose my gifts, or did I just assume he did, and he went along with it? So many questions.

Karla postures modestly. "It's nice to know you liked the gifts I picked out. I knew by the way Adam described you that you had *exquisite* taste." Karla turns her head back toward the direction we're walking.

I look at April. "Wow," I mouth.

"Exquiiiisiiiite," she replies silently with crazy eyes.

I choke on the laugh I'm trying to stifle, and Karla opens an office door, gesturing for us to enter ahead of her. All four walls are glass. So is the desktop. The chairs are chrome with leather upholstery. Copious amounts of Windex must get sprayed in here on a nightly basis.

"Are you OK?" she asks, concerned about my cough.

"Fine," I assure her. "I swallowed wrong." I sit in one of the chrome chairs.

There's a bottle of water on the desk in front of me and another in front of April. I silently thank the receptionist while I take a sip to squelch my cough-laugh.

"How do you know Adam?" I twist the cap onto the water bottle.

"His firm hired us to organize a few corporate events. He convinced the other partners to put us on retainer. His firm was our first big client. Planning their events resulted in a lot of referral business. My partner and I were grateful for that break. As a thank you, I did some personal shopping for Adam—free of charge, of course. After he left the firm last year, they decided not to renew our contract. It was a big hit to our bottom line."

"Too bad," April sympathizes.

At least, it sounds sympathetic to Karla. April sounds sweet as can be when she's sarcastic. People don't realize she's pelting them with sarcasm. That was the sweetest voice I've ever heard her use.

"Speaking of your partner," I segue, "April and I just left Wayne and Felicia."

"Oh?" Karla's eyes narrow. She looks at April. "There were no details in my calendar. I wasn't sure who you were or why you booked an appointment to see me. So, I googled you. I assumed you were here to sell me on using your bakery for our events. I'm guessing that's not why."

"No, it's not," I confirm. "First, we're sorry for your loss. Rita told us how close you and Meaghan were. This must be awful for you."

"Thank you," Karla says quietly.

"The day before Meaghan was killed, I was involved in a similar incident. The police linked the incidents, and we're talking to the people who were closest to Meaghan. We're looking for a connection she and I share, other than our name, that might explain what happened and why someone would want both of us dead."

"I'll tell you what I told that sexy Detective Sloane." Karla inhales dramatically, like a bored teenager. "Rita did it."

In one sentence, she accuses Rita of murder and objectifies Eric. I'm tempted to remind her that just because their genders are reversed doesn't mean her comment isn't inappropriate.

To calm me, April reaches for my hand. Karla misreads the gesture. Her facial expression softens, and she smirks at April and me.

"Is this why you and Adam are married, 'sort of'?" Karla asks, complete with air quotes around the "sort of."

"We're just friends," I clarify.

"You and Adam or you and April?" she asks teasingly, then laughs.

"Yes," I reply, unimpressed.

I remind myself mentally that Karla's best friend and business partner just died. Her bad week might be reflected in the way she interacts with others. I take a deep cleansing breath.

April leans forward in her chair. "Why do you think Rita did it? She loves Meaghan like a daughter."

"She's also seventy-something years old and spent her entire life living for the moment and not planning for her future. Her house is the only thing she owns, and it has a mortgage on it. The rest of her life was subsidized by Meaghan." Karla sounds bitter.

She might be a tad jealous of Meaghan and Rita's relationship.

How much money does this business make? Meaghan contributed to her own household's income and Rita's. That's a lot of financial pressure.

"It wouldn't make sense for Rita to kill her if she relies on Meaghan for financial support," April insists.

"It does when you consider Rita inherits fifty percent of *Just Task Me!*" Karla looks at us smugly, seemingly pleased by our shocked expressions.

"She didn't leave it to Wayne?" I ask.

Karla shakes her head. "They had marital problems a few years back. Their relationship was touch-and-go for a while. Frankly, I'm surprised she stayed. Meaghan changed her will to prepare for the worst—divorce—and she never changed it back."

"Rita mentioned their marital issues. She said they were happy and trying for a baby, then all of a sudden, they weren't. She said she was worried they'd divorce. She also said that's when Meaghan really started to focus on *Just Task Me!*" I stop talking and try to gauge Karla's expression. Nothing. I wouldn't want to play poker with her. "We assume the marriage issue and the sudden focus on her career are related, but we aren't sure how."

She takes a deep breath, and for the first time, when I look at Karla's face, I catch a glimpse of a micro-expression I can interpret. She's conflicted. She wants to tell us, but she doesn't want to betray Meaghan's trust or privacy. She might not be as mean as she comes across.

"You don't have to tell us," I say, and I mean it. "I know you and Meaghan were close. And talking about her when she's not here feels like you're betraying her trust. Don't tell us anything you aren't comfortable disclosing."

April shoots me a sideways glance that telepathically screams, "Are you crazy?"

Karla takes a deep breath and blows it out loudly. "Rita's right. Meaghan and Wayne tried to have a baby. Meaghan always wanted kids. When we met in college, she had a list of names picked out for her future sons and daughters. Wayne knew how important it was to her. They talked about it a lot before they got married. One of the reasons they married quickly and started trying right away was because Wayne wasn't getting any younger. He's fifteen years older than her. She was thirty, and they decided it was time to seize the moment."

"I guess it didn't happen for them?" I'm sad for other-Meaghan. Sad that she didn't get to fulfil her dream of having a baby.

"No, it didn't," Karla confirms. "Meaghan went to doctors. She had head-to-toe exams. She had her hormone levels checked. She had diagnostic imaging tests. The doctors told her they found no reason to suspect she had fertility issues. They suggested Wayne should make an appointment."

"Did he?"

Karla shakes her head. "He said he already has two kids, so there's no way the problem could be him."

"That doesn't sound very supportive," April says.

"It gets worse," Karla warns us. "One day when Meaghan and Wayne's ex-wife met to exchange the kids—because Meaghan always did that by the way—she worked up the nerve to ask his ex-wife if they'd had problems conceiving the boys. The ex-wife said they had no trouble at all. Well, this made Meaghan cry."

"Poor Meaghan," I interject. "She must've been devastated and blamed herself for their fertility issues."

"Not for long," Karla corrects me with a hint of hot anger in her voice. "The ex-wife asked Meaghan if she and Wayne were having fertility issues. Meaghan told her that yes, they were. His ex-wife said, 'Oh, I didn't know Wayne had his vasectomy reversed.'"

Karla sits back in her chair, raises her eyebrows, and purses her lips. She watches while April and I connect the dots.

"Let me guess," I offer. "Meaghan didn't know about Wayne's vasectomy."

Karla touches the tip of her index finger to the tip of her nose. I'm right.

CHAPTER 23

"Poor Meaghan." April brings her hand to her mouth in shock.

"Did she confront him?"

Karla nods. "After she took a couple of days to process what his ex-wife said. Meaghan told Wayne that Rita wasn't well, and she was staying with her, but she was really across the street staying at my house. When she confronted him about his vasectomy, he admitted it. He said he didn't want more children at his age. He said he knew if he told her, she wouldn't have married him. He told Meaghan he hoped when she didn't get pregnant, she'd assume it wasn't meant to be and would just let it go. Then he told her it wasn't really a lie because she never asked him outright if he'd had a vasectomy. Apparently if she'd asked him directly, he would have told her."

"Wait!" I raise my hand in a stop motion. "Wayne told Meaghan it was *her* fault *he* never mentioned *his* vasectomy because *she* never asked?" Gaslighting and victim blaming doesn't sound like the Wayne I just met.

"Yup." The anger emanating from Karla shrouds the entire office.

I'm angry and sad for Meaghan. I can't imagine being betrayed twice; once by being lied to, and again by being gaslighted for being upset about being lied to.

"That's a big betrayal to forgive," April says. "How did she do it?"

"Therapy," Karla replies. "So much therapy." She shakes her head. "Even after all the therapy, I'm not sure she ever really forgave him. I feel like there was still resentment there."

Karla pauses to call the receptionist and order a bottle of water.

"She should have left," Karla declares after she hangs up the phone. "If she left, maybe she would've met someone else, someone who wanted to have kids with her and wouldn't mess her around. But she loved Wayne. She loved his kids. She wanted to make it work, so she stayed. And I love her and wanted her to be happy, so I supported her. The company became her baby. She poured all her energy into *Just Task Me!* That's why I'm working this week. Meaghan would've wanted us to stay open and carry on business as usual. This company meant everything to her. It's her legacy."

A gentle tap on the glass door and Karla breaks into a wide grin like she knows a secret. She makes a come-hither gesture with the first two fingers of her hand.

"Thank you, Rico," Karla purrs, accepting the bottle of water he hands her. "Ladies, this is Rico. He's one of the best concierges we have. And the handsomest. If you ever need tickets to a sold-out sporting event, Rico is your man." She winks at him flirtatiously and crosses her legs, letting her stiletto heel dangle seductively from the toe of her foot.

This is awkward for April and I, who feel like we're intruding on an intimate moment we shouldn't see. And would rather not see.

This is the second time she's objectified a man. This time a co-worker. In his presence. Rico's pretty young, thirty-ish, maybe he needs a quick primer on sexual harassment and his rights.

"No problem, Karla," Rico replies. "Listen, can I have a word with you before you leave? About *the thing*?"

"You got it," Karla replies, stroking her bottom lip and tongue provocatively with the end of her pen.

April looks at me. She feels it too. We're stuck in the middle of Karla and Rico's weird foreplay ritual.

It's like watching one of those nature documentaries where one gender of the species preens and shows off to attract the other gender of the species, but the potential mate is either oblivious or ignores the overt attempts to seduce them.

"Boyfriend?" I ask after Rico escapes.

"He wishes," Karla replies. "He's just a colleague." She crinkles her nose and waves away my question. "He flirts with everyone."

I only noticed Karla flirting, unless I missed something.

"If you need to discuss '*the thing*' with him, April and I can leave. We've taken a lot of your time already…"

"No, it's fine," Karla interrupts before I can finish my sentence. "I'm trying to avoid talking about *the thing*. At least with you here, I don't have to."

"What is '*the thing?*'" April asks what we're both curious to know.

"Rico wants to buy into the business," Karla explains. "Not as an equal partner, but he wants a small stake. Meaghan was against it. She wasn't willing to share the company beyond her and me."

"But you're not against it?" I hazard a guess.

"I'm not sure I want him to have an ownership stake, but Rico deserves financial recognition beyond his salary, and beyond the other concierges."

"Why?" I ask, hoping the answer isn't because he's the most handsome.

"He brings a lot to the table," Karla discloses quietly.

Am I prepared to hear what Rico brings to the table? I'm not sure, but I brace myself for potential intimate details, and ask, "Like what?"

"He's our sports guy. He used to work security for professional sports teams. He knows people. He can get tickets to anything. Rico gives us an advantage over the competition. If we don't give him something extra to recognize that, he'll go to another company and take his sports connections with him."

"What are you going to offer him?"

"That's the problem. I'm not sure I can offer him anything. Meaghan and I didn't finish discussing it before…." Karla's voice trails off before she finishes her sentence, and she clears her throat then sips her water.

"If Rita is your partner now, wouldn't she have to agree to whatever you decide to offer Rico?" April asks.

"Rita's my partner *for* now," Karla clarifies. "I'll buy her out as soon as the insurance comes through." She shrugs. "I'm sure Rita doesn't want to run a business, and frankly, I need someone who can commit full-time hours. Meaghan worked constantly and handled most of the administration. She also pursued a lot of accounts and brought in most of our retainer clients. I can't do all that and my own job by myself."

"Insurance?" I ask. "You and Meaghan have a buy-sell agreement?"

Karla nods. "It's all laid out in our partnership agreement."

A buy-sell agreement is a clause that specifies the terms of a buyout in the event one partner dies, gets divorced, or retires. It's not only a good idea but is also necessary if the partnership needs a bank loan or a lease, like the lease for these lovely offices. It assures the landlord the business will remain viable if something happens to one of the partners. The simplest way to structure a buy-sell agreement between two partners is for each partner to have an insurance policy naming the other partner beneficiary.

"Meaghan's decision to leave her half of the business to Rita was probably calculated," April theorizes. "Rita's future income will be secure when you purchase half of *Just Task Me!* from her." She looks at Karla. "And you'll end up the sole owner of the company. Two of the people she loved most taken care of in one transaction."

"Where does that leave Wayne?" I ask.

April shrugs. "He has the photography business. He'll be fine."

"Is that what he told you?" Karla laughs.

"Not exactly," April replies. "It's what we assumed. He seems busy with bookings and makes enough to pay for Felicia. And their house is gorgeous."

Karla shakes her head. "He has you fooled."

"How?" I ask.

"Wayne works as little as possible," Karla alleges. "He avoids work like he's allergic to it. The only gigs he gets are the bookings we give him. *Just Task Me!* is his only client. Besides, working would interfere with his golf habit."

It's obvious Karla doesn't like Wayne. She doesn't even bother trying to mask her contempt for him. To be fair, it seems to go both ways, recalling the way Wayne quickly corrected me when I suggested Karla was other-Meaghan's best friend instead of him.

"If he hardly works, why does he need Felicia?" April asks.

"If it weren't for Felicia, he wouldn't do any work at all. She keeps him organized, does all the work before the shoot, and all the work after the shoot. She helps around the house and with his kids. I'm telling you, Wayne does bupkis! When Meaghan told Wayne to either book enough shoots to pay Felicia's salary or let her go by the end of July, he went nuts. They had a huge argument about it."

April and I look at each other, stunned.

"Let me guess, he didn't mention that either?" Karla asks, sarcastically.

"He did not," I confirm.

Karla takes a deep breath. "I'm going to tell you something no one else knows. I don't think even the police have figured it out yet. I'm sure if they did, Sloane would've mentioned it when he was here earlier."

My interest is piqued.

"What is it?" April asks.

"Meaghan was skimming money from the company. I think the pressure of supporting everyone financially caught up with her. She must've been desperate, or she would never have done it."

"Why not mention this to the police?" I ask.

"I don't want to sully her reputation," Karla replies. "It's bad enough she was murdered. She'll always be remembered as the woman who was shot in the motel parking lot. I don't want her to be remembered as the woman who embezzled money from her company."

That's not the only reason Karla hasn't mentioned this to the police. She's a smart woman and knows the buy-sell agreement, combined with the misappropriation of funds, gives her a huge motive to kill Meaghan.

"You have proof?" I ask.

"Do you consider financial statements proof?" she asks.

I nod. "Did your accountant bring this to your attention?"

"Meaghan maintains our books. She uses an online program. It automatically integrates all our bank account and credit card transactions. We only use an accountant for taxes."

"How did you notice the missing money? Did you suspect Meaghan was skimming?"

Karla shakes her head. "Never," she insists. "I would never suspect that. It's completely out of character for Meaghan to do something like this."

Karla stops talking and opens a drawer in the cabinet beside her desk. She pulls her laptop out of the drawer, and I catch a glimpse of bright coral yarn.

"You have yarn in your drawer!" I declare.

"This?" She pulls a stuffed, hand-knit letter K out of her drawer.

"Yes. Where did you get that?" The last thing I expected to find in Karla Bell's office is yarn.

"I made it." She shrugs. "I went through a knitting phase a couple of years ago. Rita taught me. I was going to knit my whole name and display the letters on my desk. I only got as far as **K**. Turns out knitting bores me." She tosses the **K** back in the drawer and closes it. She opens the laptop, taps at the keyboard for a minute, and spins the device so April and I can see the screen. "See these subcategories hidden within these miscellaneous categories?"

I nod. "Yes. They're large amounts of money and the descriptions are vague. I can see why they got your attention."

"Right? I was looking at the books because I wanted to suggest to Meaghan that we offer Rico a quarterly bonus instead of a piece of the company. I was trying to figure out how much we could give him. I came across these transactions and followed the money trail all the way to the *Martelle Photography* bank account. Not as payment for jobs Wayne did for us. Not for anything."

"What did Meaghan say when you confronted her?" April asks. "You did confront her, right?"

"She was stunned," Karla replies. "She was shocked. Surprised that I caught her. She had this deer-in-the-headlights reaction. She even opened her laptop and looked at the transactions as if they were news to her. Finally, she said, 'I'm sorry, Karla. I'll take care of it. I'll put it all back.'"

"How was she intending to pay it back?" I ask.

"I don't know," Karla admits. "This all went down last

week. Before we could discuss it further, she was killed. I only know she told Wayne his business had to pay for Felicia, or she had to go at the end of July. And I was like, thanks for the warning, Felicia's not coming to live with me again when Wayne lets her go."

"Felicia lived with you?" April asks.

"For eight months," Karla confirms. "She broke up with a boyfriend last year. It was a nasty break up. Meaghan asked me to take her in for a couple of weeks. Felicia was really depressed about the breakup, so I said yes. Two weeks turned into eight months. Never again."

"Who booked Meaghan's appointment at the Hav-a-nap Motel on the day she died?" I'm hoping the question takes her off guard.

Karla shakes her head and shrugs. "I assumed Meaghan booked it. She was in charge of business development. She pursued clients, not me. I'm more comfortable with customer retention and managing things here."

"You do know that Meaghan didn't book it, right? Someone, a woman, booked it for her and wrote it in her planner."

"I didn't know that," Karla says. "How do you know that?"

"I know the manager of the motel," I explain.

"I'll check with the receptionist for you, but Meaghan was pretty protective of her schedule."

"We've taken up way too much of your time," I say, picking my tote bag up from the floor. "Thank you so much for sharing what you know with us." I reach for my phone and unlock it. "Did the police show you a photo of this man?" I hold out my phone with Hayden Lee's photo on it.

"Hayden? Yeah. I identified him for Detective Hotty."

"You mean, Sloane?" April corrects her.

"Isn't that what I said?" Karla waggles her eyebrows.

"You know Hayden Lee?" I confirm.

"Uh-huh, he cuts my grass and shovels my snow. Sometimes I hire him for event setups and teardowns. He's a general labourer, the type that'll do any job for the right money."

"How long have you known him?" April asks.

"He kind of came with my house. He worked for the previous owners, and I kept him on when I bought the place. Nice guy. Reliable. Hard worker."

I don't think she knows he's dead.

"When was the last time you talked to him or saw him?"

"He mowed my lawn on Sunday morning."

The morning Rita's car was stolen.

BY THE TIME April and I leave the *Just Task Me!* offices, it's almost 5:30 P.M.

When we leave, it looks like Rico is the only person, other than Karla, still at the office. On the way to the car, I silently hope he's OK alone with her.

"Think she's chasing him around a desk yet?" I swear April can read my mind.

"I hope not, but unfortunately, I wouldn't put it past her," I reply. "What do you think?" I glance at April.

"I don't like her," April replies. "She's vengeful."

"Why do you say that?"

"Why did she feel the need to tell you she picked out your necklace? And your Louis Vuitton bag? Because when Adam left, the firm didn't renew their contract, and she's bitter."

"Maybe," I concede. "But is she vengeful enough to kill her business partner and best friend for stealing from their business?"

"She had nothing nice to say about Rita, Wayne, or Felicia," April points out. "In fact, she didn't seem to like anyone except Rico. Oh, and Detective Hotty."

"Don't get me started," I warn. "She lied by omission to

the police. I have to tell Eric to look at the company books. If Karla is telling the truth about Meaghan stealing from the company, it changes everything. It gives everyone a motive. By killing Meaghan, Karla would stop the skimming and own the entire business. If Rita did it, it would set her up for life financially. Felicia's motive would be keeping her job. There's no way Wayne could let her go, not if he's as useless as he appears to be."

"What would be Wayne's motivation?" April wonders aloud. "Do you think Meaghan was threatening to leave him? She was thirty-five years old, and Karla said there was still resentment about Wayne's betrayal. Maybe she was ready to leave him and find a partner who wants a family."

"Possibly," I shrug. "Or he did it to stop his wife from telling everyone that he was the person who embezzled money from *Just Task Me!*"

"You think it's possible that Wayne was stealing money from his wife's company?"

"Oh, I think it's entirely possible," I reply.

CHAPTER 24

FRIDAY, July 10th

Me: Just got to Adam's office. Meet at the house in an hour?

Eric: For sure. C U then.

After I dropped off April yesterday, I rushed to Knitorious to pick up Sophie and relieve Connie and Marla so they wouldn't have to close the store. Then Sophie and I rushed to the Animal Centre to pick up Hannah from work. Talking to people all day was exhausting. I was too tired to make dinner, so Hannah and I warmed up leftover Chinese food. She went to the beach after dinner for a bonfire with her friends, and I had a long soak in a hot bubble bath, followed by knitting and an early night.

Eric worked late last night, and I'm not scheduled to work until after lunch today, so I asked him to meet me this morning to talk about April's and my visit to Harmony Hills yesterday.

I text Adam to let him know I'm here, then turn off the engine and step into the already-suffocating early morning heat.

In the foyer of the restored Victorian house, I wave to Lin, the receptionist. She's talking into her headset and typing so quickly her fingers are a blur.

"Hey, Meg." Adam descends the stairs, and we exchange a cheek kiss. "Coffee?"

"No thanks," I reply, following him up the ornate wooden staircase that leads to his office.

"What's up?" he asks, settling into his chair after closing the office door behind us.

"You'll never guess who I met yesterday." I adjust myself in the chair across from his desk.

"If I'll never guess, why don't you just tell me?" He smiles.

Fine, we'll do it his way. "Do you remember Karla Bell?"

After a few seconds, a gleam of recognition crosses his face. "Karla! She planned events at the firm. I remember her. And Rico! I miss Rico. He could get tickets to anything."

"Small world," I say. "Karla Bell was other-Meaghan's business partner and best friend."

"Really? That is a small world. I don't think I ever met other-Meaghan though. I only dealt with Karla and occasionally Rico. But speaking of small worlds, I googled other-Meaghan last night and realized I know Wayne."

"You know Wayne?" This isn't what I came here to talk about, but I'll put my own agenda aside to hear this.

Adam nods. "He's a member at the club. I've golfed with him a few times to make up a foursome. I knew his name was Wayne, but I didn't know his last name was Martelle. He was also the photographer who did our corporate head shots each year at the firm. Karla organized them."

The club is The Harmony Hills Golf & Country Club. We have a family membership that covers Adam, me, and Hannah, and somehow now also includes Eric. I haven't been there in a few years, but Adam's an enthusiastic golfer so he's there regularly during golf season. Eric sometimes joins him for a round.

"When was the last time you saw him?" I ask.

Adam raises his eyebrows and takes a deep breath. "I'm not sure. In the last two weeks for sure. The last time I golfed during the week. Wayne's there every weekday, according to the club rumour mill."

"Every weekday? Like for an entire round of golf or something shorter?" It takes about four hours to golf eighteen holes.

"As far as I know, he golfs at least one round a day. Sometimes two. He's part of a clique. They all show up every day and golf together."

If Wayne spends four to eight hours each day golfing, that doesn't leave much time for his photography business. It sounds like Karla might be right about him not doing much work.

"You mentioned this to Eric, right?" I ask.

"I texted him last night. He was busy and said he'd call me today." Adam straightens and adjusts the family photos on his desk, then looks at me. "Is that why you came to see me? To tell me you met Karla?"

"Kind of," I say, fidgeting with my floating heart necklace that I intentionally wore today. "She said she picked out this necklace. And some other gifts you gave me over the years?"

"Probably." Adam shrugs, nonplussed.

"I thought you and Hannah picked this out." Despite trying to sound unaffected, I hear the disappointment in my voice.

"I don't think I explicitly said that." A very lawyerly answer.

"No, you didn't. I assumed it. It's a reasonable assumption, *Adam*, that when someone buys their wife a gift, they choose it themselves. One of the reasons I love this necklace is because of the thought I believed went into it. I didn't realize you delegated it to someone who didn't know me. What other parts of our marriage did you outsource? And did you outsource me five years ago because you'd already given up on our marriage? Because five years ago, I thought we were still in a pretty OK place." I stop venting and take a breath.

"Are you done? Is it my turn to speak?" He uses his calm voice, and it sounds condescending.

I cross my arms in front of my chest and nod sharply at him to continue.

"I didn't outsource every gift. When we were first married, we couldn't afford a personal shopper, and once Hannah was old enough to shop, I stopped using Karla." With his palm down, he moves his hand side-to-side in a see-saw motion. "Only about three years of your gifts were purchased by someone else." He stops talking and looks at me. I say nothing. I won't speak first. He continues, "It didn't occur to me at the time that you would feel it would make the gift less personal. In my mind, it was the same as buying you flowers."

"What does that mean? How are flowers the same thing?"

"When I gave you flowers, you liked them. You knew Phillip chose the flowers and arranged them. You knew I didn't find a field of flowers and pick them myself. In my mind, hiring a personal shopper was the same thing. I'm sorry if I got it wrong."

"Fine. Thank you for explaining it to me." I don't know why I'm upset about a few gifts he gave me over five years ago.

"To answer your other questions," Adam says, "I did not, as you say, outsource any part of our marriage. Except the occasional dinner reservation or event tickets. I had not given up on our marriage five years ago. I didn't give up until the spring of Hannah's senior year of high school when you told me you were ready to give up. I think we've established that throughout our marriage, I made some bad choices and wasn't always the most engaged or present husband and father. I'm sorry for that. If I had another chance, I would make it up to you and Hannah. In a heartbeat."

It sounds like he's saying he'd want another chance if it was offered to him, but I interpret it as, he'd do it differently if he could do it again. Because I'm sure that's what he means. Regardless, the statement hangs uncomfortably in the air between us, so I decide to break the tension with a different and equally uncomfortable topic.

"Do you outsource gifts for your girlfriend?"

"I don't have a girlfriend, Meg." He pinches the bridge of his nose between his thumb and index finger. This wouldn't be the first time one of our conversations gives one of us a headache.

"Hannah says you do," I say quietly.

"Hannah? She told you this?"

I nod. "She says you have a girlfriend who stays over. She says your girlfriend's toothbrush is in your toothbrush holder. And according to the stray hairs Hannah has found, your girlfriend has very long strawberry blonde or possibly light auburn hair."

He shakes his head. "Oh my God, she's just like you."

"I hope you're referring to Hannah," I joke.

"Of course, I am," he snaps. "She's not my girlfriend. We're seeing each other, but it's not serious."

I wonder if the mystery woman knows it's not serious. Never mind, not my concern.

"Then why the secrecy? Why hide her from your family?" I ask, remembering the last time Adam had a secret girlfriend, and two people were killed.

"Because it's not serious." He shrugs, palms up. "I don't want to introduce our daughter to someone who isn't permanent."

"I get that," I tell him.

"Hannah's only home for a few months a year now that she's in university. Between her job and her friends, I don't get to spend enough time with her as it is. Also, the three of us are in a pretty good place right now. We've found our groove as a separated family, and I don't want to upset that delicate balance by introducing another person."

"You should tell this to Hannah," I suggest. "So, she doesn't comb through your life, looking for clues about who this woman is or how serious your relationship is. Also, she's smarter than us. She knows when we aren't telling her something."

He nods. "Maybe I'll talk to her at brunch on Sunday."

"Or you could take her out for dinner," I suggest. "You want more time alone with Hannah, maybe you can set up a weekly father-daughter dinner for the last six weeks of her summer break." I reach into my tote bag and pull out the business card Karla gave me yesterday. "Here you go." I place the card on Adam's desk. "In case you want to purchase your non-girlfriend a gift."

"I WAS CRAVING one of these. Thank you!" I take the coffee Frappuccino with extra whipped cream from Eric's hand and immediately take a sip.

"Sounds like you and April were busy yesterday," Eric says after I give him the list of stops April and I made. "You forgot to mention Carlo, though. You saw him too."

"At Latte Da," I confirm, then have another sip of my Frappuccino. "Did he tell you?"

"He didn't have to," Eric replies. "He used the phrase 'other-Meaghan' twice when I was talking to him yesterday. I doubt he came up with it himself." He winks, and my insides flutter a bit.

I shrug. "I think I just missed you at Karla's office yester-day, and April and I left Wayne's house before you were due to arrive at four…"

Before I finish my sentence, my phone dings. I unlock the screen and look at the notification.

"Oh," I utter. "I don't know what to do with this."

"What is it?" Eric asks.

"I just got a Facebook friend request from Wayne."

"Oh," he utters. "Do you want to accept it?"

"Well, I'd like to snoop through his timeline and friends list, but if I accept that means he'll see my timeline and friend's list."

"You don't want him to see that?" Eric asks.

"He'll see *you*," I explain. "I didn't tell any of them that you and I know each other personally. I didn't want to put you in an awkward position."

"I see," he replies. "I haven't told them about us either. I never talk about my personal life with witnesses." He smiles. "Except one time when the witness was a cute yarn store owner that I had a crush on. I ended up falling in love with her." He laughs.

I smack his shoulder, jokingly. "Stop distracting me. What should I do?"

Sophie yelps when I smack Eric's shoulder. She rushes over to referee our pretend fight. "Sophie thinks it was funny." He pets her, which she interprets as an invitation to jump up onto the sofa and lie on his lap.

My phone dings again. "Now I'm getting an Instagram request from Felicia."

"The timing is suspicious," he confirms. "Do you think they're together?"

"Maybe. They seem really close, and I did get the sense that Wayne is doing some sleuthing on his own to find his wife's killer."

"Ignore it," Eric suggests. "You don't have to accept either request right away."

"You're right," I agree. "If they ask, I'll just tell them I've been too busy to go on social media."

Another ding. I check my phone. "They sent follow requests to April too."

I reply to her text explaining why I'm choosing to ignore both requests. She texts me back to let me know that she's taking the same approach.

Now, I'm sure Wayne is investigating something. Either his wife's murder or April and me. He wants to snoop through mine and April's timelines and friends lists as badly as I want to snoop through his and Felicia's.

"Everyone other-Meaghan loved has a motive to kill her," I reply when Eric asks me my overall impression of my visit to Harmony Hills yesterday.

"Let's explore that," he says, opening his notebook and clicking the top of his pen with his thumb. "Why would Rita want other-Meaghan dead?"

"Because it would secure her financial future," I reply. "She inherits other-Meaghan's half of *Just Task Me!* which Karla will purchase from her at a predetermined price, using the life insurance proceeds."

"But Meaghan was already helping Rita financially," Eric counters. "Other-Meaghan doted on Rita like they were mother and daughter. She might benefit financially, but when other-Meaghan died all the non-financial support died with her."

"True," I ponder, "but Rita has a sister and nieces and nephews, so maybe her non-financial needs are met else-where. Or maybe she's happy to pay for that kind of support."

"How does Felicia benefit from other-Meaghan's death?" Eric puts his pen down and looks at me.

"She gets to keep her job," I reply. "At least for now. You know other-Meaghan planned to let her go at the end of the month if Wayne couldn't pay Felicia's salary from the photography business, right?"

Eric nods.

"Felicia told me how much she enjoys working there. Maybe she enjoys it so much, she'd kill to stay. Especially if she assumed Wayne would inherit other-Meaghan's share of *Just Task Me!* I know I was shocked when I found out he didn't. Also, she claims to not recognize Hayden Lee, but she lived with Karla for eight months. Surely, she would have noticed him at least once when he was there mowing or shovelling. Did other-Meaghan have any other life insurance policies? Other than the one for the buy-sell agreement, I mean? With Wayne as beneficiary?"

"No, she had no other insurance policies," Eric confirms. "I didn't know Karla and Felicia lived together. Karla told you about the buy-sell agreement? I'm impressed. It's hard to get her to talk at all. She seems almost inanimate. Like she has no feelings. She's very cold toward me."

"Really?" I'm surprised. "She seemed pretty warm toward you when April and I were there." I tell him about Karla calling him sexy and hot. And how she commented on Rico's handsomeness while Rico was in the room. He looks shocked. He rubs the back of his neck with his hand the way he does when he blushes.

"Did she disclose anything else to you?" Eric asks.

"She disclosed *everything else* to us," I confirm. "Under the cold, hard-to-like persona she projects onto the world, I think she really loved other-Meaghan. Other-Meaghan might've been the only person she really let in."

I tell Eric what Karla disclosed to April and me about Wayne's vasectomy.

"Wow. He never mentioned this," Eric replies.

"Why would he?" I ask. "It makes him look bad, and it

was five years ago. He might not think it's relevant to her murder. Also, I think Karla is the only other person who knows. Well, Karla and his ex-wife."

"Do you think Karla was pointing the finger at Wayne?" he asks.

I shake my head. "No. She flat out told us she thinks Rita did it to secure her financial future. But I think if it does turn out to be Wayne, Karla wouldn't be disappointed. Let's not forget, Karla has her own motives. With other-Meaghan out of the way, she becomes the sole owner of *Just Task Me!* and doesn't have to share any of the profits with a partner. She would also be the sole decision maker and wouldn't have to butt heads with other-Meaghan about giving Rico a bonus. April noticed that Karla has a vengeful streak when she said something to me that was clearly out of anger about something else. And she was angry at other-Meaghan for stealing from the company. Killing other-Meaghan would stop the embezzlement."

"So, Karla knows about that...." Eric's gaze drifts off to the distance.

"I wasn't sure you knew about that," I say. "Karla said she didn't mention it to the police because she was afraid of sullying other-Meaghan's memory."

"Oh, we know about it." He looks at me. "Business partners are tied with spouses for most likely suspects. We went through the company books carefully. We even traced the IP address. All the questionable transactions originated from the Martelle's home."

"That doesn't surprise me," I admit. "I think Wayne was skimming the money, not other-Meaghan."

"Why?" Eric puts down his pen and sits back, sinking into the sofa.

"Because Karla said other-Meaghan was 'like a deer in the headlights' when confronted with the transactions. She said it was like other-Meaghan was 'seeing them for the first time.'

She even looked at them on the computer. Why would she be shocked by transactions she input? Karla also said other-Meaghan would never embezzle money from their business. And I think of all four suspects, Karla knew other-Meaghan best. Also, when I was in other-Meaghan's home office, I noticed her desk is set up for someone who's left-handed. Except her computer mouse. It was on the right. Wayne confirmed that other-Meaghan was left-handed. I know some left-handed people use their right hand for some things, but the mouse stood out to me. My first thought was that someone else used her computer."

"Would Wayne kill his wife to hide that he was stealing money from her company?"

I shrug. "Yesterday before I met Karla, I would've said no. But after hearing how he allegedly lied to his wife about his vasectomy, then blamed her for his lie, I'm not sure anymore."

Eric thinks for a moment then says, "He definitely likes to give the impression that his photography business is successful, and he enjoys the finer things, but I'm not sure Wayne's capable of pulling off a premeditated murder. And whoever lured other-Meaghan to Harmony Lake was a woman. I doubt Wayne could fake a woman's voice and a woman's giggle on the phone for an entire conversation."

"April said the same thing," I tell him. "She thinks Wayne is too lazy to kill someone. And let's face it, he doesn't seem to do much. Felicia admits to practically running his business for him. She helps with the kids and house as needed, and other-Meaghan managed the house and the back and forth of the kids with Wayne's ex-wife. Karla says the only photography bookings he gets are from *Just Task Me!* In her words, Wayne is 'allergic to work,' and according to Adam, Wayne golfs every weekday at the club, which would leave him little time to work."

We stop talking while Eric makes notes, and I drink my Frappuccino.

"Did you get the forensics report back yet for the yarn you showed me?" I ask when he puts his pen down.

"Partial," he replies. "You were right about it being a fibre blend. The soil was sent for more analysis. I hope to hear from them today or tomorrow."

"Soil?" I ask. "Do you mean the brown clumps of dried dirt on the yarn and in the bag?"

He nods. "And inside and around the car the murderer used."

"Karla has the same yarn in her desk."

Eric sits upright at full attention. "Are you sure?"

"More than 90% sure. She has a knitted letter **K** in her drawer. It looks like the same yarn. She said it's from when Rita taught her to knit a couple of years ago. She doesn't knit anymore, though."

"I can't link any one piece of evidence to only one suspect. Everything is linked to multiple people." He looks at me. "It's possible more than one of the suspects worked together to murder other-Meaghan."

We discuss it further and draw a few charts. We determine that partnerships between Rita and Karla, or Wayne and Felicia would be the most likely pairings of suspects.

"What is everyone's alibi?" I ask. "Did any two people alibi each other?"

"No." Eric shakes his head. "Wayne was golfing. There are lots of witnesses who saw him, and the club has security camera footage of his van arriving and leaving. Rita was with her sister. Again, lots of witnesses but she doesn't have a cell phone to track. Felicia was at Princess Diana Botanical Gardens. We have her parking receipt and video footage of her car arriving and leaving. We also have her cell phone location. Karla was at the Harmony Hills Mall. We have footage of her car entering and leaving the mall parking lot, but very little footage of her inside the mall. There was a problem with the mall's security system, and they took various cameras offline that day to fix it. But we do have her cell phone location."

"When was the getaway car stolen and from where?"

"Shortly before other-Meaghan's death, from the parking lot at Harmony Hills Mall. We have no camera footage of the car leaving the lot because it was parked in an area monitored by one of the camera's that was taken offline."

Bad luck.

"Let me get this straight," I say. "The getaway car was stolen from the parking lot of the mall where Karla was, and across the street from the entrance to the parking lot for Princess Diana Park, where Felicia was. And Princess Diana Park just happens to back onto the fourteenth and fifteenth holes of the golf course at the Harmony Hills Golf and Country Club where Wayne was." I pause and wait for Eric to confirm I'm correct. "Do you think all four of them were working together?" As soon as I ask, a shiver runs down my spine.

I can't imagine the four people I love most conspiring to kill me to profit from my death.

He shakes his head. He looks exhausted. I slide across the sofa and snuggle up beside him, nuzzling my head into his chest. "I wish I could help. Is there anything I can do?"

He squeezes me tightly. "Can you find the murder weapon? It's probably the key to solving this case. It's like the earth just swallowed it up."

"This is for Mrs. Roblin." Connie holds up a skein of forest green worsted weight yarn. "She phoned this morning and asked me to put it aside." She tosses it to me.

"Got it." I catch the skein of yarn and stash it on the shelf under the cash register. "What's this?" I ask, picking up a stickie note I notice on the floor behind the counter. It has Wayne M scrawled on it with a phone number.

"Marla took that message before she left," Connie recalls. "That man, Wayne, phoned here looking for you this morning. He'd like you to call him. She stuck it to the cash register, but it must have fallen off. Those off-brand stickie notes aren't worth it. They don't stick to anything. We're better off paying more for the name-brand ones."

Half listening to Connie's rant about the inferiority of off-brand office supplies, I wonder what Wayne wants and whether I should call him back. I assume Wayne M is Wayne Martelle. I don't know another Wayne M.

The store phone rings, putting an end to my internal debate about whether to call Wayne back. The call display says: *Martelle, W.* It's him.

"Thank you for calling Knitorious, Megan speaking."

"Hi, Megan. It's Wayne Martelle."

"Hi Wayne. How are you?" Dumb question. His wife died three days ago! "I mean, it's nice to hear from you. Is everything OK?"

"Yes, everything is fine. We're planning a sort of memorial gathering for my wife. This Sunday. Family and close friends only. Meaghan won't be here, of course. The police haven't released her yet. But Felicia, and Rita, and I would like to invite you and April. I understand if it's short notice."

"Well, I can't speak for April, but I'll be there."

"I tried to connect with you and April on Facebook earlier to send you an invitation online, but I didn't hear back from either of you."

That explains the flurry of social media requests.

"I apologize, Wayne, I don't go on social media very often, and Fridays are busy at the store this time of year. April's bakery is just as hectic. I'll pass along the invitation to her if you'd like."

"That would be great, Megan. Thank you."

Wayne gives me the time for the memorial gathering, and I jot it down quickly in my planner.

SOPHIE and I hang around after the store closes. I tidy the shelves, sweep the floor, and wait for Mrs. Roblin, who is running late to pick up the skein of yarn Connie put aside for her.

As I wander the store, returning mislaid skeins of yarn to their rightful shelves, something Eric said earlier nags at me. His comment about the murder weapon, and how it's like the earth just swallowed it up, keeps popping back into my head. It feels significant, like it's related to something else that's on the tip of my brain, but I can't quite grasp.

I flop onto the sofa and text April to let her know about the memorial gathering for other-Meaghan on Sunday. She texts me back to let me know she's going but is holding off until after the memorial to accept Wayne and Felicia's social media requests.

Sophie's bark startles me, and I nearly jump out of my skin. "Who's here, Soph?" I wave to Mrs. Roblin through the window as I unlock the door and let her in.

"Thank goodness you had another skein of this yarn!" she declares, squeezing it against her cheek. "I bought it six months ago. I just need enough to finish the sleeves of my husband's new sweater. I know I have two more skeins of it. They're buried somewhere in my craft room, and I can't find them. It's like my stash just swallowed them up." She laughs.

Mrs. Roblin's simile triggers something in my brain, and I realize why Eric's comment was lingering in my thoughts.

I ring up Mrs. Roblin's skein of yarn and wish her a good day. After I lock the door behind her, I resume my seat on the sofa and text Eric.

196

Me: I think I might know where the murder weapon is.
Eric: Where are you?
Me: Work.
Eric: I'll be there in ten minutes.

"It's too bad you aren't one of those sniffer dogs, Sophie," I tell her on my way to the kitchenette to fix her dinner. "Maybe we should train you to sniff out murder weapons."

"WE'VE ALREADY SEARCHED Princess Diana Park," Eric reminds me as I sink deeper into his leather sofa.

"But have you searched *under* the park?" I ask.

"That is a massive undertaking," he explains. "It's over 400 acres. I'd never get approval."

"That's why it's such a good hiding place," I observe. "Look at the evidence. You found mud in and around the get-away car. You found mud on the yarn inside the get-away car. Felicia was banging mud off a pair of rain boots yesterday. She handed me a box of kids' toys that were caked in dried mud, including a toy shovel. And three of the four suspects were either at or adjacent to that park when other-Meaghan was killed."

"If Wayne, Felicia, or Karla did it, or some combination of them, they left their phone behind to make it look like they never left the scene of their alibi," Eric points out. "So far, the forensics people haven't found anything unique about the soil to link it to a specific place or type of plant. I was hoping there would be something that would narrow the search to a specific area of the park."

"If you get a sample of the mud from the toy shovel and the boots, could they match it to the mud from the yarn and the getaway car?"

"Possibly," Eric replies, "but it wouldn't prove that the car and the boots and the shovel got muddy at the same time." He shrugs. "It could have been days apart."

"It hasn't rained for almost two weeks. There aren't many places around where one can get mud on one's boots," I point out.

Eric looks at his watch. "Don't you have to pick up Hannah?"

I shake my head. "Adam's picking her up. Do you have time for dinner?"

Eric nods. "I'd like that. Then I have to go back to work and figure out how to justify digging up an entire park."

CHAPTER 26

<small>SATURDAY</small>, July 11th

Eric: Did Wayne mention a memorial gathering for other-Meaghan?

Me: Yes. Tomorrow. He invited April and me.

Eric: You going?

Me: Was planning to. Are you going? I won't go if you're going.

Eric: I'm not going.

Me: K.

Eric: Do you know what a sting operation is?

Me: I think so. Why?

Eric: Do you want to help with one?

Me: YEEESSSSSS!!!!!

CHAPTER 27

SUNDAY, July 12th

"Are you sure you're comfortable with this? You don't have to do it. You can change your mind." Eric's brow is furrowed. He looks worried. He's having doubts.

"I want to help. I want this case solved as much as you do," I remind him. "If you aren't comfortable with me helping, why did you ask me?"

"Darby convinced me to ask you. You're the best person for the job because these people trust you. I know he's right, but that doesn't mean I like it. Operation Twisted Stitches is going down in Harmony Hills, in Darby's jurisdiction. His people need to be part of it, and they have input into how this plays out."

I think it's adorable that they gave the sting operation a knitting-related name. There is a knitting slant to the case, after all. I'm a knitter and yarn store owner, Rita's a knitter and yarn dyer, and Karla took knitting for a test drive a couple of years ago.

"How do I look? Appropriate for a memorial gathering?" I spin around and show off my black, sleeveless, fit and flare dress with a V-neck and V-back.

Despite having an extensive summer dress collection, only two of them are black. I wore the first one on Thursday, and the second one today. If I need to attend another function for other-Meaghan, I either have to re-wear one of these two black dresses or wear something that isn't black.

"You look beautiful." This is Eric's standard reply no matter what I'm wearing. He once told me I look beautiful in a sock monkey-themed onesie.

"It's not too casual? Maybe I should Facetime April quickly and get her opinion."

"Honestly, you look perfect," Eric insists. "Speaking of April, you haven't told her about this right?"

"No." I roll my eyes. "When would I? You texted me yesterday at the store on the busiest day of the week, we stayed up late last night going over everything with Darby, and we got up early this morning to go over it all again. I haven't had time to tell anyone anything."

"But you did text her about taking separate cars?" he asks.

I nod. "She was fine with it. We'll meet outside Wayne's house and go in together. She's bringing something from the bakery from both of us."

"Darby will be there. There will also be two other non-uniform officers mingling in the crowd. They know who you are. I sent them your picture. They'll introduce themselves to you. I want you to know who they are, in case you have a problem and need help."

"Won't introducing themselves ruin their cover?"

"They won't tell you they're cops. They'll tell you their first name and mention Sophie in their first sentence. Just shake their hand and they'll walk away." He shrugs.

"If this gathering is just friends and family, won't Wayne wonder who they are?"

"Wayne knows. This is standard procedure. We have his permission to be there. What photo did you choose as my contact photo in your phone?"

"One of the selfies we took at your brother's wedding last month." I unlock my phone and show him the photo of us outside the reception venue. "It's a good one because it's a closeup and your face takes up most of the screen. It's easy to recognize you. And I changed your contact name from Eric to Eric Sloane, so there will be no doubt it's you."

"Perfect," he confirms. "You can change it back later. After you're safely out of there."

I shrug. "I might leave the photo. It's a good picture of us, but I'll definitely remove your last name."

"Let's go over everything one more time," he suggests.

I shake my head. "Relax. I've got it. Everything will be fine," I reassure him. He pulls me in for a hug and kisses the top of my head. "Shouldn't this be the other way around? Shouldn't you, the cop, be reassuring me, the civilian?" I tease.

"Stay with the crowd," Eric reminds me. "Don't go anywhere alone with any of them."

"Got it."

"2:00 P.M.," he reiterates.

"2:00 P.M." I nod.

"You look Megalicious!" April compliments me as I climb down from the giant SUV.

I can't wait until my car is fixed.

There are already several vehicles in the Martelle's driveway and in front of the house, forcing April and me to park up the street.

"Thank you," I reply. "As usual, you're stunning!" I give her a hug and she holds the white confectionery box she's carrying at arm's length, where I can't crush it. "What are we bringing?" I point to the box.

"Red velvet mini cakes," she replies. "Want one?"

"Yes, please!"

Carefully, April opens the white box and reveals the small, round, red velvet layer cakes.

"The icing is a whipped cream and cream cheese mixture," she explains.

Gently, I ease one of the cakes from the box. April places the box on the hood of her car and rearranges the remaining cakes to make the missing cake less obvious.

There are two layers of cake with a thick layer of icing in between and an icing flower on top. The icing flower is embellished with a chocolate curl and a gold-coloured candy button.

"T is so talented." I admire the gorgeous pastry. "I can never decide if her creations are the most beautiful, or the yummiest, I've ever had."

"Both," April attests.

"You're right," I mutter with my mouth full of cake.

I open my phone and check my face in the camera, making sure there are no crumbs or icing left behind. I freshen up my lipstick and take a deep breath.

"Ready?" April asks.

"Ready."

The woman who opens the door and invites us in, introduces herself as Wayne's first wife. April and I introduce ourselves as family friends.

I'm careful to introduce myself using only my first name today, because I don't want to freak out any of the mourners. Wayne's first wife relieves April of the confectionery box, then flags down a server, and hands it to him. Dutifully, he takes it and disappears toward the kitchen area.

The main floor of Wayne's house is crowded. There are at least fifty people here. Other-Meaghan has a lot of close friends and family.

A few feet into the space and we're approached by a

server carrying a tray of drinks. "Champagne on the left, ginger ale on the right," she says.

I'm driving, so I take a ginger ale. April also takes a ginger ale. "Champagne at a memorial service?" April whispers as the server walks away.

I shrug. "I guess if we're celebrating her life, it makes sense?"

"Megan! April! Did you get some champagne?" Rita threads her way through the crowd toward us. "It was Meaghan's favourite. Everything they're serving today are Meaghan's favourites."

I hug Rita. "That's a lovely tribute."

April hugs Rita. Rita points to a large photo collage of other-Meaghan on display above the fireplace. Rita and Wayne's sons made it yesterday and this morning. Rita beams with pride as she shows it to us. The collage is a labour of love.

Seeing Rita bask in the glow of so much love for her beloved Meaghan is a reminder to me that these types of gatherings aren't for the deceased, but for the people who are left behind. To remind them that they aren't alone in their grief, and their loved one made an impact while they were alive and left a legacy of people who were touched by them and love them.

"Megan, right?" I turn away from Rita and April toward the voice beside me.

"Right," I extend my hand and shake his meaty hand, noting his strong grip.

"Nate," he says as though he's reminding me. "You're a friend of Sophie's, right? I think we met at her place a few months ago."

"I remember now," I say, realizing Nate is one of the plain-clothed police officers Eric told me about. "It's nice to see you again." I commit his round face, moustache, and dark hair with a slight receding hairline to memory.

"You too. Take care. Hopefully we'll catch up later." And just as quickly as he appeared, Nate is gone, blending into the crowd.

I turn back to April and Rita. April gives me a quizzical side eye and I smile.

Rita continues telling us stories behind the photos in other-Meaghan's collage. I finish my ginger ale and turn to place it on the tray of a passing server when a tall woman with a white pixie cut appears in front of me.

"Hi, Megan," she says, extending her hand.

"Hi," I say shaking her long, thin hand.

"I haven't seen you since Sophie's birthday dinner." She places her hand on her chest. "Alex, remember?" Ah, the other non-uniform officer.

"Right, of course. It's good to see you again, Alex. Your lashes are fabulous, by the way." Alex has large blue eyes and her lashes are distractingly thick and long. I have lash envy.

"They're mink." She winks. "I'll see you around." And just like her colleague, she disappears into the sea of people.

When I turn back to Rita and April, Rita is gone. "Where did Rita go?"

"She saw someone she needed to talk to," April replies. She tips her champagne flute into her mouth and drains the remaining ginger ale. "I had no idea Sophie has such a rich and full social life. When does she find time to host all these parties?"

"You heard that?"

She nods.

"I have to use the washroom," I say.

"Let's go."

I don't have to use the washroom, but I need to give April an explanation for Sophie's popularity, and the washroom is the only place I can think of that will give us any privacy.

"They're cops," I whisper as April locks the door behind her, and I turn on the faucet to drown out our voices. "Sophie is the code word, so I know who they are. Eric said they're here to watch and listen. There's another one here too. Remember Detective Morris? From Rita's driveway?"

"Why do you need to know who they are?" April whispers so quietly, I can hardly hear her.

"I'm helping them with something," I reply. She looks at me to explain further. "I *really* want to tell you more, but I can't. Trust me, I'll tell you everything after we leave."

She nods. "OK. I'll be discreet. I won't even look at the cops."

"Actually, I could use some help if you're interested."

"Of course, I'm interested." She moves in closer.

"Help me get Wayne, Rita, Felicia, and Karla in the same place at 2:00 P.M. But it has to seem organic."

April winks. "I'm on it."

I turn off the faucet, then open the door.

"I KNEW you two were more than friends!" Karla is standing outside the washroom, waiting for her turn.

"Hi, Karla." Shockingly, she moves in for a hug. I'd never have guessed she's a hugger.

"Your secret is safe with me," she whispers during the gentle, quick hug.

"We're just friends," I insist as she hugs April.

"Whatever you say, ladies!" she says, grinning as she walks through April and I into the washroom and closes the door behind her.

"I'm flattered." I look up at April. "You're way out of my league."

CHAPTER 28

TRYING to stifle our giggles over Karla's misguided impression of our friendship, and maintain a mood more appropriate to the occasion, we decide to find Wayne and say hello.

"Over there." April cranes her long neck above the crowd. "Near the back door."

We navigate through clusters of people toward the French doors at the back of the house. By the time we get there, Wayne is on the other side of the door, standing on the back deck talking to a group of men. His golf buddies, I assume, because they're miming golf strokes and proper golf posture, despite not having golf clubs in their hands.

One man imitates driving a golf ball off the tee, then the other men take turns critiquing his form. To illustrate a point he's making, Wayne imitates a golf drive, and I notice his stance differs from his friends. He golfs left. Is Wayne left-handed? Only ten percent of the population is left-handed. What are the odds that Wayne and his wife are both lefties? If he is left-handed, it's unlikely he would move her computer mouse to the right side of her desk to embezzle money from her business.

"Megan! April! I'm so glad you could both make it."

Noticing us, Wayne excuses himself from his friends and joins us.

"Nice form," I compliment his pretend tee shot. "I didn't realize you're a southpaw."

"Lots of practice," he jokes. "Yes, I'm a southpaw. Something else my lovely wife and I had in common. Thank you for coming." He stoops over and kisses my cheek. He straightens up and leans toward April, kissing her cheek. "It means a lot."

We didn't know Wayne until two days ago, but apparently our friendship has already levelled up to cheek-kissing status.

"We're honoured to be invited," April replies.

"I know you never got to meet her," he says, "and we've only known each other a few days." He gestures among the three of us. "But your visit the other day meant a lot to me, and I know you've been a great comfort to Rita."

"I feel like your wife and I would've been friends if we had the chance," I say.

"I agree with you." He smiles.

Someone else comes outside and approaches Wayne to offer their condolences, so April and I move along to give them some privacy.

"Think back," I say quietly to April. "Is Rita left or right-handed?"

"Why?"

"We have this theory that the killer is right-handed," I explain.

"Isn't most of the world right-handed?"

"I think so, but weirdly Wayne and other-Meaghan are both lefties."

"Let me think." April gazes into the distance and starts counting down with her fingers. "I'm sure the first time we went to her house she handed me a glass of iced tea with her right hand. And when she was on the phone hearing about other-Meaghan's death, the phone was in her right hand."

"And when we went back the next day, she picked up her joint from the ashtray with her right hand," I add.

"Right-handed," we say in unison.

"You think Rita did it?" April whispers. "You'll need more evidence than a trait she shares with ninety percent of the planet."

"I doubt she did it," I clarify. "Whoever did it is also computer-savvy enough to do basic banking and accounting online."

April shakes her head. "Rita's not your woman. She doesn't even have a cell phone, and I didn't see a computer, or tablet, or anything at her house. The computer age left her behind."

"I think you're right," I agree.

Beginning to wilt in the heat, April and I seek refuge in the air-conditioned house. Gratefully, we each take another flute of ginger ale from the next server who ventures within our arms' reach.

"There you are!" Felicia declares with her arms outstretched. "Karla said you were here. Thank you for coming," she says during our three-way hug.

"Of course," I reply. "Did you throw all of this together?" I gesture around us.

"It was a group effort," Felicia replies. "Rita and the boys made the collage and created the playlist of Meaghan's favourite music, Karla arranged the caterers and gave them a menu of Meaghan's favourite foods and drinks, and I cleaned the house, created the event in Wayne's Facebook account, and sent out the invitations. Wayne called the guests who aren't on Facebook and invited them personally. The four of us are a good team!"

"Wayne mentioned you and he tried to reach us on social media," I explain. "It's tourist season in Harmony Lake and there isn't much time for social media right now."

"No problem," Felicia says. "You made it here, and that's

all that matters. I reached out to you on Instagram. I post a lot of my photography work there, including my shots from Harmony Lake."

"I'll be sure to follow you back when I get home." I haven't decided yet if this is true or not. We'll have to see how the rest of the afternoon plays out first.

"The photo you like of the Harmony Lake Pier is here," Felicia declares. "It's in the basement. Do you want to come downstairs and take a look?"

Remembering what Eric said about not getting separated from the herd, I look at April. "What do you think?"

"I'd love to," April replies.

Felicia descends the stairs first. She's about halfway down, and I'm about a quarter of the way down. April is about to step onto the top step when a muffled voice calls her name. We all stop and turn around.

"Did you make these?" Karla garbles with a mouthful of food while pointing at the half eaten red velvet mini cake in her hand.

"My wife, Tamara did," April replies. "Yummy, aren't they?"

Karla shoves the rest of the mini cake in her mouth and rubs her hands together to wipe away the crumbs. "We need to talk. Do you cater?" Her words are distorted by the mouthful of cake she's chewing. She takes April's arm. "C'mon," she mumbles and jerks her head away from the basement.

"I guess I'll catch up." April smiles.

So much for not going anywhere alone with anyone.

Felicia and I look at each other. She shrugs, turns her head, and continues down the stairs. I follow.

We're alone in the basement. I thought Wayne's sons might be down here because I haven't seen them yet, but there's no one else down here.

"In Wayne's office," Felicia says, leading the way down the hall.

The framed photograph is leaning against the wall with several other photographs.

"It's beautiful, Felicia." I would want to reframe it, but mentally, I've already picked out the perfect spot for it in my dining room.

"Are the ones behind it yours too?"

Felicia nods.

"May I look through them?"

She nods again.

Carefully I flip through the framed photographs of places that are both comfortingly familiar, yet at the same time brand new. I stop when I get to a black-and-white photograph of the Harmony Lake Police Station. It's a photo of the original entrance, a large, weathered, wooden door surrounded by the original stone-clad wall. The word, POLICE is above the door in simple carved letters. This entrance isn't used anymore. I think when the new station was built, this part of the original station was left intact as a nod to the town's past and for the sake of posterity.

"Can you do me a favour?" I turn and look at Felicia. "Can you write down the prices for the photos of the pier and the police station?" A certain detective sergeant I know would like the police station photo.

"I can text them to you if it's easier."

"Actually, if you could write them on the back of one of your business cards, that would be ideal." I smile.

Felicia picks up a business card from the top of Wayne's filing cabinet, then she walks over to Wayne's desk, and picks up a pen. From the corner of my eye, I watch as she flips over the business card and starts writing. With her right hand.

"Here you go." She hands me the card and I slip it into my bag.

"Is it OK if I get back to you in a couple of days?" I ask.

"Absolutely," she replies.

I can tell she's excited about a potential sale.

"We should get back upstairs," I say with one foot already outside the office.

Turning the corner toward the stairs, I notice the clock on the wall says 1:45 P.M. I have fifteen minutes to get everyone into place.

Darby Morris is hovering around at the top of the stairs, looking at his phone.

"Nice to see you Detective Morris," I greet him with a smile when I reach the main floor.

"Likewise, Ms. Martel." He nods. "Quite a heatwave we're having, isn't it?"

"It sure is." I smile as I walk past him.

I scan the open space looking for April. Where are you, April? The crowd is thinning. People have either started to leave or they're spilling onto the back deck.

I decide to check the washroom before the back deck, to delay exposing myself to the extreme heat outside.

The door is open, and the light is on. I peek my head into the all-white washroom.

"She stepped onto the front porch to take a call." Karla looks at me in the washroom mirror, where she's touching up her lipstick. With her left hand, I think. "I assume you're looking for April?"

I do a double take, in case watching her in the mirror confuses my perspective. The mirror is messing with me. She's using her right hand.

"I am. Looking for April. Thanks," I reply distractedly while I continue to watch her touch up her lips, confirming again that she's definitely right-handed.

"Can I help you with something else?" Karla asks, still looking at me in the mirror.

I snap back to the here and now. "That shade of lipstick is

great," I say. "I was just trying to picture it on me. I think I'm too fair, though. It would be too harsh."

"Actually," she says, turning to look at me directly. "You could use a pop of colour. Want to try it?" She extends the uncapped lipstick toward me.

I could use a pop of colour. Really? There's nothing wrong with my neutral lipstick, thank you very much.

"No thanks," I reply. "Now that I look closely, bright colours tend to have an aging effect." I smile and turn to leave.

Should I have stooped to her level? No. Do I regret that I did? Also, no.

CHAPTER 29

WALKING TOWARD THE BACK DOOR, I pull my phone from my bag and check the time. Five minutes. I look up from my phone, and my smart, beautiful best friend, April, is standing at the kitchen island, holding court surrounded by Wayne, Rita, and Felicia.

"There you are, Megabear! Where did you go?"

"I was looking for you," I reply.

"Now we just need Karla!" April declares loudly.

"Need me for what?" Karla replies from behind me.

"Wayne, Felicia, and Rita have kindly agreed to taste test the red velvet mini cakes. It's a new recipe, and T, my wife, always second guesses new recipes. She's hesitant to add them to the menu at the bakery. We know Megan loves them, but an honest opinion from people she doesn't know would go a long way to convince her these are worthy of a spot in our glass display case."

I make a mental note to tell April how incredibly brilliant and amazing she is each and every time I talk to her, forever. She hands each of us a napkin. Then she opens the white box and extends it to each of us so we can take a mini cake.

"You already know how I feel about them, darling," Karla

says, reaching into the box. "But I never say no to a good piece of cake."

Darling? Really?

"Now, be honest. Good, bad, whatever your first impression is, I want the truth," April reminds us, then she takes a bite of her piece of cake.

Deftly, I place my phone face up on the island where everyone can see it, then bite into my piece of red velvet heaven.

Everyone is chewing, nodding, and complimenting T's baking skills when my phone begins ringing and moving around randomly on the kitchen island because of the vibration. I pretend I don't notice.

"Megan, is that your phone?" Wayne asks.

"I'm sorry?" I look at him.

"Your phone," Felicia says. "It's ringing."

"Oh, shoot," I reply. "I was so distracted by the cake that I forgot I put my phone down. I assumed someone else's phone was ringing."

I laugh. They laugh awkwardly. I put my cake on the counter and wipe my hands.

I pick up the phone and accept the call. "Eric?"

"Was that Detective Sloane's name and picture on her call display?" Wayne asks the others as I take one step away from the group. Far enough to create the illusion of wanting privacy, but close enough to ensure they can still hear me.

"Everything going as planned?" Eric asks.

"Yup," I reply chipperly.

"Darby texted me to tell me you got them all together. Nicely done."

"Okaaaay," I reply.

"That means you should be able to get out of there within a couple of minutes of us hanging up, right?"

"It sure does." I look around and notice all three plain-clothed officers are loitering nearby.

We pause while Eric says nothing, and I occasionally mutter, "Mm-hmm," and "OK."

"Text me when you're safely in the car," Eric finally speaks.

"Don't worry about it," I say as per the script. "If it means you'll make an arrest tonight, it'll be worth it. I'm used to you cancelling plans to arrest a killer."

"I'll meet you where we agreed," he says on the other end of the phone.

The group behind me is silent. They're listening intently to my half of the conversation.

"OK, well be careful." I pause briefly, then continue, "Of course not. You know I won't say anything to anyone. I never do."

"Please be safe. I love you," he says.

"I love you too." I end the call.

"Sorry about that!" I pick up the rest of my red velvet mini cake and pop it into my mouth.

"Was that Detective Sloane?" Wayne asks.

I nod. "Uh-huh."

"You know him?" Karla asks.

I swallow the mouthful of cake. "Detective Hotty?" I wink at her. "I thought it was common knowledge. He called to tell me he has to work late tonight. We had plans, but there's a break in the case—oops!" I stop talking abruptly and bring my hand to my mouth.

"In Meaghan's case?" Wayne asks urgently. "What kind of break?"

I look around as if to ensure no one else can hear me. I lean into the kitchen island. They all lean in with me. "You didn't hear it from me," I begin in a loud whisper. "Eric says a witness came forward. Someone who saw the killer with the murder weapon. This person says they can lead the police to where the weapon is hidden and identify the killer. Eric says he has a good feeling about it."

"Did he say where?" Karla asks.

"Or who the witness is?" Felicia adds.

"No," I reply. "He said the police aren't allowed to go to the location until he gets a warrant. A warrant takes about an hour. Then the witness will show them where to unearth the gun." It might not be an Oscar-worthy performance, but I'm pretty pleased with myself.

"That's wonderful news!" Rita touches my arm. Her eyes are wet with tears of relief.

I check the time on my phone. "Actually, I have to get going," I tell everyone. "I have to get back to Harmony Lake." It's not a lie. I have to get back there, eventually.

April announces that she should also get going, and together we make our way to the front door.

"Would you mind giving me a ride home, Megan? If it's not too much trouble or out of your way?" Rita's hand is on my arm.

"Of course," I reply. "As long as you're leaving now."

She smiles and nods.

"CALL me as soon as you get home," April demands as we part ways at our cars.

"I promise." We hug goodbye.

She and Rita say goodbye, and I walk Rita around to the passenger side of the giant SUV where I hold her purse and a photo album dedicated to other-Meaghan she brought to the memorial with her.

"It's a steep climb," I warn her, spotting her and hoping she doesn't fall and hurt herself.

"I've climbed steeper," she replies.

I hand her purse to her and put the photo album in the backseat with my bag.

"Just a second, Rita. I told Eric I'd text him from the car."

Me: In the car. Rita is with me. I'm dropping her off at home.

Eric: Rita wasn't part of the plan. I'll meet you at her house instead.

Me: K.

I lock my phone and plug it into the console.

"Ready?" I ask, buckling my seatbelt.

"I knew you and that detective were a couple." Rita grins proudly.

"Really? How did you know?" I ask, pulling away from the curb.

"After you left on Thursday, he came by with a picture of yarn and asked me if I recognized it. It was bright coral, like the yarn you asked me about." She gives me an exaggerated wink. "I let him look through my colour samples, and he asked some educated questions about yarn. I asked him if he knits or crochets and he said he doesn't, but he has a good source who does. I asked him if you were his source."

"What did he say?" I ask, turning out of Wayne's subdivision.

"He changed the subject. But he blushed and rubbed the back of his neck. That's how I knew."

"You're perceptive," I say.

"Yes, I am. And I perceive that your phone call back there was a part of a scheme. You and your detective are up to something."

"It was just a phone call," I assure her.

"He thinks one of us did it, doesn't he?"

"They always start with the people closest to the victim and eliminate them first. The four of you were closest to Meaghan." I answer her question without answering her question.

"Is he really hoping to make an arrest today?"

"He hopes to make an arrest every day." It's like we're speaking in riddles. "I'm sorry I can't answer your questions.

I know you want whoever did this to get caught. I don't know who did it or when they'll get arrested, but I know they *will* be arrested. The police are determined to solve this."

"I know dear." Rita touches my arm gently. "You remind me of my Meaghan. You get shit done." She smiles sweetly, in that innocent way only the very young and the elderly can pull off.

"That's quite a compliment, thank you." I try to hide my shock at her use of profanity.

With a confused look on her face, Rita says, "I could've sworn Connie said you were married to a lawyer."

I nod. "Adam. We're…" I'm about to say *in the process of getting divorced*, but Rita interrupts me before I can finish my sentence.

"You have a husband *and* a boyfriend? You go, girl." Rita presents her fist for a fist bump. Not wanting to leave her hanging, I extend my fist and let her bump me.

I'm sure of two things: this is my first fist bump, and Rita is a seasoned fist bumper.

"We're not together anymore," I correct her. "We're almost divorced, actually."

"OK, dear." She smiles knowingly and pats my arm. I think she prefers her interpretation.

"ARE you sure you don't mind if I leave my car in your driveway? I can park on the street." I put the giant SUV in park and unbuckle my seatbelt.

"No! Park here. That way I'll know when you come back to pick it up, and I can ask you what happened."

"Deal," I say, turning off the engine. "He's here." In the rearview, I see Eric's car pull up across the bottom of the driveway. "Stay there, I'll help you down."

I unplug my phone, grab my tote, and dismount the vehicle. I open the passenger side door and take Rita's hand as she carefully steps down.

"Hello, detective!" Rita waves as she approaches Eric's car.

He lowers the passenger side window. "Hi, Ms. McConnell." Eric waves then reaches into his back seat and extends a Kevlar vest toward the open passenger side window. "Put this on," he says.

I step forward and take the bullet-proof vest from him. Rita holds my tote while I slip the vest over my dress and fasten the Velcro straps.

"You've done that before," she observes, handing my bag back to me.

"I had lessons this morning before I left for brunch," I reply.

I get in the car and buckle my seatbelt.

"Ready?" Eric asks.

I nod.

"Good luck! Be careful!" Rita waves as we pull away from her driveway.

"Did you tell her anything?"

"No," I assure him. "She figured out the phone call was part of a setup. I denied it, but she didn't believe me."

"I can't believe I let you talk me into bringing you along."

I get to watch the takedown. I negotiated it with Eric and Darby when we met last night to go over the plan. Eric was adamant that I shouldn't be there, but Darby was more open to compromise. I have to wear a vest and stay in the car. I can live with that. Darby has a lot of influence because this is happening in Harmony Hills, his jurisdiction. If it were happening in Harmony Lake, Eric's jurisdiction, I wouldn't be in the car right now.

"I was wrong about Wayne embezzling the money," I say.

"Who do you think it was?"

I tell him my theory. We have the same suspect in mind,

but for different reasons. In a few minutes, we should know for sure.

"Two on the move," Eric says. He has an earpiece to communicate with the other cops. "Not including Rita. She's still at home where you left her."

"So, it's narrowed down to two," I say.

We're convinced the killer buried the murder weapon at Princess Diana Park. Unfortunately, all the suspects had access to the park and proximity to it around the time other-Meaghan was killed and the murder weapon was disposed of. Since digging up a 400-acre botanical garden isn't a practical option, Eric and Darby are hoping to trick the murderer into leading them to the weapon. The fake phone conversation between Eric and me at the memorial gathering was to make the murderer—or murderers—believe someone who saw them hide the murder weapon has come forward. We want the murderer to believe they have one hour to retrieve the weapon before the witness leads the police to it. I left immediately after the staged phone call, and police are following the four suspects hoping that one of them leads to the murder weapon.

We pull into a busy parking lot in a strip plaza near Princess Diana Park and wait. If we get to the park before the murderer, and they see a police presence when they arrive, it will spook them. There are already police there disguised as groundskeepers and civilians, but no uniformed officers and no patrol cars.

In the event the murder weapon isn't at Princess Diana Park, each suspect is being followed. If they lead their police officer to a different location, their police officer can communicate with the rest of the team, so everyone can get to the other location or split up if two suspects go to two different locations.

"Another suspect is grocery shopping," Eric says. "At Shop'n'Save."

"There's only one suspect still in motion?"

He nods. "And they're heading in the direction of PDP."

PDP is Princess Diana Park.

After a few minutes of anxious waiting—anxious for me, Eric is cool, calm, and collected because chasing bad guys is his happy place—he says something into his microphone and puts the car in gear. Here we go.

"Stay. In. The. Car," he reminds me as we approach the gates to the park.

"I already promised I will," I reply.

"You've never stayed in the car. Ever. Today, I really need you to stay in the car."

"I will. You don't have to worry."

CHAPTER 30

"THERE ARE binoculars in the glove compartment. I'll leave the car running so the AC stays on. Don't leave the car." He throws the car in park, gets out, and runs down the path that leads from the parking lot to the gardens.

Four patrol cars pull into the parking lot. They surround a four-door compact car, and one of the cops tapes off the area around the car with police tape. I recognize the car. I helped its owner organize the trunk on Thursday. Felicia's here, or at least her car is.

I open the glove compartment and rifle around until I find the binoculars. Digital binoculars! They have a screen that flips open and buttons to take photos of what you're looking at or even film what you're looking at. There are slots for SD cards and dials to tune the image. I just want to look through them. When did binoculars go high-tech?

While I'm trying to figure out how to use the binoculars without breaking them, the driver's side door opens.

"Alex with the awesome lashes," I say as she closes the door and aims an air-conditioning vent toward her face.

"I thought you might like some audio to go with the visual." She hands me an earpiece and leans toward me.

I lean into her and put the earpiece in my left ear, tethering Alex and I together by the short, coiled cord that connects the earpiece to her vest. "I have no visual," I explain. "The binoculars are too advanced for me."

She takes the binoculars from me, holds them up to her face, flips a few switches, turns a few dials, and hands them back to me. She's so cool.

"They work," I confirm, holding them up to my eyes. "Thank you."

I can't see much beyond the trees that line the path leading out of the parking lot. There's a crowd of people beyond the trees, but I have to settle for partial glimpses when they momentarily position themselves between branches and tree trunks. Indistinguishable voices in my earpiece crackle and say words I don't understand. Cop speak. After a few moments, the word "secured" is bantered around a lot, and the crowd I'm watching through the binoculars becomes less active. They start moving toward the parking lot.

"They have her?" I ask Alex.

She nods. "And the gun."

"Mission accomplished. Congratulations," I say.

"You were great," Alex compliments me. "We don't like to involve civilians, but you did a fabulous job."

"Thank you." I think I'm blushing. "About your lashes, are they falsies or extensions? I love them. They give me lash envy."

"Magnetic," she replies. "Watch this." Leaning into me because we're still tethered by the cord on my earpiece, she pinches her right lashes with her thumb and forefinger and pulls them away from her eyes. Then she lets go and they snap back into place perfectly.

"Amazing," I remark, mesmerized.

Alex tugs the cord of the earpiece, removing it from my

ear and separating us. She winks, then opens the car door, and leaves.

A group of people emerges from the path leading to the park. There's a police officer on either side of Felicia, each gripping one of her arms. Her hands are cuffed behind her back. More officers, including Eric and Darby, surround them. Eric clutches plastic evidence bags in his hand.

I press what I hope is the power button and return the binoculars to the glove compartment.

Did Felicia and Hayden Lee work together to try to kill me? Why? Was I part of their plot or an innocent bystander? I need answers.

I get out of the car and walk to the front. With my butt resting against the hood, I cross my arms in front of my chest, which feels less satisfying than it sounds because of the added bulk of the bulletproof vest.

"Megan!" Felicia says with the same expression she had the first time she saw me, like she's looking at a ghost.

"Why?" I ask. "Why did you and Hayden Lee try to kill me?"

"It was a mistake," she calls as the police march her past me. "I'm sorry!"

Darby says something, and her entourage stops walking. They turn her to face me.

"Hayden was an idiot. He misspelled Meaghan's name. He was so stupid that he didn't realize you were the wrong target, even though he had a picture of the right target. I'm sorry. You seem nice and you were pulled into this by accident."

She apologizes as though almost killing me was a minor inconvenience. Like she scratched my car or shoplifted from my store, not like she almost ended my life and left my daughter motherless.

She does seem remorseful, though, which takes me by surprise. I expected Felicia to be angry about being caught and full of resentment and excuses about how none of this was her fault.

"So, you killed Hayden because he shot at the wrong Megan?" I ask.

"No," Felicia clarifies. "I killed Hayden because he was a liability. When he realized you were the wrong target, he panicked. He found a quiet place to park the car and called me. He told me what happened. He assumed I would pay him, anyway. Can you believe that? He was so dumb. I went along with it. I told him I'd meet him and bring him the payment in cash. He believed me. He really thought I would pay him for a botched hit!" Felicia lets out a nervous laugh. "I met him. I made sure he gave me the gun and the phone before I gave him the money. Then I told him I wasn't paying him for an incomplete job. I told him the cops were all over Harmony Hills looking for him and Rita's car. He said if I didn't pay him, he'd turn himself in and rat me out. He said because he didn't actually kill you, he could probably get a deal and do minimal time if he testified against me." She shrugs. "I had to kill him. I shot him."

"The money you embezzled from *Just Task Me!* was to pay Hayden?" I ask. "You funnelled it through Wayne's account so it would look like Wayne paid Hayden to murder his wife?"

"You don't get it! I never intended to pay Hayden," Felicia explains. "I always planned to kill him. It was supposed to look like a murder-suicide. If he hadn't messed up, and killed the right Meaghan, he'd be able to use it against me whenever he wanted. I wasn't prepared to live the rest of my life waiting for Hayden Lee to blackmail me for more money."

I never thought I'd feel sorry for the man who tried to kill me, but here I am feeling bad that Hayden was destined to end up dead no matter what he did or didn't do.

Darby says something, and the entourage starts walking again.

"The money was for me," Felicia blurts out. The entourage stops again. "She wanted rid of me. Did you know that? Meaghan told Wayne he had until the end of the month to let me go, or she'd do it herself. Do you know how much I do for that family? Do you know how many times I've gone above and beyond my duties as a photography assistant? Do you know how little they pay me? And she was just going to discard me? They owe me. That money was for me. I deserve it. I knew I could funnel it through Wayne's account because *I* do all the banking and bookkeeping for his business. He *never* looks at it. I was supposed to be long gone by the time anyone noticed the money was missing from *Just Task Me!* Meaghan only does the books at the end of each month. I should've had until the end of July to move enough money over, cash it out, and disappear. Karla messed that up by looking at the books. Something she never does. She trusted Meaghan implicitly with the company money."

"So, Meaghan had to die because she found out about the embezzlement before you had a chance to finish stealing money and disappear?" I clarify.

Felicia nods. "If she believed it wasn't Wayne, she would've realized it was me. Everything was messed up. Killing Meaghan before Wayne could convince her it wasn't him was the only way I could avoid being caught."

Let me get this straight, she'd rather risk getting arrested for double murder than for embezzlement. Not very logical, but is murder ever logical?

"But Hayden used Rita's car, and you planted yarn in the car you used when you killed Meaghan. Why try to frame Rita when you already had Wayne in the frame?"

She shakes her head vigorously, and bits of grass and leaves fly out of her pink hair. "Not Rita! KARLA! It was supposed to lead to KARLA!" She yells. "I knew Wayne had an alibi for Meaghan's murder. He was golfing. He's always golfing. Rita's car was across the street from Karla's house. It was easily recognizable because of the bumper sticker. I found the yarn in Rita's trunk when I met Hayden. There were bags and boxes of yarn in her trunk. Rita is a yarn hoarder. When I saw the orange yarn, I recognized it as the same yarn she gave to Karla when she taught Karla to knit. I knew Karla kept that stupid letter **K**. It was the only thing she ever knitted. She hated knitting, but she was proud of that letter **K**. She kept talking about turning it into a key chain or something. I knew she kept it. I thought it was on her desk at work. I thought Rita's car and the yarn would lead back to Karla. You guys messed that one up, not me."

"It was you who wrote the appointment at the Hav-a-nap Motel in Meaghan's planner, right?"

"Yes," she admits. "After Hayden messed up the only job he had, time was of the essence. I had to get rid of Meaghan before Wayne could convince her that it wasn't him who stole the money from *Just Task Me!* It was their week with the boys, which meant Meaghan wouldn't work late. I knew she'd be home in time to cook dinner and eat with the boys. I also knew she'd put her planner on the desk in her office and plug in her phone next to it. She wouldn't go back to her office until the boys went to bed, if at all.

"While the family ate dinner, I worked in Wayne's office. I used my phone to call Meaghan's phone, but I blocked my number. I answered her phone and left the line open for a few minutes, so if she checked her calls, she'd see there really was a call during dinner. When I hung up, I wrote the fake appointment in her planner. After the family finished dinner, I told her I heard her phone ring while she was eating. She told me she heard it but ignored it. I told her I answered it for her and spoke to the manager of the Hav-a-nap Motel. I told her he was keen to put *Just Task Me!* on retainer to provide concierge services to their guests. She was grateful to me for answering her phone.

"But Carlo said someone actually called him and tried to

book an appointment. That had to be you. Why did you bother phoning him if the appointment wasn't real?" This has been niggling at me since the beginning.

"I needed the manager's name, and I needed to confirm they don't already have a concierge service. It wasn't on their website. Meaghan solicits hotels and motels all the time. She probably already knew the manager's name, and whether the motel has a concierge service. It had to look like a real appointment."

"The only reason you chose the Hav-a-nap was because it's a motel that doesn't currently provide concierge services?"

"That and the highway ramp is right there. I knew I could get on the highway and have a decent head start before the police arrived at the scene. Also, it's not in Harmony Hills. I hoped if she died in a different town, it would take a while for the police to connect her death to Hayden's death and your close call."

"How did you get there and back without anyone seeing you?"

"I told Wayne I was going to Princess Diana Park to scout locations for yesterday's wedding shoot. He didn't care. I'm not even sure it registered. He would be golfing, and that's all he cared about. When I arrived at the park, I had a backpack with extra clothes, the gun, the burner phones, and a toy shovel. I walked along the path until I found a wooded area where no one was likely to see me. I buried one of the burner phones and my phone. Not too deep, though, because I needed to find them again, and I had to be sure my phone didn't lose its signal. Then I changed my clothes and put on a sunhat with a wide brim to cover my pink hair. I walked out of the park close to a group of other walkers. On the security camera footage at the entrance, it probably looks like I was part of their group. I even made small talk with them, so I'd look like I belonged."

Felicia's sunhat was a smart disguise, though. It's been so hot and sunny lately that a wide-brimmed hat would help her blend in with a group of people spending the day outside. It had the added benefits of shielding her face and her distinct pink hair from the cameras.

"I walked across the street to the mall and stole a car," Felicia continues. "I left my hat on so the security cameras at the mall wouldn't see my face. Once I was out of the mall parking lot, I pulled onto a side street and changed again, into sweatpants and a hoodie. Then I drove to the motel. Meaghan was so eager to close the deal she got there early. I was hoping to shoot her before she went inside, but I had to wait in the car until she came back. When she got in the car, I called her name before she closed the door. I walked up to her and killed her. Then I got back in the car and got out of there."

My stomach turns when I realize other-Meaghan probably recognized Felicia's voice and her face.

Felicia continues, "I found a quiet street, parked the car, changed out of the sweatpants and hoodie, and into my outfit with the hat. I tied the sweats and hoodie in a plastic bag and shoved the bag in my backpack. I abandoned the car, walked to the main road, and used the other burner phone to call a cab. I took the cab back to the park. I found the spot in the wooded area where I'd buried my phone and the other burner phone. I dug up my phone, dug a deeper hole, and buried the gun and both burners. Then, I changed into the clothes I was wearing when I arrived in my own car. When I left, I made sure the security cameras at the entrance saw my face. I dumped the bag with the sweatpants and hoodie in a dumpster on Karla's street. There's a house under renovation there, and they have a dumpster in the driveway."

"Wow," I say. "That took a lot of planning."

Felicia smiles. I think she's mistaken my comment for praise. I don't bother to correct her.

"Did you know Karla was at the mall, or was that a fluke?"

"She has a standing massage therapy appointment every Tuesday," Felicia explains. "We used to be roommates. I know her routine. People are creatures of habit. I assumed she still went there every Tuesday. I also know that Karla can't just walk into a mall and walk out. She's a shopper. Something between the car and the massage clinic would have caught her eye, and she would have stopped. Her one-hour massage appointments always last two hours because of her shopping hobby."

Eric says something to Darby, and Darby gets the entourage moving again. I watch as the officers duck Felicia into the back of a patrol car, and the door closes. She watches me from the back of the car.

"Way to stay in the car." Eric is smirking when I look up at him.

"I did stay in the car. I didn't get out of the car until you were back in the parking lot."

"I know. I'm teasing you. You did an awesome job." He positions himself between me and the patrol car Felicia is in. "Don't look at her. It's what she wants. She doesn't deserve any more of your attention. She tried to kill you."

I nod then look up at him. "Such a waste," I point out. "Two lives senselessly lost, and she'll spend the rest of her life in prison."

"Almost three lives lost," he reminds me. "It could've been much worse." He hugs me with his free arm.

"Whatcha got?" I nod toward the evidence bags he's carrying.

"One murder weapon and two burner phones." He holds up the clear plastic bags.

"Nice job," I commend him.

"Ditto," he replies.

"You're a pro, Megan!" Darby's voice booms as he

approaches Eric and me. "Have you ever considered a career change?"

"Thank you," I bow slightly. "I had two amazing coaches. And I think one cop in the family is enough."

Eric and Darby talk about logistics, who will take the murder weapon and phones to forensics for processing since all three items are evidence for two murders in two jurisdictions. While they figure it out, I take off the bullet-proof vest I'm wearing and take a deep breath.

"There you are." Rita is out of her house and halfway down her driveway before I unbuckle my seatbelt.

"Hi, Rita," I say, getting out of Eric's car. She has her purse over her shoulder and is carrying two foil baking trays. "Where are you off to?"

"Karla's," she replies. "Now that Felicia has been arrested, Wayne will need us. We're going over there to be with him."

"How did you find out it was Felicia?" Eric asks.

"Well, I knew it wasn't me," Rita explains. "Karla got home almost an hour ago with a trunk full of groceries, and I was talking to Wayne on the phone not twenty minutes ago."

Nothing gets by her. She reminds me of Connie.

"These are for you." Rita hands each of us a foil baking tray. "Brownies." She taps the foil lids in unison. "They have nuts. Be sure to warn the people you share them with in case they have a nut allergy."

"Got it," I assure her, slightly shocked that nuts are the only ingredient she's worried about providing a warning for.

"I have to go. Thank you both for everything." Rita looks at me and waggles her finger at me. "Save some of these for Connie. She loves my brownies." She winks and smiles sweetly, then walks across the street toward Karla's house.

"She always smiles and winks like she knows something I don't," I comment to Eric.

"I'm starving!" Eric begins to peel back the foil lid of his brownie tray.

I touch his hand, stopping him from opening the tray. "Nuts might not be the only extra ingredient," I caution.

He cracks the foil lid, raises the tray to his nose, and sniffs. "Pot."

I nod.

"I'll stop at a drive thru." He secures the foil lid to the tray of brownies.

I offer to take them off his hands, unlock the giant SUV, and put both trays on the passenger seat along with my tote bag.

"I'll be late tonight," he says, pulling me into his arms. "I need to visit Wayne and explain what happened. Then I have a mountain of paperwork and administrivia."

"Do you want me to visit Wayne with you? I don't mind."

"You've done enough police work for one day but thank you. Go home and take it easy. I'll text you when I get home."

I look up at him. "Will you be texting me from the family room or the kitchen?" I ask, hoping it doesn't come across as sarcastic.

"From my apartment."

"Really?" I'm shocked.

"All three cases are solved. Anyone who had any part in trying to hurt you is either dead or in a cell. You don't need me to protect you. Besides, I get the feeling you miss your space."

"It's not that I don't like it when you stay over..." I slide my hands up his back.

"I know," he interrupts me. "I understand." He kisses me. "If you need me, just call or text."

CHAPTER 31

I called April from the car yesterday when I was on my way home from Harmony Hills. I filled her in on Operation Twisted Stitches and thanked her for her help. Like the rest of us, she was relieved it's over and shocked it was Felicia. We're both amazed at what seemingly kind people can be capable of doing. April and Tamara have a meeting booked with Karla. Artsy Tartsy might sign a catering contract with *Just Task Me!* April's not sure if she wants to work with Karla on a regular basis, and I don't blame her.

When I got home, I told Hannah everything, and she told me she was proud of me for helping and even uttered the words every mother longs to hear from their eighteen-year-old daughter, "You're pretty cool for a mum." I might embroider that quote on a wall hanging to memorialize it.

After dinner, I called Connie. I thanked her for keeping the store running smoothly while I was mostly absent for four days during our busy season. Of course, she insisted she was more than happy to do it and even admitted she sometimes misses working there full-time. She's upset we haven't spent any time together this week, so I'm going to her condo for breakfast today.

I plan to give a similar thank you speech to Marla when I see her at work tomorrow.

It finally rained overnight. It's still hot, but the rain provided some relief from the humidity, making my morning walk with Sophie much more enjoyable than it has been lately. We even hung out at the park for a while and said hi to the other dogs and their owners.

Approaching the lobby of the condo building, the security guard buzzes me in.

"Thank you, Ivan." I smile. "Pot brownie?" I gesture to the foil trays I'm carrying.

"No, thank you," he waves away my offer. "Mr. Martel or Ms. Coulson?"

"Ms. Coulson, please," I reply.

Adam and Connie live in separate buildings that are connected by a main lobby. Ivan and I get to see each other whenever I visit either Connie or Adam. While I wait for Ivan to confirm with Connie that she's expecting me, and grant me access to the elevators, a familiar voice turns my head. Adam is getting off the elevator. I check the time on the clock behind Ivan. It's earlier than I thought. He's on his way to pick up Hannah and take her to work. His arm is around a woman. His non-girlfriend. Awkward!

Flustered, and before I can get a clear look at her, I drop the brownie trays on Ivan's desk and jump behind the Areca palm tree in the corner.

Ivan looks at me, concerned.

"Can you see me?" I hiss at him, panicked.

I lunge from behind the plant to Ivan's desk. Half under and half behind the desk, I crouch beside his legs. Alarmed, he rolls his chair slightly away from me and points his knees in the opposite direction. He looks down at me. "I'm not here," I mouth, shaking my head.

The inner door opens.

"Good morning, Ivan!" Adam's voice.

"Hi, Ivan." Her voice.

I recognize that voice!

"Good morning." Ivan's voice.

The outer door opens and closes. I wait a few seconds, then stand up, and return to the side of the desk I should be on.

Squinting, I stand on my tippy toes to catch a glimpse of Adam's non-girlfriend and confirm her voice belongs to whom I think it belongs to.

"Thanks, Ivan. I'm sorry if I invaded your personal space."

He smiles and nods. He glances from me to the brownie trays and back to me.

"I haven't had any of these. You can check." I thrust the trays toward him.

"It's OK," he says.

"Normally, I would remain visible and say hi, but I haven't met Adam's…. friend… yet. His choice not mine," I overshare with the security guard. "If he'd seen me, it would've been awkward and uncomfortable for everyone. This way, it was only awkward and uncomfortable for you and me."

"Yes," he agrees, nodding. "You can go up now." He buzzes me into the elevators.

"Thank you." I smile and pick up the brownie trays.

"COURTESY OF RITA." I hold the trays out to Connie.

"I'll call her later and thank her." Connie puts the trays on the table next to her and gives me a big hug with lots of maternal swaying and back rubbing. "It's amazing you're still alive," she says, pulling away and checking me over from head to toe.

"Of course, I'm alive. I told you that bullet wasn't meant for me."

"I'm not sure bullets know who they're intended to harm, my dear. You might be giving the bullet too much credit." She picks up the brownie trays.

I pick up Harlow, who's winding himself between my ankles, and I follow Connie to the kitchen.

Harlow is Connie's cat. He lived at Knitorious for years until Connie moved in with Archie last fall. Now, Harlow and I see each other when I visit the condo, or when Connie and Archie travel and Harlow stays at the store with me.

ARCHIE HAS LEFT for the day. He and Ryan—his son—are working on a job that will take them most of the day to complete.

While Connie makes French toast, and while we eat, I tell her about Operation Twisted Stitches and Felicia's confession.

"I know these things happen, my dear. I'm not naïve about how the world works, but it seems like you find yourself in the middle of these situations more often than the rest of us," Connie observes this while she cuts up the brownies and puts each piece in a small freezer bag.

"I had no idea you indulge in *special* brownies," I say.

She looks at me. "Only occasionally. Very occasionally, in fact. They do wonders for my arthritis and guarantee me a good night's sleep." She moves the empty tray aside and begins cutting up the brownies in the second tray. "Besides, they aren't illegal."

"I'm not judging you," I assure her as I load the dishwasher. "I'm just surprised there are still things I don't know about you."

After a nice, overdue visit talking about anything and

everything, I ask, "If I go to Harmony Hills today, do you need anything?"

"No thank you, my dear." She smiles and finds space in the freezer for the last freezer bag.

"Good," I reply. "I feel like I've spent more time in Harmony Hills this week than Harmony Lake. I think I'll skip my usual errands today and stay close to home."

Ivan and I wave awkwardly to each other on my way to the parking lot.

ADAM: *Can I call you?*

Uh-oh. Did he see me behind the palm tree in the lobby? Or hiding behind Ivan's desk?

Me: Sure.

A moment later my phone rings. "Hi."

"Hey, Meg. How are you?" He's in the car.

"Good. How are you?" I fold the last piece of clean laundry and add it the basket.

"Good. Listen, the insurance company called. The police released your car. It should be fixed by the end of this week or the beginning of next week at the latest."

"I can't wait. The courtesy car is nice, but I miss my car. And it'll be nice to let Hannah use my car instead of having to drive her everywhere. Thank you for letting me know."

"No problem," he replies. "Is it all right with you if I pick up Hannah from work tonight? We're going out for dinner."

"Of course. I'm happy you're spending more time together. Are you coming here first so she can change?"

"I think that's the plan. Why don't you join us?"

"Thank you, but I'll pass this time. I'm looking forward to a quiet evening in."

"Yeah, I heard you had quite a day yesterday. You and April are Harmony Lake's version of Cagney and Lacey."

Cagney and Lacey is an 80s TV show about two female crime-fighting detectives. Adam thinks he's funny.

I roll my eyes. "Who told you about Operation Twisted Stitches?"

"There are no secrets in this town, Meg."

"No, there aren't," I agree. "Speaking of secrets. I know you're seeing Jessica Kline."

Silence. I can't even hear him breathing.

Jessica Kline is the hygienist at our dentist's office.

"How?" Adam finally asks.

"I saw you," I admit. "I was hiding under Ivan's desk when you left this morning."

"What? Why?"

"I was on my way to visit Connie. I saw you getting off the elevator. I panicked and wanted to respect your boundaries around not meeting her. So, I hid. I may have crossed a few of Ivan's boundaries in the process, but I don't always make the best decisions on the fly."

Adam laughs hysterically. "Poor, Ivan," he says when he finally comes up for air.

"I'm glad you're amused," I say stoically. "You wouldn't be laughing if I didn't hide, would you?"

"I'm sorry." More laughter. "I'm just picturing you under Ivan's desk. And the fear Ivan must've felt." More laughter. I can practically hear the tears rolling down his cheeks.

While I wait for Adam to compose himself, I get a text.

Eric: I'm outside. Can I come in?

Me: Of course!

"Adam, I have to go. Someone's at the door."

"OK." He catches his breath. "I'm sorry for laughing. I really appreciate you not ambushing us this morning." He clears his throat to hold back a laugh. "Seriously, Meg, thank you."

I end the call, drop my phone on the table, and meet Eric

at the door. As soon as he steps inside, I notice he's not wearing his sidearm.

"You're not working today?" I ask.

He kisses me hello, then crouches down to rub Sophie. "I took the day off. I have so much time owing, and last week was long."

"I hope you did something fun and relaxing."

"I golfed with your husband this morning, and I have an exciting afternoon of laundry planned. That's why I'm here. To see how you're doing and to pick up my stuff."

"I wish you wouldn't call him that."

"In less than three months, I'll call him your ex-husband. Besides, he tells people at the club that I'm his wife's boyfriend."

"You two are sick and twisted." I shake my head. "And you have no dirty laundry here. I did all the laundry. Everything is washed, dried, and folded. Not ironed, though. I hate ironing."

"You didn't have to do that but thank you." He kisses my forehead.

"It was the least I could do. You made me feel safe after what happened. And you figured out who did it and why. I probably owe you a few more loads of laundry," I joke.

"*We* figured out who did it and why," he corrects me. "Thanks to you, I have nothing to do today. You want to see a movie or something?"

I nod and snuggle up next to him on the sofa. "I'm not ready for us to live together," I blurt.

"I know. I didn't mean to pressure you. I honestly just wanted to keep you safe," he says softly as he strokes my hair. "I like kissing you goodnight instead of kissing you goodbye, and I let myself get too comfortable with our temporary arrangement. I've deleted the apps you gave me access to. Let's go back to normal."

"How about a new normal?" I propose. "You keep the

apps so you can come and go from the house, and you keep some stuff here for when we both want you to stay. I already have a few things at your place, so it seems fair."

"I don't want to rush you, Megan. I know I sulked a bit when you pulled back this week, but that's my problem, not yours. It won't work if we both aren't ready. I love you, and I really want this to work."

"I don't feel rushed," I insist. "I've been thinking about it a lot. We'll probably spend more time apart than together while Hannah's home from school. She's still getting used to the divorce, and I don't want to push anymore change on her."

"Whatever you want. You call the shots. We go at your speed. I'll take as much or as little as you're ready to give."

"Let's try this new normal, then talk about it again after the divorce is final?"

Before Eric can answer, my phone rings, and I get up to retrieve it from the kitchen table. I don't recognize the number on the call display. It's probably a telemarketer. But it's a local number. What if it's Hannah?

"Hello?"

"Megan? It's Rita!" she yells, like we're talking through two tin cans connected by string instead of a 5G cell network.

"Hi, Rita!" Now I'm yelling and I'm not sure why. "Did you get a cell phone?"

"Heavens no! I'm using Wayne's phone. I think I left my photo album in your car yesterday. Would it be OK if Wayne drives me over to get it? That album means a lot to me."

"Of course. Hang on, I'll make sure it's in the car."

I put the call on hold while I pop to the garage and check the back seat of the giant SUV. On my way there and back, I tell Eric why Rita's calling, and why it sounds like I'm shouting at her.

"It's here," I tell her when I return from the garage with the album.

"That's a relief. We're already on the highway. We can be there in fifteen minutes."

I give Rita the address, and we end the call.

Eric and I rush around tidying up and moving the baskets of clean laundry out of site, when his phone dings.

"Work?" I ask.

"Some of the forensics results are back from yesterday." He reads the email intently.

"Anything interesting?"

He nods. "I'm sure Wayne will think so."

CHAPTER 32

"WE DON'T WANT you to leave without it," I say, handing Rita the photo album she left behind yesterday.

"Thank you, dear!" She puts the album in her knitting bag and continues knitting on the sock she brought with her.

While Eric gets lemonade and blueberry squares, Rita and I debate toe-up versus cuff-down sock construction, and Wayne feigns polite interest in our conversation while petting Sophie, who is nestled beside him on his chair.

Eric places a tray on the coffee table and joins me on the sofa. Rita tucks her knitting into her bag, and we help ourselves to lemonade and blueberry squares.

"It worked out well that Rita forgot her photo album," Wayne says between bites and sips. "I wanted to see you, Megan, to thank you for everything you've done this week. Eric told us about the role you played in finding the gun and encouraging Felicia's confession."

"I'm sorry it was necessary. And I'm sorry it turned out to be someone you trusted," I sympathize.

Wayne shakes his head. "We did trust her. We trusted her with my boys. We trusted her with everything."

"Karla couldn't join us today," Rita explains, "but she

asked us to thank you on her behalf. She was quite impressed with you. She said to tell you she's sorry she underestimated you, and you're obviously more intelligent than you let on."

Another insult thinly veiled by a compliment from Karla, delivered second hand, nonetheless. Backhanded compliments are Karla's superpower.

"Please tell her that after talking to her, I feel more intelligent." I can't believe I said that out loud. I bring my hand to my mouth, then lower it again. "Actually, please don't say that. Just tell her I'm sorry for her loss." I smile.

Eric muffles a laugh.

Wayne laughs, then shakes his head. "Don't worry about it. Karla has that effect on people."

"She does like you, Megan," Rita insists. "She only complisults people she respects. She must consider you a friend."

"Complisult?" I ask

"Yes, it's what my Meaghan called Karla's form of banter. A cross between a compliment and an insult." Rita smiles sweetly.

"That's brilliant!" I say.

Rita nods. "My Meaghan was soft on the outside and strong on the inside. Like you. Karla is the opposite. She's strong on the outside and soft on the inside. That's why they had such a good partnership."

"Speaking of Karla," Rita says as though something has just occurred to her. "She says I should get a lawyer to assist with the buy-sell agreement. She'll be purchasing Meaghan's share of the business from me. Would either of you know a good, honest lawyer?"

I get up and walk into the dining room where I shuffle through a drawer until I find one of Adam's business cards. "If he can't help you, he'll refer you to a lawyer who can," I explain, handing her the card.

"Your husband?" she asks coyly.

"Not anymore," I correct her. "We talked about this, remember?"

Rita nods with a wink and smiles knowingly.

"Have there been any new developments in my wife's case since we spoke with you yesterday?" Wayne asks, looking at Eric.

"A few," Eric nods. "Do you want to talk now, or would you rather do it later?"

Even on his day off, Eric can't avoid work.

Wayne and Rita indicate they'd like to hear about any new developments as soon as they happen.

Eric tells them the gun was confirmed to be the gun that shot other-Meaghan, Hayden Lee, and my car. Felicia's fingerprints and Hayden's fingerprints were both recovered from the gun. Felicia's fingerprints were also found on both burner phones, while Hayden's fingerprints were found on one phone.

The sweatpants and hoodie Felicia wore when she shot other-Meaghan were recovered from the dumpster on Karla and Rita's street. In a tied-up plastic bag, just as she described. Blood splatter on the clothes is a match for other-Meaghan.

Despite using burner phones to communicate, Felicia and Hayden used a code to refer to other-Meaghan. They referred to her as M2, likely a reference to her first and last initials both being M. Eric speculates that having not seen her name in writing, when left to his own devices, Hayden misspelled it, which erroneously led him to me instead of his intended target.

"We traced the money transfers from the *Just Task Me!* bank account to the *Martelle Photography* account," Eric explains. "They happened from your house. From your wife's computer, Wayne, but they all happened while you were golfing, and your wife was at work. Even if Felicia hadn't admitted to the misappropriation of funds, the trail of digital evidence would have implicated her."

This last development seems to hit Wayne the hardest. He becomes emotional and needs a moment to collect himself. While Rita rubs his back and arm, I get him a box of tissue.

"I'm sorry," Wayne says when he's recomposed. "The hardest part of all of this is that my wife died believing I stole from her."

"I'm sure deep down she knew you didn't do it, dear," Rita assures him.

"No, she believed it to her core. And it's my fault," Wayne insists.

Sensing where this is going, I'm fixing to change the subject, but Wayne continues talking.

Looking back and forth from me to Eric, he says, "You see, when Meaghan and I first got married, I lied to her about something. Something huge. I've regretted it every day since, but it destroyed her trust in me. She didn't leave me, and she said she forgave me, but I don't think the trust was ever really rebuilt. That lie, five years ago, left enough doubt that she didn't believe me about the stolen money. If I had known there was a digital trail of evidence that could prove to her it wasn't me, and would implicate Felicia, my wife might still be alive."

"Wayne," I implore, "you cannot accept responsibility for the actions of a double murderer. This is not your fault. The only people to blame here are Felicia and Hayden. Not you."

"That's not how it feels," he states.

"The coroner released Meaghan's body to the funeral home today," Rita announces, changing the subject.

Strangely, this new topic is more upbeat than the previous one.

"Mourning Glory?" I ask, doing my part to change the subject.

"Yes," Rita replies. "Mort and I are good friends. We go way back."

Mourning Glory is the funeral home in Harmony Hills. Mort is the funeral director.

Rita winks, making me wonder exactly how close she and Mort are and how far back they go. Does she make special brownies for him too? Focus, Megan.

"We should probably get going," Wayne says. "We have an appointment with Mort."

As we make our way to the door, Wayne turns to me and snaps his fingers. "I have something for you! I'll be right back."

Wayne leaves through the front door and returns a moment later with two framed photos. The ones I was planning to purchase from Felicia if she turned out not to be the killer.

"For you." He hands me the framed photos.

"Wayne, are these yours to give?" I ask.

"Yes," he replies. "Felicia took those photos with my camera. As per her employment agreement, I own the rights to any photography she takes with my equipment. I can show you the contract. Anyway, before your pretend phone conversation yesterday, she came upstairs from the basement and told me you were interested in purchasing them." He gestures to the photographs. "I gave her verbal permission to sell them to you. After everything that's happened since then, I want you to have them. Regardless of who took them, they're beautiful pieces of fine art. In fact, I'll be taking all the fine art photography that I own the rights to and auctioning them off at a charity auction. The proceeds will benefit my wife's favourite charities. I'm working with the golf club to secure a venue and date. Some good must come from this."

"Well, in that case, I'd like to pay for them so Meaghan's favourite causes will benefit."

Wayne waves away my offer. "I've already taken care of it. Please accept them."

"Thank you." I kiss Wayne's cheek, then kiss Rita's cheek, and give her a hug.

I close the door behind them and sigh audibly.

"I'm sorry you had to do that on your day off." Where did he go? "Eric?"

Sophie leads me to the dining room where I find Eric. The framed photographs are on the dining room table, and he's admiring them.

"Is this the pier where we walk Sophie sometimes?" he asks.

I nod.

"These are incredible," he comments. "I love this shot of the old police station."

"I'm glad," I reply. "It was supposed to be your birthday gift."

He looks at me.

"Surprise," I say with jazz hands.

"My birthday isn't until September," he points out.

"I know, I was planning to hide it until then. I thought of you when I saw it."

"It's perfect. Thank you."

"Don't thank me, thank Wayne. I assumed they wouldn't be available after Felicia was arrested. Even if they were, I'm not sure how I feel about hanging her work in my home. It's like having a piece of her here, looking at me. I don't know if I'll ever be able to look at it without thinking about everything that happened this week."

"I get it. It's hard to separate the art from the artist." He puts his arm around my shoulder and kisses the top of my head. "Want me to hide them?"

"Hide them?"

"I'll take them with me when I leave and hide them. You won't have to look at them. Later, I can bring them back and you can see if you feel differently. We can add it to the list of things to revisit after your divorce is final."

"That's a good idea, let's do it."

Eric collects the framed art from the dining room table and leans them against the wall by the front door, turned backwards.

"What movie should we see?" he asks.

"Not a murder mystery," I reply. "I'm ready for a break from solving mysteries."

I usually love mysteries, but frankly they feel a little close to real life right now.

Eric gives me a tight squeeze. "It has been a busy year," he chuckles. "I mean, how many suspicious deaths can one tiny town have? I have a feeling you've helped solve your last murder."

I wish I had that feeling.

Son of a Stitch

REAGAN DAVIS

COPYRIGHT

ISBN: 978-1-7772359-3-2 (ebook)

ISBN: 978-1-7772359-2-5 (print)

FOREWORD

Dear Reader,

Despite several layers of editing and proofreading, occasionally a typo or grammar mistake is so stubborn that it manages to thwart my editing efforts and camouflage itself amongst the words in the book.

If you encounter one of these obstinate typos or errors in this book, please let me know by contacting me at Hello@ReaganDavis.com.

Hopefully, together we can exterminate the annoying pests.

Thank you!

Reagan Davis

CHAPTER 1

Friday, October 2nd

Six across. Jolt from Joe, eight letters. Easy! C-A-F-F-E-I-N-E. My drug of choice.

"Murder!"

I clutch the crossword puzzle to my chest and turn around. "You startled me!" I scold. "Murder?"

"Four down."

I hold up the puzzle where we can both see it.

"A collection of crows is called a murder," Eric says, pointing to four down. "I didn't mean to scare you."

"I know. You can't help that you're freakishly light on your feet for such a big guy."

"It's my superpower," he winks and kisses my forehead. "Maple pecan latte with extra whipped cream and a drizzle of chocolate." Eric hands me a to-go cup from the local coffee shop, Latte Da. "Hope I got it right."

I put down the crossword puzzle. "Thank you," I say, giddy with anticipation and caffeine withdrawal. I take the cup from him and take a sip. "It's perfect."

Eric Sloane is my boyfriend and tenant. He lives in the apartment above my yarn store, Knitorious. We met last year when the Harmony Lake police department borrowed him from a nearby police force to investigate our town's first murder. He solved the murder, then accepted a job offer from Harmony Lake PD and relocated here. We've been dating since the end of January.

Eric and his cup of dark roast double-double position themselves behind the counter. He never stands on the business side of the counter.

"Are you alone again today?" he asks.

I nod. "Connie is still taking care of Archie and his new hip, and Marla is helping at Artsy Tartsy."

Connie is my mother-friend. She's the original owner of Knitorious. I worked for her part-time until she semi-retired last year and passed the store onto me. She moved out of the upstairs apartment and into a condo with her boyfriend, Archie. Now, we've come full circle. I own the store, and she works here part-time. Archie had his hip replaced last week, and Connie took time away from the store to care for him.

My other part-time employee, Marla, is helping at Artsy Tartsy, the local bakery that my best friend April and her wife, Tamara, own.

"How's April's dad? Any news?" Eric asks, bending down to rub my corgi, Sophie, who's pawing at his knees in a desperate attempt to get him to notice her.

"They're hopeful the surgery he had yesterday was the last one. She expects the doctor to discharge him tomorrow."

April's dad fell off a ladder while tending to his eaves troughs. He broke a leg, shoulder, and his collarbone. April rushed out of town to help her mum look after him. Since Tamara can't bake and work the front counter at the same time, Marla and I decided she would work at Artsy Tartsy this week instead of Knitorious. We're a small community, but we're tight-knit and look out for each other.

"You have no sidekicks this week," he teases.

"I have you and Sophie," I remind him.

"I have a meeting with my boss late this afternoon, but until then, I'm all yours. Put me to work!"

His boss is the chief of police, Charmaine Solomon.

"What do you mean?" I ask, confused. "You're working from the store today?" Not that I mind, but even in small doses, Eric's six-plus-foot muscular hotness messes with my concentration. To say he's a distraction is an understatement. I don't know how I'd be able to focus with him here all day.

"No," he clarifies, "I'm working *at* the store today and tomorrow. You're alone all week, and I have a ton of personal time I have to use. It makes sense." He shrugs and smiles. The honey-coloured flecks in his brown eyes momentarily side-track me, and my insides flutter.

Focus, Megan.

"You don't knit," I point out, coming to my senses. "Knito-rious is a yarn store. We cater to knitters and crocheters. It's really sweet that you want to help…"

"I don't have to know how to knit to help," he interrupts. "Megan, you've helped me with my job, and you're not a cop."

I can't argue with that, so I pick up a random skein of yarn from the nearest shelf and drop it on the counter. "I'd like to purchase this, please."

"Of course, ma'am." Eric smiles, picks up the skein of yarn and proceeds to process the transaction. I'm shocked. I pay for the yarn with the app on my phone. He places the skein in a bag with my receipt and hands it to me across the counter with a smile. "Have a nice day."

"I'm impressed! I didn't realize you pay attention when you pop in and out of the store."

"I'm not just a pretty face, you know." He winks.

Oh, I know.

I drop the bag of yarn on the counter. "I'd like to return this, please."

Processing the refund takes more focus than the purchase,

but he does it. The money reappears in my account and I return the skein of yarn to its shelf.

"You're hired," I say, "but there probably won't be much to do. October is one of the slowest months of the year. You might be so bored, you'll beg to go back to the station."

Harmony Lake is nestled snugly between the lake to the south and the Harmony Hills mountain range to the north. Nature left no room for expansion but provided the town with the perfect foundation for a tourism-based economy.

Between the two ski resorts in the Harmony Hills mountains, and all the rental cottages in and around town, Harmony Lake is full of skiing and snowboarding tourists in the winter. In the summer, city-escapees flock here for the lake and the small-town living experience.

During the busiest weeks, there are more visitors than locals in Harmony Lake. This is not one of those weeks. The summer tourists have returned home to their normal lives of school and work, and the winter tourists won't descend on us until December. Right now, the town is blissfully quiet and doesn't belong to anyone except us locals.

"I doubt it," he replies. "There's nowhere else I'd rather be."

Eric is prone to say romantic things that sometimes verge on sappy. It comes naturally to him, unlike me, who needs several days' notice to think up a reply that could be considered even vaguely romantic. If, however, a comment requires a quick reply that's either awkward or sarcastic, I'm your woman.

Taking her position as greeter seriously, Sophie springs into action immediately upon hearing the jingle of the bell. She trots to the door and meets my almost-ex-husband before he has both feet inside the store.

"There's nothing else to do, Meg. She's practically dead," Adam announces, closing the door behind him.

"Well, it was a longshot. Thanks for trying. I guess it's time to put her out of her misery."

Adam places the terminally ill laptop on the counter and squats down to greet Sophie properly. Shamelessly, she rolls onto her back and exposes her fluffy belly for him to rub. "Do you want me to pick up a new one? I don't mind."

New technology is Adam's happy place. He has yet to meet a new gadget or device he doesn't love.

"I'll take care of it," I respond. "Knitorious is my store, my responsibility. Thank you, though. But can you give me a list of features and specs I need? You know, techy stuff like RAM, and Gigs, and whatever."

I return the laptop to its place under the counter and plug it in. For what good it'll do.

Technology might be Adam's happy place, but it isn't mine. I can think of a dozen things I'd rather do than research and comparison shop for a new laptop. Normally, I'd be thrilled to let him choose a replacement. But our divorce will be finalized this month, and we need to establish a few boundaries. This laptop is a good start. It's high time I step outside my technological comfort zone.

Because we live in the same small town, our lives are more enmeshed than most divorced couples. We share a nineteen-year-old daughter, Hannah, and have brunch together every Sunday. I do the bookkeeping for his law practice, and he provides tech support for my personal life and the store.

During our almost-twenty-year marriage, Adam was a workaholic. He was a partner at a large law firm in the city, and his sixty-hour weeks meant we hardly saw each other. That was then. After we separated, Adam left the firm and started a small practice right here in Harmony Lake. We've seen each other more in the last twelve months than we did during the last five years of our marriage. His constant presence in our tiny hometown and my life makes our situation complicated.

We've had to learn to spend time together as friends while working out the details of the divorce and keeping our family intact; something we both want for our daughter.

Adam and I have known each other our entire adult lives. I can't imagine not being in each other's lives in some capacity. We met at university when I was eighteen. By the time I was twenty, we were married, and I became unexpectedly pregnant with Hannah a few months later.

"I'll text you some computer specs later today, Meg." Adam moves toward the door and puts one hand on the doorknob.

"Thanks." I smile and busy myself with gathering online orders that need to go to the post office.

He glances around the empty store. Why is he lingering? He looks at me awkwardly with his hand still on the doorknob. I pretend I don't notice that he's working up the nerve to say something. I won't take the bait.

"Do you guys have plans tonight?" Adam finally asks.

Eric and I look at each other and shrug.

"I don't think so, why?" I ask.

Adam takes a deep breath and exhales slowly. "I'm thinking of inviting Jess to Thanksgiving dinner, and I'd like you to get to know each other first, before she meets Hannah. I was hoping the four of us could have dinner tonight."

Jessica Kline is the hygienist from our dentist's office. She and Adam have been dating for about five months. Adam is secretive about their relationship. He even denied they were seeing each other at first until he couldn't deny it anymore. A few months ago—completely by accident—I saw them together, and that's when Jess went from his secret girlfriend to his not-so-secret girlfriend. Only Eric and I know about them. If he wants her to meet Hannah, they must be getting serious.

"Jess isn't spending Thanksgiving with her kids?" I ask.

Jess was married to our dentist, Dr. Arnie Kline. They

have three teenagers. They've been divorced for almost ten years, a fact I didn't know until she and Adam started dating. I already like Jess. She's been cleaning my teeth every six months since we moved to Harmony Lake almost eighteen years ago. But we've never gotten to know each other beyond discussing the weather, how quickly our kids grow up, and how effective my flossing habits are.

"They're going to BC with their dad to visit his side of the family," Adam explains.

BC is British Colombia, the western-most province in Canada.

"We'd love to," Eric intervenes, putting Adam out of his misery.

Relief washes over Adam's face.

In an unexpected and strange turn of events, Eric and Adam are friends. Eric was new to town and didn't know anyone, and Adam was a local resident without any local friends because he was always at his office in the city. They bonded over a mutual love of golf, and now they're friends. Is it weird that they have a relationship with each other that doesn't include me? Yes, but it's far from the weirdest situation in this cozy, quirky town.

"I was thinking we could meet at the pub after you close the store. Sound good?" Adam asks.

"Great. We're looking forward to it," Eric replies.

Should be an interesting dinner.

"What do you think, Sophie?" I ask after Adam leaves. "Are you ready to meet Adam's girlfriend at Thanksgiving dinner?"

Sophie thumps her little corgi tail in response and twitches her eyebrows at me.

ERIC IS GOOD FOR BUSINESS, I'll give him that. We're busier than usual for October, and customers stay in the store longer than they usually do, lingering in whichever section Eric currently occupies. Knitters who never ask my opinion on anything yarn related have a sudden, urgent need for Eric's opinion on which shade of blue matches their eyes or which yarn would be "most huggable" as a sweater. At least two knitters have offered him private knitting lessons, and one asked him about the size of his gun. He's had a few opportunities to show off his cash register skills ringing up sales.

"You said it wouldn't be busy," he says, holding the door for a customer as she leaves.

"I suspect word got around about the handsome new associate at Knitorious," I respond.

The speed at which the Harmony Lake gossip network spreads news rivals high-speed internet.

"I wouldn't call you handsome, beautiful for sure, but not handsome." Another romantically, corny comment from Eric while he checks his phone. "I need to leave to meet Charmaine. Will you able to cope on your own?"

I know he's teasing. "I think I'll be OK. If I can't handle the rush, I'll text you. I'll meet you at the pub later."

"It's a date." He pulls me into a hug. "A double date with your ex. Is that awkward for you?"

"Yes," I admit, "but I'm trying to go with the flow."

"Better you than me," Eric says. "I wouldn't have dinner with my ex-wife ever again. Not for any reason."

"AFTER OUR WALK, I'll take you upstairs and you can wait in Eric's apartment until we get back from dinner. I promise to tell you all about Jess." I explain how the evening will unfold to Sophie as I attach her leash at the back door.

I go over my mental checklist before we leave. Turn the

OPEN sign to CLOSED. Check. Lock the front door. Check. Turn off the store lights. Check. Feed Sophie dinner. Check.

Sophie and I step into the parking lot, and when I lock the back door, the thud of a car door closing catches my ear.

"Hi, Megan!"

"Jess?" Why is she here? "Hi!"

"I'm glad I ran into you. Adam suggested I park here. I hope it's OK. I can move the car…"

I wave away her comment, cutting her off mid-sentence. "Of course. There's no chance of finding a spot at the pub on a Friday night. You can park here whenever you want."

"Thanks. Could we walk to the pub together?"

"Sure! If you don't mind a quick walk with Sophie first?"

"Not at all. I was hoping to get you alone. There's something I want to talk to you about."

What could Adam's not-so-secret girlfriend want to talk to me about?

CHAPTER 2

WE WALK AND TALK, stopping at every tree, bench, and rock bordering our path so Sophie can sniff and mark her territory.

The conversation starts with the obligatory weather chat. We catch each other up with how our kids are doing, while pretending there isn't an air of tension hanging between us because of whatever she wants to talk to me about.

"Megan, I just want to say thank you for being so open to meeting me and being supportive of Adam and me." Jess says, finally addressing the elephant in the room.

"Of course!" I reply. "You're both great people, I hope it works out for you. And I'm not just saying that because I dread finding a new dentist if it doesn't." I'm kidding about the last part. Sort of.

Jess giggles and flippantly flicks her wrist. "I've got your back. If it doesn't work out with Adam and me, he has to find a new dentist, and I get to keep you and Hannah. I've already told him, so don't worry."

In addition to being friendly and easy to talk to, Jess has a wicked sense of humour, and she's gorgeous.

Her long, straight, strawberry blonde hair looks almost rose gold in the light of the setting sun. She has perfect teeth—she's a walking billboard for her dental practice—and her sea-foam green eyes are captivating. Like me, she has fair skin, except hers is dotted with clusters of reddish freckles. I'm the Veronica to Jess's Betty. My hair is brown and curly, my eyes are hazel, and I have a curvy hourglass figure, whereas Jess is lean and muscular. I don't know if she works out, but she looks like she does.

The only physical feature we have in common is our lack of height. To be honest, our physical dissimilarity is a relief. The only other relationship Adam embarked on since our separation was with someone who resembled me. It was unnerving and ended in murder.

"But seriously," Jess adds, "I know how awkward it is to meet your ex's new partner. I was so nervous the first time I met Arnie's new wife. She didn't do anything to make me uncomfortable, but it was still stressful. I hope you don't feel like that. I have no expectations. You and I don't have to be friends, but I'd love it if we were. If not, I hope we can at least get along for the sake of our families."

Wow. Such a brave and vulnerable statement. How am I supposed to not love her?

I stop walking and look at her, summoning the most serious facial expression I can muster. "I already like you more than Adam."

We both burst out laughing.

With the awkwardness out of the way, Jess and I spend the rest of our walk getting to know each other better. We're both from Toronto. Though she's eight years older than me—I'd never have guessed she's forty-eight—we have similar taste in music. We were at the same concert twice, Beastie Boys and The Rolling Stones. We both read mysteries, watch true crime documentaries, and have perfectionist tendencies. She finds the same satisfaction from dislodging a huge nugget of tartar from a tooth that I find in fixing a knitting mistake that other knitters say isn't fixable. We don't look alike, but we have a lot in common.

"ARE YOU READY FOR THIS?" I ask Jess as I'm about to open the large wooden door to The Irish Embassy. "This is as public as it gets. Five minutes after we join Adam and Eric, the entire town will know about your relationship. You're about to become the most talked-about person in Harmony Lake."

Jess nods, then giggles. "I'm ready. Adam warned me about the rumour mill in this town. Hopefully, something else big will happen, and our relationship won't be the trending topic for very long."

"If nothing else gossip-worthy happens by dessert, I'll text Connie and ask her to start a rumour to take the heat off." I wink.

It's a joke, but I'm sure Connie would gladly accept the challenge.

We giggle as I open the door and gesture for Jess to go ahead of me.

The Irish Embassy—known simply as the embassy or the pub to locals—is one of the largest buildings in Harmony Lake and one of the few businesses on the south side of Water Street. The main floor has a double-sided bar in the centre with bar stools lining both sides. The bar is surrounded by various types of seating, booths along the walls, tables and chairs in the centre, and a couple of cozy sitting areas with sofas and club chairs around the fireplaces. Out back, there's a patio overlooking the lake.

During tourist season, it would be standing room only on a Friday night, but this isn't tourist season. Most of the booths and tables are occupied, but it's not crowded.

Scanning the room, Eric catches my eye and waves to me from one of the semi-circular booths.

"Over here." I nudge Jess.

"What took you so long?" Adam asks. "The store closed almost an hour ago. We were getting worried. You didn't answer my texts."

"We took Sophie for a walk, dropped her off, then walked over," Jess explains. "We took our time." She slides into the booth next to Adam while digging through her purse. "Shoot! I left my phone in my car."

Adam offers to retrieve her phone, but Jess declines. I offer her my phone so she can text her kids and let them know they can reach her at my number. She accepts and sends a quick text from my phone, which I leave on the table where we can both see it.

After an order of Irish nachos, plus two orders of steak and mushroom pie, and two of fish and chips, we're all full to bursting. Jess and I polish off a bottle of wine and order another, lamenting that we both have to work tomorrow and should have planned to have dinner on a Saturday night instead.

I can leave my car at the store and stagger home from the pub, but Jess lives and works in Harmony Hills, a half hour drive from here. So, we decide Adam will be her designated driver, and she'll pick up her car from Knitorious tomorrow.

The laughter and wine flow freely until someone touches my shoulder.

"Hey, Jamila! How are you?"

Jamila Jagger owns Bits and Bytes, Harmony Lake's electronics store. She's a tech wizard, and I trust her to guide me toward the perfect laptop for my store. I debated going to Electric Avenue, one of the big-box electronics stores in Harmony Hills, but I try to support local whenever possible. We small business owners need to stick together.

"Hi, Megan," Jamila smiles. "I just popped over to tell you I'm not ignoring you. I know you left me a message today. I didn't have time to call you back, but I'll call you tomorrow."

"No worries, Jamila! I'm glad Bits and Bytes is busy!" If I'm more enthusiastic than this conversation merits, I blame the wine.

"Hi, I'm Jamila," Jamila introduces herself to Jess and extends her hand for Jess to shake.

Ah! The real reason Jamila stopped by our booth—to check out Adam's girlfriend up close.

"Hi, Jamila." Jess shakes Jamila's hand. "I'm Jess." She flashes Jamila a wide, toothy smile and lets out a small hiccup. "If you'll 'scuse me, I hafta visit the ladies' room now." She slides out of the booth, takes a moment to confirm her footing, then walks a bit unsteadily toward the ladies' room.

I gesture for Jamila to take Jess's vacated seat. She slides into the booth next to Adam and leans over the table toward me.

"I need a laptop," I tell her. "I have specs." I pick up my phone, open my text thread with Adam, and forward the text with the computer specs to Jamila.

"Leave it with me," Jamila says. "I'll look at your text and my inventory and call you sometime tomorrow."

"Thank you," I reply. "Who are you here with? Do you want to join us?" Apparently, slightly drunk Megan is extra welcoming.

"I'm waiting for the Solomons. I was just at their house for dinner. We decided to meet here for a drink. They'll be here any second. I should get back to our table before someone takes it." Jamila smiles.

Charmaine Solomon is the chief of police. Her husband, Dr. Emory Solomon, is a local psychotherapist who specializes in family therapy. His office and Adam's office are in the same building.

"You have good taste in girlfriends." I wink at Adam and take a sip of wine.

"And you were worried they wouldn't like each other." Eric grips Adam's shoulder in that friendly way men do.

After finding her way back from the ladies' room, Jess slides into the booth.

"You were worried we wouldn't like each other?" she asks, rubbing what I hope is Adam's knee under the table.

"I had two worst-case scenarios," Adam explains. "You either wouldn't get along at all, or you'd get along too well and gang up on me."

"We promise we'll only gang up on you sometimes," Jess assures him.

"Welcome to your worst-case scenario," I add.

As we near the end of our second bottle of wine, Jess remembers her phone is in the car and announces her intention to walk to Knitorious to get it. Adam suggests he should go with her because he's steadier on his feet. Eric, also sober, agrees with Adam, but Jess rejects his offer of assistance and instead decides she and I can retrieve her phone together. The semi-intoxicated leading the intoxicated. What could go wrong?

Stepping out of the stuffy, loud pub into the crisp October night is a breath of fresh air. Literally. I inhale deeply and revel in the coolness. I glance up the alley beside the pub. Two people are standing close together in the midst of what appears to be an animated discussion. I can't hear what they're saying, but their spirited gesticulations make me think that whatever they're discussing, they don't agree on it. As my eyes adjust to the darkness, I realize the two people who are arguing are women. Then I realize one of them is Jamila. I recognize her high ponytail bobbing when she speaks. The other woman is Charmaine Solomon. What would they be arguing about? Didn't Jamila say they had dinner together tonight? I didn't realize they knew each other well enough to have dinner parties and argue in dark laneways.

"Let's go!" Jess shouts. She locks her arm in mine, and zigzagging, we amble up Water Street toward Knitorious.

She entertains me with dental-hygiene stories. Like the patient who would only brush the teeth they wanted to keep, the patient who has names for each of their teeth, and the patient who insists on being called "Your Highness" since getting their dental crown.

By the time we're close to the store, we're laughing so hard I'm afraid I might pee.

"Nice parking job, jerk!" Jess shouts, nudging me.

When I look up, there's a white Tesla parked in front of my store with its passenger-side tires on the sidewalk.

"Oh my," I say, suddenly feeling more sober. "It looks like they hit the lamp post."

Approaching slowly and assuming the vehicle is empty, we take in the scene. The car isn't wrapped around the pole, so I don't think the driver was going very fast when they hit it.

"Do you think they were drunk?" Jess asks.

"I don't know," I reply, inching closer to the car.

The car is silent, but it's electric, so that doesn't mean it's not running. The headlights and rear running lights are on, so it could be running. Could the driver be inside?

"People who drive luxury cars are so entitled!" Jess yells with a slur. "Like, how entitled are you if you think you can park like that jus' cuz you have an essspensive car?"

Her comment makes me laugh.

"Whasso funny?" she asks, starting to giggle without knowing why.

"Your boyfriend drives a JAGUAR!" I blurt out between fits of laughter.

Laughing so hard she bends forward, I reach out to steady Jess, and we approach the Tesla. Someone is in the driver's seat.

I knock on the window. "Hello?" I knock again. "Are you OK?"

The realization that someone could be hurt focusses Jess on the task at hand. Squinting, and with her nose pressed against the window, she says, "His eyes are open. I think he's all right." She raps on the window with her car key. "We'll get you help, sir."

The driver's head is turned mostly toward the passenger side of the car, so we can't see his entire face. We jog around the back of the car to the passenger window. With her hands cupping the sides of her face, Jess looks inside. "It's Dr. Armistead." She knocks with her fist. "Dr. Armistead? Look at me!" She turns to me. "Why won't he look at me?"

I squint and put my face up to the window next to hers. "Because he's dead."

CHAPTER 3

I REACH for my phone in my back pocket and panic when I realize it's not there. "Darn it! I left my phone on the table at the pub!"

"Mine's in the car!" Jess and I race toward the parking lot behind the store as she repeatedly presses the remote on her key chain. The car is blinking and chirping when we turn the corner. "Do you really think he's dead?" she asks, grabbing her phone from the passenger seat.

"Yes," I reply, nodding.

"9-1-1?" she asks, trying to unlock her phone with her fingerprint. Her hand is shaky, and the phone won't unlock. I place my hand over hers to stop the device from moving while she concentrates on steadying her thumb over the sensor until it unlocks. "Here." She thrusts the unlocked phone at me. "I can't," she says, shaking her head.

Jess sits on the pavement beside her car. I think she's about to throw up, but I can't worry about that now.

A text from Adam appears on her screen.

Adam: What's taking so long? You and Meg find a body or what?

Adam likes to poke fun at my knack for finding dead bodies. This will teach him to make light of dark situations.

Me responding on Jess's phone: Yes.

I swipe out of her text messages and dial 9-1-1. I'm about to hit *talk* when the phone rings. Unknown number. But I recognize it. Eric.

"Hello?"

"Where are you?" A thudding sound in the background. He's running.

"Parking lot. I have to call 9-1-1." I'm about to end the call, but he speaks again.

"Adam's calling them. Stay on the line with me. I'm almost there."

"A car. On Water Street. In front of Knitorious."

"Are you hurt? Is Jess hurt?"

I can hear him in stereo now. He's within earshot.

"No. The man in the car is hurt." I end the call.

"Megan!" Eric runs around the corner.

"Sorry, I hung up." I'm crouched beside Jess now, rubbing her back and listening to her whisper, "Don't puke" to herself repeatedly under her breath.

"Stay here! Adam's right behind me!" he shouts, then disappears around the corner.

I assume he's running toward the Tesla, toward Dr. Armistead.

"Let it out," I advise Jess, twisting her long hair and gathering it in my fist. "You'll feel better. You can freshen up upstairs."

Jess nods in agreement, lurches forward, and proceeds to heave while I hold her hair back.

As she wipes her mouth with a tissue from her purse, I gently steer Jess toward Knitorious.

"Your phone is in your bag!" Adam is beside us now, thrusting my forest-green tote bag toward me.

Instead of taking the bag from him, I reach in and grope

around for my keys. I unlock the door and hold it ajar with my foot while I drop my keys inside my bag and take it from Adam. All the while keeping my arm supportively around Jess. "Can you text Eric and tell him we're upstairs?"

"Of course," Adam replies, holding the door open while I usher Jess inside.

Still supporting her with my arm, and with Adam behind us prepared to catch her if she falls, Jess and I wobble slowly up the stairs.

I situate Jess on the sofa and use the hair elastic on my wrist to pre-emptively secure her hair in a messy bun in case she needs to throw up again.

"Thank you," she mumbles.

"Don't thank me until you see it," I reply. "It might be the messiest messy bun I've ever made."

She chuckles under her breath and reaches up to touch the monstrous pile of hair on her head. "I think my hair is the least of our problems right now."

Adam hands me a glass of water, then hands one to Jess and sits next to her on the sofa, rubbing her back.

Pointing, I show Jess where the washroom is and tell her she'll find washcloths and towels in the linen closet behind the washroom door. "There's toothpaste and mouthwash in the drawer on the right," I explain.

Nodding, she starts to get up. Adam helps her to her feet, and she walks gingerly toward the washroom.

"It's not just the alcohol, she's in shock," I explain quietly to Adam after Jess clicks the washroom door.

I sink into the chair next to the sofa, and Sophie jumps onto my lap, excited to see me and oblivious to the chaos happening downstairs.

"She's not the only one," he responds. "Are you OK?"

I nod. "Definitely much more sober now."

"What happened?" he asks. "Did you guys see the car hit the pole?"

SON OF A STITCH

I explain what happened, leaving out Jess's remarks about luxury car drivers being entitled, and my comment about her boyfriend—Adam—falling into that category.

"Dr. Armistead?" he asks. "The same Dr. Armistead we went to for marriage counselling a few years ago?"

I nod. "I didn't recognize him at first. Jess recognized him. Then I remembered their offices are in the same medical building in Harmony Hills. She probably runs into him all the time, so of course she recognizes him."

From inside my bag, my phone dings almost constantly. Word has gotten around about the incident outside my store. Red and blue flashing lights reflect off the walls inside Eric's apartment. The accident scene is directly below his living room window.

I retrieve my phone and unlock the screen without scrolling through the dozens of unread messages that pop up.

I type a text to the Modern Family group chat.

Me: A car hit a pole outside Knitorious. We're all fine. Will update you soon.

The Modern Family group chat is a text thread Eric started a few months ago when I was in a car accident, and he was inundated with texts about my wellbeing. Originally, it included me, Eric, Adam, April, and Connie. It quickly grew to include Connie's boyfriend Archie, Archie's son Ryan, and Ryan's girlfriend Lin. April also added her wife, Tamara.

Now that the people who matter most know what's going on and that everyone is safe—everyone except Dr. Armistead—I lock the screen and toss my phone onto the coffee table.

"How are you feeling?" Adam asks Jess upon her return from the washroom.

"I've been better," she replies, resuming her seat on the sofa next to Adam and taking small, cautious sips from her glass of water.

"Did you know Dr. Armistead well?" I ask.

She shrugs. "Kind of. We've worked in the same medical

275

building forever. He's a patient at the dental practice, and years ago, Arnie and I went to him for marriage counselling. He was a nice man. I think he's between wives right now. He has a son, about Hannah's age or a year or two older."

Between wives. What an odd way to describe someone's marital status. It gives the impression that Dr. Armistead has had several wives. I'm about to probe Jess for more details about his relationship situation when she continues speaking.

"Poor Dr. Armistead." Jess shakes her head. "If it weren't for bad luck, he'd have no luck at all this week."

"What else happened to him this week?" I ask.

"His office was robbed on Monday. The whole place was turned over. In the middle of the day."

"Wow," I respond. "That's awful." I'm about to ask what was taken, but Adam beats me to it with his question.

"I wonder why he was in Harmony Lake tonight?" he asks. "I've never seen him around town before."

"I have no idea." Jess shakes her head.

The thud of footsteps makes us stop talking and turn our heads toward the apartment door. The thudding grows louder until the door opens.

"How's everyone doing?" Eric asks, holding the door for one of his uniformed colleagues. "We need to speak to each of you briefly"—he looks back and forth from me to Jess—"then we'll get more detailed statements in the morning when you're not under the influence."

Jess and I nod.

"We'll each take one and split up?" Eric's colleague asks. "One up, one down?"

Eric nods.

"I'll go downstairs, I should take Sophie outside anyway," I offer, less out of concern for Sophie and more out of concern for Jess navigating the stairs again.

I INHALE DEEPLY and savour the crisp night air when Sophie, Eric, and I step into the parking lot. After a long, silent hug, we walk north into the residential streets behind the store, instead of crossing Water Street and walking through the waterfront park, like we normally would. To the best of my alcohol-clouded recollection, I tell Eric everything that happened from the moment Jess and I left the pub until he called me on Jess's cell phone.

"Do you think he had a medical episode?" I ask.

"Possibly. It's too early to tell," Eric replies. "But we have to treat it like a crime scene until foul play is ruled out."

"Maybe he fell asleep at the wheel, or maybe he was using the self-driving feature Teslas have, and it steered him into the pole," I suggest.

"At this point, it could be anything." Eric shrugs. "When I saw him earlier, he seemed fine. I didn't notice any signs of medical distress."

We stop walking while Sophie investigates a fire hydrant. I look up at Eric. "You saw him earlier today? Where?"

"Who's questioning who?" he teases. "He showed up at Charmaine's house as I was leaving. He was one of the Solomon's dinner guests tonight."

"You were at the Solomon's house? Is that where you met with Charmaine? Not at the station?"

"She asked if we could meet at her house because she had to get ready for a dinner party tonight. She prepared duchess potatoes while we talked. I wasn't there very long. When I was leaving, Dr. Armistead was arriving. We said hello and goodbye at the door on my way out."

"Duchesse potatoes, mmm, yummy," I observe.

"They looked good. She piped them and put them in the fridge, so she could put them in the oven when the chateaubriand was almost done."

"Chateaubriand with duchess potatoes. Now, I'm hungry. I bet she made chateaubriand sauce too. With mushrooms."

"Apparently Emory makes that. It's one of his specialties. Along with the sautéed brussels sprouts. But we're getting off track." Eric steers our conversation back to the issue at hand.

"Sorry, I'm looking for a distraction from the dead body in front of my store," I explain.

"I know," he says, taking my hand. "Are you sure you're all right? Finding a dead body is traumatic, even if it's not your first time."

I nod. "I think I'm fine. I'll know for sure when the rest of the alcohol wears off. Jess was quite shaken, though. She might need some extra support. Did you tell Chief Solomon that one of her dinner guests is dead?"

"Yeah. By text," Eric replies. "Not ideal, but I wanted to tell her personally instead of sending a patrol car. And I couldn't leave the scene since I'm the only detective in town."

"That's awkward, having to question your boss," I point out. "But aren't you a witness too? Since you saw the victim a few hours before he died?"

"Yup, among other reasons," he agrees.

I assume he's referring to the fact that the scene of Dr. Armistead's death is outside his front door.

We arrive back at the store and I pause before opening the door. "Are we done? I'd like to go home."

"We do have to talk. I need to ask you some more questions, and I need to tell you some stuff, but it's best to wait until you're completely sober."

"I'll walk home, for obvious reasons, and leave my car here. I just need to go upstairs and get my phone and bag. I guess you won't be working at the store tomorrow after all. Your new fan club will be disappointed."

"A patrol car will drive you home. I have to get back to work. I'll talk to you in the morning." Eric kisses me goodnight.

"I don't mind walking. The fresh air is good for me."

"You're still under the influence, and there's a small

chance this wasn't an accident. Please humour me and let a patrol car drive you home?"

"Fine," I agree.

"Text me when you get there. Lock the doors and turn on the alarm. I love you," he reminds me as he turns the corner.

Watching Eric disappear toward what I hope is an accident scene, the knot in my stomach swells and tries to convince me Dr. Armistead's death isn't an accident at all, but murder. I try to ignore the knot, and my instincts, but it's hard because they haven't been wrong yet.

CHAPTER 4

"I go away for a few days and you replace me, Megawatt? The rumour mill is buzzing with stories about the dead body you and your new bestie found outside Knitorious."

April likes to come up with punny nicknames for me. Apparently, this morning I'm Megawatt. She's done it since we met seventeen years ago at a mummy-and-me playgroup with our girls.

"It would be impossible to replace you," I reassure her, even though I know she's teasing. "But Jess is cool, you'll like her." I stop walking while Sophie sniffs a tree. We're only a few driveways away from home. At this rate, we'll never get to work. "How's your dad feeling?"

"Grumpy," April replies. "My mum says it means he's getting better. She says he's happiest when he's crotchety and complaining. He hates it when we fuss over him. Honestly, I love him to death, but he doesn't make it easy."

"To be fair, if I had three broken bones, I'd be grumpy too," I tell her, adjusting my AirPods. "Don't worry about anything in Harmony Lake, just focus on your parents. Marla is filling in for you at Artsy Tartsy, and Zach is helping out between school and hockey. Connie and Ryan take turns chauffeuring him to and from hockey when T has to work."

Zach is April and Tamara's son. He's a sixteen-year-old hockey player with a massive appetite. They also have a daughter, Rachel, who's the same age as my Hannah. Rachel and Hannah are best friends and attend university together in Toronto.

"I know. T says everyone is supportive and amazing. She makes it sound like everything is running so smoothly without me that I never have to come back."

T is short for Tamara.

"She just doesn't want you to worry. We all want you back, we just don't want you to worry about what's happening here while you're helping your parents. We miss you!"

"I miss you too. I'll be home by next weekend. There's no way I'm missing Thanksgiving dinner if Jess is making her debut. I'll bring my parents with me if I have to." We laugh. "So, you and Adam knew this Dr. Armistead guy?" April asks.

"Weird, right? He was the marriage counselor we went to a few years ago in Harmony Hills. He was a nice man. What are the odds he'd show up dead outside my store?"

"Why did you and Adam go all the way to Harmony Hills for marriage counselling? Why not stay local and see Dr. Solomon?" April asks. It's a fair question.

"You know what it's like here," I remind her. "Everyone knows everyone else's business. We didn't want to broadcast our marital issues, and we didn't want Hannah to find out. If anyone saw us coming or going from Dr. Solomon's office, it would have spread through Harmony Lake faster than a viral infection."

"It's true," April agrees.

April and I chat until I arrive at the store. We end our call, and I walk to the front of the store to make sure the Tesla and

Dr. Armistead are gone. They are, but crime scene tape cordons off most of the sidewalk in front of Knitorious, and a police officer and his patrol car direct traffic around the now-crooked lamppost.

Water Street is to Harmony Lake what Main Street is to other small towns. It's our main drag. Most of Harmony Lake's stores and businesses are on the north side of Water Street. The south side has a narrow park in front of the water-front—the park where I walk Sophie before the store opens. Water Street is charming and picturesque. It's old with limited on-street parking and no new architecture at all. But I think this adds to its charm.

On the way to the back door, I notice that in addition to Jess's car and my car, Eric's car is still here, as well as a couple of cars I don't recognize. Strange. When Eric has a case, he's usually out the door early, interviewing people and gathering evidence. Hopefully, the fact that he's home means the coroner has already determined the cause of death and ruled out foul play. But if that were the case, he would've mentioned it when we texted earlier this morning. Something's not right. Something else is going on.

I detach Sophie's leash and freshen her bowl of water. After checking the clock on the cash register, I realize there's more than enough time to walk to Latte Da and get a maple pecan latte before it's time to open the store. Phone in hand, I stash my bag under the counter and head toward the back door. I'll text Eric on my way and ask him if he wants anything.

"I was just thinking about you," I say when he comes down the stairs and intercepts me at the back door.

"Good thoughts I hope." He smiles and kisses my forehead.

Eric is almost a foot taller than me. I get a lot of forehead kisses.

"I'm going to Latte Da. Do you want a coffee?" I ask.

"I'd love one," a familiar, deep voice booms from the top of the stairs. "Dark roast, two milks, please, Megan."

"Hi, Darby. What are you doing here?" Darby and I hug and exchange a cheek kiss.

Darby Morris is a friend of Eric's and a detective with the Harmony Hills police department. He doesn't belong here; this isn't his jurisdiction. Now I *know* something is going on.

"Darby is here to work the Armistead case," Eric explains. "There are too many conflicts of interest. The HLPD can't investigate it."

HLPD is the Harmony Lake Police Department.

"Does this mean Dr. Armistead was murdered?" I ask.

Eric shakes his head and shrugs. "There's no evidence to suggest it was murder, but until the coroner officially says otherwise, it's a suspicious death. That's why Darby is here."

I take a step back and realize Eric is wearing the same clothes he wore last night. He hasn't shaved, and his eyes are bloodshot and heavy.

"Have you been up all night?" I ask.

He nods.

"Who wants to tell me what's going on?" I demand. "I don't like secrets."

"Why don't I go to Latte Da and leave you two to talk," Darby announces. "Text me your orders."

Before either of us can respond, Darby leaves, closing the back door behind him.

Eric and I take a seat at the wooden harvest table at the back of the store. I wait while he texts our coffee order to Darby, then gives Sophie some love before she explodes from trying to get his attention.

"If you and I are witnesses, shouldn't we be separated until Darby questions us individually?" I ask, drawing on my unfortunate previous crime scene experience.

"He already questioned me, and he has your preliminary statement from last night. It's fine." Eric takes my hands.

"Remember last night when I told you I saw Dr. Armistead at Charmaine's house yesterday evening?"

I nod. "He was arriving for dinner as you were leaving after your meeting with Charmaine."

"That wasn't the first time Dr. Armistead and I met. My ex and I went to him for marriage counselling right before we split up."

"You too?" I ask. "It's like he's the only marriage counselor in the world."

"Why do you say that?" Eric looks confused.

"You went to him for marriage counselling, Adam and I went to him for marriage counselling, and last night Jess said she and her ex-husband went to Dr. Armistead for marriage counselling too."

"Huh, that is a coincidence," Eric agrees. "And of all three couples, none of them stayed together."

"You're right," I acknowledge, shocked by the realization of Dr. Armistead's unfortunate track record. "I hope the three of us aren't indicative of his overall success rate. Is that the only reason Harmony Hills PD was called in?"

Eric shakes his head. "No. Charmaine is a witness. She was one of the last people to see Armistead alive. He was at her house for dinner. I can't question her impartially because she's my boss. In fact, she's everyone's boss, so there would be a conflict of interest if any cop with the HLPD investigates the case. Last night, we secured the scene, notified the coroner, and took preliminary statements. When Darby got here, I handed off the case to him, and he questioned me. By the time we finished, it was so late, or early depending on your perspective, that I decided to stay up and talk to you."

"Are you OK with Darby taking over?" I'm sure Eric isn't happy about being shut out of a case in his own jurisdiction.

"I'm not thrilled," he admits, "but if it has to be anyone, I'm glad it's Darby. Armistead probably died of natural causes, but if his death does turn into a murder investigation, the case is in good hands."

"What will you do now?" I ask. "Will you work on other cases?" Harmony Lake is so small, there probably are no other cases.

"I'm sticking to my original plan," Eric replies. "I'll use the time I have owing to help at the store until Connie and Marla come back. I'll fill in as your sidekick." He grins.

"Before you do anything, you should get some sleep," I suggest.

"And a shower," he adds, smiling weakly.

I don't hear the back door, and Sophie doesn't make a sound, so I'm shocked to find Darby suddenly beside us. It's hard to imagine Darby sneaking anywhere without being noticed. It's not just his voice that's big; he's a big man all around. He's as tall as Eric and thicker. It's amazing how stealth-like these huge men are when they walk in and out of Knitorious.

"One maple pecan latte with extra whipped cream and a drizzle of chocolate sauce." He pulls a cup from the tray and places it in front of me. "And one dark roast double-double." He pulls a second cup and sets it in front of Eric. "And one whipped cream for Sophie." Darby pulls a third cup from the tray and puts in in front of me.

"It's nice of you to think of Sophie," I say, cracking the lid on the whipped cream.

"I didn't," Darby admits. "When I placed your very specific order, the cashier asked me if it was for you. When I said it was, she insisted on giving me whipped cream for Sophie."

"Small town service." I smile and put the cup on the floor for Sophie.

"Do you think we have time to talk before you open the store?" Darby asks me.

I check the time on my phone. "I think so. I can open a few

minutes late if necessary. I expect the store will have more nosy neighbours than knitters and crocheters today, anyway."

By now, everyone in town knows Jess and I discovered Dr. Armistead and his car outside the store last night. Lots of "well-wishers" and "concerned neighbours" will show up with questions. Some will pretend they're shopping for yarn and knitting supplies, and some will just mill around the store talking to other customers and listening for gossip.

"I'll leave you to it," Eric says, standing up and pushing his chair in. "I'll grab a quick shower then come downstairs. If you and Darby aren't finished, you can use my apartment, and I'll watch the store."

"Or you can get some sleep. Darby and I will figure something out if we aren't finished when it's time to open the store."

Eric nods. "You and I aren't finished talking," he says, looking at me. "There's another conflict of interest I need to tell you about with this case."

"There probably isn't a case," Darby reminds him. "Poor Dr. A probably had a heart attack, or a stroke, or something."

Eric's footsteps disappear up the stairs in the back room, and Darby takes a seat across from me at the harvest table.

"Tell me, Megan, why do all murders seem to lead back to you?" he asks lightheartedly and winks while he opens his leather folio.

"I wish I knew," I reply, watching Darby uncap a fountain pen.

While we sip our coffees, I tell Darby everything that happened last night, starting from the moment Jess declared her intention to walk from the pub to Knitorious to retrieve her phone, until I went outside with Eric and Sophie to give Eric my statement.

Recalling the events with a sober mind, I also tell him I noticed Jamila Jagger and Charmaine Solomon having a lively discussion in the dark alley beside the pub—a detail I'd forgotten last night when I spoke to Eric.

"Are you one hundred percent certain it was them? I mean, it was dark, and you'd been drinking."

"One hundred percent sure it was Jamila, and at least ninety percent sure about Charmaine," I reply.

"Are Ms. Jagger and Chief Solomon close?" Darby asks.

I shrug. "You should probably ask them that. Harmony Lake is a small town. Everybody knows everybody to some extent, but until last night, I didn't realize they were friendly enough to have dinner parties and private conversations in dark alleys."

"They have dinner parties?" Darby asks while making notes in his folio.

"I assume so," I reply. "When Jamila visited our booth, she said she'd just had dinner at the Solomon's house."

"She did? You're certain?"

"I'm certain." I nod.

Why doesn't Darby know Jamila was at the Solomon's house for dinner last night? Wouldn't Charmaine or Dr. Solomon have told him? Or Eric?

"I'm surprised Eric didn't mention it in his statement," I say. "I'm sure I remember my conversation with Jamila correctly."

"He mentioned that Ms. Jagger joined your table briefly, but said he couldn't hear your conversation. He assumed you were talking about a laptop."

That makes sense. The pub was busy and noisy and Jamila doesn't have the loudest voice. She had to lean toward me so I could hear her.

"He's right," I confirm. "Jamila came to talk to me because I left a message for her earlier yesterday about a laptop. The store laptop finally died, and I'm hoping she has one at her store to replace it."

"And which whimsically named store does Ms. Jagger own?"

I tell him Jamila owns Bits'n'Bytes, then I disclose to him the previous, professional relationship Adam and I had with Dr. Armistead.

"About three to four years ago," I reply when Darby asks me when we last saw Dr. Armistead for marriage counselling.

I also mention to Darby that, according to Jess, Dr. Armistead's office was broken into on Monday.

"I'm aware," he says, acknowledging the break in.

We stop talking when we hear the back door open, then close.

"Good morning, my dear," Connie sings. "Oh, you have company. How nice. You carry on, and I'll open up."

"Connie Coulson, this is Darby Morris. Darby is a friend of Eric's and a detective with the Harmony Hills Police Department."

"A pleasure to finally meet you, Mr. Morris." Connie and Darby shake hands, and as I walk toward the front door to unlock it and switch the sign from CLOSED to OPEN, I hear Connie thank Darby for his "hard work on Megan's unfortunate car accident a few months ago." Connie refers to my "unfortunate car accident" as though it were a minor fender bender when it was actually a planned, almost-successful attempt to murder me. Connie still tears up if I mention it. I think calling it an accident makes it sound less scary and easier for her to deal with.

I unlock the door, and the first few customers—or nosy neighbours—of the day file into the store. Connie excuses herself from Darby and rushes to the front to take the lead on crowd control.

"Do you need me for anything else?" I ask, returning to Darby.

"Not right now, but I might need to speak to you again soon," he replies.

"Darby, sometimes the locals are...hesitant to talk to outsiders," I explain as quietly and tactfully as possible. "It takes a while for residents to warm up to new people. It's not personal. Eric had the same problem at first. I'm sure if you ask him, he'll tell you about it. If you need help, I'm happy to do whatever I can. Eric found that having a community liaison helped witnesses feel more comfortable disclosing things."

Harmony Lake residents spend months each year inundated with tourists who are looking to exchange their city lives for an authentic small-town living experience. We've learned to give tourists what they want while still protecting the core of our community and preserving it for just us. We accomplish this by being cautious of outsiders and not opening up to them more than absolutely necessary.

"I understand what you're saying, Megan. And I appreciate your offer. But I'm hoping the coroner will phone any minute and tell me Dr. A died of natural causes. Then, I can close the file and go back to Harmony Hills where I belong." He laughs.

Darby's not the only one hoping the coroner will conclude Dr. Armistead's death wasn't the result of foul play.

CHAPTER 5

TOGETHER, Connie and I manage the flow of questions about what happened last night. I answer honestly and briefly.

Yes, a man drove his Tesla into the light post outside the store.

No, I didn't get a good look at him.

No, the police don't think it was murder.

No, he wasn't local.

Yes, I was with Adam's new girlfriend.

No, our divorce isn't final yet.

Her name is Jess.

No, she's not local, either.

Yes, we were slightly drunk—this might be an understatement.

Yes, I like her.

The truth must be less exciting than the rumours because, within an hour, the masses stop gathering at Knitorious.

The first few visitors likely spread the word that there's nothing exciting to see or hear. Also, the crooked lamppost means driving on Water Street is a nightmare today with a police officer directing traffic in both directions on the one lane that's still open.

With the store now empty, Connie and I make ourselves comfortable on one of the sofas in the cozy sitting area and pick up our knitting.

"This is the first time I've picked up my needles since Thursday," I remark, starting a new row of the cardigan I'm working on.

"Well, you've had a lot going on, my dear," Connie responds.

"Why are you here?" I ask. "Aren't you supposed to be doting over Archie and his new hip?"

She dips her chin and looks at me over the top of her stylish reading glasses. "Ryan is on Archie-duty this morning." She smiles and tucks a few strands of her sleek silver bob behind her ear. "I wanted to make sure you're OK and help you manage the nosy neighbours. I figured with Eric having to work because of this chaos, and Marla helping at Artsy Tartsy, you'd be outnumbered. I didn't think you should be alone."

"That's very sweet, thank you. But Eric is upstairs, and the local busybodies have already lost interest, so if you want to get back to Archie, I completely understand."

"It's nice for Archie and me to have a break from each other," Connie explains. "And it's nice for Ryan to have some quality time with his father. I'm quite happy to stay here and spend some time with you. Now tell me, why isn't Eric at work, and why is Darby walking around town asking lots of questions, hmmm?"

I tell Connie about the various conflicts of interest with Harmony Lake PD working this case. I also tell her the dead man's name and how Adam and I, Jess and her ex-husband, and Eric and his ex-wife, all knew him professionally. Then I tell her that Darby didn't know Jamila was also a guest at the Solomon's dinner party last night.

"Well, Charmaine will *not* like having her name dragged into any of this!" Connie declares. "Her term as chief of police is almost over, and according to the rumour mill, the mayor doesn't intend to renew Charmaine's mandate."

"Really?" I ask, laying my knitting on my lap and giving Connie my full attention. "I haven't heard about this."

Connie nods. "You have to remember, my dear, Harmony Lake went from no murders in the town's history to more than our share of murders since Charmaine's appointment as chief of police. If the mayor renews Charmaine's mandate, she'll lose the next election for sure."

"I guess," I respond. "But is it fair to blame Charmaine Solomon for the murders? In her defence, the town has no unsolved cases, and she created the Major Crimes Unit and hired Eric to head it up."

"Exactly," Connie concurs. "Rumour has it Eric is at the top of the list to replace Charmaine as the new chief of police."

"If that's true, Eric would have mentioned it, and he hasn't said a word to me about it."

Before he went upstairs, Eric said we weren't finished talking. Could this be what he meant?

Except for the occasional interruption when I get up to help a customer, Connie and I pass the rest of the morning knitting and chatting about anything and everything until she gets a text from Ryan.

"Ryan has to leave Archie. He has to fix a furnace," Connie says, looking at her phone screen. "I have to go." She looks at me. "Will you be all right here on your own, my dear?"

"Absolutely," I assure her. "Thank you for being here today, but I'll be fine. How about you? Can I bring dinner to the condo tonight for you and Archie? Or can I cook something? You deserve a break from looking after everyone."

"That's a lovely offer, my dear." Connie opens her arms and we meet halfway for a hug. "But I won't be home at dinnertime. If Ryan's furnace emergency is over, I'm driving Zachary to his hockey game in Harmony Hills tonight."

"What if Ryan's furnace emergency isn't over?" I ask, about to suggest that I can take Zach to his game.

"Why don't I take him?" Eric offers, entering the store from the back room. "I love watching Zach's team play, they're great. I can pick up Archie, and he can come with us."

"Thank you, Eric!" Connie walks toward Eric with her arms open for a hug. "It'll do Archie a world of good to spend time with someone other than me or Ryan."

"I'm happy to do it," Eric says. "Text me the details."

Connie gives Eric a few highlights of what he's getting himself into with Archie and his walker, then, excited about having an evening to herself, she composes a text message inviting her fellow book club members to an impromptu meeting this evening at her place.

"The mayor is a member of the book club," she whispers when I walk her to the back door. "I'll see what I can uncover." She winks.

Much like a certain long-running, procedural-crime TV show, Harmony Lake is influenced by two separate yet equally important groups: The Book Club that meets twice monthly under the guise of reading best-selling fiction, and The Charity Knitting Guild that assembles on Wednesday afternoons at Knitorious. Dun dun.

Both groups have eyes and ears all over town, and through networks of carefully placed members and allies, they make it their business to know the ins and outs of anything that might affect the town as a whole.

Connie and Marla—who both happen to work for me— are crossover members who belong to both clubs.

The two groups are neither competitive nor harbour any animosity toward one another. They operate independently and have separate yet complimentary agendas.

Occasionally, when a serious situation threatens the delicate equilibrium within Harmony Lake, the two groups will join forces and almost invisibly take action to restore the town's natural balance.

While I'm not privy to the organizational structure or inner workings of either group, they seem to have a matriarchal hierarchy. The older, wiser women of the town are in charge and train the next generation to take the reins and continue the tradition when necessary.

Harmony Lake might have a democratically elected town council and mayor, but everyone knows it's the women of The Book Club and The Charity Knitting Guild who wield the real power.

"Thank you for doing that," I say to Eric.

"It's not a big deal. I get to watch a hockey game and spend some time with Archie. I'm sure it'll be fun."

Clearly, we have different ideas of fun.

"You look better," I observe. "Were you able to get some sleep?"

"A couple of hours," Eric replies. "Enough to take the edge off."

"Can I ask you something?" I ask.

"Of course." He furrows his brow, and a look of concern takes over his face.

"Connie said there's a rumour that Charmaine's mandate as chief of police won't be renewed by the mayor, and you could be in contention to replace her. Is it true?"

"I only found out last night," he admits. "It's the reason Charmaine wanted to meet with me. She believes the mayor won't renew her contract. She wants to know how I'd feel if she put my name forward as a potential candidate for her job."

"Wow," I say. "Good for her for recognizing your hard work."

If the mayor is unhappy with Charmaine's performance as chief, why would she listen to Charmaine's recommendation for a replacement? Why would the mayor value Charmaine's opinion? And why would Charmaine care who replaces her?

"I was going to tell you after dinner last night, but Armistead died, and everything's been crazy since then."

"I understand," I tell him. "Do you want to be chief of police?"

"Chief of paperwork?" He chuckles. "Not really. I became a cop to catch bad guys and help people, not manage budgets and get stuck in the middle of local politics."

"Is Charmaine angry about not being renewed?" I ask.

Eric shrugs. "She didn't sound angry. She sounded… resigned to it. But I don't know how long she's had to process it. Maybe she's known for a while."

"What will she do next?" I ask. "I can't imagine there are a lot of police-chief positions around. Each police force only has one, so she'd probably have to relocate if she found another job."

"She hinted that she and Emory might move away from Harmony Lake. She said they don't have any family connections here. They've been fixing up the house lately. I think they might be getting it ready to sell."

"If they leave town, what would happen to Dr. Solomon's patients? Maybe last night's dinner was to talk to Dr. Armistead about taking over Dr. Solomon's patients," I wonder out loud.

"Why would Jamila be there?" Eric asks.

I shrug. "Tech support? If patient files and such are digital nowadays, maybe she'd facilitate the transfer or help them merge everything? I don't know." I shake my head. "I'm just thinking out loud." I smile. "What did you tell Charmaine when she asked if she could put your name forward?"

"I told her I need to think about it. I wanted to talk to you," he replies. "I can't talk to her about it now. I can't talk to her about anything until the coroner determines Armistead's cause of death and the case is closed."

"When you can talk to her, what will you say?"

"I don't know. I'll tell her I'm honoured to be considered. I guess it would be all right to put my name forward and see what happens. I don't have to accept, and the mayor might have other candidates in mind, anyway. What do you think?"

"I think it's your career, and you should do what makes you happy. You have my support whatever you do."

"There's something else…" Eric says, his voice trailing off before he finishes his sentence.

He takes a deep breath and exhales slowly. The last time he acted this nervous was when he asked me on our first date.

"Heavy shoulders, long arms," I remind him. "I'll lock the door and put up the BACK IN TEN MINUTES sign." I get the feeling this is important.

"Heavy shoulders, long arms" is a mantra I learned in a yoga class years ago. I take deep breaths and repeat it when I'm stressed or overwhelmed. It helps relieve the tension in my neck and shoulders.

I join him at the harvest table at the back of the store where we're out of sight of anyone who might look through the window.

He takes my hand. "I hate thinking about this, never mind talking about it."

"I'm listening," I say.

"Being a former patient isn't the only connection I have to Armistead." He pauses and takes another breath. "When my ex-wife and I were his patients, Armistead's sixteen-year-old son was arrested and charged with driving under the influence. He was a new driver. He'd only been licensed for a few weeks, and he was drinking underage. It was a serious situation. Armistead called me and asked if I could help him out with the charges."

"Does 'help him out' mean make the charges go away?" I clarify.

"That's how I interpreted it," Eric replies. "He suggested if I helped him out, our counselling sessions would be free."

"Bribery," I observe. "Did you do it?"

"No!" he insists, then pauses. "You know I'd never do that." Another pause. "But I did a background check on him. To see if Armistead had a criminal record or had tried anything like this before. I didn't know if I should just tell him I couldn't help him and pretend it never happened, or if I should report it to someone. I looked him up to see what kind of person I was dealing with."

"And?" I urge.

"I found out he'd been married four times and one of his wives had a restraining order against him. Apparently, he would call her dozens of times every day in an attempt to reconcile with her."

"Are you telling me Dr. Armistead was giving relationship advice even though he had *four* failed marriages, was harassing one of his exes, and tried to bribe the police?" I'm incredulous.

The movie line, "*I guide others to a treasure I cannot possess*" comes to mind.

Eric nods. "That's exactly what I'm saying."

"So, what happened? What did you do with this information?"

"I told my ex-wife Armistead offered us free counselling in exchange for helping his son's situation, and she went berserk. First, she insisted I misunderstood what he meant, then she accused me of lying about it even happening. She said he would never do that, and accused me of making it up to sabotage our counselling sessions. To try to convince her I was telling the truth, I told her about the background check. About his four marriages and the restraining order."

"Did she believe you?"

"I don't know." He shrugs. "She was so angry at me for checking up on him that whether it was true was irrelevant.

Anyway, I refused to see him again, so she went to our next appointment alone and told him what I did and what I found out."

"Why did she throw you under the bus like that?" I ask.

"She said it was another example of me being a cop first and a husband last. And she decided it was proof I wanted a divorce and was purposely sabotaging any attempts to fix our marriage."

"I'm so sorry this happened to you." I squeeze his hand.

"Armistead reported me."

"To your superiors?"

Eric nods. "I was given an official reprimand. It's in my file."

"Reprimand for what?"

"For the background check. He wasn't part of any cases I was working on. We aren't supposed to look up random people. Cops do it all the time, but we're not supposed to do it."

"Did you tell whoever reprimanded you about Dr. Armistead trying to bribe you?"

"Yes. Armistead denied it, of course. The attempted bribery was his word against mine, but there was proof of his accusation against me, a digital trail of the search."

"What happened with you and your ex after Dr. Armistead reported you?"

"I moved out within a week."

"Can I ask you a really personal question?" I ask. "It's totally fine if you don't want to answer. I understand completely."

This is the most Eric has ever talked about his marriage. Before today, he's only ever mentioned his ex-wife's name is Karen, she's a chiropractor, and she still lives in the city. She knew he was a cop when they met, but his job caused stress in their marriage, and she wanted him to leave the force and work for her father's heating and air conditioning company. Eric refused. He wanted to be a cop since he was a little boy.

"Of course. Ask me anything," he says.

"If this situation with Dr. Armistead didn't happen, do you think you and Karen would've worked it out?"

"No," he confirms, shaking his head. "She was right about one thing, I wanted a divorce. I think her goal for therapy was to get the therapist to help her convince me to change careers, and my goal was to get the therapist to help her see our marriage wasn't worth saving."

"Thank you for trusting me enough to tell me this. I know you don't like to talk about when you were married."

"I want you to hear it from me. It's unlikely, but if Armistead's death turns out to be murder, this situation could come up, and I don't want you to think I kept it from you. No secrets."

"No secrets," I repeat after him. "But you're entitled to privacy. Privacy and secrets aren't the same."

Honestly, I don't want to know the details of Eric's past relationships.

Sometimes the past is better left there.

CHAPTER 6

THE JINGLE when I open the door at Bits'n'Bytes sounds similar to the bell over the door at Knitorious. But that's where the similarities end. Bits'n'Bytes is futuristic and sleek. Everything is white, smooth, and shiny. A completely different atmosphere than my cozy yarn store.

"I'll be right with you, Megan!" Jamila's smiling face pokes around a doorway at the back of the store.

"No worries, Jamila, take your time," I call out.

I catch sight of myself on a security monitor just below the ceiling and try to tame a few unruly curls. Other than the local jewellery store and the bank, Bits'n'Bytes is the only other business I'm aware of in Harmony Lake with a security system.

When I wander from the wall of laptops to the wall of tablets, I glance toward the back room and glimpse the back of Jamila's head. She moves toward the back door, and the rest of her body comes into view. Her back is to me. She unlocks the door and moves aside. Someone else comes into view and joins Jamila at the back door. It's Charmaine Solomon again. I've never seen Charmaine and Jamila in the same place at the same time, and now I've seen them together twice in two days. Both times, they're huddled together conspiratorially. Both women speak and nod repeatedly until Charmaine finally leaves, and Jamila closes the door and locks it.

I book it to the front window, hoping to see Charmaine's car drive out of the parking lot behind the store, so I can confirm it's her.

"Sorry to make you wait, Megan."

I turn away from the window and look at Jamila. "No problem. Your text said to stop by whenever, but I practically ran here because the laptop at the store is completely dead."

"Right!" Jamila holds up her index finger. "Give me one more minute to get it. It's in the back."

When Jamila disappears again, I run back to the window, hoping I didn't miss Charmaine's car.

Bingo!

There she is, waiting to turn left out of the driveway that connects the parking lot behind the store to Water Street. I knew it was her.

"Let's take a look!" Jamila places the laptop on one of the shiny, white, round tables in the showroom. She sits in a shiny, white chair, and I sit across from her.

Jamila gives me a tour of the laptop and lists its various tech specs and such. I nod and smile but don't actually understand what most of it means. She assures me it's fast, has enough memory, and plenty of storage for everything I need. She says it's compatible with the programs I use to run Knitorious.

"It sounds perfect. I'll take it," I say confidently, not feeling at all confident.

"Great! Do you mind leaving your phone here for a couple of hours?"

"My phone? Why?"

Jamila explains that because the laptop at the store is dead, but my cell phone, home computer, and store computer sync the same information, she can use my cell phone to set up the new laptop.

"You'll set it up for me?" This makes me happier than it reasonably should. I dread setting it up myself.

"It's part of the service," she explains. "To stay competitive, I have to offer something the big-box stores don't." She shrugs. "I offer free set up."

Jamila taps on the keyboard and occasionally spins the laptop toward me for a fingerprint or to set up a password.

"How are you feeling today, Jamila?" I spin the laptop toward her after setting up my fingerprint. "I mean, since learning that Dr. Armistead died last night."

"Dr. Armistead?" she asks without looking up from the screen.

"Yes, Dr. Armistead. Didn't you have dinner with him last night at the Solomon's?"

"Oh, you mean, Mac?"

Dr. Armistead's first name is Malcolm, or as I'm now learning from Jamila, Mac for short.

"I found him," I tell her.

She stops tapping on the keyboard and looks at me. "I'm sorry to hear that. It must've been awful."

"It wasn't pleasant," I agree. "Probably as unpleasant as finding out someone you just shared a meal with suddenly died."

She nods somberly. "He was a nice man. He was fine when I left the Solomon's. It's hard to believe that less than an hour after I said goodbye to him, he died."

"Did you know him well?"

"I was his tech support. Not very often, because he was pretty technically astute, but I did some tech stuff for him over the years."

"How did he find you? I was told he lived and worked in Harmony Hills."

"He did," Jamila confirms. "Emory referred him to me. I provide tech support for Emory's therapy practice too."

"Well, I'm sorry you've lost a friend, or client, or both."

"Thanks." Jamila's gaze returns to the laptop screen, and she continues typing.

"How are the Solomons doing today? They must be in shock after what happened to their friend."

"I haven't spoken to either of them since last night at the pub," Jamila replies. "Eric texted Charmaine, and she stepped outside to call him back. When she came back, she told Emory she had a work emergency, and they had to leave. I found out about Mac early this morning from a police officer."

Lie. I just saw Jamila and Charmaine together in the back room.

"I haven't spoken to them either," I admit. "And I'm not sure when I'll be able to give them my condolences. Charmaine is Eric's boss, and he says he can't talk to her right now —something about conflicts of interest. I don't want to put either of them in an awkward position, so I haven't reached out to the Solomons. If you speak to them, would you tell them I'm sorry for their loss?"

"Sure." Jamila nods. "Did the police question you?"

I nod. "Detective Morris questioned me this morning."

"Me too," she says, "but he said he doesn't think Mac was murdered. Why is he questioning people if it wasn't murder?"

It takes me a moment to remember that Mac is Dr. Armistead. I'm not used to hearing him called by his first name.

"Detective Morris says every death is treated as suspicious until the coroner confirms it isn't."

Jamila lets out a sigh of relief.

I know how she feels, I've been there. It's unnerving to think that something as horrible as murder could happen in your hometown. A place where you feel safe and trust the people around you. It unsettles your mind, body, and soul. It makes you second guess everything.

THE JINGLE of the bell startles the ladies who are sitting on the sofas, knitting.

"Hi, Megan," the two ladies say in unison as I enter the store.

"Hi, Megan." Eric waves from his seat, next to one of the women.

"Hello, everyone," I say, crouching down to greet Sophie and fighting back a laugh at Eric's obvious awkwardness.

"He was all alone," Mrs. Roblin says, patting Eric's knee.

"Helpless," Mrs. Vogel adds. "What if someone came in with an urgent knitting problem?"

"He wouldn't know what to do!" Mrs. Roblin continues. "Lucky for him, we came along. We decided we should keep him company and help with any knitting emergencies that might come up."

"It's the neighbourly thing to do," Mrs. Vogel justifies.

Never in my life have I encountered what I would consider a life-or-death knitting emergency.

"Thank you, ladies! I appreciate it. I'm a bit stuck this week with Connie looking after Archie and Marla helping at Artsy Tartsy."

Mrs. Roblin and Mrs. Vogel ask about Archie's hip replacement surgery, then they ask how April's father is doing. Soon they're telling Eric and me about friends and family who have had hip replacements and ladder-related accidents.

"Thank you for coming to my rescue this afternoon, ladies." Eric gives each of them a wide smile and stands up. "Now that the boss is back, I think I'll go upstairs for lunch." He gives them a wink.

Amidst cries of how he shouldn't have to make his own lunch, and if Mrs. Vogel had known, she would have brought him a sandwich, and if Mrs. Roblin had known she would have brought him a casserole, Eric escapes to the sanctuary of his apartment.

Within minutes of his departure, Mrs. Roblin and Mrs. Vogel pack up their knitting bags and leave the store.

"Are they gone?" Eric asks cautiously, his eyes darting from one yarn section to another upon re-entering the store.

"Yes, they left right after you. If you want me to call them and let them know you're back, I'm more than happy to. I'll even run another errand if you want them to hang around for a while," I tease.

"No, thank you! They're lovely ladies, but too much of a good thing is not good."

Eric goes to the backroom/kitchenette and reappears with two plates.

"Lunch," he announces, putting the plates on the harvest table. "Chicken Caesar salad wraps."

"Thank you," I say, joining him at the table. "I'm starving."

I explain how I left my phone with Jamila so she can set up the new laptop. "She said she'll call me on the landline when it's ready."

"Tell me about the new laptop," he replies.

To the best of my ability, I tell him the handful of specs I can remember and describe its appearance. I'm far more comfortable describing its appearance than the specs.

"You really don't know a lot about computers, do you?" He laughs.

"No, I don't. I'm what's called 'an end user'." I take a sip of water. "Charmaine Solomon was there."

"At Bits'n'Bytes?" Eric asks.

With my mouth full of food, I nod.

"Did you speak to her?" he asks.

I swallow before I reply. "No. She doesn't know I saw her. She was in the back room with Jamila. I happened to look up when Charmaine was leaving through the back door. I watched her car turn onto Water Street to make sure it was her." Eric looks down and to the left. He does this when he concentrates. "What?" I ask.

"I wonder if either of them disclosed this visit to Darby?"

I shrug. "I don't know about Darby, but Jamila didn't disclose the visit to me. I asked her outright if she's spoken to the Solomons since Dr. Armistead died, and she said, 'no'."

"Why would she lie?" he wonders out loud.

"It's possible Charmaine was checking on Jamila. Jamila's probably never had dinner with someone who died right after the last course. Also, Charmaine might've wanted to see Jamila with her own eyes to reassure herself that it wasn't food poisoning that killed Dr. Armistead. If one of my dinner guests died, it would cross my mind."

"Possibly," Eric agrees, nodding. "It still doesn't explain why Jamila would lie about it."

I shrug. "Maybe she thought I was being nosy. Connie and I had our share of nosy neighbours this morning. Maybe when they left here, they went to Bits'n'Bytes, and now Jamila is cautious about telling anyone anything. But I remembered something else this morning when Darby questioned me. Something I forgot to mention to you last night."

I tell him about Jamila and Charmaine's conversation in the alley beside the pub.

"Even when you're drunk, you have above average observation skills."

Slightly drunk. Tipsy.

CHAPTER 7

THE BELL above the door turns my attention from the yoke of the sweater I'm knitting. "Jess!" I declare, putting my knitting on the coffee table in front of me. "How are you?" We hug.

"Still in shock, I think, but I'm OK. How about you?" she asks.

"I'm OK."

"Megan, this is my friend Karen Porter. She works at the medical centre too. She drove me here to pick up my car."

"Hi, Karen, it's nice to meet you." I extend my hand.

"You too." Karen shakes my hand weakly.

Karen has been crying. Her face is splotchy, and her large brown eyes are red and swollen. Her dark hair is pulled back into a low ponytail, and a few escaped wisps stick out around her face. She has that raw, tired look that only comes from crying yourself to exhaustion.

"Have a seat," I say.

"There's another reason Karen drove me here today," Jess explains. "She was friends with Dr. Armistead. She was really shaken when she found out what happened. She has some questions about how we found him. I've answered them to the best of my ability, but between the shock and the chardonnay, I'm not sure I'm recalling everything correctly."

"I don't think we're supposed to talk about this together," I say. "Have you given a statement?"

"Earlier today." Jess nods. "I told the detective what happened and answered a lot of questions for him."

I'm hesitant to have this conversation without asking Darby first. My phone is still with Jamila, so I can't text him, and Eric is walking Sophie, so he's not here to ask.

"I was married to a cop," Karen pipes in. "I'm sure it would be fine, as long as we're all honest about what we talk about if the police ask."

I chew the inside of my cheek, still hesitant. Karen is obviously chomping at the bit to talk about it. She seems more distraught than I'd expect from a co-worker. Exactly how well did she know Dr. Armistead?

"Were you and Dr. Armistead close, Karen?"

Her eyes fill with moisture, and she swallows hard. She opens her mouth to speak, but no sound comes out, and she nods sharply instead.

I hand her a box of tissue, and Jess rubs her upper back.

"You loved him," I say softly. Her grief is palpable. "I'm sorry for your loss."

Karen nods again and dabs at the tears streaming down her cheeks. "Did he look…" She pauses while she finds the right word. "Peaceful?"

"It was dark, and I only saw him through the car window for a moment. He didn't look injured or in pain. It didn't look like he suffered."

I have no idea whether he suffered or not, but I know it's what Karen needs to hear, and it's probably what Dr. Armistead would want her to hear.

"Karen, I had no idea you and Dr. Armistead were together," Jess says. "Why didn't you tell me?"

We sit quietly and wait while Karen composes herself enough to speak.

"We didn't tell anyone," Karen explains, looking at Jess. "It was a secret."

"Why?" Jess asks.

"I was his patient," Karen admits. "His profession has a five-year rule. He has to wait five years before dating a former patient. We didn't wait five years."

"How long did you wait?" I ask.

"We've been dating for about a year, and I was his patient between three and four years ago."

"Oh my," Jess says, looking at me. Then she looks at Karen. "You told the police about your relationship, right?"

Karen shakes her head. "I haven't talked to the police. They don't know I exist."

"You have to tell them," Jess advises.

Good advice, Jess.

"Uh-uh." Karen shakes her head. "No way. I don't want to damage Mac's reputation. People will judge him. They'll say he took advantage of me, and he didn't. It wasn't like that. We only had a couple of sessions years ago. We lost touch until I left my practice in the city and joined the practice in Harmony Hills. We met again and had a connection. Why should we wait two more years? We're adults." Her voice becomes louder, and her tone more defensive as she speaks.

"I get it," I say, hoping to calm Karen's emotional state. "The police think he died of natural causes. If they're right, there won't be an investigation into Dr. A—Mac's death, and you won't have to say anything. The case will be closed."

"But if they're wrong," Jess adds, "and his death is investigated, you, me, or Megan will have to tell the police about your relationship."

Karen's silent tears become sobs. I get her a glass of water and place it on the table in front of her.

"Karen, do any of your friends or family know about you

and Mac?" I ask.

She shakes her head and sips the water.

"If you tell them, they can support you. Right now, everyone assumes you've lost a co-worker, not your life part-ner. If your people know the truth about your relationship, they'll understand, and you won't have the extra burden of keeping this secret and hiding your grief."

"Megan's right," Jess agrees. "It's something to think about."

Jess continues to comfort Karen until Karen asks me where she can freshen up.

"Back of the store," I direct. "Turn left in the kitchenette. There's a small hallway. The washroom is on the right."

Karen goes to the washroom, taking the tissue box with her.

Once we're alone, Jess looks at me wide-eyed. "I had no idea she was in a relationship with Dr. Armistead, I swear," she whispers. "I just assumed she's one of those super-sensi-tive people. I can't believe I didn't see it."

"In hindsight, were there any clues?" I whisper.

Jess opens her mouth to answer, but we're interrupted by the jingle of the door and the sudden appearance of Sophie.

"Hi, Sophie." Jess rubs the corgi's head. "Hi, Eric."

"Hey, Jess. How are you?"

Eric and Jess exchange pleasantries, then Eric looks at me. "Jamila stopped me outside Bits'n'Bytes. The laptop is ready."

"Listen," I hiss. "Jess's friend is here. She's in the wash-room. She told us she's Dr. Armistead's secret girlfriend."

Eric's mouth forms a very small o. "I'll leave you to talk, and I'll pick up your laptop and phone."

I nod. Eric puts Sophie's leash on the counter and leaves through the front door.

I give Jess a brief explanation about the conflict of interest with the HLPD and Dr. Armistead's investigation.

Jess takes a deep breath. "Before Eric and Sophie came in, you asked me about hindsight. Now that I think about it, Karen and Dr. Armistead had lunch together almost every day but always in his office. They never went out unless it was part of a group. And when his office was robbed on Monday, she helped him sort through the mess. It took them hours. She said they were there all night. I should've seen it."

"You saw what they wanted you to see," I tell her.

"What are you talking about?" Karen asks upon her return from the washroom.

"Jess was just telling me that Dr. Armistead's office was broken into on Monday. She said they made a huge mess."

Karen sighs and nods. "They did. They emptied every drawer, filing cabinets were flipped over, paper was scattered everywhere. It took hours to sort through."

"Did they take anything?" I ask.

Karen shakes her head. "Not even his laptop."

"The office door and his filing cabinets weren't locked?" Jess asks.

"They were," Karen confirms. "The robbers picked the locks."

"Whatever they were looking for, they must've wanted it badly," I observe.

"The police said they were probably looking for drugs."

"In a therapist's office?" It sounds like Jess doesn't buy it. "Dr. Armistead doesn't write prescriptions. He wouldn't have drug samples in his office. If they wanted drugs, there's a pharmacy in the lobby and a dozen other medical offices in the building that have drugs in them."

"But Mac's office was the only one that was empty," Karen explains. "The police think the robbers lurked around waiting for an opportunity, and when they saw Mac leave his office and lock the door, they knew it was empty. The police think the robbers were angry when they realized there were no drugs, and they trashed the office."

Jess looks at me and shrugs. I get the feeling she's still not convinced.

"Karen," Jess says gently, "is your secret relationship the reason you and Dr. Armistead ate lunch in his office every day and never went out? Were you afraid people would realize you were more than friends?"

"It was difficult for Mac to enjoy eating out with his allergy."

"Allergy?" I probe.

"He had a severe caffeine allergy. Very rare but deadly. He kept an EpiPen with him at all times. He also kept one in his car. You'd be amazed how many foods contain caffeine. Foods you'd never expect. He was conditioned to bring his own food, or he would eat at a handful of specific restaurants where he was comfortable."

While Jess and Karen talk about food allergies, I think back to the conversation Eric and I had last night about his meeting with Charmaine. She was preparing duchess potatoes and chateaubriand with sauce and brussels sprouts. I wonder what they had for dessert. Could any of those dishes have inadvertently contained caffeine? Poor Charmaine! I can't imagine worrying that I may have accidentally poisoned someone.

Did Dr. Armistead have any visible symptoms of allergic reaction when Jess and I found him? I only saw his face. I'm sure I would have noticed hives or severe swelling. But it was dark. The streetlight wasn't working because of the accident. Think Megan, think! Stupid chardonnay, clouding my recollection.

I'm vaguely aware when the bell over the door jingles, but I'm so focused on my thoughts that it doesn't distract me.

"WHY ARE YOU HERE?" Karen's shout brings me back to the here and now.

"Karen?" Eric sounds shocked.

He closes the door behind him but doesn't come any

closer.

As my brain begins to connect the mental dots, I gasp and bring my hand to my mouth.

Is this the same Karen who was married to Eric? She said she was married to a cop. She works in a medical centre. Chiropractors sometimes work in medical centres. She moved from the city about a year ago. Oh my gosh, it's her. I know it's her. The pit in my stomach and the expressions on Eric and Karen's faces confirm it's her.

"Why is my ex-wife here?" Eric asks quietly, looking at me.

He sounds calm, but I can see the panic and confusion in his eyes.

At a loss for words, I shake my head and shrug.

"Why am *I* here? Why are *you* here? What are you doing in a knitting store?" Karen demands. "Don't tell me you're the one working Mac's case?!"

"I don't know what you're talking about, Karen," Eric replies calmly. "Who's Mac?"

I'm on my feet now, standing halfway between the sofa where Karen is sitting and the front door where Eric is standing.

"Leave!" Karen demands. She looks at Jess. "Make him leave." Her voice is shaky now, and her chin is quivering.

"I live here, Karen," Eric states matter-of-factly.

"Fine! I'll leave!" Karen starts to get up, but Jess stops her by placing a hand on her shoulder.

"This is my fault," Jess interjects. "I brought Karen here. I didn't realize you two…know each other."

"None of us did," I add, walking to the front door.

I reach behind Eric to lock the door and turn the sign from OPEN to CLOSED. I don't think the BACK IN TEN MINUTES sign will be sufficient for this situation.

"Thank you," I say quietly to Eric as I attempt to pry the laptop box and my cell phone from his hand. I can't loosen the death grip he has on them. He appears calm and composed, but it's an illusion. Up close, every muscle in his body is tense. He's stiff as a board. His jaw muscles clench and unclench constantly. I take his stiff, free hand and lead him to the back room. I close the door behind us.

"Let go," I grunt, tugging at the box.

He loosens his grip on the laptop box and my phone. I put them on the counter in the kitchenette, then point to the stairs that lead to his apartment. "Sit down," I suggest gently.

Eric sits on one of the steps, takes a deep breath, runs both hands through his hair, and drops his chin to his chest. He's staring at the floor between his feet. He's in shock. Possibly speechless.

I kneel on the floor in front of him so I'm low enough to see his face. "Eric, I'm sorry. I had no idea Karen is your ex-wife. I would never ambush you like this. Jess didn't know either."

"Why is she here?" He looks at me.

I tell him that Karen drove Jess to Harmony Lake so Jess could pick up her car. And that Karen wanted to talk to me because I was with Jess when we found Dr. Armistead.

"She works in the same building as Jess and Dr. Armistead, but I didn't know she's a chiropractor. Her last name isn't Sloane, it's Porter. I've never seen a picture of your ex-wife, and you said she lives and works in the city. I honestly didn't make the connection. I wish I had. I would've made sure you weren't blindsided."

He looks at me. "It's OK. It's no one's fault."

"I know she was mean and shouty, but that's not all because of you. She's grieving. She's an emotional mess right now."

"Grieving who?" he asks, confused.

"Dr. Armistead."

Comprehension flashes across his face. "Is she the same woman who was in the washroom earlier? The one who is

Armistead's secret girlfriend? Mac and Armistead are the same person?"

I nod. "Yes."

He inhales deeply and lets it out slowly. "Not my monkey, not my circus. None of this is my problem," he says, putting his hands on his knees and standing up. He reaches with both hands. I take his hands, and he pulls me to my feet.

I climb the first two stairs, so we're close to eye level. "Are you sure you're all right?"

I genuinely can't tell. He seems fine, but he's good at hiding how he feels and what he's thinking. It's a cop thing—conceal, don't feel.

"I'm fine. I was in shock, but I'm OK now."

I wrap my arms around him and rest my head on his shoulder. Some of the tension leaves his body, and I feel him relax. "I'm so sorry this happened."

"It's not your fault. It's no one's fault." He kisses me. "I should leave. Connie says it takes up to half an hour for Archie and his walker to get from the condo to the car." He smiles.

"You don't have to go," I tell him. "You've had a rough day. I'll take Zach to his game or find someone else. You can chill at home."

"I want to go," Eric insists. "I'm going upstairs to get a jacket, then I'll leave through the back door. It sounds like Karen has quieted down, and I don't want to get her started again."

"OK."

I trust Jess has filled in the gaps for Karen and explained that Eric lives here, works in Harmony Lake, and that he and I are together.

I grab my phone from the counter in the kitchenette. Before I open the door to the store, I take a deep breath and brace myself for whatever awkward conversation I'm about to have with my boyfriend's ex-wife.

CHAPTER 8

Sᴜɴᴅᴀʏ, October 4ᵗʰ

Adam: Be there in 10 minutes.

Me: Just leaving to walk Sophie. Let yourself in.

Adam replies with a thumbs-up emoji.

Adam, Hannah, and I have brunch together every Sunday. We alternate between his place and mine, but Adam always cooks. Hannah joins us from school via Facetime. Brunch is at my place this week.

"Good morning, gorgeous! I miss you!" I shove my phone in my pocket as I talk with April while leaving the house with Sophie in tow.

"Good morning, Megalodon! Did the coroner decide the marriage counselor died of natural causes?" April asks.

"Not yet," I reply. "But he's only been dead for a day, and I'm not sure the coroner works on weekends. Do you know?"

"I have no idea, but it doesn't sound like a nine-to-five job. People die at night and on weekends too," April speculates.

Fair enough.

"I'll let you know as soon as I hear anything. But I think I might know how he died," I tell her.

"Spill," she demands.

I tell April about Jess and Karen's visit to Knitorious yesterday. "What a horrible allergy. Life would be so boring without coffee and chocolate," I observe.

"Can we back up to the part where everyone realizes Karen is Eric's ex-wife?" April knows which details are important.

I explain how none of us realized who Karen was until it was too late, then tell April about Karen and Eric's reactions when they saw each other.

"How is Eric now?" April asks.

I stop and wait while Sophie greets an elderly couple sitting on a bench. "He seems fine. He was his normal self after Zach's hockey game last night, and our texts this morning were the same as usual. He wasn't OK when it happened. He was in shock. He shut down and went into cop mode."

"What does Karen look like?"

"Hang on." I pull my phone from my pocket and open the browser. A quick web search of Karen's name, the medical centre where she works, and Harmony Hills leads to her chiropractic practice's website. I find her head shot, and text it to April. "I just texted you her pic."

"She's pretty," April comments.

"Very," I agree. "And she was really nice until she saw Eric. Then she returned to being nice after he left. I think they're an example of a couple who are nice people individually but don't work together."

"Did she say how she felt about Dr. Armistead keeping their relationship a secret?"

"She defended him. She told Jess and I that she wouldn't disclose it to the police because she didn't want anyone to think badly of him or to view her as a victim."

"She is a victim, Megastar. He was her therapist. He knows her most personal stuff. It creates a power imbalance. He was in a position of influence over her. There's a five-year rule for dating former patients for a reason." April makes several good points.

"I know," I agree. "Karen said they started dating three years after their last therapy appointment. And she's a health-care professional too. She knew about the five-year rule when they started dating. I don't know enough about the situation to have an opinion on how inappropriate it was, but it was inappropriate enough for them to keep it a secret, and secrets make me uncomfortable."

We change the subject several times, catching up on anything and everything in our lives.

April updates me on her dad's recovery and how he's settling in at home since the hospital discharged him yester-day. "He's obsessed with those flipping eaves troughs," she vents. "He has three broken bones and his biggest concern about the whole situation is that the stupid eaves troughs still aren't fixed."

"That's frustrating," I sympathize.

"I'm calling a company first thing tomorrow morning to come and fix them, so he can find something new to complain about."

We talk until Sophie and I make our way back to the front door.

"It smells amazing!" Warm comfort and cinnamon surrounds me when I walk into the house.

"Thanks!" Adam emerges from the kitchen, rapidly stir-ring something in a mixing bowl. He's wearing my ruffled apron with the cherry pattern which is much too small for his large frame "It's Apple Fritter Breakfast Casserole. I prepared it in advance and put it in the oven when I got here." He stops stirring and tips the bowl toward me. "This is the glaze."

"It's yummy. I love it."

"You haven't tried it yet."

"It smells like dessert. I love dessert," I reason, following him toward the kitchen.

"It'll be ready in ten minutes."

I nod and pick up my tablet to Facetime Hannah. "Are you going to talk to Hannah about inviting Jess to Thanksgiving dinner?"

"Yeah, if you're still good with it," Adam replies, setting the table.

"Of course, I am. I'm sure Hannah will be too."

I unlock the tablet and open the messaging app. Because my devices are "automagically" connected by the wonderful yet mysterious force known as *the cloud*, the last text I sent pops up on the screen.

"Who's that?" Adam asks. Still stirring briskly, he lifts his chin toward Karen's photo on the screen.

I tell him how Karen, Jess, Eric, and I unwittingly ended up in the same room yesterday.

"Jess told me," Adam says. He puts the mixing bowl on the counter and wipes his hand on the apron. Then he picks up my tablet and examines Karen's photo. "I've never met Karen, but I've heard about her. She's one of Jess's work friends." He looks at me, then hands my tablet to me. "But I recognize her."

"From the medical centre where Jess works?" I venture a logical guess.

Adam shakes his head, and I notice the grey around his temples is more pronounced than it used to be. It really stands out against his dark hair and enhances the laugh lines around his blue eyes. "No. From my office. Well, the building where my office is located."

"Oh? Is she there often?"

Adam's office is in a large, renovated Victorian house. He's one of four professional tenants. There's also a financial planner, an insurance broker, and a therapist—Emory Solomon.

"I've seen her a few times waiting for Emory."

Karen Porter is Emory's patient? But Emory and Dr. Armistead were friends. At least, I assume they were friends since the Solomons invited Dr. Armistead to their house for dinner on Friday. Wouldn't it be a conflict of interest for Emory to treat his friend's girlfriend? Did Karen know Emory and Dr. Armistead were friends? Does Emory know Karen was dating his friend, Dr. Armistead?

"That arrangement would be too cozy for my liking," I comment.

"Me too," Adam agrees. "Even if they all know, it crosses a line."

"And I thought we had boundary issues," I mutter.

"What?"

I know he heard me.

"What?" I answer his question with a question.

We Facetime with Hannah while Adam serves breakfast. We catch up with our daughter and hear about her life in the big city. Next weekend is Thanksgiving, and Hannah will be here in person for brunch. We haven't seen her in six weeks, and I can't wait to hug her.

"I told you she'd be fine with Jess coming to Thanksgiving. Have you invited her yet?"

He doles out another serving of casserole to me, then himself. "No. I wanted to make sure Hannah was comfortable first. I'll ask her today."

"Since I'm hosting this year, do you want me to invite Jess? You know, so she knows we all want her here."

"I'll invite her, and I'll tell her you and Hannah are on board. Thank you, though." Adam smiles.

I sense he wants to say more, but he's hesitant.

"Well, if Jess offers to bring something, say no. The rest of us are bringing enough food to feed a small town. Or she can bring those little loot bags she hands out after she cleans our teeth, and everyone can take care of their dental hygiene after dinner," I joke.

We laugh and Adam makes another joke about all of us speaking to her with our mouths open, to make her more comfortable.

"I'm happy you and Jess hit it off," he says. "And thank you for looking out for her when you guys found Dr. Armistead."

"Of course," I reply. "You always had good taste in partners."

"You guys have been texting pretty regularly," Adam says. "And she stopped by the store with Karen yesterday, when she could've just picked up her car and left."

"We get along well. She's great. Would it make you uncomfortable if Jess and I are friends?" I ask Adam the question he never asked me before he befriended Eric.

He sits back in his chair. "I didn't think so, but it's... awkward knowing you and Jess have your own relationship that doesn't include me. I don't know how to describe it. Do you know what I mean?"

"I have no idea." My voice practically drips with sarcasm.

"I get it now, Meg. I didn't get it before, but now I do. It didn't occur to me that my friendship with Eric might be uncomfortable for you. I should've talked to you about it a long time ago. I'm sorry I didn't."

"Eric and I talked about it," I tell him. "It's all good."

"While we're on the subject"—Adam leans forward and puts his elbows on the table—"Eric is my friend, but you're my family. You're Hannah's mother, and we've known each other forever. I will always have your back. Whatever happens between you and Eric, or me and Eric, or whatever. I'm on your side. Every time."

"I know." I put my hand on top of his. "Ditto."

Navigating our new post-marriage friendship is like walking a tightrope. It's all about balance and planning the next step carefully. Some days we're wobblier than others, but for the most part, we haven't fallen off yet, even though we might be tempted to give each other a little shove sometimes.

"How's the new laptop?" Adam asks, changing the subject.

"It's purple!" I reply, telling him my favourite feature.

"How does it function?"

"I brought it home to show it to you." I leave the table and return a moment later, clutching the laptop to my chest. I shove the dirty dishes to the far end of the table and place the laptop in front of him. "Ta-da!"

"Very nice," Adam says, running a finger along the edge of the device and admiring my first-ever, solo technological purchase. "May I?" he asks, opening the laptop a smidge.

"Of course," I reply. "You should get acquainted with it since you provide all the tech support."

"Same password?" he asks.

I nod.

Adam types in the password and icons fill the screen.

"Have you used it? Everything running OK?"

"It seems fine. But I just got it yesterday afternoon, so I haven't really used it. Just played with it."

"Jamila didn't install the anti-virus software?" Adam asks, furrowing his thick eyebrows.

I shrug. "I have no idea. She said it would sync with my other devices."

Adam installs a cyber security software on all our devices. It scans everything we open and keeps out viruses, and spyware, and such. It works silently in the background of the computer, so I'm unaware of it most of the time. When it comes to my relationship with technology, out of sight is out of mind.

"I'll install it," he says without looking up.

He taps a few keys, we wait a few moments, then he declares the laptop safe from virtual intruders and closes it.

On the table between us, my tablet dings. I unlock the screen with my fingerprint.

Eric: Armistead died of anaphylactic shock.

"That's a relief," I say to Adam as I type a response to Eric.

"Not for Dr. Armistead," Adam responds.

Me: Case closed?

It'll be nice not to have Dr. Armistead's unfortunate death hanging over us.

Eric: Case upgraded from suspicious death to homicide.

"What?" Adam and I say in unison.

CHAPTER 9

ADAM LEAVES, and I text the Modern Family group chat to update everyone on Dr. Armistead's status. Then I load the dishwasher and wipe the counters and table while I wait for Eric to get here. He said he'd be here in ten minutes. This feels like the longest ten minutes ever.

Finally, Sophie yelps and runs to the door. It's impossible to sneak into this house with Sophie on constant surveillance.

"Hey, Soph!" Eric crouches down and rubs her corgi head. "Hey," he says again, giving me a hug and a kiss.

We sit in the family room. Sophie jumps onto the sofa and parks herself between us.

"Murder?"

"Murder," Eric confirms.

"What if he ate something caffeinated by accident at the Solomon's dinner party? Surely if it was unintentional, it isn't murder. Caffeine is hidden in so many foods…"

"Whoa." Eric raises his hand in a stop motion. "Why are you convinced it was a caffeine allergy?"

I forgot Eric doesn't have access to all the information about the case. I'm so used to him being the investigating detective that I forgot he wasn't.

"I think I should talk to Darby," I say after I tell him about Karen's revelation that Dr. Armistead was deathly allergic to caffeine.

"I think you're right," Eric agrees.

DARBY SITS on the living room sofa, and Sophie sits at attention by his feet. Darby leans forward and opens his leather folio to an empty page then uncaps his fountain pen.

"I take it you've heard about Dr. Armistead's cause of death?"

"Allergic reaction." I nod. "Caffeine?" I ask.

Darby looks at me and tilts his head. "Why would you ask that, Megan?" He grins.

"Because Ka—his girlfriend mentioned that Dr. Armistead had a severe caffeine allergy."

I'm uncomfortable mentioning Karen's name in front of Eric. I'm scared he'll freeze again, or hearing her name will upset him.

"You met Dr. Armistead's girlfriend? I wish I was a fly on that wall," Darby chuckles as his crinkled eyes dart back and forth between me and Eric.

Obviously, he knows Dr. Armistead had a girlfriend and that his girlfriend happened to be Eric's ex-wife.

"You know about Dr. Armistead's girlfriend?" I answer his question with a question. "She said you don't know about her."

"I went through his phone," Darby explains.

"Ah," I respond.

It's difficult to keep secrets in the age of technology.

"How did you meet Karen?" he asks.

I tell him about Jess and Karen's visit to Knitorious, without mentioning the bit about Karen and Eric's unfortunate reactions to seeing each other.

"But earlier in the day," I add, "before their visit, I went to Bits'n'Bytes to talk to Jamila about my new laptop, and Charmaine Solomon was there."

"Are you sure it was Charmaine Solomon?" Darby asks. He makes a note I'm unable to decipher because I'm too far away, and leaning forward and squinting would be too obvious. Also, from my vantage point, his writing is upside down.

"Certain," I affirm with confidence. "I even watched her car leave the parking lot to be extra sure. It's not so much that she was there, it's that Jamila lied about it. She told me she hadn't spoken to either of the Solomons since the night before. I've thought about it a lot, and I think Charmaine's visit to Bits'n'Bytes was a surprise to Jamila. I don't think it was prearranged."

"Why do you say that?" Darby asks.

"Because Jamila's text said I should come to her store anytime. If she knew Charmaine was coming and wanted to have a private conversation with her, she would have told me to come at a specific time or after a specific time."

Darby asks me what time I went to Bits'n'Bytes yesterday, and I tell him. Eric is able to confirm the time because he watched Knitorious while I was gone.

I ask Darby if it would be considered murder if someone inadvertently fed caffeine to Dr. Armistead without realizing it. "It could happen, right? I'm sure lots of foods and drinks contain caffeine, but people who don't have a caffeine allergy or sensitivity wouldn't realize it."

Darby caps his pen and closes his folio, then looks at me. "Dr. Armistead had at least one gram of caffeine in his system. That's the equivalent of more than five cups of coffee. He ingested it very quickly or all at once. More quickly than he could drink five cups of coffee.

"Oh," I respond. "How is that possible? What food has that much caffeine?"

"It probably wasn't a specific food. It was likely added to

something he ate or drank. Caffeine is readily available in pill, liquid, and powder form."

Now, I understand why the coroner concluded that Dr. Armistead was murdered.

"How long does it take for caffeine to kill someone with an allergy?" I ask. "Maybe he ingested it earlier in the day, and it didn't take effect until after dinner," I suggest, grasping for reasons to exclude the suspects who live and work in Harmony Lake.

"The coroner says it was ingested within an hour of his death," Darby explains.

"Ka—his girlfriend said Dr. Armistead carried an EpiPen with him at all times and kept one in his car. Did he try to use it before he died?"

An EpiPen is an auto-injectable device that delivers epinephrine, a life-saving medication for life-threatening allergic reactions. An allergic person uses it if they are exposed to whatever they're allergic to and experiences anaphylaxis, a severe allergic reaction that often results in death.

"I believe when he hit the lamp post, he was pulling over to use his EpiPen but ran out of time."

I adjust uncomfortably in my chair and try to banish the mental image of Dr. Armistead trying to stop his car and reach his EpiPen before it was too late. He must have been full of fear and panic.

"Karen is Emory Solomon's patient." I can't tiptoe around her name forever. I glance quickly toward Eric and notice no reaction from him when I say her name.

"Really?" Darby straightens his spine and sits up at attention. "Did you hear this from a reputable source or the small-town rumour mill?"

Darby is a cop, and cops like tangible evidence, so I don't bother to explain to him that Harmony Lake's rumour mill has a shockingly high accuracy rate.

"A reliable source," I assure him. "Someone in a position to see it for themselves."

I'm sure Adam wouldn't mind if I named him as my source, but I'd rather warn him first.

"Innnnteresting," Darby remarks, re-opening his folio and once again uncapping his pen to jot down a note.

"Now that you know Dr. Armistead was murdered, do you think the burglary at his office on Monday could be related to his death?" I ask.

"There's no evidence linking the two incidents," Darby replies matter-of-factly.

From the corner of my eye, I notice Eric shift uneasily in his chair. I look at him and smile. He smiles back. He wants to tell me something, I can sense it. Sophie senses something, too, and jumps onto his lap. She settles there, and he rubs her.

"Anything you'd like to add, Eric?" Darby asks.

Clearly, he also noticed Eric's sudden unease.

Eric shakes his head. "Nope. I'm good."

"You're very quiet," Darby observes.

"I'm listening," Eric responds. "Listening and learning."

He definitely has something to say. I'm sure he'll tell me when Darby leaves.

"Getting back to the break-in at Dr. Armistead's office," I interject, redirecting the conversation back to the topic at hand. "You mean there's no evidence linking the break-in to Dr. Armistead's murder *yet*, right? Karen said you told Dr. Armistead that it was probably kids looking for drugs. But yesterday, Jess said if they were looking for drugs, they wouldn't target a psychotherapist's office when there are so many other sources for drugs in the building…"

"Hold up," Darby interrupts me and drops his pen onto his folio. "The full impact of your visit yesterday with Jess and Karen is just hitting me." He pauses and crosses his hands on his lap. "Yesterday, you're sitting in your yarn store, casually chatting with your husband's girlfriend and your boyfriend's ex-wife. The three of you were comparing notes on the murder of a marriage counselor you were all patients of." He quirks an eyebrow and smirks. His expression is a combination of amusement and shock.

I take a deep breath and let it out. "When you say it like that, it sounds a lot weirder than it actually is," I reply. "Also, Adam is my *ex*-husband, and none of us *knew* at the time that Karen is Eric's *ex*-wife, and we were discussing Dr. Armistead's *death*, not his murder. Until this morning, we believed he died of natural causes."

"C'mon," Darby pleads, still grinning. "You have to admit it's unconventional."

"Fiiine," I acquiesce with a sigh, so we can move on and get back to talking about the break-in. "It's unconventional. You know what else is unconventional? Drug addicts leaving behind a perfectly good computer they could've sold for drug money."

"Who told you what was or was not stolen from Dr. Armistead's office?"

"The person who helped him clean up the mess."

I don't think he knew Karen was there and helped Dr. Armistead clean up after the break-in.

"We're still looking into the break-in," Darby says. "It's an open case."

'It's an open case,' is cop speak for 'I'm not telling you anything, so you may as well stop asking'.

"As usual, it's been educational and delightful, Megan." Darby and I exchange a cheek kiss at the door on his way out.

"When this is settled, the four of us should get together for dinner," I suggest, referring to Darby and his wife, and Eric and me. "I promise I won't serve anything you're allergic to." I gasp and cover my mouth with my hand. Next to me, Eric stifles a laugh. "I'm sorry," I blurt out. "It was too soon and in poor taste."

"Are you sure you aren't a cop?" Darby teases. "Dark humour is a common coping strategy for cops."

"I tell her that all the time," Eric concurs.

I say goodbye to Darby, then go to the back door and put Sophie outside while he and Eric talk.

"You've been busy," Eric says after closing the door behind Darby.

"Not really." I shrug. "Most of the time information finds me, not the other way around," I clarify.

It's true. Mostly. Granted, I seem to emit an energy, telling the universe I'm open to receiving the information, but it's not like I can turn that off. And if I could, I'm not sure I'd want to.

"You can say Karen's name, you know," Eric says. "It's fine. It's not a trigger or anything. I was caught off guard yesterday, but I'm fine now."

"OK." I nod. "Now that Darby's gone, can you tell me what made you squirm when we talked about the break-in at Dr. Armistead's office?"

"That was the first I've heard about it," Eric explains. "You said it happened on Monday?"

I nod. "Right."

"This past Monday? The twenty-eighth?"

I nod again. "Right. Your birthday."

Where is he going with this?

"Do you happen to know what time it happened?"

"Lunchtime," I reply.

"Remember when I cancelled lunch with you on Monday because I couldn't get away from work?"

"I remember."

Eric and I planned to go out for lunch on Monday to celebrate his thirty-ninth birthday. We planned to go to the pub, then he was going golfing. But something came up and he couldn't leave work, so his birthday lunch became a birthday dinner, and he missed his tee-off time.

"The reason I was stuck at work was because Charmaine had a dental emergency. She broke a tooth snacking on popcorn. I had to take her place in a meeting and a conference call while Emory took her to the dentist."

"Okaaayy." I'm not sure why this is relevant to anything related to Dr. Armistead.

"Her dentist is in Harmony Hills," he explains. "I know this because I offered to have a patrol car drive her. But she wanted Emory to take her instead. She would've been at the dentist office around lunchtime."

"Do you know which dental office she went to?" I ask, starting to understand why this might be significant.

He shakes his head. "There are quite a few dental offices in Harmony Hills."

What are the odds she was at Jess's dental office in Dr. Armistead's building? Are dental offices subject to the same standards of patient confidentiality as doctor's offices?

"Would Charmaine be able to pick a lock?" I ask.

Eric nods.

CHAPTER 10

Surveying the tables and booths, I see a lot of people I know, but not the people I was hoping to see. The sign by the door says, WELCOME TO TIFFANY'S, PLEASE SEAT YOUR-SELF. I scrutinize the available seating and choose a booth with a relatively unobstructed view of the door so I can keep watch discreetly.

I position myself in the booth and pull out my knitting. I'm at the easy part of the sweater, working stitch after stitch in plain stockinette. I can knit without having to look down at my needles. I want to keep my hands busy, but I don't want to miss them if they show up.

"Connie!" I drop my knitting onto my lap and wave over my head to get her attention.

"Good morning, my dear!" She bends over and we exchange cheek kisses, then she settles across from me in the booth. "This is nice. We hardly ever get together for breakfast. I can't remember the last time I had breakfast at Tiffany's."

We scan the menu and discuss what looks good. Connie says she only has an hour for breakfast before she has to leave

332

to take Archie to a physiotherapy appointment. We place our orders and sip our coffees. I knit intermittently on my sweater, and, as if on autopilot, Connie knits on a sock she keeps in her purse.

"You seem distracted, my dear." Connie puts her coffee on the table and resumes knitting. "Is it this nasty murder business with the marriage counselor?"

"Kind of," I admit. "It happened right outside Knitorious. It's almost like he *wanted* me to be the person who found him."

"Just because it happened outside your store, doesn't make it your responsibility," Connie advises. "You don't always have to fix everything for everyone. This murder has nothing to do with you. It's not your job to right all the wrongs in the world."

No, but I feel like it's my job to right all the wrongs in my little corner of the world if I can.

"It's too late now," I respond.

"What does that mean?"

I explain how Jess introduced me to Karen, and the eye-opening conversation that followed. Then I tell her about Jamila and Charmaine's furtive meetings before and after Jess and I found Dr. Armistead's body.

"I wonder if these clandestine meetings with Jamila are related to whatever happened between Charmaine and the mayor?"

The server brings our breakfast, and I stash my knitting in my tote bag, safely away from the poached eggs. Egg yolk gets right into the fibres of cashmere-merino yarn and is harder to get out than you'd think. I speak from experience. Learn from my mistakes, people!

"Something happened between Charmaine and the mayor?" I quietly ask after the server leaves.

"I don't know the details," she whispers, leaning over her

plate of scrambled eggs so I can hear her. "The mayor wouldn't tell me. Even after two margaritas, she managed to stay tight-lipped. And that's not like her."

"Then how do you know something happened?"

"Remember, I invited the book club to that impromptu meeting on Saturday night? When Eric and Archie went to the hockey game?"

I nod until I swallow a mouthful of food. "You said you'd ask the mayor if there's any truth to the rumour she isn't renewing Charmaine's mandate as police chief, and who she's considering to fill the position."

"Right. And I did. According to the mayor, Charmaine left her no choice. She said the increased murder rate in Harmony Lake is only part of the reason Charmaine has to go. The mayor says Charmaine overstepped in her role as police chief and interfered in town business. I don't know what happened, but they both want to keep it hush-hush."

"Interesting," I say.

Why would Charmaine insert herself in town business? Maybe it's revenge because she knows the mayor isn't renewing her contract. Maybe she's working on behalf of someone who plans to run against the mayor. But no one ever runs against our mayor. She's run uncontested in every election since I've lived in Harmony Lake. Unless... Could Charmaine have set her sights on the mayor's job? The mayor would not like that.

"Anyway," Connie continues, "she did confirm that she's interested in talking to Eric about becoming the new police chief. She says she's impressed by his track record and how quickly the locals warmed up to him."

"Speak of the devil." I nod toward the front door where Emory and Charmaine Solomon are stepping into the restaurant. I recognize her short, platinum-blonde shaggy pixie cut immediately.

Connie turns and looks toward the door, then turns back to me.

"Coincidence?" she asks. "Or were you hoping to run into them?"

"Yes," I reply to both questions.

The Solomons have breakfast at Tiffany's regularly. It's one of the reasons Eric and I rarely come here—he doesn't want to get stuck sitting with his boss and her husband.

I smile and make eye contact with Charmaine as she walks toward our booth, presumably on the way to an empty booth or table behind us.

"Megan! It's lovely to see you. Actually, I'm glad we bumped into you. How's Eric doing?" Charmaine and Emory stop at our booth.

"Hi, Charmaine," I reply with a smile. "It's nice to run into you too. I was hoping to ask you something. Eric is fine, if not a bit bored helping at Knitorious." We laugh. "Emory, I was sorry to hear about your friend, Dr. Armistead. It must have been quite a shock. I wanted to reach out earlier, but I was afraid it might be inappropriate given all the conflicts of interest involved."

"Thank you for the sympathy, Megan. It really is a shame. He was so young. Dr. Armistead and I were more like colleagues than friends. We've known each other for years, but in a professional capacity. Still, a shocking death is a shocking death, whether it's a friend or a colleague."

Am I the only one who notices Emory's attempt to distance himself from the victim? I understand you don't have to be friends with someone to have dinner with them. Goodness knows I hosted and attended more dinner parties than I can count with Adam's colleagues during our marriage, but I didn't intentionally distinguish them as colleagues instead of friends if someone made the assumption.

"How's Archie doing since his hip replacement?" Charmaine asks, looking at Connie.

While she updates the Solomons on Archie's recovery, Connie shifts over and taps the Tiffany-blue pleather seat, gesturing for Charmaine and Emory to join us. I follow her lead, also sliding over to create space.

"Just for a minute," Charmaine stipulates, sliding into the booth next to Connie.

"You catch up with your friends. I'll claim that table before someone else takes it and order our coffees," Emory suggests to his wife, nudging the bridge of his glasses with his index finger.

Emory is a couple of inches shorter than his wife, Charmaine, and though they're close in age, his salt-and-pepper hair and stomach paunch make him look older than his fit, carefully groomed wife. Charmaine's trendy clothing and hairstyle also contribute to the illusion. In contrast, Emory looks like someone who's dressed up for Halloween as a university professor—complete with a dark turtleneck under his tweed sports jacket with elbow patches. Whenever I see him, his hair has a windswept look, regardless of the wind situation that day.

Charmaine smiles and nods at him.

"Ladies, it was nice running into you." Emory smiles and looks from Connie to me, giving his glasses another small nudge.

"You, too, Emory," I reply.

"Take care, Emory." Connie smiles.

"I'm glad we ran into you, Megan," Charmaine says quietly, leaning across the table. "You might be able to save me a phone call. Does Adam handle criminal law? The lawyer we have now is *meh*. We called the first lawyer who came to mind, but we'd like someone who specializes in criminal law. Also, our guy is all the way in the city, and we'd like someone closer."

The Solomon's have lawyered-up? Consciously, I smile and focus on my breath in an attempt to hide my shock. Are they being prudent, or do they have something to hide?

I dig through my bag and find my phone, then, leaning across the table toward Charmaine, I unlock the screen and open the text app.

"I'll text you Adam's number," I say quietly as my thumbs type. "If he can't help you, he'll refer you to someone who can."

"Thank you," Charmaine whispers. "Who is Eric using?"

Why would Eric need a lawyer? Oh my god, does Eric need a lawyer? Is he a suspect? He saw Dr. Armistead in passing before dinner, but not alone, and not for longer than a minute, according to Eric. They have a history of confrontation, but that was a long time ago. Dr. Armistead was dating Eric's ex-wife, but Eric didn't know about that until after Dr. Armistead died.

I shake my head and shrug one shoulder. "I'm not sure."

"Surely, Eric doesn't need a lawyer," Connie insists. "If everyone hires a lawyer, that would slow down the investigation and drag out this unpleasantness even longer."

Picking up on my surprise at the question, Charmaine lays one of her hands atop of mine. "Not because he did anything wrong," she reassures me with a smile. "Lawyers aren't only for guilty people. It's a good idea for everyone involved to protect their own interests."

I nod. I know what lawyers are for, but I appreciate Charmaine's attempt to reassure me, nonetheless.

"What do you think happened to Dr. Armistead, Charmaine?" Connie blurts out.

Thank you, Connie! I've been biting my lip on this very question since Charmaine got here. I'm scared if I ask, it might cross a line into one of the many conflicts of interest surrounding this case. I can always rely on Connie to ferret out information in a nonchalant manner.

Charmaine purses her lips and shrugs. "I'm not sure." She shakes her head. "I suspect he ate or drank something after he left our house, or somehow, someone injected him with it. Our lawyer is trying to get a detailed inventory of the contents of Mac's car. The source of the caffeine might be there. Like a water bottle or something."

Connie and I nod. "Who would want to kill him?" Connie asks, intuitively sensing what I want to know.

Again, Charmaine shrugs. "He had four ex-wives," she points out.

Unfortunately, previous experience has taught me that the spouse, or ex-spouse, is usually the prime suspect. In Dr. Armistead's case, there are four to choose from. Not including his current partner, Karen. Murder investigations are kind of like a series of nested circles surrounding the victim. The police start with the smallest circle, the people closest to the victim. They either eliminate them, or investigate them, then move outward to the next circle of people in the victim's life.

"Did Jamila lawyer-up, too?" I wonder out loud.

I don't expect Charmaine to answer me. Sometimes my thoughts escape from my mouth when I'm deep in thought.

"I don't know," Charmaine replies. "Jamila and I haven't spoken since Friday night."

Lie.

"I saw her yesterday," I volunteer. "She sold me a laptop."

"How was she?" Charmaine asks.

Her blue eyes narrow into slits as if she's trying to bring my face into focus.

I shrug. "As well as can be expected. She was in shock and sad about what happened. She didn't say much. I got the feeling she didn't want to talk about it."

"What did you want to ask me?"

"I'm sorry?" I reply, confused.

"When Emory and I got here, you said you were glad to see me because you want to ask me something."

Right! I'd contrived an excuse to talk to Charmaine if she showed up, but I didn't need it because she came to me.

"Your mouth!" I exclaim, remembering my fake reason. "Eric said you had a dental emergency last Monday. How's your mouth?"

"It's fine now. I cracked a tooth on a popcorn kernel. Who knew one little kernel could cause such a big inconvenience? Thanks for asking. That's what you wanted to ask me about?"

"Sort of," I say. "Who's your dentist? I'm kind of in the market for a new dentist, and yours seemed to take you right away after your kernel-issue. If you're happy with them, would you mind passing along their name and number to me?"

I'm not in the market for a new dentist. I'm quite happy with the Klines, but I'm trying to determine if Charmaine was in the medical centre where both Kline Family Dentistry and Dr. Armistead's offices are located on the day and time that Dr. Armistead's office was broken into.

"I don't think I can help you," Charmaine replies. She leans forward again, and Connie and I lean forward, too, meeting her in the middle. "I assume you're trying to put some distance between yourself and the dental hygienist your ex is dating?" she whispers.

"Something like that," I agree quietly.

"I go to the same dentist. The Klines have been our dentist since Emory and I moved here."

"It was worth a try," I say, leaning back into a normal sitting position.

"I heard you and the hygienist were getting along well," Charmaine observes. "Or is that just a rumour?"

"Oh, we do get along well," I say, setting the record straight. "I like Jess. But a few boundaries might be a good idea."

"I get it." Charmaine winks at me. "If you want to discuss

boundary issues, you should book an appointment with my husband. Relationship issues are his thing."

I know she's kidding, and I laugh along with her, but maybe she's right. Maybe I should book an appointment with Emory.

CHAPTER 11

"I THINK you're overlooking the most obvious suspect," April says as we have our morning phone call while I walk home from *Tiffany's* after breakfast.

"Who?" I ask. "Only three other people were there. Charmaine, Emory, and Jamila. It has to be one of them or a combination of them."

"What about Karen?" April asks. "Maybe she was tired of being Dr Armistead's secret girlfriend, or maybe she found out he was friends with her shrink, Emory. Maybe he broke up with her. Maybe they were never even a couple. Maybe she was his stalker. Without him alive to tell his side of the story, we can't know for sure. She can say whatever she wants. There are no friends or family to confirm anything because no one knew about them."

"Darby said he found out about Karen and Dr. Armistead's relationship when he went through Dr. Armistead's phone," I remind her. "So, at the very least, they were a couple. You're right about everything else, though. But, when and how did Karen have the opportunity to give Dr. Armistead the caffeine?"

Truth time: It would be convenient if Karen is the killer. I

REAGAN DAVIS

don't know her, so I wouldn't constantly look back in hindsight, searching for signs that she was capable of murder. Also, she's not local. I wouldn't have to live with knowing I regularly greeted her with a smile on the streets of my sweet, cozy hometown without realizing she was a monster. Collectively, the residents of Harmony Lake wouldn't have to deal with the emotional fallout of a killer living among us and blending in without being noticed. If the killer is a local resident, it could really harm our sense of trust and community spirit. And let's not forget that one of the suspects is the highest-ranking police officer in town, and another is a trusted psychotherapist—both positions of trust.

While Karen being the murderer might be the best possible outcome, if there is such a thing in a murder investigation, I don't really want it to be Karen because I don't want to believe that Eric could unknowingly marry a murderer. He'd blame himself for not seeing her for what she was. And would he ever trust his cop-instincts again? If it turns out that Karen did kill Dr. Armistead, I'm worried the revelation could unravel him.

April and I continue to talk about anything and everything until our conversation is cut short when she gets a call from an eaves trough company.

"Hey, Soph!" I lock the door behind me and crouch down to greet the happy corgi. "I'm happy to see you too."

A familiar *swoosh* grabs my attention. Pipes.

"Water," I say, looking down at Sophie. "Is something leaking, Soph? Did I leave a tap running?"

If Sophie knows the answer, she's not telling. She looks up at me with her mouth slightly open and her corgi tail wagging.

"Shoot! I hope it's not a leak," I mumble, checking the laundry room, then rushing to check the kitchen.

Nothing. Not even a drippy faucet. As I hurry toward my

bedroom, the *swooshing* grows louder. It's coming from my ensuite washroom.

I burst into the bedroom, and humid, steamy air gets thicker as I get closer to the half-open washroom door. The shower is running, and Eric's phone is plugged into the charger beside the bed. Mystery solved.

Why is Eric here? And why isn't his car in the driveway? It has to be Eric. That's definitely his phone, and if a stranger were in the house, Sophie wouldn't be this calm and happy. Also, who else would come over and use the shower?

"A heads up would've been nice, Sophie," I teasingly chastise.

Sophie doesn't care. She's sprawled comfortably on the bed, ready for a nap.

It's Monday. Knitorious is closed on Mondays, and I usually run errands and do housework. So, while I'm in here, I may as well collect the dirty laundry and take it to the laundry room. I slip into the steamy washroom and find Eric's sweaty running clothes on top of the dirty laundry in the hamper. Another mystery solved; his car isn't in the driveway because he ran here.

I walk around the house, collecting kitchen linens and sofa blankets to add to the laundry pile, then put the first load in the washer.

"Another one for the pile," Eric says.

I pop my head out of the washing machine, and he drops the towel into the sink.

"Hey, handsome. What are you doing here? I thought you were going to the driving range this morning." I give in to the urge to hug him and lean into his strong, solid chest and inhale deeply. Eric always smells good, but I especially love the way he smells right after a shower.

"Change of plans," he says, then kisses the top of my head. "I met with Darby this morning instead."

While I toss a pod in the machine and turn it on, Eric asks

me about breakfast with Connie and my morning phone call with April. I provide general answers to his general questions and, for now, leave out my sort-of chance encounter with the Solomons and April's theory about Karen being the prime suspect in Dr. Armistead's murder.

We move to the family room where Sophie has already positioned herself on the sofa.

"Why did you meet with Darby?" I ask.

"I told him about Charmaine's dental emergency last Monday, and he wanted to ask me a few questions," Eric explains. "And I gave him permission to search my apartment."

"Search it for what?" The panic in my voice reflects the panic in my body. "Are you a suspect?"

"For evidence." He shrugs. "And I don't know if I'm a suspect, but I'm definitely a person of interest. I saw the victim shortly before his death, the victim and I have a history of confrontation, and it's no secret that I didn't like Armistead. Darby has to eliminate me."

"Are they searching it now?" I ask. "Are they searching the store too?"

"Darby said they'd search it today and finish as quickly as they can. They're not searching the store. I can't give permission for that, and he didn't indicate he was interested in the store, anyway. I also gave him permission to search my car and left it for him. I ran ten K, then came over here to shower and change. The search was my idea, Megan. I offered."

"You offered? Why?"

"I have nothing to hide. Anyway, he'll have to search my place, eventually. Same with the Solomons and probably Jamila's place too. Today is the perfect day, so I made him a deal. I gave him permission and saved him the trouble of getting a warrant, and he agreed to do it today while both Water Street and the store are closed."

"Water Street is closed?" I ask.

My travels to Tiffany's and back didn't take me near Knitorious or that part of Water Street.

"There's a hydro crew fixing the streetlight that Armistead's car hit. They closed Water Street around it, and there's a cop detouring traffic. As far as police searches go, this is as low profile as it gets."

"Stay here until this is over," I suggest. "You have enough stuff here for at least a few days."

I wouldn't look forward to going home after people I don't know—whether they're cops or not—touched everything, opened my drawers and cabinets, and rummaged through my personal belongings. Just thinking about it makes me feel violated. Also, if anything else happens, if Eric and I are under the same roof, we might be able to alibi each other.

"Don't worry," Eric assures me. "The only caffeine Darby and his officers will find in my apartment are my coffee pods and your chocolate stash."

"I don't have a chocolate stash at your apartment," I clarify.

I don't have a chocolate stash anywhere. I tell myself if it's not in the house, I can't eat it. I don't let that stop me though. When I get a craving, I go out and buy some. Also, my best friend and her wife own a bakery, so chocolate and other sweet treats find their way to my kitchen on a regular basis, with no effort on my part.

"Yes, you do," he asserts. "I maintain it, but it's your stash. For those days when you don't feel well and complain that you have no chocolate in the house." Eric shrugs. "The stash has saved me a lot of trips to the store."

"You keep a stash of PMS chocolate for me? Eric, that's so sweet." I'm so touched I might cry.

No one has ever kept a chocolate stash for me before.

"Where is it?" I ask, nuzzling up to him.

"I'm not telling." He smiles.

"Do you have a lawyer?" I ask, changing the subject.

345

"I don't need a lawyer. I told you, I have nothing to hide."

"Charmaine says you should get a lawyer," I argue. "She and Emory lawyered up."

"You spoke to Charmaine?" He raises one eyebrow slightly and sits up a little straighter.

I nod. "Connie and I ran into her and Emory at breakfast."

"You went to Tiffany's?" Eric asks. "I told you the Solomons go there for breakfast. You clever little sneak. Did you run into them accidentally-on-purpose?"

How can he be so flippant? He's a person of interest in a murder investigation.

"Remember when you told me you were reprimanded for looking up Dr. Armistead?"

Eric nods.

"Charmaine would know about that, right? She's your boss, so she has access to your employee file?" I ask.

"Sure," Eric replies.

"Have you considered that Charmaine met with you at her house on Friday intentionally so she could place you in the frame for Dr. Armistead's murder?"

"Uh-uh." Eric shakes his head. "No way. Charmaine would never do that. Armistead showed up for dinner early, and we happened to pass each other at her front door. It was an unfortunate coincidence."

"Was it?" I ask. "Or did he show up exactly when he was told. Think about it. Charmaine knows you and Dr. Armistead have an unpleasant history, but she put you in a position where you could potentially bump into each other. And he happened to die shortly after."

"Coincidence," Eric insists.

Charmaine Solomon is a smart woman. You don't climb up the ranks to police chief without strategically planning your career path. I suspect Eric's chance encounter with Dr. Armistead was carefully orchestrated.

"Last Monday, Charmaine was at the medical centre

REAGAN DAVIS

"I don't need a lawyer. I told you, I have nothing to hide."

"Charmaine says you should get a lawyer," I argue. "She and Emory lawyered up."

"You spoke to Charmaine?" He raises one eyebrow slightly and sits up a little straighter.

I nod. "Connie and I ran into her and Emory at breakfast."

"You went to Tiffany's?" Eric asks. "I told you the Solomons go there for breakfast. You clever little sneak. Did you run into them accidentally-on-purpose?"

How can he be so flippant? He's a person of interest in a murder investigation.

"Remember when you told me you were reprimanded for looking up Dr. Armistead?"

Eric nods.

"Charmaine would know about that, right? She's your boss, so she has access to your employee file?" I ask.

"Sure," Eric replies.

"Have you considered that Charmaine met with you at her house on Friday intentionally so she could place you in the frame for Dr. Armistead's murder?"

"Uh-uh." Eric shakes his head. "No way. Charmaine would never do that. Armistead showed up for dinner early, and we happened to pass each other at her front door. It was an unfortunate coincidence."

"Was it?" I ask. "Or did he show up exactly when he was told. Think about it. Charmaine knows you and Dr. Armistead have an unpleasant history, but she put you in a position where you could potentially bump into each other. And he happened to die shortly after."

"Coincidence," Eric insists.

Charmaine Solomon is a smart woman. You don't climb up the ranks to police chief without strategically planning your career path. I suspect Eric's chance encounter with Dr. Armistead was carefully orchestrated.

"Last Monday, Charmaine was at the medical centre

346

where Dr. Armistead's office is located. At lunch time. When Dr. Armistead's office was broken into. She was in the building, Eric."

"You know this for sure?" Eric asks.

I nod. "She told me."

He shakes his head again. "I'm telling you, Megan, she wouldn't do that. Charmaine is totally above board. I trust her with my life."

I wish I had as much faith in anything as Eric has in the Harmony Lake Police Department and its leader.

Eric considers Charmaine a mentor. He looks up to her and admires her achievements. No one wants to believe someone they respect so highly would do something unethical and illegal.

I'm debating whether now is the right time to tell him about April's theory that Karen is a prime suspect in Armistead's murder when my phone dings.

Connie: Check your email.

I tilt the screen to show Eric the message, then I open the email app on my phone. There's an email from a generic email address I don't recognize: *truthfinder234093@freemail.com.* The subject line says, *Dr. Armistead.*

I open it, and the body of the email is a link.

"Should I click it?" I ask, looking at Eric.

"I'm not sure," he replies, "but I just got the same email."

"I'm clicking it," I say.

The link leads to a simple webpage with an alphabetized list of Dr. Armistead's patients. I scroll down to the M's and find *Martel, Adam and Megan.* It's a long list. Are these just his past patients, or are his current patients listed too? Why would someone post this?

Scrolling through the hundreds of patient names, I recognize dozens of them. I'm shocked so many Harmony Lake residents travel to Harmony Hills for therapy when Emory is right here in town. Like Adam and me, I guess they were hesitant to go to someone local and risk having their personal business become fodder for the town gossip network.

Eric mutters a curse word under his breath.

I'm sure he scrolled down the list to S and found his and Karen's names. I scroll down to S and look for his name, but there are no patients with the last name Sloane.

"You and Karen aren't listed," I observe. "But Adam and I are listed, and Jess and her ex-husband are listed."

"We're listed," he confirms. "Look under P for Porter."

"Right," I say, scrolling up to P and finding *Porter, Karen and Sloane, Eric*. "Who sent this?" I ask rhetorically.

"That's for Darby to figure out," Eric replies. "I just forwarded him the email."

Within five minutes, my phone starts dinging constantly as people all over town receive the link either from the anonymous email address or from a friend. Everyone is speculating what it could mean, who posted it, and why it was posted. Above all, everyone is shocked they recognize so many names on the list.

"Is this list even real?" I ask, dumbfounded that someone would post this and send out the link. "Why would someone do this?"

"The killer might be trying to create a distraction," Eric speculates, "or maybe someone who knows something is trying to give the investigators a clue."

"Could it be a warning?" I ask. "If the poster has this information, they might have more information, like Armistead's notes and such. Maybe this is a warning. Back off or they'll post more information. Maybe someone on the list knows something, and this is a warning to keep quiet if they don't want the notes their therapist took posted on the worldwide web for everyone to see."

"Anything is possible," Eric concurs. "The question is, who has access to this information?"

"Dr. Armistead," I reply, stating the obvious. "An

assistant. Did he have an assistant? I don't remember anyone else in the office when we were his patients, but an assistant would probably have access to his files."

"Whoever provides his tech support," Eric adds.

"Jamila," I elaborate. I pause briefly and take a breath. "His girlfriend might have access to his files," I suggest delicately.

"Karen?" he asks.

I nod. "She helped him clean up his office after the break-in, which means she had access to his physical files. Maybe she had access to his electronic files too."

Careful not to throw anymore shade on Charmaine, I silently wonder if she could've used her influence as police chief to access Armistead's files? How hard would it be to influence an officer working on the case to access them for her?

CHAPTER 12

TUESDAY, October 6th

Thanks to Darby's quick intervention, the webpage disappeared almost as quickly as it appeared. Less than an hour after I first clicked the link, it was dead.

Dr. Armistead's patient list might be erased from the internet, but it's not erased from the minds of the residents of Harmony Lake. My phone lit up all night with texts about the list, and people are still talking about it today. Some people took screen shots. The link might be dead, but I'm afraid the list will live on forever.

"So, you and your new best friend, Jess, need relationship counselling with Emory Solomon," April teases during our morning phone call.

I just told her about my plan to rope Jess into coming with me to question Emory.

"I'd rather go to therapy with you, but you're not here," I jokingly reassure her.

"I'm not sure if that makes me feel better or worse," she responds.

While April and I catch up on the last twenty-four hours of our lives, Sophie and I meander through the park across from the store. The first fallen leaves of the season crunch beneath our feet and paws. The air is crisp, and the changing leaves on the trees makes Harmony Lake even prettier and cozier than usual. Fall is my favourite season, and I bask in it every chance I get. I love our morning walks; the world is still relatively quiet, and there's something about a new day that's fresh and full of potential. Our first walk of the day is meditative and helps me get into the right headspace to tackle whatever else happens throughout the day.

"Keviiiiin! I'm coming, Keviiin! Daddy's here!"

Phillip's voice jolts me out of the zone I'm in with April. Sophie and I stop walking, and I turn to see Phillip Wilde helplessly banging on the front door of Wilde Flowers.

Phillip is my neighbour. His florist shop, Wilde Flowers, shares a wall and a parking lot with Knitorious, and he also lives next door to me.

"April, umm... Can I call you back? Phillip needs help with something." We end our call, and I shove my phone in the back pocket of my black skinny jeans.

"Uh-oh, Soph!" I give the leash a gentle tug, and she looks up at me. "Let's go."

We hustle to the sidewalk and cross the street.

"Phillip, what's wrong?"

"I locked my stupid keys in the store!" He grabs the door handle and jiggles it so vigorously, the force rattles the windows of his florist shop. "Kevin's in there *alone*!" Phillip looks at me pleadingly. His eyes are open wide, and the inner corners of his eyebrows almost meet, forming an inverted V. His desperation is painful to watch. "He won't understand. He'll think I left him." He cups his hands on either side of his face and peers into the window. "It's OK, Kevin. Daddy's here. Daddy will save you."

Kevin is Phillip's chihuahua. They go everywhere together.

I copy Phillip and cup my hands on either side of my eyes and squint into the window next to him.

Granted, Kevin and I don't know each other very well, but he looks fine to me. He's atop his royal blue velvet pillow. The one with gold piping and gold tassels. Kevin is lying down with his wee head resting on his tiny paws. I think he might be asleep, but his face is so small, I can't tell for sure.

"Kevin has *terrible* separation anxiety. He won't be able to cope." Beads of perspiration dot Phillip's forehead, and his breath is fast and shallow; he's on the verge of hyperventilating.

Kevin has separation anxiety? Got it. Apparently, Kevin has the anxiety, but Phillip suffers the symptoms.

"Who has a spare key?" I ask.

"Noah!" Phillip blurts without looking away from the window.

Noah is Phillip's shop assistant and florist apprentice.

"Where does Noah live?" I ask. "I'll drive there and get his key."

"We don't have time for that. He lives all the way in Harmony Hills. Anyway, he's not home. He switched his usual day off from yesterday to today because he has an appointment this morning." Phillip looks at me. "Unless you can pick a lock, I'm throwing a brick through the window and saving Kevin."

A brick seems hasty, considering Kevin appears to be the most comfortable and content of all of us right now, but I doubt Phillip would agree.

"Ryan!" I exclaim, already pulling out my cell phone and typing a text to the local handyman-slash-locksmith.

"Good idea, Megan!" Phillip resumes watching Kevin through the window. "We're going to get you out, buddy. Stay brave. You're such a brave boy, Kevin."

I peer into the window again. Kevin is definitely asleep.

My phone dings. "Ryan's working a job in the city. He won't be back until tonight."

"Can Eric pick a lock?" Phillip asks, looking at the ground around our feet, presumably for something he can use to break the glass in the door.

"Eric isn't around. He's at the driving range, then he's getting a haircut. He won't be back until late morning."

"Have you tried the back door?" I ask.

Phillip nods. "Locked."

Phillip paces up and down the sidewalk with his gaze glued to the ground, scouring for something to hurl through the window.

"Did you lose something, Phillip?" Jamila's gaze also scans the pavement, despite not knowing what she's looking for.

Phillip fills her in about his keys, Kevin's separation anxiety, and the downside of being someone who diligently locks his doors.

"Hang on," Jamila replies, reaching behind her head and pulling two hairpins from her chignon. Her smooth, shiny, black locks fall gracefully around her shoulders as she bends and twists the hairpins until they no longer resemble hairpins. "No promises." She crouches in front of the locked door and fiddles with the straightened hairpins and the lock. "I haven't done this in years." She looks up at us briefly. "Hopefully locks haven't changed much." More fiddling with the hairpins and jiggling the door handle. "I think that's it," she mumbles. She turns the handle, gives the door a push, and it opens.

"Wow, Jamila," I say. "That's impressive. Where did you learn to do that?"

"By-product of my misspent youth," she chuckles.

"Oh." Still shocked by Jamila's lock-picking prowess, now I'm doubly shocked by what she just said.

"I'm kidding." Jamila laughs and touches my arm gently.

"My brothers were into magic, and they taught me to pick locks so I could be their magician's assistant." She shrugs. "It was fun. We used to have races to see who could pick a lock fastest." She grins nostalgically. "I usually won. Our parents hated it. We'd pick every lock in the house, and sometimes other people's locks too."

"It's amazing! Thankfully you remembered, after all these years." Unless she brushed up her lock-picking skills last Monday at Dr. Armistead's office.

"It is," she agrees. "I don't think I've picked a lock since I was a teenager."

"Oh, Jamila! Thank you! Thank you! Kevin and I are forever in your debt." A relieved Phillip appears with a sleepy Kevin in his arms.

Did Jamila pick the locks on Dr. Armistead's office door and filing cabinets? Would hiding caffeine and secretly adding it to someone's food be considered a magic trick?

"Slow, how?" Adam asks, opening the laptop.

Something's wrong with my new laptop. I tried to use it this morning to check the store email and process the online orders that came in over the weekend, but it's so slow, I couldn't finish either task and had to use my phone instead. I've brought the machine to Adam's office so he can look at it and hopefully fix it.

"Nothing loads. I can't check email or search the web. I bought a dud."

"It could be something simple," Adam says. "It was fine when you showed it to me on Sunday."

"It was fine before you installed the cyber security app-program-thingy. Could that be the problem?" I speculate.

"Let's see." He opens the laptop and types in the password.

"So, what do you think of this patient-list scandal?" I ask while we wait for whatever Adam launched to open.

"I've been getting calls all morning from people on the list. They want to know who they can sue for breeching their privacy."

"Really?" I ask, wide-eyed and wondering who called him. "Who knew the residents of Harmony Lake are so litigious."

"People are angry, Meg. They feel violated. Frankly, I don't blame them. I feel violated too. Our names are on that list."

"I know," I sympathize. "It's not pleasant, but at least whoever did it, didn't post anything else, like Dr. Armistead's notes, observations, or diagnoses."

"Do you think they have all that information?" Adam sounds concerned.

"I have no idea." I shrug. "But if they were able to get an extensive patient list, you have to wonder what else they have access to."

"Let's hope the police find out who did it before they post anything else," Adam says.

"It should be easy for the police to find them, right?" I ask. "Computers leave digital trails? IP addresses and things like that?"

"Someone who knows what they're doing can hide their digital footprint," Adam explains. "They can use VPNs and other masking technology to make it appear as though they're posting from a different computer at a different location. They can make it look like they're anywhere in the world."

"Oh," I respond.

Adam continues to explain the different ways computer-savvy people hide their identities, locations, and crimes.

I was under the misguided impression that technology makes it *more* difficult for people to hide, but for criminals who are technically inclined, technology actually makes it easier for them to avoid detection and get away with their bad deeds.

Adam's monologue is interrupted when his phone rings. He answers the call and puts the caller on hold.

"I have to take this, Meg. It's about a case that's going to court next week."

"No worries," I assure him. "I'll leave the laptop with you. Look at it whenever you have time, and let me know when I can pick it up."

"Sounds good," Adam says.

I get up from my chair and leave his office. I close his office door quietly behind me and hear Adam resume his phone call.

When I reach the bottom of the stairs, the receptionist, Lin, is on the phone. I smile, wave, and mouth a silent goodbye to her on my way to the door.

"Megan!"

I turn back to the waiting area, and Jess is standing up, smiling at me.

"Hey, Jess! What are you doing here?" We hug and kiss cheeks.

"I'm taking my favourite lawyer out for lunch," she explains. "It's an apology lunch. Adam and I had plans last night, but I had to cancel because my youngest was in his first car accident."

"Oh no! Is he OK?"

"Adam or my son?"

Ha!

"I'm sure Adam is fine. How's your son?"

"He's OK, thank goodness. It was his first fender bender. He was more shaken than anything. My fender is the real victim here."

"That first year or so after they start driving is the most stressful year of parenting," I commiserate.

"It is. Thankfully, this is my last teenage driver. If I can get through his new-driver-phase, I'm in the clear. What are you doing here?"

"I dropped off a laptop for your favourite lawyer to look at."

"Your new laptop?" Jess asks. "The one you just bought?"

"The very same," I reply.

"We've had a stressful few days," Jess observes. "First, we found a body, then you, me, and Karen had that awkward visit, then the list was posted, and now your new computer is on the fritz! We deserve a drink."

"Isn't that how this started?" I tease. "You, me, and a couple of bottles of wine?"

"You're right," Jess replies. "We need a new vice."

"Well, if we choose chocolate, I have a lead on a chocolate stash in the apartment above the store." I tell Jess about Eric's confession that he keeps chocolate in his apartment to appease my cravings.

"He's a keeper," she replies.

"Did Adam talk to you about Thanksgiving?" I hope I'm not overstepping by asking.

"Yes! I can't wait to meet everyone. Are you sure I can't bring anything?"

After a few minutes of polite banter, where I insist she shouldn't bring anything, and she insists she should, we finally agree that Jess will bring an appetizer.

"I should go," I say, checking the time on my phone. "Eric's alone at the store."

"I wonder what's keeping Adam?" she asks. "He knows I'm here."

"He had to take a call," I explain. "I'm sure he'll be right down."

"Are you ready, Karen?" We turn toward Emory Solomon's voice.

"Karen!" Jess and I exclaim in unison as Karen puts down

the magazine she was holding in front of her face and stands up.

"I didn't see you there," Jess declares, giving Karen a quick hug.

"Hi, Karen," I say, "It's nice to see you again." I look at Emory. "Hi, Emory."

He smiles and nods at me.

"I didn't see you ladies, either. I was lost in my own thoughts. It's been a rough few days."

Jess and I nod sympathetically.

Was she lost in her own thoughts? Or was Karen holding up that magazine to hide from Jess and me? Perhaps she doesn't want us to know she's a patient of Dr. Solomon, or maybe she'd like to avoid another uncomfortable conversation with her ex-husband's new girlfriend. Either reason is understandable.

"I'll see you later, I don't want to keep Dr. Solomon waiting," Karen says as she follows Emory upstairs to his second-floor office.

"What the heck?!" Jess blurts out after we hear Emory's office door close.

"I found out on Sunday. From your favourite lawyer." I tell Jess that Adam recognized Karen's photo as one of Emory's patients.

"That can't be right." Jess sounds concerned. "Surely it's a conflict of interest."

"Like Karen's personal relationship with Dr. Armistead was a conflict of interest," I remind her.

"I'd love to ask Dr. Solomon a few questions," Jess mutters, still looking up the stairs toward Emory's office.

"Me too," I respond.

I move closer to Jess so Lin won't overhear. I tell Jess I'm considering booking an appointment as an excuse to ask him about Dr. Armistead.

Jess looks at me with an expression somewhere between

shocked and impressed. "He's a suspect. You shouldn't see him alone," she whispers. "Do you think we would benefit from joint therapy?" she whispers, gesturing between us.

"Totally," I agree.

"Why are you together, and what are you whispering about?" Adam is halfway down the stairs.

The crease between his brows is extra deep. He looks worried.

"Don't worry," Jess says, taking his hand. "We aren't ganging up on you."

"It's a pleasant coincidence," I add. "Jess was arriving as I was leaving."

Adam's facial muscles relax a little.

I turn to leave, and Jess touches my arm. "Leave it with me. I'll make the arrangements and text you," she says quietly, then smiles and nods.

CHAPTER 13

"Dark roast, double-double," I announce, placing Eric's coffee on the counter, then bending down to Sophie's level to give her some love.

"Thank you," Eric says from somewhere deep in the store.

This is backwards. Eric usually brings me a coffee during the day, not the other way around. This whole week has been a role reversal with him working at Knitorious while I pound the pavement trying to solve Dr. Armistead's murder.

"Hi, Megan." A chorus of slightly out-of-sync voices greets me when I stand up.

The charity knitters are here. They're seated around the harvest table at the back of the store. I thought I heard the low clicking of knitting needles, but I assumed it was psychosomatic because I associate the sound with Knitorious. Like how I occasionally think I feel my phone vibrating in my pocket even when it's not in my pocket.

"Hi, ladies," I say with a wave. "You don't usually grace us with your presence on a Tuesday."

"Well, we heard you weren't here and thought Eric could use some company," one of them replies.

"Would you like a date square, Megan?" another one asks. "I made them for Eric, but there's enough for everyone."

"On Saturday, I mentioned I like date squares. They remembered and made some. Isn't that nice?" Eric asks.

"There are carrot muffins too," Mrs. Roblin adds, nodding toward the centre of the table. "Help yourself."

"Not right now, thank you," I reply, politely declining their offers. "It's thoughtful of the Charity Knitting Guild to think about Eric and keep him company."

"It sure is," Eric concurs in a perky voice. He gets up from his seat at the table and retrieves his coffee from the counter. He flashes his fan club a wide, toothy smile. "Thank you for the pleasure of your company, ladies, but now that Megan's back, I think I'll go upstairs and phone my parents to see how their Thanksgiving preparations are coming along."

Accompanied by a chorus of "Bye, Eric," he makes a swift exit.

After the charity knitters discuss amongst themselves what a caring and doting son he is, and how proud his parents must be, they ask me if Eric phones his parents often, and when I think he might be back.

"A couple of times a week," I reply. "I don't know when he'll come downstairs. His mum is pretty chatty. He could be gone a while." I shrug. "I'm here until the store closes, so he might talk to her for the rest of the afternoon."

After reminding me to wrap and store the date squares and carrot muffins, the charity knitters decide it's time to pack up their knitting and leave.

"Is it clear?" Eric asks after he cautiously scans the store.

I nod. "I told them your mum is chatty."

"Thank you. It's not that I'm not appreciative of the knit-ters, they're sweet and very doting," he explains. "But there are so many of them, and they're almost competitive with their attention."

"They like you," I respond. "You seem to be one of their projects."

"I've been thinking about that list of Dr. Armistead's patients," Eric says, changing the subject. "You could be right. The list could be a warning."

"You think one of his patients knows something?"

"Possibly," he replies. "Or it could be a warning to an amateur sleuth who is snooping around and asking questions."

"Just say it. You mean me."

"I mean you."

"A warning that they'll post more information? Or that I could be next?" I ask.

"Both. Either. I don't know." Eric shrugs. "But either way do you want to risk it?"

"I've risked it before," I remind him.

"Those were my cases, Megan. I was the investigator. I had access to all the information. I have none of the information on Armistead's case. I haven't interviewed anyone. I have no sense of what kind of suspect we're dealing with, or how to gauge how much risk you're taking."

"If I back down, they win."

"And if you back down, I win because you stay alive and safe."

"I'll be fine," I assure him. "The killer's MO is feeding the victim something the victim is allergic to. I don't have any food allergies."

"That's not funny." He's not smiling. In fact, he looks dead serious.

"You always say a sense of humour helps to deal with murder."

"In general." He takes my hands. "But it's not funny when it's you."

"I'm sorry."

"I can't tell you what to do, but I'd feel better if you let this go and let Darby handle it," he says. "I know people come to you and drop evidence into your lap, but maybe this time you don't have to actively look for it."

Now is not the time to tell him about the therapy appointment Jess and I are planning.

"I want to fix this for you," I admit. "You helped me once when I was tangled up in a murder investigation, and now I want to help you."

Saved by the bell.

"Oh my, Phillip! Let me help you." I rush out from behind the counter and relieve Phillip of the huge floral arrangement he's carrying. "How did you find your way over here with this?" It's massive, I can't see through it, and I can't see around it.

"You get used to it after a couple of decades," he replies. "Full light, sweetie. Over here."

Phillip guides me to the cozy seating area and I carefully place the arrangement on the coffee table. Literally nothing else will fit on the coffee table now. I'll take them home with me tonight. They'll look gorgeous in the living room window.

"It's beautiful!" And smells delightful.

"Thank you," he replies, fussing over a few individual blooms that shifted on the short walk between our stores. "It's your October bouquet. I wanted to do something extra special after the help you gave Kevin and me this morning."

Back in January, Eric and I attended a fundraiser. It was kind of our first date. Phillip donated a year's worth of monthly floral arrangements to the silent auction, and Eric had the winning bid. So, now I get a beautiful seasonal floral arrangement delivered each month.

"I didn't do anything. Jamila saved the day," I remind him. "If anyone deserves thank-you flowers, it's her."

"She's next on my list," Phillip assures me. "Her arrangement is gorgeous. All white to match her store."

"What did I miss this morning?" Eric asks.

Phillip tells him how Jamila's latent lock picking skills saved the day, and saved Kevin's life, after he almost died of separation anxiety because he was left unattended in the shop for fifteen minutes.

"You should leave a spare key with someone nearby," Eric suggests.

"Great minds think alike!" Phillip reaches into his pocket and hands me a key on an enamel, flower-shaped key chain. "I had a spare key cut. Would you mind keeping it safe for me?"

"Of course," I reply taking the key from him. "It'll be in the cash register, under the tray."

Eric opens the till and I hand him the key. He lifts the tray, drops the key, and closes the till.

"How is Kevin? Has he recovered from being locked in the store?" I'm sure Kevin is fine. It's Phillip who might be feeling the aftereffects.

"He's emotionally exhausted," Phillip replies. "But he's a brave boy and doesn't let it show. He doesn't like to upset me. He's very sensitive to other people's feelings, you know. But I can tell he was scared."

"I'm glad you're both OK," I tell him.

"Can you pick a lock?" I ask Eric after Phillip leaves.

"I know how," he replies. "I haven't done it in ages though, and lock picking is one of those use-it-or-lose-it skills."

"How so?" I ask, remembering that Jamila said she hasn't picked a lock since she was a teenager, which would be at least fifteen years ago.

"It takes practice to develop the muscle memory you need to maneuver delicately around the tumblers inside the lock. And your hands learn to recognize the subtle changes that happen inside the lock. You can't see inside it, so you have to rely on the way the lock reacts to the pick."

"I didn't realize lock picking is such a subtle, sensitive skill," I comment. "Does it come in handy at work?"

"No," he replies. "We call a locksmith. Unless it's urgent, then we smash a window or break down the door because it's faster than picking the lock."

"Jamila picked Phillip's lock in about two minutes," I tell him. "She said it was the first time she'd done it in years."

"Hmmm," he replies.

I can practically see the wheels spinning inside his head.

"HI, DARBY." I put down my knitting and stand up.

Darby closes the door behind him. "Good afternoon, Megan!" he booms, surveying the store. "Are we alone? Is now a good time to talk?"

"Eric's in the back somewhere, but other than that, it's just us." I gesture for him to join me in the cozy sitting area.

I offer Darby a drink, which he declines. He opens his folio and uncaps his fountain pen.

"TWO OH NINE!" Eric bellows from the back room.

"GOT IT!" I shout back, making a note of the numbers in my planner on the sofa next to me. "GOOD JOB, HONEY!"

"Two hundred and nine what?" Darby asks.

"Two minutes and nine seconds," I clarify. "Jamila picked a lock this morning. It took her less than two minutes—at least it felt like less than two minutes—despite insisting that she hasn't picked a lock since she was a teenager. Eric is trying to beat her time. His personal best so far is two minutes and nine seconds."

"Right," Darby says nodding. "What lock is he picking?"

"I'm not sure. The back door. His apartment door. The back door at Wilde Flowers." I shrug. "He's bored, but he won't admit it. I told him to go back to work, but he insists on helping at the store until Connie and Marla are back next week. Have you had any luck finding the person who posted Dr. Armistead's patient list online?"

"Not yet," Darby shakes his head. "The suspect used an elaborate network of proxies to hide their location and identity. The cyber-crimes division has traced it from Germany to India to Mexico, to France, so far. They're still working on it, but I'm confident they'll track down the person or persons responsible."

This is what Adam explained to me earlier. The cybercriminal bounces their signal off servers all over the world, hiding their true location and the identity of the computer they use. How many people would know how to do that? Is this a skill an average computer user would have? I don't have it, but I'm neither technically inclined nor technically interested in computers, beyond how I can use them to shop online and find funny pet videos.

"I hope so," I say. "People around here are nervous. They're worried whoever has the list has other, more personal information and might post it."

Let me clarify. *Most* people are worried, but a few are *hoping* the hacker will post personal information about their friends and neighbours so they can read it.

"So, Ms. Jagger can pick a lock. That's interesting, isn't it?" Changing the subject, Darby turns to a blank page in his folio and makes a note. "Did you see this firsthand, or did someone tell you about it?"

I tell Darby about the heroic role Jamila played in Phillip and Kevin's harrowing ordeal. "You know who else can pick a lock?" I ask.

"Eric?" Darby answers my question with a question.

"Charmaine Solomon," I tell him.

"You're telling me this like it's relevant to Dr. Armistead's murder investigation."

"It's relevant to the break-in at his office last week," I explain. "And the break-in at his office could be relevant to his murder, no?"

"We haven't found any evidence linking the two incidents."

A standard-issue cop response.

"Charmaine and Emory Solomon were in the building at the same time Dr. Armistead's office was broken into," I point out.

"Now, how do you know that, Megan?"

"Charmaine told me," I reply.

"You spoke with the Solomons about the case?"

"I spoke with Charmaine," I correct him. "We ran into each other at a local restaurant."

"Coincidentally, of course," he adds.

"Of course," I confirm.

"ONE FIVE EIGHT! WOOHOO!" Eric yells from what sounds like the parking lot.

I note the time in my planner under the last entry.

"GOT IT!" I yell in response. "YAY! YOU DID IT!"

"Well done, detective sergeant!" Darby booms.

The bass tone of his voice is so deep, it makes my insides rumble. And I don't think he was shouting.

"I'd like you to look at something for me, Megan." Darby unzips the large pocket at the back of his folio and pulls out an iPad. "A video." He unlocks the screen and taps a few times, then hands me the device.

"What am I looking for?" I ask.

"Anyone or anything you think you recognize. If you see something or someone, pause the video by touching the screen and show me."

I nod. "Got it."

Eric comes into the store and says hi to Darby. He suggests that Darby and I use his apartment and offers to stay down here and watch the store.

CHAPTER 14

THE LEATHER SOFA in the upstairs apartment wheezes when I sink into it. I tap the iPad screen, making the video footage start. It's the main entrance to the medical building where Dr. Armistead's office is located. Specifically, the area between the front door and the elevators.

According to the date and time stamps at the top of the screen, it's from the day Dr. Armistead's office was broken into. The video quality isn't great. It's black and white, grainy, and kind of far away from the people being filmed.

I tap the screen. "Here," I extend the device toward Darby and point at the image. "That's Charmaine Solomon, and her husband, Emory, behind her." The Solomons are entering the building. Charmaine cups her jaw with one hand, and Emory holds the door open for her as she enters the building.

Darby reaches over and takes a screenshot of the paused video then nudges it toward me.

"Again?" I ask.

Darby nods.

I tap the screen and watch anonymous, grainy people come and go from the lobby of the building.

"There," I tap the screen. "That's Dr. Armistead, in the lower left, leaving the building."

I pass the device to Darby and he takes another screen shot and hands it back.

"More?" I ask.

"A little more," he replies.

I tap the screen and watch the video. It's lunchtime, and the lobby is busy. After a few more minutes of watching, the video skips ahead by almost an hour. Edited by the police, no doubt.

"The Solomons," I say, tapping the screen.

This time, they're leaving the building. I hand the device to Darby so he can take a screenshot. He hands it back.

I tap the screen and watch. The video skips ahead again. "Dr. Armistead," I touch the screen to pause the video. "He's entering the building."

Darby takes a screenshot, then uses his finger to find a specific location in the footage.

"Watch this part again." He passes the device to me.

I look at the footage, searching for a familiar face. The crowd around the elevator makes it difficult to pick out specific people. It gets harder when the elevator door opens and even more people file into the lobby.

"Sorry," I say, handing the iPad back to Darby. "Nothing."

"Don't be sorry, Megan." He taps on the screen a few times then holds up a screenshot from the video footage. The screen shot has been enhanced. It's a grainy close-up of someone from the crowded lobby wearing a dark baseball cap and looking down, away from the camera. The person is wearing a dark hoodie, but the hood is down showing hair in a low chignon. A glint of light grey near the face catches my eye.

"Jamila Jagger," I say confidently. "I couldn't pick her out of the crowd in the moving footage, but I'm sure this is her."

"Why are you sure?" Darby asks.

"Her hair," I reply. "Jamila always wears her hair either in a high ponytail or a low chignon. Also, the long, thin neck. That glint on the side of her face is the light reflecting off Jamila's nose ring."

"How sure are you," Darby asks, "as a percentage?"

"At least eighty-five percent. I'd bet money on it, but not all of my money, if you know what I mean."

"Now, if I told you that I have video footage of Ms. Jagger at a different location at the same time this footage was filmed, would that change your answer? Would that make you less certain it's Ms. Jagger?"

"It looks like Jamila to me," I say shrugging, not sure what he's hoping I'll say. "Are you sure the timestamp on the footage is correct? Is it possible the other footage and this footage have the same time stamp but are actually from different dates or times?"

"We've done our due diligence," Darby replies.

What the heck does that mean? He's confirmed the time-stamps? His image forensics people said it's all good? I hate cop speak, it's so vague.

"How does Jamila explain being in two places at once?" I ask.

Darby purses his lips into a tight line.

I see what's happening. Darby doesn't know Jamila's explanation because he can't question her whenever he wants since she lawyered up. Same for the Solomons. I've probably talked to the witnesses more extensively than Darby has.

This image of Jamila is the whole point of this video footage exercise. Darby was hoping I'd pick Jamila out of the crowd but didn't want to make his focus obvious, so he also made me look at footage of the people who are easily recognizable.

"Can I see the other footage?" I ask, expecting to be told no.

Darby taps the iPad screen a few times and hands it to me.

This footage is from Bits'n'Bytes. The video quality is better than the other footage; it isn't grainy and it's in colour. Jamila sits at one of the round, shiny, white tables in the showroom, working on a computer. The computer is covered in stickers and decals, so I assume it's her personal computer and not a computer she's selling.

"It looks like she's doing administrivia," I say.

Jamila has the same bored, glazed-over look on her face that I get when I'm bogged down with administrative tasks, and last Monday was the twenty-eighth, so she could be getting a head start on her month end or quarter end paperwork.

The longer I watch the bigger the knot in my stomach gets. There's something in front of me that I'm missing. "Something isn't right, but I can't figure out what." The video ends. I look up at Darby. "May I watch it again?"

"Absolutely," he replies.

The angle of the camera also shows the front window of the store, so I'm occasionally distracted by a car or person passing by, and I'm afraid I missed something in the store because I'm watching the window. I re-watch the footage, and my sense of cognitive dissonance grows. What's wrong with this footage? What am I missing?

I ask Darby if I can have a copy to watch again later. He says no, which is what I totally expect his answer to be. He waits patiently while I watch the video one more time, trying to find the part that makes my stomach hurt.

A knock at the apartment door brings me back to the here and now. Eric opens the door just enough to poke his head inside.

"Adam's on the phone," he says looking at me. "He says it's urgent."

I pick up my phone from the coffee table. No missed calls. "My phone's here."

"He called the landline," Eric clarifies.

My heart pounds so fast and hard I can hear it. I force myself to swallow. Something's wrong. Adam hasn't called the landline at the store or the house in forever. I didn't think he even knew the phone number for Knitorious. I lunge the iPad at Darby and jump to my feet.

"Is it Hannah?" I ask, racing toward the door.

"He didn't say," Eric replies as I rush past him and run down the stairs.

"Adam? Is Hannah OK?" I inhale sharply and brace myself for his answer.

"Hannah's fine, Meg. I'm not calling about Hannah." I exhale and my shoulders drop about three inches from the tension they release.

"Why are you calling the landline? You never call the landline."

"I'm not sure it's safe to call your cell phone."

"Why wouldn't it be safe to call my cell phone?" I ask.

"Because of what I found on your computer..."

"Adam," I interrupt him. "Darby Morris is here. Should he hear this? Should I put you on speakerphone?"

"Definitely, and yes."

In the quietest whisper possible, Eric asks me if Hannah is OK. I nod. If she wasn't, I wouldn't be this calm.

"Adam found something on my computer," I say, looking at Darby. He says you should hear this. I'm putting him on speakerphone.

Darby nods. I put the call on speakerphone and hang up the receiver. Eric locks the front door and puts up the BACK IN TEN MINUTES sign. We've gotten more use out of that sign this week than the entire time I've worked here.

"We're listening, Adam," I say.

"When you dropped off the laptop, you said it worked fine before I installed the security software."

"Right," I agree, nodding, even though he can't see me.

"You were right," Adam confirms. "The security software

is the reason it slowed down. The security software was trying to disarm and uninstall the spyware on your laptop. In response, the spyware was trying to shut down the security software. The battle between the two programs used up so much processing power that it brought the computer to a standstill."

I don't follow most of what he said, but I'm pretty sure the spyware is the important part.

"How did the spyware get there?" I ask.

"Someone who had access to the laptop installed it."

"I've only had the thing since Saturday. It sat, unused, at my house until this morning," I say. "The only people who had access to it are you, me, and Jamila."

Jamila!

"Listen to me, Meg."

"I'm listening," I respond.

"All your devices are connected. And Jamila had your phone when she set up the laptop, right? The spyware could be spying on all your devices. That's why I didn't text or call your cell phone. It might've tipped off whoever is monitoring you."

"Why would anyone want to monitor me? What kind of stuff can they monitor?"

I feel violated. Violated and nauseous.

"I'm not very familiar with spyware," Adam disclaims. "But they might be able to read your emails, access your passwords, read your texts. They could pretend to be you."

"Did you uninstall it?" I ask.

"Don't uninstall it!" Darby shouts, leaning toward the phone on the counter. "Don't alter the computer in any way, Adam." He looks at me. "Cyber-crimes will need to look at your computer," he says quietly. "Will you give me permission to take it?"

I nod. "Adam, Darby will pick up the laptop."

"OK," Adam replies. "Meg, listen to me carefully." He

knows I zone out when he talks about tech stuff. "You need to get your hands on another computer, someone else's computer that doesn't sync with your stuff, and change your passwords. As soon as possible."

"All of them?" I ask, flipping to the page in the back of my planner where I keep my passwords.

They're encrypted in a code my friends and I made up in middle school, so we could pass notes in class without worrying about the teachers reading them if they were intercepted.

"All of them," he replies.

That's a lot of passwords.

"She can use my laptop," Eric says behind me.

"But if I suddenly stop using my devices, won't that tip off Jamila?"

We decide that Eric will create a Modern Family 2 group chat with everyone from the original Modern Family group chat except me. Then, he'll send a text explaining that my computer was hacked, and they should call me on a landline if they need me.

Darby and Adam also offer to send me occasional, innocuous text messages. I'll reply to them so whoever is watching me won't suspect I stopped using my devices because we discovered the spyware.

"Can you send me proof?" I ask Adam.

"I'll use my phone to take some photos of your computer screen, and I'll text them to Eric. I don't want to take screen shots with your laptop in case whoever is spying on you sees them."

"That makes sense," I respond. "Thank you."

"Darby, you can pick up the laptop at my office," Adam says.

"Thank you, Adam," Darby responds.

"Adam, before you go. Can they hear my phone calls? Or see my Facetime calls?"

"I don't know, Meg. Darby's cyber-crimes people will be able to tell you that."

"OK. One more thing. Jess is supposed to text me some information. Can you tell her to either call me on a landline or text Eric?"

"Sure thing," he replies.

We hang up, and I drop my weary, overwhelmed self into one of the Parsons chairs at the harvest table. While I try to process everything that just happened, Eric rubs my shoulders.

Darby sits in the chair across from me.

"Jamila installed the spyware. You know that, right?" It's a statement of fact, not a question.

"We have no evi…"

I raise my hand in a stop motion, cutting him off mid-sentence. "Don't. Just don't. No more cop speak." I lower my hand. "Jamila Jagger is spying on me, and I want to know why."

"I'll look into it," Darby says. "Leave it with me."

This could explain how someone got hold of Dr. Armistead's patient list.

"Did you find spyware on Dr. Armistead's computer? Jamila did tech support for him. She told me."

"There was no spyware on Dr. Armistead's computer," Darby replies. "Megan, why are you concerned about someone accessing your phone calls and Facetime calls?"

"I talk to April at least once a day. Every day," I explain. "We talk about everything. Personal stuff. Other people. Dr. Armistead's murder. If Jamila is listening in, she knows everything I know."

"I know it's early," Eric interjects, "but let's go home, eat pot roast, and change your passwords."

On the way to Adam's office to drop off the laptop earlier, I stopped at home and put a pot roast in the Crock-Pot for dinner. I'm glad I did. I need comfort food right now.

I nod. "I have to drop off the online orders at the post office first."

Darby leaves to pick up the laptop, and Eric insists on dropping off the online orders for me.

"I'll take Sophie with me and take her for a walk after I drop off the orders." He attaches her leash, then stands up and kisses my forehead. "Relax for a few minutes and knit. I'll be back soon."

I nod and lock the door behind them. Then I grab my keys from my bag and my phone from the counter. I leave Knitorious, lock the door behind me, and storm off in the direction of Bits'n'Bytes.

CHAPTER 15

THE DOOR IS LOCKED, and the lights are off at Bits'n'Bytes. The neon OPEN sign in the window is off. I'm not the only store owner who closed early today. I rap my knuckles loudly on the door, then on the glass window. Nothing. I peer in the window. Everything is dark. Still determined, I march up the alley beside the store to the parking lot. Empty. Jamila's car isn't here. My quest for answers will have to wait until tomorrow.

On the way back to Knitorious, I look in Jamila's window one more time and spy the green light of her security camera looking back at me. If she checks the footage, she'll know I was here. I don't want her to know that I'm on to her yet, so I unlock my cell phone and type a text to her as I walk up Water Street.

Me: Hey Jamila! I stopped by the store, but you closed early. I hope everything's OK! I'm looking for a laptop sleeve for my new computer. I'll try to stop by tomorrow and see if you have anything. Have a great evening

It's much easier to be fake-nice in a text than it is in person.

"Hi, Megan."

The key is in the lock, and I'm just about to turn it. I was seconds away from avoiding another human interaction today.

"Karen! Hi." I force a small smile, convinced this day will never end. "Are you looking for me?"

"Yes. Can we talk for a minute?" Her voice and demeanour are a combination of sad and apprehensive.

I might be having a bad day, but Karen's is worse. Dr. Armistead was murdered four days ago, and most of the world thinks she lost a co-worker, not her true love. I wouldn't switch places with her for anything in the world.

"Sure," I smile. "Come in." I lock the door behind us and gesture for her to sit in the cozy sitting area. "What brings you to Harmony Lake?" Surely her appointment with Dr. Solomon ended hours ago.

"I want to apologize to you," she says.

"For what?"

"My behaviour on Saturday when Eric showed up. I was in a bad place, and I wasn't expecting to see him..."

I touch her hand. "It's OK, Karen. I get it. I understand. The last few days have been horrible for you, and honestly, under the circumstances, I'm amazed how well you're coping. You don't have to explain."

"I don't want you to think that's who I am. I'm not like that. No matter what Eric says."

"Eric hasn't said anything," I tell her truthfully. "He rarely mentions you." I shrug.

If I wasn't so tired and frazzled after a long day, I would have stopped myself from saying that last sentence. It sounded more insensitive than I intended. I have no desire to talk about Eric with her, and I need to shut this down.

"I'm glad he's not bitter," she smiles weakly.

"Are the police keeping you apprised of the investigation?" Time to change the subject.

"Which investigation?" Karen answers my question with a question. "The break-in or Mac's murder?"

"Both," I reply.

"Not really," she admits. "I didn't have any official standing in his life. And now I don't have any official standing in his death." Karen's voice hitches on the last word, and her eyes fill with tears.

I hand her a box of tissues. She pulls one out and the tears flow. Unable to restrain myself, I put my arms around her and rub her back while she sobs on my shoulder. We stay like this for a few minutes until Sophie comes charging into the store from the back room and puts her paws on Karen's knees.

Eric's back! Thank goodness he used the back door.

"Hi, Sophie," Karen says, her voice thick with sobs. She scratches Sophie between the ears.

"I'll be right back, Karen," I say, untangling myself from her. "Sophie will keep you company."

I speed walk to the back room and close the door. Where's Eric? I check the storage room, the washroom, then look up the stairs. His apartment door is open. I'm about to go up, when he appears at the top of the stairs.

"Just getting my laptop," he says, closing his apartment door behind him. "And some chocolate from your stash. It's been one of those days. Ready to go?"

"Karen's here," I whisper when he reaches the main floor.

"Why?" he hisses, narrowing his eyes.

"She showed up unannounced. She wanted to apologize for Saturday."

"To you or me?"

"Me. I don't think she knows you're here."

"Can you tell her you have to leave?"

I shake my head. "She's crying. It's not a good idea to send her away when she's this emotional."

Eric sighs. "Are you making friends with my ex-wife?"

"Are you serious?" I ask. "You are literally best friends with my ex-husband."

"That's different. *You're* friends with your ex-husband. Karen and I are *not* friends."

"No, Karen and I aren't friends! Why would you even think that?"

"You have a way of making friends quickly."

"She's grieving for goodness' sake. Who else does she have to cry with, Eric? It's me or Jess, and Jess isn't here," I whisper-yell.

He puts his laptop and the chocolate on the stairs and puts his hands on my shoulders. "Megan, it's not your problem that Karen agreed to be Armistead's dirty little secret instead of choosing a partner who was willing to date her publicly."

At a loss for words, I huff. Twice. "That's harsh, Eric." I huff again and throw up my hands in frustration, forcing his hands from my shoulders. "I've never seen you so insensitive. We kept our relationship a secret at first, remember? Was I your dirty little secret? I know you have issues with her but come on! Where's your compassion?"

"It's not the same, Megan, and you know it. You wanted to keep us quiet so we could get to know each other without being the talk of the town. And we kept it on the down low for a few weeks, not over a year. And neither of us was breaking any rules or professional codes of conduct."

I sigh. "It's been a long day. I don't want us to argue about your ex-wife." I'm too tired and defeated for this.

Also, I'd rather have this discussion when we can speak with our normal voices instead of whisper-yelling at each other.

"You're right." He rubs my upper arms. "I'm sorry. I'll go home and roast some vegetables for the pot roast. Do you want me to take Sophie?"

I shake my head. "No, thank you. I'll take her. I'll be home before dinner is ready."

I stand on my tippy toes and kiss him goodbye, determined not to let his unresolved issues with his ex-wife interfere in our relationship.

"Sorry about that," I say, resuming my seat on the sofa.

I offer Karen a glass of water. She declines. Sophie is half on Karen's lap and half on the sofa. Karen is stroking her, and Sophie is loving the attention.

"She's sweet," Karen comments.

"She has a calming effect," I agree.

"Was that Eric?" she asks.

I nod. "He left. He went home."

"Doesn't he live here?"

"He does. Like eighty percent of the time," I explain.

"Mac used to stay over at my house all the time. A lot of his stuff is still there. I don't know who to give it to."

"I'm sure if you ask Darby, he can help you with that."

"I'll do that."

"Karen, remember when you told me whoever turned over Mac's office didn't take anything? Do you believe it was a crime of opportunity, and they were looking for drugs? What do you think they were looking for?"

"I have no idea, but they probably got frustrated trying to find it. I jokingly told Mac that's why they tossed his office, because they were frustrated with his horrible filing system." She chuckles under her breath. "On the surface it looks organized, but inside those drawers are a mess. Well, they *were* a mess. After the break in, I helped him organize it properly. I doubt he would have maintained it, though."

"A mess how?" I ask.

"Take the O-P drawer for example. It wasn't just for patient files. Anything starting with those letters was in those drawers. P for phone bill. P for property taxes. O for owner manuals. Then within each file everything was misfiled. The latest phone bill might be filed in the phone bill folder, but it more likely landed in one of the five files around the phone bill file. You see what I mean?"

"I do." I nod. "He could've used an assistant to keep him organized."

"I suggested that," Karen says. "But he said he didn't have enough work to keep an assistant busy. Almost everything is electronic now. Patients don't have paper files anymore. And his electronic files were way more organized than his paper files."

She could only know that if she had access to his electronic files.

Darby said no spyware was found on Dr. Armistead's computer, but I wonder if they searched Karen's computer. She said Dr. Armistead stayed over at her house regularly. Maybe he used her computer while he was there.

Karen tells me a few stories about her and Dr. Armistead. Their first date, practical jokes they played on each other, and how good he was at making her laugh. Now that her mood has improved, and she's not crying, I think it's safe to send her out into the world.

"It's been nice talking with you, Karen, but I have to get Sophie home for dinner," I say as I stand up and brush some corgi hair from my lap.

"I'm sure you want to get home to Eric," she says. "It's OK, I'm not angry or bitter anymore. You're really nice. I hope you and Eric are happy together."

She's not bitter *anymore*!

"Thank you, Karen. That means a lot coming from you."

"We were a bad match from the start," she explains.

"That's too bad," I sympathize. Please don't let this be the beginning of a long post-mortem discussion of their marriage.

"I hated that he was a cop," Karen says. "It's not a job, you know, it's a lifestyle." It sounds more like a warning than a statement of fact.

I nod. "I know. My ex-husband was a workaholic."

"Well, I'm happy you got a different version of Eric."

What a strange thing to say. Deep breath. Give her some grace, Megan, her world imploded this week, and her life partner was murdered.

"How do you know what Eric is like now? You haven't spoken to him since you split."

"He walks your dog, he helps in your yarn store, he sees you during the day, and he even keeps a stash of PMS chocolate for you. The Eric I was married to didn't do those things."

She overheard me tell Jess about the chocolate stash. It didn't occur to me that Karen heard us talking while she waited for Emory. In my head, I quickly replay Jess's and my conversation, making sure we didn't say anything about Dr. Armistead's murder. I'm sure we didn't mention it until Karen and Emory were in his office.

"Karen, you know that Mac was at the Solomon's house for dinner the night he died, right?"

She nods. "I know. That's why I met with Emory today. He told me about the last few hours of Mac's life."

"That was nice of him. Is today the first time you met Emory?"

She nods again. "Yes. I got his contact information from Mac's address book. He told me he was having dinner at his friend Emory's house."

Dr. Armistead told Karen that he and Emory were friends, but Emory insists they were just colleagues.

Adam is sure he's seen Karen in the reception area waiting for Emory, but she says today is the first time she met him. I believe Adam over Karen.

Who is Karen trying to protect with her lie? Herself, her dead boyfriend, or Emory? And why?

What else is she lying about?

CHAPTER 16

"How can we be sure your landline isn't bugged?" April asks when I explain why I'm calling her from the landline at the store this morning.

"Only customers and telemarketers call the landline. Would it even occur to someone to hack a landline nowadays?"

"Well, if it is bugged, we can always use smoke signals. Or two tin cans and a long piece of string."

"How about two tin cans and a piece of yarn?" I ask. "Would that work? Between the store inventory and my personal stash, I might have several thousand kilometres of the stuff."

I tell April about my long, hectic day yesterday. "I'd send you a pic of the beautiful floral arrangement Phillip made, but I'm avoiding my phone until I know for sure it's not spying on me."

"I will never buy another thing from Jamila Jagger again!" April declares angrily.

"I don't think I will, either," I concur. "The worst part is, now the police have the laptop, and it's stuck in evidence. By

384

the time I get it back, laptops will probably be a thing of the past."

"I'm glad she wasn't there when you went to Bits'n'Bytes last night," April says. "If you confronted her and she's the killer, she might have snapped and killed you too."

"I know," I admit. "I realize that now. I felt angry and violated at the time. I didn't think it through. I won't go back unless someone is with me. That way if she snaps and goes homicidal, whoever is with me can escape and make sure she's held accountable for killing me."

"That's funny, not funny, Megapop. Death jokes are only funny when they're about bad people or people we don't love."

"Sorry, not sorry," I say.

"*Are* you and Karen friends?" April asks after I tell her about Karen's surprise visit and the whisper-yelling argument Eric and I had in the back room.

"No," I state firmly. "She lied to my face. I can't be friends with someone who lies to me. And it was a risky lie. She knows Harmony Lake is a small town, and everyone knows everyone else. She knows there's a high likelihood someone I know has seen her at Emory's office. Also, she has a habit of steering our conversations toward Eric, and I don't want to talk about him with her. Or about her with him."

"Do we hate her now?" April asks.

"No." I reply with a sigh. "We don't hate her, but we don't trust her."

"Got it."

"Is everything OK with you and Eric after the whisper-yelling argument?"

"Totally," I assure her. "We talked after dinner while I changed my passwords. Karen's sudden appearance in Harmony Lake rattled him. The Karen he knows is spiteful, and he's afraid she'll try to sabotage our relationship. We're on the same page now. He promises to trust my judgement about dealing with his ex-wife, and I promise not to befriend her and invite her to Thanksgiving dinner."

I came to the store early to phone April. To give us some privacy during our call, Eric stayed home. He says he'll clean out the shower drain, vacuum the dryer vent, and put the winter cover on the air-conditioning unit. Despite reaching the fix-stuff-around-the-house level of boredom, he still insists on using his time off to help me at the store. I think what he's really doing is avoiding work because it's too diffi-cult for him to watch someone else investigate a murder that happened on his doorstep—literally and figuratively.

While I putter around the store before it opens, April and I talk, and talk, and talk until my cell phone dings.

"It's Jamila," I say, picking up the phone.

"Sneaky computer hacker," April says. "What does she want?"

I read Jamila's text out loud.

Jamila: I have loads in stock. Come by whenever.

"Loads of what?" April asks.

I tell her about the text I sent to Jamila when I realized she would see me on her camera footage banging on her door like a crazy woman.

"But you won't go alone, right?" she reminds me.

"Right," I agree. "I promise."

Me: Great! I'll stop by later this morning.

"Good morning, ladies!" I smile at Mrs. Roblin and Mrs. Vogel. The rest of the Charity Knitting Guild files into the store behind them. "I wasn't expecting you until this after-noon," I remark.

The charity knitters come by the store on Wednesday afternoons to knit, plan their projects, and order yarn for upcoming charity knitting endeavours.

"We thought Eric was working," Mrs. Vogel says while Mrs. Roblin stands next to her, craning her neck and surveying the store for any sign of Eric.

"He'll be in later this morning," I advise them. "But you're welcome to stay. I'll put the kettle on."

"It's OK, Megan. Don't go to any trouble. We'll come back at our usual time." Mrs. Roblin smiles at me. "He's not here, ladies," she tells the rest of them as she turns back toward the door. I hear a faint chorus of disappointed groans as the group of knitters turns and files out of the store.

"I think Eric is more popular than us," I say to Sophie after the door closes behind them. She sits at the door patiently, staring and waiting, hoping her friends will come back. "They'll be back later, Soph. Try not to take it personally." The last sentence was for both of us.

To distract Sophie from feeling dejected, I convince her to follow me into the kitchenette where I give her some dog treats even though it isn't snack time. I put the last treat on the floor and, like one of Pavlov's dogs, rush back to the store when the bell over the door jingles.

"Good morning, my dear," Connie sings.

"Good morning," I say, hugging her. "This is a nice surprise."

"Did I just see the back ends of the charity knitters marching down Water Street?" she asks.

I nod.

"It's not like them to congregate this early in the day. What's going on?"

I tell Connie about the group's shared disappointment that Eric isn't here.

"Yes, I hear they're fond of him," Connie says. "Apparently, he's very charming and attentive to them when they're here." She sits on the sofa and opens her knitting bag. "He's a novelty. It'll wear off."

"It'll have to," I agree. "He's going back to work next

week. Eric working here is good for business, though. So far, this is the busiest October we've ever had, and most of the sales happen when Eric is here alone. How's Archie doing?"

"His recovery is going very well, and he's ready to spend a few hours alone," Connie explains. "I thought I'd visit you for a while and tell you some gossip."

The book club calls the intelligence they gather "gossip".

"Oooh," I say, joining her on the sofa. "What kind of gossip?"

"The mayoral kind," Connie discloses. "The mayor brought Archie a care package, and the three of us had a chat."

"Did you ply her with margaritas?" I ask.

"Margaritas are for book club meetings only," she reminds me. "We had gin and tonic. One each."

"Right," I say, nodding.

"Anyway, the mayor has had a change of heart. She's renewing Charmaine's mandate. If Charmaine wants it."

"That's an about-face," I comment.

"Yes, it is," Connie agrees. "Especially when you consider how insistent she was when she told me Charmaine had to go."

"Did she explain her change of heart?" I ask.

"Nope," Connie replies shaking her head. "She said it was all a big misunderstanding, and everything is fine now."

"Interesting," I say.

At least Eric doesn't have to feel conflicted anymore about whether he wants to be considered for Charmaine's job.

Sophie joins us on the sofa while Connie and I knit together for a while. She knits on a shawl she's making for a friend, and I work on my sweater, until Connie packs up her knitting and announces she's going down the street to Artsy Tartsy to visit Marla and Tamara before she has to get back to Archie.

Almost as soon as she leaves, Eric and Adam enter the store. Together.

"Double trouble," I say, taking the coffee Eric hands me. "Thank you." I immediately crack the lid and inhale the glorious maple-pecan aroma.

They're deep in conversation about something sports related, so I sit on the sofa and knit while I wait for them to finish. As they talk, Sophie approaches Eric, then Adam, and instinctively they each bend down to rub her. Watching them gives me an idea for an experiment. If sales are good with one hot guy in the store, would sales double with two attractive men?

"Meg, did you hear me?"

"I'm sorry, I was distracted." I put down my knitting and look at Adam.

"This is Hannah's old laptop. It was in her bedroom at my place. I thought you could use it at the store until the police return yours."

"Thanks," I say. I take the laptop to the counter and plug it in. "Why are you two together, anyway?"

"We ran into each other at Latte Da," Eric explains.

"I was on my way here to give you the laptop and check your other devices."

"Right, I almost forgot," I say. "Here's my phone." I unlock the screen and hand it to him, then reach into my bag, pull out my tablet, and put it on the counter.

Adam called me at home last night and offered to check my other devices for spyware. I'd already looked and didn't find anything, but a second set of eyes can't hurt, so I took him up on his offer.

"I don't see anything on your phone." He hands me the phone, and I unlock the tablet for him.

I sip my coffee and wait for his verdict.

"Nothing," Adam declares, placing the device on the counter. "But I'm not familiar with spyware. For all I know, she only had to install it on one device. Also, your emails, texts, and photos automatically sync to all of your devices, so she can see those even if they don't happen on your laptop."

"Got it," I say. "Thank you for checking. I won't use my phone or tablet until Darby tells me it's safe." I rub my hands together and flash them a wide smile. "Who wants to come with me to visit Jamila?" I ask as if it will be fun. It won't.

"I can't go with you," Eric replies. "I'm not on duty, but I'm still a cop. Jamila has a lawyer. It could look like I'm trying to question her without her lawyer present."

I nod and look at Adam.

"If I say no, will you go alone?"

I nod.

"Fine. I'll go. But I want it on the record that I don't think it's a good idea, Meg."

"Duly noted," I say. "Do you still have the photos of the spyware on your phone?"

Adam nods.

Armed with my cell phone and coffee, I open the door and gesture for Adam to leave ahead of me.

"Please be careful," Eric says.

"Always," I respond. "You won't be alone long. As soon as your fan club hears I've left, and you're here alone, they'll rush over." I grin at him and leave.

CHAPTER 17

"I AGREE WITH YOU, but Darby says there was no spyware on Dr. Armistead's computer," I say to Adam on the walk to Bits'n'Bytes.

"I don't buy it," he says. "Maybe she was able to remove the spyware remotely, without getting her hands on his computer," he suggests. "It makes perfect sense. Jamila admits she provided tech support for him, and she installed spyware on your computer, which means she's capable of installing it on his. And she was one of the last people to see Armistead alive. What do you think she found on his computer?"

"Other than his patient list, I don't know," I say.

"Before I forget," Adam says, snapping his fingers, "Jess asked me to tell you she'll see you at noon tomorrow, and she'll meet you there. She said you'll know where 'there' is."

"Tell her thank you, and I'll see her tomorrow."

"Do I want to know where you and Jess are going?" he asks cautiously.

"Ask Jess," I reply.

"I did. She said it's a surprise."

I get the feeling Jess likes to keep Adam guessing. I'm not

sure if it's a quirky part of their dynamic, or if it's mean, but either way it's none of my business.

"It's not my place to tell you if she won't," I say.

Talking about Jess makes me think of the medical centre where she works, which makes me think of Karen. I stop walking and open my phone. I find the photo of Karen that I sent to April and hold it up to Adam.

"Are you sure this is the same woman you've seen waiting in the reception area for Emory?"

He looks at my phone. "Positive. I already told you I'm certain it's her."

I nod. "I believe you, but I have to double check because Karen told me yesterday was the first time she met Emory."

"Does she have a twin?" Adam asks.

The question catches me off guard. I'm about to say no but realize I have no idea. I know literally nothing about Karen except what she disclosed the two times we met.

"I don't think so," I reply hesitantly.

"Then it's her."

"OK," I say, and we resume walking.

"Emory's office is directly across the hall from mine," Adam explains, "and he doesn't use it very often, so when he has a patient, I notice. Unless I'm on the phone or with a client, I keep my door open—the air circulation is awful in those old Victorians—and I tend to notice the few times he comes and goes from his office."

"Does he work part-time? Or does he divide his time between multiple locations?" I wonder out loud.

"I don't think he has many patients," Adam replies. "We have an office lunch once a month, and at one of the lunches, he mentioned how challenging it is to build a practice in a small town. He said no one wants to be seen entering or leaving their therapist's office. He said people in Harmony Lake go to Harmony Hills for therapy. He hoped setting up an office in a building with other professionals would help him grow his practice because his patients would blend in with everyone else's clients."

"That's exactly why we went to Dr. Armistead in Harmony Hills," I remind him.

"I know. I didn't tell him that, though."

"Well, I'm sure he knows since Dr. Armistead's patient list was posted online."

Adam holds the door, and I enter Bits'n'Bytes first.

Jamila pops her head out of the back room. "Just a sec," she says with a smile.

"You don't have to say anything," I tell Adam quietly. "I just need a witness in case this goes off the rails."

He nods.

Jamila comes out of the back room with a stack of laptop sleeves and places them on the shiny, white table closest to Adam and I. "Hi guys," she says cheerfully.

"Hi, Jamila," Adam and I say slightly out of sync.

"All of these will fit your new laptop," she says, unstacking the sleeves and laying them next to one another.

"Actually, I think I've changed my mind about the laptop sleeve," I say. "I'd like a refund instead. And an explanation."

"A refund?" Her eyes are wide, and the inner corners of her eyebrows are squeezed so tightly together they almost meet in the middle. "I don't understand. Is there something wrong with the laptop?"

"It doesn't work," I explain. "It's super slow because the cyber security program we installed conflicts with the spyware you installed."

For a nanosecond, panic flashes across Jamila's face before it's replaced with mock concern. "Spyware? What are you talking about? I would never install malware on a computer." On the outside, her demeanour is calm, but I'm sure her insides are hectic.

"Yes, Jamila, you did. And you've been caught, so you may as well admit it."

"Hah," Jamila replies breathily and haughtily puts her hands on her hips. "Where's the computer? Let me see it." Her tone escalates from calm to defiant.

"The police have it," I explain. "I d…"

"YOU CALLED THE POLICE?" she shouts, going from defiant to full panic in the space of four words. "OH. MY GOD. Is that why HE'S here?" she points at Adam. "You brought a lawyer? What… Are you going to sue me?"

"I'm not going to sue you, Jamila," I say, trying to sound reassuring so she'll calm down. "Take a deep breath and lower your voice."

"You're not going to sue me, but you brought a lawyer? Really?"

"Well, I guess *technically* I brought a lawyer, but he's not here *as a* lawyer. He's here because he found the spyware and has proof," I explain. "And I didn't call the police, Detective Morris happened to be with me when I found out about the spyware."

Jamila drops into one of the shiny white chairs and covers her face with her hand. "OHMYGOD this is why my lawyer keeps calling me. The police KNOW." Her shoulders heave.

"Jamila, if your lawyer is trying to reach you, you should call them back," Adam advises, but I'm not sure she hears him through her sobs.

I walk behind the white shiny counter and poke my head in the back room. I find a box of tissue and drop it on the table in front of Jamila, then collapse into the chair across from her. If I'd accepted Adam's offer to find a new laptop for me, we wouldn't be here right now. If only I had a time machine.

"Why are you spying on me?" I ask. "Are you running an identity theft scam or something?"

"No, of course not." She uncovers her face and dries her eyes with a couple of tissues. "I had no choice. If I didn't install the spyware, I would have gone to jaaaaiil." The word jail evolves into a loud sob, and she's crying again. Full on crying. Ugly crying.

"Jail?" I ask. "Who would put you in jail? And why?"

"Charmaaaaaiiiine," she wails, then starts to hyperventilate, inhaling sharply after each syllable. "Be…cuz…of…the…may…yer."

"Deep breaths, Jamila." I exaggerate my own breathing hoping she'll copy me, like I used to when Hannah was a toddler having a tantrum.

"Jamila, do you want to talk to your lawyer before you say anything else?"

What did Adam just say? I look up at him and give him the stink eye. "Really?" I mouth.

"I'm an officer of the court, Meg," he reminds me, throwing up his hands.

I turn to Jamila and resume my exaggerated breathing. To my relief, she synchronizes her breathing with mine.

"Go in the back and get Jamila a glass of water, please," I instruct Adam.

This is the first time I've seen Jamila react strongly to anything. When I saw her the day after Dr. Armistead's death, and again yesterday when she picked Phillip's lock, she was cool, calm, and collected. And those were stressful situations.

By the time Adam returns with a bottle of water he found in the fridge, Jamila's breathing is back to normal, and she's able to speak.

I call upon my calmest, most reassuring voice. "Jamila, what's going on with you, Charmaine Solomon, and the mayor?"

"Jamila," Adam starts.

Jamila interrupts him before he can continue. "It's OK, Adam, I don't want to call my lawyer." She looks at me. "About two months ago, the mayor came to see me. She told me some town residents are plotting to get her out of office.

She said they're frustrated by her support of the big-box policy, and they plan to have their members run for council positions in the next election and nominate a candidate to run against her in the mayoral race. She said if they succeed, and enough of their candidates get elected, they could reverse the big-box policy."

"OK." I shrug. "This isn't news, Jamila. The town has always been divided about the big-box policy."

Harmony Lake has a policy against big-box stores and restaurants. Our quaint, family-owned businesses and restaurants are what makes our tiny town so intimate and cozy. We have no drive-thrus, no neon signs advertising corporate logos or businesses, and no multi-level parking lots. None of the corporate landscape commonly found in cities and suburbs. Tourists come to Harmony Lake to escape from that and immerse themselves in our small-town charm.

Our mayor is a loud advocate for the big-box policy. She wants to keep Harmony Lake cozy and friendly. Not everyone agrees with her. Some residents–particularly the ones who would benefit from selling land to big corporations–claim the big-box policy limits Harmony Lake's potential and stops progress. Every few years, the big-boxers push to have the policy reversed, but they never win.

"This is different," Jamila sniffles. "She said Electric Avenue is funding them. In exchange, if the big-boxers win, Electric Avenue will get first refusal on a location in Harmony Lake. Megan, I can't compete with Electric Avenue. It's a big-box computer and electronics retailer. I can't offer all the products and services they offer at discount prices. It would kill my business. I've spent twelve years building Bits'n'Bytes. If Electric Avenue comes to town, I'll end up wearing one of their orange and grey uniforms, working for minimum wage, and hoping for enough hours to pay my bills."

Oh my. If this is true, and the big-boxers have found themselves a corporate sponsor, they're really upping their game. They'd have money to pay for campaign advisors and PR people. More residents might start to take them seriously.

"Why did the mayor tell you this?" I ask. "What did she want from you?" Our mayor is sweet and grandmotherly, but she's also savvy. She hasn't been mayor for over twenty years for no reason. She knows how to play local politics to win.

"She gave me a list of big-boxers and asked me to hack their computers, so she could monitor their plans and progress."

"That was a big ask," I comment, shocked.

Jamila nods. "Some of them were my clients. Local business owners and farmers on the outskirts of town. It would be easy for me to access their computers."

Adam shifts awkwardly in the chair beside me. I can't expect him to sit here and listen to Jamila confess to committing a crime. It would put him in an awful position. I pretend to check the time on my phone.

"Adam, it's getting late. I appreciate you coming with me, but I know you have a meeting to get to. You should go. I'll text you if I need those photos."

He practically leaps out of his seat. "Are you sure, Meg?" He already has one hand on the door.

I nod. "Totally. I'll talk to you later."

I wait for the door to close behind him, then ask Jamila, "So, you did what the mayor asked?"

She nods. "I sure did. I felt sneaky and dishonest the entire time, but I did it."

"I'm guessing Charmaine found out?"

"A few weeks ago," Jamila confirms. "One of the people I was spying on realized what was happening. He went to Charmaine. He wanted to press charges." Jamila starts crying again and takes a moment to collect herself. "Charmaine confronted me, and I admitted everything. She told me she wouldn't charge me but said I owe her."

"And she made you hack into Dr. Armistead's computer?" I probe. "And post his patient list online?"

"No." She shakes her head. "That wasn't me. I don't know who did that."

Then who the heck was it?

"What did Charmaine ask you to do?"

"Nothing until a few days ago when she told me to spy on you," Jamila replies.

"Just me?" I ask.

"So far." She blows her nose. "She saw us talking at the pub on Friday night. Remember when I stopped by your booth?"

I nod. Of course, I remember. I wasn't *that* drunk. I was tipsy.

"Well, I was pretty excited about selling you a computer, and I told her about it. She was happy for me. The next day, after she found out Dr. Armistead died and you found his body, she came to the store to see me. She told me to spy on your computer. She said you have a habit of inserting yourself in police investigations. She said people confide in you. She wanted to know immediately if you found out anything about Dr. Armistead's death."

"I see," I respond.

So far, Jamila's story sounds plausible. When we spoke at the pub, Jamila mentioned she was waiting for the Solomons, so it's possible they showed up while Jamila and I were talking. Also, Charmaine was at Bits'n'Bytes the following day when I came to see the laptop Jamila picked out for me.

"When I left the pub on Friday, I saw you and Charmaine speaking in the alley beside the pub. What were you talking about?" I ask.

Jamila's shocked expression tells me it was definitely them, and she had no idea I saw them. She inhales deeply.

"Charmaine took me aside to tell me she confronted the mayor about getting me to spy on the big-boxers. She said the mayor denied it, but Charmaine wouldn't let it go. Eventually, the mayor told Charmaine her mandate as police chief will not be renewed. Charmaine tried to blackmail the mayor to renew her mandate."

"Why would Charmaine tell you that?" I ask.

"Because, according to Charmaine, if her mandate as chief isn't renewed and she loses her job, she's taking the mayor down with her. She'll expose everything."

"Including you," I point out.

"Including me," Jamila confirms. "Charmaine suggested I get a lawyer and prepare to ask for immunity in exchange for giving evidence against the mayor."

I can't fathom that my lovely little town is a hotbed of corruption and lies.

"Today, someone close to the mayor told me she changed her mind. She plans to renew Charmaine's mandate as police chief, after all."

"Charmaine won," Jamila observes, seemingly unaffected.

"So did you," I point out. "I'm sure neither of them will want anyone to know about you spying for them."

"But you know," Jamila says. "Are you going to tell?"

"I have to think about it, but I doubt it. I love this town, too, and we don't need a scandal like this."

I dare not say yes for fear of Jamila coming unhinged. I'm alone with her, and while I'm confident I would put up a good fight, I'm not certain I'd win.

"Thank you, Megan." Her eyes fill with moisture.

"Why did the Solomons invite you for dinner? What happened that night?"

Jamila shrugs one shoulder. "To make it an even number. Charmaine's funny like that. Also, I might be the only person in Harmony Lake who knows Mac. Except for all his patients."

"Have you ever met Dr. Armistead's girlfriend?" Let's toss it out there and see what happens.

"He had a girlfriend?" She shakes her head. "He never mentioned her."

I can't tell if she's lying or not. My phone dings.

Eric: Darby says it's safe to use your phone. Text me back so I know you're OK.

I type a quick reply thanking him and assuring him I'm fine.

"I have to go," I say, standing up and moving toward the door. "But I have one more question. Did spying on the big-boxers yield anything? Did you find proof they're launching a campaign and have the support of Electric Avenue?"

"No," Jamila replies, shaking her head. "But that doesn't mean it isn't true. I only spied on a few of them." She stands up and steps toward me.

I open the door, and step outside, determined to keep a safe distance from her.

"Megan, please don't tell anyone," she says before I let go of the door.

CHAPTER 18

"HI AGAIN, LADIES." I smile and close the door behind me. "Hey, Soph! Who's a good girl?" I bend down and give her a quick rub.

"You're back!" Eric says, getting up from his centre seat on the sofa and stepping around the knitters on either side of him. "How'd it go?"

I nod. "Good." My voice is too cheery and higher pitched than usual. I'm sure my anxiety is obvious to him.

"Cannelloni, Megan?" A charity knitter gestures to the plate on the table in front of her.

"No, thank you," I reply, smiling.

"I made them for Eric's lunch," she explains.

"That's sweet," I respond. "I'm glad he won't starve in my absence." I mean it sarcastically. Eric is a fully grown adult who's more than capable of feeding himself.

The sarcasm is lost on the knitters who tell me they don't mind at all, and it's a pleasure to cook for someone who appreciates it.

They bring him food every day. Sometimes multiple times each day. The fridge in the kitchenette is full. It will take hours to dispose of the leftovers and wash the containers.

"I'm glad you're here," he says slowly, like he's trying to figure out what to say next. "I need to talk to you about that order you placed. You know the order with that yarn place?"

I nod, realizing he's trying to separate me from the highly perceptive charity knitters without alerting them that something is up. "Right. The order."

Eric turns to his fan club. "Ladies, will you excuse us for a moment? There's a problem with a yarn order, and I need to talk to Megan about it in the back."

"What kind of problem?" Mrs. Roblin asks.

"They have no record of my order," I reply, making it up as I go along. "It's an order for limited edition colours. If we don't straighten it out today, we won't get *any* of it."

"Why didn't you say it's an emergency?" Mrs. Vogel asks, standing up and dropping her knitting where she was sitting. "You two go." She brushes us away with her hand as she walks toward the counter. "We'll keep an eye on the store. You get us some of that yarn!"

Eric closes the door separating the kitchenette from the store, and I sit on the stairs that lead to his apartment.

"What's wrong?" he asks. "I've never seen you this flustered."

I take a deep breath, collect my thoughts, and try to figure out where to start.

"First of all, is Karen a twin?"

"No," he replies, confused. "She has a brother, but he's two years older than her." Short pause. "Why?"

"Unless she's a twin, it's not relevant. It was just something Adam said." I shake my head. "Next," I continue, "have you thought anymore about Charmaine's job? How attached are you to maybe becoming the next chief of police?"

Eric shrugs. "I haven't really thought about it. Armistead's murder and your laptop issues have kept me preoccupied. Why?"

I tell him what Connie told me about the mayor changing

her mind and deciding to renew Charmaine's mandate as chief. Then I tell him about my conversation with Jamila.

"Adam just left you there? Alone with her?"

Of all the bombshells I just dropped, this is what he chooses to focus on? Really?

"I told Adam to leave," I explain. "There's no way Jamila would have talked with him there. She was already scared he was there because I want to sue her."

I believe part of the reason people confide in me is I don't have a stake in their story. I'm not a cop, a lawyer, or anyone else who's officially interested. I have no agenda or code of conduct to follow, except my own moral compass. I'm a neutral third party to whom they can unburden themselves.

"You told her you wouldn't go to the police with any of this?" he asks.

"I only said it to keep Jamila on an even keel. I texted Darby on my way here and asked to meet with him."

Eric nods and takes my hand. I scoot over so he can sit next to me on the narrow stair. "You did the right thing. I'm glad you got out of there safely. Did Darby text you back?"

"Not yet," I reply.

"Do you think Jamila is telling the truth?" he asks.

That's a big question.

I take a deep breath. "I believe parts of her story are true," I reply. "I believe Charmaine told her to spy on me, and I believe Charmaine found out Jamila was caught spying on someone else. I'm not sure I believe her when she said it wasn't her who accessed Dr. Armistead's patient list and posted it online. The mayor's sudden change of heart about renewing Charmaine's mandate makes sense if Charmaine blackmailed her."

Shaking his head, Eric looks at me. "I can't believe Charmaine would conceal a crime and blackmail the mayor and Jamila." His eyes are heavy with sadness. "The Charmaine Solomon I know wouldn't do that."

"It sucks when people disappoint us," I sympathize.

Eric wraps his arm around me, and I rest my head on his shoulder. We stay like this until my phone dings.

"Darby?" he asks.

I nod. "He'll come by as soon as he can."

"We should get back to the store," Eric reminds me.

"I know," I sigh. "You have cannelloni to eat, and I have to find some limited-edition yarn to order, or the charity knitters will never stop asking me about it."

BEFORE ERIC TAKES Sophie for her midday walk, he drops several fake hints that he won't be around the store much this afternoon. That's all the charity knitters need to hear to convince them that it's time to pack up their knitting and convene today's meeting.

Phillip walks past the store window with Kevin perched in the crook of his arm. Watching them go by, I get a tight knot in the pit of my stomach. It reminds me of the knot I had yesterday when I watched the security camera footage with Darby. I hope he brings it with him today, I'd like to have another look at both the footage from the medical centre and Bits'n'Bytes.

"I was just thinking about you," I say when Darby enters the store.

"I'm flattered," he replies, placing his folio on the counter. "Were you thinking anything in particular?"

"Just that I hope you bring the video footage with you today so I can watch it again."

"Great minds think alike, Megan" he says with a wink, tapping his leather folio.

While I re-watch the security footage, Darby reads something on his phone and eats a few of the left-over date squares that one of the charity knitters made for Eric. I still can't pinpoint what triggers my Spidey sense when I watch it.

Feeling frustrated that I *can't* figure it out, while at the same time obsessed with watching the footage because I *want* to figure it out, I lock the screen and close the flap on the iPad case.

"I need a break from this." I hand the iPad to Darby.

"No problem," he replies. "So, you paid a visit to Ms. Jagger?"

I'm about to tell him about my conversation with Jamila when Eric and Sophie return from their walk. Sophie rushes over to Darby and puts her two front paws on his knees. He rubs her and says nice things to her. Sophie and Darby are like two old friends who hardly see each other. Except they're like this every time they see each other which, lately, is frequently.

When the corgi finally agrees she has been sufficiently acknowledged by all who are present, I tell Darby about my visit to Bits'n'Bytes. At first, I don't mention that Adam was there. He wasn't actually present for Jamila's confession, and he doesn't need the hassle of another police interview. But then I remember Jamila has security cameras in her store, and if the police check, they'll see exactly who was there. It would look suspicious if I don't mention Adam, so I include him.

"Can you arrest her?" I ask, when my story is complete. "She admits to installing spyware on my computer and spying on other people's computers."

"As usual, Megan, our conversation has been very enlightening," Darby replies, completely ignoring my question.

"Will you at least question the mayor? And Charmaine?" I ask. "I know she denies it, but it's too much of a coincidence that Jamila was cyber-spying on so many people yet insists it wasn't her who posted Dr. Armistead's patient list online. It has to be connected. All of this somehow ties back to Dr. Armistead's murder. I just know it."

"We're looking into it."

Cop speak: lots of words but no actual information.

"Of course, you are," I say with a frustrated sigh, knowing full well that this is a one-way conversation. Darby's here to get information, not give it.

When Darby leaves, I stomp up the stairs to Eric's apartment and make lunch. Open-faced roast beef sandwiches with the leftover pot roast and gravy we had for dinner last night.

We're eating at the harvest table in the store when, for the first time since we've known each other, Eric doesn't finish a meal.

"I can't do it." He drops his fork and knife in defeat and pushes his plate away. "The knitters keep bringing me food. They go to so much trouble cooking for me, and it makes them so happy when I eat what they make that I feel guilty if I don't. I'm full all the time. I forget what hunger feels like. It's like they're determined to fatten me up, and they're aggressive about it."

"It's more likely they're following the old adage, the fastest way to a man's heart is through his stomach," I tell him.

"Actually, the fastest way to a man's heart is through the fifth left intercostal space, midclavicular line," Eric informs me. "I learned that at an autopsy I attended."

Welcome to our mealtime banter! Eric explains the most efficient methods of murder, and I explain the difference between worsted weight and fingering weight yarn. Spoiler alert: It has nothing to do with weight at all, but with diameter. The real mystery is why we aren't invited to more dinner parties.

"They mean well," I remind him. "I can put up a sign, NO OUTSIDE FOOD OR DRINKS IN THE STORE, and can take it down when you go back to work."

"No," he replies. "You're right, they mean well. And it

took so long for people around here to accept me, I don't want to ruin it."

The women have certainly accepted him, that's for sure.

While Eric sits and contemplates his distended belly, I stack the dishes and cutlery and take them back upstairs. When I re-enter the store from the back room, I'm looking down at my dishpan hands and massaging lotion into them.

"I don't think you should be here," Eric says, his voice low and monotone.

Who is he talking to? I look up.

"Hi, Charmaine. What are you doing here?"

"Hi, Megan," Charmaine greets me, looking past Eric and ignoring his words of caution. "I was hoping to speak to you." She glances at Eric, then back at me. "Alone."

I'm looking at Charmaine, and Eric is between us shaking his head with his arms crossed in front of his chest.

Right now, I don't trust Charmaine Solomon as far as I can throw her. She's obviously here because Jamila told her about our chat at Bits'n'Bytes this morning. Is she here to find out information? Or feed me information that supports her version of events? Let's find out.

CHAPTER 19

"WE CAN TALK," I tell Charmaine, "but not alone." I gesture for her to take a seat at the harvest table.

"Fine," she agrees. "But can we put our cell phones on the table, face up?"

I swear I hear a low growl emanate from Sophie when Charmaine walks past us. Sophie never growls. I look down at the corgi sitting next to me, and her upper lip is curled, revealing her tiny, sharp teeth as her steady gaze follows Charmaine.

I place my phone in the centre of the table. Charmaine places her phone in the centre of the table. We both look at Eric. Reluctantly, he places his phone on the table.

"I'll lock the door," he mutters.

Charmaine's eyes scan the ceiling and corners of the store.

"No cameras," I assure her.

"Just checking." She smiles.

It dawns on me that Charmaine has never been to Knitorious. She's not a knitter, and she doesn't crochet. There's no other reason to come here. Although there are people who occasionally stop in to visit Sophie, Charmaine isn't one of them.

"What do you want?" I cut to the chase.

"I heard about your conversation with Jamila this morning," Charmaine starts. "I want to explain a few things."

I bet she does.

"Jamila...misunderstood me. I didn't ask her to put spyware on your computer or to do anything malicious to your computer," Charmaine explains. "I asked her to talk to you and try to find out what you saw when you found Dr. Armistead on Friday night." She pauses, waiting for me to tell her what I saw on Friday night. I don't take the bait and stay quiet. She continues, "Somehow, Jamila interpreted that as me wanting her to monitor your correspondence and report back to me."

"I see," I reply. "I appreciate you clarifying that, Charmaine. Did Jamila also misunderstand you when she hacked into Dr. Armistead's computer and accessed his patient list?"

"I don't know what you're talking about, Megan," she replies matter-of-factly.

"Is the part about the mayor and the big-boxers true?" I ask.

"As far as I know, yes," Charmaine replies. "The mayor coerced Jamila into doing some...questionable things to protect her small business. However, I don't know if the story the mayor told her is true or if she made it up to manipulate Jamila."

"Either way, it's illegal," Eric points out. "You had a duty to act on that information, Charmaine."

Charmaine turns to Eric. "I did act on it," she replies. "I'm conducting an investigation into Jamila's allegations against the mayor, and the allegation against Jamila for spying on computers. The investigation is ongoing."

"Let me guess, the investigation will remain ongoing as long as the mayor renews your mandate?" Eric asks.

"That depends," Charmaine replies. "I think we can all agree the last thing this town needs is a scandal. Especially one that would destroy the confidence the townspeople have in their local government and their local police force."

She makes a good point. If the office of the mayor and the office of the police chief implode under the weight of this scandal, the big-boxers could use it to their advantage and possibly gain enough support to get one of their supporters elected.

"You know how to make this go away, right?" I ask.

"Enlighten me," Charmaine crosses her arms in front of her chest.

"Solve Dr. Armistead's murder," I reply. "That's all anyone cares about. The break-in at his office, his patient list appearing online, and the spyware on my computer are only being investigated because they could be connected to his murder."

Charmaine takes a deep breath and uncrosses her arms. "We know who killed him, but we can't prove it."

"We?" I ask.

"Emory and I."

"Who did it?"

"The girlfriend," Charmaine replies.

"Karen?" I ask.

Charmaine nods. "Karen." She lets out an audible sigh. "We invited him for dinner on Friday to warn him." Charmaine closes her eyes and rubs her forehead with her hand like she has a headache. "I can't say anymore. It would compromise my husband."

I shrug. "It's up to you." I refuse to beg her. She came to me, after all. I start to get up.

"Karen is a patient of Emory's," she explains.

I sit down again. "I know," I say.

Charmaine looks at me shocked. "How do you know?"

"People I know who work at his office have seen her coming and going from appointments for months."

"Well, Emory didn't know she was Mac's—er, Dr. Armistead's girlfriend until recently. He only knew Karen was in a relationship with someone who was breaking their professional code of ethics by dating her. He wouldn't have kept her on as a patient if he knew it was Mac."

"OK." I shrug at her justification of her husband's actions, or inaction, depending on your perspective.

"Karen wanted Dr. Armistead to go public with their relationship. Recently, she gave him an ultimatum. They go public, or she'll end their relationship. He chose to end it. Karen didn't take it well. As she came more unravelled, she said things in her sessions with Emory that made him realize her boyfriend was Dr. Armistead. She also said things that convinced Emory that Dr. Armistead was in danger."

"Then Emory should have reported it," Eric interjects. "Therapists are mandated to report if they believe their patient is a threat to themselves or others."

"Emory said the threats weren't specific enough to report, and when he probed Karen further about the threats, she retracted them."

"So, he broke Karen's confidentiality and told Dr. Armistead about the threats?" I ask, skeptical.

"Emory believed he could get the point across without actually breaking the rules," Charmaine explains.

"Hypothetically?" I ask.

"Exactly," Charmaine replies, obviously relieved she doesn't have to explain further.

I was married to a lawyer. Adam and I used to speak hypothetically when he wanted to talk about a case, or vent about a client, without breaching attorney-client privilege. He'd use hypothetical clients and hypothetical scenarios, and in return I'd ask hypothetical questions and provide hypothetical support and suggestions.

"Did Dr. Armistead pick up on the hypothetical references?" I ask.

"We couldn't tell."

"Why did you invite Jamila to dinner?"

"To be a witness," Charmaine replies. "If Emory was accused of breaking patient confidentiality, Jamila would be able to confirm that Emory never referred to Karen or anyone else by name."

I'm dubious. Her explanation doesn't sit right with me. It's too convenient.

"How and when did Karen give Dr. Armistead the caffeine?" I ask.

"That's the missing piece. It's the one thing we can't figure out, and why I was hoping to find out from Jamila what you saw that night."

I shrug one shoulder. "I didn't see anything. It was dark. I was drinking. Is that all you want from me?"

"I'm hoping to convince you not to talk to the police about your conversation with Jamila today."

There it is. Of everything Charmaine said, this is the one thing I'm certain is true.

"You're too late," I respond.

The realization she told me all this for nothing hits Charmaine immediately, and the look on her face is priceless.

She must be desperate. Eric is a cop for goodness' sake. An honest one. Even if I agree to keep quiet, there's no way he would. Unless she thought we could convince him together. Peer pressure.

"Then I should tell you that before she called me, Jamila panicked and erased the video footage of your visit to the store today," Charmaine says. "She plans to tell her lawyer and the police that you were never there. It will be your word against hers."

Even without sound, the footage wouldn't have looked good for Jamila, her panic attack and hyperventilating could be incriminating.

"I think you mean it will be Jamila's word against *ours*," I clarify.

The colour drains from Charmaine's face and her jaw drops. "Who else was there?"

"Adam." I don't mention that he left before Jamila said anything self-incriminating.

"She didn't mention that." Charmaine looks stunned.

"I'm sorry I couldn't be more help." I stand up and push my chair in. We're done here. "I have an appointment with your husband tomorrow. I decided to take your advice and see if he could help me with my boundary issues. Given the circumstances, perhaps I should cancel it."

"On the contrary," Charmaine says, while in one fluid motion, she grabs her phone from the table, slips her purse onto her shoulder, and stands up. "I think it would be good for you two to talk."

And without another word, Charmaine Solomon strides to the door, unlocks it, and leaves.

FOR A WHILE, neither Eric nor I say a word. Silently and separately, we putter around the store, tidying shelves and doing odd jobs while we process everything Charmaine said. Every so often we look at each other with an expression of shock and disbelief, and occasionally, one of us will open our mouth, then close it, and shake our head without saying anything.

"I feel like such an idiot." Eric finally breaks the silence. "How did I not see she's a corrupt, dirty cop?"

"She has everyone fooled," I assure him. "And I'm sure she wasn't always like this."

"You have an appointment with Emory tomorrow? Since when?"

"Since yesterday," I explain. "Jess and I are going together. Under the guise of blending our families and respecting each other's boundaries, or some such thing. It's not a real therapy session, it's an excuse to talk to him about Dr. Armistead."

"Are you still going?" he asks.

I can tell he'd prefer I don't.

"I think so. I want to talk to him. I'll only go if Jess goes. I won't go alone." I'm not sure how to ask my next question, other than carefully. "Do you believe what Charmaine said about Karen?"

"About her being a threat to Armistead?" he asks.

I nod. "Do you think Karen could kill someone?"

"No," he replies without hesitation, shaking his head. "I'm not Karen's biggest fan, but she's not capable of murder. The Karen I know holds a grudge. If she killed him, she wouldn't be able to punish him anymore, and punishing the target of her grudge is how she works through her anger. I believe she'd give him an ultimatum, though. She loves ultimatums."

I'd like to talk to Karen again, but she's already lied to me.

I don't know who to believe.

CHAPTER 20

"Sophie actually growled?" April asks through the speakers in my car. "I've never heard her growl. Ever."

"I know, right?" I agree. "Sophie's a lover, not a growler. Aren't you, Soph?"

I glance at the corgi next to me on the passenger seat. She looks at me briefly, then turns her attention back to watching the world pass by the car window.

April tells me her brother and his family are coming to stay with her parents, and she's coming home to Harmony Lake. She hopes to leave tomorrow.

"Good!" I say. "I miss you! And it means your dad's recovery is going well."

"I've been here a whole week. I'm ready to come home. I miss you guys, and I need a break from hearing about the stupid eaves troughs!"

"Didn't you get them fixed?" I ask, pulling into the parking lot behind Knitorious.

There's an unfamiliar car in the corner of the parking lot. Who would be here this early?

"I did," April replies. "Now he's obsessed with climbing

up there and looking for himself. He says he wants to make sure 'they did a proper job and didn't cut any corners'," she says, mimicking her father's voice. "My brother's kids have a drone. They're bringing it with them to take pictures of the eaves troughs and shut him up."

"You're a patient daughter," I commend her.

The driver's side door of the unfamiliar car opens, and Karen Porter steps out.

"Uh-oh," I sigh.

"What is it?"

"Karen's here. She's waiting for me in the parking lot, and now she's walking toward me."

"What does she want now?" April asks rhetorically.

"I'm about to find out. I have to go. I'll call you back."

"Call me as soon as she leaves so I know you're OK," April says.

We end our call, and I step out of the car, then help Sophie to the ground.

"Hi, Karen," I say when she gets within a few feet of my car.

"Hi, Megan." She bends down. "Hi, Sophie."

Sophie trots over with her bum wagging, and Karen rubs her. Sophie's enthusiastic approach to Karen is a stark contrast to yesterday when she didn't go near Charmaine.

"Are you looking for me?" I give Sophie's leash a gentle tug, and she trots back to me.

"Yes," Karen replies, standing up. "I would've phoned or texted first, but I don't have your number."

And you're not getting it.

If Karen really wanted to call first, she could look up the store number, send an email through the store website, or ask Jess to reach out to me.

"What can I do for you?" I ask, ignoring her comment about my phone number.

"Jess mentioned that you have a history of getting to the

bottom of things. She says you've even helped solve a few murders."

"OK." I shrug, neither confirming nor denying anything.

"She said if I know anything about Mac's death, or his life, that I haven't been completely forthcoming about, I should tell you. She said you might be able to help figure out who killed him."

"Are there things you haven't been forthcoming about, Karen?" I ask.

"Yes," she says quietly. "But I'm scared. Scared what I know might give people the wrong impression of Mac and scared I could get in trouble for not speaking up sooner. I hoped the police would find a smoking gun—metaphorically —and I'd be able to keep Mac's secrets to myself."

"Sophie and I are going for our morning walk. Would you like to join us?"

Karen nods, letting out an audible sigh of relief.

Just in case Charmaine is right about Karen being a killer, I keep our interaction as public as possible. A walk in the park by the lake is public enough for someone to hear me scream, but private enough for us to talk, as long as we keep an eye on our surroundings for nosy neighbours.

"The Solomons claim you killed Dr. Armistead," I say bluntly.

Karen stops walking and looks me in the eye. "I didn't."

"Why would they suspect you?"

"Because I was his partner," she surmises. "You know how cops think. They always suspect the victim's spouse or partner. The police ruled out Mac's ex-wives, so I guess I'm the next logical candidate."

She's right. The police always start with the people closest to the victim. To be fair, statistically the murderer is usually the spouse or someone closest to the victim.

"Why did you lie to me about how long you've known Emory?" I ask.

"How do you know I was lying?"

"Harmony Lake is a small town, Karen. I know everyone who works at his office. You've been visiting Emory regularly for months."

"You're right," she fesses up. "I've been his patient for almost six months. When I started going to Emory, I didn't know that he and Mac knew each other. But I was careful, just in case. I never used Mac's name. I talked about our relationship and my frustration with keeping it secret, but I never used names."

"Then how did Emory figure out Dr. Armistead was your boyfriend?"

Karen shrugs and shakes her head. "He must've used context clues. I was careful to never use Mac's name, but over the course of my sessions, it's possible I disclosed enough other non-identifying information for him to figure it out."

A gang of determined speed walkers marches toward us, and we stop talking. Karen looks pensive as we step off the path to make way for them.

"I'm so stupid," she says after the walkers have passed, and we're back on the path. "I didn't realize it at the time, but I did give him information. I mentioned that Mac was married four times. I mentioned I work in the same medical centre as my boyfriend and that we both work in Harmony Hills." She looks at me with wide, wet eyes. "I told Emory everything he needed to figure out who I was dating."

"Emory didn't confront you when he realized you and Dr. Armistead were dating?" I ask.

"No, and now that I think about it, he mined me for information."

"That's awful," I say. "Not to mention unprofessional."

"There's more," Karen says quietly.

"I'm listening."

"You know the break-in at his office? The one on Eric's birthday?" she asks.

She has a knack for bringing Eric's name into conversations that have nothing to do with him.

"I remember," I reply.

"That wasn't the first time Mac's office was broken into," Karen discloses. "He usually brought his lunch from home and ate at his desk, but on Mondays he ran errands. You know, the bank, the dry cleaner, stuff like that. Well, two Mondays before the break-in, he came back from his usual errands and was convinced someone had been in his office while he was out. He was sure of it."

"Why did he think that?"

"Because the door was unlocked. He insisted he locked it and checked it before he left. He stayed at the office late that night looking through every drawer, looking for whatever could've been stolen. Nothing was missing. I didn't think anyone had been in there. I told him if it was a robbery, they would've at least taken his laptop. I assumed he was mistaken about locking the door."

"But you no longer think he was mistaken," I clarify.

Karen nods. "About a week later, Mac found spyware on his computer. He was sure whoever broke into his office that day installed it."

This revelation makes me stop dead in my tracks.

"Did he check the security footage from the lobby?"

"He tried," Karen replies, "but the property manager wouldn't show him the footage unless he had a police report for the break in."

Darby can access that footage. I need to see that footage.

"Did he uninstall the spyware?" I ask.

"He disabled it," she claims. "He wasn't super techy, but he was techy enough to do that. He said he wanted to keep it in case it was evidence."

"But Darby said there was no spyware on Dr. Armistead's computer." I'm so confused.

"There wasn't," Karen concurs. "Not on the computer in

his office. The computer with the spyware is in the trunk of my car. I brought it with me today. After Mac found the spyware, he brought the infected laptop to my house and took his home laptop to the office instead. Both laptops look almost identical."

This makes sense.

"So, if the first break-in was to install spyware on Dr. Armistead's computer, was the second break-in to remove it?" I think aloud.

"Mac thought they were looking for a paper file," Karen replies.

"What paper file?" I ask.

"Mine and Eric's."

I look at her confused. "I don't understand."

"This is the part that makes Mac look bad," she admits. "When we started dating, Mac deleted mine and Eric's patient file from his computer and his back-ups. He wasn't supposed to do that."

"So, if anyone accused him of dating a former patient, there would be no patient record to prove it," I theorize.

"Right," Karen confirms. "The notes from our sessions are gone, but for whatever reason, our names still appeared on his patient list. I realized this when Mac's patient list was posted online."

I can see why Karen is worried about Dr. Armistead's reputation. He was shady. He dated at least one former patient, tried to bribe a police officer, and erased patient records. And these are just the things I know about.

"The hackers found you on the patient list, but couldn't find any notes with dates that would prove *when* you and Eric were Dr. Armistead's patients."

"Exactly." She sounds excited and relieved that I'm following along. "Mac thinks they were looking for a paper file when they broke in the second time. But there isn't one. He hasn't kept paper files for patients for years."

"Wow." I sit my shocked self on the next park bench we encounter. "Karen, as long as you have that computer—the one with the spyware—you're in danger. You need to give it to Darby."

"I know." She sits down next to me. "That's why I brought it today. But if I'm charged with obstructing justice, or whatever, I could lose my licence to practice as a chiropractor."

All these professional licences and professional codes of conduct really complicate things.

"Solving the murder is Darby's biggest priority. If you're telling the truth, I'm sure we can convince him to overlook you hanging onto the laptop."

"I am telling the truth, Megan."

"I want to believe you, Karen. But you've lied to me before, and everyone's version of the truth is different. It's hard to know who to trust. But the laptop will help prove your version of events," I tell her.

Karen inhales deeply, then lets it out. "OK."

Before she can change her mind, I pull out my phone and text Darby. I tell him it's urgent, and we have evidence. He replies immediately that he's on his way to Knitorious. I tell him to meet us in the parking lot and keep an eye on Karen's car. Then I text Eric to warn him his ex-wife is here. He thanks me for the warning and asks me to text him when the coast is clear.

On the walk back to the store, I ask Karen if Dr. Armistead had any theories about who broke into his office and who put the spyware on his computer.

"The lady who did his tech support. Her name starts with J."

"Jamila?" I ask, hoping I'm not leading the witness.

"That's it!" She points at me. "Her last name is Richards or something. Same as one of the Rolling Stones."

"Jagger?" I suggest, filling in the blank for her.

"Yes. Jamila Jagger."

"Why did he suspect her?" I ask.

"She saw us at the movies together a month ago," Karen explains. "Mac and I were waiting in line at the concession stand. We were hugging and kissing while we waited our turn. When we turned around with our popcorn, Jamila was in line behind us."

"Are you sure it was her?"

"That's how Mac introduced me to her. They were friendly and spoke for a minute. It was disappointing because we went to a theatre in the city so we wouldn't be seen by anyone we know, yet there she was."

I stop walking and open my phone. I find Jamila's Facebook page and Karen confirms Jamila is the woman they saw at the movies. We start walking again.

"Why did Mac go to the Solomon's house for dinner the night he died?" I ask.

"Apparently, the Solomons might be moving away from Harmony Lake," Karen replies. "Charmaine's contract is almost over, and she isn't sure if she wants to renew. Emory approached Mac and asked him if he wanted to purchase Emory's practice. The Solomons invited him for dinner to talk about it."

I don't bother telling Karen the truth about Charmaine possibly not having a choice about whether to stay on as chief of police in Harmony Lake.

"Did Dr. Armistead know Jamila would be there?" I ask.

"Jamila was there?"

I nod. "Yes, she was."

"If he knew she would be there, he would've told me," she insists.

We're about to cross Water Street, and I can see Darby standing in the driveway that leads to the parking lot. This is my last chance to ask Karen anything. As she's about to step off the curb, I grab her arm.

"Karen, did you give Dr. Armistead an ultimatum? Did

you threaten to end the relationship if he didn't make it public?"

Karen looks at me, then at her feet. She looks up at me again and nods. "I didn't mean it. I said it out of frustration." Her eyes fill with tears. "He was so stressed and anxious after we saw Jamila at the movie theatre. I mean, we were always careful, but after we ran into her, he wanted to be even more careful. Do you know how hard it is to have a relationship and pretend you hardly know each other?"

I shake my head. "It must be awful," I sympathize.

"It is," she nods. "To answer your question, yes. I gave him an ultimatum, but I regretted it immediately and took it back. I was committed to making our relationship work. We were planning to travel to Europe together next year. For at least part of the year, we would be a normal couple and not have to worry about Mac losing his job because he loved me."

We cross the street and Sophie speeds up, straining the leash when she sees her long-lost friend, Darby, waiting for her.

CHAPTER 21

"It makes sense, right?" I ask April, as I flip the CLOSED sign to OPEN and unlock the door.

"Let me get this straight," she says through my AirPods. "Jamila saw Dr. Armistead and Karen at the movies and was so determined to prove their relationship was illicit, she hacked into his computer and accessed his patient files. Have I got it right, so far?"

"Yes," I say as I tidy shelves of yarn.

"But how would Jamila know it was a secret relationship? And how would she know Karen was a past patient?" April asks.

"Good questions," I reply. "I don't know the answers, but I have a theory. Jamila did tech support for both Emory and Dr. Armistead. I think it's possible that when Dr. Armistead introduced Karen and Jamila at the movie theatre, Jamila recognized Karen's name. For all we know, she snooped through patient files when she was on their computers. Also, Jamila might have picked up on the tension when Dr. Armistead and Karen realized they'd been seen by someone who knows one of them."

"OK," April cedes. "That makes sense, but *why* would

Jamila want to expose them? Their relationship has nothing to do with her. Why would she go to so much trouble and take on so much risk to prove Dr. Armistead was dating a patient he shouldn't be dating?"

"Money," I reply. "Jamila told me she's struggling to compete with Electric Avenue and the other big-box retailers out there. She's terrified they'll run her out of business."

"So, you think she was going to blackmail him?"

"Precisely," I reply, retrieving the duster from the back room and dusting the shelves in the bulky yarn area. "But Dr. Armistead found out she hacked his computer and had proof. She broke into his office last week to find the proof and destroy it. But he hid the laptop with Karen. Maybe he threatened to expose Jamila, and she killed him."

Just like he exposed Eric for looking him up on the police database.

"If you're right, Jamila's dinner invitation on Friday night was very convenient. Too convenient," April points out.

"It was," I agree. "I wonder if Charmaine or Emory mentioned the dinner in front of her, and Jamila invited herself or dropped hints that she'd like to attend?"

"Jamila's not a pushy person, that doesn't sound like something she would do," April responds.

"Neither does cyber-spying or erasing security camera footage and denying I was at her store," I remind her.

"Touché," April concedes. "Did you tell Darby your theory?"

"The short version," I say. "He was in a hurry to get the laptop to the cyber-crimes division. He drove Karen and the laptop to the Harmony Lake Police Station and said we'll talk when he drives Karen to pick up her car after she gives a statement."

April updates me on the logistics for her return trip to Harmony Lake. She's leaving tomorrow as soon as her mother gets home from the grocery store. On her way, she'll pick up Hannah and Rachel in Toronto and bring them home for Thanksgiving weekend.

"Thank you for picking up the girls!" I'm so happy I don't have to make the nine-hour round trip tomorrow. "Adam and I will take care of driving them back on Monday so you can stay home and enjoy the day off with T."

While April and I talk about the latest episodes of our favourite shows, I put the duster away and take out my knitting. I'm determined to make some progress on the sleeves of my new sweater. I was hoping to wear it to Thanksgiving dinner on Sunday, but I'm not sure I'll be able to finish it by then.

As I knit mindlessly and chat with my best friend, I look out the front window. A familiar, powder-blue PT Cruiser drives down Water Street. Connie. She drives the only powder blue PT Cruiser in town.

Connie!

Oh my god, that's it! I have to phone Darby.

"April, I have to go. I found a hole in someone's alibi. I'll call you later."

I text Darby, telling him it's an emergency. Again. This is the second emergency text I've sent him today, and it's still morning. I send a follow-up text, reminding him to bring his iPad.

"ARE YOU SURE ABOUT THE TIMING?" Eric asks when I tell him how seeing Connie drive past the store this morning, and Phillip walking on the sidewalk with Kevin yesterday, jogged my memory about the security footage Darby showed me.

"Well done, babe!" He grins proudly. "Maybe we should switch roles. I'll run Knitorious, and you find the bad guys."

Impressing a professional investigator makes me proud and a little smug at the same time.

"The charity knitters would love that," I respond, not joking.

Just as I finish telling him about my early morning conversation with Karen, and my theory on how and why Jamila killed Dr. Armistead, Darby walks into the store.

"You're here!" I say, eager to show him what I figured out before I have to leave to meet Jess at Dr. Solomon's office at noon.

"You beckoned me, Megan, and here I am," Darby teases. "I have a couple of things to mention."

I try not to let his serious tone kill my positive vibe.

Darby bends over to greet his favourite corgi and speaks as he rubs her. "Ms. Jagger denies your version of events yesterday. She says you did not go to Bits'n'Bytes, and she provided video footage of the store at the time in question. It's almost an hour of an empty store."

"Charmaine told us Jamila erased the footage," I tell him coolly. "Adam can verify most of my version of events."

"*Charmaine* told you?"

"Oh right, we haven't told you about that. Charmaine was here yesterday. Can we bring you up to date later? I have an appointment at noon, and I want to show you this before I leave."

Darby tells me he's waiting for the property manager at the medical centre to call him back about the security footage from the first suspected break-in at Dr. Armistead's office; the one Karen told me about this morning. The one Dr. Armistead suspected was when Jamila installed the spyware on his computer.

I think I might know how to get the footage without waiting for the property manager to call back, but I don't mention it to Darby because I don't want to give him a chance to tell me not to do it.

Darby unlocks his iPad and opens the video footage from Jamila's store. The footage that disputes the medical centre footage showing her—well, someone who looks exactly like her—arriving at and leaving the medical centre during the same time frame.

He hands me the device, and I place in on the harvest table where we can all see it. I tap the screen and the video starts. Jamila is sitting in her store working on her sticker-covered laptop.

Excitedly, I bounce on the balls of my feet waiting for the first thing I remember to appear on the screen. This must be how Sophie feels when she's so excited she tippy taps her little paws.

I tap the screen.

"There!" I yell in the same voice I'd use to yell, "Bingo!" if I'd just won the jackpot, and if I played bingo,

"That man on the sidewalk is my neighbour, Phillip Wilde." I look at Darby. "You remember Phillip, right?" Phillip and Darby met in the summer when Phillip was a witness to my "car accident" as we call it.

"I remember Mr. Wilde," Darby agrees. "That looks like him and his little dog, Keith."

"Kevin," Eric and I correct him in stereo.

"Sorry. Kevin," Darby acknowledges, looking at me blankly.

"If this footage was filmed on Monday September twenty-eighth, at lunchtime, Phillip can't be there," I insist.

"Why not?"

"Because Noah is off on Mondays, and Phillip and Kevin are alone in the store. Phillip brings his lunch from home on Mondays. He only leaves the store to take Kevin outside for quick washroom breaks. Phillip would *never* wander this far down Water Street on a Monday."

"Maybe last Monday was different," Darby suggests.

I shrug. "You should ask Phillip, but I doubt it."

Fine, if he doesn't like my Phillip-evidence, I'll show him

the next one. When he sees all three, he'll have to be convinced. I tap the screen again and the video resumes.

I hover my finger over the screen when I sense the next thing is about to happen.

"Connie!" I shout, tapping the screen.

"Connie?" Darby asks.

"Connie," I confirm. "In the powder-blue PT Cruiser." I point to the car on the screen. "There's *no way* Connie drove past Bits'n'Bytes on Monday September twenty-eighth at lunchtime." I shake my head. "It's not possible."

"Because?" Darby asks.

"Because that was the day Archie had hip replacement surgery. Connie was at the hospital in Harmony Hills. All Day. The next time she drove on Water Street was Thursday of that week. Thursday was October first." I point to the paused image of Jamila on the screen. "Look how focussed Jamila is on her computer. She was probably doing her month end or quarter end books, because this was probably filmed on the first, not the twenty-eighth."

"What else have you got?"

Why isn't he impressed? I tap the screen and wait. Again.

"That's me!" I tap the screen, and point to my black, cross-over SUV. "That's my car. I wasn't there on Monday the twenty-eighth."

"Are you sure?" Darby asks.

"Positive," I reply, nodding. "The twenty-eighth was Eric's birthday. We planned to go out for lunch, but Charmaine had a dental emergency and Eric had to stay at work. We changed our lunch plans to dinner plans, and I went to the hospital to visit Archie and Connie. Connie and I had lunch together at the hospital cafeteria." I raise my index finger and signal for Darby to wait.

I retrieve my wallet from under the counter and pull out the pile of crumpled receipts I habitually stuff in the part of the wallet where paper money used to go when paper money was a thing. One by one, I smooth out each receipt, and a surprise ten-dollar bill, until I find one of the receipts I'm looking for. "My parking receipt from the hospital. Note the date and times." I hand him the receipt and continue uncrumpling. "And the receipt for lunch in the hospital cafeteria." I press the paper against the table with my palm to make it as readable as possible. "I paid for both meals." I hand it to him. "The hospital should have video footage of Connie and I coming and going from the hospital parking lot."

Finally, Darby cracks a small smile. "Thank goodness you're a receipt hoarder, Megan." His smile grows into a wide grin.

"Is this enough to prove Jamila wasn't at her store doing paperwork when Dr. Armistead's office was broken into?" I ask, hopeful that it is.

Eyes wide, Darby nods. "Definitely."

It also proves Jamila is good at altering video footage. So good, she was able to fool the cyber-crimes people.

Jamila is full of surprises: picking locks, altering security video, what other secret talents does she have?

CHAPTER 22

JESS IS WAITING outside when I arrive, and we go in together.

"Hi, Lin," we say simultaneously.

We exchange pleasantries with Lin and discuss our Thanksgiving dinner plan this weekend. Lin is part of my extended, non-traditional, modern family. Her partner is Ryan, Archie's son.

We remind Lin we're here to see Emory, not Adam, and she hands Jess and I each a clipboard with a pen tethered to it.

"Fill these out," Lin instructs. "When you're finished, bring back the clipboards and pens but keep the forms. You'll give them to Dr. Solomon."

Jess and I sit side by side on the leather sofa in the seating area and fill in our New Patient Information forms.

"I don't know how much information I want this guy to have," Jess mutters without looking up from her form.

"I know," I agree. "I think I'll put the information he already knows or is easily searchable and leave everything else."

I release the form from the clipboard and offer to take Jess's clipboard and pen back to Lin. She hands me her clipboard, and I hand her my completed form to hold until I get back.

"You didn't write penicillin in the allergies section," Jess chides.

I'm allergic to penicillin and all the other "cillins." My allergy first showed itself when I was fifteen years old and had strep throat. Our family doctor prescribed penicillin, and I ended up in the emergency room with anaphylactic shock.

The doctor told my parents anaphylactic shock is extreme for a first reaction, and they told him it was because I was an overachiever. I survived, obviously, and I should wear a medic alert bracelet, but never do.

"Why does a psychotherapist need to know I'm allergic to penicillin?"

"In case something happens while you're here and you need medical attention. He would notify the first responders or whoever treats you," Jess lectures. "It can't hurt to include it. I'll write it in for you."

Despite my inner voice telling me it's not a good idea, I let Jess take one of the tethered pens and add my penicillin allergy to the form.

"I can't believe you remembered my penicillin allergy," I say, impressed. I can't even remember what I had for dinner last night.

Jess shrugs. "I've been cleaning your teeth every six months for seventeen years. I check your patient information before each visit in case anything has changed. It's burned into my brain now. Like the pit that could turn into a cavity that we're keeping an eye on in your forty-seven."

In response to my blank stare, Jess explains that forty-seven is one of my molars, and it has a pit that attracts bacteria and could become a cavity.

"Fascinating," I respond, not fascinated.

"Did Karen get in touch with you?" Jess asks when I return from Lin's desk. "She knows more than she lets on. She won't talk to the police, so I suggested she talk to you. I hope you don't mind."

"She was at the store this morning," I reply.

In hushed tones, I tell Jess about the evidence Karen had in the trunk of her car and the highlights of our conversation.

"Did Darby get the security footage from the first suspected break in?" Jess whispers.

"He's waiting to hear from the property manager," I explain. "Karen said Dr. Armistead tried to look at it, but the property manager wouldn't show it to him without a police report."

"Leave it with me." Jess winks. "I know the property manager. Our daughters are best friends. I might have some pull." She counts silently on her fingers. "Two weeks before the twenty-eighth was the fourteenth, right? Is Karen sure about the date?"

This is exactly what I was hoping to hear. I planned to ask Jess if she could get her hands—or eyes—on that footage, but she beat me to it by offering.

"She says it was definitely Monday because Dr. Armistead always ran errands at lunchtime on Mondays."

Humans are creatures of habit. We find comfort in the familiarity of routine. It's scary how easy it is for a someone with evil intentions to use our innate inclination toward the familiar against us.

"Good afternoon, ladies."

Emory's voice shocks us out of our huddle.

"Hi, Emory." I extend my hand and he shakes it.

His hand isn't big, but it's meaty. His grip is warm and confident.

"Nice to see you again, Megan." He moves his extended hand toward Jess. "Ms. Kline." He smiles.

"Please call me Jess." She flashes a wide smile and shakes Emory's hand.

We follow Emory up the curved staircase and down the

hall. His office is across the hall from Adam's. We're brought to a halt briefly in front of Adam's open door while we wait for Emory to open his door. Jess and I smile and wave at Adam, who looks up at us with a series of micro expressions ranging from shock, to confusion, then dread. Emory gestures for us to enter his office ahead of him.

"Make yourselves comfortable," he instructs.

We sit next to each other in the middle of the simple beige sofa. He sits across from us in a wing chair, and we sit in silence while he peruses our New Patient Information Forms.

"What brings you here today?" he finally asks, smiling over his glasses, then nudging them with his index finger.

"Well…"

"We're hoping…"

Jess and I speak at the same time.

"You first," I say to Jess.

"No, you," she insists in response.

"Actually, it was your wife's idea," I tell him. "She said you know a lot about boundary issues."

"What she said." Jess laughs and jerks her head toward me.

Jess and I take turns explaining our unconventional and slightly complicated relationship situation to Emory. How we know each other, and how we each know everyone else in our modern family.

"We're trying to blend our families, be friends with each other, and respect everyone else's relationships," Jess summarizes.

"I'm tempted to draw a chart," Emory remarks.

"A chart *would* save time," I admit, "and give you something to refer to."

"And it's not just personal relationships," Jess adds. "We have a slew of professional relationships to deal with too." She shrugs. "Sometimes we find out things about each other we shouldn't know or would rather not know."

"Exactly," I agree, taking the baton from Jess. "For example, Jess and I recently learned someone we know uses information they learned in a professional capacity to their advantage."

I'm making this up as I go along. The only person Jess and I suspect may have done this is Emory, when he found out about Karen's relationship with Dr. Armistead.

"And we can't agree on the best way to deal with it," Jess adds, reclaiming the baton. "As a professional myself"—she clutches her hand to her chest—"*I* think there should be zero tolerance for trusted professionals ignoring their professional codes of conduct and acting in their own self-interest."

Jess assumes the role of bad cop in our make-believe scenario.

"And *I* think just because someone does something that appears unethical doesn't mean it's not justified. I think we should give our…friend the benefit of the doubt and ask them why they did what they did," I argue, trying to convince Emory that I'm sympathetic.

I'm worried our conversation sounds rehearsed, but I swear we're improvising.

"How do we resolve this?" Jess asks, dramatically throwing her hands in the air. "What would you do, Dr. Solomon? If you were, say, stuck between a patient and a professional colleague, for example? Would you break the patient's confidentiality and tell your colleague, or would you honour your duty to your patient and not let your colleague know you have personal information about them?"

We both look at Emory, smiling and waiting to hear his position on our hypothetical ethical dilemma.

"I'd need more information before I could answer," he replies. "It would depend on what profession we're talking about and the nature of the situation …"

A ringing phone interrupts his response.

"I'm sorry," Jess says looking at her phone. She looks at

me. "It's the insurance company. About the accident. I have to take this. Do you mind?"

"Of course not." I wave her toward the door. "Good luck."

Jess leaves the office without closing the door, intentionally I'm sure. Emory stands up and closes the door.

Alone with Emory, I remind myself Jess is right outside and will hear me if I need to be heard. Assuming I can make noise. I look at the throw cushions that line the sofa on either side of me. If he smothers me with a pillow, I won't be able to scream. Stop it, Megan! No one is going to smother me or strangle me with their meaty hands. Focus, Megan.

In an effort to distract myself and pass the time as pleasantly as possible until Jess returns, I explain about Jess's son having his first fender bender.

"Let's cut to the chase, Megan. Why are you really here? What do you want to ask me?"

CHAPTER 23

I TILT MY HEAD, feigning ignorance. "What do you mean?" I shake my head. "I'm not sure I understand."

"Charmaine visited you yesterday," Emory says. "You know Karen is my patient, and she was Dr. Armistead's girlfriend."

"Why didn't you stop seeing her as a patient? Or report him?" I ask.

"As Charmaine told you, I didn't make the connection until recently that Karen and Dr. Armistead were a couple. By the time I realized, she was struggling with his decision to end the relationship and was making veiled threats toward him. I tried to warn him." He nudges his glasses for what feels like the millionth time.

You know that torture technique where the torturers let one drop of water drip onto the victim's forehead at random intervals until the victim is driven to insanity waiting for the next drip? That's what it's like waiting for Emory Solomon's next eyeglass-nudge.

"Charmaine said you tried to warn him subtly. Why didn't you warn him directly?"

Emory sighs. "I didn't want Mac to think I was threatening him."

"I don't follow."

"If I told him I knew he was having an inappropriate relationship with a former patient, he could easily have interpreted it as me threatening to report him. Even if I never did report him, he'd always know I had this information about him and could use it against him. It would have made our personal and professional relationship awkward. Karen told me he ended the relationship. I believe her. If I didn't believe he had ended it, I would have reported him." He nudges the bridge of his glasses again.

"Did you make the realization yourself, or did Jamila Jagger tell you about Karen and Dr. Armistead's relationship?"

"How would Jamila know?" He nudges the bridge of his glasses and squints at me.

I tell him about Jamila's chance encounter with Karen and Dr. Armistead at the movies. "When she met Karen, she may have recognized her name from the patient files of either you or Dr. Armistead."

"Jamila? Interesting…" He rubs his chin with his fingers. "Why would she kill him if she caught him doing something wrong? Wouldn't it be the other way around? Wouldn't Dr. Armistead kill Jamila to stop her from exposing him?"

I give the highlights of my theory that Jamila hacked into Dr. Armistead's computer and he found out. Emory follows along, intrigued. You'd think after listening to other people's drama all day, every day, he'd be indifferent to the ins and outs of Dr. Armistead's life, but he's enthralled.

"That makes sense," Emory utters under his breath, his gaze fixed on the wall behind the sofa.

"What makes sense?" I ask.

"Hmmm?" He comes out of his trance, looks at me, and nudges his glasses.

"You said, 'that makes sense.' What did you mean?" I ask again.

"Jamila was anxious during our dinner on Friday. She had trouble sitting still. I assumed it was social anxiety. She insisted on helping in the kitchen. You know, plating the food, carrying it to the dining room, that type of thing. I *assumed* she was trying to keep busy and be helpful."

"So, you're saying Jamila had the opportunity to put caffeine in Dr. Armistead's food and drink," I state for clarification.

"Quite possibly," he says reaching for his phone. "I'm texting Charmaine to ask if she noticed the same thing." His thumbs move quickly across the keyboard on his phone. He sends the text then looks at me and nudges his glasses. *I'm* tempted to text Charmaine and ask her how she copes with Emory's incessant eyeglass-nudging. "But this would mean it wasn't Karen," he says, shaking his head. "I was sure it was Karen."

"Sorry about that," Jess says, re-entering the room. "Is everyone OK?" She looks at me, and I smile and wink.

"It's all good. I think our time is up," I say, standing up and hoisting my bag over my shoulder.

We thank each other and say our goodbyes, then Emory holds the door for Jess and me as we leave.

"Megan…" He touches my elbow as I step into the hall.

I tell Jess I'll catch up. She steps into Adam's office to wait for me, loitering near the open door.

I turn to Emory and smile. "Yes?"

He moves in uncomfortably close. "Is the computer still in Karen's trunk? It needs to be surrendered to the police," he whispers, nudging his glasses.

"It was," I assure him quietly as I shift my weight to put a bit more space between us. "Darby Morris took Karen and the computer to the Harmony Lake Police Station."

"You mean Harmony Hills," Emory corrects me. "Harmony Hills is handling the investigation."

"No, I mean Harmony Lake," I insist. "Darby said someone from HHPD would pick it up. He said taking it to HLPD was the most immediate way to secure it while he questioned Karen."

"That's a relief." Emory purses his lips into a tight smile. "Thank goodness it found its way into the right hands."

IT SMELLS WEIRD IN HERE. What is that smell? It's making my stomach roil.

"Hi, everyone." I smile and put the tray of coffee cups on the counter, then bend down to greet Sophie.

I try not to drink coffee after lunch, but today requires extra caffeine.

I stand up and reach for my coffee. The charity knitters–who never visited Knitorious on a Thursday until Eric started working here–aren't knitting. They're frozen in place with their knitting on their laps, and their needles paused mid-stitch. The tableau reminds me of the statue game we played when we were kids and would freeze and see who could hold their pose the longest. They look at me intently, like they're waiting for me to do a trick or something.

"Do I have something on my face?" I ask, thankfully distracted from the mysterious stench. I run my hand across my mouth and chin, checking for food. "Is everything OK?" I pause. They look at me, then each other. "What's going on?" I demand.

"She doesn't know," Mrs. Roblin says.

Does she mean me? She must mean me.

"What don't I know?" I ask, bracing myself for whatever it is I don't know.

Eric strolls out of the back room. We all look at him.

"Did you get my text?" he asks when he sees me.

I shake my head. "My hands were full." I nudge his coffee toward him. "And my phone is buried in my purse."

"She hasn't heard." Mrs. Vogel brings Eric up to speed.

"Charmaine was arrested in connection with the break-in at Armistead's office," Eric says calmly.

But it was Jamila. I showed Darby the proof.

I can't help but give a small gasp. "Charmaine Solomon?" I'm so stymied that I have trouble formulating a response. "It wasn't…" I shake my head as though it will make me less confused. "Who told you?"

"I heard it from Darby," he replies. "I'm not sure how everyone else found out." He gestures vaguely at the charity knitters who have now resumed knitting. Their eyes might be firmly fixed on their needles, but their ears are focussed on what Eric and I are saying.

"It's all over town," a charity knitter pipes up over the out-of-sync clicking of knitting needles.

"The texts started about twenty minutes ago," adds another one.

I reach into my bag, pull out my phone and, ignoring the slew of missed messages, check the time. Twenty minutes ago, I was in line at Latte Da waiting to order. Before that, Jess and I talked at our cars for about ten minutes after we left Emory's office. And before that, we spent about ten minutes chatting with Adam in his office.

It must have happened after Jess and I left Dr. Solomon's office. Surely, if he'd received a call or message while we were there that his wife had been arrested, he would've been too shocked to continue our session.

I take a deep breath and raise my coffee to my lips when the unpleasant stink once again assaults my nose. "Is that… cabbage?" I ask, my nostrils twitching as I try to place the odour.

"Cabbage rolls," Eric replies, nodding. "Would you like some?"

I don't like cabbage rolls. The smell is making me nauseous. I shake my head. "No, thank you."

"Mrs. Willows made them," Mrs. Roblin informs me. "There's plenty." Ah, of course, cabbage rolls are today's food offering to Eric from his fan club.

"They smell wonderful," I lie. I'm sure to someone who appreciates a good cabbage roll, Mrs. Willows's rolls smell tempting, but no cabbage roll will ever smell pleasant to me. "I ate." Another lie. "But thank you." I smile. "I have a few emails I have to respond to. I'll be in the back if anyone needs me." I shove my purse under the counter, grab the laptop, my coffee and phone, then hightail it to the back room.

The emails are a ruse. There's nothing in my inbox that requires my immediate attention. The truth is, I'm eager to prop open the back door and air out the store. I hold the door open and kick the brick in front of it to keep it open. I'm worried the cabbage-roll smell might cling to the yarn. I'm sure I'm not the only knitter who would never buy yarn that smells like over-cooked cabbage.

"Darby says Charmaine confessed," Eric explains, closing the door that separates the back room and the store. "Apparently someone caught her in the evidence locker, looking for the laptop Karen gave to Darby."

Why would Charmaine suddenly confess? So far, she has cooperated minimally with the investigation into Dr. Armistead's murder. What would cause her to go from barely cooperative to making a confession?

"Did she get the laptop?" I ask, opening the door to the store, then leading Eric to the open back door. We step outside and stand in the parking lot, careful to stay within sight of the backroom in case any curious charity knitters suddenly appear. "I don't want to close the door to the store, because I'm trying to dissipate that smell."

"Sorry about that," Eric replies. "It would be rude not to eat one. I heated it up in the microwave."

"Do you like cabbage rolls?" I've never seen him eat one, and I don't think I could stomach going home to this smell in the house.

"Meh," he says, wrinkling his nose. "They're not my favourite." He shakes his head. "Anyway, no, Charmaine didn't get her hands on the laptop. Forensics already picked it up."

"That's a relief," I say. "But it couldn't have been Charmaine who broke into Dr. Armistead's office. Could it?" Briefly, I doubt myself. "I proved it was Jamila. You saw the proof. Darby saw the proof. Jamila doctored her store's security footage, so she'd have an alibi. And she's on the footage at the medical centre at the time the break-in occurred. It doesn't make sense."

"They could be working together," Eric suggests. "If they are, the race is on for one of them to turn against the other in exchange for a deal. The truth will come out. We have to wait and let Darby do his thing."

I nod. "Trying to get to the laptop was a desperate move and isn't Charmaine's style," I theorize. "Charmaine is strategic. Every move she makes is carefully planned. It's hard to believe she'd spontaneously confess to a crime."

Something isn't right about Charmaine's confession. She gave it up too easily. If she had gotten her hands on the laptop, it would have been obvious it was her. There are cameras, locks, and procedures to keep evidence safe from prying intruders. But if she managed to erase whatever she doesn't want the police to find on that laptop, she would have been charged with evidence tampering or some such thing instead of computer hacking, stalking, or even murder. Charmaine might have decided that getting caught tampering with evidence is the lesser of two evils.

"Charmaine was at the medical centre the day of the

break-in. You saw her on the security footage. She had the opportunity to break into Armistead's office," Eric reminds me.

"You think she faked a cracked tooth? As an excuse for being at the medical centre at the same time as the break in?" I ask. "Jess told me herself that Charmaine had an emergency procedure to fix it."

Eric shrugs. "Maybe she had time to get her tooth fixed *and* turn over Armistead's office. The police will figure out the timing."

I make a mental note to text Jess and ask her exactly what time Charmaine showed up with her cracked tooth, and exactly what time she left with her fixed tooth.

"This is my fault," I confess. "I told Emory about Karen having Armistead's laptop at her house. He asked me if she gave it to the police, and I told him Darby took it to HLPD until HHPD could pick it up." I look at my feet, hanging my head in shame. "I shouldn't have told him that. Emory must've told Charmaine where it was."

"If that's the case," Eric takes my hand and tilts my chin up with his index finger, forcing me to look at him, "you helped solve it. If Charmaine didn't know the laptop was there, she wouldn't have been caught trying to get to it, and she wouldn't have confessed. She confessed to breaking into Armistead's office, she didn't confess to murdering him. His killer could still be out there." He tucks a stray curl behind my ear.

I disagree. I know the two crimes are related. The knot in my stomach insists they are.

"My gut tells me otherwise," I say.

"Are you sure it's instinct and not the smell of cabbage rolls you feel in your stomach?"

"I'm positive."

CHAPTER 24

I inhale deeply, sniffing for any trace of cabbage roll. I think it's gone. I hope it's gone. I came in early to check the odour situation at the store and air it out again if necessary.

"What do you think, Soph? Can you smell anything?" I ask as I detach her leash. "Let's leave this open just in case." I use my foot to slide the brick up against the back door, forcing it to stay open.

"Good morning, gorgeous," I say to April, answering my phone as I put Sophie's full water bowl on the floor.

"So, how's the smell?" she asks.

"It's either gone, or I'm immune to it. I propped open the back door to air out the store, just in case."

A chill from the breeze coming through the open door sends a small shiver up my spine. I gather my pumpkin-coloured, hand-knit cardigan around my neck as thunder rumbles in the distance. It's supposed to rain today, and there's a foreboding thickness in the air.

April is tending to her dad and packing while her mum runs errands. When her mum returns home, April will leave to pick up our girls. While April and I talk about the weather

445

and how it might impact her drive to Toronto, then to Harmony Lake, I put in my AirPods and get busy processing the online orders that have come in since the last time I shipped online orders.

"I can't believe Charmaine would do something like that," April says after I tell her about Charmaine's arrest and her shocking confession.

"That's what I said," I agree. "But why confess to something she didn't do? And why else would she try to tamper with the evidence?"

"I don't know," April replies. "But her connection to Dr. Armistead must be deeper than we think."

"How do you mean?" I ask. "Aieeee!" I scream, pulling away from the hand gently touching my back. "You scared the life out of me." I put my hand on my chest.

"Megnificent! Are you OK, what's going on?"

"Sorry, April. I didn't mean to scream in your ear. Eric snuck up behind me and almost gave me a heart attack." I swat playfully at his arm with the skein of yarn I'm holding. "April, I'm going to put you on hold for a sec."

"Sorry, I didn't mean to scare you," Eric apologizes, trying unsuccessfully not to laugh. He hands me a coffee and nods at the skein of yarn I just smacked him with. "Is that your weapon of choice? It's not very lethal."

"It would be if the intruder has a wool allergy," I reply, defending my pathetic choice of weaponry.

"If someone with a wool allergy is stupid enough to break into a yarn store, they deserve what they get," he chuckles.

"Why are you here?" I ask. "You said you weren't coming in until this afternoon."

"To get your keys. I'm taking your car for an oil change and tune up, remember? I wanted to get it done before you left for Toronto. Here, take my keys in case you need them." He hands me his keys.

"That's thoughtful of you," I say, digging my keys out

from the bottom of my purse. "But I'm not going to Toronto, anymore," I remind him. "April is picking up the girls on her way home."

Eric shrugs. "I know, but it's booked. I may as well go."

"I'm back," I say to April, taking our call off hold after Eric leaves.

"He loves you," April informs me when I tell her Eric booked my car for service before my road trip today. "Some people say I love you, and some people take your car for an oil change, vacuum your dryer vents, and cover your air conditioner."

"Eric does all of the above," I respond. "Mostly out of love, but partly to keep his mind off this murder case that happened on his turf, but he's not allowed to investigate."

The first sip of coffee burns my tongue. I move the cup to the far corner of the counter and place it in time-out so it can think about what it's done and cool down enough not to scald me.

"What were we talking about?" she asks.

"Charmaine's surprise confession, I think?"

"Right!" April declares. "We were trying to figure out why Charmaine Solomon would want to hack into Dr. Armistead's computer."

"Whatever the reason," I respond, "could it be serious enough for her to want to kill him?"

I glance at the window just as Eric drives by in my car.

"Charmaine isn't a murderer!" April insists.

"And I didn't think she was a blackmailer, but she is," I counter.

We bounce ideas back and forth and come up with a few weak but possible reasons to explain why Charmaine might try to access Dr. Armistead's computer. None of them are supported by evidence, and none are a strong motive for murder.

"Maybe Darby is right," I admit, "and the spyware on

447

both my computer and Dr. Armistead's have nothing to do with his murder."

"*Alleged* spyware," April reminds me. "Right now, all we have is Karen's word that Dr. Armistead found spyware on his laptop. The police haven't confirmed it yet."

"You're right," I admit. "We can't eliminate Karen as a suspect yet. If Emory is telling the truth about Dr. Armistead ending the relationship, she has the strongest motive of all."

"And she knew about Dr. Armistead's allergy and where he would be the night he died," April adds. "You know who else is a good suspect?"

"Who?" I ask.

"Emory Solomon," April replies. "He had access to whatever Dr. Armistead ate and drank that night, and he knew Dr. Armistead was having an illicit relationship. Maybe Emory killed him for making the profession look bad."

"You don't think that's far-fetched?" I ask.

"Not to a crazy person," she justifies.

"Emory is so soft-spoken and non-threatening, though," I remark. "Dr. Armistead told Karen they were having dinner to discuss Dr. Armistead possibly purchasing Emory's practice. Why would you kill someone who you hope to sell something to?"

Cautiously, I attempt another sip of coffee. Ouch! Still too hot! What the heck? Coffee from Latte Da is never this hot. Must be a new barista, or a new machine, or something.

"The dangerous ones are always non-threatening," April tells me. "It's a ruse. They use it to their advantage. Lulled into a false sense of safety, the victim lowers their defenses, and boom! The culprit strikes!"

"If we were placing bets, I'd put my money on Jamila," I say. "She knew about Karen and Dr. Armistead, she has a history of digitally stalking people, I've seen her pick a lock with my own eyes, and she deleted Adam and me from her store's security footage, then insisted we weren't there."

"I think you're right," April agrees. "Jamila makes the most sense, but Charmaine must be involved somehow, or she wouldn't have tried to compromise evidence and admitted to breaking into Dr. Armistead's office."

My phone dings and I pull it out of my pocket.

Jess: Good morning! I looked at our office security footage and the footage of the main entrance for the twenty-eighth. Charmaine came straight to our office upon entering the building and exited the building immediately after leaving our office. There's no way she had time to break into Dr. Armistead's office and destroy it.

"She's still typing," I tell April after I read her the text message from Jess.

"If Jess is right, Charmaine couldn't have broken into his office. We're back to Jamila," April points out.

Jess: But her husband left our office right after Charmaine got in the dental chair. He didn't come back until she was done. In fact, after her procedure, she sat in our waiting room for a few minutes until he came back to get her.

"Oh. My. God."

"What is it, Megastar? What did she say?"

I read the text to April.

"Emory?" I ask in disbelief. "Why? What motive would Emory Solomon have for murdering Dr. Armistead?"

April says something, but it doesn't register in my brain because I'm in shock. In shock over the realization that Emory Solomon is the break-and-enter bandit and possible murderer.

I watch anxiously as three dots bounce on the screen, indicating Jess is typing another text.

"DID YOU HEAR ME?" April shouts. "You need to contact Darby. *Now*. He needs to know *now*."

"I hear you," I respond blankly. "She's still typing. I'm waiting in case there's more?"

"More?"

"More evidence."

"Megabear, screenshot those texts and send them to me. Just in case."

"Good idea."

I do as I'm told and send the screenshots to April.

"Got them," she confirms.

Jess: I'm with the property manager. We're looking at the footage from the 14th. I only recognize one person. They enter the building after Dr. Armistead leaves, and they leave the building shortly before he comes back.

Me: Who is it?

Jess: Hang on.

"Who is it?" April asks when I read her Jess's texts.

Suddenly, or finally, because every second feels like an hour while we wait for Jess to reveal the name, a photo pops up in my text conversation with Jess. A grainy, still image from the security footage in the medical centre lobby. I click the photo and enlarge it.

"Emory!"

No way!

I'm overcome with a sudden urge to close and lock the back door.

"Are you sure?" April asks. "Send me those texts, just in case."

I send the texts and photo to April, then indulge in a brief moment of panic.

"I was in his office yesterday, April!"

"I know. Listen, you need to text Darby. Right now."

"I will. Just let me close the back door and lock it. I feel too vulnerable with it open." I slip my phone into the pocket of my cardigan and walk toward the back of the store. "What if Charmaine's arrest made him more unstable, and he's out there all…murdery…and looking for revenge?"

Halfway between the counter and the backroom, the back

door closes with its distinct click. Eric! He must have forgotten something.

Briefly, a wave of relief washes over me.

Very briefly.

Sophie starts barking.

It's not Eric. She doesn't bark at Eric. She rarely makes a noise when he shows up, except for the occasional high-pitched yelp-whine.

This isn't the friendly, excited bark that she uses for other friendly visitors either.

Each bark is punctuated with a snarl. This is a warning bark. Low growls between each snarly bark warn the intruder that Sophie means business. Her upper lip is curled back, and she's baring her small but powerful teeth. I've only seen her do this once before; earlier this week when Charmaine was here.

"Eric?" I call out, hoping Sophie is wrong.

But Sophie is never wrong.

"Not Eric."

I stop abruptly in the doorway between the store and the back room.

"You," I say, taking a backwards step away from the back room.

Away from danger.

CHAPTER 25

"ARE YOU EXPECTING SOMEONE ELSE, MEGAN?"

"Yes. Eric will be back any second." I summon my most convincing voice.

"I don't think so." Emory Solomon smirks and shakes his head. "Two old ladies knitting at Latte Da said Eric won't be here until this afternoon."

Each backwards step I take away from Emory, he takes an equal step toward me. I need to position myself with something between us. We already passed the harvest table, so the counter is my next best option.

"Megster! Is that Emory?" April asks through my AirPods.

"Yes," I say to April and Emory. "He's not working until this afternoon, but he'll be back any minute. He lives upstairs."

"I'll take my chances," Emory says, not sounding at all concerned about being interrupted by a muscle-bound, six-foot-plus cop who does hand-to-hand combat training as a hobby.

Evidently, Dr. Emory Solomon has lost his mind.

"Clear your throat if you're in danger," April says to me, before she yells to her father, demanding to know where his cell phone is.

"Ahem... hem... hmph." I bring my hand to my throat to make it look real for Emory. I also fuss with my hair and ensure my curls are covering my AirPods. If I'm going to die here and now, April will hear everything and can tell my story. I hope she heard me clearing my throat over Sophie's loud barking.

"Frog in your throat?" Emory asks, using his forefinger to nudge the bridge of his glasses closer to his face. "No worries. I have something that will clear that up."

He pulls a syringe from the pocket of his tweed sports jacket.

I hate needles and the sight of this one, in a psychotic murderer's hand, makes me shudder.

"Is that caffeine? Did you have some left over after you murdered Dr. Armistead?" I ask. "I hate to disappoint you, but I'm not allergic to caffeine. Between my coffee and chocolate habits, I probably have a much higher caffeine tolerance than most people."

Emory shakes his head. "It's not caffeine." He nudges the bridge of his glasses and smirks. "It's Benzylpenicillin."

OK, that would kill me.

Benzylpenicillin, also known as penicillin G, is the liquid form of penicillin. The form used in injections.

I knew I shouldn't have included my penicillin allergy on my New Patient Information form yesterday!

"Where did you get a vial of penicillin?" I don't care where he got it; it's a stall tactic. I need to keep him talking while I come up with a plan to get Sophie and me out of here alive.

"He has penicillin?" April whispers through the phone. "How does he know about your allergy?"

"I have my ways." He winks. It's the creepiest, most unsettling wink ever.

I glance behind me. Almost at the counter now.

"Why do you want to kill me? Wasn't killing Dr. Armistead enough?"

"Because this is all your fault," Emory hisses. "I won't allow Charmaine to take the fall for me, and if I have to go down, I'm taking you with me."

The cap is still on the syringe, a good sign. A sign that he isn't planning to kill me right away.

Can I make it to the front door, unlock it, and get out before Emory catches me? Risky. Especially in these peep-toe ankle boots. Stupid heels! What was I thinking, putting form before function?!

I could run through the display window. I'd be scratched up and bloody, but it would attract the attention of everyone around. Would I be able to burst through the window? Or does that only happen in movies and on TV? If it doesn't work, he'll jab me with the needle, and I'll probably be dead before anyone can get in here to save me. I don't want to die in the display window. I don't want to die period. Also, if I die, Emory gets what he wants. That can't happen. I won't let him win.

"It's my fault you killed Dr. Armistead?" I ask.

"No, it's your fault the case is still open, and it's your fault Charmaine was arrested and charged," Emory replies. "Armistead's murder should've been an open-and-shut case. I planned it so the evidence would point to Karen. And if by chance the police eliminated Karen, I made sure there was enough evidence to frame Jamila. But you inserted yourself into the investigation and wouldn't let it go. Now my wife's reputation is ruined, and her career is over. Because of you."

"To be fair," I say calmly with my hands in front of my chest, palms facing out, "I wouldn't have gotten involved if your wife didn't order Jamila to spy on me."

The counter is between us now.

Sophie is at my feet. When we stop walking, she stops barking. She sits at attention, intermittently curling her upper lip and emitting a low-key growl, just loud and frequent enough to remind us of her unwavering diligence. Her gaze is laser-focussed on Emory. He seems oblivious to her presence.

"I'm still here, Megapop. I'm listening and recording everything I hear. I'm calling Darby on my dad's phone. Help is coming. Whatever happens, don't hang up. I love you!"

I love you too, April.

"I understand why you're angry at me, but why did you kill Dr. Armistead? What did he do to you?" Please keep talking and leave the cap on that syringe.

"Because I'm tired of working hard, playing by the rules, and barely earning a living wage. Do you know how hard it is to watch someone—who's a bad therapist, by the way—have their patients handed to them while they break all the rules and sit back getting rich?"

"Not really," I admit quietly. "I get that Dr. Armistead broke rules when he dated a former patient. And I know he's done at least one other shady thing in the past."

Emory laughs and tosses his head back. "See?" he asks when he lowers his chin again. "That's exactly what I mean. He did whatever he wanted and got away with it. Where was karma to teach him a lesson?"

Not sure whether this is a rhetorical question, I shrug and shake my head trying to appear sympathetic. "What do you mean when you say his patients were handed to him? Did he inherit his practice or something?"

Emory puts the syringe of penicillin on the counter and places his hand on top of it. He's a little less agitated than he was a few moments ago. I need him to let his guard down a little more so I can make a run for it.

"Let me answer your question with a question, Megan."

He nudges his glasses with his finger again. He really should get them tightened.

Focus, Megan. "OK," I say.

"If Armistead weren't dead, would you and Jess have come to me or him for your appointment yesterday?"

"Um…" I don't know how to answer this. If Armistead were alive, Jess and I wouldn't have gone to either of them.

"Just tell him you hadn't thought about it," April whispers in my ear.

"To be honest, we hadn't thought about it," I reply. "I mean you were the only option so…"

"Exactly!" Emory slaps his hand on top of the syringe, keeping it securely under his palm. "I work in Harmony Lake. The residents of Harmony Lake should be *my patients*. They should come to *me* for their counselling and psychotherapy needs. Am I right??" His eyes are bulging, and he's nodding enthusiastically. "But they have this small-town paranoia that everyone is watching them and talking about them, so instead of coming to me, they go to Harmony Hills where they can see a therapist more discreetly."

"I see. That must be frustrating." By showing him some sympathy, I'm hoping he'll be less eager to kill me.

"He's completely lost it, Megan. Please be careful." This must be serious if April is calling me Megan instead of a punny nickname.

"He used to gloat about it. He'd tease me about my small-town practice and how much time I must have to pursue other interests," Emory explains. "Do you know how many referrals I've received from Dr. Armistead? Ever?"

"I have no idea."

"Guess."

"I don't know," I shrug, mentally grasping for a reasonable number.

"Just GUESS!" He slams his fist on the counter.

"TWENTY?" I shout while at the same time, April shouts, "Fifteen" in my ear.

"None. Zero. Zilch. Nada." Emory touches the tip of his thumb to the tip of his fingers, making a zero.

"Wow. That's…."

"Awful?" He finishes my sentence. "Unprofessional?" He finishes it again. "Sel-fish?" He prolongs each syllable.

"It certainly sounds unfair and frustrating," I sympathize. "So, were Dr. Armistead's patients supposed to transfer to you after he died? Was that the plan?"

"Partly," Emory admits, nudging the bridge of his glasses. "But mostly, I had to kill him because if I didn't, he would've gotten me in trouble, and he would've gotten away with it. There's no way I was going to allow him to ruin my life and walk away unscathed."

When Emory nudges the bridge of his glasses yet again, I notice how thick the lenses are. I bet he can't see a thing without them. He'd probably be defenseless and unable to chase me. Focus, Megan. Keep him talking.

"What did he threaten you with?" I ask. "I believe you, by the way. I know for a fact that a few years ago, Dr. Armistead tried to bribe a cop, and when the cop refused, he filed a complaint and got the cop in trouble. I know he was capable of doing bad things and hurting people." I want to convince Emory we're on the same side.

Emory takes a deep breath and lets it out. "When I found out he was dating Karen, I knew it could be his downfall. I became determined to prove it. This would be the thing he couldn't weasel out of. I recruited Jamila to help me. She owed my wife a favour, you see."

"Charmaine and Jamila both told me how Charmaine used her influence to prevent Jamila from being charged when she was caught hacking computers for the mayor."

"Because that's the kind of person my wife is. She's selfless and forgiving." Emory annunciates each word clearly and emphatically.

I would have said opportunistic and corrupt, but I'm not about to argue with someone who's clenching a vial of something that would kill me, so I nod and summon my most sympathetic and understanding smile.

"What did you recruit Jamila to do for you?"

Once again, he nudges the bridge of his glasses. If I had an eyeglass repair kit handy, I'd offer to tighten them for him just so I wouldn't have to watch him constantly nudge them anymore.

"She gave me the password to Mac's computer. She knows it because she's done tech support work for him."

"She didn't install spyware on his laptop?" I ask suspiciously.

"No," he replies. "That was me. But it was no use. He deleted Karen's patient file from his database. The only proof I found that she was ever his patient was an old patient list. Not enough to prove that he was breaking the rules. He would have slithered out of an accusation."

The patient list Emory just mentioned must be the same one that was posted online.

"But Dr. Armistead found the spyware and knew it was you," I say as though I already know it's true and not just a theory. "Did he threaten to expose you?"

Emory nods. "I didn't know he'd found the spyware. He didn't let on that he knew it was there or that he suspected I did it. I only intended to leave it on his computer long enough to get the evidence I needed to prove he deserved to lose his license. But the evidence wasn't there so…"

"You went back to his office on the twenty-eighth to delete the spyware, or steal the computer, or something, but it was too late. Dr. Armistead switched computers. The computer you tampered with was gone. Angry and frustrated, you destroyed his office," I say, finishing his thought. "Who taught you how to pick a lock?"

"Charmaine," he replies. "Years ago. It's a handy skill to have."

Apparently, it's also a common one. I'm starting to feel like the only person in Harmony Lake who doesn't know how to pick a lock.

"We have to learn how to pick locks," April whispers as if she's in my head.

"But Jamila was at the medical centre on the twenty-eighth. Why was she there if you were acting alone?"

"My wife was having a dental procedure. If the dental office called because Charmaine had some kind of emergency, I would have to go. Jamila was there to finish the job if I couldn't."

Very conscientious.

"Why was Dr. Armistead at your house for dinner last Friday?" I ask. "You obviously didn't like each other. Why did you invite him over?"

"That's when all of this went wrong," Emory explains, and yet again nudges his glasses. "I told him Charmaine and I might be moving away from Harmony Lake, and I invited him to dinner under the guise of discussing referring my patients to him. I planned to confront Armistead with my evidence about his relationship with Karen. In exchange for not reporting him to our regulating body, I wanted him to take his practice elsewhere and refer his clients to me when he left town."

"I take it he didn't agree," I probe.

He shakes his head. "On the contrary. He showed me his proof that I hacked into his computer and compromised his patient files. He wanted money—money we don't have—or he said he would report me. My career would be over, and I would face criminal charges. I had to stop him."

"And you just happened to have lots of caffeine lying around?"

"It's easily obtainable online. I didn't want to use it, but was prepared to use it. He left me with no choice."

There it is. His confession.

"You're doing great, Megalicious. I'm recording everything." April's reassuring voice in my ear gives me comfort and makes me less afraid.

"I put it in his pudding and his after-dinner scotch," Emory continues. "Immediately after dinner, I dispatched Jamila to save us a table at the pub, and Armistead and I had our little disagreement. I showed him my evidence, and he showed me his. He left quickly and…You know the rest." He waves toward me in a sweeping motion, then nudges the bridge of his glasses with his index finger.

Emory says he didn't want to use the caffeine but was prepared to if necessary. However, he fed it to Dr. Armistead *before* they had their after-dinner confrontation. He knew exactly what he was doing. This was premeditated murder, not a spontaneous crime of opportunity.

"Why did you post Dr. Armistead's patient list?" I ask.

"I had Jamila do that. It was intended to distract you." He nudges his glasses again. "It didn't work. When Charmaine and I ran into you at Tiffany's on Monday, she mentioned you seemed to be sleuthing and asking a lot of questions. I hoped the list would give you something else to focus on."

If I made a drinking game where I take a sip of wine every time Emory nudges his glasses, my liver would fail, and I would die.

"It almost worked," I tell him. "I was worried about more private information being posted if I kept asking questions, but I persevered. So, Charmaine doesn't know you killed Dr. Armistead?"

Emory shakes his head. "She's convinced it was Karen or possibly Jamila. I have her fooled. She'd never consider me a murderer. But she does know that I installed spyware on Armistead's computer."

"That's why she tried to find it in the evidence locker yesterday," I theorize. "And why she confessed. She was protecting you. She loves you."

"I love her too," he garbles almost intelligibly. Emory's eyes well up, and he lifts his hand off the syringe and pinches the bridge of his nose between his thumb and forefinger, lifting his glasses toward his forehead.

This is it. This is my opportunity to get away.

CHAPTER 26

WHILE MY RIGHT hand sweeps the syringe off the counter, my left hand reaches across the counter, tears the glasses from Emory's face, and tosses them toward the display window. The syringe slides along the floor and disappears under the shelves of discounted yarn.

Sophie jumps into action, adding to the chaos by barking and snapping at Emory's ankles.

Taking advantage of his semi-blind confusion, I try to run around the counter and past him. He reaches out and grabs the sleeve of my sweater. Before he can get a better grip, I wriggle my arm out of the sleeve, then rip the other sleeve from my other arm, and let the cardigan fall to the floor.

I grab the coffee from the time-out corner of the countertop and throw it at his head.

Instinctively, Emory raises both hands to his coffee-soaked face.

"Run, Soph!" I yell, running toward the back door.

Her snarling and growling get fainter as I get closer to the back door.

I stop and turn. With the hem of a pant leg in her mouth,

Sophie tugs it repeatedly and growls. She's preventing Emory from getting up. She's stopping him from coming after me.

"Come on, Soph! Let's go! Sophie!"

"Run, Megan. Get out. Sophie will be fine," April shouts in my ear.

No. I can't do it. I can't leave Sophie behind.

I tune out April's voice encouraging me to run. I look around, searching desperately for inspiration.

The brick we use to prop open the back door is on the floor just inside the door.

I run into the back room and lunge toward the brick.

It's heavier than it looks, but brick in hand, I run back to the counter.

Sophie still has Emory's pant leg clenched between her teeth. Snarling, she tugs and shakes her head vigorously while dodging his attempts to kick her away with his other foot.

If he hurts Sophie, so help me, a life sentence will be the least of his problems.

Clawing at the floor with both hands, he tries to slide his body away from the determined corgi while also frantically groping the floor in front of him, presumably in search of his glasses or the syringe of penicillin.

I run around the counter to Sophie, being careful not to get within arm's reach of Emory.

"Sophie, come!" Focussed on keeping the intruder down, she ignores me. "Soph! Let's go!" I reach down, place my hand under her belly, and slide her backwards toward me. "It's OK! Let's go!" She yanks her head away from him, tearing off a swatch of pant leg. She lets me pick her up as she releases the swatch of fabric from between her teeth.

Holding Sophie under my left arm like a football—she's also heavier than she looks—I clutch the brick in my right hand and run to the other side of the counter.

Almost on his feet, Emory lurches toward us. I leap back and avoid his reach. Sophie snarls and snaps threateningly.

He's mostly on his feet, albeit unsteadily. He's disoriented. Probably because he can't see without his glasses, or because the corgi attack combined with the unfamiliar surroundings have made him discombobulated, or all of the above. Nevertheless, Emory perseveres. He reaches for the counter to steady himself and is able to stand up all the way.

"Overhand or underhand? What's the best way to throw a brick?"

"Overhand! I don't know. Just throw it!" April instructs.

I hurl the brick toward him.

Because the brick is heavy and I am weak, it barely hits him. But it hits him nonetheless, awkwardly on the shoulder, with just enough impact to knock him off balance. He slips on my discarded sweater and the coffee covered floor, allowing Sophie and I to get away from him while he recovers.

"Great! I just gave him a brick. He has a brick!"

"Just run, Megan!" April cheers.

At the back door, I fiddle with the locks. It takes me longer than usual with only one available hand, but I manage to turn the first lock, then the second.

Sophie's barking elevates in volume and urgency, causing me to turn around.

Dragging my coffee-soaked cardigan behind him with the foot that Sophie attacked, Emory is in the doorway between the store and the back room. His left arm hangs limply at his side, and he squints hard as he flails his good arm in front of him with the brick gripped tightly in his hand.

Still looking behind me in case Emory lobs the brick at us, I throw the back door open and run.

I make it two steps when I run into a wall of... person?

Without taking his eyes off Emory, Eric puts one hand on each of my arms, lifts Sophie and I off the ground, moves us out of his way, and runs inside.

When he places us on the ground, I lose my balance on the uneven asphalt in these impractical heels. I stumble backward, struggling to stay upright and not drop Sophie. I stagger backwards into the corner of the door frame and come to a stop when it digs into my upper back. At least I didn't fall and injure Sophie and I in the process.

"Ouch!" I blurt.

Distracted by my outcry, Eric turns and looks at me with his left fist clenching the lapel of Emory's tweed sport jacket. Emory raises the brick above him; he's about to smash it into Eric's head.

"Eric! Brick!" I shout, pointing behind him with my free hand.

"Eric, turn around!" Connie is beside me. Where did she come from?

Eric releases Emory's lapel, raises his hand, and grabs the brick, blocking Emory's attempt to smash Eric in the head.

Despite having only two fully functional limbs and impaired eyesight, Emory doesn't let go of the brick and struggles to regain control of it from Eric.

Eric makes a fist with his right hand and delivers an upper cut to Emory's jaw. The thud of fist against bone is followed by a grunt from Emory, who immediately drops to his knees and releases his grip on the brick. His head hangs low, with his chin almost resting on his chest.

Eric lowers the brick to his hip, then tosses it aside.

Connie wraps her arm protectively around me, digging her fingers into my shoulder and pulling me close to her. I wince slightly because my back hurts where it hit the door frame.

Still on his knees, Emory raises his head and looks up at Eric. His jaw bulges where Eric punched him. His misaligned jaw, limp arm, and damaged leg are all on the same side, making him look more like a stroke victim than a freakishly determined, maniacal killer. He wriggles. I think he's trying to get up. Emory's determination is resolute. I wish I was as committed to anything as Emory is to not staying down.

When he sees the door, Emory lunges his upper body toward Connie, Sophie, and me. Instinctively, Connie and I cringe and lean away from him. Instinctively, Sophie barks and growls while making doggy paddle movements with her front paws as if she's trying to swim toward our attacker. Sophie and I have very different instincts when it comes to how we react to danger.

Eric once again grabs Emory by the lapel and restrains him. Eric makes a fist with his right hand while lifting Emory up slowly by his lapel. Eric pulls back his fist. Oh my god, he's going to punch Emory again!

"Eric, No! Enough!" I yell.

"Finish him off, Eric!" Connie shouts beside me, pumping a fist in solidarity with Eric.

Connie and I have very different instincts when it comes to how we react to violence.

Darby Morris sweeps past us so quickly the breeze he leaves in his wake moves my hair.

He grabs Eric's fist and positions himself between Eric and Emory.

Eric lets go of Emory's lapel and steps back. Emory collapses forward.

A flurry of blue police uniforms descends on the store and the parking lot. Too many voices speaking at the same time, the clomping of boots on pavement, and the idling engines of patrol cars drown out the thumping of my racing heart.

"Finish him off?" I ask, looking at Connie. "Really?"

"Yes. That horrible man deserves everything he got and more!" Connie insists.

With Darby on Emory-duty, Eric turns away from them. The white-hot anger emanating from him is palpable. He looks agitated. His brow is furrowed. His jaw is clenched. His fists are clenched. Everything is clenched.

I follow Eric's gaze as he takes in the scene around him. We make eye contact, and he narrows his eyes and moves aggressively toward us. Reflexively, Connie and I recoil in unison. Eric puts his hands up in front of him like he's surrendering.

"It's OK. It's over," Eric says.

Poof! His anger is gone.

Sophie makes that high-pitched yelp-whine she only makes for him. I can feel her tail wagging under my arm. I shift my weight and switch Sophie to my other arm because the one I've been holding her with is cramping. Eric holds his hands out to take her from me, and Sophie practically leaps into his arms. I shake out my arms and stretch my neck. Connie brushes my hair away from my face and tucks it behind my ear, her hand grazing my AirPod.

I forgot about April!

"April! April? I lost her." I pat my hips and butt area, searching for my phone, then remember where I put it. "My phone is in the pocket of my cardigan." I'm too far away and the AirPods lost the Bluetooth connection to my phone.

I'll miss my pumpkin-coloured cardigan. I've worn it every fall for the last five years.

"It's OK, my dear. We'll call her from my phone," Connie replies.

Since they're no use to me without my phone, I remove my AirPods and place them in Connie's waiting hand. She drops them in her purse and takes out her phone. "I'll call April and fill her in." Connie gives me a quick, tight shoulder-squeeze, and I try not to grimace when it hurts my back. She steps away from the commotion to talk to April.

"Is your back OK? I'm so sorry." Eric's eyes are full of worry and regret. "I can't believe I hurt you. I didn't mean to. I *would never*…"

I reach out and touch his forearm. "It's fine," I say, interrupting him before he can finish his sentence. "You didn't do

467

it. I lost my balance and stumbled into the corner of the doorway." I point to my cute but non-functional ankle boots. "I wore the wrong footwear to outrun a killer."

"I'm so sorry," he starts to apologize again, shaking his head. I wave away his comment. "We'll get the paramedics to check you over and look at your back."

"I think he needs the paramedics more than me." I point to Emory who is face down on the floor with his hands secured behind his back.

"Hi, Megan."

"Hi, Amy."

Amy is a police officer with the Harmony Lake Police Department. Seeing another friendly face, I'm suddenly overwhelmed. My throat is thick, and my eyes fill with tears. I take a minute to compose myself.

"Would you like to sit down?" Amy asks. "My patrol car is right here."

A few minutes alone to process what happened sounds like a good idea.

"Thank you, Amy, we'll wait upstairs. The apartment isn't part of the crime scene." Eric looks at me. "Is it?"

I shake my head.

"April is fine. I told her you'll call her as soon as you and your phone are reunited," Connie says, approaching us.

"Amy, do you think I'd be allowed to leave for a little while?" My question raises multiple objections from both Connie and Eric. "I want to take Sophie to the vet. She seems fine, but I'd like to have her examined, anyway. She put up quite a fight."

"Let me call the Animal Centre. I'm sure when they find out it's for Sophie, they'll be more than happy to make a house call."

"Thank you, Amy. That would be great."

Amy winks and rubs Sophie's head before she walks to her patrol car.

The Animal Centre is Harmony Lake's all-in-one animal shelter, veterinary hospital, animal sanctuary, and wildlife education centre. Sophie's previous owner was the founder and executive director. Sophie has a special relationship with the staff and volunteers.

Eric cuts a path through the horde of police officers so we can make our way inside to the stairs. He positions himself between the stairs and Emory, so Emory and I can't see each other. Though I highly doubt Emory can see much of anything without his glasses.

Eric places Sophie on one of the steps, and she races up the stairs to the apartment. Connie follows her, and I follow Connie.

CHAPTER 27

AFTER CHECKING MY VITAL SIGNS, the paramedic examines my back. She says there's no visible mark or swelling. It's tender when she pokes around, but not as tender as it was earlier. Together, we decide it's a minor bruise or soft tissue damage, and I'll bounce back in a day or two.

A uniformed officer comes upstairs to tell us the vet is here. Eric offers to take Sophie downstairs instead of bringing the veterinarian upstairs to his crowded apartment. Connie insists she'll go in his place and calls for Sophie to follow her downstairs. The paramedics pack up their gear and leave shortly after.

"I need a coffee so bad," I say, pulling away from Eric's tight embrace. "Want one?"

He shakes his head. "I saw your first coffee all over the floor of the store. The store's a mess, Megan. It looks like ten people had a struggle, not two. Are you sure you weren't hurt?"

"I'm fine, honestly," I assure him as I put a pod in the coffee machine and close the lid.

"I'm sorry I wasn't here." His eyes and face are downcast. He's blaming himself.

"None of this is your fault," I remind him. "You couldn't have known a deranged psychotherapist would walk into my closed store determined to kill me. No one could've known. Trust me, if I thought it was even a tiny possibility, I would have worn different shoes and left my pumpkin-coloured cardigan at home."

"I think I might've killed him if he hurt you," he confesses, looking relieved to say it out loud.

I nod. "I was scared you were going to punch him again."

"I wasn't, I swear," he insists. "I wanted to scare him. To make him feel as scared as you felt when he trapped you."

"I think it worked," I confirm. "For all of us."

"I'm sorry." He sounds defeated. "I didn't mean to scare you or Connie. I would *never* hurt you. Or threaten you..."

"I know," I interrupt before he launches into a long list of all the things he'd never do. I retrieve the mug of coffee and hesitantly take a small sip. Once burnt, twice shy, as they say. The temperature is perfect, so I take a bigger sip and put the mug on the counter. "This is the first time I've ever seen you angry. It was a shock. I mean, I've seen you annoyed and frustrated, but not angry. Not like this."

It was also the first time I've ever witnessed a real-life punch. The only punches I've seen before today were in movies or TV shows. They're scarier in real life.

"I wasn't angry," Eric corrects me. "I was scared. He was a mess, and I was terrified you were in worse shape."

If that's what scared-Eric looks like, I don't think I want to see what angry-Eric looks like.

I take his hand, and he winces and sucks in his breath.

"The paramedics should've checked you over," I say, looking at his red, swollen knuckles. How could this hand that gently rubs Sophie and delicately tucks my hair behind my ear almost break a man's face? If I hadn't seen it with my own eyes, I wouldn't believe it.

"I'll be OK. Nothing is broken," he says. "Battle scars." He smiles and winks, then raises my hand and kisses it.

"Why did you come back, anyway?" I ask. "You weren't gone long enough for an oil change and tune up."

"Your car never made it into the service bay," Eric confirms. "One of the charity knitters phoned me just as I arrived at the dealership."

"Lucky they have your phone number," I respond.

"Yeah, how did they get it?"

"They have their ways," I reply.

"Anyway, she said two knitters saw Emory at Latte Da, and he was acting strangely. They mobilized their forces and kept eyes on him while he wandered around Water Street. They called me when they saw him loitering behind the store. I came back right away."

"Thank you for coming to my rescue," I say, standing on my tippy toes to give him a kiss. "Again."

"I didn't rescue you," Eric insists. "You saved yourself. I just restrained him until Darby arrived. I might have saved Emory, though. I'm not sure he would have survived another round with you and Sophie." He smirks, then adds sheepishly, "But if you insist on thanking me, I won't stop you."

"Do you hear that?" I ask, mid-kiss.

I hear it again and recognize Sophie's distinct scratch on the apartment door.

"She might be your fearless defender, but Sophie's timing sucks," Eric jokes on his way to let her in.

Darby follows Sophie into the apartment. They make themselves comfortable in an overstuffed leather chair.

After a few pleasantries and Darby declines our offer of a beverage, he leans forward and opens his leather folio on the coffee table.

"The vet said to assure you that Sophie is fine, and in light of her heroic actions, she should get extra treats today," he says, scratching under her chin. She loves it and raises her head to give him better access.

"That's a relief," I say with a sigh.

"I'm taking her to the butcher later so she can pick out her own steak," Eric adds.

Darby asks about my back and any other injuries I have, then uncaps his fountain pen, lays it on his folio, and looks at me.

"What the hell happened down there, Megan? The store looks like a war zone, and Dr. Solomon's injuries are severe enough that he had to go to the hospital for treatment."

I shake my head and shrug.

"Was anyone else there with you?" Darby asks.

"Nope," I reply. "Just me and Sophie."

She perks up and wags her tail when she hears her name.

Darby points from Sophie to me. "You two did that to him? By yourselves?"

"Though she be but little, she is fierce," Eric says, quoting Shakespeare.

Is he talking about me or Sophie?

"Let's start at the top and work our way down," Darby suggests.

The top of what? I nod.

"Dr. Solomon wears glasses. He can barely see without them. Where are his glasses?"

"Somewhere near the display window or cozy seating area," I reply.

"And they got there how?"

I explain about the glasses while Darby takes notes.

"Can you explain the burn marks on Dr. Solomon's face?"

"I think there's a new barista at Latte Da," I reply. "Or a new machine, or something."

"I don't follow, Megan."

I explain how my coffee burnt me not once, but twice and was relegated to the time-out corner.

"So, that's why there's coffee all over the floor," Darby says. "What happened to Dr. Solomon's jaw? It's dislocated and possibly broken."

Eric raises his hand. "That one is on me," he confesses. "Self-defense. Emory was about to brain me with a brick."

"The brick we found nearby?" Darby clarifies.

We nod.

"And how did Dr. Solomon's shoulder get dislocated?"

"His shoulder is dislocated?" I'm stunned. "I swear the brick didn't hit him that hard!"

Eric tries unsuccessfully to stifle a laugh.

"Maybe when he slipped on my sweater on the wet floor, he fell in such a way that his shoulder dislocated?" I theorize.

"Good," Darby responds, writing in his book. "That explains how Dr. Solomon got hold of the brick he threatened Eric with. Do you always keep a brick in your yarn store?"

"We use it to prop open the back door when we're bringing in deliveries or airing out the cabbage smell."

"Of course, you do," Darby remarks.

"Now, what can you tell me about Dr. Solomon's shredded pant leg?"

I point to Sophie. I was hoping to leave her out of this. Our jurisdiction has tough dog biting laws. I'm afraid the authorities will quarantine her, or even put her down for biting Emory.

"She won't be in trouble for biting, will she, Darby? She was defending herself and me. If it weren't for her, we wouldn't have escaped, and at least one of us—me—would be dead. You know she's a good dog, Darby. She's gentle. She's never hurt anyone before. Ever. If anyone gets in trouble, Emory should be charged for trying to kick her..."

Darby raises his hand in a stop motion, and I cease my rambling defense of Sophie's actions. "Sophie's not in trouble, and she's not going anywhere. Did she sprain his ankle too?"

"He has a sprained ankle? I have no idea how that

happened unless he did it when he slipped on the wet floor." I shrug.

Darby reaches into his suit pocket and pulls out a small evidence bag containing a pill bottle.

"Did Dr. Solomon force you to take any of these? They were in the pocket of his sports jacket."

I shake my head.

"Did he force you to take anything else? Or did you witness him taking anything?"

I shake my head. "I've never seen those. What are they?"

"Sleeping pills. A lot of them."

"Maybe they were for another victim?" I suggest. "He planned to kill me with the syringe of penicillin."

"We didn't find a syringe of penicillin with Dr. Solomon," Darby interrupts loudly.

"Because it's under the shelves of discounted yarn," I tell him, then explain how it ended up there.

I wonder who the sleeping pills were for? Who else was on Emory Solomon's kill list?

CHAPTER 28

Button-up sweater, eight letters. Simple. C-A-R-D-I-G-A-N.

Speaking of cardigans, I finished my new sweater in time to wear it to Thanksgiving dinner, after all.

Last Friday, I wasn't allowed back in the store until the police finished gathering evidence, so instead of waiting upstairs, Sophie and I went home, and I finished the sleeves. Then I washed it and blocked it. By Sunday it was dry and ready to wear.

When Darby finally released the store on Friday, Connie asked him to wait an hour before notifying me so she, Phillip, and Marla could clean it. I have the most amazing friends. Connie even opened for a couple of hours when they were done. She was able to deal with the initial rush of nosy neighbours so when I came in the next morning, I didn't have to dodge as many questions as I was expecting.

The situation is public knowledge now. Everyone in town knows Emory killed Dr. Armistead.

They know Charmaine tried to tamper with evidence that implicated her husband, and they know Charmaine and the mayor were secretly hacking computers, spying on people, and using the information to blackmail people.

Unfortunately, the part that hasn't become public knowledge is the role Jamila played in the scandal.

Jamila was able to negotiate immunity from any charges in exchange for her cooperation. Somehow, the residents of Harmony Lake interpret this to mean that Jamila is some sort of cyber superhero who used her tech skills to expose the mayor, Charmaine, and Emory and bring down the corrupt pillars of our small community.

Rumour has it Jamila was a police informant and the intelligence she gathered was so sensitive, that not even the chief of police, Charmaine, knew what Jamila was up to. It's not my place to correct the rumours, and I would never say anything that could jeopardize Jamila's cooperation with the police.

Despite being viewed as a local hero, Jamila is gone. She left town to visit her family for Thanksgiving weekend and didn't come back. Her brother came back in her place. He's staying in her house and taking care of the store. According to him, Jamila wanted to spend some time with their parents, and he offered to take care of Bits'n'Bytes until she comes back. I have a feeling she won't be back.

It sounds like the mayor won't be back either. By the time everything hit the fan last Friday, the mayor and her husband were in Boca Raton, Florida where they apparently have a second home that no one in Harmony Lake knew about.

Citing health reasons, the mayor sent an open email to the town, tendering her resignation effective immediately. It turns out she's a dual Canadian-US citizen, and she and her husband won't be back. Good riddance.

They say things happen in threes, and the third person to disappear when the scandal broke was Charmaine Solomon. Within minutes of being relieved of her duties, she packed a bag and hit the road. As far as I know, no one has heard from her, and yesterday a FOR SALE sign appeared on her and Emory's lawn.

"So, if no one else comes forward, this candidate runs unchallenged? Or do they win by default, and we skip the campaign and election?" April asks Connie.

"I have no idea." Connie shrugs. "In the history of Harmony Lake, this has never happened. We're in uncharted territory."

Because of the vacancy left by the mayor's sudden resignation, Harmony Lake is having its first ever mayoral by-election! The window for potential mayoral candidates to hand in their nomination packages and get their name on the ballot opened at noon yesterday. So far, the only candidate is a big-boxer. We don't know if this is part of the big-box plot the mayor was trying to uncover with Jamila's help, or if the big-boxers are opportunists who are using the corruption scandal to make a power play.

I put down the crossword puzzle and pick up my phone. "According to the internet, if a candidate is unopposed, they'll be acclaimed on the day the election was scheduled to happen," I say, putting my phone on the counter.

"That won't happen," Connie says confidently, with a chuckle. "We're working on a plan." Nodding, she winks and lays her finger aside her nose.

"We?" April and I ask in unison.

Connie checks her watch. "We've called an emergency joint meeting of the charity knitters and the book club. There will be no corporate interference in my cozy little town. Not on my watch. Unless it's over my dead body."

I'm not usually a superstitious person, but I wish Connie hadn't made that last comment. No need to tempt fate.

April and I gasp. A meeting between the readers and the knitters is huge.

The campaign period only officially started at noon yesterday, but I already can't wait for this election to be over. Once we have a new mayor and a permanent chief of police, the people of Harmony Lake can lay this scandal to rest, and our tight-knit community can go back to being the hotbed of rest I know and love.

Adam: Lunch?

Me: Sure.

Adam: Pub at 1 p.m.?

Me: Sounds good.

"Anything important, my dear?" What Connie really means is, who are you texting and about what.

"No," I reply, smiling. "Just making lunch plans with Adam."

"Today?" April asks, giving Sophie a dog treat.

"Yup. Today," I confirm.

"Won't that be…awkward?" Connie asks.

I shrug. "I don't expect it will be more awkward than usual. It feels right somehow to see him today. Is that why you're both here? Are you checking on me?"

"Kind of," April admits. "How are you feeling?"

I shrug. "Bittersweet," I reply. "Sad it had to end, but happy we came through it in one piece."

"Are you sure you're all right, my dear?"

"I'm fine," I reply. "I truly believe we'll all be happier this way. It helps that we're both moving on. I'm with Eric now, and Adam is with Jess."

"Jess is lovely!" Connie interjects. "They're a beautiful couple."

Jess's Thanksgiving debut was a success. I think Jess was nervous at first, but she fit in immediately. Who wouldn't be nervous about Thanksgiving dinner with twelve new people? Jess and Hannah got along great. So well, in fact, that Jess and Adam drove the girls back to school the next day. It gave Hannah and Jess a chance to get to know each other and gave me the chance to avoid another day-long road trip. Everyone was a winner.

The thud of the back-door closing makes me jump. I check the time on my phone. A week ago today, almost to the minute, Emory Solomon closed the back door, locked it, and tried to kill me.

"Good morning, ladies," Eric says, entering the store and seeing Connie and April on the sofa. "A lady in the parking lot asked me to give this to you." He hands me a squishy plastic envelope.

"Yarn," I say, squeezing the package. I find a pair of scissors and open the envelope. Three skeins of yarn tumble on to the coffee table.

"These are lovely." Connie compliments the yarn while automatically petting and squeezing it.

"Custom, limited edition colours," I tell her. "This one is inspired by the colour of the lake." I point to the blue-green variegated skein. "This one is inspired by the mountains in the winter." I point to the brown yarn with cream speckles. "And this one is inspired by the Knitorious logo." I point to the purple-green self-striping yarn.

"What a wonderful idea! How did this come about?"

"Well, I kind of told the charity knitters I was working on getting some limited-edition yarn. It was a lie of convenience, but I want to be true to my word, so I commissioned these from a local dyer. My plan is to donate the proceeds from the sales of these skeins to the charity knitters to help fund their projects. I have to decide which colours and how many to order."

"Well, it's nice to see you, Eric, but we were just leaving," Connie announces, nudging April's elbow and standing up.

"We were?" April asks, then she looks at me and shrugs. "I guess we were." She smiles.

Connie kisses my cheek. "I'll pop by later, my dear."

"Text me if you need me." April winks and gives me a hug.

Eric hands me a maple pecan latte with extra whipped

cream and a drizzle of chocolate and locks the door behind them.

"Thank you," I say, cracking the lid. "Where's yours?"

"I had one at the office already."

He's already been to the office and back? It's barely 8:00 a.m.

"You didn't have to leave work just to bring me a coffee," I tell him. "You could've sent someone else. Now that you're Chief of Police, don't you have people who run these types of errands for you?" I tease.

"*Interim* chief of police," Eric corrects me. "I want to be here when Darby comes by with your laptop. And visiting you isn't an errand." He smiles.

Harmony Lake's octogenarian deputy mayor is now mayor until the election in the new year. Her first order of business was to contact Eric on Saturday and invite him to her house for tea on Tuesday. She asked him to step in as interim chief until the new mayor can recruit a permanent chief of police. Eric was hesitant to accept, but the deputy mayor is very grandmotherly and very persuasive. She plied him with tea and guilt until he gave in.

"Are there turkey sandwiches in the fridge for me for lunch?" Eric asks, jerking his thumb toward the back room.

As usual, there was more food than people at Thanksgiving dinner. Everyone left with leftovers. Since Sunday, I've made turkey pot pie, open-faced turkey sandwiches with gravy, turkey casserole, and too many turkey sandwiches to count.

"We're out of turkey," I reply.

"Yes!" he mumbles and pumps his fist triumphantly. "I almost answered the phone yesterday with 'Gobble Gobble' instead of 'Hello'."

I gather the plastic envelope from the custom yarn and toss it in the garbage pail under the counter.

"How are you feeling?" Eric asks.

"Fine," I reply.

"I know what day it is. I know what happens today."

"You mean the enrollment window for mayoral candidates to submit their nomination packages?" I ask, knowing this isn't what he means.

"Yes, that's exactly what I mean," he replies sarcastically. "That and your divorce will be finalized today."

"Oh, that," I respond. "I'm fine. I'm happy and sad, but I'm fine."

"Well, I'm here for whatever you need. And I just re-stocked your chocolate stash. We can go out for dinner, we can stay in. We can do whatever you want. If you want to be alone, I understand. Just let me know how to show up for you today."

"Thank you." I give him a hug.

Sophie runs to the back door as though she recognizes Darby's knock. Maybe she does, what do I know?

Darby puts his messenger bag on the counter and opens it. He slides my laptop out of the bag and places it on the counter. "Our tech people said it's completely spyware-free and safe to use."

"Thanks," I say, not sure I'm emotionally ready to trust this computer.

"Also, we solved the mystery of who the sleeping pills in Dr. Solomon's pocket were intended for."

"Oh?" My interest is piqued. "Who?"

"Himself," Darby replies. "Dr. Solomon emailed a long, rambling suicide note and confession to Charmaine. He used a delay feature, so it wouldn't send until the next day, when he thought he'd be dead."

"Wow," I say, then drop into a chair while I process what Darby just said.

I guess I should've realized this was a possibility when Emory said, "If I have to go down, I'm taking you with me." I assumed he meant if he had to go to prison, he would make it worth his while, not that he was planning a murder-suicide.

Darby reaches into his bag, pulls out an envelope, and hands it to me. "From Karen Porter," he explains.

In neat penmanship, the envelope is addressed to Megan and Eric.

While Darby congratulates Eric on his appointment to Interim Chief of Police, and they talk about cop stuff, I open the envelope and read the notecard inside.

It's a thank you note. In lovely handwriting, Karen thanks me for believing her when she came to me with the truth and for helping find Dr. Armistead's killer. She goes on to say that she hopes Eric and I will be happy together and to look her up if I ever need a chiropractic adjustment.

Karen is leaving for Europe. She's taking the trip she and Dr. Armistead were planning to take next year. Apparently, he left her his house in his will. She'll be away for six months, then decide what she wants to do with the house when she gets back. She ends the note by asking me to give Sophie some rubs for her.

I'll show Eric later.

As soon as I turn the sign from CLOSED to OPEN and unlock the door, my phone is abuzz with news of the two most powerful groups in Harmony Lake combining forces. Apparently, the charity knitters and book club are meeting right now, upstairs at the pub.

As the entire town waits in awe to find out how the powers that be will keep our town safe from corporate invaders, people wander up and down Water Street, in and out of stores, collecting and sharing information.

There is no shortage of speculation and rumours. While no one knows anything for sure, we all agree on one thing: this is historic. There are events in a town's history that are so monumental, future generations refer to time as before-the-thing-happened and after-the-thing-happened. This is one of those events.

Marla races through the door.

"Marla! Why are you here? Shouldn't you be at the meeting?"

"I've been dispatched to relieve you, Megan. You've been summoned."

"Summoned? Me? Why?"

What did I do? What could they want with me?

"There's no time to explain." Marla shoves my bag and cell phone into my arms and turns me toward the back room. "They're at the pub. Upstairs. Drive. It'll be faster than walking. They saved a parking spot for you by the door." She prods me to the back room and out the back door.

As I PULL up to the pub, a book club member zooms out of a parking space and a charity knitter standing nearby gestures for me to pull in. I guess this is what Marla meant when she said they reserved a spot for me by the door.

The charity knitter who gestured for me to pull into the parking spot holds the outer door for me. A book club member opens the inner door, allowing me to stride through without stopping. At the bottom of the stairs, a charity knitter moves the velvet rope aside so I can climb the stairs.

The upstairs area of the pub is available by reservation only. There are two function rooms, an office, and extra washrooms. The velvet rope at the bottom of the stairs keeps regular patrons from going upstairs looking for extra seating.

"Thank you," I mumble to each of them as I pass by.

At the top of the stairs is an open reception area with an ornate wooden railing overlooking the pub below.

I'm quickly able to determine which function room they're in when I see a charity knitter on one side of the closed door working on a baby bootie, and a book club member on the other side engrossed in, *The President Is Missing* by James Patterson.

"Good morning, ladies," I say with a smile.

"Good morning, Megan," the charity knitter says as the book club member knocks on the door.

"Someone will be right with you," the book club member says without looking up from her book.

The door handle turns from the other side. I take a deep breath and brace myself. I'm excited and nervous, like when I was seven years old and Katie Humphries was about to let me into her clubhouse for the very first time, but only if I did the secret knock perfectly.

"There you are, my dear! I knew you'd get here quickly." Connie puts a hand on my shoulder, kisses my cheek, and guides me into the room.

There's a mahogany board table surrounded by mahogany chairs with dark-green leather trim. Connie resumes her seat at the table. She is flanked by the former-deputy-now-current mayor on one side and another book club member on her other side. Across from them, Mrs. Roblin and Mrs. Vogel look up at me and smile without breaking the rhythm of their knitting. Eric sits between them. He looks up at me and smiles with a small wave. Why is he here? Adam is at the head of the table. Why is he here?

Am I being ambushed?

"Is this an intervention?" I ask meekly, slightly afraid I've found one dead body too many, and now the unofficial leaders of the town have taken it upon themselves to intercede.

"Of course not, Megan. Don't be silly. We only do those at the library," Mrs. Roblin assures me after everyone stops laughing at my question.

I think she's serious.

"Have a seat, my dear." Connie gestures for me to sit at the other end of the table. "And don't look so worried."

I sit and a charity knitter appears from nowhere offering me a glass of water. "Thank you," I say when she finishes pouring.

She disappears into the corner where she waits with a book club member.

"Time is of the essence, so I'll get right to the point," Connie says. "Adam has agreed to run for mayor on the condition that Eric agrees to accept the chief of police job on a permanent basis. We think they're our best chance at defeating the big-boxers."

"Adam would be a great mayor," I respond. "He's politically inclined, he's local, and his values are in line with most of the town's residents."

The knitters and readers sound like a leaky air mattress when they breathe a collective sigh of relief.

"We were hoping you'd say that," Connie says, smiling widely.

Adam pulls himself up to his full-seated height and clears his throat. "I have zero interest in recruiting a new chief of police," he begins, "especially when the best person for the job is already doing the job on a temporary basis."

I look at Eric.

"I want to talk to you first," Eric says.

Eric and I step across the hall to the other, unoccupied function room and close the door.

"You said you don't want to be 'chief of paperwork'," I start.

"I don't. But I don't want to risk working for another corrupt boss, either. You know what this town is like, Megan. After what happened with Charmaine, they'll never trust an outsider. If I say no, an outsider will be the only option. If I support Adam and make it clear to the town that I won't work for a pro-big-box mayor, it could help Adam's campaign and keep the big-box stores out of Harmony Lake."

He's right.

I tell Eric he has my support whatever he decides, and with that sorted, we re-join the meeting across the hall.

Adam signs a few pieces of paper, and the rest of us sign forms as his nominators. Connie and Mrs. Roblin think it will strengthen Adam's position if they, Eric, and I show our support by being nominators.

The meeting is adjourned, and Connie and Mrs. Roblin leave to hand deliver Adam's documents to the town hall.

With the knitters and readers gone, I close the door and turn to Adam and Eric.

"Are you sure about this?" I ask Adam.

"No." He shakes his head. "But look at the alternative, Meg. Harmony Lake would be full of drive-thrus and Mega-Marts in a year."

"Real estate prices would skyrocket because of corporations buying land, and the next generation of residents would never be able to afford to settle down here and raise families," Eric adds.

"And you have to admit, we're a great team." Adam smiles.

I assume he's talking about him and Eric.

"I know you're right," I agree. "But I have a feeling this election could get messy. With the mayor gone, and the scandal that just happened, this is a big opportunity for the big-boxers. There's no telling what they might do to win."

"C'mon, Meg!" Adam says, chuckling. "This is small-town politics that we're talking about. Really small. How nasty can it get? It's not like anyone would kill to fix the election," he says confidently, then laughs.

Wouldn't they?

I don't laugh with him because I'm not so sure.

A Knitorious Murder Mystery Book 6

Crime Skein

REAGAN DAVIS

COPYRIGHT

ISBN: 978-1-7772359-4-9 (ebook)

ISBN: 978-1-7772359-5-6 (print)

FOREWORD

Dear Reader,

Despite several layers of editing and proofreading, occasionally a typo or grammar mistake is so stubborn that it manages to thwart my editing efforts and camouflage itself amongst the words in the book.

If you encounter one of these obstinate typos or errors in this book, please let me know by contacting me at Hello@ReaganDavis.com.

Hopefully, together we can exterminate the annoying pests.

Thank you!

Reagan Davis

CHAPTER 1

THURSDAY, January 14th

Tomorrow morning, Harmony Lake will either stay the cozy, sweet town I know and love, or become a soon-to-be tacky resort town on the cusp of a corporate coup.

I'm hoping for the former, not the latter.

Harmony Lake isn't like other towns. We have a big-box policy to protect us from corporate invasion. I support the big-box policy. I don't want big business to commercialize our lovely little lakeside sanctuary. Residents who *oppose* the big-box policy, and want to see our town overrun with drive-thrus and giant warehouse stores, are known as big-boxers. They are a loud minority, made up of residents who would benefit from selling land to the corporate invaders.

Our quaint, family-owned businesses and restaurants make Harmony Lake the intimate and cozy refuge we call home. There are no drive-thrus, no neon signs advertising corporate logos, and no multi-level parking structures. Our town is a blissful oasis, free from the corporate landscape found in most cities and suburbs. The reason tourists flock here is to escape the hustle and bustle of their day-to-day lives and immerse themselves in our small-town charm.

"Is that a cat toy for the Animal Centre?" Sheamus asks, pointing to my knitting.

"Yes," I reply, nodding. "Nothing like knitting for a worthy cause."

Sheamus isn't a knitter, so I'm surprised he knows about the cat toy initiative for the Animal Centre.

Our local charity knitting guild is collecting knitted cat toys to benefit The Vanity Fur Centre for Animal Health & Wellness—known to locals as the Animal Centre. It's our local, all-in-one animal shelter, veterinary hospital, animal sanctuary, and animal education centre. The donated cat toys will be sold in their gift shop and online store.

"No need to ask who you voted for, I take it?" Sheamus shouts over the buzz of the crowd, as he stands next to our booth at the Irish Embassy Pub.

"What gave it away?" I reply teasingly.

I brush aside my brown curls and point to the MARTEL FOR MAYOR button affixed to the front of my hand-knit sweater.

Today is election day in Harmony Lake's first ever mayoral by-election, a historic event in our tiny town.

Harmony Lake was a reliable hotbed of political rest, then our town's predictable political balance was thrown into upheaval by a scandal so shocking that the former mayor and police chief were forced to leave town in a cloud of corruption and disgrace.

Today, the residents of Harmony Lake will choose between two potential leaders, and the future of our cozy town hangs in the balance. Everything is on the line.

"What did Sheamus say?" April leans over and asks in my ear.

April is my best friend. We thought a quiet post-ballot dinner at the Irish Embassy Pub would be a nice way to commemorate the end of the mayoral campaign. Apparently, the rest of the town had the same idea, and the pub is packed. Standing room only.

"He asked me who I voted for," I reply directly into her ear.

April smiles and nods. Her blue eyes sparkle, and she tucks a few long, blonde strands of hair behind the ear I'm speaking into. Her year-round, sun-kissed glow gives her the appearance of someone who just returned from a sunny getaway down south. All winter long, people assume she's fresh off a plane from some sun-filled destination or other and are shocked when she tells them she has been nowhere. No one makes that mistake with me. My hazel eyes and fair, alabaster skin are more likely to elicit questions about what type of anemia I have. I don't have anemia; this is just how I look.

April leans forward and turns her head so her wife, Tamara, can yell into her ear next.

"He asked who Megan voted for," April shouts in response to her wife's question, while nudging her head toward me. Tamara nods and smiles, leans back in her seat, and gives us a thumbs-up.

Sheamus is leaning away from me now and speaking into Eric's ear. I don't know what he's saying, but his full head of shocking red hair bobs up and down as he speaks. Whatever he's saying, Eric isn't very enthusiastic about it. He replies with the occasional shrug and a few uncertain smiles.

Eric Sloane is my boyfriend. We met over a year ago when the Harmony Lake Police Department borrowed him from another police force to investigate the first murder in our town's history. He solved the case—and a few more since—and moved here after accepting a detective sergeant position with the Harmony Lake Police Department. Eric is also my tenant; he lives in the apartment above my yarn store, Knitorious. We've been dating for almost a year. In fact, the anniversary of our first date is next week. Eric is planning something special to celebrate it, but whenever I ask him for details, he tells me it's a surprise.

Sheamus leans toward me and jerks his thumb toward Eric. "Megan, convince yer man, here, to come by my place later for a bit of poker, will ya?" he yells with a hint of Irish brogue, flashing me a wide grin.

"I'll see what I can do," I shout back with a wink.

Sheamus is wearing a lovely hand-knit scarf. It looks like two strands of bulky weight yarn held together. One yarn looks to be a variegated combination of greens and rusts, and the other is a complimentary solid cream. I want to reach out and touch it, but over the years, I've learned that non-knitters think it's weird when knitters randomly reach out and pet their clothing. Or get within an inch to inspect the stitches. Or sniff it. When knitters spot hand knits in the wild, personal space protocols go out the window. I speak from experience.

I file away a mental image of the scarf and make a mental note to ask Sheamus about it when we find ourselves in circumstances more conducive to conversation. Sheamus finishes speaking to Eric and moves along to spread his unique brand of blarney to a group of tourists at the next booth.

Sheamus O'Brien is the second-generation owner of The Irish Embassy, known as The Pub, or The Embassy to us locals. The embassy is as close to a genuine Irish pub experience as you can get without hopping on a plane and flying to Ireland.

"Ready to go?" Eric mouths to me from across the table.

His phone buzzes and vibrates. When he picks it up to check it, I notice how tired he looks. His eyes are heavy, and his posture is more limp than normal, like he's wilting. Even the honey-coloured flecks in his brown eyes seem duller than normal.

"Sure," I say, nodding.

He puts down his phone, winks, and gives me a warm smile that makes the butterflies in my stomach wake up and start fluttering.

I lean over and tell April that Eric and I are heading out. She informs me that she and Tamara won't be far behind us.

We pay the bill and wrap ourselves in our winter woollies because it's freezing outside. The temperature is at least minus ten with the windchill, and we're supposed to have a snowstorm tonight. Environment Canada issued a snowfall warning saying we should expect up to fifteen centimetres before morning.

We're about to get up from the booth when Adam waves to me from the door. I gesture for him to come over. Adam Martel is my ex-husband and the mayor presumptive of Harmony Lake. By the time the residents of Harmony Lake wake up tomorrow morning to shovel their driveways, Adam will hopefully be our new mayor. Our big-box policy will remain securely in place for the duration of his term in office.

Adam and I were married for almost twenty years. We finalized our divorce in October. Our daughter, Hannah, is nineteen and goes to university in Toronto. We have a virtual brunch with her every Sunday. I'm proud of how Adam and I handled our divorce. We were careful to make sure the implosion of our marriage had a minimal effect on the people we love, and we redefined our relationship and learned how to be friends. We're not married anymore, but we're still family.

Adam is Harmony Lake's local lawyer. He's politically inclined and passionate about the small town where we live and raised our daughter; he'll be an amazing mayor.

"Good evening, Your Worship," I greet him playfully.

Your Worship is the appropriate way to address a mayor. He better not get used to it. I don't intend to call him Your Worship ever again.

"It might be premature for that," he chuckles, then bends down, and we exchange a double-cheek kiss.

Adam turns to Eric and asks him if he's going to Shea-mus's place later to play cards. When Eric says he doubts he'll go, Adam tries to persuade him.

Yes, my ex-husband and boyfriend are friends. Good friends. Eric was new in town and didn't know anyone in Harmony Lake, and despite living here most of his adult life, Adam didn't have many close relationships in Harmony Lake either. Before opening his own practice, Adam was a workaholic senior partner at a law firm in the city. They bonded over a mutual love of golf, and the rest is history. Sometimes it's weird that they're friends, but no weirder than the friendship I have with Adam's new part-ner, Jess.

Jess and I kiss cheeks, and April and I shove over in the booth so she can slide in with us.

"I'm surprised you're here tonight," I say to Jess. "With the snowstorm coming, I didn't think you'd risk the drive."

Jess lives and works forty-five minutes away in Harmony Hills. She takes off her toque and shakes out her long, straw-berry-blond hair.

"I wanted to be here tonight for Adam," she explains. "I won't stay long. I plan to get on the road before the worst of the snow starts."

"Full house tonight." Adam scans the pub, searching for an available table or booth.

"We're just leaving," Eric says. "Why don't you sit here?"

With that decided, Eric and I vacate the booth, giving Adam and Jess our seats.

Stepping into the cool night air is a relief. It took us at least ten minutes to get from the booth to the door. We stopped at almost every table and booth to say hi to friends and neigh-bours—one hazard of living in a small town where everyone knows everyone else. Stopping to chat while wearing two layers of clothes, a down-filled winter coat, a thick hand-knit ear warmer, cowl, and mittens is a recipe for overheating.

"Are you going to play cards with the guys?" I ask Eric as we walk up Water Street toward Knitorious.

"I don't think so," he replies. "I'm tired, and they always play on a weeknight when I have to work the next day."

"Maybe you're tired because you're working two jobs," I suggest. "It's pretty much a done deal that Adam will win this election. Tomorrow, he'll appoint you as the permanent chief of police. You can't be police chief and Harmony Lake PD's only detective. It's too much. Have you given any more thought to hiring a detective to replace you?"

After the scandal that shook our town to its core, the deputy mayor asked Eric to step in as interim chief of police until the newly elected mayor could choose a permanent replacement. He's been doing two jobs for three months, and it's taking a toll.

When Adam was approached to run for mayor, he made it a condition that he would only enter the race if, upon his election, Eric agreed to become the chief of police permanently. Eric accepted because he knows the locals—who are skeptical of outsiders on a good day—will hesitate to accept a police chief recruited from elsewhere.

"I haven't had much time to think about it because I'm so busy." Eric gathers his scarf around his neck and takes my hand. From inside his coat pocket, his phone makes the notification sounds that have become the soundtrack to our lives lately. "I hope to promote someone from within because I don't think the town is ready to accept any new people, especially someone in a position of authority."

I keep my face down and look at my feet to avoid the sharp sting of the frigid January air on my face.

"Ms. Martel, Police Chief Sloane, so lovely to see you both."

I look up when I hear my name.

Saxon Renaud. Ugh! What an unpleasant way to end the day.

Eric looks up at the same time as me and utters a curse word under his breath, then plasters a fake smile on his handsome face.

"Mr. Renaud." I nod, intending to continue walking.

"Saxon," Eric nods, also still walking.

Saxon steps in front of us, forcing us to stop.

"Hi, Rick," I say with a smile to Saxon's hired henchman, Rick Ransan.

"H-hi, Megan," Rick smiles.

Rick is such a pleasant person. Why does he hang around with someone as insufferable as Saxon Renaud?

"Rick." Eric nods.

"H-h-i, Chief S-Sloane." Rick returns the nod.

In what qualifies as the weirdest thing I've seen today, Saxon uses the long metal tip of his whangee bamboo handle umbrella to draw a line in the snow that's beginning to accumulate on the sidewalk. A line between where Eric and I stand and where Saxon and Rick stand. Is it some kind of metaphorical or literal battle line?

Watching Saxon scrape the tip of his umbrella along the sidewalk, I notice that instead of wearing boots, which would be a practical footwear choice for a night like tonight, he's wearing his signature penny loafers. Complete with pennies, even though we haven't made pennies in this country for years, and rubber overshoes with no insulation value.

Saxon Renaud carrying an umbrella during a blizzard isn't strange to me. He carries his umbrella with him everywhere he goes, all the time, no matter the weather situation. It's like an extension of his right arm; the umbrella is Saxon's quirk.

Using it to draw a line in the snow, however, is new. At least it's new to me. I've never seen him do it before. He's also fond of using his umbrella as a cattle prod to protect his personal space and make people—women—jump out of his way. I've been on the receiving end of his prodding, and it's infuriating. Saxon Renaud is a hard person to like.

I sigh. "What's up, Saxon?" I ask, since he has made no attempt to tell us why he stopped us or to explain the weird line he drew in the snow.

I'm tempted to use the toe of my boot to erase his stupid line, but I resist the urge. The snow is falling faster now, and the line is already disappearing, anyway.

"Chief Sloane, I was hoping to run into you," Saxon says, ignoring me and my question, and looking up at Eric. "I'm willing to give you one more chance to change your mind and accept the permanent chief of police position when I'm confirmed as mayor tomorrow."

Eric shakes his head, rolls his eyes, and chuckles breathily. "No thank you, Saxon," he replies, still shaking his head. "I told you, I would *never* be police chief in a town that would have you as mayor."

"Are you sure?" Saxon asks again. "I suspect you might regret it tomorrow morning."

"A risk I'm willing to take." Eric grins. "Now if you'll excuse us, gentlemen, it's chilly out here." Eric tightens his grip on my hand and walks straight at them, forcing them to part and let us through.

I glance behind us to make sure Saxon and Rick are out of earshot, then quicken my pace to keep up with Eric. He's almost a foot taller than me, and his strides are longer than mine. "The only way Saxon Renaud might win this mayoral election is by cheating," I assert with confidence.

"He won't win," Eric agrees. "There's no way. I'd bet my life on it."

I know he wouldn't *literally* bet his life on it, but I wish he wouldn't tempt fate by saying that.

We both turn to check one more time and make sure the two men haven't doubled back and are walking behind us, listening to our conversation. We glimpse them disappearing into the pub.

"It looks like we left just in time," I remark.

"Yep," Eric concurs. "It might get pretty heated in the pub tonight with both candidates there."

CHAPTER 2

"REMIND me again why we vote today but don't get the results until tomorrow?" Eric asks as I unleash Sophie and take off her sweater after our walk.

Sophie is my corgi. She comes to work with me every day. If Eric and I go out after work, she hangs out in his apartment until we get home. Sophie has a full suite of toys, food, dishes, sweaters, and even a bed here. Knitorious and Eric's apartment are her homes away from home.

"Well," I start, "this year it's due to the weather. Because of the snowfall warning, voting hours were extended until 10 p.m. to give residents who commute enough time to get home to Harmony Lake and cast their votes."

"And in previous years?" he asks.

I shrug. "I don't know. Tradition, I guess? You know how much this town likes tradition."

It's snowing heavily now, and visibility is bad. A fresh layer of white covers everything like a blanket and makes our already-picturesque town look even more postcard worthy. The glow from the slivered fraction of the waxing moon, and the streetlights reflecting off the new-fallen snow, makes the light coming in the windows brighter than usual for a January night.

I hem and haw about whether to go home or stay at Eric's apartment for the night. He convinces me to stay by warming my favourite flannel pyjamas in the dryer and showing me his PVR full of mindless TV shows we like to watch.

There are advantages to dating my tenant; I sleep above the store when the weather is bad, and my morning commute is only thirty seconds.

"MEGAN." Eric gently nudges my shoulder. "Babe, wake up. We fell asleep watching TV. It's late, go to bed."

Disoriented and groggy, I take a deep breath and force open my heavy eyes. Overwhelmed by the harsh glare of artificial light, I shut them again. The last thing I remember is knitting a mouse ear and trying to stay awake for the big reveal on the home renovation reality show we were watching. Eric fell asleep checking his email on his phone within ten minutes of the opening credits and was snoring softly on the sofa next to me. I felt myself being lulled to sleep by his rhythmic breathing and fought to stay awake. I guess I failed.

"Why are you dressed?" I ask, squinting while my eyes adjust to being awake. "Is everything OK?"

"I was called into work," he replies. "They called me to a hit and run out on Lake Access Road."

"In a snowstorm?" I asked, still confused, but better able to focus and take in my surroundings.

"Not everything shuts down because of terrible weather." Eric smiles and holds out his hands. "I'll be back as soon as I can."

I take his hands and let him pull me to my feet. I walk him to the door and wrap him in hand knits until I'm satisfied he's protected from the cold and wind, remind him to drive safely, and kiss him good night. After locking the door behind him, Sophie and I trudge off to bed.

SOPHIE'S SHRILL bark startles me awake, and I jolt upright to a sitting position.

"What's the matter, Soph? Do you need to go outside?"

Without looking at me, the corgi barks again and launches herself off the bed. Her paws don't touch the floor until she lands in the hallway outside the bedroom. She scampers off toward the apartment door.

Turning on lights as I go, I follow Sophie and find her whining and scratching at the apartment door. Then I hear it. Someone is pounding on the outside door, downstairs. It's the middle of the night. I squint at the clock on the stove. 1:12 a.m. Eric hasn't been gone very long. I can't believe I fell asleep so fast. Who's knocking at this hour?

Sophie and I descend the stairs while the pounding continues. Sophie, having twice as many legs as me and being built for speed, gets to the bottom first and yelps, then scratches the back of the door. This is her friendly yelp, the one she uses for friends. She knows and likes whoever is on the other side of the door.

I'm about to pick up the brick we use to prop open the back door, just in case, when I hear a familiar voice.

"Sophie? Is that you? Meg? Are you there? It's me!"

Adam. What the heck is he doing here?

"Adam?" I ask through the closed door.

"Yes, it's me. Can you open the door, please?"

I open the door, and there stands Adam, his hands shoved in his pockets, the collar of his navy-blue pea coat turned up against the wind, and his hair and shoulders covered in a dusting of big, fluffy snowflakes. He blinks a few snowflakes from his eyelashes, and I step aside so he can come in.

"What's wrong?" I ask.

Adam kicks the brick wall next to the door to knock the excess snow off his boots, then steps inside.

"I'm stranded," Adam replies, using his bare hand to shake the snow from his salt-and-pepper hair.

"How are you stranded?" I ask, "You live ten minutes away." Dramatic much?

I use my bare hand to dust snow from the shoulders of his coat. He's not wearing a hat, a scarf, or mittens. He's inadequately dressed for regular January weather, never mind a blizzard.

"I can't find my keys," Adam explains. "I think they fell out of my coat pocket at Sheamus's house. I can't start my car, and my phone is dead. Even if I walk home, I can't unlock the door."

"Did you go back to Sheamus's house to see if your keys are there?"

He nods. "I searched around outside the house, and the path from the front door to my car, but nothing. For all I know, they fell in the snow. Sheamus isn't there. No one's there. The poker game ended abruptly, and we cleared out in a hurry. I lost my keys in the commotion. I was hoping Eric could drive me to your place, so I can get the spare set of keys, pick up my car, and go home."

"Eric's not here," I explain. "He went to work because of a car accident or something."

"Can you drive me to get the spare set of keys?" Adam asks.

I shake my head. "My car isn't here. I walked to work this morning—yesterday morning—whenever."

Adam huffs in frustration, rubs his hands together vigorously, and uses them to cup his red ears.

"Crash in the spare room." I jerk my head toward the stairs. "It's too late and snowy to do anything tonight. We'll find your keys in the morning."

Adam agrees, and after lending him one of Eric's t-shirts and a pair of sweatpants, I set him up in the small spare room. When Sophie and I check the door to make sure it's locked, I notice Adam's dead phone on the breakfast bar. I plug it into the phone charger in the kitchen, then Sophie and I shuffle off to bed. Again.

Drifting off to sleep for the third time tonight, I replay my conversation with Adam in my head. Why did the poker game end abruptly? And why did they leave Sheamus's house in a hurry? What did he mean when he said he lost his keys in the commotion? What commotion? Between being dazed from waking up prematurely, and shocked at finding Adam on the doorstep in the middle of the night, it didn't occur to me to ask questions. As sleep takes over my brain, I make a mental list of questions I want to ask him in the morning.

Friday, January 15th

I'm a morning person. This time of year, I'm awake before the sun is up. I know everyone isn't an early riser and try to be considerate.

That's why, after I shower and dress, I tiptoe around the small apartment, trying to make as little noise as possible. The door to the spare bedroom is still closed, and I don't want to wake Adam.

Eric isn't home yet from wherever he went in the middle of the night. He must be exhausted. Intending to text him and see how he's doing, I grab my phone, quietly close the apartment door, and sneak downstairs with Sophie to get ready for our morning walk.

"Which sweater do you want to wear today, Soph?" I ask, holding up a sweater in each hand.

If Sophie prefers one sweater over the other, she doesn't

share it with me, so I choose for her. I bundle myself up, then help Sophie into her purple, cabled, turtleneck sweater and unlock the back door.

Walking through the park, I'm grateful the windchill has eased, and it's less frigid this morning. The world is still and silent, except for the occasional echo of a branch in the distance cracking under the weight of last night's snowfall, and the snow crunching beneath our feet and paws as we walk. The snow is smooth and untouched, shimmering in the pre-dawn light. Tree branches curve toward the ground, reaching lower than usual, yielding to the weight of the snow on top of them. My heart is bursting with gratitude because I live in the prettiest town on earth!

"I was just about to text you," I say when I see Eric getting out of his car in the parking lot behind Knitorious.

"How'd you sleep?" he asks, then kisses me hello.

"Interrupted and not long enough," I reply, walking through the back door he's holding for Sophie and me.

I unleash Sophie and take off her sweater, then take off my winter gear, and put everything away.

"I'm going upstairs to grab a quick shower, then I have to go back to work," Eric says, heading toward the stairs. "After my shower, I'll tell you about the hit and run I attended last night. It was a doozy."

"Adam slept in the spare room last night. Be quiet because I think he's still asleep," I warn him.

Eric stops and turns to me, his eyes narrow and focussed. Hot intensity emanates from him. "Adam's here?" He steps toward me and narrows his eyes even more. "Why? What time did he show up? Where's his car? It's not in the parking lot."

He's using his cop voice, and I feel like I'm being interrogated.

"Am I a witness or something?" I ask, confused.

"We've been looking for Adam for hours. He's not at

home, he's not at his office, he's not with Jess, and his phone is off."

"*We*? Are the police looking for Adam? Why?" I demand.

An anxious knot forms in my stomach. My heart pounds against my ribs. I feel panicky, and I'm not sure why.

Heavy shoulders, long arms, I remind myself and take a deep breath. Heavy shoulders, long arms is a mantra I learned in a yoga class once upon a time. It reminds me to let go of the tension in my neck and shoulders.

"Someone saw his car driving away from the hit and run," Eric replies. "His car isn't in his parking spot at the condo, it's not at his office, it's not anywhere."

"It's at Sheamus's house," I inform him. "But the witness must be mistaken," I insist, wondering who the witness is.

Eric mumbles something about already checking Sheamus's house while he unlocks his phone and starts typing with his thumbs.

"Adam showed up here after you left," I say. "He lost his keys. He couldn't have been driving on Lake Access Road."

Eric pauses his thumbs mid-type, looks up at me, and says, "LAWYRUP," then looks down at his phone again and resumes typing, presumably to dispatch a patrol car to Sheamus's house.

LAWYRUP is the lawyer-themed vanity license plate Adam bought himself years ago when he got the job at the firm in the city. Everyone in town knows his plate.

"The witness was close enough to read Adam's license plate in a blizzard?" I ask, dubious.

Adam drives the only late model maroon Jaguar sedan in town. But I'm sure lots of cars would resemble his car, right? Most sedans look the same to me, anyway, and at night, in a blizzard, one sedan must look like another.

Eric fights back a yawn, musses his short, dark hair with one hand, and turns to climb the stairs. I follow him, and

Sophie follows me, but she zooms past both of us and reaches the apartment door first.

"Adam's not here," Eric booms from the spare room. "What time did he leave?"

I shrug. "I'm not sure. I haven't seen him since he closed the bedroom door." I rack my brain, trying to remember if Adam's coat and boots were downstairs, when Sophie and I got ready for our morning walk. I can't remember. I turn toward the charger on the breakfast bar where I plugged in Adam's dead phone last night. Just a charging cable, no phone. Was his phone plugged in this morning after my shower? I didn't notice.

"He took his phone," I mutter. I look at Eric. "I'm sorry, I don't know when he left. I'm usually more observant than this. I don't know why I'm off my game today. He took his phone, and it's charged. Try texting him."

"It's not your job to be observant, babe, it's OK," he reassures me. "You had a long night, and you're tired."

Eric texts, then calls Adam's cell phone while he paces the living room.

He drops the hand with the phone in it to his side and exhales loudly. I assume Adam didn't answer.

I feed Sophie breakfast and drop a pod in the coffee maker.

Our phones ding in unison.

"He's acclaimed," Eric says, reading the text. "Adam is officially the mayor of Harmony Lake."

I got the same text. It's from Connie, my mother-friend. She sent it to the Modern Family group chat, a group text chat with me, Eric, Adam and his girlfriend, Jess, April and her wife, Tamara, Connie and her boyfriend, Archie, and Ryan and Lin who are Archie's son and his partner.

"I'm sure Saxon Renaud is already on his way to the town hall to contest the results and demand a recount," I remark.

"I doubt it," Eric says. "Saxon Renaud is dead."

CHAPTER 3

"DEAD? How? We just saw him last night walking into the pub. Was it a heart attack or something?" I ask, hopeful that Saxon's death was because of natural causes.

Eric leads me to the leather club chair in the living room and coaxes me to sit. I look up at him, stunned. He squats, making us close to eye level.

"Saxon was the victim of the hit and run I attended," he explains.

I slouch deeper into the chair. After taking a moment to process what he just said, I pull myself up and sit up straight.

"Was he wearing a seatbelt? And why was Saxon on Lake Access Road in the middle of the night?" I ask.

Saxon Renaud owned a lot of property in and around Harmony Lake. It's the reason he wanted to become mayor. If he could reverse the big-box policy, he stood to make a lot of money selling land to developers and corporations. As far as I know, though, he didn't own property near Lake Access Road, and he didn't live there; no one does. Lake Access Road is a secluded, dirt road on the far side of the lake that leads to a slipway boaters use to move their boats in and out of the water. It's deserted this time of year.

"He wasn't in a car," Eric clarifies. "As far as we can tell, he was in the middle of the road when the car hit him."

Eric retrieves my coffee from the coffee maker, adds the sweetener I like, and brings it to me.

"In a snowstorm?" I shake my head as if it will help this story make sense. It doesn't. "You're saying Saxon Renaud *walked* all the way to Lake Access Road in a blizzard, wearing his penny loafers, and was walking down the middle of the remote, poorly lit road when a car ran over him." I pause. "And the driver didn't bother to stop or call for help?"

Eric nods. "Pretty much. I know it makes little sense now, but after the coroner examines the body and provides more details, and after I trace Saxon's movements in the days before he died, and when we locate the vehicle that hit him, I'll be able to piece it together, and it'll make more sense."

The back door closes with a thud downstairs, distracting Sophie from her bowl of food and making her yelp.

"Adam," I say to Eric.

"We haven't notified Saxon's next of kin, yet. We're still trying to locate them," Eric explains quietly. "His death isn't public knowledge."

"I understand," I whisper, nodding. "I won't say anything."

"Meg, I don't know what your drink of choice is lately, but the barista told me you'd want a white chocolate and peppermint latte with extra whipped cream and a sprinkle of white chocolate shavings," Adam says without looking up, as he closes the apartment door behind him. "Hey, Eric," he says when he looks up. "I didn't know you were here, or I would've picked up a coffee for you."

"It's OK," I say. "Eric has a coffee." I hand Eric my mug and, mouth watering, liberate my latte from the tray. "Thank you, Mayor Martel," I say, raising the to-go cup in a toasting gesture.

"You saw the text?" Adam asks, sheepishly.

I think he's blushing. Adam doesn't blush easily.

"Congratulations, Adam." Eric extends his hand. "The best candidate won."

Adam and Eric's over-pumped handshake morphs into one of those half-hug-half-handshakes that men do where they slap each other on the shoulder.

While they shake hands, I send a quick text to Hannah to let her know her dad is officially the new mayor of Harmony Lake. I doubt she's awake yet, but she'll see it when she gets up.

"Megan mentioned you lost your keys last night?" Eric asks Adam.

I take my coffee to the leather club chair, cross my legs with my feet tucked under my butt, and settle in, ready to hear what happened at Sheamus's card game last night.

"I'm sure they're on the floor somewhere at Sheamus's house," Adam begins.

According to Adam, after Eric and I left the pub, Saxon Renaud and Rick Ransan showed up. We already knew that, but Eric doesn't interrupt Adam to mention it, and I don't either.

Adam says when Saxon arrived, the atmosphere at the pub changed. He said it went from relaxed and happy to tense and fractious. He says Saxon recommended that people congratulate him on being the next mayor of Harmony Lake, and even suggested they should buy him a drink to celebrate. Apparently, some residents booed at Saxon's comments, and others left the pub altogether. Adam thinks this annoyed or offended Saxon—or both. He reacted by telling everyone that this time next year, Harmony Lake would be a different town, a better town, and everyone would thank him. He said everyone who didn't vote for him would be sorry.

"We decided it was time to go to Sheamus's house to play cards," Adam explains. "Sheamus had to finish up a few things at the pub before he could leave, but he gave Pete his house key and the rest of us headed over there."

Pete is Pete Feeney. Pete was born and raised in Harmony Lake. The Feeney family is a town fixture. Pete's mum was the interim mayor until this morning when Adam was acclaimed as the new mayor, and his dad was the fire chief of the Harmony Lake Fire Department for many years.

"Other than you, Sheamus, and Pete, who else went to Sheamus's house?" Eric probes.

"The usual," Adam replies, shrugging. Then he counts people on his fingers. "Sheamus, me, Pete, Ryan, and because you weren't there"—he nods toward Eric—"Sheamus invited Rick Ransan so we'd have five players. You know how Sheamus is, he only likes to play if we have at least five players."

Ryan is Ryan Wright. He's part of my non-traditional modern family. His dad, Archie, is Connie's partner. Connie is like a mother to me, and Ryan jokes that he and I are stepsiblings.

"He invited Rick?" Eric sounds shocked. "Rick has never played cards with us before."

"He still hasn't played cards with us," Adam explains, shaking his head. "He didn't show up. Rick had an emergency and had to back out. He sent Saxon Renaud in his place."

Did I hear him correctly?

"Saxon Renaud?" I ask, certain I misheard Adam.

Adam nods. "Saxon Renaud," he confirms. "You should've seen everyone's face when Sheamus opened the door, and we all saw Saxon and his stupid umbrella standing on the doorstep. He had the nerve to tell us he was doing us a favour because if he hadn't offered to take Rick's place, we would only have four players."

"Wow." I shake my head in disbelief, then sip my latte.

"I'm glad I missed it," Eric remarks.

"Dude, if you'd showed up, Saxon wouldn't have been there, and the game wouldn't have ended with fisticuffs and a search for a missing person."

"Tell me everything," Eric instructs.

Yes, Adam, tell us everything! Who got into a fight? Who went missing? I have so many questions.

I check the time on my phone. The store opens in just over an hour, but Connie is opening for me today, so I can be late if necessary. I don't want to miss anything Adam says about last night.

Adam speaks but is interrupted by a notification sound from Eric's phone. Eric glances at his phone, then places it screen-down on the breakfast bar.

"We're listening," I say encouragingly. I sip my latte and shift position in the oversize chair, so my knees are against my chest.

"Things were fine at first," Adam tells us. "Before we played the first hand, we agreed not to discuss politics, real estate, big-box stores, or anything else that could be controversial. We talked about the weather and hockey. It wasn't as much fun as usual, but it was tolerable." He shrugs.

"Fast forward to the fight," Eric urges.

Hearing nothing else, I'm already convinced Saxon was involved in the fight. I swear that man looked for trouble.

"Ryan was drinking Diet Coke, and Saxon was drinking rum and Coke. Sheamus's drinking glasses are all identical, so both drinks look the same. Saxon was sitting beside Ryan at the dining room table," Adam says as he provides background details relevant to the altercation. "Ryan picked up his glass and took a sip, then this funny look came over his face. He sniffed the glass and took another sip, then spat it out. He had picked up Saxon's glass by accident. The glass with rum and coke."

I gasp, my eyes wide with shock and concern. "Was Ryan OK?" I demand.

Adam shakes his head. "Not really. He pushed his chair away from the table and stood up. He accused Saxon of switching the drinks on purpose."

Ryan is a recovering alcoholic. His sobriety is important to him, and he works his program to avoid a relapse into active addiction. This could be a serious setback for him.

"Then what happened?" I ask, almost scared to find out the answer.

"Sheamus and I told Ryan we were proud of him for spitting it out when he realized it was alcohol. We told him it was a difficult thing to do, but he did it. We took him into the living room, away from the alcohol, and asked him if he wanted to call his sponsor," Adam replies.

"Good job." I take a deep breath, relieved. "Thank goodness you two were there for him."

"But we heard Pete and Saxon arguing in the dining room, so we went back in there," Adam continues. "Pete was accusing Saxon of switching the drinks on purpose. Sheamus always puts a wedge of lime in Ryan's diet coke, to avoid this situation."

"It's true," Eric agrees, nodding and looking at me. "Sheamus makes a point of reminding Ryan the wedge of lime is there to distinguish his drink from the alcoholic drinks."

"Did Sheamus forget the lime this time?" I ask.

"No," Adam shakes his head. "Pete held up the drink with the lime and Sheamus and I sniffed it. It was the rum and Coke. Pete suspects that when no one was looking, Saxon took the lime from the Diet Coke and put it in the rum and Coke to trick Ryan into drinking alcohol. We couldn't think of another explanation for how the lime got there. Ryan had already finished half of his diet coke. If the rum had been there before, he would've noticed earlier."

"That's awful." My eyes are welling up with tears.

I can't believe anyone would do such a thing, even

someone as mean and bitter as Saxon Renaud. What joy could he get from tormenting Ryan and putting his sobriety at risk?

Could Ryan have been angry enough to kill Saxon?

"Who threw the first punch?" Eric asks, refocusing Adam and me on the purpose of the story.

"No one," Adam informs us. "But Ryan grabbed Saxon by the shirt collar and shoved him into the living room. Saxon tried to shove back, but Ryan shoved him again, harder. Our coats were laying over the chair in the living room. Ryan pushed Saxon into the chair so hard, our coats fell to the floor, and the chair slid across the room. When Saxon tried to get up and push back, his feet just pushed the coats around. My coat ended up under the sofa. In hindsight, my keys probably fell out of my pocket. Pete and Sheamus picked up the coats but must not have noticed my keys."

"How did the altercation stop? Who went missing?" Eric's notebook is open on the breakfast bar, and he's taking notes.

"After Ryan shoved Saxon the second time, I positioned myself between them," Adam replies. "Ryan couldn't get to Saxon without going through me. While Sheamus and Pete picked up the coats and put the furniture back, I turned around and suggested to Saxon it was time for him to leave. With none of us watching Ryan, he grabbed his coat and took off. It was more than a minute before we realized he had left, but as soon as we did, we grabbed our coats and went after him. We were worried he might be tempted to go somewhere and drink. When I got to my car, I discovered my keys weren't in my pocket. I checked all my pockets and the ground around my feet. By the time I realized I was stranded, everyone else was long gone."

"Where did Ryan go?" I ask.

I assume someone found him safe and sound, and sober, otherwise my phone would have blown up with calls and texts from the modern family group chat.

Adam shrugs. "I don't know where he went, but as soon

as I woke up, I found my phone—thank you for charging it, Meg—and there was a text from Archie to everyone at the card game. It said we could stop searching because Ryan was safe."

"Thank goodness," I remark, exhaling a long breath I'd been holding onto.

"What did you do when you realized you didn't have your keys?" Eric asks.

"Panicked," Adam replies. "I checked my coat pockets, my pants pockets, and I retraced my steps from Sheamus's house to my car, in case I'd dropped the keys on the way. I didn't find them. It was snowing, and I thought maybe they had sunk into the snow. I used the flashlight on my phone to search through the snow but didn't find them. I finally stopped looking when my phone died, and I lost the flashlight. I walked around for a while to stay warm, then walked back to Sheamus's house, hoping he'd come home, and I could go inside and look for my keys. His car wasn't there, and I was freezing. I went to the pub in case Sheamus was there, but it was closed. Nothing else in town is open that late. I was stranded."

"Was your car at Sheamus's house when you went back?" Eric asks.

"Where else would it be?" Adam shrugs. "That's where I left it. But now that you mention it, everything was snow covered. I can't say for certain I saw my car when I went back." His gaze drifts off into the distance while he recalls the events of last night and whether he can be certain his car was there when he returned to Sheamus's house.

"So, that's when you came here," Eric concludes, distracting Adam from his thoughts.

"Right," Adam confirms. "Your place was close, and I was hoping you'd drive me to Meg's house because she has my spare keys. But you were at work, and her car was at home, so I crashed in your spare room."

"Where's your car now?" Eric asks.

"Parked across the street from Sheamus's house," Adam insists.

Eric shakes his head. "Your car isn't there, Adam. I sent a patrol car to check. The officer texted me a few minutes ago. There's no sign of your car."

"It has to be there," Adam maintains. "I texted Sheamus earlier to explain why I left my car there all night. I told him I was worried a snowplow might hit it, and he said he looked out the window and my car was fine. He said he'd look around for my keys."

To prove he's telling the truth, Adam unlocks his phone and shows Eric the text conversation he had with Sheamus earlier this morning.

"Sheamus isn't home," Eric informs him. "His truck isn't there, and the snow on his driveway is still fresh. My officers suspect Sheamus hasn't been home since last night."

Where is Sheamus, and why did he pretend to be home when Adam texted him?

Where is Adam's car, and what time did Adam leave this apartment this morning?

The knot in my stomach is growing bigger by the minute.

CHAPTER 4

"ERIC, if my car isn't on the street outside Sheamus's house, it was stolen, and I need to file a report." Adam's voice is laced with either urgency, or fear, or both; I can't quite tell.

"Adam, we believe your car was involved in a serious incident overnight on Lake Access Road. I've been looking for you and your car all night, but it never occurred to me to check my apartment."

Before Adam can respond, his phone rings, startling him and me.

"It's Hannah," he says, looking at the screen.

"I texted her earlier to tell her you're the new mayor," I say.

"I'm answering it. Everyone act normal."

If there's something Adam and I do well together, it's act normal. When our marriage was unravelling, we separated emotionally before we separated physically. For the sake of Hannah's senior year of high school, and to give ourselves time to work out the details of our separation, we lived under the same roof and maintained the pretense of a happily married couple for months before we told anyone we were splitting up.

Adam answers the call and puts our daughter on speakerphone. She congratulates him on being elected mayor and jokingly asks if she should call him Your Worship instead of Dad for the next four years.

The three of us laugh and play along, pretending there isn't a mess of a murder investigation unfolding around our family. We keep the tone of the conversation light and happy. We tell Hannah about the snowstorm and how pretty Harmony Lake is this morning.

Hannah wants to ask Adam a question about a paper she's working on for one of her law classes—she's studying pre-law—and Adam takes her off speaker and raises the phone to his ear to speak to her. I use the opportunity to talk to Eric alone and gesture for him to follow me downstairs to the store.

"Wow," I declare when we're alone.

Eric nods. "There's so much information to sort out."

"When you tell Adam that Saxon is dead, I think Jess, or me, or someone should be with him in case he freaks out. He's never been the last person to speak to someone before they died. It'll be a shock. It'll be an even bigger shock if it turns out his car was involved." Eric nods and envelops me in a hug and a kiss. I lean into him, inhaling his scent and listening to his heartbeat through his sweater. We both relax a little. "Adam's car should be easy to find," I theorize. "His fancy car comes with a fancy app that shows him where his car is and even shows him how it got there. You should be able to trace the route it drove last night."

Eric nods. "That's next." He sighs. "When I go upstairs, I'll ask him to show me the app." We cuddle on the sofa, in the cozy sitting area near the front of the store. "Do you know anything about Saxon's family?" Eric asks. "We need to notify his next of kin, but we don't know who to notify." He rubs Sophie when she jumps onto the sofa next to him.

"I would ask Rick," I suggest. "He's the only person who

seemed to like Saxon. Other than that, he must have a lawyer. I mean, someone helped him close all those real estate deals."

"I have an officer looking into that," Eric says. "She's tracking down his lawyer as we speak."

Hearing him mention that he's delegated someone to find Saxon's lawyer reminds me that today is a big day for Eric too. Besides a new mayor, Harmony Lake gets a new permanent chief of police today.

"Congratulations," I say, nuzzling into his neck. "Today, you're the permanent chief of police. I know Adam's victory party is tonight, but how do you want to celebrate your achievement? Do you want me to plan something?"

"Thank you," he replies, squeezing me tightly. "I don't feel very celebratory right now. Can we put it on the back burner for a while?"

"Totally," I agree, relieved.

I'm not feeling festive either, and I'm wondering if it's appropriate to have Adam's victory party tonight, considering his opponent died today, suddenly and suspiciously.

"Do you think given the circumstances we should postpone Adam's victory party?" I ask.

"Absolutely not," Eric replies without hesitation. "Everyone from the card game will be there. Along with other people who might have hated Saxon Renaud enough to want him dead. This party could lead to a break in the case. Also, all the friends and volunteers who helped with Adam's campaign deserve recognition for their contributions, regardless of what happened on Lake Access Road last night."

Eric returns to his apartment to continue talking to Adam, and I pull out my phone to text Connie.

Me: Good morning! I hear Ryan had a rough night. If you need to stay home today, I totally understand.

Connie: Ryan is fine. Archie will tend to him. Besides, I've already put my face on! I'll be there soon.

I should have known it would take more than a snowstorm and her stepson's near-relapse to keep Connie away from Knitorious.

Connie was the original owner of Knitorious. She passed it on to me before she semi-retired with Archie. Before that, I worked for her part-time for five years. Now, we've switched roles; I own the store, and Connie works here part-time. Connie *is* Knitorious, without her the store wouldn't exist.

We met after Adam, Hannah, and I moved to Harmony Lake eighteen years ago. I was a young, recently married, new mother, living in a town where I didn't know anyone. If that wasn't enough to deal with, my mum died just before we moved here. Between missing my mum and an ambitious husband who was working all hours to build a career, I was overwhelmed.

I coped by knitting through my grief during Hannah's naps and after we put her to bed at night. One day, realizing I'd grief-knitted through my entire yarn stash, I pushed the stroller into Knitorious and met Connie. Our connection was instant. Connie took Hannah and I under her wing, filling the mother and grandmother-shaped holes in our hearts. We became friends, then quickly became family. She calls me her daughter-friend, and I call her my mother-friend.

"Good morning, my dear!" Connie sings as she breezes into the store from the back room.

At seventy-one years young, Connie is the most sophisticated, beautiful woman I know.

"Good morning," I say as Connie hugs me.

Her sleek silver bob tickles my cheek, and she smells like lilac, comfort and unconditional love.

"Your car isn't in the parking lot," she observes. "Did you and Sophie walk to work in the snow?"

"No," I reply. "We walked to work yesterday and spent the night upstairs."

"Very practical," Connie commends. "I'm glad you decided not to drive in this."

Says the woman who drove through the snow to get here.

"How's Ryan?" I ask.

Connie sighs and, knitting in hand, joins Sophie on the sofa. "He's all right. It was touch and go for a while, but he's using all his tools to stay on track."

"Thank goodness. Do you think it would be OK if I text him to tell him I'm rooting for him? I don't want to upset him or pressure him."

"Oh, I'm sure he'd love that, my dear! How did you hear about his unfortunate incident?"

Connie has a charming tendency to refer to everything she finds disagreeable as either "unpleasant" or "unfortunate."

"Adam mentioned it," I reply, pursing my lips into a tight smile and fighting the urge to tell her everything that has happened since last night.

"Have you heard anything about the unpleasantness on Lake Access Road?" Connie asks nonchalantly.

"There was some kind of car accident." I shrug. "Eric went there in the middle of the night."

She stops knitting, puts her needles on her lap, and looks at me over the top of her reading glasses. "Did he tell you what happened or who was involved?"

"We haven't really seen each other." It's not a lie. "Adam slept in the spare room last night, and Eric and I bumped into each other when I walked Sophie this morning."

I avoid answering Connie's question directly because I can't lie to her. I'm not a good liar. Lying gives me anxiety, and I'll do anything to avoid feeling anxious.

"Why did Adam sleep here last night?" she asks.

"He lost his keys and couldn't get into his car or condo. Eric was at Lake Access Road, and my car wasn't here. The easiest solution was for Adam to crash in the spare room."

"Did he find his keys?" Connie asks.

I can tell she's suspicious. She knows there's more to the

story. Even though I'm not lying to her, Connie knows I'm not being completely honest.

Saved by the bell, my phone dings, and I rush to the counter to fetch it.

Eric: Found Adam's car. On our way there now.

Me: Where is it?

Eric: Your house.

My house? Why? How did it get there?

"Is everything all right, my dear?" Connie asks, bringing me back to the here and now.

I nod, typing one more quick text to Eric.

Me: Drive safely. Let me know what happens.

Connie cranes her neck and looks toward the back of the store where the distant, muffled thumping of large, booted man-feet are clumping on the stairs. We both hear the familiar thud of the back door closing, then she looks at me expectantly.

"That was Eric and Adam," I explain. "Eric is taking Adam to find his keys." Connie continues to look at me, her facial expression unchanged. Her blue eyes wide with waiting. "Adam thinks he may have dropped them at Sheamus's house in the rush to leave last night to find Ryan."

Satisfied with my explanation, Connie opens her mouth in a silent "Ah," nods with a smile, and resumes knitting. "I hope he finds them," she remarks. "I've heard replacement keys for those luxury cars are very expensive. In fact, I'm told all the costs related to luxury cars are unnecessarily high."

Relieved at the change in topic, I nod encouragingly while Connie educates me about the inflated costs of everything related to luxury vehicles until it's time to unlock the front door and turn the sign from CLOSED to OPEN.

Within minutes of opening the store, my phone blows up with texts. People are asking if I'm all right, and curious to know why there are police cruisers and crime-scene tape around Adam's car in my driveway.

CHAPTER 5

ERIC: *It's here!*

Me: *So I'm told.*

People are even texting me photos of the scene in my driveway. I assume a crowd has gathered on the street in front of chez Martel, as my house is affectionately known locally.

I send a quick text to my confused and concerned best friend, April, explaining that everyone is OK and promising to phone her soon. Apparently, the brief text explanation isn't good enough, and she replies with a photo of her faux, fur-cuffed, rated-for-minus-forty-degrees winter boots standing in the snow outside Artsy Tartsy. This means her booted feet are marching toward Knitorious right now and will walk through the door any second.

Artsy Tartsy is the bakery April and her wife, Tamara, own. Tamara is a talented pastry chef, and her creations are locally famous. Artsy Tartsy is down the street from Knitorious.

I look at Connie and smile. She looks back at me, matching my smile.

"I'll wait until April gets here," she says, "so you won't have to repeat yourself."

I nod. How does she know April is coming? Did April text her, or is Connie freakishly intuitive? I decide not to ask.

Thanks to the fresh snow from last night's storm, the skiers and snowboarders will spend the day on the slopes and are unlikely to venture down from the mountain resorts to shop. Business will be slow today, which means I won't have any customers to use as an excuse when Connie and April ask me questions I want to answer but know I shouldn't. Like, was anyone hurt on Lake Access Road? And why is there front-end damage to Adam's car? And how did his car get to my house if Adam was here with me?

April walks through the door, carrying one of my favourite things: a white confectionery box with the Artsy Tartsy logo on the lid.

"You are a real-life snow angel!" I declare, relieving her of the box while she pulls down her white, faux, fur-lined hood and takes off her white puffy winter coat. "I'm starving!"

Whatever is in this box is fresh-from-the-oven warm and smells glorious. It's making my mouth water.

"I'll plug in the kettle and get plates," Connie announces as she crosses the threshold from the store to the back room.

"It's not a treat," April clarifies as we hug, "It's a bribe. Something big is going on, and you know the details. Pastries for information. That's the deal, Megnificent." She winks as we pull apart.

April likes to call me random nicknames that are puns of my actual name. This morning I'm Megnificent.

April and I have been best friends since we met at a mummy-and-me group with our daughters eighteen years ago. Our daughters are the same age and are best friends. They even attend university together in Toronto. Besides their daughter, Rachel, April and Tamara also have a son, Zach who's sixteen.

Connie pops her head out of the back room. "Don't start without me."

We give her a thumbs-up.

April greets Sophie with rubs and tells her there's a treat in the confectionery box for her, then opens the box and pulls out a small white bag. At the sight of the bag, Sophie's ears perk up to full attention and her entire back end, not just her tail, wags with enthusiasm.

Besides yummy treats for humans, Tamara also makes pet treats under the brand name, The Barkery: Gourmet Treats For Well-Heeled Pets.

April puts her hand in the bag and pulls out what looks like a Sophie-sized bagel. "Peanut butter dog doughnut with carob icing," she explains to Sophie and me.

Because she's a good girl, Sophie contains her obvious excitement, sits, and waits patiently for April to put the treat on the floor in front of her. She eats it so fast, I wonder if she bothered to chew the thing.

"Start at the beginning, my dear," Connie urges, as she places the tea tray on the coffee table.

In between bites of my pomegranate-seed and cream cheese-topped puff pastry, I explain how Eric woke me in the middle of the night to tell me he had to go into work, then, after he left, a semi-frozen Adam knocked on the back door, looking for a ride to my house to get his spare set of keys because he lost his original set at Sheamus's house.

"Is that when Adam told you about Ryan?" Connie asks.

I shake my head. "No, I didn't ask for any details, and Adam didn't offer. We were both too exhausted for conversation. I found some pyjamas for him, and we went to sleep in our respective rooms."

"What happened to Ryan?" April asks, worried. "Was he involved in that accident everyone is talking about? The one on Lake Access Road?"

The Harmony Lake gossip network's dedication to spreading news is matched only by their speed. If I didn't know better, I'd swear they use telepathy to communicate because it feels like news travels throughout our community at the speed of thought. Even news about incidents that happen on remote roads in the middle of the night during a snowstorm. They have eyes and ears everywhere, all the time.

"Haven't you heard?" Connie asks April.

Wide-eyed, April shakes her head, and Connie tells her about Ryan's "unpleasant experience" at the card game when, by accident, he sipped an alcoholic drink.

Upon hearing that Saxon was among the poker-night participants, April looks at me and asks, "Do we think it was an accident, or do we think it was Saxon being Saxon?"

I shrug. "Adam believes it was intentional. He says everyone else who was there believes it was intentional too." I tell her and Connie what Adam told Eric and me about the lime wedge mysteriously moving from one drink to another.

A low, animalistic growl emanates from the back of April's throat, and she rolls her eyes. "That man is infuriating!" Though she doesn't refer to him by name, I know she means Saxon Renaud. He evokes this reaction from people. "I swear causing trouble for other people is how he entertains himself. He collects enemies the way some people collect stamps."

I'm about to correct April's present tense statement by replacing the verbs with their past tenses, but stop myself by biting my lips. His death isn't public knowledge yet, and I promised Eric I wouldn't say anything. It's difficult, though, because I tell April and Connie everything. I remind myself it's only temporary until the police notify Saxon's next of kin.

"What were you about to say, my dear?" Connie asks, raising her eyebrows and nodding at my forcefully closed mouth.

"Just that it would be a strange coincidence, if the only time Ryan accidentally confuses an alcoholic drink with his non-alcoholic drink is the one time Saxon is there and seated next to him." It's a quasi-lie. I would've said this *after* I corrected April's remarks and made them past tense.

"How did Adam's car end up at your house if Adam wasn't driving it?" April asks.

I shake my head and shrug. "That's the million-dollar question," I reply. "Adam thinks he lost his keys in the rush to leave Sheamus's house and look for Ryan. He said when he walked away from Sheamus's house, his car was parked across the street. If it's not there now, it was stolen."

"Someone else must have found his keys," Connie surmises.

April nods. "Adam's car has a decent security system. It would be difficult to steal without the keys."

I nod in agreement.

We finish our tea and pastries while we discuss how uncommon auto theft is in Harmony Lake. To the best of Connie's recollection, the last time a car was stolen was the mid 90s. A coach's car was taken for a joy ride by the players from a rival hockey team in Harmony Hills. The rival team plastered the coach's car in Harmony Hills Hockey Association bumper stickers before abandoning it on the side of the highway.

"Are you suggesting a rival lawyer stole Adam's car and took it for a joyride?" I ask jokingly when Connie finishes her story. "Or a rival mayor?"

"If they covered it in bumper stickers, Adam will go berserk!" April laughs with that contagious laugh she has, making Connie and I laugh with her.

We're interrupted when Connie's cell phone rings. April and I suppress our giggles while Connie steps away from the cozy sitting area to answer the call.

I can't hear most of what she says because Connie gravitates away from us and toward the back room. She straightens and fusses with random skeins of yarn on the shelves as she moves through the store and talks quietly on her phone. The few words I hear are imbued with a tone of worry. And when she glances at us, her facial expression matches the concern in her voice. Her eyes are wide, and her mouth, which usually smiles, is pressed into a thin, tense line.

"What's going on?" April whispers.

"I don't know, but it's not good," I reply.

"Do you think it's Ryan?" she asks.

"I hope not."

Connie hangs up and, looking stunned, pulls out one of the Parsons chairs from the harvest table and sits down. April, Sophie, and I join her.

"Connie, what's wrong?" April asks, sitting in the chair beside her. "Did something happen?"

"Whatever it is, we're here for you," I remind Connie as I sit in the chair on the other side of her.

"That was Archie," Connie tells us, referring to her boyfriend. "He said a police officer came and took Ryan to the station for questioning."

Ryan is Archie's son.

"Questioning about what?" I ask, wondering if the officer said Ryan was being questioned about Saxon Renaud's death.

"Archie doesn't know." Connie's concern is morphing into fear. I can hear it in her voice and see it on her face. "What if Saxon is pressing charges against Ryan because of their shoving match last night?" Connie looks at April, then at me. "Ryan has a record. This could be really bad for him."

Several years ago, when Ryan was a young man with a drinking problem, he moved to Ottawa to work for his uncle's construction company. While he was there, he made some bad decisions. He caught some of his co-workers stealing supplies from the construction site, and instead of turning them in, he agreed to look the other way for a cut of the proceeds from the sale of the stolen goods. Unbeknownst to Ryan, one of the co-workers involved in the scheme was an informant who was working with the police to bring down the theft ring. When the takedown happened, Ryan was arrested and charged, even though he didn't steal or resell anything. Benefitting from the theft was enough to get him convicted. He spent a few months in jail, followed by a few years on probation. The experience was a wake-up call for him, and he got sober and made better decisions.

Ryan has been an upstanding member of our community since. He moved back to Harmony Lake and started working with his dad. They own the handyman company, The Wright Men For The Job. Ryan is a one-man operation nowadays because Archie is semi-retired and only works occasionally. I trust Ryan, and so do most of the other town residents. He's in and out of our homes and businesses regularly, fixing things, installing things, and keeping our town running smoothly. I would trust Ryan with my life. I would trust him with Hannah's life. I don't believe for a moment that Ryan could kill Saxon Renaud, no matter what Saxon did to provoke him.

"I don't think Saxon filed a complaint about Ryan to the police." I can't stand to see the tears welling up in Connie's eyes. I need to reassure her there's no way Saxon filed a complaint against Ryan.

"But you don't know that for sure," Connie responds. "How could you?"

"Trust me," I say, putting my hand on top of hers.

"You know what Saxon is like," Connie says. "Maybe when he found out he lost the election, he went looking for someone to take out his frustration on and set his sights on Ryan. Saxon Renaud could be at the police station right now, spinning a web of lies about what happened between him and Ryan last night."

"Saxon Renaud is not at the police station," I insist confidently, shaking my head.

"How do you know?"

"Because Saxon Renaud is dead." Adam is standing in the doorway between the store and the back room.

CHAPTER 6

"ADAM?!" I say, not sure if I'm more surprised by his sudden appearance or his use of the back door.

Adam never uses the back door at Knitorious, and this is the fifth time he's used it in less than twelve hours.

He steps into the store and joins us at the harvest table. "Saxon died last night in the incident on Lake Access Road."

Connie doesn't seem reassured by this explanation, and I understand why. She's already concerned that Ryan is being questioned about shoving Saxon, and now she realizes it's possible he's being questioned in relation to Saxon's death. A much more serious crime, with much more serious consequences.

"Is Saxon's death public knowledge?" I ask quietly, looking at Adam.

Adam nods. "Eric said it's fine. They found a brother to notify."

"Oh," I say.

The four of us sit together in silence while Connie and April process what they just heard. I break the silence when I notice Jess standing in the back room. She must've come in with Adam. I'm glad she's here with him.

"Hi, Jess." I greet her with a hug, and she joins us at the harvest table.

"Hi, everyone," she mumbles. "What a day, huh?"

Connie asks Adam to go to the police station as Ryan's lawyer and stay with him while they interview Ryan. Adam explains that he can't do that because he's also a person of interest in the case and offers to refer Ryan to another lawyer.

Connie decides she should be with Archie, so they can anxiously wait for Ryan together. We all offer to drive her home. In fact we try to insist that someone should drive her home and stay with them, but she won't accept any of our offers and insists she will drive herself. She promises to call if she or Archie need anything.

After giving everyone the opportunity to hug her and reassure her that Ryan did nothing wrong and will probably be home before lunchtime, Connie goes to the back door and puts on her coat. I follow her and ask one more time if she'll let me take her home.

"No, my dear, I'll be fine. I promise." She brushes a stray curl away from my face then puts on her gloves. "I need you to be my eyes and ears," she whispers. "Find out everything you can about how Saxon died, so we can prove Ryan and Adam had nothing to do with this unpleasantness."

I nod. "I'll do my best."

We kiss cheeks, and I close the door behind her after she leaves.

Adam takes out his phone and shows us some photos of the front-end damage on his car. They parked the car at the bottom of my driveway.

"You'd think hitting a grown person would cause more damage to the car," I observe, looking at the photos.

"That's what I said," Adam agrees. "But Eric thinks Saxon was already lying on the road when my car ran over him."

Why would Saxon be lying in several inches of snow, on the road, in the middle of the night? Did the killer render

Saxon unconscious, then run him over? Was Saxon drugged? Is it possible Saxon was already dead? But if he was already dead, why bother running over him at all?

Maybe whoever ran over him wanted to cover up the fact that Saxon was already dead and his actual cause of death. Or maybe they wanted to make it look like Adam killed Saxon. I wonder if Eric has heard from the coroner yet. I resist the urge to text him with all my questions because he's probably questioning Ryan, and I don't want to interrupt them.

"So, it was your car that hit Saxon?" I ask. "The police know for sure?"

"Not one hundred percent," Adam replies, "but according to the app, my car was on Lake Access Road last night. It took a rather indirect route to get there, but it was there, and my car's movements coincide with the 9-1-1 call from the anonymous witness who said they saw my car leaving the scene. We're waiting for forensics to confirm it, but it's safe to assume it was my car."

Jess, April, and I exhale almost in unison.

"Are you a suspect?" Jess asks Adam.

Adam nods.

"How?" April asks, then she points to the ceiling. "You were asleep upstairs. How could you drive from Lake Access Road to Megan's house, dump your car, lose your keys, and walk to Eric's apartment in that short time?"

"Also," I add, "didn't you say you stopped at the pub to see if Sheamus was there? Before you came here?" If he stopped in at the pub, someone would have seen him and can confirm he was there and not in his car near Lake Access Road.

"I went there, but the pub was closed," Adam clarifies.

"They're open until 2 a.m.," Jess counters.

Adam shrugs. "I guess they closed early because of the weather."

He looks exhausted and defeated. I ask him if I can have another look at the photos on his phone.

"They parked your car at the very bottom of my driveway," I point out. "The back end overhangs the driveway." I look at Adam. "Don't you think that's strange?"

"I think this whole situation is strange, Meg," he replies. "Eric checked the security footage, and the cameras didn't pick up my car at all. He thinks whoever left my car there knew about the security system and parked like this to avoid the cameras."

While you'd think this information would narrow down the number of potential suspects, it doesn't. Harmony Lake is a tiny town, and everyone knows about the state-of-the-art security system at my house. Adam had it installed before he moved out because someone broke in, laid in wait for me, and tried to kill me.

Eric can check the camera footage because he has access to the app that came with the security system. He can lock and unlock the house, arm and disarm the security system, and view the camera footage.

"Who cleared the snow from the driveway?" I ask, although I'm sure I already know the answer.

"Who do you think?" Adam answers my question with a question.

"Phillip," April and I answer in stereo.

Phillip Wilde is my next-door neighbour at home and at work. His florist shop, Wilde Flowers, shares a wall and a parking lot with Knitorious. Phillip is a thoughtful, diligent neighbour who likes to ensure the curb appeal of the neighbourhood meets a certain minimum standard. If I don't clear my snow quickly enough, Phillip will clear it for me— and the other driveways in the immediate vicinity of his house—when he clears his own driveway with his snowblower.

He's wonderfully thorough about it too. Looking at these

photos, there isn't one flake of snow left on my driveway. Or on Adam's car.

"Did he clean the snow off your car too?" I ask.

"He sure did," Adam confirms with a hint of exasperation in his voice. "He said there was no point in doing the driveway if I was going to come along and just brush the snow from my car onto the freshly cleared driveway."

"Of course, he did," I commiserate, realizing Phillip might have also unwittingly erased critical evidence like footprints in the snow, hair, or other DNA that might have fallen off the culprit when they abandoned the car. "He meant well, Adam. Phillip couldn't have known he was disturbing a crime scene."

"I know," Adam acknowledges somberly. "I thanked him for doing it."

"Did you get your spare keys while you were there?" April asks.

"Yes, and the ones he lost were in the ignition of his car," Jess replies. "The police have them now to check them for evidence, but at least we know where they are. But I think it's a good idea to change his locks, anyway. What if they made copies?"

"Jess is right, Adam," April advises. "Maybe you should call Ryan and get him to change the locks at your office and condo."

An uncomfortable silence follows the mention of Ryan's name. We're all reminded that a crime has taken place, and two members of our modern family are persons of interest.

Jess looks at Adam with a concerned expression on her thin, fair face. Her seafoam green eyes are heavy with worry, and her mouth is frowning. She rubs Adam's arm.

"Why don't we get you home? You haven't eaten yet today, and you look like you could use a nap before tonight," Jess suggests to Adam.

Adam rolls his eyes. "I forgot about tonight." He looks

back and forth from me to Jess. "We should postpone the victory party," he says.

Jess and I look at each other. She shrugs.

"I talked to Eric about postponing it," I tell everyone. "He wants it to continue as planned. He's hoping a room full of people who didn't like Saxon Renaud might yield some clues or information about what happened last night."

"Makes sense." Adam nods and gets up from his chair. He buttons up his navy peacoat and looks at Jess. "What do you think?"

Jess also stands up. She nods. "Whatever it takes to clear your name and put this behind us."

The four of us exchange hugs, and April and I tell Jess and Adam to call us if they need anything.

"This puts a damper on his first day as mayor, doesn't it?" April asks, after Adam and Jess have left.

"It sure does," I agree. "Even in death, Saxon Renaud can ruin everyone's day."

I feel bad as soon as I hear the words pass my lips. As much as I didn't like Saxon, he's not here to defend himself, and I shouldn't speak ill of the dead.

"Ryan and Adam had nothing to do with this," April proclaims.

"I know," I agree, nodding. "But unless the coroner concludes that Saxon's death was caused by either an accident or natural causes, someone killed Saxon Renaud. Someone local."

I know the murderer isn't Adam or Ryan, but to prove it and clear their names, I need to find the killer.

CHAPTER 7

"Hı, Marla."

"Hi, Megan."

I place the mouse tail I'm knitting on the coffee table in front of me and watch my part-time employee take off her coat while she hurries through the store to the back room.

We've only had two customers in the two hours since the store opened, and neither of them bought anything. I think one of them came in to escape from the cold for a few minutes, and the other made a beeline for the front window where Sophie was having her morning nap. She said she saw Sophie in the window and couldn't resist coming in to pet her. Neither person was familiar to me. I'm sure they were tourists.

After April left to get back to the bakery, I texted Marla and told her she was welcome to take the day off because last night's snowstorm brought today's business to a halt. Marla insisted she'd be here, and true to her word, here she is, right on time.

Like Connie, Marla was born and raised in Harmony Lake. She's the same age as Connie, and they've known each other all their lives.

"Did you hear what happened?" Marla asks, still trying to catch her breath as she smooths her salt-and-pepper pixie cut into place.

"Can you be more specific?" I ask. "It's been a busy day for news. Are you referring to the election results? The accident on Lake Acce…"

"Saxon Renaud is dead!" The words explode out of Marla's mouth like there's a prize for the first person to say them. "And so far, Ryan, Adam, Sheamus, and Pete are being questioned by the police."

I nod. "Yes, I heard about that. Sad. We don't know for sure they're being questioned about Saxon's death, though," I remind her.

"Why else would the police want to talk to them?"

She makes a good point. Time to change the subject.

"Saxon went to your church, didn't he?" I ask. "Did you know him well?"

Marla nods and joins me in the cozy sitting area with her knitting.

"He was a very polite, proper gentleman," Marla says, lowering her reading glasses from the top of her head to her eyes.

"Really?" I ask, skeptical at the suggestion Saxon Renaud had any redeeming qualities. "I hear he has a brother somewhere. Did Saxon ever talk to you about his family?"

Marla screws up her face and shrugs. "Saxon had a way of revealing nothing about himself, yet talking to you in a way that made you feel you knew each other well. He learned a lot about everyone else while revealing nothing about himself."

"So, he was a private person," I surmise.

Marla puts down her needles and considers my comment. "Not private. Secretive." Satisfied with her response, she picks up her needles and resumes knitting.

"What's the difference?" I ask, confused about the distinction.

"Well," Marla pauses, once again lowering her knitting to her lap, "privacy is passive, and secrecy is active."

"Go on," I urge.

I'm intrigued. Nothing about Saxon Renaud has ever intrigued me before, but this has my interest piqued.

"Private people don't hide information, but they don't broadcast it either. It's there, they just don't bring attention to it. Secretive people keep information hidden intentionally, out of fear. They're afraid if they reveal their information, something bad will happen. Saxon was secretive."

"That's deep, Marla. How do you have so much insight into Saxon? Did he tell you his secrets?"

She shakes her head and chuckles. "No. But after seven decades of people watching, you notice a few things."

"Did you notice anything else about Saxon?" I ask. "Anything that might help to piece together his last moments? Can you think of any reason he'd be on Lake Access Road?"

Marla shrugs and shakes her head. "I wish I could help, Megan, but I didn't know Saxon very well. We were acquaintances."

I smile, thank Marla for trying, and make a mental note to mention our conversation to Eric. Maybe Saxon had other friends in his church community who know more about him than Marla.

Marla and I knit in comfortable silence until we're interrupted by the jingle of the bell over the door.

"Cold enough for you?" The postal carrier asks as she drops a stack of mail on the counter.

The three of us make small talk about the weather until the postal carrier overheats underneath her winter gear and needs to escape to the cold air outside.

Sifting through the stack of mail, I find two items addressed to Wilde Flowers.

"Marla, will you be all right on your own while I pop next door and drop off Phillip's mail?"

"Of course," Marla insists, "take your time."

I nip into the kitchenette and grab the white confectionery bag that contains the last remaining peanut butter dog doughnut.

"Why, Megan Martel, where on earth is your coat?" Phillip asks melodramatically with one hand on his hip and the other waggling a finger at me scoldingly.

"I'm feeling impetuous," I tease, closing the door behind me. "With reckless abandon, I risked walking the few metres between our doors coatless." I mock gasp and bring my hand to my mouth.

"Scandalous," he replies sarcastically, clutching pretend pearls. "What will the neighbours think?"

We giggle, and I drop the envelopes on the counter of the florist shop.

"Some of your mail was delivered to Knitorious." I hold up the white confectionery bag and shake the contents. "And I have an extra dog treat from The Barkery. May Kevin have it?"

"Kevin, would you like a treat?" Phillip asks.

Kevin is Phillip's chihuahua. They go everywhere together. Kevin is perched regally atop his royal blue velvet pillow with gold piping and tassels. I let Kevin sniff my hand. After I pass his smell test, he positions his head so I can scratch between his ears.

I place the doggie doughnut on the velvet pillow. Kevin sniffs it cautiously, then takes small, chihuahua-sized bites.

"Thank you for clearing my driveway this morning," I say to Phillip, who's opening the mail I left on his counter.

"Anytime." He flicks his wrist dismissively and puts down the mail. "What's the deal with Adam's car?" he asks.

"It was stolen," I explain. "Sometime last night, someone

either found or stole his keys and took his car. Adam didn't realize it was missing until this morning, and I spent the night at Eric's, so we didn't know it was in my driveway until this morning."

"I saw some front-end damage when I brushed the snow off his car," Phillip explains. "Any idea what happened to it?"

"Not exactly," I reply honestly. "The forensics people have the car. They should have some answers soon."

"It was involved in the accident on Lake Access Road, wasn't it? Everyone's talking about it. Saxon Renaud died."

I nod. "So I've heard."

"I thought it was odd that Adam's car was there when you weren't home," Phillip observes. "And odder still, it was parked at the very foot of your driveway. Adam never parks like that. It makes sense now that you say someone stole the car."

"How did you know I wasn't home when you noticed Adam's car?" I ask.

It's not like I check in with Phillip when I spend the night away from home, and my car is always in the garage this time of year, making it more difficult to tell whether I'm home.

"Sophie," he explains. "When I clear your snow, or pull a few weeds from your garden, or water your plants, or whatever, Sophie watches me from the living room window. No Sophie, no Megan." Phillip shrugs.

"Ahhh," I say, "very observant of you."

As much as I want to ask more questions about how often Phillip tends to the garden and snow maintenance at my house, I stop myself, because who am I kidding? If it weren't for Phillip Wilde, my house would have no curb appeal. We both know he does at least half the work.

"I should get back," I say. "Marla is on her own, and it's time for Sophie's midday walk."

"Before you go," Phillip rushes around from behind the counter. "I think this rightfully belongs to you."

He reaches into his pants pocket and produces a shiny, copper penny.

"A penny?" I ask.

"A penny saved is a penny earned, as my mother used to say." Phillip presses the penny into my palm and closes my fingers around it.

"Thank you?" I'm confused. "But why is it rightfully mine?"

"I found it on your property," he explains. "It fell off Adam's back bumper when I was brushing the snow off his car. It's amazing I noticed it in all that snow. I would've missed it if it wasn't so shiny. It must be a lucky penny."

"It must be," I agree, looking down at the shiny penny in my hand.

"You know what they say." Phillip waggles his index finger at me. "See a penny, pick it up, and all day long you'll have good luck." He smiles.

"Thank you," I say, holding up the penny between my thumb and forefinger as I walk to the door.

Once upon a time, finding a penny was an everyday occurrence, but Canada hasn't had pennies in circulation since 2012. This one-cent coin is a relic from the past. These days, the only places to find pennies in Harmony Lake are old piggy banks, and the coin slots of Saxon Renaud's penny loafers. How did this penny end up on the rear bumper of Adam's car? If this penny is a clue in Saxon's murder, maybe it really is a lucky penny. Lucky for me, unlucky for Saxon's killer.

"MARLA, I'm taking Sophie for a walk, then I have to run an errand."

"No problem, Megan. Take as long as you want. If it's OK with you, I'm going to move some yarn around to display the reds, pinks, and purples for Valentine's day next month."

"Brilliant idea!" I tell her as I collect my bag from underneath the counter.

I put the penny Phillip gave me in the zippered coin slot of my wallet.

I bundle up myself and Sophie, put my Airpods in my ears under my ear warmer, and put my playlist on shuffle. With Adele's sultry vocal stylings crooning *Hello* in my ear, I warn Sophie to brace herself for the chilly walk home.

According to the text updates I've received from most of the town, the scene in my driveway has cleared up. With the crime-scene tape gone, and Adam's car towed away by the police, I can get my car out of the garage. My plan is to leave Sophie at home for the afternoon, drive to the police station to drop off the penny to Eric, then drive back to Knitorious and relieve Marla.

If this penny is from Saxon's penny loafer, how did it find its way onto Adam's back bumper? In the photos I've seen, there was no damage to the rear of his car, so it's unlikely Adam's car backed up over Saxon's body. And if the penny was there since the car left Lake Access Road, how did it get all the way to my house without blowing off the bumper? Maybe this penny isn't evidence after all, maybe it's a coincidence. I sigh. Whether the penny is relevant to Saxon's murder isn't for me to decide, it's for the police to determine.

While I'm deep in thought, my phone rings, startling me back to the here and now.

I reach under my ear warmer and tap my right Airpod to answer the call. "Hello?"

"Hey, babe! How's your day?"

The familiar echo tells me that Eric is in his car.

"Less eventful than yours," I reply. "Are you in the car? I thought you were interviewing witnesses."

"Another officer is helping me with the interviews. I'm on

my way home to have the shower I didn't get to have earlier. If you haven't walked Sophie yet, maybe you can wait for me and we can walk her together?"

"You're too late, Chief! Sophie and I are walking as we speak."

"Are you at the park? I can meet you."

"Nope, we're on our way home to pick up my car," I respond. "If you meet me there, I'll make you lunch and maybe give you some evidence for dessert."

"What kind of evidence?"

"It's a surprise," I tease.

Most women probably surprise their partners with fancy meals or sentimental gifts. Not us, we give each other clues and evidence. The gifts that keep on giving.

"Give me a hint," Eric pleads. "What size evidence bag should I bring?"

"The smallest one you have."

CHAPTER 8

I MAKE a quick omelette for Eric and me with some leftover ham and chopped onion I find in the fridge.

Eric hasn't put down his phone since he walked through the door. His thumbs are forever typing and have been since he accepted the interim chief of police position three months ago. His phone has a bigger presence in our lives than it ever did before; it's like an unwanted third person in our relationship. Even when he's not at work, he's invisibly tethered to the station thanks to the magic of Wi-Fi and 5G cell phone networks. Days off don't exist for him anymore.

Before he was chief, Eric's phone was only this active when he was working a case, but now it never stops. It rings, dings, vibrates, beeps, and buzzes twenty-four hours a day, seven days a week. At first, I told myself it was a transitional phase, and the need to be constantly reachable would slow down once he settled into his new role. Now, I'm not sure. I'm having flashbacks to being married to Adam, and look how that turned out.

"Thank you," he says, without looking up from his phone when I put his plate in front of him.

Finally, he turns the blasted thing upside down and pushes it to the other end of the table.

"Can I ask you something?" I push some omelette around my plate with my fork.

"Of course," Eric replies, "you can ask me anything." He bites into his toast.

"When you found Saxon, did both of his penny loafers have pennies in them?"

"You found it?" Eric garbles, still chewing. His eyebrows almost disappear into his hairline, and he swallows with a loud gulp. "Where did you find it?"

I shrug one shoulder. "I didn't find it. It found me. Phillip gave it to me. He didn't seem to realize it might be evidence."

"He didn't think it was evidence?" Eric sounds dubious. "What did he think it was? Where did he find it?"

"He thought it was good luck," I reply, and I recite the little rhyme Phillip told me when he gave the penny to me earlier. "Look at it from Phillip's perspective," I suggest. "When Phillip cleared the snow earlier, he didn't know about the accident on Lake Access Road or about Saxon's death. It didn't occur to him that Adam's car was a crime scene or that he might come across evidence."

"Phillip thought finding a shoe with a penny in it was good luck?" Eric clarifies, suspiciously.

I think we're talking about different things.

"No, he thinks the penny he found on the rear bumper of Adam's car was good luck. He thinks it's a lucky penny," I explain. Then I realize what I'm missing. "Was Saxon missing an entire shoe? Not just the penny?" I ask.

Eric puts down his fork. His phone has been buzzing the entire time we've been talking, and he glances over at it. I can tell he wants to pick it up. He restrains himself.

"The shoe is a holdback," Eric tells me.

A holdback is a piece of evidence from the scene of a crime the police don't disclose to the public. Something only the culprit or someone with inside knowledge of the crime would know about. The holdback is used to confirm a suspect's confession or expose a false confession. According to Eric, false confessions happen more than you'd think.

"I won't tell anyone," I assure him.

"I know." He takes my hand. "The umbrella is a holdback too. We can't locate it, either."

"His umbrella is missing?" I swallow to suppress a smile. There's poetic justice in Saxon Renaud being separated from his beloved umbrella. "Do you think he poked the wrong person with it, and they killed him?" I'm half-joking, half-serious. "Or he drew another battle line in the snow, and it made someone angry?"

"Maybe," Eric replies. "Based on the coroner's preliminary findings, Saxon was already dead when Adam's car ran over him. He was likely murdered somewhere else, then transported to Lake Access Road. The cause of death is strangulation. The coroner isn't sure if the killer yoked him from behind, or did it face-to-face, but Saxon's neck was compressed with a straight, blunt object."

A straight, blunt object like an umbrella, maybe?

"And now you can't find his umbrella. You suspect the cause of death is strangulation, and the manner of death is the umbrella," I deduce.

Eric nods.

In cop speak, the cause of death is how the victim died, and the manner of death is how the cause of death was delivered.

So, the killer—or killers—put Saxon's dead body in Adam's car, drove to Lake Access Road, removed Saxon's body from the car, positioned it in the road, and drove over it. Why? We're either looking for one very strong person, or multiple average-strength people. Lugging a dead body around isn't easy.

We finish eating, and while Eric clears the dishes from the

table, I retrieve the penny from my wallet and meet him in the family room.

"I haven't ruled out anyone yet," Eric says as he seals the evidence bag with the penny in it. "Everyone at the card game last night is a suspect. And if Adam lost his keys *outside* Sheamus's house, the pool of potential suspects gets even bigger."

I cozy up next to him on the sofa and pull the blanket over our legs. He yawns and sinks deeper into the sofa. Because yawns are contagious, I yawn too. His eyes are tired and bleary. Can he even see me clearly?

"Adam said his car took an indirect route to Lake Access Road," I say. "Could the murder scene be somewhere along that route? The killer either brought Adam's car to Saxon's body or brought Saxon's body to Adam's car. The former would be easier and less conspicuous than the latter."

"Officers are searching the route inch by inch," Eric explains. "So far, there's no indication of a murder scene. They haven't found a shoe or an umbrella, either. I think the indirect route might have been a tactic the killer used to avoid being recognized while driving Adam's car."

"That confirms my suspicions that whoever killed Saxon is a local," I conclude.

"Why? What else makes you think the killer is local?" Eric asks, pulling away to look me in the eye.

"Well, they knew about Lake Access Road," I begin. "Only people who live in Harmony Lake or visit frequently would know about it and how to get there. Also, we were having a snowstorm, and you wouldn't be here in a blizzard if you didn't live here. Harmony Lake is too remote to enter and exit in terrible weather. And they left Adam's car at my house. They associated this address with him and wanted his car to get back to him. It all screams local to me."

"The last part is the part that bothers me," Eric reveals. "It doesn't make sense to leave Adam's car at your house." He looks at me. "Why not abandon it at Adam's office? Or the parking lot at the pub? Or in front of Sheamus's house, where they found it? All of those places would have been lower risk than your house because none of them have security cameras. They chose the only house in town with security cameras. And they knew about your cameras because they parked the car to avoid them. There's a reason the killer left the car here, and if I can figure it out, it might lead us to the killer."

"The only thing I can think of," I say, trying to help, "is that all the places you listed are either too high traffic or too remote."

"Everything in this town is downtown or remote," Eric points out. "There's no in between."

"Adam's office and condo are both at the eastern most point of town. If the killer didn't have another car handy, it would be a long walk in a snowstorm to get anywhere," I reason. "The pub parking lot is busy and well-lit, even during a snowstorm. It snows here six months of the year. The residents of this town are used to snow. They won't let a blizzard stop them from a night at the pub. If the killer didn't know the pub closed early because of the storm, they would avoid the parking lot for fear of being seen dropping off Adam's car. Same with Sheamus's house. He lives right behind Water Street, and his street gets a lot of foot traffic when people stumble home from the pub."

"Those are good points," Eric cedes, then yawns again, "but it doesn't explain why they chose this specific house." He gestures around himself.

"Either their car was near here, or my house is walking distance to wherever they went next," I speculate. "And I live on a quiet street, far enough away from Water Street that it was unlikely anyone would recognize them walking up the street in a blizzard."

"We don't even know which direction they went after they left the car." He sounds dejected.

"The falling snow covered up any footprints or tire tracks they left, and Phillip's dedication to snow removal blew away any evidence the killer might have left near the car."

"Except the lucky penny," I remind him. "And maybe the forensics team will find something inside Adam's car that will help identify whoever did this."

"Let's hope," Eric mutters.

Could one of my neighbours be a murderer? The thought makes me visibly shudder. Eric squeezes me tighter, and I pull the blanket up to my shoulders.

Eric's phone is in his other hand again, and he's scrolling through messages.

"Why did Sheamus lie about being home when Adam texted him this morning?" I ask.

Eric sighs. "I don't know. I can't verify Sheamus's alibi." He stops typing and puts his phone on the armrest of the sofa. He blinks rapidly and rubs his eyes with his free hand. "He says he was driving around looking for Ryan, and when he got the text saying Ryan was found and was safe, he parked at the pub and walked home. He claims he turned off his phone and went to bed. Which would explain why Adam didn't see Sheamus's truck in the driveway when he went back to his house."

"Why would Sheamus park at the pub and walk home?" I ask. "His house is only a short drive from the pub."

"He blamed the weather," Eric explains. "He said visibility was terrible, and he didn't want to drive."

"Sheamus drives a huge four-wheel-drive pickup truck with a snowplow attachment in the winter. But he didn't want to drive for five minutes in the snow? OK," I say, with sarcasm oozing from each word.

"I know, babe, but I can't prove Sheamus is lying. His truck was in the parking lot where he said it would be, and it was covered in several hours' worth of snow accumulation."

I look up at him, and his eyes are tired and bloodshot.

"Will you do something for me?" I ask.

"I'd do anything for you," he replies, once again looking at his phone. "What do you want me to do?"

"Take a nap."

"A nap?" he asks, returning his phone to the armrest.

I nod.

"You want me to sleep?" He looks at me. "Now?"

I nod again. "With your phone turned off."

"It's day one of a murder investigation. I can't take a nap," Eric reasons. "And I can't just turn off my phone."

I take a deep breath and prepare to make my case. "Honey, it's a day and a half past your bedtime," I tell him. "You've slept less than two hours out of the last thirty, and you still have Adam's victory party tonight because *you* insisted that it continue as planned, so you could observe the suspects in the same room at the same time."

"Can I nap with my phone on?" he counters, attempting to negotiate.

I shake my head. "It never stops, and you won't sleep. The world won't end if you unplug for a few hours."

"What if you have an emergency and need to reach me?" He's grasping for reasons to keep his phone on.

"Nap here. If I need you, I'll call the landline," I propose, shutting down his argument. "I'll wake you in plenty of time to shower and get dressed for tonight," I assure him, making it more difficult to find a reason not to nap. I make one last plea and try to appeal to his sense of duty. "You'll be a more effective investigator if you recharge your battery." I rest my case.

"I have to take the lucky penny to forensics." He shrugs, smirking triumphantly.

I didn't expect this argument.

"I'll drop off the penny on my way to the store. Just tell me who to give it to." Ha! Argue with that, Sloane!

"Fine," he surrenders with a sigh.

I tuck in Eric and Sophie for a nap, plug his phone into a charger in another room, and turn it off before the lucky penny and I get in the car and head to the Harmony Lake Police Station.

CHAPTER 9

TODAY REQUIRES extra caffeine if I'm going to stay awake long enough to attend Adam's victory party tonight. At least, this is what I tell myself to justify having two coffees today. I was going to justify it by getting one for Marla and telling myself I may as well get one for myself while I'm here, but I texted Marla, and she said it's too late in the day for her to have coffee.

While I stand in line at Latte Da, waiting for the barista to finish making my white chocolate and peppermint latte with extra whipped cream and a sprinkle of white chocolate shavings, I text Connie to make sure she, Archie, and Ryan are OK. She insists everyone is fine, and they're still planning to attend the victory celebration tonight. It will reassure me to see them in person and gauge for myself that Ryan is OK.

Coffee in hand, I lower my sunglasses from the top of my head to my face and step onto the sidewalk. A sunny day after a fresh snowfall is always brighter than usual because the sunlight reflecting off the snow makes everything appear brighter. A sunny, winter day can be brighter, and harder on the eyes, than a sunny summer day.

Sheamus O'Brien is loitering on the sidewalk outside

Hairway to Heaven. Is he peering in the window? I get the impression he's trying to look discreet about it, but his awkward attempt to appear nonchalant makes his vibe more creepy-stalker than casual passerby. I guess it's hard to be inconspicuous with a head of bright red hair and pale Irish complexion. When tourists at the pub comment on Sheamus's stereotypical Irish pigmentation and ginger hair, he jokingly tells them it's because of the lack of sunlight inside pubs.

Hairway to Heaven is the hair salon next door to Latte Da, and across the street from the pub. The owner, Kelly, is my hairdresser and good friend.

Curious to see how this plays out, I hang back for a few minutes and watch what Sheamus does next. Leaning against the wall between the two stores, I sip my latte and watch Sheamus spy on whatever is happening inside Hairway to Heaven.

He's wearing that scarf again; the chunky hand-knit one he wore last night. The yarn is even more beautiful in the daylight, and I'm dying to ask him about it.

"Hi, Megan," Sheamus says when he notices me. "Cold enough for ya?"

"Hi, Sheamus." I smile. "Whatcha doin'?"

He shrugs. "Nothing much." He fidgets when I push myself off the wall and crane my neck to look at the window he was just peeping through, then look back at him. "I was thinking of getting a haircut," he explains, "but it looks like they're busy. They probably won't be able to fit me in." He shrugs again and self-consciously shifts his weight from one foot to the other.

I nod. Why is he uneasy? He's not usually uneasy; he's usually laid back and relaxed.

Sheamus doesn't look like he's due for a haircut. The longest hair on his ginger head appears to be only an inch long. I cup my free hand against my temple and squint, looking in the window. Two stylists sit at the reception desk, chatting and giggling.

"Doesn't look busy to me," I observe.

Sheamus shoves his ungloved hands in his jeans pocket and rocks back and forth on his heels. "Kelly's busy though. I only like Kelly to do my hair."

I look in the window again and scan the salon for Kelly. Sure enough, there she is with her back to the window, leaning over a sink, washing a client's hair.

"Me too," I admit. "Kelly is the only hairdresser who's touched my hair in a dozen years." I smile.

"She's the best." Seamus grins widely and blushes.

"May I touch your scarf?" I ask, proud of myself for checking first, instead of just reaching out and petting it, like I'm tempted to do.

"Absolutely," he replies, pulling the rest of his scarf out from inside his zippered coat. "A special friend made it for me," he explains. "She said she chose the yarn because the colours remind her of Ireland. She paired it with white yarn. It reminds me of the Irish flag."

"Yes, it looks a bit like the Irish flag," I agree, enjoying the squishiness of the stitches. "Alpaca?" I ask, already certain it is.

The soft, spongy texture and the fuzzy haze surrounding the fabric is a dead giveaway that this yarn is mostly, if not entirely, alpaca.

Sheamus nods. "Yes. Her aunt has an alpaca farm and spins and dyes the fibre herself. The whitish yarn is natural, undyed, and the yarn with reddish and green flecks is called *Ashes to Ashes, Rust to Rust*."

"It's beautiful," I say, smoothing the scarf against Sheamus's coat and taking a step back. "You know a lot about your scarf. Most non-knitters aren't as well-informed about their hand-knit gifts."

"Well," he blushes, "it's my favourite scarf." He tucks the ends back inside his coat.

"Sheamus," I start hesitantly, "what happened last night?"

We stroll toward Knitorious, and I sip my latte while Sheamus recounts his version of events. The details of his story are almost identical to Adam's description of what happened.

"At the height of the storm, visibility was awful, Megan. I parked my truck and walked home."

"It must have been bad," I sympathize. "But when Adam texted you this morning, you told him his car was still outside your house and you said it was untouched. Why did you tell him that? His car disappeared hours before he texted you."

Sheamus sighs. "I was still asleep when Adam texted me. His text woke me up. I was groggy and looked out the window to ease his mind because I could tell he was worried a snowplow had hit his car. There were two snow-covered cars parked on my street. The snow was smooth and untouched." He shrugs. "I assumed one of them must be Adam's Jag, so I texted him back and told him his car was fine."

That makes sense, except for the part where Adam's text woke up Sheamus. I'm sure Eric told me that, in his statement, Sheamus said he turned off his phone before he went to bed. If his phone was off, a text message couldn't have woken him.

Is Sheamus lying to me, or did he lie in his statement to the police? Or is the status of his cell phone a minor, insignificant detail that he's confused about?

"Hello?" I already know who it is because my phone has call display.

"It's dead here!" April declares. "It wasn't worth opening

the bakery today. T and I should have gone tobogganing instead."

"You and T go tobogganing?" I ask. "I had no idea."

"Sometimes," April replies. I can picture her shrugging as she says it, even though we're talking on the phone. "You should come with us next time. It's fun."

"Yes, please!" I used to love tobogganing. I haven't done it since my daughter was little. "I still have Hannah's old sled in the rafters of the garage."

"The reason I'm calling," April says, as if she's ever needed a reason to call me, "is to ask if we can bring a lot of baked goods to the party tonight. T baked them fresh for all the customers we didn't have today. Do you think it would be OK?"

"It has nothing to do with me," I remind her. "It's Adam's event. He and Jess planned it with Sheamus."

A loud sigh comes through my AirPods. "Sometimes, for whatever reason, I still think of you and Adam as a single unit," April admits quietly. "I'm sorry, Megapixel."

"No worries," I assure her. "Twenty-year habits are hard to break." Slightly uncomfortable pause. "But check with Jess about the baked goods, I think she chose the menu for tonight," I add, changing the subject. "And check with Sheamus, too, since he's catering." I look around the store, even though I know I'm the only person here because Marla left to take her break. "Speaking of Sheamus…"

"Have you seen him? Did you ask him about last night?" April gasps. "You *did*!" How does she know when I haven't answered her question yet? I swear this woman can read my mind. "Tell me everything," she demands.

"Sheamus is a friend, and I want to believe he's telling the truth," I conclude at the end of my story.

"But you aren't sure if you believe him?" April asks. "I'm not sure I believe him either, Megnolia. I've seen Sheamus drive his truck in all kinds of bad weather. Heck, I've seen him use his snowplow attachment to clear snow when it's too snowy for the real snowplows to come out. And if he couldn't tell for sure if one of the snow-covered cars outside his house was Adam's, he should've said so instead of lying and saying he could see Adam's car. His story doesn't feel right."

"That's what I thought," I admit, relieved I'm not the only one who thinks Sheamus might be lying or leaving out an important detail or two.

CHAPTER 10

When I get home after work, I'm relieved to hear water *whooshing* through the pipes because it means Eric is in the shower. When I called the landline earlier to wake him, he was so drowsy I thought he might roll over and go back to sleep as soon as he hung up the phone.

According to Jess, tonight's event will have appetizers, finger food, and—thanks to the snowstorm keeping skiers and snowboarders in the mountains and out of Artsy Tartsy—a lot more pastries than were on the original menu

"I won't be late tonight, Soph," I explain to the corgi while I fix myself a small plate of cheese and crackers to sustain me until the party.

I don't want to eat a full dinner because I know I won't be able to resist the siren song of Tamara's delicious desserts, and I plan to indulge my sweet tooth to the fullest extent possible. After all, it is a celebration.

"Are you hungry, Sophie? Do you want dinner?" I wash a handful of grapes and add them to the plate of cheese and crackers, then dry my hands on a towel.

"Don't fall for her hungry dog act." Eric winks from the

561

kitchen doorway where he's rubbing Sophie. "I fed and walked Sophie before my shower."

"Thank you," I say, extending my plate toward him. "Snack?"

He takes two pieces of cheese and a few grapes. "I warmed up the last piece of lasagna while Sophie was eating," he explains.

For me, tonight's function is a party, but for Eric, it's a work event. While I nibble, he explains that there will be a few non-uniformed officers at the party, watching and listening for anything that might pertain to Saxon Renaud's death and the incident on Lake Access Road. Eric says he hopes to glean some insight from watching the card game participants, in particular, and how they interact with one another.

"Do you need me to do anything?" I ask.

"Just enjoy yourself," Eric replies and puts his hands on my hips. "I'm sorry I have to work this event. I wish we could go together as a proper couple."

"It's fine," I assure him. "If it leads to a break in the case, it will be worth it." I hug him. "How was your nap?"

He kisses my forehead. "About my nap," he says. "Now that I've had some rest, I realize how overtired I was. I feel much better, and the world didn't fall apart without me for a few hours. Thank you. You were right."

"I usually am," I tease. "You just forget sometimes." I stand on my tippy toes and kiss him.

I mentally debate whether now is the right time to tell him about my conversation with Sheamus, but Eric checks his watch and announces that we should get going. He wants to be early, so he can talk to his colleagues before the guests start to arrive.

"I'll take my car and meet you there," I suggest. "I need to change and freshen up. Also, I told April and T that I'll meet them outside, and we'll go in together."

THERE'S no point trying to park at the pub because I already know the small parking lot will be full. Instead, I park behind Knitorious, beside Phillip's white floral-wrapped delivery van. April is already here, sitting in her warm car, waiting for me.

"Where's T?" I ask when April gets out of her car alone.

"I dropped her off at the pub," she explains as we hug hello. "I helped her carry the baked goods inside, and she stayed to organize and plate them. I drove here to park the car and meet you."

We walk from the store to the pub, and I'm grateful the sidewalks were plowed and are clear of snow, allowing me to wear my stiletto heels. I hate wearing boots to a function and going through the hassle of changing into my shoes when I get there.

Approaching the pub, I see Jess standing outside talking on her phone. Her gesticulations and facial expressions are familiar to me. I recognize a fellow mum arguing with a teenager when I see one. I've made those same faces and thrown around those same hand gestures when bickering with Hannah. Jess has three kids; her youngest is seventeen years old and recently started driving. Raising one teenager was stressful enough, I can't imagine raising three, especially when they're as close in age as Jess's kids are.

I give her a sympathetic smile, and she holds up her index finger telling me to wait as she puts the call on hold.

April gets a text from T who needs help plating pastries in the kitchen. I tell April to go inside and help her wife, and we'll see each other later.

Jess takes a deep cleansing breath. "Teenagers!" She rolls her eyes. "This one insists that I promised him two weeks ago that he could have two friends sleep over at our house tonight. There's no way I promised that. I would never approve a sleepover and allow three teenagers in my house when I'm not there to monitor it."

"Oh my," I sympathize. "Is there anything I can do?"

"Would you rather deal with an irrational teenager or with Adam's anxiety? I can't decide which one is less fun," she says. Her voice has a teasing tone, but her face is tense and serious.

"Adam is anxious?" I ask, knitting my brows together. "About what?"

Adam is one of the most poised people I've ever met. Even when he's stressed, most people would never know because his steady demeanour is usually unflappable.

"Nerves, I think." Jess shrugs. "He's freaking out about his speech."

"Really?" I reply, at a loss for words. "Huh."

The Adam I know loves an audience. I've watched him give speeches, keynote addresses, toasts, and emcee large events without ever breaking a sweat. Charming a room is his happy place.

Jess nods and holds up her phone. "Let me finish dealing with this teenage drama, and I'll join you inside when I'm done." She smiles.

"Good luck," I say opening the outer door to the pub.

I suspect the true source of Adam's stress isn't his speech, but the stress of Saxon's murder, on top of being elected mayor, and having his car stolen; it would be a lot to handle for anyone.

Inside the pub, it's business as usual downstairs with tourists and locals laughing and having a good time. The jovial atmosphere is accompanied by a DJ mixing music and an alcohol-induced, cheerful buzz in the air. Tonight's party is on the second floor in one of the function rooms, so I weave my way through the crowd toward the stairs. At the bottom of the stairs, an employee moves the velvet rope aside, I thank him, and begin my ascent.

At the top, I pause and look and take in the scene. They have converted one of the smaller offices into a coat-check room for the night, so I head over there to check my coat. As I take off my coat and hand it to the attendant, Adam approaches me from the side.

"There you are!" He looks flustered. "When Eric showed up without you, I panicked. I thought you weren't coming. Where were you?"

Jess wasn't kidding. Adam is definitely anxious.

I've only seen Adam anxious four times in the entire twenty-two years we've known each other: when he proposed to me, when I was in labour with Hannah, when he was waiting to find out if he made partner at the firm, and when we were separating and he had to tell me we were being blackmailed because he was having an affair with a married colleague.

"I'm here now," I assure him. "What's wrong?"

"My speech. It's all wrong. It's a mess. Everything's a mess. Can you go over my speech with me?" Adam isn't a fast talker. His usual tone is calm and authoritative, but right now his voice is urgent and uncertain. "This is the first speech I've written without your help. What if my jokes are inappropriate?"

He has a point; Adam's sense of humour can be a little raunchy for an all-ages audience. But I'm sure Jess would've helped him tone it down.

I thank the coat-check attendant when they hand me my ticket, then take Adam by the arm, and lead him to a quiet corner where we can speak privately. The rest of the town's residents need not see their newly elected mayor having a meltdown.

"Didn't Jess listen to your speech already? I thought you practiced with her."

"Yes," he admits. "She listened, and she made a few suggestions, but it's not the same. Meg, I need your help." He shakes his head and adds, "This is a mistake! Why did I do this? I shouldn't be mayor."

"Adam, you'll do great. You always give great speeches. You're a natural public speaker. You've done this hundreds of times, and it's always gone off without a hitch. Tonight will be no different."

I did not expect this evening's festivities would begin with me giving my ex-husband a pre-speech pep talk, but here we are.

I point toward the large function room where his guests are waiting to congratulate him and celebrate his victory. "Everyone in that room voted for you because they believe in you. They voted for you because they *want* you to be mayor. They are our friends and neighbours, and they knew what they were getting when they voted for you. If you can speak to a room full of hundreds of lawyers, you can speak to them."

"That's the problem Meg," he explains, throwing his hands up in frustration. "I'm used to speaking to lawyers and law societies, not friends and neighbours who are depending on me to keep our town happy and safe. Outside of Harmony Lake, I'm Adam the lawyer, and I know how to do that, but inside Harmony Lake, I was always Megan's husband or Hannah's dad. Now I'm just Adam Martel, and people don't know me. They know *you* and like *you*, not me. Don't you get it? Your nice personality offsets my egotistical personality. Without you to soften me and make me more likeable, everyone will see me for the arrogant fraud that I am." Adam catches his breath, loosens his tie, and undoes the top button of his shirt. Beads of sweat dot his brow.

Shocked by Adam's sudden capacity for self-insight, and starting to feel anxious myself after watching his anxiety-fuelled rant, I decide to try to calm down both of us.

"Heavy shoulders, long arms." I take a deep breath.

Adam nods and takes a couple of deep breaths.

"Calm down. We'll figure this out," I say comfortingly. "You're usually the calm, rational Martel, and I'm usually the emotional Martel."

"Well, we're switching roles tonight, Meg! Tonight, I get to be the emotional Martel, and you get to be the calm one!"

I reach out and turn the doorknob to Sheamus's office. It's unlocked. I open the door and gesture for Adam to follow me inside.

"Go ahead. Let it out. I'll stay with you until you feel better." I hand him a tissue from my clutch purse.

Adam paces around the crowded office, dabbing his sweaty brow, until he calms down. After he composes himself, he recites his speech to me, and it sounds great. I make a few small suggestions to tone down a couple of his jokes, and I remind him that less humour might be better considering his political opponent was murdered today. Adam wrote the speech before Saxon's death and admits that, because of today's chaos, he didn't think to change it to reflect a more sombre mood.

While Adam types into his phone, changing his speech, I sit in a chair across from Sheamus's desk and look around the cluttered room.

Sheamus's office is more like a storage locker than a functional office. The lighting is dim, and there are no windows to provide natural light. There are spare bar stools stacked in one corner with boxes of unopened straws, napkins, and toothpicks stacked precariously on top of the barstools like a real-life game of Jenga: Irish Pub Edition. Against another wall, folding chairs and tables lean against each other, along with the A-frame sign that Sheamus puts outside the pub in the warmer weather with the day's specials written in chalk.

There are piles of folded table linens, white bar towels, and old menus on top of the filing cabinets. Leaning against the wall in the corner farthest from where I'm sitting is... a whangee-handled, black umbrella? Are my eyes playing tricks on me? I blink and do a double take, in case the dim light is messing with my vision. Could that be Saxon's missing umbrella? Without taking my eyes off the umbrella, I open my clutch purse, take out my phone, and snap a quick photo.

The flash distracts Adam from his speech, and he looks at me quizzically.

"Oops," I say. "I didn't mean to do that." I hate lying, but the umbrella is a holdback, and I don't want to make up a bigger lie to explain why I'm taking a photo.

"What do you think?" Adam asks, handing me his phone with his speech open.

I skim it, make a few small edits, and hand it back to him.

While he reads the changes and commits them to memory, I do up the top button of his shirt, then tighten and straighten his tie.

"Do you feel better?" I ask.

Adam nods and gives me a small smile. "Thank you, Meg. I'm fine now. I don't know what I would do without you."

I smooth his lapels and step away, looking him up and down to make sure he's stage ready, when Jess pokes her head in the door.

"There you are! I looked everywhere for you. What are you doing in here?"

"We went over Adam's speech, made a few minor changes to reflect today's events, and removed a couple of jokes that may or may not have been inappropriate for the audience," I reply. "I'm off to join the party. I told April I'd meet her, and Eric will wonder where I am." I smile, pick up my purse from the chair, and leave.

I close the office door behind me and pull out my cell phone. I text the photo of the umbrella to Eric.

Me: Found this in Sheamus's office.

CHAPTER 11

INSIDE THE FUNCTION ROOM, I am but one drop in a sea of familiar faces. I pause, take a breath, and survey the room, looking for Connie, Archie, or Ryan, but don't find them in my initial scan of the crowd.

"You look beautiful," Eric says, then kisses me hello. "Wow! That dress is flattering and kind of distracting."

I'm wearing my navy-blue wrap dress. It has long sleeves and a lapel collar. My favourite features are the pockets! The wide-belted waist flatters my curves. I have an hourglass figure, and I learned a long time ago that I feel more comfortable in clothes that flatter my shape than in clothes that try to hide my shape. It's easier to work with what I have than to try to make myself into something I'm not. I don't have a long, willowy body like April, but I'm pretty happy with the body I was born with. I'm happiest when I wear clothes that work with me instead of against me.

"Thank you," I reply, squeezing his hand. "Did you get my text?"

Eric nods. "I've already asked Sheamus if we can take the umbrella. He said yes. I sent an officer to secure it."

A server comes by with a tray of sparkling drinks. "Champagne?" she asks.

"I'm tempted, but I'm driving," I reply, the disappointment obvious in my voice.

"Ginger ale?" the server asks, pointing to one of the champagne flutes on her tray.

"Thank you." I smile and take the ginger ale.

Eric furrows his brow. "You're not staying at my place tonight?" he asks when the server moves on to the next cluster of guests.

"I have to go home. Sophie's there."

"Can I stay over?" he asks.

"Always," I reply. "But I'll probably leave before you, so I'll drive myself home and meet you there."

"I can drive you home and come back," he suggests.

Why is he in bodyguard mode?

"Why are you being so protective? Did something happen you haven't told me about?"

"Megan, someone, who is likely a murderer, left a stolen car in your driveway last night and avoided your security cameras. I'd feel better if I took you home myself."

Eric has a talent for saying things in a way that makes them sound scarier than I think they are.

He's here to do a job, and I don't want to distract him with an argument, so we agree to discuss it later. He goes on his way, eavesdropping and watching everything around him.

"Have you seen Ryan yet?" I ask April when we find each other and after we ooh and aah over how amazing we both look.

She shakes her head. "I don't think they're here yet." April slouches so her mouth is closer to my ear. "Kelly's here," she hisses at me in a loud whisper. "She said she wasn't coming, but she's here."

Our friend, Kelly, hasn't been out and about much since her husband passed away just over a year ago; it was his murder that brought Eric to Harmony Lake. Since her husband's death, Kelly has kept to herself. We've tried to encourage her to come out, socialize, and have fun, but she just wasn't ready yet.

I follow April's gaze to Kelly, who is smiling and chatting with a group of people that includes Sheamus.

"It's such a relief to see her happy," I say blinking tears out of my eyes. "I was beginning to think we'd never see her laugh again."

"Well, if anyone can make her smile again, Sheamus is the guy to do it. He's the most outgoing and extroverted person we know," April observes.

"It's true," I say, nodding.

Watching the small group of people interact, I notice Sheamus is wearing that scarf again. Isn't he warm? He's wearing a thick alpaca scarf inside a crowded upstairs room of a pub. I guess he wasn't kidding when he said it was his favourite scarf.

Kelly spots us looking at her. She smiles and waves, then comes over. We exchange hugs and hellos.

"It's so great to see you here, Kelly," I tell her. "We've missed you!"

"If we knew you were coming, we could've come together," April says.

"Thanks, ladies," Kelly smiles and nods. "It feels good to see everyone again. I'm glad I came. It was a last-minute decision. A couple of my stylists were coming, and I wanted to congratulate Adam in person. Thank goodness he beat Saxon and saved us from the big-box stores."

Kelly, April, and I chat until someone approaches Kelly from behind and taps her on the shoulder. She turns around to say hello to them, then turns back to us.

"Ladies, I'm going to mingle and catch up with people I haven't seen in forever." Kelly points at me. "Don't forget our appointment next week."

"Never," I respond. "My hair and I need to spend some time with you. See you on Monday."

Kelly wanders over to another group of people, which again includes Sheamus because he somehow is everywhere all the time. April and I watch Kelly smile and laugh. We comment that seeing Kelly enjoy herself again makes us feel warm inside.

"Do you sense a spark between them?" April asks.

"Between Kelly and Sheamus?" I ask.

April nods slowly. "The heat between them is so hot I can feel it from here."

"You think?" I watch Sheamus and Kelly. April's right, There's chemistry. "Kelly has barely left her house for over a year," I remind her. "I don't think she's started dating yet."

"I don't know if they're dating, but I know chemistry when I feel it, Megapop," April says.

The clinking of glasses grows louder than the collective murmur of the crowd, and everyone turns toward the stage where Adam is ready to give his speech.

I make my way to the buffet table and fix a plate of pastries to eat while I listen. I notice Eric standing near the buffet table, deep in conversation with Pete Feeney. I wonder what they're talking about, and whether Eric is learning anything that could help solve Saxon's murder.

April and I find a spot close to the stage, and I eat pastries while Adam speaks.

When his speech is over, the room cheers and gives Adam a round of applause. As the crowd disperses and everyone divides themselves into cliques, I overhear several comments about how good his speech was and how relieved and happy people are that Adam is the new mayor of Harmony Lake.

To his credit, Adam said some lovely words about Saxon which couldn't have been easy. He also announced that the flags at the Harmony Lake town hall will be at half-mast for the next three days in Saxon's honour. He must've added the part about the flags after I edited his speech because I don't recall it being there before.

Eric and Pete are still talking, and I'm contemplating casually drifting toward them until I'm within eavesdropping range, when a light touch on my shoulder makes me flinch.

"Ryan!" I say when I spin around and realize it's him. I throw my arms around him and give him a hug. "It's so good to see you."

"It's good to be seen," he replies jokingly.

I let go of him and hug his partner, Lin. Then I hug both Connie and Archie. When I stand back and look at them as a group, it's obvious they're uptight and tense. But other than that, everybody seems fine, and most important, Ryan is sober.

We talk for a while, limiting our conversation to small talk. We don't venture beyond anything more interesting than the weather, or what each of us is wearing, because we're aware of the many eyes and ears around us.

"Is it OK if I come by the store tomorrow morning to change the locks?" Ryan asks.

"Why do you want to change the locks?" I answer his question with a question.

"Adam asked me to take care of it because he had a spare key on the key chain that went missing with his car," Ryan explains.

"Come by whenever, someone will be there all day." I forgot Adam had a spare key to Knitorious.

April and Tamara and I work the room for a while, stopping to talk to friends and neighbours. I make sure to gently steer us in the general direction of the buffet table, so I can have a few more cheesecake bites before I leave.

We finally reach the buffet table, and someone stops Tamara to compliment her mini Black Forest cupcakes. While a fellow-pastry lover tries to coax the recipe out of Tamara, I quietly say goodbye to April, interrupt Tamara to give her a quick hug goodbye, and start the process of saying goodbye to friends and neighbours on my way to the coat check.

"I'm tired," I say when I approach Eric. "I think I'll go home now."

"I'll drive you." It's a statement, not a question or a suggestion.

"I'll be fine," I insist. "I'll text you as soon as I get home."

"At least let me walk you to your car," Eric negotiates.

"If you leave, you might miss something important," I rationalize. "You need to stay here and find clues to solve Saxon's murder. This investigation is making everybody crazy. I've never seen the people I love so stressed and worried." I tell him about Adam's breakdown, and how tense Connie, Archie, and Ryan are.

"Good evening, you gorgeous couple," Philip says, giving me a double-cheek kiss and exchanging an air kiss with Eric.

Philip takes my hand and looks me up and down. "Sweetie, you are throwing off serious Jane Russell vibes in that dress, and I *love* it!"

"Thank you," I say demurely, slightly embarrassed at the attention.

"Megan, am I to understand you're leaving now?" Philip asks, then looks at Eric. "Why don't I see Megan home safely, and you can stay here and do what you do best. I'm leaving now, anyway. I have an early delivery at the shop." He looks at me. "Baby's breath and roses for a bridal bouquet."

"Were you eavesdropping on our conversation, Phillip?" I ask.

"Only half of it," he replies. "Eric's half. You speak too quietly."

Well, at least he's honest.

"It would be great if we could walk to our cars together," I say. "I parked next to you."

"Perfect! I'll follow you home in my van and make sure you arrive at chez Martel safe and sound."

We both look at Eric. "Are you comfortable with this arrangement?" I ask.

He nods. "Thank you, Phillip."

Phillip flicks his wrist casually. "It's the least I can do since I might've blown away all your evidence with my snowblower." He extends his hand, palm up, and looks at me. "Give me your coat-check ticket, sweetie. I'll get our coats while you say goodbye to lover boy."

I give Phillip my coat-check ticket, and he turns and leaves.

"I'll likely be asleep when you get home," I tell Eric, and stretch to my tallest height to kiss him. "Good night, I love you. I'll see you tomorrow."

"I love you too. Please text me when you get home. Remember to lock the doors and arm the security system."

On my way out, I stop and say goodbye to friends and neighbours as I pass them.

"Your speech was great. I told you it would go off without a hitch," I tell Adam when I encounter him and Jess.

"Thanks, Meg. And thanks for coming tonight," he replies.

"Thank you for doing Adam-management while I dealt with my teen troubles," Jess says, hugging me.

"No problem," I reply. "I think I got the easier of the two tasks."

We wish each other good night and remind each other to drive safely. I head out of the function room and into the large open area. I don't see Phillip anywhere.

"Meg! Wait a sec," Adam hisses, jogging to catch up with me.

I turn around. "What's wrong?"

"Nothing," Adam replies, coming to a stop in front of me. "Thank you, again. If you hadn't shown up, I don't think I would've been able to go in there and give the speech." He smiles.

"No problem," I say. "You'd do the same for me." I turn to walk away.

"You look beautiful, by the way," Adam calls after me. "That's one of my favourite dresses. You bought it in Montreal when we were there for my parents' forty-fifth wedding anniversary, remember?"

I remember, but I'm surprised Adam does. In our two decades of marriage, he never once said anything about what I wore to various events, let alone mentioned where I bought it or whether he liked it. Is the stress of this investigation making him snap? Is he having some kind of breakdown? Or is this a midlife crisis? Whatever it is, it's weird. The quicker we rid ourselves of this murder investigation and get back to normal, the better.

"Thank you." I smile. "Enjoy the rest of your party."

With no sign of Phillip upstairs, I decide to head downstairs and see if he's waiting for me by the door. Sure enough, I spot him by the door talking to Rick Ransan.

"Sorry I kept you waiting, Phillip," I say, then I look over at Rick and smile. "Hi, Rick."

"H-hi, Megan. You look nice," Rick responds.

"Thank you," I reply.

Before I can tell Rick I'm sorry that his friend Saxon died, Phillip is behind me, saying goodbye to Rick and slipping my coat sleeves over my arms. The next thing I know, I'm dressed for the outdoors. I blurt a quick goodbye to Rick as Phillip pulls me by the hand through the inner doors of the pub, then the outer doors, not letting go until we're standing on the sidewalk where I finish buttoning my coat.

"I had to get out of there," Phillip explains, taking a deep breath and lowering the zipper of his coat to expose his neck. "It's too hot and stuffy in that crowded bar when I'm wearing this goose down-filled coat." He extends his elbow, offering me his arm.

"I understand," I sympathize, hooking my arm through

his. "Are you and Rick Ransan close friends?" I ask as we meander down Water Street.

"No," Phillip replies. "I'm closer to Trudy than Rick, but because Rick and Trudy are close, I guess that kind of makes Rick and me friends."

Trudy Nakata is an elderly resident of Harmony Lake. She's active in our community and a member of the book club. She and Rick Ransan are neighbours; Rick dotes on Trudy and helps her live independently in her home.

"I didn't know you and Trudy are close," I say.

"Oh, yes, Trudy and my mum were good friends back in the day," Phillip explains. "And Trudy looks after Kevin when I'm not home. Tonight, she took Kevin outside to do his business and gave him his bedtime snack." He looks around to make sure no one is listening, then tilts his head toward me and adds quietly, "Aaaaand, Trudy is Rick's alibi for when Saxon was killed."

"Really?" I ask, shocked. "I didn't know that." In a quieter voice, I add, "Tell me more."

It didn't occur to me that Saxon Renaud's only friend could also be his murderer. But I guess it makes sense that he would be a person of interest. Rick was one of the last people seen with Saxon. He backed out of the poker game at the last minute, and who knows where Rick went after he dropped off Saxon at Sheamus's house.

"Well, according to Trudy, when Saxon was murdered, Rick was rescuing Cat Benatar," Phillip explains. "She said she spent hours looking for Cat Benatar when she heard his meows coming from the ceiling. The cat found its way up there but couldn't find its way out. She phoned Rick in a panic, and he rushed over to rescue the cat. Rick had to drill holes and everything. Trudy says it was an awful mess but was worth it because Cat Benatar got out unharmed."

Cat Benatar is Trudy's cat, and he's a climber.

"How did Cat Benatar get up there?" I ask.

"Loose ceiling tile in the laundry room," Phillip replies. "Trudy says Rick fixed all the holes he made and the loose ceiling tile, so Cat Benatar couldn't climb up there again. She says Rick was there all night."

Rick sounds like a good person. He cares for his elderly neighbour, saves her cat, and stays up all night repairing the damage he made saving the cat to ensure it won't get stuck again. What could Rick Ransan and Saxon Renaud have in common?

"Why would a nice person like Rick hang around with someone like Saxon Renaud?" I wonder out loud.

"I don't know," Phillip replies with a shrug. "I know Rick worked for Saxon, but why they were friends beyond that is a mystery to me."

It's a mystery to me too. For now.

CHAPTER 12

Saturday, January 16th
Saturday, January 16th

I take one of the hand-knit display scarves and wrap it around my neck, then hug myself with my hand-knit cardigan, and shiver. It's freezing in the store because Ryan has the door open while he changes the lock. Even Sophie is chilly; she's curled up in a tight little ball on her dog bed, still wearing her purple and white argyle sweater.

"Thanks for coming in early to meet me, Megan," Ryan says as he works on the front door.

"No problem," I reply. "I'm an early riser, so I was up, anyway." I smile. "So, how are you feeling Ryan? I mean, how are you doing after Friday night?"

"You mean when I accidentally drank Saxon's rum and Coke?" He answers my question with a question. "It's OK, Megan, you can mention it. It's not a trigger for me."

"OK," I respond. "If you're sure... What happened after you drank the rum and Coke and confronted Saxon? Where did you go?"

Ryan tells me from his perspective how the evening played out. His story is remarkably similar to both Adam and

579

Sheamus's versions of events. At least everyone agrees on the events that led up to Saxon's murder.

Ryan tells me that when he left Sheamus's house, he got in his car and drove with no particular destination in mind.

"I wanted to put as much distance as possible between me and that rum and Coke. Finally, I decided to drive either to Harmony Hills or the city and find a twelve-step meeting." Ryan finishes with the front door, closes it, locks it, and joins me in the cozy sitting area where he continues his story. "Driving was horrible. There was no visibility, and the roads were covered in snow. I realized it would take hours to get anywhere, and I wouldn't find a meeting anyway, not in this weather."

"So, what did you do?" I ask.

"I pulled into the parking lot at the Hav-a-nap motel," Ryan replies.

The Hav-a-nap motel is on the west side of town, near the ramp to the highway, and, coincidentally, near Lake Access Road. Could Ryan be the witness who reported seeing Adam's car leaving Lake Access Road?

"Is that where Pete Feeney found you?" I asked.

"Pete didn't find me." Ryan shakes his head. "No one found me. I called my sponsor from my cell phone. After a while, he talked me off the ledge. Then I called my dad, and he stayed on the phone with me while I drove home."

By process of elimination, I assumed Pete Feeney found Ryan. I knew it wasn't Adam because he had no car and showed up on Eric's doorstep. Sheamus said he went home when he got a text saying that Ryan was safe. Rick was at Trudy's house tracking Cat Benetar through the ceiling to rescue him. I figured it couldn't be Saxon because he was murdered, and who are we kidding, it's doubtful Saxon would have been concerned enough about Ryan's well-being to help look for him, anyway. That left Pete Feeney. If Pete didn't find Ryan, where was he when Ryan parked at the Hav-a-nap motel?

"When you parked at the motel, were you parked where you could see Lake Access Road, by chance? Did you see Adam's car near there?"

Ryan shakes his head. "My car was facing the opposite direction," Ryan explains. "And the snowfall was too heavy. Snow started accumulating on my windshield as soon as I put the car in park. I couldn't see anything, and I'm sure no one would have been able to see me, either."

This proves my point. Unless they were super close to it, how would a witness have been able to see Adam's car clearly enough to identify it?

I smile. "We were all relieved that you were OK," I tell him.

"Thanks, Megan." Ryan gets up, picks up his toolbox, and gestures for me to follow him to the back of the store.

I sit on the stairs that lead to the apartment while Ryan gets to work changing the lock on the back door.

Ryan stops working and looks up at me. "I didn't kill Saxon Renaud," he says, making what feels like deliberate eye contact with me. "I didn't like him, and I'm not sad he's dead, especially after what he did to me on Friday night. But I didn't kill him. I wouldn't kill anybody."

"I know," I reply. "No one thinks you did it. And we'll prove it by finding out who did."

"You should have a lot of suspects to choose from," Ryan observes as he resumes working on the lock. "Few people liked Saxon, and he owed many people money."

"What?" I ask, correcting my posture and sitting at full attention. This is the first I've heard about Saxon owing money to anyone. "Who does Saxon owe money to? Who told you about his debt?"

Money is a common motive for murder; maybe an angry creditor killed Saxon.

"Jay Singh told me," Ryan explains.

Jay Singh is Ryan's friend, and a local money lender, though he prefers to call himself an alternate lender. In exchange for a higher rate of interest than one would pay at a bank or other traditional lending institution, Jay will discreetly lend money with no questions asked. His job often makes him privy to intimate details of his clients' lives. Details his clients would prefer to keep private. Once, when I was a person of interest in a murder investigation, Jay helped me by sharing a tidbit of information with me to help clear my name.

It surprised me when Jay told me he counts several residents of Harmony Lake among his clientele. It's the paradox of this tight-knit community; while it seems like everyone knows everything about their friends and neighbours, our town is still full of secrets.

"Did Saxon owe money to Jay?" I ask.

"That's what Jay told me," Ryan replies. "He said Saxon owed money to other lenders too. Jay said Saxon was overextended." Ryan puts air quotes around *overextended*. "Jay didn't come out and say it, but I got the feeling Saxon was behind on his repayments. Jay hates that."

"I'm sure he does," I agree, nodding.

To look at Saxon, you wouldn't think he had financial difficulties. He drove a newer mid-range car, he wore designer, albeit older clothes, he carried that expensive umbrella everywhere he went, and he conducted himself with an air of self-importance. Not to mention all the property he owned around Harmony lake. Combined, his property holdings must be worth a lot of money.

If Ryan is correct, and Saxon was over-leveraged, he hid it behind a carefully cultivated image of affluence.

Saxon wouldn't be the first person who looks wealthy but isn't. It's possible to be asset-rich and income-poor. Owning lots of property doesn't mean lots of cash flow. It's feasible that the income from Saxon's real estate investments wasn't enough to cover his expenses. Also, some of his properties were older and likely required expensive maintenance.

The sound of someone knocking at the front door, followed by Sophie's excited yelps, distracts me from my thoughts, and I check the time. Only a few minutes until it's time to open the store. I bet Marla is knocking, wondering why her key doesn't work. I remind Ryan that I need a few extra keys, excuse myself, and rush to the front door.

"My key doesn't work," Marla says, holding up the offending key as evidence.

"Sorry about that," I respond. "Ryan just changed the lock. We lost a spare key to the store yesterday."

"Oh my," Marla says, her eyes wide.

I leave the front door unlocked and turn the sign from CLOSED to OPEN.

A few minutes later, Ryan finishes working at the back door and gives me the keys on his way out. After he leaves, Connie arrives and the three of us take turns serving customers and ringing up sales.

Knitorious is busy today, which isn't a surprise because we're in the middle of the winter tourist season, and the ski resorts in the Harmony Hills mountains are booked solid. The skiers and snowboarders like to wander into town on Saturdays to soak up the ambience, eat at our fabulous restaurants, and shop at our local stores.

Between customers, Connie, Marla, and I talk about last night's party. We chat about who was there and who wasn't, review the food, and inevitably find ourselves talking about who killed Saxon Renaud.

According to Marla, the rumour mill favours either Adam or Ryan as the prime suspects in Saxon's murder. Adam's alleged motive was to eliminate his political rival, and Ryan's supposed motive was revenge after Saxon tricked him into drinking alcohol.

Connie tells us she heard mumblings last night that Sheamus might be the murderer. Sheamus is vehemently opposed to any big-box stores or restaurants in Harmony Lake. The rumour mill speculates that Sheamus would have more to lose than many small businesses because big-box restaurants and sports bars would likely be among the first new inhabitants of our small town under a Saxon Renaud-led town council.

"It's true, big-box restaurants and sports bars would be tough competition for the Irish Embassy Pub," I agree. "But using that logic, every business owner in Harmony Lake is a suspect." I bring my hand to my chest. "*I* would be a suspect." I laugh, and Connie and Marla laugh with me.

"Well, there are other rumours about other potential suspects," Connie teases.

"Who?" I ask.

"Rick Ransan is a favourite choice among the charity knitters," she replies.

"Connie's right," Marla confirms. "Some of the charity knitters talked about it last night."

The Charity Knitting Guild is a local organization whose outward mission is to use knitting to raise money and awareness for good causes.

We also have a book club. The book club is a local group of book lovers whose outward mission is to read and discuss best-selling fiction.

I say outward mission because the whole town knows the inward mission of both groups—the true reason they exist—is to preserve Harmony Lake's small-town charm by eliminating anything that threatens it.

The membership of both groups comprises many of Harmony Lake's older, wiser, female residents. The groups have a matriarchal hierarchy with the elder, more experienced members training the younger members to eventually take over.

Harmony Lake might have a democratically elected mayor and town council, but everyone in town knows the knitters and the readers wield the real power.

In fact, Adam ran for mayor because the knitters and the readers joined forces to recruit him. They spearheaded his campaign and used their influence to keep the big-boxers out of power. Never have two groups of sweet, nurturing women been so loved and so feared at the same time.

Connie and Marla are the only two crossover members; they belong to both groups. I don't belong to either group, but the charity knitters meet at Knitorious every Wednesday afternoon to knit and plan their upcoming projects, so I interact with them regularly.

"The book club thinks Rick might be the killer too," Connie adds, "but they don't dare talk about it in front of Trudy."

"Of course." I nod.

Trudy is a member of the book club, and Rick Ransan's neighbour. They look after each other. She wouldn't like to hear the other readers accuse him of murder.

"Why would Rick want to kill his friend, Saxon?" I ask. "I mean, neither of them seemed to have any other friends."

"Rick was Saxon's employee, he did odd jobs and helped maintain Saxon's properties," Marla reminds me. "But people say Saxon was mean to Rick. They say they've heard Saxon call Rick nasty names and make fun of his stutter. Maybe Rick was sick and tired of Saxon's abuse. Maybe Rick finally snapped and ran over Saxon with Adam's car."

The accuracy rate of the Harmony Lake rumour mill is shockingly high, and knowing Saxon, it's believable that he might have bullied and verbally abused Rick. That being said, I can't imagine Rick would murder Saxon to make it stop. This is the same man who gave up a night's sleep to save a cat from a ceiling, for goodness' sake. People who save cats don't commit murder, right?

CHAPTER 13

COMING IN FROM THE COLD, dry outside air, I sniffle. What's that splendid smell? When I inhale again, my nostrils twitch, then flare to maximum capacity to let in as much of the glorious aroma as possible.

"It smells like coffee in here, Soph," I mutter as I detach her leash after our midday walk. "My coffee. White chocolate and peppermint latte," I elaborate, taking off her sweater.

"With extra whipped cream and a sprinkle of white chocolate shavings."

Who said that? Is Eric here? I look up, shocked to see Eric sitting at the table in the kitchenette, his face focussed on his phone screen as his thumbs type so fast they appear to hover over the keyboard. He'll get repetitive stress syndrome if he's not careful.

"Hey, handsome! What are you doing here?" I ask, joining him at the table and cracking the lid on my coffee.

"I was nearby, so I stopped by to say hi and bring you a coffee." He smiles, laying his phone face down on the table.

"Thank you," I say, taking a small sip. "You must have used the front door," I speculate.

We keep the back door locked, even when the store is open.

He tilts his head and looks at me inquisitively. "I did. I came from Latte Da, so I came in the front door and said hi to Marla and Connie," Eric confirms. "How did you know that?" He rubs Sophie's head when she puts her front paws on his knees.

I set my coffee on the table and raise my index finger. "Stay here. I have something for you."

"Is it an early anniversary gift?" he calls after me as I walk out of the back room.

A surprising thing I've learned about Eric as our relationship grows is that he's a hopeless romantic. He's prone to romantic gestures so sweet, they verge on corny. As someone who is more practical than sentimental, I wasn't sure at first how to respond to his increasingly frequent romantic words and gestures, but now I think it's one of his most endearing qualities. On the outside, Eric is a hunky, muscle-bound man who carries a gun, but on the inside, he's a soft, sentimental, gentle soul who tears up at the end of romantic comedies. I admire his ability to deal with horrible situations and criminals every day at work, without letting it harden him and make him emotionally unavailable. If sentimentality and romanticism are his coping mechanisms, I'll embrace it.

"Not an anniversary gift," I say when I return a moment later and place a key on the table in front of him. "Ryan changed the locks this morning," I explain. "Your key wouldn't have worked if you tried to come in the back door." I explain to Eric that a spare key to Knitorious was on Adam's stolen key chain.

"Speaking of keys," Eric responds. "The forensics people didn't find any fingerprints or DNA on Adam's keys. Whoever stole them wiped them clean before abandoning them with the car."

My sigh conveys the defeat I feel. "I was hoping the killer

left evidence in the car," I explain. "Evidence that would lead straight to them, so this fiasco would end." I wrap my hands around my coffee cup and take comfort in the warmth.

"Don't give up hope," Eric says, enveloping my hands and coffee cup with his big, warm hands. "I'm on my way to meet with forensics and get the report for the rest of the car. Maybe they found something we can use."

"Don't they usually email forensics reports to you?" I ask, sipping my latte.

Eric nods. "They want to show me something. They said it's visual." He shrugs. "But they did email me a report about the umbrella you found in Sheamus's office last night."

"And?" I ask.

"It's not one of Saxon's umbrellas," Eric replies, flipping his phone over and quickly checking his notifications, before turning it face down again.

"One of? Saxon had multiple umbrellas?" I ask.

"We found multiple umbrellas when we searched his house," Eric explains. "It seems he kept back-up umbrellas. They're all identical. Same manufacturer too. Anyway, the one in Sheamus's office isn't the same, and they recovered no fingerprints or DNA from it to prove Saxon ever touched it. Sheamus said a customer left it at the pub about four months ago and never came back for it. He said his office is the informal lost-and-found for the pub. We questioned the server who found it four months ago, and she corroborated Sheamus's story."

Now I feel bad that Sheamus had to go through being questioned again, and have one of his employees questioned, because I hastily mis-identified an umbrella in his dimly lit office.

I lean in and speak quietly, so anyone hanging around the door to the back room won't hear me. "If Saxon had multiple umbrellas, could the umbrella you're looking for, the holdback," I mouth the word holdback, "be amongst the umbrellas you found at his house?" I ask.

Eric shakes his head. "It's a good thought, but forensics checked," he replies. "The umbrellas we found at his house were brand new. They were sealed in plastic from the manufacturer and had tags on them."

"Did he have multiple pairs of penny loafers too?" I ask rhetorically, my voice thick with sarcasm.

"He did. They were still in boxes with store tags on them," Eric says.

"I was talking with Ryan this morning, and he mentioned that he parked near Lake Access Road around the time Saxon was killed. He said there was no visibility. How did the witness who identified Adam's car actually *see* Adam's car?" I ask.

"I don't know, babe. I'd love to question that witness, but I don't know who it is."

"The 9-1-1 dispatcher couldn't trace the call?" I ask.

Eric shakes his head.

"Is there a tape of the call?" I plead, hopeful. "Maybe if I listen to it, I'll recognize the caller's voice."

He shakes his head again. "The witness didn't call 9-1-1, they called the tip line at the station."

"I didn't know the tip line is still a thing," I retort.

Several years ago, most police departments in our area set up toll-free tip lines. These tip lines encouraged anyone who had any information about any crime to come forward anonymously. The tip line doesn't have call display to reveal the phone number the tipster is calling from, and calls are neither traced nor recorded. The caller's anonymity is guaranteed.

"It's a thing," Eric confirms, "and the witness used it on Friday night, er, Saturday morning."

"Unless they were at the scene, there's no way they saw Adam's car," I insist.

"Agreed." Eric nods, then whispers, "I think the witness

who called the tip line is likely the killer."

My mind is blown. I sip my latte and take a moment to let what he said sink in.

Finally, barely above a whisper, I ask, "Why would the killer report themself to the police? If they drove away and returned Adam's car to where they found it, in front of Sheamus's house, Saxon's body probably wouldn't have been discovered until spring thaw. Saxon would have been presumed missing, and the killer would have gotten away with murder. For now."

"I have a couple of theories," Eric leans closer and lowers his voice. "Either the killer has a conscience and couldn't live with abandoning Saxon's dead, damaged body to freeze and go unfound until spring, or they saw Adam walking alone after he'd lost his keys and realized he had no alibi, so made the call to frame him." He sits up and in his normal speaking voice, adds, "But it's impossible to get inside the head of someone unhinged enough to commit murder."

Eric picks up his phone to check the time and gets distracted by the notifications that have accumulated since he put it down a few minutes ago. "I have to get going," he says, standing up. "Dinner later? I'll make a reservation at Pastabilities." He pulls me in for a hug and bends down to kiss me.

"Pastabilities sounds amazing," I say, thinking about their shrimp and mushroom risotto. "I'm not sure we'll get a table with a same day reservation, though. Not on a Saturday night during tourist season."

Eric winks. "I'll turn on the charm."

"In that case, we'll get a table for sure," I tease. "Remember to make the reservation for three."

Eric looks down at me. "Three?" he asks, confused.

"You, me, and your phone," I reply.

"Ha Ha... hilarious!" He kisses me again. "I'll text you with the time." He winks, then disappears through the back door.

CHAPTER 14

"Hɪ, Mᴀʏᴏʀ Fᴇᴇɴᴇʏ." Is that the correct way to address a former mayor? I make a mental note to look it up later. "It's nice to see you. Are you starting a new project?" I ask.

"Hello, Megan," Mayor Feeney smiles sweetly. "I was just telling Connie and Marla how excited I am to have the time to indulge my hobbies now that I'm retired. I'd like to knit my youngest grandson this lovely sweater." She holds up an aged and tattered paper pattern that's flimsy from being folded and unfolded many times.

Mayor Feeney is a tiny, wrinkled octogenarian, who smells like lavender and cedar, and has a saccharine-like sweetness to her voice. Her short blue-grey hair is treated with a blue rinse every two weeks and a perm every four months. She is a walking, talking stereotype of the ideal grandmother. Except this grandmother is a force to be reckoned with. Alice Feeney has been a fixture in Harmony Lake's local political scene for the better part of fifty years. Prior to her twenty years as deputy mayor, she was a member of the town council, a school board trustee, and before that, Alice Feeney was Harmony Lake's first ever female police constable. She did all

591

these things while also being married and raising four children. Her husband was the fire chief of the Harmony Lake Fire Department for many years. She's a pioneer who blazed a trail for the generations of strong Harmony Lake women who followed in her footsteps.

"It's lovely," I say in response to the paper pattern. "Have you decided which yarn you'd like to use?"

"Connie was just getting some samples for me to choose from." Mayor Feeney squints and points toward the back half of the store. "I think I like that baby blue yarn over there." She walks toward it before she finishes her sentence.

With Connie in tow, Mayor Feeney makes her way over to the baby blue yarn in the worsted weight section, and I notice her son, Pete, sitting in the cozy sitting area, scrolling his phone while he waits for his mum.

Pete is one of those people whose hair greyed prematurely. As a result, though he's only in his early fifties, his hair has already gone through the various stages of grey, and is already pure white. The whiteness of his hair matches the whiteness of his teeth. The contrast of his white hair and teeth against his blue eyes is captivating when you meet him for the first time. Somehow, Pete's white hair doesn't age him at all. In fact, his healthy physique and smooth skin make him appear younger than his actual age.

"Hi, Pete," I say, making my way to join him in the cozy sitting area. "Are you shopping for yarn too?"

I'm teasing. Pete doesn't knit, at least not that I know of. Pete's probably too busy to knit. Between his full-time job as a firefighter and his part-time job as a real estate agent, I can't imagine he has much time for hobbies.

"Oh, hi, Megan," he says, smiling and looking up from his phone. "No," he chuckles, "I'm on chauffeur duty today. My mum's mind might be sharp as a tack, but her reflexes aren't what they used to be, no matter what she tells you. We try to save her the trouble of driving, when she lets us. Especially in poor weather. Which means we get to be at her beck and call at least six months of the year."

"She's lucky to have you," I comment, and sit down next to him on the sofa. Pete slips his phone into the pocket of his black pea coat. "Listen, Pete, thank you for the other night."

"The other night?" Pete asks with an expression stuck somewhere between shock and confusion.

"Yes, thank you for looking out for Ryan at Sheamus's card game the other night. We appreciate you searching for him despite the weather and hazardous road conditions."

"Oh, that," Pete says, nodding. "There's no need to thank me, Megan. I really didn't do anything. In fact, I had to abandon the search and rush to my parents' house to remove a squirrel that got stuck in their chimney."

"Oh?" I asked. "In the middle of the night? That's what I call good service. If a squirrel gets itself stuck in my chimney in the middle of the night, I know who I'll call." I smile and we both laugh.

"I had no choice," Pete explains. "The thing was chattering, and scratching, and making all sorts of noises. My parents couldn't sleep, and my mother was afraid it might be injured or possibly die."

"Was the squirrel OK?" I ask.

"Yes, I'm pleased to report the squirrel came through the entire incident without a scratch. I put it in a box with an old blanket and some peanuts until I could release it yesterday morning."

"I'm glad it worked out for everyone involved." I pause while I figure out how to broach the subject of Saxon's murder without sounding nosy or confrontational. "So," I say, smiling. "How about all those rumours about Saxon Renaud's murder?" Pete nods in acknowledgement. "Which one of the many rumours do you subscribe to?" I ask.

Pete sits back and brings his right ankle to his left knee, holding it there with his right hand. "Have you heard the one about the money lender?" he asks.

"Yes, I have," I reply.

Pete tilts his head toward me and in a lower voice says, "Well, I know his lawyer—we've done a few real estate transactions together—and he says the money lender, Jay Singh, started legal proceedings to force the sale of some of Saxon's properties. The money lender isn't happy, and It wouldn't surprise me if he took out Saxon to set an example to his other clients." He raises his eyebrows and nods.

Does Pete mean he knows Saxon's lawyer, or Jay's lawyer? It makes little sense to me to kill someone who owes you money. It's more difficult, and expensive, to collect money from a dead person than a living one. Estates can take years to settle; it would be more efficient to deal with the debtor instead of their estate.

I help Connie and Mayor Feeney by finding the size of knitting needles the pattern calls for to get gauge. Then, when Mayor Feeney and Connie have gathered all the yarn and notions that she'll need to complete her project, I ring up the sale.

"If you don't mind waiting until tonight to start your sweater, Mayor Feeney, we can wind the yarn for you in the store, and I can drop it off at your house on my way home tonight," I offer.

"That's sweet, Megan, but I don't want to be any trouble."

"It's no trouble, Alice," Connie interjects, using Mayor Feeney's first name. "Megan lives around the corner from you. She has to drive past your house to get home."

I nod. "We're practically neighbours," I confirm.

"That's right," Mayor Feeney responds. "I forgot you and I live in the same neighbourhood." She smiles. "In that case, thank you. I'd love it if you would wind the yarn for me."

"I'll drop it off around 6 p.m.," I tell her as I place the needles she purchased in a bag. "If you don't get gauge with these needles, Mayor Feeney, be sure to bring them back, and we'll exchange them for a different size." I put her receipt in the bag and hand it to her across the counter.

"Thank you, Megan. I'm sure these will be fine. I always get gauge. It's a natural gift."

If I had a nickel for every time a knitter told me that, I'd be the wealthiest woman in town.

Mayor Feeney and Pete turn to leave, and Pete turns back, looking at me and snapping his fingers.

"Megan, before I forget," he says, pointing at me, "can you tell Eric that I printed those listings for him? I forgot them at home, but I'll drop them off over the next day or two."

"I'll tell him." I'm sure the tone of my voice conveys my confusion. "What listings did Eric ask you to print?"

"He wants to see what's available in Harmony Lake, you know, to get a feel for the market," Pete explains. "I was telling him how I expect to be busy in the next few weeks because of the spring market, and he mentioned he'd like to buy a house now that his position as chief is permanent. So, I told him I'd print some listings. I forgot to bring them with me. I left them at home on top of my printer." He rolls his eyes and smiles.

Pete turns to leave and flips up the collar of his black pea coat in an almost identical way that Adam does. Pete opens the store door for his mum, takes her shopping bag from her, and gestures for her to leave first. Such a doting son.

"What's this about Eric moving, my dear?" Connie asks, concerned.

Dumbfounded, I shake my head. "I have no idea. It must be a misunderstanding. If Eric was planning to move, he would've mentioned it to me."

I'm sure he would've mentioned it to me. I know he's

eager for us to move in together, but he wouldn't go house hunting without discussing it with me first. He knows I'm not ready for us to live together yet. He says he understands, and except for an occasional hint disguised as a joke, he's supportive and patient. Has his patience run out?

CHAPTER 15

CONNIE AND MARLA take turns going on break, and the time passes quickly. But by mid-afternoon, traffic has slowed down, and we have time to putter around the store, straightening and organizing. I take this opportunity to organize the back room and make space for new stock we're expecting next week.

"Megan?"

"In here, Marla," I call from the storage closet.

"There's someone here to see you," she says.

"Who?" I ask, gathering my curls into a messy ponytail with the hair elastic I always keep on my wrist.

"Rick Ransan," Marla replies. "He asked for Eric first. I told him Eric isn't here, and he asked to see you."

My curiosity is piqued.

"You can send him back here, Marla. Thank you." I smile.

My initial instinct is to talk to Rick in the store, but he asked for Eric first, making me think he might want to talk about Saxon or Saxon's murder, so I decide it's best if we speak in the back where it's more private.

"Are you sure that's a good idea, Megan?" Marla sounds worried.

"I'll be fine, Marla. You and Connie know we're back here, and I won't close the door all the way. I'll make sure I have an escape route available."

"If we see the door to the back room close all the way, we'll call for help," she tells me.

I nod.

Satisfied with our plan, Marla smiles and nods, then turns and rushes back to the store to get Rick. I step out of the back room, brush off my clothes, and make my ponytail a little less messy. I sit at the table in the kitchenette, choosing the chair closest to the door.

"Over here, Rick," I say when his head pokes through the doorway.

"There you are! H-h-hi, Megan. I've never been in a knitting store before." Rick looks at the kitchenette and back room with fascination.

I study his facial expression as he beholds the room in awe, and for a microsecond, I glimpse the curious little boy he once was.

Rick is a large, hefty man. Everything about him is thick. He has a thick neck, thick torso, and thick fingers. His light brown hair is thick and curly, with curls looser than mine. His beard is short, but thick, and he dresses like Ryan, which makes sense, I guess, since they're both handymen. I don't see Rick often, but when I do, he's wearing broken-in jeans, work boots, and a flannel shirt.

"How are you, Rick?" I ask, gesturing for him to take the chair opposite me.

"I am fine, Megan. How are you?" he asks, smiling.

"Very well, thank you," I reply. "I didn't get a chance last night to tell you I'm sorry for your loss. I understand that you and Saxon were friends, and I'm sorry you lost a friend."

"Thanks, Megan," he responds. "To be honest, w-w-we weren't as close as people seem to think. He was my employer. He didn't h-have any friends, and I don't have any friends, so we just kind of hung out friendless and alone together."

"Friendless and alone together" might be the saddest description of a relationship I've ever heard.

"Oh." I'm not sure how to respond to his disclosure. "Well, you've lost someone significant in your life, and for that, you have my condolences." I give him a small smile. "What will you do now that your employer is… gone?" I ask.

"Don't worry about me, M-Megan. I'll be all right. I own a few rental properties around the lake and two condos."

I didn't know Rick was a property investor. It must not be common knowledge, or I'm sure I would've heard about it from the rumour mill. I'm glad he has something to fall back on and won't struggle while he looks for another job. He continues to tell me about his rental properties and mentions that the cottages he owns "around the lake" are on the same side of the lake as Lake Access Road. Coincidence? Eric always says investigators don't like coincidences in murder investigations.

"Good for you!" I say.

"I paid close attention when I worked for Saxon. Watching him and some of the mistakes he made was more valuable than the wages he paid me." Rick chuckles. "I learned what to do and what not to do."

I offer Rick a cup of tea, but he declines.

"Saxon's death is why I'm here," Rick discloses. "I phoned Chief Sloane, but he hasn't gotten back to me, yet. I didn't know what else to do, so I came here to see if he's home, but he's not."

I shake my head. "Eric is at work today. I don't know when he'll be home. Is there anything I can help you with?"

"I hope so," Rick replies. "I'm worried about Clawdia."

I search my memory bank for anyone named Clawdia but come up blank.

"Who is Clawdia?" I ask.

"Saxon's cat," Rick replies.

"Saxon had a cat?" I blurt louder than I intend.

I can't imagine Saxon Renaud having any love or affection for another living being.

Rick nods. "He s-sure did. I'm worried about her. Is she still in his house? Did the police take her somewhere? If she's there, is she alone, scared, and hungry?"

Oh, my. Now, I'm worried about Clawdia too. I do some quick mental math and realize that Saxon has been dead for thirty-six hours; a long time to go without fresh water, food, or a clean litter box.

"Did you mention Clawdia to the police when they questioned you?" I ask.

Rick shakes his head. "I was nervous and didn't think about her until after," he replies. "I have a key to Saxon's house, and I went there, but there's police tape on the door, so I didn't go in."

I hate to admit it, but I might not have been as truthful in Rick's situation. If I was worried about the health and welfare of an animal, I might've just moved the tape, let myself in, then re-sealed the tape on my way out.

"You want to ask Eric if you can enter Saxon's house to check on Clawdia?" I ask.

He nods. "I want to get Clawdia. And maybe her food and litter box, too, if Chief Sloane will let me. I can take her back to my house. I don't mind taking care of her. She's a shy cat. She hides from strangers, and she probably hid when the police searched the house. She would have been terrified. Or worse, maybe she got scared and escaped while they were searching. It's freezing outside, Megan, and goodness knows where she is…"

Rick's voice is panicky, and his words increase in speed as he speaks. His concern is palpable, and I notice that over the course of our conversation, his stutter has almost disappeared. I raise my hand in a stop motion, and Rick stops talking and takes a breath.

"Let me see if I can get hold of Eric," I suggest, unlocking my phone screen.

I know even if he's in a meeting, Eric will reply to my text, but I don't tell Rick that.

"Megan, if he says I'm allowed to pick up Clawdia, would you come with me? It feels weird going to Saxon's house alone, now that he's… you know… and I don't have anyone else to ask."

I nod. "Of course, I will," I respond.

Me: Did you know Saxon had a cat? Rick wants to enter Saxon's house to get Clawdia and take her back to his house.

Eric: Are you with Rick right now? Is he at the store?

Me: Yes and yes. He was looking for you.

Eric: We know about the cat. I assigned an officer to feed the cat and scoop the litter. Saxon's brother has until Monday to get the cat, otherwise someone from the Animal Centre will pick it up.

My inner animal advocate doesn't like this. If Saxon's brother doesn't pick up Clawdia, she'll be alone for almost ninety-six hours. What if she's scared and doesn't understand why her human isn't coming back?

I read Eric's last text to Rick, and we're of the same mind; we'd both prefer for Clawdia to stay with him. Rick tells me he doubts that Saxon's brother will want Clawdia.

"Saxon had hardly any contact with his family. He wasn't close to them. I doubt they'll come all the way to Harmony Lake just to get his cat. But if I'm wrong, and his brother wants the cat, I'll give her to him. In the meantime, I think Clawdia would be happier staying with me. Other than Saxon, I'm the only person she knows."

"Let's see what we can do," I say to Rick while looking at my phone and typing a text to Eric.

Me: Can Rick pick up Clawdia? He has a key. If Saxon's

brother wants the cat, he can just as easily get her from Rick's house as he can from Saxon's house.

"Three dots," I say to Rick. "He's typing a reply."

The three dots disappear, and I startle when my phone rings.

"It's Eric," I tell Rick as I answer the call.

"Hello?" I stand up, stepping away from the table and walking toward the stairs for privacy.

"Hey, babe. Is Rick still there?"

"Yes," I reply, nodding even though Eric can't see me. "I'm sorry to interrupt you at work, but Clawdia isn't used to being alone, and we're worried about her."

"Can you go somewhere quiet with Rick and put me on speaker?"

I return to the table and put Eric on speaker.

"We can hear you," I say.

"Hi, Chief Sloane," Rick says, waving as if Eric can see him.

"Hi, Rick, I'm sorry I haven't called you back. I've been in meetings all day. Does the cat have any health issues? Does it require medication or anything?"

"Not that I'm aware of," Rick replies. "And I think Saxon would have mentioned it. He talked about Clawdia a lot."

Eric sighs. "Rick, I'll have an officer meet you at Saxon's house in one hour. You can take the cat, her food, and her litter box. You cannot remove anything else from the house. The officer will take photos of everything you take."

"Thanks, Chief Sloane, we'll be there," Rick replies.

"We?" Eric asks. "Megan, are you going with him?"

"Yes," I reply.

"Can you take me off speaker now, please?"

I take the call off speaker, and once again wander toward the stairs.

"If I tell you I'm uncomfortable with this, are you going to go anyway?" Eric asks.

"I think so," I reply honestly.

Another deep sigh from his end of the phone.

"An officer will be with you. I'll tell them to make sure you aren't alone with Rick." It's another one of those statements that is neither a suggestion nor a question.

I thought the police confirmed Rick's alibi. If they eliminated him as a suspect in Saxon's murder, why is Eric uncomfortable with me being alone with him? I want to ask but know that Rick is only about ten feet away, so I save my question for later.

"I understand," I say.

"I'm a phone call away if you need anything. I love you."

"I love you too," I say.

"Dinner is at 7 p.m."

"I can't wait," I reply.

We end our call, and I tell Rick I'll meet him at Saxon's house in an hour. He thanks me for helping him and Clawdia, then leaves through the back door, mumbling something about borrowing Cat Benatar's kitty carrier from Trudy.

CHAPTER 16

CONNIE AND MARLA insisting they'll be fine without me at Knitorious makes me feel better about leaving to meet Rick at Saxon's house.

Before I left, Connie and Marla tried to think of anyone they know of, other than Rick, who has been inside Saxon's house. They couldn't come up with anyone. They're curious and excited about my visit, and I'm under strict orders to report back to them. They tried to convince me to take photos, but I can't do that. It feels too much like violating someone's personal space, even if that someone is dead.

If the way Saxon presented himself indicates what his home is like, I expect a tidy, organized space with carefully chosen, tasteful, and collectible antique furniture and knickknacks.

I roll to a stop, pulling up behind Rick's car, outside Saxon's house on Mountain Road. Mountain Road is one of the oldest streets in Harmony Lake. It's on the east side of town and is one of only two roads that leads to the resorts in the Harmony Hills mountains.

The lots are large with mature, shady trees and large Victorian-era homes setback far from the street. Old-timey reproduction, Victorian-era streetlights add to the charm of the neighbourhood.

Saxon owns several houses on this street. Most of them were renovated and repurposed from their original single-family-residential status, to either professional office spaces or multi-residential rental properties. I've never been inside Saxon's home, but I believe he lives in a renovated duplex.

Rick and I exit our cars at the same time. We look around, then at each other, and shrug. There isn't any sign of a police car nearby.

"I guess the police officer who's accompanying us isn't here yet," I observe.

"I guess not," Rick agrees.

I check the time on my phone, and we're a few minutes early. We stand by our cars while we wait for the officer to arrive. Today is less frigid and windy than the last few days. I use this opportunity to ask Rick a few more questions about Saxon. Maybe he can give me some insight into Saxon's life, a clue about who killed him or why.

"Rick, earlier when you told me about your job with Saxon, you said you learned a lot from watching him. You said you learned what not to do. What did you mean by that?"

"It's like my mum always said," Rick replies. "You'll catch more flies with honey than with vinegar. Saxon was all vinegar and no honey."

"You mean he wasn't very nice to people?" I clarify.

"Exactly," Rick says. "Saxon was nasty. Sometimes, it seemed like he was mean and difficult on purpose." Rick shrugs one shoulder. "He made his life more difficult than it had to be. If he was nicer to people, life would have been easier for him."

"Easier how?" I ask.

"Saxon was always fighting with someone. He was always threatening to sue someone, or someone was threatening to sue him. For example, he owed a lot of people money and was always late making repayments. He wouldn't apologize when his payments were late. He would try to come up with a reason that it wasn't his fault. Nothing was ever his fault, if you asked him. Saxon was always the victim of other people's choices."

This is the third time today someone has mentioned that Saxon had a debt problem. First Ryan told me that Saxon owed money to Jay Singh, then Pete, and now Rick.

"Why did Saxon have so much debt?" I ask.

"Saxon's properties are mortgaged to the hilt," Rick explains. "He bought them on spec. He never planned to keep them. Saxon's plan was to buy as much real estate as he could, then sell it for a profit to investors and developers who want to build in Harmony Lake. He underestimated how difficult it would be to get around the big-box policy. He protested the policy for years, but the town council and most of the residents are opposed to big-box companies coming here. Saxon got stuck with these properties. His payments were so high, the rental income barely covered the expenses. As the value of a property would go up, he would increase the mortgage against it and use the borrowed money to keep himself afloat."

"You can only do that for so long," I conclude. "Eventually, you've borrowed as much as any lender will allow, and your monthly payments are so large you can't maintain them. Never mind the costs of maintaining the properties on top of the regular expenses."

"Exactly!" Rick says. "Saxon's only hope to dig himself out of debt was to win the mayoral election and reverse the big-box policy. Then he could sell his properties to the investors and come out of it with money in his pocket."

If this is true, this election was Saxon's last hope, his Hail Mary pass. Saxon's entire financial future depended on him winning the mayoral by-election.

"What was his backup plan?" I ask. "What was Saxon planning to do if he lost the election?"

Rick shakes his head. "I don't know, Megan. He never mentioned a backup plan. I think in his mind he had no other option."

"What do you think of the big-box policy?" I ask, assuming Rick would be of the same opinion as Saxon. "If the policy were reversed, would you sell your properties to developers and walk away with a profit?"

"I voted for Adam," Rick divulges. "I like Harmony Lake the way it is, small and uncommercialized. Judging by the landslide results, most of the town's residents feel the same way."

I'm shocked at Rick's disclosure. He spent so much time with Saxon, I just assumed they were of the same opinion about the big-box policy. That'll teach me to go around making assumptions. Could Rick feel so strongly about it he killed Saxon to make sure if he won the election the policy wouldn't be reversed?

"Who do you think killed him?" I ask.

"I don't know for sure," Rick replies. "But Saxon and Pete Feeney had quite a few meetings together in the weeks leading up to the election. Secret meetings."

"If they were secret, how do you know about them?" I ask. "Do you know what they talked about?"

"Saxon would tell me he was meeting with Pete, but he wouldn't tell me what they were meeting about. They would meet on FaceTime."

I wonder what they were meeting about? Pete is a fire-fighter and a real estate agent. It's unlikely they met multiple times to discuss fire safety. Was Saxon so confident about winning the election that he was already arranging for Pete to sell his properties? Odd that Pete didn't mention this earlier when we talked about Saxon's death. I wonder if he disclosed these meetings to Eric? I add it to the mental list

I'm keeping called, things-to-mention-to-Eric. The list is getting long.

"I hear you saved Cat Benatar's life on Thursday night," I say changing the subject. "It was nice of you to give up a whole night to save Trudy's cat."

"It was as much for me as it was for Trudy," Rick explains, chuckling. "It was the third time this winter Cat Benatar found his way into the ceiling and got stuck there. I closed off every hole I could find so I wouldn't have to save him again." We laugh.

"You're a really nice person, Rick," I tell him. "I don't think many people realize how nice you are because you're quiet, and you spent so much time with Saxon. People might've assumed because you were friends with him, that you and he were alike, but you're not."

"It isn't easy for me to make friends, Megan," Rick confides. "I have bad social anxiety. It's difficult for me to hang out in groups. And when I was growing up, I was teased and bullied because of my stutter. A mean group of popular boys tormented me about it for years. So now, when I'm around smart guys like Adam, athletic guys like Eric, or funny, confident guys like Sheamus and Ryan, I feel like that bullied kid again. I get uncomfortable, and my stutter gets worse, which makes me more anxious, and it becomes a vicious cycle. It's easier to avoid those situations."

"I'm sorry that happened to you," I say. "But the people you mentioned aren't like that. Adam, Eric, Sheamus, and Ryan would never tease you or bully you because you stutter. Trust me, I wouldn't be friends with people like that. Also, I notice when you and I talk one-on-one your stutter disappears."

"It's not as prevalent when I'm speaking with one person, especially someone like you, who's easy to talk to. I know Saxon was one reason I don't have many friends," Rick admits. "I think on some level it worked for me. As long as I hung around with Saxon, I didn't have to worry about being socially awkward because everyone avoided me."

"Is it true that Saxon was a jerk to you?" I ask. "I heard he said some unkind things to you sometimes."

Rick nods. "It's true," he admits. "Saxon had a short temper and, sometimes, I was the closest person he could take out his frustrations on."

Maybe Marla is right; maybe Rick got fed up with how Saxon treated him and killed him in a fit of rage or revenge. But how could Rick be the murderer when he was at Trudy's house, saving Cat Benetar from the ceiling?

"Well, without Saxon around," I respond, "it'll be more difficult to hide that you're a nice, funny person who's pleasant to be around, and people might want to be your friend," I warn him.

"I hope so," Rick admits. "I think I'm ready to extend my friend group beyond Trudy, Cat Benatar, and Clawdia." He laughs.

We're interrupted when the patrol car shows up. Rick collects the kitty carrier from his car, and we follow the officer to the front door where he removes the crime-scene tape blocking the keyhole. Rick uses his key to unlock the door, and the three of us step inside.

The inside of Saxon's house is not what I was expecting. Instead of the tidy, organized space I imagined, I'm standing in a space not comfortable enough to call a home. The furnishings are sparse and barely functional. There's a small, dented, metal folding table with two folding chairs that I assume was Saxon's kitchen table. A TV so old it has a picture tube sits on top of a stack of two sideways milk crates that house a record collection. Across from the TV is an old floral sofa with three sunk-in seat cushions that look like they have almost no padding left. The velour upholstery is worn so thin, it's see-through in some spots.

The lighting in the house hasn't been updated, so there are

few overhead lights. Instead there are lamps on the floor throughout, and the heavy velvet draperies are pulled closed, preventing any natural light from coming in.

The walls near the windows are water-stained, and the wood floors are about thirty years overdue for refinishing. A litter box sits in one corner of the kitchen, and a bowl of kibble and a bowl of water are in the opposite corner. Scattered cat toys dot the floor.

Rick walks through the space, making kissing sounds and calling Clawdia's name. He alternates the kissing sounds with *ssspssssp* sounds.

"I think I know where she's hiding," Rick whispers to me.

The police officer and I follow him down the hall, then up the stairs. We enter what I assume was Saxon's bedroom. He didn't even have a proper bed; he slept on a mattress on the floor. Maybe this wasn't Saxon's bedroom. It doesn't look very lived in. But when Rick opens the closet door, I see a whangee handle umbrella leaning against the wall and several identical shoeboxes lining the shelf above the clothing rack. I know this was Saxon's bedroom. Rick shoves the shoeboxes aside, exposing a small, very timid, wide-eyed kitty.

"There you are Miss Clawdia," Rick coos to the small cat.

He reaches up and pulls Clawdia from the shelf, bundling her in his arms and rubbing her head with his bearded chin. When she nuzzles into his neck, it's obvious she knows him and is happy and relieved to see him. Rick and Clawdia are old friends.

I pick up the kitty carrier and open the door, holding it toward Rick so he can slide Clawdia inside. Loud, guttural meows fill the room. She does not like the kitty carrier and registers her dislike verbally.

The police officer follows Rick and I downstairs. In the kitchen, I collect the bag of kitty kibble and Clawdia's food dishes. I dump the water out of the water dish, and I gather a few of the cat toys that are scattered on the floor. The police officer collects her litter box and the unopened box of fresh litter. The three of us take Clawdia and her accessories to Rick's car, then return to the front door so Rick can lock it, and the officer can re-seal the keyhole.

"Thank you for coming with me today, Megan. I appreciate it," Rick says as he closes the trunk with the litter box inside.

"No problem," I reply. "I'm glad I could help. Clawdia is lucky to have you looking out for her. I don't think anyone else in town knows she exists."

"I'm happy to take her," Rick says. "She's a sweet cat. Hopefully she's not a climber and doesn't find her way into the ceiling like Cat Benatar," he jokes.

After Rick drives away, I knock on the passenger side window of the patrol car. The young officer lowers the window, and I thank him for his time and help. On my way to Knitorious, I prepare myself to answer tons of questions from Connie and Marla about the inside of Saxon Renaud's home.

CHAPTER 17

ON MY TIPPY TOES, I scan the Pastabilities dining room for Eric. I don't see him, but because of how the tables and booths are arranged, it's difficult to see who occupies them. I know he's here somewhere; he sent me a text a few minutes ago to let me know he was seated. Also, he's never late when we meet. Ever.

Even when Pastabilities is fully booked, it's neither loud nor crowded. They configured the restaurant for intimacy with tables and booths spaced farther apart than most restaurants. The sense of seclusion is further enforced with strategically placed coat racks and floor plants that double as privacy screens.

The maître d' spots me waiting, smiles, and comes over. He teasingly chides me for being late, though I'm less than ten minutes late, and gestures for me to follow him. We pass several coat racks and floor plants before I spot Eric, laser focussed on his phone, in a quiet semi-circular booth in the corner. We're seated at one of the best tables in the restaurant, a bit big for a party of two but definitely a premium location.

"I'm sorry I'm late," I apologize as I slide into the semi-circular booth next to him. "I stopped at Mayor Feeney's house to drop off some yarn she purchased. We started talking, and you know how it is," I explain.

"No worries," he says with a smile. "I've waited way longer for way less." His wink makes my tummy flutter like a charm of hummingbirds just took flight inside me.

I sense Eric is about to lean over and kiss me, but we're interrupted when the maître d', still standing next to our table, speaks.

The maître d' congratulates Eric on his appointment as police chief and tells him it's an honour to have the chief of police dine in their humble establishment. After much smiling and thank yous by all three of us, the maître d' takes our drink order, leaves us with menus, and disappears.

Finally alone, Eric leans over to kiss me hello, then holds up his cell phone between us, opens my bag, and drops the phone inside.

"No phone until after dinner," he declares. "You first, then work."

"Wow," I say in response to his gesture. "Are you sure? What if there's a break in the case and they need to reach you?"

"It can wait an hour," he insists, then adds, "besides, if something big happens, word will get to us through the rumour mill before the official channels, anyway."

We laugh because it's true.

"Thank you," I say. "I was starting to forget what it's like to spend time together without your phone providing a constant digital soundtrack."

"I know, and I'm sorry." He covers my hand in his and strokes my knuckles with his thumb. "You've been so patient the last few months while I figure out how to do this police chief job. Starting tonight, I'm implementing a daily detox of at least an hour with no phone and no computer."

The server arrives with our drinks and attempts to take our order, but we haven't opened our menus yet. She gives us a few more minutes and leaves. Before we open our menus, I already know what I'm having. Shrimp and mushroom risotto with spinach salad. It's my favourite dish at Pastabilities. Eric decides on the chicken Asiago, chicken breast stuffed with Asiago cheese, spinach, and caramelized onions. To start, we order the antipasto plate.

"How was your visit to Saxon's house?" Eric asks after the server leaves with our orders.

"It was… educational," I reply.

"I'm listening," Eric says.

I tell Eric about my visit to Saxon's house, starting with pulling up behind Rick's car before the officer arrived. I tell him how shocked I was at the inside of the house and the conditions in which Saxon lived. Then I tell him Rick's disclosure to me about his relationship with Saxon and what he observed during the time they spent together.

"My instincts tell me Rick didn't murder Saxon," I say. "But I have to admit, he had a lot of motive. As if wanting revenge against Saxon for the mean abusive things he said to Rick wasn't enough, it turns out Rick didn't even vote for Saxon because he didn't want the big-box policy to be reversed."

"There's a hole in Rick's alibi," Eric reveals. "That's why I was uncomfortable with you going to Saxon's house with him today. Rick is an unlikely suspect, but he's a suspect. There's at least an hour-long gap in his alibi. Trudy fell asleep and can't vouch for Rick's whereabouts. She can't even confirm how long she slept."

"But Rick was at her house before Trudy fell asleep and then still there when she woke up?" I ask.

Eric nods. "That's right, but there's a large enough gap of time unaccounted for that I can't rule him out as a suspect."

"Speaking of holes," I make a play on words, "Rick created several holes when he was chasing Cat Benetar through the ceiling. Also, Trudy's laundry room has ceiling tiles. It was because of a loose ceiling tile that Cat Benetar could get into the ceiling."

"And?" Eric urges.

"And it would've been easy for Rick to shove something in those holes before he sealed them."

"Ah," Eric says. "You mean like an umbrella or penny loafer."

I nod. "It's worth a look, isn't it?"

"We asked. Trudy doesn't want us poking around in her ceiling. I'd have to get a warrant, and I'm trying to avoid it if possible. I don't want to upset her or get blamed if Cat Benetar gets lost in the ceiling again."

"When I asked Rick if he had any theories about who killed Saxon, he named Pete Feeney." I watch Eric's face for a reaction, but he gives nothing away.

"Did he say *why* he thinks Pete would kill Saxon?" Eric asks.

"Rick said Saxon and Pete had several secret meetings together over the last few weeks. Rick said they met over FaceTime. He said Saxon wouldn't tell him what they talked about."

"Interesting." Eric looks down and to the left, something he does when he's thinking. "Pete didn't mention these meetings in his statement."

"He didn't mention them to me either," I say.

"You spoke with Pete?" Eric asks, wide eyed. "My goodness, you have had a busy day."

I nod. "He was in the store earlier with his mum. She was shopping for yarn, and he was her driver, so I sat with him while he waited, and we talked."

I tell Eric about my conversation with Pete, and how Pete suspects that a money lender might be behind Saxon's murder.

"We're beginning to get a picture of Saxon's financial situation," Eric discloses. He shakes his head. "It wasn't good.

Saxon had a lot of debt. He was in over his head, behind in payments to everybody, and his income was less than his expenses."

"It wasn't a very well-kept secret," I tell him. "Today alone, three different people have told me that Saxon was in debt and was behind on his repayments."

"Did you learn anything else from your conversation with Pete?" Eric asks, taking a sip of his drink.

"I did," I reply. "He asked me to pass on a message to you." Eric raises his eyebrows with interest. "He wants me to tell you he printed the listings you asked about, but he forgot them on top of his printer. He said he'll drop them off in the next day or so." I look at Eric and wait for a response. Nothing. His facial expression gives nothing away. "Are you moving, Eric?" I finally ask.

"Only if you're evicting me," he replies playfully.

"Why does Pete think you want to buy a house?"

"I think Pete misunderstood the conversation we had at Adam's victory party last night," Eric explains. "I was standing by the buffet table, and Pete was telling me how busy he is every year between January and April with buyers and sellers hoping to move in the spring. I told him I miss having my own home. I mentioned that I'd like to own a house again, someday. That's all I said. Being the salesman he is, Pete jumped on it and decided he should sell me a house."

"So, you aren't house hunting?" I clarify.

"No, I wouldn't do something like that without talking to you first," Eric replies, using his finger to sweep a stray curl from my face. "But one day, I want to own a home again," he admits. "The apartment above the store was supposed to be temporary, until I figured out if I liked living and working in this town enough to stay here, and until I could convince the cute yarn store owner I had a crush on to go on a date with me." He smiles, and I'm sure I'm blushing. "It's been over a year now. I love my life here, and I'm still sitting on the money from my divorce settlement. I set aside that money to buy my next home."

"So, you're not fed up with waiting for me to be ready for us to live together? You haven't given up and moved on without me?"

"Never," Eric insists. "Pete misunderstood our conversation. I didn't realize he was so keen to make a sale. I'll have a word with him and make sure he understands I'm not in the market for a house."

When I saw Eric and Pete by the buffet table at Adam's party, I assumed they were talking about Saxon's murder, but I guess Pete was trying to sell Eric a house.

"I know you're ready for us to live together," I say, rubbing Eric's knee, "and I really appreciate you not pressuring me, while you patiently wait for me to catch up." I take a deep breath and admit, "I want us to live together, too, but I don't want to move. I know it sounds selfish, but I raised my daughter in this house, and I have good memories there. I live on a great street, my neighbours are fantastic, I love my gardens and the southern exposure, and I'm just not ready to sell it and leave."

"You think I want you to sell your house?" he asks. "You don't have to sell your house. If you want us to live in your house, I'm happy with that."

"Seriously?" I'm shocked. I'm not sure I'd live in a house Eric shared with his ex-wife. "When I imagine us living together, I imagine us in a home we choose together. A fresh start in a house where neither of us has a past. It never occurred to me that you'd want to live at chez Martel."

"Babe, I don't care where we live," Eric explains. "I agree with everything you said about your house. It's a great house in a great neighbourhood, and it's Hannah's home. I understand why you'd want to keep it. I also understand if you don't want me to live there with you, but for the record, I'd move in with you in a heartbeat."

"Can I think about it?" I ask. "I'm not procrastinating, I just want to make sure we make the right decision at the right time. If we do this, I want it to work."

"I'm not going anywhere," Eric assures me, then sighs deeply. "I can't tell you how relieved I am that location is what's holding you back. I was scared you were hesitating because you have doubts about us."

"No doubts," I reassure him, leaning in and nuzzling his neck. "Thank you for not rushing me." Eric kisses the top of my head.

"Maybe there's a compromise," he suggests. "We could renovate your home and make it our home. Whenever we watch those home-reno shows, you say there are things you'd like to change about your house. We could do that. We could time it for when Hannah is at school, so she's not inconvenienced while she's home. And we can stay at my apartment when the renovations are in progress, so we aren't living in a construction zone."

This is a brilliant idea.

"You might be onto something," I say, then bite my lip thinking about the possibilities.

Proud of himself, Eric grins widely. "We can take it one project at a time," he suggests. "We can renovate as fast or slow as we want so neither of us feels rushed."

He uses the phrase, "neither of us" liberally. We both know he means me. I'm pretty sure if I booked a church and chose a wedding dress, Eric wouldn't feel rushed.

The server brings our appetizer, and we decide not to talk about Saxon's murder or real estate for the duration of our meal. Instead, we talk about gloriously mundane things like the TV shows we watch together, the weather, and what's going on with his family back east.

"Do you miss your phone yet?" I ask over our shared tiramisu.

"Not at all," Eric replies. "But after dinner, I want to show you a photo I took today when I met with forensics."

"A photo of something they found in Adam's car?" I put down my fork and nudge the plate with the remaining tiramisu toward Eric.

I wipe my mouth with my napkin and leave the napkin on the table like a flag of surrender. An official signal that I can't eat another bite. Everything was so delicious that I stuffed myself until I couldn't possibly swallow another crumb.

Eric nods with a mouth full of cake. Why doesn't he ever get full?

"They didn't find much in Adam's car," he says, managing my expectations. "No fingerprints at all. The steering wheel, seatbelt, gearshift, and door handles were wiped clean. At the very least, forensics expected to find Adam's fingerprints, but they didn't. They found trace DNA belonging to Adam, and they're running DNA on a few long strawberry blonde strands of hair recovered from the front passenger side of the vehicle. I assume they'll come back as belonging to Jess. And a few long brown curly strands I assume will come back as Hannah's."

"This is enough to eliminate Adam as a suspect, right?" I coax. "First, he has an alibi. He was in your apartment with me when Saxon died. Second, it wouldn't make sense for Adam to wipe his own fingerprints from his own vehicle when it would be expected for them to be there. Obviously, somebody who isn't Adam killed Saxon Renaud."

"I don't believe Adam is the killer," Eric says, using his gentle voice.

I recognize this tone of voice; he's about to say something I don't want to hear, something like Adam is still a suspect.

"But…" I argue prematurely.

"I can't eliminate him as a suspect," he says, interrupting me. "You can't be sure he was in my apartment all night. I have to assume he showed up to give himself an alibi, snuck out while you were sleeping so he could clean and dispose of the car, then snuck in again before you woke up."

I can't argue with that. I can't confirm what did or didn't happen or who was or wasn't in the apartment while I slept, but if Adam left and came back while I was asleep, Sophie would have alerted me to it. I mention this to Eric, but he says Sophie's lack of bark is neither admissible evidence nor reliable testimony, and not sufficient to verify Adam's whereabouts the night someone killed Saxon.

"We suspect the killer is the same height as Adam or very close. The driver's seat and mirrors weren't moved. Or, if the killer adjusted them, they re-adjusted them to the original settings before they abandoned the car in your driveway. Either that, or they couldn't figure out the seat and mirror controls and gave up."

"Pretty much anyone who attended the card game could be a suspect if height is a requirement," I counter. "Even you could be a suspect using that criteria. You, Adam, Pete, and Rick are within about an inch of each other's height. Sheamus and Ryan are both a little shorter, maybe five foot nine and five foot ten. Does this eliminate Sheamus and Ryan because they're a few inches shorter than whoever may have driven the car?"

"No, they're both close enough in height that they would be able to drive the car without changing the settings," Eric explains. "The evidence found in the trunk rules out Saxon as a driver and confirms what we've suspected all along—he was killed elsewhere, then transported to Lake Access Road."

"You thought Saxon might've driven the car?" I don't understand how Saxon could be a suspect in his own murder.

"I couldn't rule out the possibility that whoever killed Saxon forced him to drive to Lake Access Road, then killed him and ran over him. But thanks to the evidence we found in the trunk I've eliminated that possibility."

"What did you find in the trunk?" I ask.

He shrugs. "A few strands of Saxon's hair, some fibres from his clothes, and a few other unidentified fibres. Those are the photos I want to show you, the unidentified fibres."

I spy our server in the distance and raise my hand to get her attention. When she looks at me and smiles, I smile back and make a check mark with my thumb and forefinger to indicate we're ready for the bill. I want to get out of here and see the fibre evidence from Adam's trunk.

CHAPTER 18

WHILE ERIC LOVES up Sophie and reacquaints himself with his phone, I change into my pyjamas, wash my face, and brush my teeth. No longer able to deny that I've become one of those people who, more often than not, falls asleep with their knitting in their lap watching TV after dinner, I've embraced it and get ready for bed before I get settled on the sofa.

"The forensics team found some unidentified fibres in the trunk of Adam's car and around the driver's seat. They found similar fibres on Saxon's coat and in his hair." Eric opens his messenger bag and hands me a plastic evidence bag with a few kinky, frizzy strands of fibre. "They determined that the fibres from Saxon's coat and head, the driver's seat, and Adam's trunk originate from the same source…"

"Animal fibre," I interrupt. I hold the bag closer to my face to look at the fibres as closely as possible. "This is haze. From yarn." I look at him.

Haze is the halo of fuzz that surrounds certain animal fibres like cashmere and alpaca.

"I knew you'd recognize it." He sounds equal parts impressed and astonished.

"Mohair? Cashmere?" I ask, once again inspecting the fibre through the plastic barrier of the evidence bag.

"Alpaca," Eric replies.

I furrow my brow. Why is this familiar? I'm having one of those déjà vu moments. Even though I'm not touching the fibre directly, I feel like I've touched it before. I remember feeling the squishy, soft stitches between my fingers.

"What is it?" Eric asks. "Do you recognize this fibre? Do you know where it came from?"

I shake my head. "I'm not sure. I touch alpaca every day at the store. Maybe it reminds me of something we have in stock." I squint at the strands of fibre. "It might help if I know what colour it is."

Was the murderer wearing something made with alpaca yarn from my store? The thought makes me momentarily queasy.

Eric unlocks his phone and opens the camera roll. "I have photos of microscopic images of the fibres," he explains. "There are multiple colours. Some were white, like this one. The forensics report said the white ones are undyed." He hands me his phone and shows me a fuzzy picture of what he says is an undyed alpaca fibre, then he takes it back and swipes to another photo. "Some are dyed one of two solid colours, and some are dyed with both colours. I told the forensics guy that the term for that is variegated, and he was pretty impressed with my yarn knowledge."

As soon as Eric says the word variegated, I flashback to Sheamus walking from table to table at the pub on Thursday evening after the election. He was wearing that hand-knit, bulky scarf. The next day, when I saw him outside Hairway To Heaven, he was wearing the scarf again, and he let me touch it while he told me about the variegated colours. Later that night, at Adam's party, Sheamus wore the scarf again, and I remember thinking it was too hot for such a thick scarf.

"Anyway, the other two colours are..."

"Red and green." I finish his sentence. "Or should I say, *Ashes to Ashes, Rust to Rust*," I add, recalling the name Sheamus used for the variegated yarn.

"Babe, do you remember who bought this yarn?"

I shake my head. "No, I didn't sell it to anyone."

In shock, I feel behind me to make sure the sofa is there before I sit down.

Sheamus O'Brien killed Saxon Renaud? Sheamus can't be a murderer, he's my friend. Heck, he's everyone's friend. He's the friendliest, happy-go-luckiest person in town. No way.

"Can you find the purchasers on the store computer?" Eric asks.

I shake my head again. "No, we don't sell it at Knitorious. I'm told this yarn was hand spun and hand dyed by someone who owns an alpaca farm," I explain.

Eric sits down next to me. "Told by who?" he asks.

"Sheamus," I reply. "The fibres are from his scarf."

"Are you sure?" He looks as shocked as I feel.

I nod. "As sure as I can be."

Eric curses out loud. "His alibi is unverified."

"What does that mean?" I ask.

"He was alone when Saxon was murdered. There's no evidence to prove or disprove his whereabouts." Eric shrugs. "He may as well have no alibi at all."

"That reminds me." I pivot so my body faces Eric. "Did you say Sheamus turned *off* his phone before he went to sleep on Thursday night?"

"That's right," Eric replies, nodding. "That's why we couldn't get a location on his cell phone." He narrows his eyes. "Why? Did you hear something different?"

"Sheamus told me he was asleep when Adam texted him to check on his car on Friday morning. He said Adam's text woke him up, and he was confused when he said he saw Adam's car in front of his house."

"How can a powered-off cell phone wake you up?" Eric asks rhetorically.

"Exactly," I reply.

"The officer who went to Sheamus's house on Friday morning to look for Adam's car said it looked like Sheamus hadn't been home all night. The snow was undisturbed, and he didn't respond when my officer knocked on the door. He said he was in the shower, but again, I can't verify it."

"I don't believe Sheamus is a murderer," I say. "It doesn't feel right. The evidence against him is circumstantial, right?"

"Right," Eric says. "I'm not sure we have enough to charge him, but there's enough for me to question him again and ask him to surrender his scarf for examination."

I pivot more toward Eric, and bring my feet up onto the sofa, crossing them in front of me.

"Here's the thing about alpaca." I begin my fibre lecture. "The haze is always shedding, and it sticks to everything. It's like a bad rash or craft glitter—just when you think you got rid of it, and you haven't seen it in months, it suddenly reappears, stuck to you, and you realize you can never get rid of it."

"OK," Eric says. "How is this relevant to Saxon's murder?"

"Saxon was at Sheamus's house. It would be reasonable for Saxon to have alpaca haze on him." I wave my hand in front of me. "Scratch that. It would be reasonable for everyone at the card game to have alpaca haze on them. And they likely transferred it to their cars. And depending where Sheamus's scarf was located when Saxon and Ryan had their shoving match, lots of haze could have been disturbed and become airborne, landing on whoever and whatever was nearby."

"If the scarf was with the pile of coats, the coats could have picked up some of the fibre," Eric speculates.

"Precisely," I say, poking his arm.

"So, the haze on Saxon might not be from the killer, he could've picked it up before he was killed," Eric surmises.

"And," I think out loud, "it means the killer wasn't necessarily at the card game. Saxon could have transferred haze to his murderer when he was strangled or when the killer moved his body. Then the killer could have transferred some of the haze to the driver's seat of Adam's car. The stuff can move from person to person like a cold virus."

"So, I could use this alpaca fibre as evidence against the killer, and the killer could use the same fibre as evidence of their innocence," Eric concludes, unlocking his phone. His thumbs move back and forth across the keyboard at record speed.

"What next?" I ask.

"I need to make sure Sheamus's scarf is, in fact, the source of these fibres, and I need to ask everyone who was at the card game to provide the clothes and coats they wore on Friday night for examination." He types on his phone again.

Anyone at the card game could have found Adam's keys and used his car to run down Saxon. Even someone who wasn't at the card game could have done it. If Adam dropped his keys on his way to his car, someone else could have found them. Maybe someone saw him searching in the snow for them, waited for Adam to give up searching and leave, then found them. Instead of eliminating suspects, the list of potential suspects is growing.

CHAPTER 19

APRIL: *We're supposed to get two more inches of the white stuff tonight! Want to go sledding with T and me tomorrow?*

Me: Yes! When and where?

April: Whenever you finish brunch, at Harmony Lake Elementary School

Me: See you there!

CHAPTER 20

SUNDAY, January 17th

I slept in this morning, if you can call it that. Sleeping in for me means until sunrise, but it was still nice to have the extra sleep. The last few days were hectic and overwhelming.

When I get off the elevator, a savory aroma invades my nostrils. The glorious smell gets stronger as I get closer to Adam's door.

"Good morning." Adam and I kiss cheeks.

"Good morning. What is that amazing smell?" I step inside and close the door behind me.

"Brunch," he states the obvious. "It's almost ready. I just need to clear the table so we have somewhere to eat."

Adam closes his laptop and gathers the papers and folders scattered across the top of the table.

"I'll do that," I offer. "You finish making breakfast, and I'll clear and set the table." I swoop in and take over gathering and shuffling the papers while Adam rushes to the kitchen.

Adam brings out two plates of bacon and egg sandwiches and puts one in front of me. Breakfast looks as good as it smells.

"It looks yummy," I say, picking up my sandwich. I take a

bite without waiting for him to sit down. "Mmmm," I moan, rolling my eyes in bliss. "Is this your mum's recipe?" I ask with my mouth full of food, forgetting my manners.

Adam nods and smiles proudly. "It is," he confirms. "It's her recipe for bacon and egg sandwiches with smoky barbeque relish. I know how much you and Hannah like it, so I asked her for the recipe."

Adam's mum is an amazing cook. She used to make this for breakfast when we would visit them in Montreal. For Hannah and me, breakfast was always one of the culinary highlights of the trip; a simple yet traditional breakfast with a twist—the twist being her secret smoky barbeque relish.

"You did an outstanding job following her recipe," I tell him. "Next time I talk to her, I'll tell her. She'll be very proud." Then I add, "I can't believe you convinced her to give you the recipe. I've been asking her for it for years, and she wouldn't give it up. She told me she'd leave it to me in her will."

"Well, she's so happy I'm finally learning to cook that she'll do anything to encourage it, even if it means sharing a few of her secret recipes."

Adam unlocks his tablet and FaceTimes Hannah. While we eat, the three of us catch up and talk about our lives. Hannah has heard about Saxon's murder, and she has questions. I'm not surprised she's heard about it. She has a lot of friends in Harmony Lake, and our rumour mill would win the gold medal for speed if such an event existed. We answer her questions honestly and reassure her that her dad isn't a suspect, even though he and I know he is. The last thing we need is for Hannah to sit in her dorm room four-and-a-half hours away, worried about something she can't control, when Adam and I are perfectly capable of worrying enough for all three of us. We keep the tone and mood of the conversation relaxed and upbeat.

Hannah is jealous when I show her my sandwich with her

grandma's smoky barbeque relish, and Adam promises to make it for her the next time she's home.

When we end our call with Hannah, I help Adam clear the table and load the dishwasher. I'm about to thank him for breakfast and get ready to leave when, out of the blue, he asks me if Eric and I are planning to buy a house together.

"Why would you ask that?" I ask, taken aback.

Adam shrugs. "Pete mentioned that Eric is looking to buy a house, so I assumed you were looking with him."

"No one is buying a house," I begin.

I stop myself from explaining the misunderstanding between Pete and Eric and remind myself that I don't owe Adam an explanation about anything; we're divorced. "I wouldn't make a big decision like that without discussing it with Hannah first." The last sentence sounds more defensive than I intended.

I'm sure he's asking as a concerned parent. It's a big decision, and it would affect our daughter.

"Just asking," he says with his hands in front of his shoulders in a surrender-like gesture. "But while we're talking about buying houses, can I run something past you?"

"Sure," I say, resuming my seat at the dining table. "What's up?"

"I hear through the grapevine that Saxon Renaud was having financial difficulties before he died," Adam says, picking up his laptop and pile of papers and carrying them to the table. "This could be an opportunity, Meg."

"An opportunity for whom?" I ask.

"For us, and for Harmony Lake as a whole," he replies. "Saxon's creditors will want their money sooner rather than later. If someone offered to take these properties off their hands and pay off the debt, I'm sure the creditors and the executors of the estate would be very grateful."

"Why would we do this?" I ask, biting my lip and

CRIME SKEIN

wondering how taking over Saxon's troublesome properties could possibly benefit our family.

"Well, for starters, it would be a good investment," Adam replies. "And purchasing a few key properties could be a more effective way of protecting Harmony lake from big-box developers than our current strategy of winning elections every four years. I can't be the mayor of Harmony Lake forever, Meg, and at least we'd know the properties we own would never be sold to developers."

Though we're divorced, and live mostly separate lives, Adam and I still have a few financial connections. I do the bookkeeping for Adam's law practice, and his car is in my name. Adam still manages the insurance for my house, his condo, his law practice, Knitorious, and both vehicles, and we still share a few joint investments.

I stop biting my lip. "Are you suggesting that by strategically choosing which properties we purchase, the remaining properties would be less desirable to investors?"

Most of the properties in Harmony Lake are too small to be useful to developers or big-box corporations. They would need to purchase groups of connected properties to build anything worthwhile. I think Adam is suggesting we choose properties that would break up the most desirable clusters of lots. We could thwart any future development plans we don't like by refusing to sell our lots. This is the type of strategic plan I would expect from Adam's brilliant mind.

"Exactly!" Adam declares. "Earlier this morning, I was looking at a map of Harmony Lake and marking off the properties I know Saxon owns. I also looked at our investments, and I think if we pool our resources, choose the locations carefully, and take advantage of Saxon's estate's desire to settle his affairs quickly, we could do something beneficial for us and for the town's future."

I take a deep breath. "There's a lot of risk in owning so much real estate," I say. "I mean, look how it worked out for

Saxon. All our financial eggs in one basket. It would tie up all of our money in real estate. I'm not comfortable with that."

"I get it," Adam says with forced cheerfulness. The undertone of disappointment in his voice betrays the smile plastered on his face. "I thought I would suggest it. No harm in talking about it."

While my initial instinct is that this would be too risky for Adam and me alone, he makes valid points about the advantages of such a strategy.

"What if we form a syndicate," I suggest, thinking out loud. "It would reduce our risk and give other people who love this town the opportunity to take part in preserving it."

Adam tilts his head. "It could work," he responds. "Who are you thinking of?"

I shrug. "I don't know. Connie and Archie, maybe Eric."

"Can you run some numbers?" Adam asks. "Maybe you could talk to Pete and get an idea of how much Saxon's various properties are worth."

I've always handled our investments. When we were married, Adam and I made big investment decisions together, but I did the research, executed the decisions, and monitored everything. I was happy to do it. My educational background is economics and accounting, so spreadsheets are my happy place, and since I was a stay-at-home mum for most of our marriage, managing our money kept me intellectually engaged. Also, Adam worked so much, he didn't have time for the minutiae of our household finances.

"Sure," I reply. "If you'll do something for me."

"What do you want me to do, Meg?"

"Invite Rick Ransan to your next guy thing," I reply. "You know, the next card game, or night at the pub watching hockey, or whatever."

"Why?" Adam sneers and raises one thick eyebrow.

"Because he just lost his only friend," I explain. "And he's a nice guy. He's kind of shy and doesn't make friends easily.

I'm not asking you to invite him to *everything*. I'm just asking you to give him a chance."

"It's a deal. I'll see what I can do." Adam extends his hand and I shake it.

"Thank you," I say.

Adam's phone dings, and he reaches into his pocket to retrieve it.

"It's Eric," he says, reading the screen. "He's sending a cop over here to pick up the coat and clothing I wore on Thursday night." Adam looks up at me. "What's that about?"

"It's not just you," I reassure him. "Everyone at the card game is receiving the same text. He wants to do a fibre analysis or something." Adam's facial muscles tense, and the creases in his forehead are suddenly deeper than usual. "It's not a big deal," I tell him. "No one thinks you killed Saxon Renaud."

Adam sighs. "I'm not worried about what people think, I'm worried about where the evidence is pointing."

So am I.

CHAPTER 21

APRIL WAS RIGHT, Harmony Lake received two more inches of fresh snow overnight.

At the elementary school, sledders are lining up at the top of the hill, waiting their turn to barrel down to the bottom.

"If you and Adam go ahead with this real estate scheme, T and I might like to take part too," April says over the swishing of our snow pants as we climb the hill to join the queue and wait our turn. "I'll talk to her about it later, and let you know for sure."

I tell her I'll keep her informed, then Tamara runs up behind us, toboggan in hand, and the three of us trudge up the hill together.

"Have you decided what to get Eric for your anniversary yet?" April asks as we inch forward in line.

"I'm working on it," I reply. "He said something at dinner last night that gave me an idea."

"No pressure," Tamara interjects. "But he put a lot of thought into your anniversary. It means a lot to him."

April shoots her wife a look that silently screams, *stop talking!*

"What do you mean? What's he planning?" I ask, my

eyes darting back and forth between April and Tamara. I glare at each of them equally hard and for an equal amount of time, applying the same amount of pressure to both of them.

"We don't know what he's planning," April says slowly and clearly. Then she looks at Tamara. "*Do we, T?*" she asks through clenched teeth.

Tamara shakes her head exaggeratedly. "Nope. We know nothing. Pretend I never said anything." She purses her lips into a tight, thin line, raises her eyebrows, and pretends to zip her lips with her gloved thumb and forefinger.

"You know, and you won't tell meeeee?" I whine so loudly the two kindergarten-aged kids in line ahead of us turn and look up at me.

"If we say anything, Connie will kill us." April sounds serious and her eyes are wide.

"You mean she'll kill *you*," Tamara clarifies. "It was you who was told in confidence, not me."

"Someone tell me something!" I demand, interrupting their domestic dispute.

"No way," April responds, shaking her head. "Have you seen Connie angry? She's scary."

"One hint," Tamara holds up her gloved index finger. "Do you remember what you wore on your first date with Eric?" she asks.

"I think so," I reply cautiously.

Actually, I remember *exactly* what I wore. I wore my Lane-splitter skirt from the fall 2010 edition of Knitty, a black T-shirt, my black leather moto jacket, and black knee-high boots with heels.

"You should wear it again this Thursday," Tamara suggests with a wink. "It'll be a nice touch."

The two little kids ahead of us are next. As they position themselves on their runner sled, I remind them to hold on tight, and they turn to look at me. Twins. I know these kids.

"Hey, you're Jacob and Justin Singh," I say. "Are your mum and dad here with you?"

Twin number one nods. Twin number two points at the bottom of the hill and says, "Our dad's over there." The boys wave to their dad, and he waves back, then gives them a thumbs-up.

The twins finish arranging themselves and their sled, and I give them a little nudge to get them started. As they careen down the hill, I glance down at their waiting father. When we make eye contact, I smile, and wave; he reciprocates, smiling and waving in return. Their dad is Jay Singh, the money lender to whom Saxon was allegedly behind in making repayments.

When the twins are a safe distance ahead of me, I sit on my knees on Hannah's old saucer sled and push off down the hill. I zoom down the hill, veering toward Jay Singh with questions swirling in my head.

"Well, well, well, if it isn't the first lady of Harmony Lake." Jay bows with mock formality.

"I'm not the first lady of Harmony Lake," I correct him. "Mayor Martel and I finalized our divorce months ago."

"Details," Jay says, sweeping away my comment. "Everyone in town knows you two are still tight, and your boyfriend is the chief of police. If those connections don't make you the first lady of Harmony Lake, I don't know what does."

I decide not to argue because I have more pressing things to discuss with him. After the obligatory pleasantries and small talk, I get to the point.

"I hear our town's latest murder victim owed you a lot of money."

Jay smiles and waves to his boys, who are once again waiting in line at the top of the hill. "It's true," he corroborates. "Saxon was into me for a lot of money. He was behind on his repayments, and I suspect he'd reached the point where he couldn't catch up. My lawyer started paperwork last week to force the sale of some of Saxon's properties."

"I bet Saxon didn't like that," I venture a guess.

"He sure didn't." Jay chuckles. "I have a phone full of angry voicemails from Saxon detailing how much he didn't like it."

"Did you share those voicemails with the police?" I ask.

"Of course I did, Megan. What kind of person do you think I am? I am an upstanding, legitimate businessperson."

"I know," I assure him. "You don't have to convince me. I think your business model is brilliant."

Jay fights an uphill battle regarding his reputation. Despite counting several of Harmony Lake's residents among his clientele, at least that's what he tells me, his reputation is akin to that of a mafia-style loan shark like the violent, intimidating money mongers portrayed in Hollywood mobster movies. But in actuality, Jay provides a legitimate service and is transparent about the terms and conditions of his loans. He provides full disclosure on his website.

"You're one of the few people around here who gets it," he says. "And before you ask, I was out of town with my family until Friday afternoon. Me, Jenna, and the kids drove into the city on Thursday to have dinner with her parents and ended up staying overnight because of the snowstorm. I already told Eric, and he verified my alibi."

"I didn't think you were a good suspect," I confide. "You're too smart to kill someone who owes you money."

"Right?!" He shrugs with his hands in front of him. "Why don't people get that? Why don't they see that it would be bad for business if I went around killing my clients?"

I shrug.

"I can tell you this." Jay looks around, then moves closer to me, putting some extra distance between us and the cluster of elementary school-aged children standing nearby. "I'm not the only lender Saxon owed money to. He was in over his head. Things would've come crashing down around him in the next few weeks if he hadn't died."

"So I hear," I say. "Who do you think killed him and why?"

"I don't know who," Jay replies. "But I have a theory about why. Have you talked to whoever was helping him fix the election?"

What? Did I hear him correctly? Saxon Renaud was plotting to fix the election?

"Who was helping him fix the election? And how do you know he was trying to fix the election?" I hiss in a whisper-yell.

If this is true, Saxon's election-fixing scam failed. He didn't win. He didn't even come close to winning.

"I don't know, and he told me." Jay's voice is low and calm.

"Keep talking," I urge.

"I don't know if he was lying or not, and I don't know any details," Jay qualifies what he's about to tell me with a disclaimer and I nod in acknowledgement. "It's possible he was so desperate, he said whatever he thought might buy him more time, but Saxon begged me not to contact my lawyer until after the election. He told me he was going to win. He said it was a sure thing. He told me someone owed him a favour, and his winning the election was a done deal. He said his properties would be sold, and he would pay me in full within thirty days of the election."

Mind blown, I'm speechless.

"You better close your mouth before you catch flies, Megadoodle," April calls from the bottom of the hill where she, Tamara, and Jay's twins march toward us, dragging their sleds behind them.

I close my mouth and look at Jay. He raises his index finger to his mouth and makes a silent *shhh* gesture as April, Tamara, and the twins get closer. I nod.

I glance behind Jay, and they're still a good thirty feet away. I whisper, "You told the police about this, right?"

Jay shakes his head. "I have no proof, and my lawyer advised me not to tell the police more than they ask."

Lucky for me, I'm not the police.

CHAPTER 22

MONDAY, January 18th

Knitorious is closed on Mondays, so Monday is the day I run errands, clean the house, and get caught up on the not-so-fun maintenance tasks of my life.

I pull into the parking lot behind Knitorious and choose the spot closest to the back door. I check the time on the dashboard of the car. Fifteen minutes. I have fifteen minutes to get these groceries upstairs, put them away, and get to my appointment with Kelly at Hairway to Heaven. I should have left Eric's groceries at my house when I stopped at home to put away my own groceries and take Sophie for her midday walk. I could have gone back to get them later and skipped this game of beat-the-clock.

Before hitting up the grocery store, I went shopping for Eric's gift, which took longer than I expected. Then, I found myself grocery shopping for two houses because, while I was cruising the aisles at the Shop'n'Save, I remembered a bunch of stuff that Eric is out of at his apartment. I don't normally do Eric's grocery shopping for him, but I know how busy he is with Saxon's case. A lot of the stuff he was out of is stuff I use, so it behooved me to pick up his groceries too.

Before I knew it, the day was half over, and now, I'm dangerously close to being late for my hair appointment with Kelly.

"Megan!"

I spin when I hear my name. "Oh, hi, Pete." I Look down at the grocery bags in my hands and shrug. "I'd wave, but you know," I joke.

"Yes, you've got your hands full." He secures the letter size manila envelope he's carrying under his arm, nods toward the bags in my hands, and says, "Can I help you with those?"

"No thank you," I reply. "They're not heavy, just awkward."

"At least let me get the trunk for you," Pete offers, then he reaches up and closes the trunk of my SUV.

"Thank you," I say. "Are you looking for me?" I assume he is; otherwise, why would he be here? "Knitorious is closed on Mondays. Is there a problem with the yarn your mum purchased on Saturday?"

"Oh no, nothing like that. I was hoping to see you or Eric," Pete replies.

"Eric is at work," I tell him. "But here I am. What can I help you with?"

Pete pulls the manila envelope from under his arm and holds it up. "These are the listings I promised to drop off for Eric," he explains. "If you have a few minutes, I'd be happy to come inside and go over them with you."

I guess Eric hasn't talked to Pete and cleared up the misunderstanding about Eric buying a house. But to be fair, this case is occupying all his time and attention, and Pete's listings are probably at the bottom of his priority list.

"It's nice of you to offer, Pete, but I have to be at an appointment in less than fifteen minutes, and I need to put away these groceries before I leave."

"I understand, Megan," he responds. "Is there a convenient time when you'd both be available? I am happy to come back."

"I'm not sure," I answer. "Eric is working all hours on the Saxon Renaud case, and I have no idea when I'll see him again." Pete sighs and frowns, his disappointment obvious. "Why don't you leave the listings with me," I suggest. "I'll be sure Eric gets them, and we'll call you if we have questions."

"That would be great, Megan, thank you." His disappointed facial expression is replaced with a happier one. "Speaking of Saxon's murder," Pete says, "have there been any developments? Is Eric close to making an arrest?"

I'm not sure if Pete is asking out of idle curiosity, civic concern, or to gauge a timeline for when Eric might be available to look at houses.

"I'm not sure," I reply. "He's confident he'll make an arrest, but I don't know when."

Pete holds out the envelope, not sure where to put it since I'm fresh out of hands. I tilt my head toward the shoulder with my tote bag.

"You can drop it in there," I instruct. Pete delicately opens my tote bag and slips the envelope inside. "Why paper?" I ask. "Why not send the listings in an email? Wouldn't it be easier and save time?"

"Probably," Pete replies. "But I prefer the personal touch of delivering tangible listings. I make a few notes of things for you to consider about each property, and clients like to have somewhere to jot down questions or comments they have."

"Makes sense," I say. "Well, thanks for coming by to drop these off, Pete, but I have to get a wiggle on, or I'll be late for my appointment."

We say goodbye, and while Pete walks across the parking lot and climbs into his pickup truck, I unlock the back door and race upstairs to put the groceries away.

"I'M NOT LATE!" I pant, as a charge into Hairway to Heaven after speed walking down Water Street from Knitorious.

"You're right on time, hun." Kelly smiles and gives me a tight hug.

Have I mentioned that Kelly is beautiful? She bears a strong resemblance to Grace Kelly and has the same refined demeanour.

She's taller than me, most people are, but shorter than April, with a delicate, thin figure. Her blonde hair is always perfectly coiffed, her makeup is on point—neither too heavy, nor too light—and her hands are forever flawlessly mani-cured. She's a walking testimonial to the services her salon provides.

But Kelly's beauty goes beyond her aesthetic. She's one of those women who is effortlessly elegant. Her movements are so smooth, she appears to almost float. Her voice isn't soft or loud, but confident and warm. Kelly has beautiful taste; her clothes are classically stylish—no trendy fashion fads for her—and her jewelry is understated and chic.

Taking off my coat and hanging it on the coat rack, I'm aware as Kelly takes a step back and appraises my hair situation.

When she crosses her hands in front of her chest, I notice Kelly isn't wearing her wedding ring, and I try not to react. It's been sixteen months since her husband's murder, and this is the first time I've seen Kelly without her wedding ring.

"How are you?" I ask as she guides me to a sink.

"Not as flustered as you seem to be," she replies, smiling.

Kelly drapes a black nylon cape over me and closes the snap at the back of the neck. I cinch the black nylon belt around my waist while she tucks a black towel into the neck-band and gestures for me to sit at one of the black enamel sinks. I sit down, and she eases the chair into a reclined posi-tion, so my head is in the sink. We're making small talk while

Kelly runs the water and tests the temperature with her hand, adjusting the ratio of hot to cold as necessary.

"Oof!" Kelly releases a breathy grunt, and with her lips puckered and her brows knitted together, she turns off the water. "We need to put an OUT OF ORDER sign on this sink," she calls to the employee sitting at the reception desk. She looks down at me and returns my chair to its upright position. "Sorry, hun, we have to move to the next sink. This one's clogged. I called Ryan to fix it, but he's so busy that he had to put me on his waiting list."

"No problem," I say, shuffling sideways to the next chair. "Since Archie retired, Ryan sometimes has more work than he can keep up with."

I'm pleased to report that the next sink is clog-free, and my hair appointment continues as scheduled.

Few things feel as indulgent as someone else washing your hair. I close my eyes and breathe deeply, enjoying the luxurious scalp massage and giving silent thanks to the universe for blessing Kelly with such skilled fingers.

When I'm settled in her stylist chair, I arrange the excess cape around myself, and Kelly runs her fingers through my hair and assesses what we're dealing with. We decide that Kelly will clean up my split ends and re-establish my layers, then with her comb in one hand and scissors in the other, she gets to work, and bits of my hair rain onto the shiny, white floor.

While Kelly skilfully sections and snips my hair, I tell her how nice it was to see her at the party on Friday night.

"I hope you had fun," I tell her. "When you're ready, you, me, and April should have a girl's night."

"I'd love that," Kelly replies. "I've missed you guys."

We talk a little more, and Kelly asks me about business at Knitorious, which steers the conversation toward knitting. Kelly is a knitter. Activities that require both hands and both sides of the brain are her thing.

"Did I tell you my uncle and his wife bought a hobby farm?" Kelly asks.

"No, you didn't," I reply. "Do they have sheep?"

"Not sheep, but something just as good." She stops snipping and looks at me in the mirror. "Alpacas!" she says wide-eyed and grinning.

"Is your uncle a knitter?" I ask.

Kelly shakes her head and resumes trimming my hair. "No, but his wife is. She also spins and dyes her own yarn."

I'm struck with a sense of déjà vu. Again. This is the second time I've had déjà vu this week, and it unsettles me. I'm sure I've heard this story before.

"Does she sell it?" I ask, partly out of curiosity and partly on behalf of my yarn store.

"Not yet," Kelly replies. "But I keep telling her she should. Her yarn is beautiful, Megan. She gave me some to give to you."

"I can't wait to see it and squish it," I respond, making a squishing motion with my hands underneath my cape.

"And I can't wait to show it to you." Kelly places her comb and scissors on the counter in front of me and raises her index finger. "I'll be right back." And with that, Kelly disappears into the back room, and I hear her delicate footsteps race up the stairs toward her apartment.

Moments later, Kelly returns carrying three project bags. "First," she says, opening one bag and tilting it so I can see inside, "cat toys. I heard the charity knitters are working on cat toys for the Animal Centre to sell in the gift shop, so I made some with scrap yarn." She holds up a puffy, heart-shaped, stuffed toy and shakes it. The bell she stuffed inside jingles, and she returns it to the project bag, zips it shut, and hands it to me.

I toss the bag of toys toward my tote bag on the empty stylist chair next to me. I miss, and the bag of toys lands on the chair behind my bag. "Thank you," I say. "The charity knitters will love these."

Kelly opens the second project bag and holds up two skeins of yarn, one is a solid, undyed cream, and the other a variegated black and grey.

I free my hands from under the black nylon cape and reach for the skeins of yarn. They're bulky weight, wonderfully soft, and scrumptiously squishy. They're also familiar in a way that makes me anxious. The more I pet them, the larger the knot in my stomach gets. Yarn *never* makes me anxious; yarn is my happy place, it's where I go to escape anxious feelings. What is it about this yarn that makes me feel this way?

While I continue to pet the skeins of yarn and contemplate my complicated feelings about them, Kelly unzips the third project bag and pulls out her current knitting project. It's a hat. A hat that is an exact match for Sheamus's scarf. Same colours, same stitch pattern, same yarn!

CHAPTER 23

KELLY IS THE "SPECIAL FRIEND" who made Sheamus's favourite scarf? She's the friend who Sheamus said had an aunt who spins and dyes fibre on an alpaca farm. Kelly said her uncle and his wife bought an alpaca farm, and her uncle's wife is a dyer and spinner. Technically, her uncle's wife would be her aunt. Are Sheamus and Kelly dating?

Unable to hide my shocked reaction, Kelly misinterprets my stunned facial expression for admiration.

"I know, it's beautiful right? Kind of leaves you speechless, doesn't it?" she asks.

"It really does," I reply truthfully.

I extend my hand to return the two skeins of yarn I've been petting, and she waves me off.

"Those are for you," Kelly says. "I'm hoping if you knit with them and like them, your feedback might help convince my uncle's wife that her yarn belongs in yarn stores."

"Thank you, Kelly. And please thank your uncle's wife for me." I toss the skeins of yarn on top of my bag.

"That's a beautiful hat," I say, gesturing toward the hat-in-progress in her hand. "Is it for you?"

Kelly looks down at the hat and shoves it back inside the

project bag. "No, it's for a friend. It matches a scarf I made him."

I knew it!

How many bulky, alpaca, hand-dyed, slip-stitch patterned scarves can there be in Harmony Lake? Especially ones made with the Ashes to Ashes, Rust to Rust colour? Answer... One, and I've seen it wrapped around Sheamus O'Brien's neck three times in two days.

"The colours kind of remind me of the Irish flag," I observe, watching Kelly's face for a reaction. Nothing.

"That's what I thought too," Kelly agrees. "That's why I chose it. The friend I'm making it for is of Irish heritage."

It's Sheamus; it has to be. I'd bet my yarn stash on it.

"As much as I'd love to sit and talk about yarn all day," Kelly announces, "I better finish cutting your hair before it dries and curls up on us." She zips the project bag and tosses it onto an empty stylist chair.

While Kelly sections and snips, we talk about this and that and share stories about some of our favourite shared customers, but I can't stop thinking about that yarn and about Sheamus's scarf.

Kelly always straightens my hair. First with a big round brush and blow dryer, then with a flat iron. She says it helps her to make sure she cut it evenly because the curls can complicate things, but I secretly think she enjoys the challenge of forcing my rebellious curls into submission. I don't mind. I rarely straighten it myself because of the time commitment, and I'm happy to spend the extra time in Kelly's chair, laughing and chatting with her.

When she pulls the flat iron from its slot, she asks me how Eric is doing. I decide this might be the best opportunity I'll get to steer the conversation toward intimate relationships and ask whether Kelly is involved in one.

"He's great. The chief of police job keeps him busy, but I think it makes him happy," I say in response to her question.

"How about you, Kelly? Now that you're starting to socialize, do you think you might start dating soon?"

Her posture becomes more rigid, and the muscles around her eyes and mouth tighten. She looks at me in the mirror and sighs.

"When Paul died, I didn't think I would ever date," Kelly confesses. "I couldn't imagine being with anyone except him, and that was fine with me." She looks down at my hair and runs the flat iron through a long section of it.

Paul is Kelly's late husband.

"That's understandable, Kelly. You don't have to date. You don't have to do anything that doesn't feel right for you," I assure her. Maybe my instincts are wrong about her and Sheamus. Maybe they're just friends. Friends with chemistry.

She stops ironing again and looks at me in the mirror. "I don't feel that way anymore," she explains. "I don't want to be alone forever, and I don't think Paul would want that for me, either. If I have feelings for someone else, it doesn't mean I didn't love Paul."

"That's right," I agree. "You'll always love Paul, even if you love someone else."

"I realize that now," she says, obliterating another ringlet with her flat iron.

I furrow my brow and squint, looking at her in the mirror. "Kelly, are you seeing someone?" I ask quietly.

She nods and her eyes fill with moisture. Oh, no! What have I done? The last thing I want is to upset my widowed friend and make her cry!

"I'm sorry, Kelly. I shouldn't have asked. Ignore me, I'm being nosy. Please don't cry." I pull some tissues from the box on the counter in front of me and pass them to her behind me.

"Tears of joy," she explains with a shy smile. With her free hand, Kelly fans her damp eyes while she tries to blink the tears away. "I haven't been this happy since before Paul died." She stops waving at her face and rests her hand on my shoulder.

"That's wonderful." I place my hand on top of hers. "You deserve to be happy. Everyone wants you to be happy."

Smiling and nodding, Kelly resumes sectioning and ironing my hair.

It's obvious Kelly is in a delicate place emotionally. I don't want to make her uncomfortable, but I have a feeling she could help eliminate a suspect in Saxon's murder, so I ask my next question but proceed with extreme caution, asking quietly and gently.

"May I ask who is responsible for your tears of joy?"

"Not yet," she replies, smiling and shaking her head. "I'm not ready to share it yet. I'm still getting used to this new relationship, and we're still getting to know each other. But Megan, he's funny, and sweet, and patient."

"Take your time. No pressure," I say and mean it.

I remember how fragile I felt when I first started dating Eric after my separation. We kept our relationship quiet at first, too, while we got to know each other. The last thing I want to do is scare Kelly back into seclusion, so I'll respect her privacy and won't ask her anything else. Instead, I'll focus on being grateful she's found happiness again, and I'll find another way to get my questions answered.

ME: Tacos for dinner at my place?

It's mid-afternoon, and I haven't had lunch yet. My tummy is rumbling, and my thoughts keep turning to food. I'm standing on the sidewalk outside Hairway to Heaven, debating whether to cross the street to get something to eat at the pub and talk to Sheamus, or skip the pub—and Sheamus—until tomorrow, and give my thoughts about my conversation with Kelly a chance to marinate overnight.

Eric: I wish! I'm working on getting a pile of warrants. It'll be a late night.

Warrants? Arrest warrants or search warrants?

Me: Is the warrant for a person or a thing?

Eric: Yes. For a person who would not submit a thing, and a few other searches.

Time to take this conversation off text. I dial Eric's number.

"Hey, babe! How's your day?"

"Let me guess," I dive right in, ignoring Eric's pleasant greeting, "At least one of your warrants involves Sheamus's inconsistent alibi and his scarf?"

Silence. Brief pause. Sigh. "You're very intuitive," Eric answers my question without actually answering my question.

"Can it wait?" I plead. "Can you move that warrant to the bottom of your pile? I have a hunch, and if I'm right, you won't need to pick up Sheamus."

"When will you know if your hunch is correct?" Eric asks.

"Soon," I assure him. "Today."

"Can you give me a hint?"

"Not until I confirm I'm onto something. If you wait, I promise I'll personally deliver a full explanation and a hot meal," I negotiate.

Monday's special at the pub is Irish stew, and it's one of Eric's favourites.

Another sigh. "Can you deliver both in the next couple of hours?" he asks. "I'm starving."

"Yup!"

I guess I'll talk to Sheamus today.

ASIDE FROM A FEW booths of tourists from the ski resorts, and the regulars who sit at the bar, nursing their beers and watching the giant TV, the pub is empty. I hope Sheamus is here.

"Takeout?" the bartender asks when I approach the cash register at the bar.

"Yes, please." I smile, and she produces a menu from under the bar and hands it to me. I don't need a menu, but I take it and say thank you to be polite. "Is Sheamus around?" I ask.

"He's upstairs in the office," the bartender replies. "Would you like me to call him?"

This conversation will require privacy. "No, thank you, I'll go up and see him." I sense the bartender is about to object because she points to the velvet rope that signifies the stairs are a no-go-zone and opens her mouth as if to speak, but I don't give her the chance. "Can I have two orders of Irish stew to go, please? With garlic bread." I give back the unopened menu and smile, then turn and walk away, slipping behind one of the silver, ball-top stanchions at the bottom of the stairs.

Sheamus's office door is ajar. I peek inside to make sure he's alone and not on the phone, then tap lightly on the door.

"Megan," Sheamus says when he looks up at me. "I didn't recognize you for a second. You got your hair done." He gestures toward my straightened hair, then closes his laptop and beckons me inside with his hand.

He's wearing the scarf. It's draped over his shoulders.

"Hi, Sheamus." I bend and he gets up, and we meet halfway for a quick hug, then I sit in the chair across from him. "I'm waiting for a takeout order and wanted to talk to you for a minute."

"Irish stew for Eric?" he guesses with a hint of Irish lilt.

"Yes," I confirm. "He's working late and loves your stew." I raise my index finger to my lips. "But don't tell him because it's a surprise," I joke.

"Your secret is safe with me, lass." Sheamus winks.

I'm sure it is. It would seem Sheamus excels at keeping secrets.

"Your hair looks good straight," he comments. "Did Kelly do it?"

"Yes, she's amazing. She makes my hair look better than I can."

"Yup, she's mad talented," he agrees, nodding and with a hint of pride in his voice. "So, what can I do for ya?"

Sheamus's last sentence goes in one ear and out the other because I'm distracted by the corner behind him, remembering the whangee handle umbrella I saw there on Friday night before Adam's victory party. I owe Sheamus an apology for that debacle.

"Earth to Megan."

"Sorry, Sheamus," I say, shaking my head as though it will help me organize my thoughts. I look at him. "I owe you an apology…"

The landline on Sheamus's desk rings, interrupting me mid-sentence.

"One sec." He picks up the receiver, mumbles a few acknowledgements, then moves the phone away from his ear and covers the speaker with his hand. "We ran out of stew at lunch, and the next batch is almost ready. Can you wait about twenty minutes, or do you want to order something else?"

"It'll be worth it," I reply. "I'll wait for fresh stew."

He hangs up, apologizes for the interruption, and says, "What were we talking about?"

"I was about to apologize to you," I remind him. "On Friday night, I saw the umbrella in the corner. I knew the police were looking for a similar umbrella, so I told Eric it was here. Apparently, it wasn't the umbrella they were looking for, and you and one of your employees had to endure being questioned for no reason. I'm sorry."

"Were you snooping around in my office?" he asks rightfully, but with a hint of amusement.

"No. Absolutely not," I insist. "The door was open. Adam and I came in here so he could practice his speech before the party."

"I was joking," Sheamus says. "I know you wouldn't snoop."

Is he joking again? I can't tell. Because I feel like it's common knowledge that I enjoy an occasional snoop.

"I regret that I didn't ask you about the umbrella before I mentioned it to Eric. We're friends, and I shouldn't have gone behind your back."

"*Pshaw*," he says. "You did the right thing, Megan. No need to apologize. Is that what you wanted to talk to me about? Do you want me to have a drink brought up for you while you wait for your order?" He unbuttons his cuffs and rolls up his shirt sleeves, revealing his pale forearms.

I shake my head. "No, thank you, I'm fine." I take a deep breath and prepare to ask him about personal things, things that are none of my business. "Can I ask you something, Sheamus?" I pause, waiting for permission. He nods, and I continue, "Remember when we bumped into each other on Friday, and you told me how Adam's text woke you up and you were half-asleep and confused when you texted him back?"

"I remember," he confirms.

"You told other people that you turned off your phone before you went to bed. How did Adam's text wake you up if your phone wasn't on?"

"Ah, I can see how that would confuse you." He grins and leans forward, putting his muscular forearms on the desk. "I woke up, turned on my phone to check the time, rolled over, and went back to sleep."

"That makes sense," I admit. "Did the text wake up Kelly too?"

CHAPTER 24

I DIDN'T THINK it would be possible for Sheamus's pallor to have less colour than it already has, but his face drains of what little colour it had before my comment, and his clear blue eyes are wide with shock.

"Wh... ho... I... Excuse me?"

"I know about you and Kelly," I say confidently, not feeling at all confident.

He blinks three times in rapid succession with his mouth agape and shakes his head in disbelief. "Megan," he huffs my name. "I'm not sure what you think you know, or who's spreading rumours..."

"I know Kelly is the 'special friend'" who made your scarf," I interrupt him with my circumstantial evidence, and put finger quotes before and after *special friend*.

I don't mention the matching hat she's making, because if it's a surprise, I don't want to spoil it. It's infuriating to spend ten hours of your life knitting a surprise for someone just to have someone else come along and ruin the surprise. I refuse to be that person.

"That doesn't mean we're a couple," he hisses as though

there's someone nearby who might hear us. "Friends are allowed to knit scarves for each other."

So, I was right about the scarf.

"Sheamus." I lean forward and put my arms on his desk, mirroring his pose, and place one of my hands gently on his forearm. "I think you left the card game after the fiasco, got in your truck, and searched for Ryan. Then, when you received Archie's text calling off the search, you parked in the lot behind the pub, turned off your phone, and walked across the street to Kelly's apartment where you spent the night. That's why the snow around your house was undisturbed, and the police officer who went to your house and knocked on your door twice on Friday morning said it appeared you hadn't been home. It also explains why you didn't see Adam's car across the street from your house when you looked out your window, because you weren't home to look through your own window."

Sheamus pulls his arm away from my hand, stands up, and walks around the desk. He closes his office door all the way, then returns to the chair behind his desk. He inhales deeply, holds it for a second, then exhales.

"You can't prove it."

"You're right," I acknowledge, "I can't prove where you were when Saxon Renaud was murdered, but neither can you. Your version of your alibi can't be verified and having an unverifiable alibi is the same as having no alibi at all."

"I didn't Kill Saxon Renaud," he exclaims.

"I know," I affirm. "And if you tell the truth about where you were when he died, Kelly can verify it, and eliminate you as a suspect. It'll be over."

He shakes his head. "I refuse to bring her into this, Megan. Do you remember what Kelly went through when Paul was murdered? She was a suspect. The police questioned her relentlessly. She couldn't grieve her husband's death properly because of the investigation. I won't let them re-traumatize her. I won't. If I have to be a murder suspect to protect Kelly, so be it. I'm sure that, eventually, Eric will find the actual killer and exonerate me without having to involve Kelly."

I remember the investigation into Paul's murder vividly because I was a suspect too. It was a traumatic experience that created a bond between Kelly and me that's hard to describe but is only shared between people who have survived a tragic experience together.

"The last thing anyone wants is to hurt Kelly," I remind him. "We all love her. But don't you think it will traumatize her if the investigation into Saxon's murder drags on with you as a suspect? Or if the police charge you because you lied about your alibi, or obstructed the investigation, or something? How will you comfort and protect Kelly if you're defending yourself in court or serving time in prison?"

With tears in his eyes, Sheamus raises his hand to his forehead and rests his elbow on the desk. Great! In the last hour I've made two friends cry. A new personal best.

"Sheamus, I'm sorry, I wasn't trying to upset you…"

He raises his hand in a stop motion. "You're right," he says. "My approach could be worse for Kelly in the long run. And if the tables were turned, and I could help eliminate her as a murder suspect, I'd be angry if she denied me the chance to help."

Huzzah! He gets it! I let out a sigh of relief.

"Is that why you wouldn't give your scarf to the police?" I ask.

He nods and grips one end of the alpaca scarf. "It would lead back to Kelly. They would want to ask her about it."

The landline on his desk rings again, and we pause our conversation while he answers it. He tells the caller we'll be right down and returns the receiver to the base.

"Your order is ready," he says, rising from his chair.

Downstairs, I wait near the bar with my wallet in hand while Sheamus goes into the kitchen to get my order. When he returns, he's carrying an insulated food bag and a paper bag, and wearing his coat. Noticeably absent: his scarf.

As he gets closer, he points to my wallet and says, "Put it away, it's on the house."

"Don't be silly," I argue. "I told you I didn't mind waiting."

He approaches me, and instead of handing me the insulated food bag, he presses his hand into my back and continues walking toward the door. "I insist," he says while we walk. "It's the least I can do."

Outside on the sidewalk, I stop walking. "Where are we going?"

"To drop off Eric's stew," Sheamus replies like it's a foregone conclusion.

"I ordered takeout, not delivery," I remind him.

"We can go together, and while I'm there, I'll amend my statement, give Eric my scarf"—he holds up the paper bag—"then I'll go to the salon and talk to Kelly, so she's not surprised when the police contact her."

"How about this?" I take the insulated food bag and the paper bag from him. "I'll deliver the stew and your scarf. You go to the salon and talk to Kelly *before* you amend your statement, so there's zero chance she'll be unprepared when the police contact her."

"Is that legal?" Sheamus asks as we step off the curb and cross Water Street. "I don't think I'm supposed to talk to Kelly about my statement before I change it."

I shrug. "I don't know, I'm not a cop. You and I talked about your statement, was that wrong?"

Was it? I'm sure if it was, the newly appointed chief of police will educate me when I tell him about it. We're now standing in front of Hairway to Heaven and move next door to Latte Da so Kelly won't see us and come outside to say hi.

"Megan, thank you for helping me see sense," Sheamus says.

"You'd do the same for me." I know this to be true. "I won't tell anyone other than Eric about you and Kelly," I promise. "Kelly doesn't even know I know."

"How is that possible?" he asks.

"I guessed based on some things she said while she was doing my hair," I explain. "She's still fragile, and I didn't want to pressure her, so I went to the pub and pressured you instead."

"And I appreciate it," he says with a chuckle.

We part ways, and while I hustle toward my car in the Knitorious parking lot, I use the remote key chain to start my car so it's warm when I get there. I need to deliver this stew before it gets cold and before Eric files the paperwork for those warrants.

THE FOOD IS in an insulated bag, but I turn on the seat warmer on the passenger seat anyway to ensure the stew stays warm during the short drive to the Harmony Lake Police Station.

Me: I'm here.

Eric: I'll be right out.

"Hi," I say to the familiar-looking, young officer behind the counter in the lobby.

"Hi," he says. "Delivery? You can leave it over there." He points to a chair next to the secure inner door. "Who's it for? I'll page them and let them know it's here."

He thinks I'm a delivery person. I guess I am, sort of.

"Eric," I say through the small round speaker in the bullet-resistant acrylic barrier between us.

"Eric who?" he asks.

"Eric Sloane," I specify. "He's expecting me."

"Hey, you're the lady from the cat house."

A look of recognition flashes across the cop's face at the same moment it flashes across mine; he's the officer who accompanied Rick and I into Saxon's house when Rick rescued Clawdia.

"You're the officer who carried the kitty litter."

He smiles and nods enthusiastically. "Yeah. How's Clawdia doing? Is she happy in her new home?" he asks.

"I don't know yet," I reply. "It's on my to-do list for tomorrow."

Looking slightly confused, probably because I'm still here, he asks me if I'm waiting to be paid for the delivery. I shake my head, and before I can explain that I'm waiting for Eric to come to the lobby and let me in, the secure door opens, and Eric is standing next to me.

"Your hair looks nice," he says, tucking a section of my extra shiny, straight hair behind my ear.

"Thank you," I say, leaning into his touch.

Eric takes the insulated food bag, and when he tries to take the paper bag, I pull my hand back.

"It's a surprise," I say.

"An early anniversary gift?" he asks.

"I guess you could call it that," I reply, shrugging.

Eric takes my free hand in his, and the young officer behind the desk rushes to the locked inner door and opens it for us from the inside.

"You aren't a delivery person, are you?" the young officer asks me quietly.

I shake my head. "Why? Is Eric this friendly with everyone who makes deliveries to the station?" I joke.

He's not amused. In fact, the young man, a rookie cop, looks mortified.

To make up for it, I put in a good word for him.

"This is the officer who helped Rick and me when we picked up Clawdia. He was very helpful and very professional."

Eric looks at the rookie's name tag, then commends, and thanks him.

Eric's police-chief office differs from his detective-sergeant office. His new office is bigger, has nicer furniture, and a window. It's still minimalist, though. Other than two fine art photographs I gave him for his birthday hanging on the wall, and the Newton's cradle on his desk, there are no personal items at all. It's the polar opposite of Adam's office, which has so many photos and knickknacks there's barely enough space on his desk to work.

"What first, stew or this?" I hold up the paper bag and give it a gentle shake.

"Are the contents of the paper bag edible?" he asks.

"Definitely not," I reply, hoping I'm right.

I probably should have opened it to make sure Sheamus's scarf is actually inside. I'll look pretty dumb if this is a bag of condiments, or napkins, or something.

"Food first," he decides, placing the insulated bag on his desk and opening it. "Oooh, extra garlic bread." Eric is easily pleased, foodwise.

While we eat, I tell him about my hair appointment and my revelation that Kelly and Sheamus are in a relationship.

"Are you sure?" he asks. "There was no evidence of relationship-type text messages between him and anyone on his phone."

"Did you check his social media accounts?" I ask. "Sometimes people private message each other on social media when they want to keep their relationship secret."

Next, I tell him about my visit to the pub and the enlightening conversation Sheamus and I had.

"Let me make sure I understand," Eric says, soaking up my remaining Irish stew with a piece of garlic bread; the serving sizes at the pub are huge, and I'm rarely able to finish anything. "Sheamus wants to amend his current, inconsistent statement to include a witness who can verify his whereabouts, but you don't want me to talk to the witness who can verify his alibi?"

"Why do you rephrase things to make them sound sketchier than they are?" I ask. "Obviously, Kelly *can* verify the details of Sheamus's alibi, but it would be less stressful for her if she didn't have to."

"I'll see what I can do," he says, stacking the empty takeout containers. "But we'll have to talk to her, and when the time comes, I'll personally take her statement and make it as stress-free as possible."

"Thank you," I say.

"Can I see what's in the bag now?" he asks, rubbing his hands together in anticipation.

"If you want to touch it, you'll need a rubber glove," I warn him.

"Why?" Eric looks concerned. "Is it sharp? Does it bite? It's not alive, is it, babe?"

"No, it's not alive." I laugh.

"Then why do I need gloves?" he asks, pulling a disposable glove from one of his desk drawers.

I shrug. "Because you always wear gloves when you touch evidence, so I assume it's a requirement."

"There's evidence in that bag?" he asks loudly, pointing at the bag like I just told him it's radioactive. "You're just driving around town with murder evidence in your car?"

"How else was I supposed to get it here?" I ask.

"If you called me, I would have had it picked up," Eric replies. "Chain of custody and protection from contamination are important."

"I'm a civilian," I remind him. Sometimes he forgets.

"I know," he says, kissing me. "And you're still a better cop than some real cops I know." With his gloved hand, he opens the paper bag and peers inside. "Is that Sheamus's scarf?" he asks, sounding impressed.

"You're welcome," I say.

"Thank you. You're incredible." After another kiss, he jokingly asks, "Sheamus knows you have it, right?"

"I'm not a thief." I swat his arm playfully. "He wants his scarf back as soon as possible." Eric nods in acknowledgement. "His revised statement will eliminate Sheamus as a suspect, right?" I ask.

Eric nods. "If his story checks out, and there's no forensic evidence to contradict it, Sheamus is off the suspect list."

"Who else is off the suspect list?" I ask.

"Pete," Eric replies. "His parents verified that he was at their house removing a squirrel from the chimney, and we tracked his cell phone. It was at their house when the anonymous witness called the tip line. Ryan was eliminated because he was on the phone the entire time he was unaccounted for. First, he spoke with his sponsor, then with his dad. I don't see how it would be possible for him to murder Saxon, move his body, run over the body, hide the murder weapon and a penny loafer, then drop off Adam's car at your house, walk back to his own car, and drive home while carrying on an uninterrupted conversation."

"That only leaves Adam and Rick," I conclude. "And I'd bet my life it wasn't Adam."

"We're pursuing other lines of inquiry." Eric rubs my shoulders.

I know he's trying to reassure me, but I hate it when he uses cop speak with me.

"What other lines of inquiry?" I ask.

Eric sighs. "Saxon Renaud had a lot of enemies. Every time we question someone, they lead us to someone else who had a grudge against him."

"Like who?" I ask.

Eric counts on his fingers. "People he owed money to, disgruntled tenants, people he had political differences of opinion with, people he offended…"

"OK, I get it," I interrupt him. "You have a lot of leads."

Eric nods, then there's a knock at the door.

"Come in," Eric says loudly.

The officer who helped Rick and me with Clawdia opens the door halfway. "Sheamus O'Brien is here to see you, Chief.

I tried to call you, but your phone is set to DO NOT DISTURB."

"I'll be right there," Eric says, smiling at the rookie.

The rookie closes the office door and returns to his post.

The rookie cop's comment makes me realize that I haven't heard Eric's cell phone make a sound the entire time I've been here.

"Is your cell phone on DO NOT DISTURB too?" I ask.

He nods and opens a desk drawer. "I told you I'm unplugging for at least an hour a day," he reminds me as he takes his cell phone from the drawer and slips it into his pocket.

Eric and I say our goodbyes in the privacy of his office before we walk to the lobby, so he can unlock the secure door to let me out and let Sheamus in.

"Thanks for the stew," he says. "By the time I finish work tonight, most places will be closed, and I haven't had time to pick up groceries. I would've gone home hungry to an empty kitchen."

"No, you wouldn't," I tell him, shaking my head. "I picked up groceries and restocked your fridge and pantry this morning."

"I don't deserve you," he says, hugging me. "Because of you, I won't starve," he jokes.

"Because of me, your kitchen is full of *my* favourite foods," I joke back.

Sheamus and Kelly are in the lobby when we get there. They're sitting side by side, holding hands. So much for Kelly's desire to keep their relationship under wraps. Half of Harmony Lake will know by now, and the other half will know before sunset. I'm not surprised to see her here. I'm sure when Sheamus explained the situation to her, Kelly insisted on accompanying him to the police station to support him.

When Eric gestures for Sheamus to follow him to his

office, I remind Sheamus to take his insulated bag with him when he leaves.

"Do you want me to wait with you? I don't mind," I offer, lowering myself into the chair that Sheamus just vacated, next to Kelly.

"Thank you, hun, but I'm OK," Kelly responds. "Can you believe he was willing to be a murder suspect to protect me?"

I nod. "I can," I reply. "Sheamus is a stand-up guy, and he obviously cares about you. A lot. He wants to protect you."

"I know," Kelly says, smiling shyly. "I hope Eric understands, and Sheamus doesn't get into trouble for lying."

"I'm sure it'll be fine," I reassure her. "And I didn't tell Sheamus about the hat, in case it's a surprise."

"Oh, good! Thank you, hun! It *is* a surprise." Kelly reaches into her bag and pulls out the project bag with the hat-in-progress inside. She opens the bag and starts knitting. "You left the bag of cat toys at the salon earlier. I'll bring them by Knitorious tomorrow," she says. "It'll give me an excuse to look at the spring yarn colours."

I offer once more to wait with her, but Kelly shoos me away. "You only have to tell me twice," I tease as I exit the police station.

"Excuse me! Ma'am!"

I'm only a few feet from the door when the rookie cop calls after me.

"Hi." I smile. "Megan Martel," I introduce myself and extend my hand for the rookie cop to shake. "Call me Megan."

"Lucas Butler," he reciprocates. "I'm sorry I didn't know who you were when you got here," he apologizes. "We get a lot of deliveries, and you had a delivery bag, so I assumed you were a delivery person."

"Don't worry about it," I tell him. "It was an honest mistake, and I *was* delivering something. Are you new to the department?"

He nods. "I've only been here a month. I'm still learning who everyone is."

"How do you like it so far?" I ask.

Lucas shrugs. "So far, so good," he replies. "I'm the new guy, so they give me the jobs no one else wants to do, but I don't mind paying my dues."

"You mean jobs like working the front desk and carrying cat litter?" I tease.

"Pretty much." Lucas nods. "But I got to answer a call on the tip line on Friday night. That was exciting. It's the closest I've gotten to a real murder investigation."

Does he mean the call from the witness who said they saw Adam's car leaving the hit-and-run on Lake Access Road?

"The one from the witness who reported the hit and run on Lake Access Road?" I ask.

"That's the one," Lucas replies. "I was working the front desk, so I was responsible for the phones."

"I don't suppose you recognized the caller's voice?" I ask, knowing it's a longshot.

He shakes his head. "No," he replies. "I'm sure it was a man, though. And it echoed like he was in a car. And he was nervous."

"Did he tell you he was nervous, or did he say something that led you to believe he was nervous?" I ask.

"It wasn't what he said, it was how he said it," Lucas explains.

"How?" I ask.

"The caller had a stutter," Lucas reveals. "Some people stutter when they're nervous, right?"

I know at least one person who does.

CHAPTER 26

TUESDAY, January 19th

Sophie scurries, losing traction on the wood floor, when she hears the back door thud shut.

"Good morning, Soph," I hear Eric say.

Moments later, he hands me a white chocolate and peppermint latte with extra whipped cream, white chocolate shavings, and a drizzle of chocolate syrup.

"Good morning, handsome." I give him a kiss and relieve him of the coffee cup. "Thank you."

"I'm sorry we didn't see each other last night. I was up to my eyeballs in paperwork, and by the time I left the station, you were asleep."

"Don't worry about it," I insist. "I hope you're getting enough sleep and eating properly."

"I'll catch up on sleep and healthy food when we solve this case," he says. "Taking Sheamus's revised statement and talking to Kelly took longer than I thought."

"I understand," I assure him. "Speaking of the case," I segue, "remember the witness who called the anonymous tip line?" Eric nods, so I proceed. "You didn't mention the caller had a stutter. Is the stutter a holdback?"

The look of confusion on his face tells me this is the first Eric has heard about the caller's alleged stutter.

"Who told you the caller had a stutter?" he asks.

"The officer who answered the call," I reply, hoping I'm not about to get Lucas Butler in trouble.

"The new guy?" Eric asks. "Butler?"

I nod. "We had a brief conversation when I was leaving the station yesterday, and he mentioned he answered the call from the tipster. I asked him if the caller's voice was familiar. He didn't recognize the voice, because he's new in town, but he said the caller's stutter made him sound nervous."

Eric's jaw muscles clench and unclench—something he does when he's angry—and his gaze drifts to his lower left. Something he does when he's thinking.

"Be nice," I say, interrupting both his jaw clenching and his thoughts.

"What do you mean?" he asks. "I'm always nice."

"Don't go charging into the station and yell at Lucas because he didn't mention the stutter before," I explain. "I can tell you're angry."

"I won't yell," he promises, "but I will have to mention it to him. This is too significant of a detail not to mention it until yesterday."

"Does the call to the tip line coincide with the hole in Rick's alibi that Trudy couldn't verify because she fell asleep?" I ask.

"Yes." Eric nods.

Eric leaves for work, and I resume getting the online orders ready for shipping.

"Good morning, my dear," Connie sings as she enters the store a few minutes after I unlock the door and turn the sign to OPEN.

"Good morning," I respond. "How was your weekend?"

"It was lovely, my dear. How was yours?"

"Busy and informative," I reply.

Connie stops in her tracks and looks at me with one of her eyebrows raised higher than the other. "Hold that thought, my dear, while I make some tea," Connie instructs. "Then I want to hear everything!"

While Connie makes tea, I text April and ask her to come to the store, so I can tell both of them what I've learned, and we can brainstorm what it might mean. Three heads are better than one!

April arrives carrying a white confectionery box.

"What treats did you bring for us?" I ask, sniffing in the direction of the box.

It smells delicious, and I detect a hint of cinnamon, but I can't distinguish what's in the box.

"Apple cider doughnut holes and mini caramel pecan pies with cinnamon roll pie crust," she replies.

I swallow hard because my mouth begins to water.

I take the box from April while she takes off her coat.

"We didn't forget about you, Sophie," April reassures the corgi.

Sophie is already sitting at attention, like a good girl, waiting for her treat. Clearly, I'm not the only one who gets excited when April shows up with a white confectionery box.

April opens the box and removes a small, white, confectionery bag. "Carrot cake dog treats," she says, removing two bone-shaped cookies from inside the bag.

Connie, April, and I settle in the cozy sitting area with our warm drinks, freshly baked treats, and knitting.

Connie and I are Knitters with an uppercase K; we embrace knitting as a lifestyle. April is a knitter with a lower-case k; she knows how to knit, and she knits occasionally, but knitting isn't essential to her everyday life.

Despite being a lower-case k knitter, April has been knitting like a fiend lately. So far, she has made almost a dozen cat toys for the Charity Knitting Guild's cat toy initiative.

"Four more mice," April says, handing me the knitted cat

toys from her knitting bag. "These toys have catnip in the stuffing."

"Thank you," I say. "The charity knitters are coming to the store tomorrow to pick them up." I snap my fingers. "That reminds me. Kelly made some toys, too, but I forgot them at the salon yesterday. She said she'd drop them off today." I get up and jot down a quick reminder in my planner to pick up the toys if Kelly doesn't drop them off.

"Speaking of Kelly," April coos coyly, "I hate to say I told you so about her and Sheamus, but I told you so." She smiles smugly.

"Yes, I heard they're seeing each other," Connie interjects. "I can't think of a nicer couple. I think he'll make Kelly very happy, and goodness knows, she deserves some happiness."

I smile and nod.

April narrows her eyes and glares at me. "You aren't surprised," she declares. "You already knew, and didn't tell us, Megnolia?"

"I only found out late yesterday," I state defensively, then look at Connie. "And I agree with Connie, I think they'll be happy together."

"*Hmph*," April grunts under her breath, miffed that I knew but didn't tell her. "I hope it works out for them. This is the happiest we've seen Kelly since Paul died."

"Speaking of secrets," I say, changing the subject, "Saxon Renaud allegedly told someone he had a plan to fix the election so he would win."

Connie drops her knitting in her lap. "Nonsense." She picks up her teacup. "Either your source is lying, or Saxon lied to them."

"Maybe," I reply. "All I know is what I was told. Saxon allegedly told one of his creditors the election would be fixed, and he would be the next mayor. He told them he would reverse the big-box policy, sell his properties, and repay his debts in full."

"If he had a plan, it failed," Connie concludes. "Adam won the election by a landslide."

"How on earth would he fix a municipal election?" April asks. "Especially by himself. I mean he didn't seem to have any friends, and you would need at least one trusted friend to help you pull off something that big."

"Well," Connie says, dipping her chin and looking back and forth between April and me over her reading glasses, "he had one friend."

"One friend who's alibi has a big hole in it," I comment.

"I heard Trudy Nakata is Rick's alibi for the night Saxon died," April says.

"Kind of," I say, giving her a half-smile and making a seesaw motion with my hand.

"Kind of?" Connie asks.

I explain to April and Connie how Trudy fell asleep for an undetermined amount of time while Rick was repairing the holes in her ceiling, after he rescued Cat Benetar.

We discuss how the holes in his alibi, and his relationship with Saxon, make Rick a good suspect for Saxon's murder. I don't mention that the person who called the tip line stuttered because Eric hasn't confirmed it yet.

"I don't know," I admit my misgivings. "Rick and I have spent some time together since Saxon died, and the Rick I know is a nice, funny, caring man. You should see him with Clawdia, he's so sweet. And Trudy always talks about how helpful Rick is and says she doesn't know what she'd do without him."

"Neighbours always say that about serial killers," April reminds me. "They say, 'he was such a good neighbour. He was so quiet. He would do anything for anyone.' It's part of their plan to get people to trust them and not suspect them. They're always the last person anyone suspects."

She's not wrong.

The jingle of the bell over the door interrupts our brainstorming session.

"Good morning, Phillip!" I stand up from my seat at the sofa and leave my knitting on the sofa cushion. "How are you?"

"Frustrated," Phillip replies, holding up half of a key.

"Oh no, Phillip, what happened?" Connie asks.

"My key snapped when I tried to unlock the back door," he explains. "I had to bring in the deliveries through the front door, and I can't get the broken piece of key out of the lock."

"How can we help?" I ask.

It's just gone on 10 a.m., but he's already having a bad day.

Phillip sighs. "Ryan isn't sure he'll have time to fix it today. Can I have my emergency store key? I'll bring it back after I get another one cut."

"This is why you gave me a spare key," I reply, opening the cash register and retrieving Phillip's spare key from under the till. "Here you go." I smile.

Phillip gives me a weak smile. "Thanks." He takes the key.

"Maybe we can fix it," April suggests. "There are loads of YouTube videos showing how to get a broken key out of a lock." She gestures for Phillip to sit next to her, and they search for a video on April's cell phone.

"With Archie retired, Ryan needs to hire a helper," I whisper to Connie.

"Ryan needs to find the time to hire a helper," Connie replies. "I've suggested that Archie help Ryan hire someone, but Ryan wants to do it himself. I'll suggest it again."

Connie and I resume knitting while April and Phillip watch their third or fourth video tutorial about removing broken keys from locks.

"My turn," Connie says, getting up when the bell over the door jingles again. "Hello, Rick. What brings you to Knitorious today?"

My head snaps up from my knitting at the sound of Rick's name. "Hi, Rick," I say, craning my head to see him in the doorway.

"H-hi, Megan," Rick responds, walking toward me.

I gesture for him to sit down. He sits in the oversized chair at the end of the sofa.

"I was going to text you later today," I tell him, finishing my row and putting down my knitting. "How's Clawdia settling in?"

"I was w-w-walking by your store and came in to g-give you an update," he replies. "She's doing gr-great. Saxon's brother didn't phone or show u-up to get her, but I knew he w-wouldn't."

Rick pulls his cell phone from his coat pocket and opens the photos app on his phone. He shows me several photos he's taken of Clawdia since taking her home on Saturday.

While I scroll through photos of Clawdia on her new scratch post, Clawdia watching the birdfeeder through the window, and Clawdia sleeping on a windowsill, I lean toward Rick and ask quietly, "Do you know if Saxon had a plan to fix the mayoral election so he would win?"

A surprised expression flashes across Rick's face. I'm not sure if he's surprised at Saxon possibly planning to fix the election, or if he's surprised I know about the plan.

"He j-joked about it, but it was j-just a joke," Rick replies. "I'm sure h-he wished he could do it, but he c-couldn't do something like that, especially without help."

"Aren't we the hub of social activity this morning?" Connie mutters as she once again puts down her knitting and stands up to greet our newest arrival.

"Kelly! It's so nice to see you!" Connie gives Kelly a quick hug.

"Excuse me, Rick." I hand him his phone. "I'll be right back." I stand up but abandon my plan when I realize Kelly is almost right in front of me.

"Hi, Kelly," I say, re-settling into my seat on the sofa.

"Hi, hun. Here are the cat toys you left at the salon yesterday." The small zippered bag jingles and crackles when I take it from her.

"Thank you. The cats will love these," I tell her. "They love the toys with bells and tissue paper inside."

"I know it's a longshot," Kelly says, "but do you have a slitherer I could borrow?"

What's a slitherer? Is it some newfangled knitting tool I've never heard of? I furrow my brow and tilt my head, trying to figure out what she means.

"Can you be more specific?" I ask.

"You know, one of those slithery things?" She puts her hands together in front of her and slithers them toward me. "You shove it down the drain to unclog the sink."

"A snake!" Rick interjects so loudly we all look at him, and April and Phillip even pause the video they're watching.

"Yes! A snake!" Kelly points and hops excitedly when Rick guesses her charade.

"Do you have a c-clog, Kelly?" Rick asks.

Kelly tells Rick about the clogged hair sink at the salon, and Rick tells her he has a snake and can look at the sink for her. She offers to pay him, but he waves away her offer, insisting it will only take a few minutes of his time. She insists on paying him somehow, and after a short, friendly negotiation, it's decided that Rick will unclog the hair sink in exchange for a haircut, which Kelly insists he needs.

"How are you with broken keys?" Phillip asks, holding up his broken key so Rick can see it.

"I'm a trained locksmith," Rick replies. "I have a set of key extractors in my truck." He jerks his thumb behind him, toward Water Street. "I can look at it. It'll only take a few minutes."

Phillip jumps up from the sofa and thanks Rick profusely.

April locks her phone screen and drops the device in her knitting bag.

"Are you sure you have time?" Phillip asks. "I don't want to inconvenience you. This is so last minute."

Rick sweeps the suggestion away with his hand. "It's not like I have anything better to do," he says. "I've been at loose ends since my employer died."

And with the mention of Saxon's death, the upbeat mood in Knitorious turns uncomfortable and sullen as we're collectively reminded that his unsolved murder still hangs over our town like a rain cloud.

CHAPTER 27

WEDNESDAY, January 20th

> *April: Want to come with me to Rick's house?*
>
> *Me: Why are you going to Rick's house?*
>
> *April: To drop off treats for him and Clawdia. Rick jump-started T's car yesterday and we want to thank him.*
>
> *Me: I'm alone at the store until noon, then I have to walk Sophie. 1:00 p.m.?*
>
> *April: Works for me. I'll pick you up.*

Rick Ransan's sudden spate of good deeds are earning him a lot of goodwill among the residents of Harmony Lake. He said he's bored now that he's unemployed, which makes sense, but could there be other reasons for Rick's sudden neighbourliness? Maybe he hopes ingratiating himself with his neighbours will distract everyone from the fact that he's a murder suspect. Maybe he misses his only friend and is trying to keep his mind off his loss. Or maybe Rick has a guilty conscience, and these acts of kindness are his way of making amends.

"IF RICK HADN'T BEEN THERE, T might have waited hours for roadside assistance to show up." April brakes at the stop sign and looks both ways.

Yesterday, when Tamara closed the bakery and left to go home, her car wouldn't start. She'd left the lights on all day, and the battery was drained. April was in Harmony Hills with their teenage son, Zach, attending his hockey game. Thankfully, Harmony Lake's hero-of-the-day, Rick Ransan, was nearby and had his jumper cables in the back of his truck.

"It was lucky timing that Rick parked behind Artsy Tartsy and just happened to return to his truck at the very moment T realized her car battery died," I reply.

"Do I detect a hint of skepticism in your voice, Megapixel?" April taunts. "In case you forget how this works, *I'm* the skeptical friend, and *you're* the optimistic friend."

"Sorry," I apologize. "I forgot." We laugh.

"You don't think it was a coincidence that Rick came along precisely when T needed help?" April asks, sounding as dubious as I do.

I shake my head. "I don't know what to think," I admit. "It seems like Rick is out and about more since Saxon died, more than he ever was before, and has morphed from an introvert to an extrovert."

April shrugs without taking her hands off the steering wheel. "Maybe without Saxon here to use up Rick's time and energy, Rick can finally be himself. Maybe he was always a friendly, sociable, kind person, but we couldn't see it because Saxon's overbearing, toxic personality overshadowed him."

"You're probably right," I concede. "And if you are, I should encourage Rick to come out of his shell and get involved in the community, instead of doubting his intentions."

April pulls into Rick's driveway and parks alongside his pickup truck. She collects a white confectionery box from the back seat and walks around to the passenger side of the car, where she waits for me to finish signing the *welcome home* greeting card that goes with the knitted mouse toys that I brought for Clawdia.

I made fifteen hand-knit mice for the charity knitting initiative and gave three of them to Clawdia as a house-warming gift. There must be over two hundred hand-knit cat toys for the gift shop at the Animal Centre. I'm sure no one will notice if I give three of the mice that I made to Clawdia.

"Is Rick expecting us, or are we showing up unannounced?" I ask.

"I texted him, and he replied. He knows we're coming," April informs me as we walk up the driveway.

Next door, the curtains in Trudy Nakata's front room twitch. April and I smile and wave at the twitchy curtains.

"Do you think Trudy or Cat Benetar is the curtain twitcher?" April asks.

"Both?" I guess, shrugging one shoulder.

Rick lives in a small, older bungalow. A snow shovel and bag of rock salt lean against the porch wall next to the screen door. I ring the doorbell and we wait. Out of the corner of my eye, I notice Trudy's curtains twitch again.

"Do you think she's spying on us or Rick?" April asks.

"Yes," I reply.

We both cough to suppress our giggles.

Living in a small town where your friends and neighbours watch you more closely than surveillance cameras ever could isn't as annoying as most people think. In fact, it's oddly comforting. I'm grateful I get to live in a community where the residents care about their friends and neighbours so much that they go out of their way to be involved in each other's lives.

To outsiders, we're a community of small-minded, nosy busybodies with too much time on our hands, but that's a misconception; we're actually a close-knit community of friends and neighbours who care deeply about each other and the town we call home.

"H-hi, April." Rick beams. "Oh, and hi t-to you, too, Megan. This is a pleasant surprise, like finding a d-double yolk in your egg when you only expect one yolk."

To the best of my recollection, this is the first time someone has likened April and me to an egg. Rick invites us inside, and next thing we know, April and I are slipping off our winter boots in his foyer.

While April thanks Rick for jump-starting Tamara's car yesterday and gives him a box of snowball cookies and cranberry-orange-banana bread, I glance around Rick's small, cozy home and get a feel for his space.

Rick's home is cozy. It's clean and tidy, yet lived in. His furnishings are neither old nor new, and a few antique collectibles stand out. Family heirlooms, I assume. Judging by the shelf of cookbooks and the extensive herb and spice collection in his kitchen, Rick is a culinary hobbyist. I wonder who he cooks for?

"And we couldn't forget Clawdia," April says, pulling a white confectionery bag from her coat pocket. "Sardine flavoured," she divulges, handing Rick the bag.

Ewww. Sardine cookies sound gross to me, but I'm sure to a cat they sound *pawsitively purrfect*.

"Oh, I brought Clawdia a small housewarming gift too," I add, handing Rick the gift bag of knitted mice.

"Thank you, both!" Rick responds. "Why don't you sit down, and I'll make us some coffee to have with these treats."

We offer to help make the coffee, or plate the sweet treats, but Rick insists he's fine and directs us to the living room. On the sofa, April discreetly nudges my leg with her knee.

"What?" I mouth, looking at her.

She raises her eyebrows and nods toward the dining room. I follow her gaze to a suitcase. It's upright against the wall beside the hutch. There's something on top of the suitcase. I stand up and take two quiet steps toward the dining room to get a better look. It's a passport.

As I take two quiet steps backward toward the sofa, my phone dings. I sink back into the sofa next to April and take my phone out of my bag.

April: Is that a passport? Do you think he's going on the lam?

She's texting me from the next sofa cushion. I turn my head and look at her in disbelief.

"What?" she whispers. "It's not like I could say it out loud."

"I'm not sure how you take your coffee, so I brought everything." Rick places a tray with three mugs of coffee, spoons, and coffee condiments.

"Is Clawdia settled in?" I ask, then sip my coffee.

Rick nods while he chews a snowball cookie.

"Are you getting used to each other?" April adds.

"She's been here less than a week, but it feels like she's always been here," Rick replies. Then he calls for the cat. "Miss Clawdia! Come here, Miss Claaaawdia. *Sssspsssssp.*"

To my surprise, Clawdia bounds into the room from the hall that leads to the bedrooms.

"Here she is," April says, lowering her hand to cat-level and rubbing her fingertips against her thumb, hoping to coax Clawdia to come within stroking distance.

It's hard to believe this is the same small, timid cat Rick and I rescued from Saxon's house. She looks the same, but she acts completely different. This version of Clawdia is friendly and confident. She visits each of us, making certain everyone has a chance to rub her, then jumps onto Rick's lap, puts her front paws on his chest, and headbutts his beard, before coiling herself into a content pile of furry warmth on his lap.

Sophie has taught me that animals have a knack for seeing the essence of who people really are. Animals are neither fooled nor impressed by the facade many people project when they are out in the world. Surely, if Rick were a cold-blooded murderer, Clawdia wouldn't be this comfortable with him. I'm not a cat, but I get a calm, peaceful vibe from Rick too. I just can't believe he's a heartless killer.

"Your hair looks great," I compliment Rick on his new *do*. "Kelly is a great hairdresser, isn't she?"

Rick looks cleaner and more put together with his new style. Before Kelly worked her magic, Rick's head of thick brown curls resembled a curly helmet. Now, the sides and back are super short, and the curls on top of his head are shaped to complement his rugged features. He looks like a different person.

"I hardly recognize myself when I look in the mirror," Rick responds with a chuckle. "But I expect I'll get used to it." He runs his hand through his curls.

We chat about the weather, the best places to buy pet food and supplies, and other generic topics. I drink my coffee, nibble at my slice of cranberry-orange-banana bread, and wait patiently for an opportunity to ask Rick about the suit-case and passport in the next room.

"Who will take care of Clawdia while you're away?" April asks, as if she can read my mind. Sometimes I swear she has mind- reading powers but won't admit it.

"I'm not going anywhere," Rick replies, looking confused.

"Oh," I interject. "We noticed your suitcase and passport" —I gesture toward them with my almost-empty mug—"and assumed you were going on a trip. Maybe somewhere sunny and warm to escape winter for a few days." I bring the mug to my lips and finish my coffee.

"Oh th-that," Rick replies, turning to look at the suitcase and passport. "I told Trudy I'd drop off the suitcase at the library. It's full of books and clothes and toiletries that someone donated to the book club. The book club collects d-donations for people displaced by natural disasters. They p-put together kits of clothes, toiletries, and books, then send them where they're needed. I think they're currently collecting donations for the hurricane that recently hit the Bahamas, but they take donations all year."

"I can drop off the suitcase at the library," I offer. "I have to drive past there today, anyway. I'm happy to do it."

"That's nice, Megan, thank you for the offer, but it's heavy. It's full of books. I'd h-hate if you hurt yourself. I don't mind doing it."

"Is the passport part of the donation too?" April asks.

"No," Rick laughs. "The passport is going to the bank. I keep my important papers in a safe deposit box. I renewed my passport, and the new one just arrived in the mail. I need to switch out the new passport with the expired one."

Rick's explanation makes sense, but the suitcase and passport still look suspicious, especially considering Rick is a suspect in a murder investigation.

We thank Rick for the coffee and explain that we have to get back to our respective businesses. We tell him we'll see ourselves out and insist that he not get up because neither of us can bear to disturb Clawdia who is fast asleep and purring on Rick's lap.

"Thanks again, Rick. Bye," I call as I open his front door.

"Wrap up the leftover cake or it'll dry out," April advises. "We'll see you and Clawdia soon."

"Thanks, guys. For everything. Bye," Rick calls from the living room.

"What do you think?" I ask April as we walk to the car.

"I want to believe him about the suitcase and the passport, but I'm not sure I do," she replies.

"Same," I say, nodding. "But he knew we were coming over. If he's planning to go on the run, he would've hidden the suitcase and passport before we arrived, wouldn't he?"

"I don't know," April replies. "But I think we should let the police know, just in case he's planning to skip town."

I nod. "I think you're right."

"Woohoo! Hi, Megan!" Trudy is on her porch, gathering her thick cardigan around her with one hand and waving at me with her other hand over her head.

"Hi, Trudy!" I smile and wave.

"You talk to Trudy, and I'll text Eric to tell him about Rick's suitcase and passport situation," April says. "I never get to tip him off about evidence." She sounds almost excited at the prospect.

"How are you, Trudy?" I ask, trudging across the snowy lawn toward her porch.

"I'm fine, Megan. How are you?"

"I'm well, thank you. We were just next door visiting Rick and Clawdia," I tell her. "I offered to drop off your donation suitcase at the library, but Rick wouldn't have it."

"It's for the best," Trudy says. "That suitcase is much heavier than it looks. I think it might be heavier than me." She laughs. "I couldn't even drag it across the lawn to his house. Rick had to come over here to get it."

"I didn't realize the book club takes donations all year," I say. "I know you do donation drives in response to natural disasters, but I didn't realize it was an ongoing program."

"Oh yes," Trudy responds. "We collect donations all year. The library generously stores them for us until we send them to displaced families."

"If you have a flyer or pamphlet or something to raise awareness about it, I'd be happy to post it on the community bulletin board at Knitorious," I offer.

"That would be wonderful! I have some flyers in the house. I'll get a few for you. I'll be right back." Grinning widely, Trudy holds up her index finger, reminding me to wait here, while she disappears into the house.

"What did Trudy want?" April asks when I get into her car.

I show her the flyers Trudy gave me and place two of them on the back seat for April to display at Artsy Tartsy.

"It sounds like Rick was telling the truth about the suitcase." April lets out a sigh of relief. "Eric said he'll come to Rick's house and ask about the suitcase and passport. I hope we're not wasting police time and putting Rick through another interview with the police for no reason."

I feel her remorse. I felt the same when I told Eric about the umbrella in Sheamus's office that turned out to be a false lead.

"We did the right thing by telling the police," I assure her. "It's possible Rick emptied the donated contents from the suitcase and packed it with his own clothes, or mixed evidence to the donated contents to dispose of it."

Maybe Eric will find a missing penny loafer or a few umbrella pieces stuffed in there.

CHAPTER 28

THURSDAY, January 21st

The line of caffeine addicts at Latte Da inches forward, and I inch forward with it because I'm one of the caffeine addicts waiting patiently for my first caffeine fix of the day. My phone vibrates in my pocket, and when I look at the screen, I notice a missed call notification. The call was from Eric. He tried to call me early this morning. Why isn't my phone making its usual ringing and dinging sounds?

April: Did Eric tell you what was in the suitcase?

Me: I haven't talked to him yet. I'll ask him and let you know.

I inspect my mysteriously quiet phone for the cause of its silence. Mystery solved; sometime between last night and this morning, I accidentally hit the silent switch on the side of the phone.

Why did Eric call me so early? Is everything OK? Maybe there was a break in the case. I'll text him instead of calling him, in case he's in a meeting. Now that he's the police chief, he's in a meeting more often than not.

Me: Good morning! I'm sorry I missed your call. I accidentally turned off the sound on my phone.

Eric: Happy Anniversary!

I'm a bad girlfriend, I totally forgot to wish him happy anniversary. I mean, I *know* it's our anniversary, but I haven't thought about it since waking up. I was caught up in my morning routine.

Me: Happy Anniversary! Are you in a meeting? Can I call you?

Eric: I'm not at the station right now.

Me: Where are you?

"Behind you."

I almost jump out of my skin at the sound of Eric's voice, much to the amusement of my fellow caffeine addicts.

"You scared me." I clutch my chest with one hand and swat him with the other. "Why didn't you tell me you were here?"

"I was about to, but then you texted me," he replies, laughing. "I didn't mean to scare you. I'm sorry." He's laughing so hard, I can barely make out what he's saying.

Eric joins me in line, and we inch forward.

"What are you doing here?" I ask.

"Getting you a coffee," he replies. "I wanted to see you and say happy anniversary in person."

"Happy anniversary." I stand on my tippy toes and kiss him. "Where are we going tonight?"

"It's a surprise," Eric reminds me.

"If I don't know where we're going, how am I supposed to know what to wear?" I ask.

"You always wear just the right thing," he replies. "It's one of your superpowers."

Coffee in hand, we meander up Water Street toward Knitorious, and I hook my arm through his. "Did you have time to look inside Rick's suitcase?"

"I sure did," Eric exclaims. "Kids clothes, kids shoes, kids boots, kids snowsuit, board books, story books, and a few stuffed animals."

"Oh. Another dead end." My voice sounds as disappointed as I feel.

"I prefer to think of it as eliminating one more line of inquiry."

I guess that is a more positive way to look at it. "What about the rumour that Saxon was planning to fix the election?" I ask. "Did you find any evidence to support it?"

"Nothing," he replies.

Inside Knitorious, I lock the door behind us because the store doesn't open for another fifteen minutes.

Eric and Sophie greet each other, and Eric suggests that we take her for a walk together. I tell him that Sophie and I already had our morning walk, and I need to unlock the door in a few minutes.

"It's kind of Sophie's anniversary too," he reminds me.

"You're right," I admit. "Sophie came to live with me a year ago this month." I crouch down and rub her between the ears. "We've had a big year, haven't we, Soph? Lots of big changes for both of us."

"For the better, I hope?" Eric asks.

"Definitely," I tell him just as my phone dings.

Adam: Can I borrow your escargot dishes?

Me: Sure.

"I didn't know you like escargot," Eric says when I tell him why Adam is texting me.

"I don't," I tell him. "I use escargot dishes when I make baked garlic shrimp or stuffed mushrooms."

Adam: Thanks. Can I please have your baked garlic shrimp recipe? I'm cooking for Jess tonight.

Me: Sure.

Adam: Can I pick them up around 3 p.m.?

Me: I'll be at work, but if you text me when you get to chez Martel, I'll let you in with the app.

Adam: Great! Thanks, Meg!

For the next few minutes, I use my feminine wiles to

persuade Eric to tell me where we're going tonight and what my anniversary gift is. Just as my charm is wearing down his resistance, and I'm sure he's about to tell me what I want to know, the thud of the back door closing interrupts us. He's teased me for weeks about this mystery gift, and now that the day is finally here, I want to know what it is.

"Good morning, my dear," Connie sings as she enters the store from the back room. "Good morning, Eric. It's nice to see you. It feels like we haven't seen each other in days." She gives Eric a maternal hug, complete with back rubbing and swaying.

"I haven't been around much because this case takes up most of my time," he explains, sounding apologetic.

"I'm not complaining," Connie clarifies. "Take all the time you need to clear Ryan and Adam's names."

Eric tells us he has to get back to the station, and I offer to walk him to the back door. Connie tells us to take our time, and she'll take care of opening the store. Then she smiles mischievously at us and giggles a very un-Connie-like giggle.

"Thank you for the coffee," I say when we get to the back door.

"Thank you for the happiest year of my life," Eric replies. "I'll pick you up at six o'clock. I love you."

"I'll be ready. I love you too."

I'M HELPING a customer find a wool-free yarn for her project, and she's deep into the story of how she found out she has a wool allergy, when the sound of the bell over the door gets my attention. I know Connie is at the front of the store, so I don't interrupt my customer to turn and greet the new visitor.

Moments later, a tap on my shoulder. "Phillip is here to see you, Megan," Connie informs me. "Why don't you see what he wants while I show this lovely lady the cotton-silk blend that came in last week."

I excuse myself from my customer, assuring her that Connie is Canada's foremost yarn expert, then thank Connie and leave them to it.

Phillip is fussing with a gorgeous floral arrangement on the coffee table in the cozy seating area. A gorgeous and familiar floral arrangement.

"Hi, Phillip," I say. "Hey! Am I having déjà vu, or I have seen this exact floral arrangement before?" Déjà vu used to be a rare sensation, but this week it's become a regular occurrence.

"It's not déjà vu," Phillip hints. "You've definitely seen this before."

I retrieve my phone from the counter and unlock the screen, then I swipe through the camera roll, stopping to look at each floral arrangement I received last year.

Last January, Eric and I attended a fundraiser together. One of the fundraising events was a silent auction with prizes donated by local businesses. Phillip donated a year's worth of floral arrangements, and Eric had the winning bid. As a result, every month last year I received a gorgeous, seasonal floral arrangement. I took pictures of them. They are truly works of art. Phillip is more than a florist; he's an artist whose medium is flowers.

"Found it!" I declare. "This is identical to the floral arrangement you delivered last January."

"You are a good little sleuth, aren't you?" Phillip teases. "Is there a date on that photo?" he asks, nodding toward my phone.

I bring up the information about the photo. I took this photo one year ago today. "Same floral arrangement on the same date," I observe. "Phillip, my year of floral arrangements ended last month."

"Lance Romance renewed it for another year," he explains.

I assume "Lance Romance" is Eric. "You have twelve more arrangements coming to you—well, eleven after today—and he requested that this month's arrangement be identical to last January's arrangement, and that I deliver it on the same day at the same time."

That's a lot of specific requests.

"You remember the *exact time* you delivered flowers a year ago?" I ask, astonished.

He flicks his wrist. "I have no idea. But I try to finish my deliveries before lunch, so I assume it was in the morning. He was fine with that."

"Well, thank you, Phillip. They're just as beautiful this January as they were last January."

I'm not sure Phillip heard me because he's looking past me. I follow his gaze to see what's distracting him and land upon the wool-allergic customer incessantly scratching both of her palms simultaneously.

"What's wrong with Connie's customer?" Phillip whispers.

"She must've come in contact with wool. She has a wool allergy," I whisper.

"Why would she come to a yarn store if she has a wool allergy?" he asks.

"Why do people allergic to chrysanthemums go to Wilde Flowers?" I retort.

"Touché," Phillip replies without taking his eyes off the itchy customer.

Believe it or not, this isn't uncommon. Lots of knitters are allergic to wool or other common knitting fibres. We keep a box of antihistamines under the counter for just such occurrences.

I walk around the counter and dig out the antihistamines to offer them to the itchy knitter.

"While you're near the cash register, here's the spare key for my store." Phillip reaches into his front pocket and produces the familiar, enamel key chain. "I'm glad you had it when I needed it."

I open the till and return the key to its spot under the cash drawer.

"Rick fixed the lock, I assume?"

"Oh yes," Phillip confirms. "It took him less than five minutes, and he made it look so easy! The lock is fine now, and I had another key cut. Who knew Rick Ransan is so handy?"

"Not me," I admit.

"Megan! Thank goodness you're here!" Pete Feeney exclaims before the bell above the door stops jingling.

His outburst gets everyone's attention. Even the itchy knitter stops scratching to see what's going on.

"Pete! What's wrong? Did something happen?" Phillip demands.

"I'm so glad you're here," Pete says urgently, looking at me and ignoring Phillip's question. "Do you still have the envelope I gave you on Monday? The one with the listings?"

I nod. "Uh-huh. We haven't looked at them yet."

"Have you opened the envelope?" Pete asks.

To be honest, I forgot about the envelope. It's still in my tote bag. I've been carrying it around all week. When I look in my bag to find something, I see the envelope and remind myself to take it out of my bag when I get home, then immediately forget about it again. This doesn't just happen with envelopes; my bag is a black hole of things waiting to be remembered.

I shake my head. "No," I reply. "We haven't touched it." Pete's panicked expression is replaced with relief. "Why?" I ask.

"I gave you the wrong envelope," he explains. "I just realized that I gave your listings to a young couple looking for their first home, and I gave you the envelope with the young couple's mortgage application. It has their private information on it."

"I see," I say.

"That looks uncomfortable," Phillip says to the itchy knitter when she walks in front of him.

"It is," she confirms. "I squooshed the merino roving. I couldn't help myself." She shrugs and looks Phillip in the eye. "It was worth it. I regret nothing."

"It happens to the best of us," I assure her and notice she's extended her scratching area to include the insides of both her forearms. "Pete, have a seat." I point to the cozy sitting area. "I'll be right back."

Pete opens his mouth to protest, but I pretend not to notice. I hand Connie the box of antihistamines and continue walking to the kitchenette to get our itchy customer a glass of water. Phillip follows me.

"Is it me, or does Pete seem a little too concerned about the envelope he gave you?" Phillip asks.

I'm glad I'm not the only one who thinks Pete's reaction is out of proportion to the issue at hand.

"A little," I agree, "but he has a duty to protect client information. Maybe the house-hunting couple are pressing him to produce their application."

"You're probably right." Phillip shrugs. "I should get back to the shop." We exchange a double cheek kiss. "Enjoy your flowers and enjoy your date tonight." He winks.

"You know where we're going, don't you?" I ask.

Philip pretends to zip his mouth closed with his thumb and forefinger, and before I can ask him anything else, he disappears through the back door.

The itchy knitter accepts the glass of water but declines the antihistamines because she carries a supply in her purse. While Connie rings up her purchase, I join Pete in the cozy sitting area. He stands up anxiously when he sees me approaching him.

"Is the envelope here?" he asks. "I need it."

I shake my head. "It's upstairs in the apartment. I don't have a key," I lie.

I hate lying; it gives me anxiety, but I sense there's more to this story than Pete has told me so far, and every instinct I have is telling me not to give him the envelope.

"I *really* need that envelope, Megan."

Time to call his bluff.

"OK." I shrug. "Let's call Eric. I'm sure he'll be happy to come home and get the envelope for you." I pull out my phone to show Pete that I'm serious.

"Oh, no," Pete puts out a hand to stop me. "Don't do that." He wipes beads of sweat from his brow, then wipes his palms on his thighs. "I mean, I don't want to interrupt the police chief just for an envelope. Especially not when he has a murder to solve."

I don't know what's in the envelope, but whatever it is, Pete doesn't want Eric to see it.

"Are you sure?" I ask. "What will you tell your clients?"

Pete shifts his weight from one foot to the other, looking rather uncomfortable. "It's fine." He swallows hard. "I'll put them off until tomorrow. If I come back tomorrow, can you have the envelope here?"

"For sure," I assure him.

"Promise you won't open it," he teases, chuckling awkwardly, but I sense he's genuinely concerned I might.

"Promise," I assure him, smiling and crossing my fingers behind my back.

CHAPTER 29

PETE and the itchy knitter leave at the same time. He holds the door for her on their way out, which saves her from having to pause from scratching.

While Connie takes the itchy knitter's water glass to the kitchenette, I text Eric to thank him for the flowers.

Me: Phillip just delivered my gift. They're beautiful. Thank you.

I snap a picture of the floral arrangement and text it to him.

Eric: Glad you like them, but that wasn't your gift.

If a year's supply of floral arrangements isn't my anniversary gift, then what is?

I'm about to text him with more questions, when Connie interrupts me.

"Why did you lie to Pete about having a key to the upstairs apartment? The same key opens the store and the apartment."

"You're right," I admit. "I lied because my gut told me not to give him the envelope. Did you see his reaction when I suggested we call Eric? There's something in that envelope he doesn't want anyone to see, and I'm not sure it's a house hunter's mortgage application."

Connie nods. "I had a feeling he was lying to you too," she admits. "He was more nervous than a long-tailed cat in a room full of rocking chairs."

"The envelope is in my bag," I divulge. "I think we should open it."

"Let's do it!" Connie agrees.

I find the envelope in my bag and meet Connie at the harvest table.

The envelope isn't sealed with glue; it's one of those reusable interoffice envelopes with a string you wind around the button to close it and secure the contents inside. This is a good thing, because if Pete is telling the truth, and the envelope contains a mortgage application with personal information, I'll close it, and Connie and I will pretend we never looked at it.

"Kind of thick for a mortgage application," Connie observes as I pull the stack of papers out of the envelope.

The pile of papers is about a quarter of an inch thick and held together with a binder clip. I sit in the chair next to Connie, and together, we look at the cover sheet. "S R props and comps," we read aloud in unison.

"Is that Pete's handwriting?" I ask.

Connie shrugs. "I assume it is."

We flip through the papers. Listings. Every sheet of paper is information about a property in Harmony Lake.

"Definitely not a mortgage application," I confirm.

"I think these are listings for one of Pete's real estate clients, and comparable listings for comparison," Connie theorizes. "Archie and I must have viewed a dozen properties before we bought the condo, and our agent gave us a listing for each home we viewed, and listings for comparable properties to help us judge whether the property we were viewing was fairly priced."

I flip back to the handwritten cover page. "That explains the 'props and comps,'" I say. "It must be real estate speak for properties and comparables."

"But Pete was insistent this envelope contained a mortgage application." Connie takes the papers and flips through them one by one, looking for misfiled mortgage information, for proof that Pete didn't intentionally lie about the contents of the envelope.

"Don't people complete mortgage applications online nowadays?" I speculate. "Why would he bother printing a copy?"

"I don't know," Connie says. "But most of these listings are for properties owned by Saxon Renaud. And almost all of them have handwritten notes and numbers on them."

"Pete told me he likes to print listings and make notes on them for his clients," I say.

Connie is right. This looks like a package of Saxon's properties, organized by location.

Could this explain the "S R" on the cover page? S R could be Saxon Renaud's initials.

We open the binder clip for better access to the hand-scrawled notes on the listings. Beneath the binder clip, the listings are organized into smaller groupings of three or four properties held together with a staple. My mind flashes back to Sunday brunch when Adam and I discussed strategically purchasing a few of Saxon's properties to make the remaining properties less attractive to developers and investors.

"I think Pete was bundling Saxon's properties and looking for buyers," I say.

"You might be right," Connie agrees. "Look at this." She points to a name and phone number on a listing.

"Reginald White," I mutter. "Reginald White... Why is that name familiar?" I ask.

"Reginald White is the head honcho at Mega Mart," Connie reminds me. "Remember last year when he tried to purchase land from the Animal Centre and part of the Willows's farm for one of his mega stores?"

"Aaah, right," I say, nodding. "But why would Pete be wooing big-box corporations to sell them land in Harmony Lake?" I ask, dumbfounded. "He knows we have a bylaw against it, and his mother spent most of her life advocating to keep big-box stores out of this town."

Connie shrugs. "Maybe Pete was preparing to sell the properties if Saxon won the mayoral election." Pouting, she shakes her head. "This will break Alice's heart, my dear. It would be best if she doesn't find out."

I nod. "I know, and I'm sure Pete has a perfectly reasonable explanation for this," I say with certainty, not feeling at all certain.

"According to the date on these papers, he printed them before Saxon died. He printed some of them weeks ago," Connie notices.

I wonder if this is the reason Saxon and Pete were having secret FaceTime meetings in the weeks before Saxon's murder.

"You don't think Pete and these listings had anything to do with Saxon's murder, do you, my dear?" Connie asks, her eyebrows pulled tightly together.

"Pete was eliminated as a suspect, remember?" I remind her. "And how would Pete benefit from Saxon's death? Saxon died before we knew the election results. If Saxon won the election, he would have to be alive to take office and reverse the big-box policy. Also, real estate transactions take longer if they involve the owner's estate than if the owner is alive."

If Connie and I are correct, and he was planning to sell Saxon's properties, Pete stood to earn a hefty commission from the transactions. It would be in Pete's best interest for Saxon to be alive.

When the bell above the door jingles, Connie jumps up to greet whoever is here, and I hastily gather up the listings, attach them with the binder clip, and slide them back inside their envelope.

"Hello," I greet the two ladies who are browsing through the shelves of sock yarn.

I walk to the front of the store and nonchalantly return the envelope to my bag.

"There you go, Soph," I say, pulling the purple and white fair-isle dog sweater over her head.

Sophie gives her head, then her body a good shake before she disappears into the store to see what she missed while we were out for our midday walk.

"Marla! What are you doing here?" I ask, fluffing out the curls which were matted down against my head because of my knitted hat. "Today is your day off."

"I came in so you can leave," Marla explains. "Connie and I are sending you home early, so you can get ready for your date tonight."

"That's sweet of you, thank you." I give her a hug. "Where is Connie?" I ask.

"On her break," Marla replies.

I'm about to tell Marla that I'll stay until Connie gets back from her break, when my phone dings.

Adam: Running early today. Can you let me in?
Me: Yup

I open the app on my phone and unlock the front door. Adam sends me a thumbs-up emoji to let me know he's inside the house.

Two more customers enter the store, and Marla and I divide and conquer. I'm in the back room looking for a pattern book my customer special-ordered when my phone dings again.

Adam: Where are the escargot dishes?

Me: Dining room hutch, middle door, second shelf.
Adam: Why did you move them?

They've been in the same spot for twenty years, but I don't bother explaining this to Adam.

"Here you go," I say to my customer, holding up the book they ordered.

While I ring up the book, my phone dings. Twice.

"Thanks again. Have a nice day." I smile, handing her the book and receipt.

As soon as she turns to leave, I pull my phone from my pocket.

Adam: Where's your recipe box?

Same place it's been for twenty years, Adam!

Me: Pantry, top shelf, left side.
Adam: thumbs-up emoji

I'm tidying the shelves of sock yarn when it dings again.

Adam: Can't find the recipe box.

Imagine being able to make a brilliant legal argument but being unable to find a recipe box that's been on the same shelf for two decades. Unbelievable.

Me: Look again. It's black. It might be hard to see.

Geez, should I come over later and cook it for you too?

When my phone dings again, I'm tempted to throw the thing across the store.

Adam: You know about the squirrel in the fireplace, right? Also, I still can't find the recipe box.

What squirrel? The fireplace was squirrel-free when I left this morning.

Me: Are you sure?
Adam: About the squirrel or the recipe box?
Me: I'll be home in 10 minutes.

While I grab my bag, I whistle for Sophie to follow me to the back room, then I tell Marla that I have to leave and tend to a potential squirrel situation at home.

SOPHIE TILTS HER HEAD, mesmerized by the muffled scraping sounds coming from inside the wall.

"There's definitely something in there," I say to Adam. He's on his back with a flashlight, looking up the chimney. "Adam, your suit will get covered in soot. Get out of there."

I haven't used the fireplace in years, yet I still get it cleaned every fall. There's no soot to get on Adam's custom-tailored suit, but there's still no need to risk it.

"Keep the flue closed," he instructs, wiping and straight-ening his suit. We both look at the wall when the scratching gets louder. "Or if you get a pillowcase, I'll hold it in place and you bang on the wall. Maybe we can knock it into the pillowcase and set it free."

I sigh. "Thanks, but I'll call Ryan. You have to go home and make dinner, and I have to get ready to go out tonight."

I send a quick text to Ryan, asking when he can fit my squirrel problem into his schedule.

"Ryan's rushed off his feet lately, he had to start a waiting list," Adam informs me. "I hope he can fit you in."

Me, too.

While I wait for Ryan to get back to me, I retrieve the recipe box from the top shelf of the pantry. It was in the back, out of view where Adam couldn't find it, despite being almost a foot taller than me and having a better vantage point.

I find the baked garlic shrimp recipe card and slam it triumphantly on the island in the kitchen.

"I swear, Meg, I tore that shelf apart looking, and it wasn't there."

Ding!

"I hope that's Ryan," I say, retrieving my phone from the family room. "He can come by after dinner and liberate the squirrel."

"Aren't you going out tonight?" Adam asks, taking photos of the front and back of the recipe card.

"Yes." I nod. Cancelling this date with Eric isn't an option; he's been planning it for weeks.

I type a response to Ryan, hoping we can figure out a solution.

"Ryan will come by after dinner. He'll text me when he gets here, and I'll use the app to let him in," I tell Adam.

"Perfect!" Adam responds, returning my recipe box to the top shelf of the pantry. "If Ryan has a problem, tell him to text me and I'll come over. It's the least I can do, Meg. You've gone above and beyond your ex-wife duties trying to get me eliminated as a suspect in Saxon's murder."

Trying is the operative word. But try as I might, I've only eliminated one suspect: Sheamus O'Brien. Everyone else has compelling evidence that points to them having motive, means, opportunity, or all of the above. Despite being frustrated at the lack of progress, I feel like the killer is right in front of me, but I can't see who it is. Like the squirrel stuck in my chimney, there's a clue here somewhere; I can't see it, but I know it's there. Also like the squirrel, it wants to be set free.

CHAPTER 30

"You're wearing the same outfit you wore on our first date!" Eric points out when I take off my coat at the restaurant.

"You said wearing just the right thing is one of my super-powers," I remind him, without giving Tamara credit. I don't want to throw her under the bus for giving me a hint.

We're seated in the same booth of the same restaurant where we had our first date one year ago tonight. In very sentimental and Eric-typical fashion, he recreated our first date. I hope he doesn't expect me to order the same meal because I can't remember what I ordered. I only remember being nervous and shocked that this hot guy, for whom I'd harboured a months-long secret infatuation, asked me out.

"How was your day?" he asks, taking my hand.

I tell him about the urgent visit Connie and I had from Pete Sweeney, and about the contents of the envelope Pete gave me on Monday. Then I tell him about the squirrel situation at chez Martel.

"That's why my phone is on the table." I gesture to my phone. "Ryan said he'll text me to let him into the house."

"Where is the envelope Pete gave you?" Eric asks. "Do you still have it?"

"It's at home," I reply. "Still in my tote bag."

"Mind if I look at it later?" he asks.

"Of course," I reply. "How was your day?"

"We searched two of Saxon Renaud's vacant rental properties today," Eric informs me.

"Find anything useful?" I ask.

"Counterfeit election ballots," Eric replies.

"What?!" I'm gobsmacked. "So, the rumour about Saxon fixing the election was true?"

"He might have *wanted* to fix the election," Eric explains, "but the ballots we found are fakes. His plan was not carried out."

I wonder why it wasn't carried out.

On the surface, this gives Adam even more motive than he already had. But if Adam knew about a plot to manipulate the election results, he would have exposed the plot through appropriate, official channels like the police and the media. Adam has too much respect for the law and for the democratic process to handle it any other way.

The server comes to take our drink order and deliver our menus. We decide we're not allowed to talk about work, or murder, anymore tonight.

Ironically, I order the same thing for dinner tonight that I ordered on our first date. I only know this because Eric told me after I ordered. He has an exceptionally good memory for details, especially when those details are food related.

After dinner, and before dessert, we exchange gifts. I go first and hand him a gift bag. One by one, he pulls out each item and lays it on the table. Paint swatches, a printout of a sofa, four upholstery samples, and a catalogue from a custom desk and cabinet maker.

"Are these clues?" Eric asks.

"Kind of." I shrug. "I've thought a lot about your suggestion that we renovate chez Martel to make it our home instead of my home, and I want us to do it. I thought we could start by converting the guest bedroom into a home office for you." Picking up the printout of the sofa, I say, "We'll still need your new home office to function as a guest bedroom occasionally, so I thought we could replace the bedroom furniture with a pullout sofa." I pick up the upholstery samples. "We need to choose a fabric for the sofa." I pick up the paint chips. "When we decide on a fabric, we can pick the paint colour, and finally"–I pick up the custom desk catalogue—"I thought we could get built-in cabinetry and a custom desk for you."

"OhMyGod! Are you serious, babe?" Eric asks, beaming from ear to ear. "Are you sure about this? I wasn't trying to rush you."

I nod, smiling. "Positive. Like you said, we can do it at our own pace."

"This is the best gift you've ever given me! Thank you!" He leans across the table and kisses me. "Your turn." He hands me a small gift bag.

I rummage through the tissue paper until my hand finds an envelope.

I open the envelope and unfold two pieces of paper. Concert tickets. "We're going to see Matchbox Twenty?!" I declare, more loudly than I intend. "I love that band." I rush to his side of the table and throw my arms around his neck. "Thank you!"

I slide into the booth next to him and scan the ticket, looking for the date, and realize this concert isn't anywhere near Harmony Lake. I was expecting it would be Toronto, Ottawa, or maybe Montreal, but this concert is at The Pearl in Las Vegas, Nevada.

"Ummm, the concert venue is in Vegas," I say.

"There's another envelope in the bag," he says.

I pull out the tissue paper and place it on my lap, then I tilt the empty gift bag toward him.

"It must be in the car," Eric says, reaching for his coat. "I'll be right back."

As Eric makes his way to the parking lot, I stuff the tissue paper and other gifts inside their respective bags.

"Good evening, Megan." Out of nowhere, Alice Feeney is standing next to our booth, smiling.

"Hi, Mayor Feeney," I greet her. "It's nice to see you. Is it date night for you and Mr. Feeney?" I ask.

"Heaven's no," she replies, chuckling at the notion. "I'm having dinner with my sister. This is one of our favourite restaurants. I just wanted to tell you I got gauge with the needles you sold me." She winks. "See, I told you I always get gauge."

"I guess getting gauge is your superpower," I joke. "How is your grandson's sweater coming along?" I ask.

"Swimmingly!" Mayor Feeney responds, digging her phone out from her purse. "I have a few photos of it." She hands the phone to me. "See, I finished the yoke and separated for the sleeves. Now I'm working on the body. I might have this sweater finished sometime next week."

"It's beautiful," I say, swiping through the photos, then my phone dings. "Excuse me," I say, handing her phone back to her.

Ryan: I'm here. Can you let me in?

"It's Ryan Wright," I explain to Mayor Feeney.

While I tell her about the squirrel who moved into my chimney this afternoon, and how Ryan is working late to get rid of it for me, I open the app on my phone and unlock the door at my house.

Me: Unlocked

Ryan: I'm in.

"Maybe it's the same squirrel in our chimney last week," Mayor Feeney suggests. "It's possible, we live close enough to each other." She giggles. "Maybe he's moving from chimney to chimney until he finds one where the owners won't evict him."

We laugh. "Well, I hope he doesn't move back to your chimney after Ryan frees him from mine."

"I hope so too," Mrs. Feeney agrees. "But if he does, I won't call my Pete again to get rid of him, I'll call Ryan Wright."

"Why?" I ask. "Pete removed the squirrel on Thursday, didn't he?"

"He certainly did," Mayor Feeney confirms. "But we called him on Wednesday morning. I worried the poor creature would die waiting. I know Pete is busy, between being a full-time firefighter and part-time real estate agent, he's pressed for time most days. I don't want to make extra demands on his time, but if he'd just told me on Wednesday that he couldn't get there until Thursday night—who are we kidding, it was Friday morning—I would have found someone else to take care of it."

"I thought Pete said you texted him in a panic about the squirrel late Thursday night," I say. "I must've misunderstood."

"Or it's more likely he didn't want to admit that it took him a day and a half to take care of it," Mayor Feeney retorts, with a playful huff.

"Didn't you think it was odd when he showed up in the middle of the night to take care of the squirrel in your chimney?" I ask.

She shrugs. "Not really. Firefighting isn't a nine-to-five job. Between my husband and Pete, I'm used to shift workers coming and going at all hours. But it all worked out for the best, because if it weren't for that squirrel, Pete wouldn't have found the crack in our firebox."

"Oh?" I urge. "What does that mean?"

"It means we can't use our fireplace because it's a fire hazard," Mayor Feeney explains. "It must be a hairline crack, because my husband and I can't see it with our old eyes. But Pete insists it's there, and I believe him. He's a trained fire professional. So, no cozy fires for us until Pete has time to fix it."

"No cozy fires," I agree, distracted by Mayor Feeney's version of events on Friday night. "Better safe than sorry."

The server shows up with our Black Forest cake at the same moment Eric returns from the parking lot. Mrs. Feeney gets up from the booth and greets Eric. She congratulates him on his appointment as police chief, and he congratulates her on her well-deserved retirement.

Mayor Feeney waves toward the door. "Well, I should get going, my sister is getting impatient, waiting to drive me home. Have a lovely evening, you two."

Eric takes off his coat and hands me an envelope. "It was under my seat," he explains, joining me on my side of the table. "That's what took me so long. I had to get the flashlight from my glove box and move the driver's seat to reach it."

I'm only half-listening, because I'm mentally stuck on a few things Mayor Feeney said.

"Babe, open the envelope," Eric says, bringing me back to the here and now.

"Right." I smile. I open the envelope. Two tickets to Las Vegas for the same weekend as the Matchbox twenty concert. "We're going to Las Vegas?" I ask, shocked. "I love Vegas."

"I know," he replies. "It's already arranged with everyone. Connie and Marla will run the store with Sophie, and Adam and April will take turns having Sophie overnight. You won't miss your weekly brunch with Hannah, because you can FaceTime with her and Adam from the hotel."

"Such a thoughtful gift," I say, then kiss him. "Thank you." I wave away the forkful of cake he offers me, and he redirects the fork to his own mouth.

"What's wrong?" Eric asks. "You're distracted. Did Mayor Feeney say something that upset you?"

I shake my head. "No. We talked about knitting and squirrels."

"I know that look," he says, pointing his fork at my face and speaking with food in his mouth. "You figured something out. Whatever Mayor Feeney said or did, it made you figure something out."

"Possibly," I confess.

"Can you tell me?"

"Can we talk about work?" I ask.

"Depends. Is it urgent?"

"I think I know where the murder weapon is."

"Let's talk about work." He puts his fork on the cake plate and pushes the plate away.

I tell Eric about my conversation with Mayor Feeney; a conversation I have a feeling changes everything.

CHAPTER 31

I DRIVE Eric's car home from the restaurant in Harmony Hills while he sends texts, makes phone calls, and organizes his team from the passenger seat.

I'm only privy to one side of the phone conversations, and none of the texts, but it sounds like he assigned officers to track down Pete Feeney and bring him to the station for questioning, and started the process of obtaining a warrant to search Mayor and Mr. Feeney's house.

"Where are we going?" I ask as I exit the highway in Harmony Lake.

"Your house," he replies without looking up from his phone. "I'll drop you off and pick up the envelope Pete gave you."

"Drop me off?" I ask. "Are you going to question Pete?"

Eric shakes his head, hits send, and flips his phone face down on his lap. "We can't locate Pete," he says with an exasperated sigh. "He's supposed to be on duty at the fire hall tonight, but his shift captain says he left fifteen minutes ago, claiming he didn't feel well. He didn't give any details about his symptoms, and no one knows where he went when he left."

"Is he at home or at his parents' house?" I ask, knowing the police would have already checked there.

"No and no," Eric replies. "I posted officers at each location, in case he shows up."

"Maybe Pete truly is sick," I suggest. "Have you tried the hospital? The urgent care clinic? The pharmacy?"

"We're looking everywhere and anywhere. There's a BOLO on his truck, and every available officer is out looking for him."

"BOLO?" I ask.

"Be. On. The. Lookout," Eric explains.

"Ah," I acknowledge. "I doubt he's avoiding you. I mean, how could he know the police are looking for him unless…"

"Unless what?" Eric demands urgently.

"Unless Pete spoke with his mother, and she told him about our conversation at the restaurant. In that case, he might realize she contradicted parts of his alibi."

"Change of plan," Eric says, pulling himself up to his full-seated height. "Instead of your place, we're going to Mayor Feeney's house."

"Don't you need a warrant?" I ask.

"Not if Mayor or Mr. Feeney give me permission," he explains.

I nod, and Eric phones and texts his colleagues with new instructions.

"Pull over here and turn off the lights," Eric instructs.

I do as I'm told and pull over in front of the Henderson house. The Hendersons aren't home to alert the rest of the neighbourhood to our presence outside their house; they're in Winnipeg visiting their daughter and her new husband.

"Now what?" I ask.

We're so far up the street from the Feeney residence that I

may as well have parked in my own driveway and walked here. I can't even see their driveway from here.

"Now we wait," he replies.

"For what?"

"For the team to get into position."

"Are the police surrounding the Feeney's house?" I ask. He nods. "Eric, they did nothing wrong. They're harmless octogenarians whose biggest problem right now is the crack in their firebox that's stopping them from enjoying cozy nights by the fire." I glare at him and pause for dramatic effect. "Being raided by a bunch of armed cops could cause them to have a stroke or something."

"We're also waiting for an ambulance," he assures me matter-of-factly. "It should be here any minute. It'll be nearby just in case."

"This seems over the top," I attempt to reason with him. "I'm sure if we knock on the door and calmly explain why we'd like to come in, the Feeney's would cooperate. She was a cop, like you, remember?"

"The Feeneys won't know we surrounded their house. My team is excellent. They're trained professionals." His phone rings, and Eric answers the call. After a few grunts of acknowledgement, he ends the call and unbuckles his seatbelt. "I'll be back in a few minutes with your vest." I doubt I'll need a bullet-resistant vest to protect me from the Feeneys. I open my mouth to protest, but he doesn't give me a chance to argue. "Unless you want to go home and wait there," he says, countering my unspoken protest. I shake my head. "Stay in the car. I won't be far. If you need anything, text me or yell. I'll hear you."

"Be careful," I say, trying to be supportive instead of argumentative. "I love you."

"I love you too." He closes the door softly behind him when he exits the vehicle, and I lock the doors.

The harsh glare of unnatural light reflects off the rearview mirror and into my eyes. I reach up and tilt the mirror to redirect the blinding glare. The headlights are likely from the ambulance that Eric said was en route.

Already jumpy, I flinch when the vehicle with the head-lights behind me honks its horn.

"Eric? Megan? Is everything all right? Why are you pulled over?" A familiar voice shouts from the driver's side window.

"Ryan," I mutter to myself, unbuckling my seatbelt. "I better get out and tell him we're fine. Otherwise, he'll honk again or get out of his van and come over here."

"Is everything OK? I thought you guys were in Harmony Hills tonight," Ryan says, lowering his window as I approach his van.

"We were on our way home, and Eric had to stop to visit someone about something." I gesture vaguely to the houses around me, implying he could be in any of them, not neces-sarily the Feeney's house. "Work stuff." I shrug.

"Does it have to do with Saxon's murder? Is there a break in the case?" Ryan asks.

I tilt my head and scrunch up my mouth. "Maybe," I divulge. "I don't know the details." I resist the urge to tell Ryan how the squirrel he just rescued from my chimney, and his after-hours house call might have helped to crack the case wide open. "But it could be another dead-end."

"Hopefully, it's the real deal, and we can put Saxon's murder behind us," Ryan says, then he tells me he safely removed the squirrel from my chimney. Ryan suspects the critter chewed through the mesh chimney cap his dad installed several years ago—the last time a squirrel tried to set up house in the chimney. "Weather permitting, I'll come by in the next few days and install a new mesh cap. In the mean-time, keep the flue closed."

"Thanks, Ryan," I say. "I know you're super busy, so I appreciate you fitting my squirrel into your schedule."

"That's what family is for," Ryan reminds me with a wink.

"I hear you're looking to hire a helper."

"I am," he confirms. "Do you know someone?" he asks with a chuckle.

"Maybe," I reply. "No promises, but I might know a guy. He's a trained locksmith, does basic plumbing, seems to know his way around an engine, and has experience repairing holes in drywall. Give me a few days to find out if he's available. I heard he might be planning to move." By move, I mean go to jail.

Ryan's eyebrows shoot up with interest. "Wow, he sounds great! It's more difficult to find the right person than you'd think," Ryan explains. "Most experienced handymen work for themselves. Less experienced workers need training and supervising, and I don't have time for that right now. If you know someone who would fit the bill, I'd be grateful if you'd give them my contact information."

"Leave it with me," I say.

Ryan smiles, then raises his window, and waves as he pulls away from the curb.

I wrap my arms around myself and shiver. I regret not taking my coat when I left the car. I jog back to the car, and jump inside, turning on the engine and turning up the heat to its highest setting.

Eric: Ryan just drove past the Feeney house. Did he see you?

Me: Yes. He pulled up behind the car and honked. I got out and spoke with him. I'm back in the car now.

Eric: Lock the doors and please stay in the car.

Me: thumbs-up emoji

Still shivering, I reach into the dark backseat for my coat. Instead of my puffy down-filled parka, I feel... hair? Stubble? Skin?

"Hello?" I whisper, my heart pounding so hard I can feel it in my ears.

"Don't scream, Megan."

"Pete?" I ask barely above a whisper.

"Don't scream," he instructs again. "I didn't mean to scare you."

"It's OK, I'm not scared." I'm terrified, but under the circumstances, it's best if we both remain calm. "What are you doing here? How did you get in the backseat?"

My phone is in my hand. I could unlock the screen and phone Eric in less than five seconds, but the glare of the screen would light up the interior of the car, and Pete would know I'm using my phone. Think, Megan, think!

"I was under the Henderson's giant evergreen tree. When you went to talk to Ryan, I waited until you were both distracted, then I hid under the glare of his headlights, army-crawled across the sidewalk, and snuck into the backseat. Thank goodness you left the car unlocked."

"Thank goodness," I agree. Why didn't I lock the car? Argh!!

"I was going to my parents' house," he admits, "but I can't get near it because there are police everywhere."

I can't help but think an innocent person would be concerned about a police tactical unit surrounding their elderly parents' home. If it were me, I'd want proof that my parents were OK. I'd ask if they are injured or in danger. I'd create a dramatic scene and demand answers. Pete isn't doing any of those things because Pete knows the police are here for him. I'll pretend not to know they're looking for him.

"Eric told me to pull over here," I explain. "He said he'll be right back. Something about picking something up for work. He said nothing about you or your parents."

I shouldn't feel guilty about lying, but I do. This is the second time today I've lied to Pete. He lied to me first, but two wrongs don't make a right.

"What did you say to my mother at the restaurant?" Pete asks.

I shrug. "We talked about knitting and squirrels," I reply

honestly. "She showed me photos of the sweater she's knitting for your nephew. It was a pleasant and short conversation. Why? Did your mother tell you something different?"

If Eric shows up while Pete is in the backseat, it could get ugly. Pete could take me hostage. Maybe I'm already a hostage. Am I a hostage? Pete hasn't told me I *can't* leave, but I don't feel like I *can* leave, if that makes sense. Is he armed? It doesn't matter; he's bigger and stronger than me. If there was a struggle, I'd do everything in my power to escape. I'm sure I'd put up a better fight than Pete would expect, but in the end I'd lose. Physical strength will not save me from this situation. I need to make sure Eric doesn't come back to the car.

"No, she said the same thing," Pete replies cautiously.

"Pete, do you want me to drive you to your parents' house?"

"No!" he shouts. "Megan, do not start the car. Do you understand?"

"Totally," I say, covertly sliding my phone under my leg. I'm worried if it makes a sound or lights up, Pete will see it and take it.

"Turn off the car. Disengage the engine," he orders.

"OK," I say, disengaging the engine. "Can I please have my coat? It's in the back seat with you. With the heat off, it'll get very cold very quickly."

Pete heaves my coat over the centre console, and I cover my upper body with it as if it were a blanket. Hiding my hands underneath my coat-blanket, I press and hold the side button and the volume button simultaneously on my iPhone. Adam showed Hannah and I how to do this in case we ever need to discreetly call emergency services. Besides calling 9-1-1, it will send a text to my emergency contacts letting them know I'm in trouble and telling them my location. My emergency contacts are Eric and April.

"Thank you," I say to Pete.

Under the guise of adjusting my coat-blanket, I look down

at my phone and ensure it's connected to 9-1-1. It is. Without looking, I slide the silent switch on the side of the phone to prevent the phone from making any notification sounds that would remind Pete my phone is here. I grip the phone tightly in my hand, like a lifeline.

"Where's your truck?" I ask, assuming it wasn't under the Henderson's giant evergreen tree with him.

"Why?" he snaps.

"Just curious," I assure him. "Making conversation."

"I didn't mean to snap, I'm sorry. I'm stressed."

"Stressed about what?" I ask.

"Lots of stuff," Pete replies.

"I'd feel stressed too if the police were surrounding my parents' house," I sympathize. "Are your parents OK? Did something happen?" I ask, feigning ignorance.

"The police think I killed Saxon Renaud," he blurts out. "I'm sure they're raiding every place they think I might go to."

I turn my head and crane my neck to look at him in the back seat. It's dark because we're parked between streetlights, but Pete is lying on the floor. His body is crumpled and bent to squeeze his tall, muscular frame into the too-small space. He must be uncomfortable. Looking at his unnaturally contorted body, I get the urge to straighten my spine.

"Are the police right? Did you kill Saxon?"

CHAPTER 32

I SLIDE my coat-blanket farther down my body to ensure the microphone on my phone picks up his response.

"I didn't kill him on purpose. It was an accident," Pete confesses. "I'm not a killer." He pauses, then adds quietly, "Well, I guess I am a killer, but that's not who I am. It was a one-off. A blip. I'm a firefighter. I save lives, I don't end them."

Out of the corner of my eye, the lower branches of the Henderson's giant evergreen jostle briefly, then stop. Not in a windy way, but in a someone-else-found-Pete's-hiding-spot way. I take a deep breath, feeling slightly more relaxed, knowing help is only metres away. Or maybe it's the squirrel from my chimney taking refuge in the tree's thick branches for the night, who knows, but I choose to believe it's an armed cop.

"Heavy shoulders, long arms," I mumble. "Deep breath, Megan."

"What did you say?" Pete demands urgently. "Who are you talking to?"

"Myself," I reply. Then I explain about my heavy shoulders, long arms mantra, and we do it together a few times.

"Pete, tell me what happened last Thursday night. How did Saxon die?"

"It started long before Thursday night," he says with a sarcastic chuckle. "It started weeks ago when Saxon asked me if I'd be willing to help him sell his properties when he won the election."

"What did you say?" I probe.

"I said yes," Pete replies. "I never thought I'd have to do it. I didn't think he could win. How could the most hated man in town get elected mayor?"

"I hear you," I agree. "But he was so confident. He was convinced he'd win the election and reverse the big-box policy."

"There was a reason for his confidence," Pete informs me. "He had a plan to fix the election."

"How?" I ask.

"One of his shady creditors hooked him up with a counterfeiter who could make fake ballots. Saxon filled them in, voting for himself on most of them to ensure he'd win the election."

"Did he say which creditor hooked him up?" I ask, hoping it's not Jay Singh.

"Some woman in the city," Pete replies, much to my relief. "Saxon said her and the daughter manage the lending side of the business, and the sons manage the collections side. He was terrified of the sons."

"I see," I respond. "How did Saxon pay the counterfeiter? It's common knowledge that he was in a bad way financially."

"He sold everything he could," Pete explains. "His furniture, family heirlooms, electronics, even his car."

This explains the decrepit living situation I saw at Saxon's house when Rick and I rescued Clawdia.

"His plan to fix the election didn't work," I conclude. "Saxon didn't win the election."

"He planned to hire the shady lender's sons to swap out the ballots on election night, but they wouldn't do it without a substantial down payment upfront. He couldn't afford to pay them. That's where I came in."

"Came in how?" I ask.

"Saxon wanted me to start a fire at the town hall while the ballots were being counted. A small fire. Then, when the ballot-counters exited the building, he wanted me to use my mother's keys to sneak into the room where the ballots were being counted and swap the fake ballots with the real ones."

"He wanted to take advantage of your expertise as a firefighter, and your access as the mayor's son," I sum up.

"Exactly," Pete confirms. "But I wouldn't do it. I don't start fires, I put them out, and I don't fix elections. Anyway, I would've done time for either of those crimes."

He'd rather do time for murder than arson and election tampering? Baffling.

"Saxon must've become more desperate as the election got closer," I add, trying to move the conversation forward.

"He harassed me right up until election day. He kept reminding me that if he didn't win, I'd lose out on the commissions from selling his properties. He even had developers contact me to register interest in certain properties."

This explains the notes Pete wrote on the printouts of Saxon's properties.

"Those commissions would have been a lot of money, Pete. Weren't you tempted?"

"No, I wasn't," he insists emphatically, as though the suggestion offends him. "So, after the card game, he changed tactics and came at me from a different angle."

"Tell me about the card game," I say. "If you were the focus of Saxon's attention that night, why did he swap drinks with Ryan? Did Saxon trick Ryan into almost relapsing for his own amusement, or was there another reason?"

"The trick with the lime was a distraction, so Saxon could

get me alone. The polls were about to close, and it was now or never for Saxon to implement his ridiculous plan. When Rick backed out of the game to help Trudy with Cat Benetar, Saxon saw an opportunity and seized it. He was desperate, he had nothing to lose. Saxon hoped that after Ryan took a sip of the alcoholic drink, he would rush off to a twelve-step meeting somewhere.

"Sheamus hates to play with less than five players, so the game would end early, and the rest of us would go our separate ways. Saxon could use that opportunity to ask me to drive him home, so he could get me alone. But that didn't happen. First there was a shoving match, then Ryan took off. We were scared Ryan might go somewhere and drink, so instead of going our separate ways, we each picked a direction and searched for him."

I doubt it will make Ryan feel better about what happened when he learns that he was collateral damage in Saxon's larger, twisted plot, but at least he'll have answers as to why Saxon pulled such a nasty stunt.

"Saxon didn't have a car," I point out. "It was snowing hard, and he wasn't dressed for the weather. He must've asked one of you for a lift."

"He was crouched next to my truck when I got there, hiding in the dark. He warned me to let him in or else," Pete admits. "After all, getting me alone so he could blackmail me was the reason he came to the card game."

"He blackmailed you?" Did Saxon Renaud's villainy have any limits? "With what?"

"With proof that I was working with him to reverse the big-box policy and invite huge retailers and restaurants to Harmony Lake.

"But you weren't, right?" I specify.

"Not actively," Pete elaborates. "But I had spoken with representatives from those companies, and Saxon and I had virtual meetings about it. Meetings he said he recorded."

"Those meetings would make Saxon look as guilty as you," I say.

"But Saxon had nothing to lose and didn't care what people thought of him. I have a life here. I have friends and family. If my parents thought I was involved in a scheme to destroy the town they dedicated their lives to serving, it would kill them."

"So, you killed Saxon to prevent him from exposing your role in his plan?" I clarify.

"Megan, he picked up his phone and threatened to call my mother," Pete discloses. "That phone call would have been like a nail in her coffin. It would have killed her. I didn't know what to do. I panicked. I drove around for a while, trying to talk him down, but he wouldn't hear it. Finally, I found a poorly lit side street and pulled over. Then I grabbed Saxon by the collar and dragged him out of my truck. I reached back into the truck and grabbed his stupid umbrella. I was going to drive off, leaving him and his umbrella on the side of the road. But he said if I didn't switch those ballots immediately, he would phone my mother, then post everything on social media for the entire town to see."

"What did you do?" I ask.

"I grabbed that stupid umbrella with both hands and used it to pin him against my truck by the throat."

I gasp audibly and bring my hand to my throat, which suddenly feels quite dry and constricted. "Oh, Pete."

"It was surreal. Time sped up and slowed down simultaneously. It felt like I watched his eyes for hours, waiting for the life to drain out of them. Yet, it also felt like he was gone seconds after I pinned him by the throat." Pete sits up and looks at me, placing his hand on the console between the front and back seats. "I didn't realize I was killing him. Believe me, Megan, it wasn't until I looked down and saw Saxon's feet dangling above the ground that I realized how much strength I used. And by then it was too late."

"I believe you," I assure him, gently placing my hand on top of his. I'm not sure how much of Pete's story I believe, but if he's capable of strangling a grown man with almost his bare hands, I want him to think I'm sympathetic and on his side. "Why did you take him to Lake Access Road in Adam's car? And how did you get Adam's keys?"

"I didn't plan any of this," Pete attests. "When I realized Saxon was dead, I knew I had to get rid of his body. I thought I could make it look like an accident. Visibility was awful that night because of the blizzard, and it would be easy for a driver to lose traction in the snow and accidentally veer off the road. I wasn't wearing my gloves, and my hands were cold. I lowered Saxon to the ground and leaned him against the tire of the truck. It looked like he was sitting. He didn't look dead. I shoved my hands in my coat pockets to get my gloves, and found two things, my cell phone, which I turned off, and Adam's keys. I don't know how Adam's keys got there. I suspect they fell out of his coat pocket when the coats fell on the floor during the shoving match. When Sheamus and I picked up the mess, Sheamus must've picked up Adam's keys and put them in the wrong coat. Our coats are almost identical, except Adam's is dark blue and mine is black."

This makes sense, and Adam's keys getting lost in the commotion is one theory Eric, Adam, and I considered from the beginning.

"So, when you saw the keys, you saw an opportunity to frame someone else for Saxon's murder?" I speculate.

"No," Pete shakes his head. "It wasn't like that. I wasn't thinking that far ahead. My pickup truck is big. I'm a muscular guy, but it wouldn't be easy to hoist Saxon's dead body into the back of my truck. Or into the front. My truck is just too high off the ground. Besides, I couldn't bear the thought of driving with a corpse in the passenger seat."

"Adam's car was more efficient, and less likely to injure

your back," I say, finding it harder and harder to disguise my contempt.

"Pretty much," Pete responds, shrugging. "So, I shoved Saxon's body in a snowbank and used the shovel I keep in my truck to make sure the snow completely covered him. Then I turned my phone on and drove to my parent's place and parked in their driveway. I set my phone to silent and left it in my truck. Then I walked to Sheamus's house, hoping Adam's car would still be there."

This all sounds very premeditated for something that Pete insists he didn't plan. Remembering to turn off your cell phone so your whereabouts can't be traced, then turning it on again when it can give you an alibi, doesn't sound like the actions of someone in shock because they just spontaneously committed murder.

"You recovered Saxon and his umbrella from the snowbank and put him in Adam's trunk," I suggest.

"How did you know that?" Pete asks, looking confused.

"There was forensic evidence that Saxon was in the trunk," I reply.

Pete shakes his head. "I didn't think to clean the trunk. I only cleaned the parts of the car that I touched."

"You did a good job," I tell him. "They found none of your DNA or fingerprints in the car."

The corners of Pete's mouth quirk downward smugly, as if he's pleased to hear he did a good job eliminating the evidence.

"I took back roads to and from Lake Access Road, so no one would see me driving around in Adam's car."

"Smart." I almost choke on the compliment but force it out, anyway.

"I was going to leave his umbrella with him, but when I used it to pin him against the truck, I wasn't wearing gloves. I'm sure it would've led the police straight to me. I put the umbrella in the trunk, so if I got pulled over or something, it wouldn't be visible. Thank goodness I did that, because if I didn't, I wouldn't have noticed that one of Saxon's shoes came off when I lifted him out of the trunk and was still there."

Pete must've taken the umbrella and penny loafer out of Adam's trunk in my driveway, and that's when the lucky penny fell out of the penny loafer and onto the bumper of the car.

"Why did you call the tip line after you abandoned Saxon's body?" I ask. "If you hadn't called, he probably wouldn't have been found until spring. By then, any evidence on his body probably would've been destroyed by the elements."

"I didn't want an innocent person, or even a kid, to find the body. And I knew without a body Saxon wouldn't be declared dead right away, he'd only be a missing person. His estate would be in limbo. His executors will need to sell his properties to pay off his debts. I didn't want to delay that."

It's more likely Pete was hoping to be the real estate agent who would sell Saxon's properties and didn't want to delay his commission payments.

"And the stutter you pretended to have when you called the tip line was to frame Rick Ransan for Saxon's murder?" I hypothesize.

"Look, Rick would be a suspect anyway because he and Saxon spent so much time together, and everyone knows Saxon bullied him. The stutter was less about pointing the finger at Rick and more about leading the police away from me."

"Why did you leave Adam's car at my house?" I ask. "You could've left it anywhere."

"Do you want the honest answer?" Pete asks.

Of course, I want the honest answer! Hasn't he been honest so far?

"Yes." I nod.

"I was tired," he confesses. "The whole experience left me physically and emotionally exhausted. You live around the corner from my parents' house. It's a short walk from your house to theirs. Also, I know how much Adam loves his car, and I knew he would freak out when it wasn't where he left it the night before." Pete shrugs. "I figured you'd find it when you woke up, and Adam's panic would be short-lived."

"Adam's car has a sophisticated GPS tracking system. His panic would've been short-lived, anyway."

Even in the dimly lit interior of the car, I see Pete's jaw drop, and his eyes widen with worry.

"Then why didn't he use it to track me down that night?" Pete asks.

"His phone died," I reply. "He drained the battery using the flashlight on his phone to search through the snow for his missing keys."

"That was lucky," Pete says.

"So, you walked from my house to your parents' house and disturbed your parents, so they could verify your alibi?" I presume. "Did you actually remove a squirrel from their chimney?"

"I walked from your house to my parents' house and got my phone out of my truck. I missed a group text from Archie telling us we could stop searching because Ryan was safe. I responded and told them I was glad Ryan was OK, and that I already abandoned the search because my parents were having a critter crisis." He shrugs. "It wasn't a lie. I did abandon the search, and my parents did have a critter crisis." He pauses briefly, then adds, "I really removed the squirrel. You can ask my mother, she saw it."

"When you shoved Saxon's umbrella up your parents' chimney, did you lie to them about the cracked firebox to make sure they wouldn't open the flue to start a cozy fire and watch the umbrella fall into the fireplace?"

"I shoved the umbrella and penny loafer up there first,

then I shoved a pillow up there last, so if someone opened the flue, nothing would fall out," Pete replies matter-of-factly. "How did you figure out that's where I hid the umbrella and shoe?"

The missing umbrella and penny loafer were holdbacks. Only the killer or someone with intimate knowledge of the crime would know about them. Same for Saxon's cause of death. Everyone believes he was run down by Adam's car. They don't know he was already dead when the car ran over him.

"I didn't mention the shoe, you did," I inform him. "Mayor Feeney said you found a hairline crack in the firebox when you removed the squirrel. She said that she and your dad looked for it but couldn't see it." Should I make him feel guilty for lying to his parents? He seems to have more remorse about how all of this affects them, than about taking a fellow human's life. "She blamed it on their ageing eyesight, you know. She trusts you so much that it didn't occur to her you might be lying or mistaken about the crack."

"This will break her heart, Megan. You can't tell her."

"I won't," I assure him. "The police will. They even have an ambulance on standby in case your parents need medical assistance when they find out."

"It'll be your word against mine," Pete warns.

"No, it won't." I shake my head. "My phone has been connected to 9-1-1 the entire time we've been talking."

I hope it's connected to 9-1-1. I was so caught up in Pete's confession, that I haven't checked it in a while. I can't check it now, because I sense that Pete might attack if I dare move a muscle. He has nothing left to lose, he's desperate, and desperate people do desperate things.

"You're bluffing," he challenges. His eyes narrow, and his jaw muscles clench and unclench.

"Why do you think Eric didn't come back to the car?" I

ask, hoping it's because he's been listening to our conversation remotely.

"Hand me your phone, Megan," Pete commands.

"Pete, I'm getting out of the car now."

Slowly, and without breaking eye contact with him, I move my hand out from under my coat-blanket so I can open the door.

Sensing that Pete is about to lurch forward, I brace myself and swallow hard. Suddenly, his chest and forehead light up with half a dozen tiny red dots. We notice them at the same time and look at his chest. Aim points. There are at least half-dozen guns aimed at him.

"They're on your forehead too," I whisper. "Are they on my forehead?"

Slightly unnerved at the thought of so many guns in such close proximity to me, I glance down and scan my own chest for tiny red dots. Nothing. Phew.

Pete swallows loudly and shakes his head. "No dots on your head." He raises his hands to his shoulders, palms out, in a surrender gesture. In the dim light of night, beads of sweat glisten across his brow. "Tell them not to shoot," he pleads.

Without taking my eyes off him, I slowly reach for the door handle, planning to step out of the vehicle slowly and carefully while keeping an eye on Pete. I don't know what I'll do after that, but running toward the Henderson's giant evergreen and taking shelter behind its thick trunk and dense branches is a possibility. So far, so good. Gently, I tug the handle and unlatch the door. It immediately flies open, and hands grab me by the arm and waist, yanking me out of the car.

CHAPTER 33

I CAN'T TELL if I'm walking or being swept along, but it feels like I'm calmly floating through the chaos.

The loud, frenzied scene outside the car is a stark contrast to the dark, quiet scene inside the car. A cacophony of voices, crackling radios, flashing lights, and out-of-sync boots thudding on the ground are almost loud enough to compete with the sound of my heart pounding throughout my entire body.

The officer's left arm is around my waist, and my right wrist is in his right hand. He says reassuring, comforting things, but I'm too overstimulated to process his words and respond.

Behind us, the commotion grows louder, even though we're moving farther away from it. I turn my head, but everything is a blur because we're moving too fast. The scuffling intensifies, and desperate to see what's happening, I try to break free from my unchosen chaperone. He contains me, but not before I glimpse a pile of officers cuffing and searching Pete Feeney, who is face down on the frozen asphalt.

His parents must know by now that something is happening. His poor parents! I hope someone is with them. I hope they're OK.

We continue moving forward while I crane my neck and struggle to look back.

"You're OK, Megan. You're safe now."

"Officer Butler?" I snap my head to the right.

"Call me Lucas." He halts abruptly, then helps me stop when I keep going forward because of the momentum we built up. "Everything about that was amazing. You have mad interrogation skills."

"Thank you?" I respond, hoping it was a compliment.

Lucas's enthusiasm for Pete's arrest is palpable. He's so proud and excited. I remind myself he's a rookie, and this might be his first time attending the takedown of a murder suspect.

"I've never heard a live interrogation before." Lucas shakes his head. "The way he just opened up and told you everything... The way you encouraged him to keep talking... How did you stay so calm? It was sick!"

The English language has evolved a lot in my lifetime, and I'm fairly confident the young people have redefined "sick" as a good thing. I've heard my daughter use it with friends and in social media posts. But to be sure, I better ask.

"Is 'sick' good or bad?"

"It's *good*," Lucas confirms. "It's like saying something is cool or groovy."

"Right," I acknowledge. "Thank you for pulling me from the car, Lucas. You were great." I smile.

In our previous conversation, Lucas hinted he hasn't attended many crime scenes. I want to assure him he's doing a good job.

"The chief trusted me to take care of you, and I won't let him down," he says proudly.

He guides me to a gurney, and I realize we're standing next to an ambulance. Lucas positions me in front of the gurney and applies gentle pressure to my shoulder encouraging me to sit down.

He's so young; everything about him is youthful and full of potential. He reminds me of my daughter, idealistic and determined to make the world a better place. Lucas is only three or four years older than Hannah—too young to be taking down cold-blooded murderers and seeing the worst humanity has to offer. Something about him triggers my maternal instincts. I want to ask him if he's cold and suggest he put on his gloves, and I want to make sure he had dinner, but I don't. I resist my maternal urges.

Lucas moves aside, and an EMT swoops in, fussing over me and asking me questions about my breathing, chest pain, and any injuries I might have.

"I'm fine," I assure her. "Honestly. If anything changes, I promise to seek medical attention."

"Humour me and let me check your vitals, please." She has a calming presence and a pleasant bedside manner.

She's doing her job, and I don't want to be difficult. So, I sit still, answering questions when asked, and cooperating when she tells me to take a deep breath, then let it out. I zone out, watching the red gauge wiggle back and forth on the blood pressure cuff, my mind spinning with everything Pete told me in the car.

"Megpie! Over here!"

The sound of my best friend's voice brings me back to the present.

"Thank you," I say when the EMT releases me from the cuff.

I jump off the gurney and race toward April with my arms open.

"Where are you going?" Lucas calls after me. "Megan! Hold up!" His boots thump behind me when he gives chase.

April is standing behind a barricade; she's too far away.

We wrap our arms around each other tightly, squeezing the barricade between us.

"I'm so happy to see you," I say, tearing up. "What are you doing here?"

"Your phone sent me a text with your location when you called 9-1-1," she explains. "What the heck happened? Why were you sitting on a gurney?" She pulls away and grips my shoulders. She scans me from head to toe, then back again, looking for injuries.

"I'm fine," I assure her. "They're being overly cautious."

April and I move to the end of the barricade, away from the crowd. Lucas moves with us, staying a few feet behind me. I can't see him, but I can sense his hovering.

Whispering in her ear, I give April the abridged version of everything that happened tonight, starting with the conversation Mayor Feeney and I had at the restaurant.

"Wow. I'm speechless," April says when I finish filling her in. "Thank goodness you're OK." She hugs me tightly and rubs my back. "You're shivering. Where's your coat?" she asks.

"Backseat of Eric's car," I reply. "I feel and see myself shivering, but physically, I don't feel cold." Actually, I feel kind of warm, like I was running or something.

"Adrenaline," April diagnoses. "When it wears off, you'll feel cold. Let's go over to the ambulance and borrow a blanket, then we'll ask if you can have your coat."

April's impossibly long legs step gracefully over the barricade.

"Ma'am, you can't do that. Get back behind the barricade. That's why it's there." The officer points from April to the barricade, like he's ordering a rebellious teenager to her room.

"She's fine, she's allowed to be here," Eric says, jogging toward us, taking off his coat. "There you are. I told Butler to keep you at the ambulance," he says, draping his coat over my shoulders.

"It's not Lucas's fault," I defend the rookie, shaking my head. "I ignored him and ran away." Eric wraps his arms around me and kisses the top of my head. "Lucas did a great job."

He tells me he loves me under his breath. Three times. His hug grows progressively tighter until I have to gasp for air.

"Sorry," he says, letting go and taking a step back to appraise me from head to toe like April did.

The EMT should hand out stickers that say NOT INJURED, so I can stop insisting I'm fine; it would save time.

"I'm not hurt," I assure him.

"I know," Eric says, "If you were, Pete Feeney would be full of bullet holes."

"You're trembling," he observes, drawing his eyebrows together. "Are you cold, or is it adrenaline?"

I nod, because at this point, I'm not sure.

April taps my shoulder. "Megastar, if you need me, I'll be over here." She jerks her thumb over her shoulder. "My phone is blowing up. Everyone is worried, and I need to let them know what's happening."

"Thank you," I respond. "You're the best. Tell them I'm not ignoring them. I left my phone in the car." It fell out of my hand when Lucas yanked me, but I don't say this out loud because he's within earshot, and I don't want him to feel bad.

"Butler," Eric calls the rookie, and he rushes over. "Can you please retrieve Megan's coat and phone from my car? Thank you." He smiles.

Eric takes me by the hand and leads me between two houses. It's pitch black, and we're standing in about a foot of snow. He hugs me again, but his body is more relaxed this time. His heart rate is slower, and he doesn't try to squeeze the air out of my lungs.

I pull away first this time. "It's all on tape, right? The entire 9-1-1 call was recorded? It's a good confession?"

I don't mean good as in well done or critically acclaimed. Eric distinguishes between good and bad evidence. Good evidence is evidence that will hold up in court. Bad evidence isn't admissible but helps the investigation along and usually leads to good evidence.

"It's a beautiful confession." He smiles. "It's so good, a couple of cops want the transcript to study it."

"Consider the confession part of your anniversary gift," I tease smugly.

"As great as the confession is, an even better gift would be not almost having a heart attack when your phone texted me to tell me you were in trouble, then a 9-1-1 dispatcher calling me so I could listen to you and Pete."

"I'm sorry you were scared."

"I was terrified, babe." He exhales loudly, and his eyes fill with moisture that twinkles in the moonlight. "I feel like I aged ten years in the fifteen minutes you were in the car with him."

"I didn't know what else to do," I confess. "I was afraid if you or someone else approached the car, it might push him over the edge. I felt like I could manage the situation if it was just me and him."

"You did the right thing," Eric insists. "And we had the car surrounded immediately. Pete wouldn't have been able to hurt you if he tried." I nod. "Trust me, if he tried, he would be dead. It took all my willpower not to get you out of there."

"I half-expected you would," I admit. "Why didn't you?"

"Three reasons. First, we didn't know if Pete was armed. Second, I had faith you would save yourself. It's one of your superpowers. Third, I knew he'd confess for you. You have a way of getting people to talk. If I had burst in there before Pete confessed, you might have never talked to me again."

He's right. As soon as Pete started talking, I had a feeling he would confess, and if Eric stormed in and prevented the confession, neither of us would be happy.

"Was Pete armed?" I ask.

He shakes his head. "No, thank goodness."

Eric's phone dings. "Butler. He has your coat and your

phone." I nod again, and my teeth chatter. "Are you starting to feel cold?"

"Uh-huh," I reply, thinking about how nice the heated seats in the car will feel.

"The adrenaline is wearing off. Let's get your stuff and get you home. I started the car, so it'll be nice and toasty." Eric takes my hand and leads us back into public view. "We'll take your statement tomorrow."

"April can drive me home," I suggest.

"I'll drive you," Eric responds. "April can meet us there. She can stay with you while I come back to talk to Mayor and Mr. Feeney."

"How are they?" I ask. "Do they know Pete killed Saxon?"

"I'm not sure," he replies. "Two of their children are with them, and their daughter is worried about Mr. Feeney's heart. She asked us to wait and talk to them with medical assistance nearby. Obviously, we're honouring that request. Now that the medics have checked you and Pete, we'll send them to the Feeney house, and I'll meet them there."

"I can come with you," I offer. "If you think it would help."

"It would help if you were safe and sound at home."

"I bet this will be our most memorable anniversary ever," I point out.

"I hope so," Eric responds. "I don't think my heart can handle an anniversary more exciting than this one."

CHAPTER 34

WEDNESDAY, March 3rd

It's unseasonably warm for early March, and the cloudless, sunny sky makes it feel downright spring-like. Spring doesn't officially arrive for two more weeks, but today Mother Nature is teasing us with a sneak peek of the warm days ahead.

To take advantage of the unseasonably warm day, we walked to Harmony Lake Town Hall this morning to attend Mayor Feeney's community spirit award ceremony.

The community spirit award is one of our town's highest honours and recognizes the contribution Mayor Feeney has made to the quality of life and community spirit of Harmony Lake.

It was a lovely celebration, with several residents sharing funny and touching anecdotes about her and paying tribute to her long history of civic pride and contributions to our community.

Besides a plaque, Mayor Feeney's name will be engraved on the wall of fame at the town hall alongside the previous award winners, and the town council voted to rename the waterfront playground, Alice Feeney Park.

Most of the businesses on Water Street closed, so the owners and employees could attend the ceremony. A group of us are heading back to our respective businesses, walking as leisurely as possible to maximize our time outside.

"Mayor and Mr. Feeney seemed in good spirits," April comments. "It's nice to see them out and about again and not worried that the media will ambush them."

"I know," I agree. "It almost feels like the town is back to normal."

The story about Saxon Renaud's murder, his attempt to fix the election, and Pete's arrest was picked up by a regional news outlet. They spun it like some kind of Murder She Wrote, small-town mystery, and it drew attention from other media outlets who wanted to report the story.

Pete agreed to accept a plea deal and avoid a long, drawn out trial when his siblings convinced him that the unwanted attention and stress of a trial would harm their parents' health.

In exchange for some concessions in his plea deal, Pete provided information that helped Eric track down the shady lender who hooked up Saxon with the counterfeiter. The lender was more than happy to point Eric toward the counterfeiter, for Eric not tipping off her local police department about her quasi-legal lending operation.

"Bon voyage," April says as we pass Artsy Tartsy, and she and Tamara stop to go inside.

"I'll text you," I promise, then hug them because this is the last time I'll see them until Eric and I get home from Las Vegas.

"I spoke with Phillip and gave him a key," Eric says. "He said he's fine to let the cabinet makers in and out of the house while we're away."

"Great," I say, taking his hand. "Thank you for looking after that."

The guest room renovations are underway, and by the

time we get home next week, Eric should have a fully functioning home office.

"Are we property owners yet?" Connie asks as she unlocks the door at Knitorious.

"I don't think so," I reply. "Adam said we probably won't hear anything for a couple of weeks."

"It's so exciting!" Connie says. "I hope they accept our offer."

After Saxon's murder was solved, and Adam and Ryan's names were cleared, Adam and I called a family meeting and told everyone about his idea to purchase a few of Saxon's properties. We showed everyone our research and our projections. There was more interest than we expected, and now me, Eric, Adam, Connie, Archie, Ryan, April, and Tamara have formed a property management company called Oppidum Group. Oppidum is Latin for *small town*. We submitted an offer on a few properties, and Saxon's estate is considering it. Some members of our corporation are more impatient than others.

"Hey, Soph! Did you miss us?" I crouch down and rub her. She's not used to being alone at the store during the day. I felt guilty leaving her here, but the only dogs allowed at the town hall are service dogs.

"I'm going to change out of this suit and get my luggage," Eric says. "I'll be down in a few minutes. We need to leave by noon if we're going to get to Toronto in time for dinner with Hannah."

"My luggage is already in the car." I smile.

One of the few downsides to living in a remote town is the five-hour drive to the airport. Our flight to Vegas is tomorrow, but we're driving to Toronto today and staying in a hotel tonight. Having dinner with Hannah the night before we leave, and the night we get back, is a bonus.

Sophie goes into greeter mode when the bell over the door jingles.

"Hey, Rick! How are you?"

"I'm good, Megan. How are you?" He greets Sophie then walks over to the counter.

"I take it you aren't here to buy yarn?" Connie jokes.

"No, but I have a question about knitting," he replies.

"I'm intrigued," I say. "What can I help you with?"

"Clawdia loves the knitted mice you made for her. Especially the one filled with catnip. I want to get a few more, but they're sold out at the Animal Centre. Do you sell them here?"

"I don't," I reply. "But I have ten hours' worth of car rides and ten hours' worth of flights in the next week, and I'm sure I can use that time to make a few more mice for Clawdia," I offer.

"That would be great! Thank you," Rick responds. "I'll pay you for them, of course."

"No, you won't," I correct him. "If you want to pay it forward, make a donation to the Animal Centre."

"I can do that," Rick says. "Ryan and I are doing some roof repair work there next week. I'll knock a little off their bill. It's the least I can do after you set me up with Ryan."

The Charity Knitting Guild's cat toy drive was an enormous success. Between in-person sales at the gift shop, and on-line sales through their website, they sold out of toys within a week. I think the charity knitters are planning toy drives regularly. I've already started knitting mice for the next one.

Rick and Ryan work together now. I suggested it to both of them as soon as Rick was cleared as a suspect in Saxon's murder. They have complementary skill sets, and Ryan was exhausted from all the hours he was working. For the first month, Rick was Ryan's employee, but then they became partners. Instead of calling themselves, The Wright Men For The Job, which was the name of the company when Archie and Ryan worked together, they're now called, R & R Handymen. They're tagline is: We repair & renovate while you rest & relax.

Ryan is working normal hours and taking two days off each week. He and his partner, Lin, could book a last-minute getaway a few weeks ago and spend some time together enjoying the sun and the beach. Rick is more outgoing every time I see him. He's getting to know people in the community, and they're getting to know him. He started seeing a speech therapist, and I can't remember the last time I heard him stutter.

Rick opens the door to leave and holds it for Sheamus and Kelly, who are on their way in.

"Ya still in for poker tomorrow night, fella?" Sheamus asks Rick.

"Wouldn't miss it," Rick replies, then says goodbye to everyone and leaves.

"Why, Sheamus O'Brien, I don't think we've ever had the honour of your presence at Knitorious," Connie declares.

I think she's right. I can't remember Sheamus ever being here.

"Well, my girlfriend's a knitter, so you might wanna get used to me stopping by," he retorts proudly.

"Kelly, I'm glad you're here. I want to show you the hat I made with the alpaca yarn you gave me." I rummage around under the counter and pull out the hat.

"It's beautiful," Kelly compliments. "What do you think of the yarn? Did you like it?"

"I loved it," I reply. "I gave half of each skein to Connie, so she could take it for a test drive too."

"And?" Kelly asks anxiously, looking at Connie.

"It might be the nicest bulky alpaca I've ever had the pleasure to knit with," Connie says.

Kelly claps her hands in front of her chin. "I can't wait to phone my uncle's wife and give her your feedback. She'll be so happy." I wonder if she'll be as happy as Kelly appears to be.

I'm not sure if it's the positive yarn review or Sheamus that's making Kelly downright giddy. I don't care, it's just nice to see her thrive again.

"When you talk to her, tell her I would be honoured if Knitorious was the first yarn store to carry her line of alpaca yarn."

"Really?" Kelly asks, wide-eyed and grinning. "Thank you, hun! I'll phone her as soon as I get back to the salon!"

The bell above the door jingles, and Jess and Sophie make a beeline for each other. Jess loves dogs, but two of her kids have allergies, so she hasn't had a pet since she was a child. Adam is taking Sophie home with him tonight, and Jess can't wait to pretend she has a dog. From the look of it, Sophie can't wait either.

"Hey, fella, I thought you were still schmoozing and being all political at the town hall," Sheamus says to Adam.

"I've completed my mayoral duties for today," Adam says. "After lunch, I have to put in a few hours at my law practice."

"I sent you and April a copy of Sophie's schedule," I say to Adam. "Did you get it?"

"It wasn't a schedule, it was a complicated spreadsheet," Adam replies.

At least he looked at it; otherwise, he wouldn't know it's a spreadsheet.

"Do you have questions about it?" I ask. "Sophie is routine driven. She likes to know what to expect and when to expect it."

"The dog will be fine, Meg." I sense frustration in Adam's voice. "You trusted me to take care of our child, remember? And she's still alive."

"Point made," I agree.

"Is Sophie's stuff by the back door?" Adam asks. "I'll put it in the car before I forget."

I nod. "It's piled up on the counter."

"I have a copy of the spreadsheet, too, Megan," Jess reassures me from the sofa in the cozy sitting area. "Don't worry, it's under control."

"Thank you," I mouth to her.

I'm doing a mental inventory of Sophie's stuff to make sure I didn't forget to include anything when Kelly's phone rings.

"It's her!" she declares excitedly. She answers the call, then places it on hold and looks at Sheamus. "I can't wait to tell her what Megan and Connie said about her yarn. I'll just be a minute. I'll step outside."

"Take your time, a ghrá," he says as she walks toward the door, already talking on the phone.

"A ghrá?" I ask, having never heard the word before,

"It's Gaelic," he explains. "It means, my love."

"It sounds beautiful," I respond.

Sheamus joins Jess and Connie in the cozy sitting area, and they ask him to say other terms of endearment in Gaelic.

"Are you ready for your trip, Meg?" Adam asks, returning from the parking lot and leaning on the counter next to me.

I nod. "I'm looking forward to it. Thank you for taking care of Sophie."

"I don't mind," he says, "and look how happy it makes Jess." Adam straightens up and looks toward the back room, smiling.

"Hey, Adam," Eric says, approaching the counter.

"Hey, man. We'll miss you at poker tomorrow night."

"Hello, everyone," Eric smiles at Connie, Jess, Kelly, and Sheamus.

Kelly finished her phone call and came back in when I was talking to Adam.

"Are we ready to go?" I ask, leaning into Eric.

"We can leave whenever. My suitcase is in the car."

"I know Adam and I can't take Sophie home until tonight, but would it be OK if I took her for a walk?" Jess asks.

"Sophie would love that," I reply. "I'll go in the back and get her leash."

"Actually, Meg, I think I put the leash in my car." Adam pulls his keys out of his pocket and hands them to Jess. "It's in the trunk."

"Uh-uh," she protests, giving him back his keys. "No way. I'm not going anywhere near that trunk. It's creepy."

It is creepy. The corpse of a murder victim rode around inside that trunk. I'm not sure I'd go near it either.

The insurance company repaired the damage to Adam's car and had it detailed. He seems just as attached to it as ever, but some of the locals have developed a morbid fascination with it. It's not uncommon for people to ask Adam if they can look inside his trunk or even touch it.

"Come by the station when Megan and I get back. I'll bring out the cadaver dog, and we can see if he signals on your trunk," Eric suggests to Adam.

"Yes!" Adam points to Eric and laughs. "Let's do it. I bet he'll still smell it."

"You two are twisted," I say.

"I'll fetch the dog's leash for ya, Jess," Sheamus offers, probably to escape this macabre conversation.

He takes the keys from Adam and walks toward the back door. As soon as Sheamus crosses the threshold from the store to the back room, Kelly jumps up from the sofa.

"We only have a minute," she declares. "Phones everybody and calendars open."

Not used to Kelly being this demanding, we do as we're told.

"Why do we need our calendars?" Connie asks.

"I'm planning a surprise birthday party for Sheamus," she explains. "Does Saturday April 10th work for everyone?"

We all nod and murmur out of sync.

"It doesn't interfere with Easter or with the Between The Covers Book Fair," Kelly informs us. She looks at me. "This date doesn't conflict with your dad's visit, does it, hun?"

I shake my head. "He's not scheduled to arrive until the following week. He's coming for the book fair."

"Perfect," Kelly says. "Save the date, everybody. I'll be in touch soon with the details."

"Here he comes," Connie says when the back door thuds shut.

"OK, well I should get back to the salon," Kelly announces. "Are you ready to go, sweetie?"

Sheamus nods.

"And Sophie and I will be across the street at the park for a few minutes if anyone needs us," Jess says.

"Jess, would you mind some company on your walk?" Connie asks. "I want to enjoy as much of this rare warm day as possible before it disappears."

"I would love some company." Jess smiles.

Eric and I hug each of them goodbye, and they wish us a good trip.

"Why didn't you tell me Mitchell is coming to town?" Adam demands as soon as the door closes behind everyone.

"It's in the family calendar," I inform him.

"I don't look that far ahead in the family calendar," he says as though it's a previously established fact. "You know I need lots of time to brace myself before your father comes to town."

"Wait." Eric holds up his hand. "Why are you so freaked out about Megan's dad coming for a visit? Don't you get along?"

"Mitchell *hates* me," Adam explains. "He's hated me since the day we met, and every time we see each other, he hates me even more. And it's not just me, he hated his other sons-in-law too. But he hates me the most."

"Other sons-in-law?" Eric asks, looking both confused and concerned.

"My sister's current and ex-husbands," I clarify, so he doesn't think I have skeletons in my closet that might be the remains of husbands-past I haven't told him about.

"Do you think your dad will hate me, babe?"

"*Will* hate you?" Adam asks. "You haven't met Mitchell yet?" Adam looks at me, then Eric. "How have you avoided meeting Mitchell?"

"I had a series of court dates in the city last time he was in town," Eric explains with a half-shrug. "I stayed over."

"That was lucky," Adam says. "If I were you, I'd book more court dates for the second week of April," he mutters.

"Stop trying to scare Eric," I chide Adam.

"He should be scared, Meg," Adam insists. "Every time your father comes to town, he brings trouble with him, and each incident is worse than the one before. It wouldn't surprise me if someone dropped dead during one of his visits."

"He's exaggerating," I reassure Eric.

At least I hope it's an exaggeration.

SINS & NEEDLES: A KNITORIOUS MURDER MYSTERY BOOK 7

Harmony Lake buzzes with excitement when world-famous author and avid needle felter, Claire Rivera, attends our annual book fair.

But excitement turns to shock when Claire is found dead from a freak accident with a felting needle.

And shock turns to suspicion when the police determine that Claire's seemingly accidental death is actually murder.

When another world-famous author, who happens to be my father, rockets to number one on the suspect list, I take a stab at finding the real killer.

Can I find out whodunit before my father gets stuck taking the blame?

I hope so, but with no shortage of suspects, finding the killer is like looking for a felting needle in a haystack.

Click here to read Sins & Neeldles: A Knitorious murder mystery book 7.

ABOUT THE AUTHOR

Reagan Davis doesn't really exist. She is a pen name for the real author who lives in the suburbs of Toronto with her husband, two kids, and a menagerie of pets. When she's not planning the perfect murder, she enjoys knitting, reading, eating too much chocolate, and drinking too much Diet Coke. The author is an established knitwear designer who regularly publishes individual patterns and is a contributor to many knitting books and magazines. I'd tell you her real name, but then I'd have to kill you. (Just kidding! Sort of.)

http://www.ReaganDavis.com/email

ACKNOWLEDGMENTS

I owe the biggest thanks you, dear reader. Your love and enthusiasm for the first three books in the series gives me the determination and inspiration to the series.

Thank you to Kim of Kim's Covers for another perfect cover.

Thank you to Chris and Sherry at The Editing Hall for correcting all my misplace punctuation and making the story readable.

Eternal love and gratitude to the Husbeast and Kidlets for everything.

Made in the USA
Columbia, SC
30 November 2022

72336347R00411